'What an extraordinary book. *The Ruin of Kings* is everything epic fantasy should be: rich, cruel, gorgeous, brilliant, enthralling and deeply, deeply satisfying. I loved it' **Lev Grossman**

'It was one hell of a ride' **Glen Cook**

'*The Ruin of Kings* revs up with the glitz of a high-speed, multi-level video game, with extreme magic' **Janny Wurts**

'A fantastic page-turner with a heady blend of great characters, fast-moving action and a fabulously inventive magic system . . . I loved it' **John Gwynne**

'*The Ruin of Kings* is a fascinating story about a compellingly conflicted young hero in an intriguingly complex world' **L. E. Modesitt, Jr.**

'It's impossible not to be impressed with the ambition of it all, the sheer, effervescent joy Lyons takes in the scope of her project. Sometimes you just want a larger-than-life adventure story about thieves, wizards, assassins and kings' ***New York Times***

'An impressive and highly accomplished debut' *LA Times*

'In a sprawling, magic-filled world populated by gods, dragons, krakens, witches, demons, ghosts, shape-shifters, zombies, and so much more, Lyons ties it all together seamlessly to create literary magic. Epic fantasy fans looking for a virtually un-put-down-able read should look no further' ***Kirkus*, starred review**

'Though the hero's journey structure and classical fantasy elements are familiar, the complex mysteries and revelations feel novel . . . its lore and memorable characters will leave epic fantasy fans eager for the second volume'
Publishers Weekly, **starred review**

'Lyons proves she is worthy of comparison to other masters of epic fantasy, such as Patrick Rothfuss, Stephen R. Donaldson (particularly in Grand Guignol action), and Melanie Rawn'
Booklist, **starred review**

'An enchanting epic fantasy, with a thrilling plot'   *SFBook*

THE NAME OF
ALL THINGS

Jenn Lyons lives in Atlanta, Georgia, with her husband, three cats and a nearly infinite number of opinions on anything from Sumerian mythology to the correct way to make a martini. She is a video game producer by day, and spends her evenings writing science-fiction, fantasy and paranormal mysteries. A long-time devotee of storytelling, she traces her geek roots back to playing first edition Dungeons & Dragons in grade school and reading her way from A to Z in the school's library. She is the author of *The Ruin of Kings*, *The Name of All Things* and *The Memory of Souls*.

BY JENN LYONS

A CHORUS OF DRAGONS
The Ruin of Kings
The Name of All Things
The Memory of Souls

THE
NAME
OF ALL
THINGS

JENN LYONS

TOR

First published 2019 by Tom Doherty Associates, LLC

First published in the UK 2019 by Tor

This paperback edition first published 2020 by Tor
an imprint of Pan Macmillan
The Smithson, 6 Briset Street, London EC1M 5NR
Associated companies throughout the world
www.panmacmillan.com

ISBN 978-1-5098-7955-7

1 3 5 7 9 8 6 4 2

A CIP catalogue record for this book is available from the British Library.

Typeset in Baskerville Com by Palimpsest Book Production Ltd, Falkirk, Stirlingshire
Printed and bound by CPI Group (UK) Ltd, Croydon, CR0 4YY

For Bethany,
whose faith and friendship
will always be gold.

KIRPIS
THE EMPIRE
KAZIVAR

EAMITHON

DEVORS

ZHEVEN

The
CONTINENTS
of VALA &
TYGA

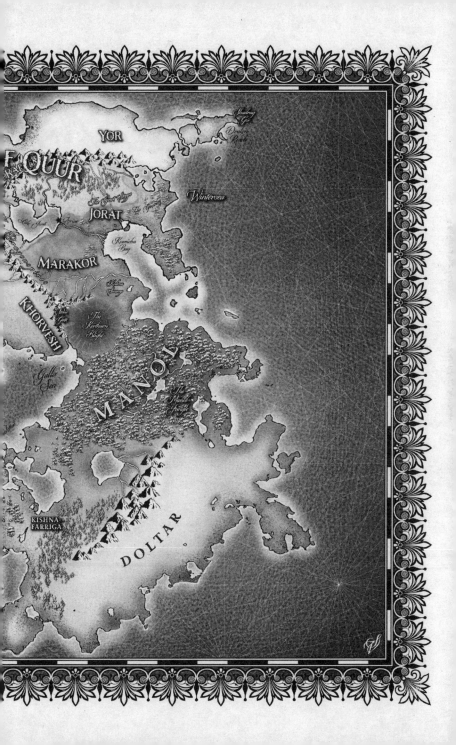

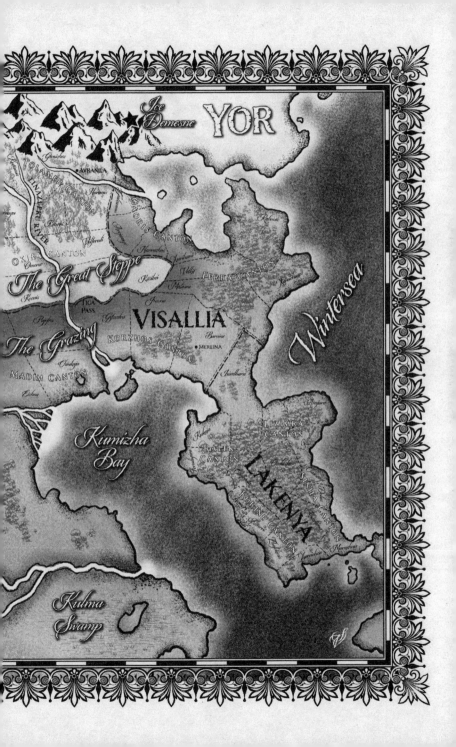

Lake
Jorat

COLLEGE
OF BANNERS

HORSE
MARKET

ATRINE
BARRACKS

TEMPLE OF
THE EIGHT

THE
PALACE

The Atrine
Gatestone

TEMPLE OF
KHORED

The Green

THE
BAZAAR

TOLAMER
APARTMENT

The
CITY
of ATRINE

BARCINE
APARTMENT

MERAT BRIDGE

*Demon
Falls*

MARAKORI SLUMS

*The Zaibur
River*

DOMINIONS OF THE EMPIRE

(in order of conquest)

Quur—Not technically a dominion, Quur was a city-state ruled by God-King Qhuaras. He was slain by Simillion (who promptly declared himself Emperor Simillion), who then expanded Quur's borders. Quur remains the capital of the empire of the same name.

Eamithon—Added to the empire in 1 QR (Quuros Reckoning) with the marriage of Emperor Simillion and the god-queen Dina. It was the only dominion added to the empire without violence, and its citizens are granted enormous privileges and latitude compared to the rest of the empire.

Khorvesh—Added to the empire by Emperor Nerikan in 5 QR, with the death of the region's previous god-king, Ynis. The native thriss population was either slaughtered or pushed out. The descendants of the Eamithonian and Quuros populations, who moved there after its annexation, have since become famous for their bravery and talent on the battlefield.

Kazivar—Conquered in 43 QR by Emperor Nerikan. This was the conclusion of a campaign that started forty-two years before. This push began with the death of the area's god-king, Nemesan, at the hands of Emperor Simillion. Most of the native population was forcibly assimilated, and the empire wouldn't expand again for over a thousand years. This was in large part due to the nonexpansionistic proclivities of Emperor Samar the Builder.

Raenena—Conquered by the empire in 1533 QR by Emperor Atrin Kandor. Whether the dominion was conquered or claimed is debatable. Most people believe Kandor killed the native dreth residents in order to have greater access to the region's ore mines.

Jorat—Conquered by the empire in 1612 QR, with the death of the god-king Khorsal. He died at the hands of Emperor Kandor. As part of the same campaign, Kandor dammed the Zaibur River to flood the Endless Canyon. This created Lake Jorat, Demon Falls, and Atrine—later embraced as the capital of Jorat.

Kirpis—Conquered by the empire in 1699 QR by Emperor Kandor, who pushed out the vané population of the Kirpis region. This included their king, Terindel. The Kirpis vané resettled in the Manol, with their Manol vané cousins. Emperor Kandor followed them in 1709 QR and was slain during the attempted invasion. His sword Urthaenriel, a.k.a. Godslayer, was lost.

Marakor—Conquered by the empire in 1962 QR by Emperor Jalore. This concluded a 240-year campaign to unite the various city-states and divided clan groups of the region. Jalore named the technically united dominion *Marakor* (a name none of the clan groups wanted or accepted). He also chained the rebellious population with extreme penalties as punishment for their prolonged disobedience.

Yor—Conquered relatively recently in 2044 QR by Emperor Gendal. Even without Urthaenriel, Gendal oversaw the deaths of the god-king rulers of Yor—Cherthog and Suless. However, to this day, the region remains inhospitable, and its citizens are still unhappy with Quuros rule. Their current duke, Azhen Kaen, is primarily Yoran. However, he's also the grandson of one of the original Quuros generals involved in the conquest.

FOREWORD

My dearest Lord Var,

Here's the account you asked for on the history behind the current situation in Jorat. I cheated and took advantage of Janel telling the story herself, but best from the source, yes? And your little brother is even in here too, which I know you'll find just delightful.

I didn't make up nearly as much as you might think—it helps when you can use an artifact to check your facts. Our friend's input was useful too. He didn't want to contribute at first, but I convinced him to see reason. I'm sure he'd have gathered his records together into a semblance of order eventually, but we don't have the time for that academic crap. No offense, but have you read his transcripts? He does love words, doesn't he?

I'm glad I decided to do this myself.

I hope you'll forgive my occasional artistic license, but if that D'Lorus brat can do it, why can't I? I've left a few of my own personal notes along the way.

Anyway, turns out you can top killing the emperor, freeing every demon, and destroying half Quur's Capital City, but then . . .

. . . you know how much I love happy endings.

Ever your faithful and obedient servant,

Senera

. . . one last thing, my lord.

I suppose I should explain what really happened in the Capital.

Long story short: this is all Gadrith's fault. Our favorite undead necromancer decided that he and he alone was the answer to all those prophecies. Thirty years of him plotting to snatch Urthaenriel away from everyone, us included, just came to a rolling boil in the Capital. It didn't work out well for Gadrith. Or for the Capital.

Gadrith needed the Stone of Shackles, which was a problem, because he had no idea where it was. We did—but he didn't ask us, did he? No, instead he plotted and schemed and recruited a couple of royals to his cause—Darzin D'Mon must have been a real coup—until he finally figured out where it was: around the neck of a High Lord's long-lost son, Kihrin.

Except that to get to that point, Darzin D'Mon's mimic Talon had killed, oh, pretty much anyone Kihrin had ever spoken to. Kihrin hated Darzin's guts. Still, Darzin claimed Kihrin was his son and laughable as that idea is, Kihrin's real father let Darzin get away with it. After that, Darzin tried to mind fuck the poor kid into giving up the Stone of Shackles, mostly using Thurvishar D'Lorus and some slave girl Kihrin was sweet on.

It didn't work. Kihrin gets no credit here. It didn't work because Talon screwed it up, as you'll find she's in the habit of doing. Talon is the one who put Kihrin on that slave ship, and ultimately who we can thank for letting the Black Brotherhood get their claws into him. And while Kihrin did come back to the Capital eventually, it was four years later, with friends, and having been trained by literally the best swordsman in the whole world. Nice job, Talon.

But Kihrin underestimated Gadrith's willingness to break the rules of polite villainy. The wizard took over the Blue Palace and started executing Kihrin's family until he finally agreed to hand over the Stone of Shackles. Which Kihrin did. After which point Gadrith promptly killed him.

Or rather, Gadrith had Darzin kill him, sacrificing Kihrin to the demon Xaltorath during what was no doubt stage 517 of Gadrith's great "conquer the world" plan. You'd think being sacrificed to a demon would be enough to kill Kihrin for good, right? Once again, we can thank Talon. Neither Gadrith nor Darzin realized Kihrin had been gaeshed while he was away. Talon knew. So she'd grabbed Kihrin's control talisman as a souvenir. Combined with our very own Janel personally escorting Kihrin's soul to the Land of Peace in the Afterlife, it was enough for Thaena to bring Kihrin back.

And that, as they say, was that.

Sure, Gadrith probably thought his plan was coming up rainbows and puppies. Xaltorath had started a Hellmarch in the Capital, luring Emperor Sandus into the open. Gadrith then tricked Sandus into killing him while Gadrith wore the Stone of Shackles. And–since that's what the stone does–that meant Sandus was now dead and Gadrith, now living in Sandus's body, was the newest emperor of Quur. Nobody could stop him–he'd killed his own daughter Tyentso when she tried and left her body to rot on the Arena floor. Everything was going great.

Funny how quickly your fortunes can change when you've just murdered one of the Goddess of Luck's favorite people. Kihrin might have been too weak to stand after being Returned, but he still managed to kill Darzin, find Urthaenriel, and destroy both the Stone of Shackles and Gadrith at the same time. Destroying the Stone broke every gaesh made using it, so that means all the demons are free now too. So's Kihrin's mother, Khaeriel. Who, by the way, killed every single member of House D'Mon Gadrith hadn't already finished off except Kihrin's father, whom she's kidnapped. Pretty sure she has no idea her son's alive. Do with that as you will.

Just to add insult to injury, remember how I said Gadrith killed his daughter? Thaena Returned her without even being asked. After Kihrin had slain Gadrith, and after the magical barriers had gone up to keep the Crown and Scepter locked away until the next Great Contest. All Tyentso had to do to crown herself emperor of Quur was reach out and grab the damn things.

So good news: we have a new emperor. One who hates the Royal Houses. I'm excited to see where that leads.

And Kihrin? Kihrin did one smart thing: he left town. I couldn't use magic to find him because of Urthaenriel, but we know he headed to Jorat next—which is where the chronicle attached picks up. Happy reading.

PART I

CONVERSATIONS
IN A STORM HOUSE

The men paused at the ramp's base to shake the rain from their sallí cloaks. Behind them, the black sky flickered, then lit up with blinding brightness. A second later, the crash of thunder rolled over them. The heavens opened to drench the ground.

"Shut that door!"

Before they could respond, Scandal, the gray fireblood mare, shouldered her way past. Her passage knocked the heavy oak barrier backward, and the high winds yanked at the unanchored door, forcing the two men to wrestle it back into position. One man closed the latch, locking it.

Stillness enveloped the men even as they heard the winds howl outside. Kihrin turned to his companion. "Why didn't we go to Atrine again?"

The other man, a large fellow with a white star-shaped birthmark on his forehead, grunted. "Too many imperial soldiers in Atrine."

"Right. That was it." Kihrin eyed the stone building's interior with suspicion. "Star, I know how much you love horses, but . . . is this a *barn*?"

As Kihrin D'Mon walked forward, the barn opened into a broad stone-lined vault nestled into the hillside. A herd of horses clustered at the rear, wide-eyed, ears flicking back at each peal of thunder. His gray fireblood, Scandal, joined them, sidling up to two large black fireblood stallions also present. Unlike

Scandal, who resembled an oversized mare, the other fire-bloods' not-a-horse natures showed themselves in red eyes and matching tiger stripes running up their legs. The other horses grouped around them like children seeking a parent's protection.

"If she winds up pregnant, she'd better not come crying to me about it," Kihrin muttered.

An old woman with piebald skin rushed to the entrance from a passage in the back. "Shut that door good, you hear me? That storm's a killer, if ever I've seen one . . ." Her voice trailed off as she took in Star's appearance.

Kihrin couldn't blame her. Star could stop a stampede with a frown. Kihrin stood taller, but Star was twice as wide and rough as the weather outside. At the brothel where Kihrin grew up, he'd have hired Star as a bouncer on the spot.

The old woman gave Star a wink.

"Aye, Mare." Star laughed as he pulled on a lock of his salt-and-pepper hair. "And you're a fine sight to see too. We need pillows and a place of honor for Hamarratus. Sorry to trot in so late. We weren't expecting the storm." He touched forefingers to forehead, then bowed from the waist.

Kihrin had never heard Star string more than two sentences together before. He'd also never seen Star bow—not to a high lord, not to anyone.

*Wait. Who is Hamarratus?**

"Oh, no problem at all." The old woman pulled up short and turned her attention to Kihrin. "Right. At least you're here. Get yourself into the shelter. She's waiting for you. Best hurry while the stew's hot."

Kihrin lowered his pack to the hay-strewn ground. "I'm sorry, ma'am, but there's been a mistake. No one here's expecting me."

---

* Apparently, Hamarratus (or Scandal to her friends) was a fireblood slave previously owned by Darzin D'Mon. Did you know Darzin had smuggled a fireblood out of Jorat? What an absolute idiot. Not related, but do you think you could raise Darzin from the dead? I'd like to kill him again.

The old woman looked surprised. "You ain't named Kihrin, then?"

The young man, who definitely *was* named Kihrin, managed not to pull out any weapons. Barely. "Who gave you that name?"

"Your woman said you'd be along."* She pointed down a tunnel leading into the hillside. "She's waiting for you. Said I should watch for a tall foreign-looking fellow with yellow hair. And that's you, right? I mean, you must be from the other side of the empire. Nobody local would dress like you." Her eyes flicked down to his misha and kef as though they were a signed confession.

"My woman?" Kihrin exchanged a look with Star. Not all his female acquaintances were friends. "Nobody knows I'm here. Hell, I don't even know where we are." Kihrin's hand found the pommel of the dagger at his belt.

"I'll settle here, see to the horses," Star offered.

"Sounds good. If you hear my dying screams, avenge me."

Star shrugged. "Not sure how. You're the one with the fancy sword."

Kihrin didn't seem armed with anything larger than a dagger. If the groom thought the comment strange, she didn't say.

"Come on, then, foal." She motioned to Star. "Help an old woman with the watering."

Kihrin walked toward what he hoped was a tavern.

The passage led from the vaulted stone stable to a wide common room, nestled so far into the hillside it was underground. Fresh air somehow still circulated to flutter the multicolored banners hanging from the ceiling.

The rainbow hues reminded him of the Capital's Royal Houses, but he suspected these colors had a different meaning here. The Royal Houses didn't have a strong presence in Jorat; Kihrin thought that spoke well of Jorat.

Kihrin noticed three exits from the main room, besides the one he'd used to arrive. He had no way to know which of them—if any of them—led back outside, but he liked to keep

---

* I assume this is an example of Joratese humor. "His woman." Ha!

his options open. The tavern also possessed a well-stocked bar, no obvious bouncer, and the aroma of roasting meat wafting out from a kitchen. *Perfect.*

Joratese townsfolk sheltered from the weather here and many were enjoying an afternoon meal. Kihrin forced himself not to stare; Joratese skin colors varied as much as their horses, with similar markings. Everyone wore their hair long and straight—loose or in intricate decorated braids. Some townsfolk shaved the sides of their heads so a single strip remained, mimicking equine manes. And all either sported plain earth-toned attire or bright clothing paired with all the jewelry they owned. Kihrin couldn't tell if the difference in styles showed rank or fulfilled some other social role, but it seemed independent of gender.*

The townsfolk's return stares were far less polite than his own. All chatter in the area died away.

"Kihrin?"

He turned to see a woman his age, standing by the fire.

Kihrin's breath caught in his throat.

She was as Joratese as everyone else in the room; she was nothing like anyone else in the room. Everything about her was red—her skin burnt sienna, her eyes ruby. He'd imagined meeting her so often that seeing her in person struck him as ludicrous. A demon prince named Xaltorath had shown her image to Kihrin once, years before. Kihrin had never been able to push her memory away. She defined the meter by which he measured all beauty.

And she was there. She was *right there.*

Impossible. The idea he'd travel to Jorat and run into his dream woman at the first ale house defied credulity. The Goddess of Luck favored him more literally than most, but there were limits.

So this must be a trick. *Bait.*

---

* Yeah, I thought it couldn't possibly signify gender roles too at first. Easy mistake, right?

He suddenly felt insulted; it wasn't even subtle bait.

She gave him a smile that outshone the sun, to his dazzled eyes. "I'm so glad you're here. Please, join us." She gestured next to her. A thin, small western Quuros man sat with her, dressed in a priest's robes and agolé. He looked like someone resigned to being an awkward third wheel.

She stopped smiling as Kihrin again placed a hand on his dagger.

"I don't believe we've met," Kihrin said. "I'm Kihrin. And you are?"

The joy drained from her eyes. "You don't remember me."

"I'll repeat myself: we've never met."

The surrounding people started grumbling. A man in the back even stood up. No doubt they felt the need to protect their own from a random outlander.

She turned to the tavern and made a shushing motion. "It's fine. He's my guest. Free drinks for the room on my tab." That earned cheers, with laughter mixed in, as if she'd said something funny. Kihrin added it to his list of reasons to distrust the situation.

"Perhaps you might sit down," said the priest. "We'll introduce ourselves and explain matters."

Kihrin moved his hand from the dagger. If she were a ruse, at least he had the small advantage of recognizing her nature. Only three entities in the universe knew what his dream girl looked like: his best friend, Teraeth; the demon Xaltorath; and the mimic Talon. Teraeth would never do something like this, but the other two? Neither of them was a friend.

But the priest struck him as an odd accompaniment to a demonic seduction. Why would Xaltorath or Talon have brought a chaperone?

Kihrin pulled a chair over and sat down.

The Joratese woman returned to her seat. "That didn't go the way I'd hoped at all. We don't have time for this."

"I told you he wouldn't remember," the priest said. "Most never do."

"You were introducing yourselves?" Kihrin pressed. "Let's start there."

"Yes," the woman said. "Of course." She placed a pitch-black hand on her chest.

Kihrin blinked. He hadn't imagined it. She wasn't wearing gloves; the color of her hands and face didn't match.

"I'm Janel Theranon. This is my dearest friend Qown, formerly—" She turned to Qown. "Is it formerly?"

The man grimaced. "My status is uncertain." To Kihrin, he said, "I'm Brother Qown, a votary of the Vishai Mysteries. It's a pleasure to meet you."

"Likewise," Kihrin said, but his stare remained locked on Janel.

Janel. He felt like an idiot. She had a name. Of course she did. In all the years since Xaltorath had forced her image into his mind, he'd never wondered what her *name* might be. Janel could even be a common name. Maybe Janels in Jorat were like Tishars in the Capital. Something meaning *pretty* or *blessed* or—in this dominion—something to do with horses.

"Janel," he said. "Why wouldn't I remember you if we've met?"

She lowered her voice. "Because you were dead."

He glanced around. People had stopped paying any attention after Janel had vouched for him. "I'd appreciate a little more detail."

Kihrin's friend Teraeth had a free visitor's pass to and from the Afterlife, thanks to his mother, who just happened to be Thaena, Goddess of Death.* And Thaena often brought others back to life—himself, for example, just two days before. The idea he'd been dead when they met *was* possible.

Unnerving, but possible.

"Very well," Janel said. "I have the ability to travel between the Living World and the Afterlife. I was in the latter when

---

* Her real name's Khaemezra, right? Not that I plan to run into her anytime soon . . .

you were sacrificed to Xaltorath, two days ago. I helped you fight your way past the demons hunting you, so you could Return to the Living World."

His mouth dried. "And how did you know I'd be . . . here?"

The priest, Qown, turned to her. "Janel, I don't think—"

"Shh," Janel said before returning to Kihrin. "When we met in the Afterlife, you told me your story. You'd died trying to stop Gadrith D'Lorus, whom you suspected of plotting to kill the emperor. On waking, I discovered the emperor was dead. Gadrith was dead. And someone had broken the Stone of Shackles, which freed all gaeshed slaves—but likewise freed all gaeshed *demons*. And I know destroying a Cornerstone like the Stone of Shackles requires the sword Urthaenriel, also known as Godslayer."

Kihrin managed not to swallow. She'd hit the major points. "All very interesting, but I'm not hearing an explanation."

She lifted her chin. "I was looking for you, but I couldn't *find* you." Janel lowered her voice again. "*Magic* couldn't find you. And since I'd used a Cornerstone to search, the easiest explanation for why it failed was that you must be holding Godslayer.* It's somewhere on you, right now. Since we had no way to track you, we took a chance that sooner or later you'd try to use the gate system."

"And . . . ?" Kihrin motioned for her to continue.

"And we bribed the Gatekeepers Guild to watch for you."

"That way they would link you here to *this* Gatestone rather than your original destination," Qown added.

"Jorat."

Janel tilted her head. "Excuse me?"

"I was already coming here. To Jorat. Because I need to—" Kihrin stopped himself.

Because I need to find the Black Knight, Kihrin thought. *Because a single person isn't going to fulfill the prophecies as the Hellwarrior.*

---

* Yeah, okay. I was going to mock her for assuming it had to be Urthaenriel, but a Cornerstone *can* find another Cornerstone, so . . . fair point.

We suspect they refer to a quartet, with only three accounted for so far: Therin's son, Doc's son, and Sandus's son.

*Which means there's one more son to go.**

Kihrin realized she still waited on him to finish explaining why he was there. Instead, he smiled and asked, "Where are we in Jorat, anyway?"

"Avranila," Janel said. "A town in the northeast." She sighed. "I'd hoped you might make it here sooner. What delayed you?"

"I needed a bath," Kihrin said.

She didn't seem to find that funny.

Kihrin sighed. "There was a Hellmarch going on in the Capital. Refugees swamped any Gatestone within ten miles of the Capital, and we had to walk because Scandal wasn't about to let anyone ride her. We ended up traveling another thirty miles to reach the next available gate. And I wondered at how easy it was to bribe that Gatekeeper; he must have been taking extra metal to follow your orders."

Janel cleared her throat. "Just as well. We worried some enterprising Gatekeeper would try to play it both ways."

Brother Qown added, "There is a reward offered by House D'Mon for your 'safe return.'"

"I'm not surprised. I'd been missing for a few years. No one's had a chance to take down the 'lost pet' notices." Kihrin raised a hand to catch the bartender's attention. "Hey, can I get a cider over here? And whatever your special is."

Janel touched her fingers on his wrist. "We don't have time for food. That's what I'm trying to explain. Your help is needed elsewhere right away. That's why we brought you here."

A large banging echoed down the corridor. The crowd froze, and several townsfolk stood to get a better view of the new arrivals.

But there were no new arrivals. Instead, Star and the old

---

* Love the assumptions he's making here. Yes, because all the Hellwarriors simply must be *men*. Oh, how I hate Quuros misogyny.

groom who had been helping with the horses walked into the main tavern.

The woman wiped her hands on her apron. "I hope no one had any important plans. We've had to lock up the storm door."

Groans filled the room.

Janel stood again. "We'll leave as soon as one more person arrives."

The groom shook her head. "No, you won't. Nobody's coming or going. Tempest outside's gone into murder mode. You won't survive five minutes if you go out there right now. So sit down and enjoy the company until the worst blows over." The old woman gave Janel a sharp look. "That last person you're waiting on? Sorry, but he's missing the party."

"He's late," Janel conceded. "He was supposed to be here by now."

"Yeah? Well, I was supposed to be the Markreev of Alvaros, so we don't always get what we want. Anyhow, what with demons starting Hellmarches from one side of Quur to the other, your friend showing up at all, storm or no storm, was always a bit on the iffy side." The old woman turned and headed to the bar, seating herself on a chair and shouting for a bottle. To Kihrin's surprise, Star followed her, bypassing Kihrin's table.

Kihrin startled. "Wait, did she say *Hellmarches*? Plural?"

Janel and Qown both stared at him.

"Uh, that's not a trick question."

Janel smoothed her trousers, which she wore tucked into hard riding boots. "Yes, Hellmarches. Xaltorath has roamed free since before you broke the Stone of Shackles. She's been busy inviting her friends to the party ever since."

Despite having ordered food, he felt sick to his stomach. "I . . . I didn't realize."

"Not all is lost," Janel said. "The Eight Immortals fight to keep the demons too occupied to overrun the Living World. They've pushed them back before. I've every faith they'll do so again."

And Kihrin had every faith in her naïveté.* "Fine. You've gone through a lot of effort to find me." He looked Janel in the eyes. "Why?"

She answered, "We want to slay a dragon."

Kihrin blinked at her.

"A dragon? A *dragon*?"

Janel blushed. "Please lower your voice."

"A dragon," Kihrin repeated a third time. "Do you have any clue—? No, wait. Look, I applaud your ambition or greed or whatever reason you have for thinking this is a good idea. Let me assure you—this is a terrible idea."

"It matters not if it is or it isn't—"

"No. I'm sorry. 'Let's go kill a dragon' ranks among the worst of ideas. It's right above invading the Manol in summer and right below freeing Vol Karoth 'just for a little while.' Do you know why parents don't warn their children not to attack dragons? Because no parent wants to think their kids are that *stupid*. A dragon would annihilate me before I got close enough to hurt its feelings, let alone do any real damage to it."

Janel raised an eyebrow at Kihrin. "Are you quite finished?"

"No," Kihrin said. "I want to know who told you to enlist me into this ludicrous scheme, so I can find that person and shove my—"

"A quarter million people are currently in Atrine," Janel interrupted. "And they have no idea they're about to be attacked by the largest dragon ever known."

That stopped him cold. He ignored the bartender—doing double duty as waitstaff—as she shoved another mug of cider onto the table. She followed that with a bowl of rice and vegetables covered in a thick paste. Without asking if anyone needed anything else, she retreated to the bar.

Kihrin pushed aside the food. "What?"

---

* Yeah, me too. And never mind that calling them *the Eight Immortals* hasn't technically been accurate for a while. They still haven't had to do this job in millennia. I bet they're out of practice.

Musicians and storytellers in the Capital loved to talk about Atrine. What wasn't to love? Atrine was a literally magical city, crafted of poetry and marble, built by Emperor Atrin Kandor in a single day. Ironically, Kihrin had never met anyone who'd actually been there; it was everyone's favorite city from a distance.

"You heard me quite well," Janel said, no longer smiling. "Now, as *I* decided to recruit you for this plan, just what, pray tell, are you planning to shove, and where? Would you care to elaborate?"

Kihrin turned red. He exhaled and turned to the priest. "How are you involved in this?"

"Oh, I'm uh . . ." Qown floundered. "I used to be . . . that is to say . . ." He scowled, flustered. "It's complicated," he finished.

"As Qown mentioned earlier, he's a votary of the Vishai Mysteries," Janel said. "He's also a qualified physicker and my best friend."

Qown looked uncomfortable. Kihrin wondered what part of Janel's description had upset the priest—his religion or his status as a Royal House licensed healer. Being called *dearest friend* hadn't bothered him earlier.

"And you're fine with this 'Let's go kill a dragon' plan? Because you don't strike me as the type to throw away your life."

"With all respect," Qown replied, "my approval or disapproval is irrelevant. Once Morios surfaces from underneath Lake Jorat, he'll attack Atrine. Thousands will die. Normally, the emperor would handle the problem, or the Eight Immortals themselves, but Emperor Sandus is dead, and the gods . . ." He held out his hands.

"The gods are busy battling demons," Janel finished.

Kihrin looked around the room. Everything seemed normal, or what passed as such in this corner of the empire. Star and that old groom were at the bar. The crowd was making the best of the storm and had started a sing-along.

Kihrin turned back to the two reckless would-be heroes. Xaltorath clearly hadn't set a trap here.

The demon prince wouldn't have invented a scheme this implausible.

As far as Kihrin knew, the last dragon attack on a city in the Empire of Quur had taken place during the Age of God-Kings, thousands of years ago. Kihrin had always assumed dragons were nothing but a story: a myth the minstrels trotted out whenever they wanted to sing the first emperor's praises. At least that's what Kihrin had believed until he'd met a real dragon—the Old Man, Sharanakal. He had no desire to repeat the experience.

Kihrin scrubbed a hand over his face. "Do you two mind if I eat while we talk? I haven't had food since west of the Dragonspires."

Janel agreed with an aristocratic finger twirl.

Kihrin wondered if those red eyes meant she was Ogenra—the name the Royal Houses gave to bastards lucky enough to show the god-touched marks of their bloodlines.

For example, House D'Talus red eyes—or his own House D'Mon blue.

"Okay, so you . . . fine. You have my attention. At least until the storm clears." He nudged around the food in the bowl. The rice appeared unflavored. The vegetables looked blanched. The thick paste on top seemed edible, but the white goo was a mystery.*

Joratese cuisine had been all the rage back in the Capital. Kihrin's heart sank at the prospect of eating more of what he remembered being flavorless garbage.

Brother Qown took pity on him. He walked over to a table, said a quick "Pardon, pardon," and swiped a pot of bright red paste. "They have chili sauces." The priest set the jar in front of Kihrin. "But they don't bring them out for outsiders unless you ask. If you're liberal with the peppers, it's not bad."

"Not bad?" Janel raised an eyebrow.

"It will never beat my vanoizi-spiced eggplant," Qown said.

---

* Cheese. I know, I know, but they make it differently in Jorat. I've become quite fond of their version, honestly.

"I'm sorry, but that's a fact. You Joratese can't be expected to compare your cuisine to perfection."

Janel slapped Qown's shoulder. "Stop it. Priests are supposed to be humble."

"Humility is a virtue much to be desired by those who walk in the light," Qown agreed, beaming. "But then, so is honesty."

Kihrin chuckled as he opened the jar and sniffed. The priest seemed much more relaxed when talking about food instead of dragons. Kihrin's eyes watered—a good sign. He mixed in a large spoonful. "We'll assume for the moment you're serious. What's the plan if this dragon—what was his name?"

"Morios."

"Fine. Morios. How are you proposing to kill—" Kihrin stopped himself from laughing. "I'm sorry. How is this supposed to work? Humor me."

"We're waiting for another person." Janel gave an anxious glance to the tunnel leading to the tavern entrance.

"Who?" Kihrin asked. "And how do you know this dragon—Morios—is about to go on a rampage all over this dominion's capital? Did he send you a letter?"

Janel and Qown shared a look.

Janel said, "That's . . . complicated."

Kihrin possessed a well-honed sense of caution thanks to a childhood spent with criminals. This entire scenario smelled like a con. His adoptive mother, Ola, had taught him the best way to avoid ending up a mark: never stick around long enough to end up on the hook.

Kihrin dropped his spoon and grabbed his pack. "All right. I'm out of here. Good luck with your dragon hunt. It's been a pleasure meeting you." He yelled across the room. "Hey, Star, we're leaving! Right now!"

The other man looked up from his drink in surprise. "We're *what*?"

Janel stood. "You can't leave. The storm outside—"

"I'll risk it." He decided not to wait for Star as he dodged around chairs on his way to the exit. The Joratese horseman was exactly where Kihrin had promised to take him: Jorat. He didn't assume Star's loyalty ran any deeper than that.

Kihrin retraced his steps through the tunnel. Lanterns hung from the passage rafters, lighting his way back to the stables and the entrance—where a heavy wooden crossbeam stretched across the latched door. It rattled as though a giant stood on the other side, shaking it for entry. When he moved to shift the bar, Scandal whinnied at him. Kihrin didn't speak fireblood, but the tone suggested something like "You're not going out in *this* weather, are you?"

"Sorry, Scandal, but you're back in Jorat just like I promised. Star can take it from here." He'd made a mistake coming here. Kihrin should have stayed with Teraeth. He'd then have been blissfully ignorant of the body count attached to his deeds. He'd triggered *Hellmarches* . . .

So many people had died. All because he'd figured out a clever way to circumvent the Stone of Shackles' power in order to kill Gadrith. How could he have known the damn artifact was responsible for binding demons? He'd had no idea.

"Hail to thee, Lawbreaker. Hail to thee, Prince of Swords." He whispered Xaltorath's mocking words to himself. He'd done just what Xaltorath had wanted: freed the demons. He'd also slain the emperor. Then he'd reclaimed the sword Urthaenriel, the Ruin of Kings. And according to the Devoran Prophecies, what was in store for the person who accomplished those things? That lucky bastard would go on to destroy the Quuros Empire—and quite possibly the world.

Did it make a difference if Kihrin didn't want to?*

How many people did he know who'd tried to escape the game of prophecies played by demons, dragons, and gods? Didn't matter. They ended up involved, anyway. The Eight Immortals had personally dropped Kihrin into this mess in the hope of subverting the prophecies. Yet he wondered if they had really known what they were doing. The demons seemed to be winning.

* No, not really. Tough luck, kid.

Hail to thee, Thief of Souls.

He set down his pack and put a shoulder to the crossbeam over the door. The heavy wood groaned before it finally pulled free, and he dropped it to one side.

The moment he opened the latch, the outer door crashed open. The wind howled like a dragon's roar. Kihrin could only make out silhouettes of the town's nearby buildings as the storm turned the afternoon into night. But Kihrin didn't care if the weather was unsafe for man or beast.

He started to step outside.

Started to. Then he heard a ferocious whistling. A massive white blur flew overhead; the shape flipped around and landed with a thunderous boom. Wood from nearby—houses, tents, buildings—cracked and splintered. Stone crushed and scattered.

Lightning outlined the draconic shape before him. It wasn't Sharanakal, the volcanic dragon who had sought to keep him prisoner. This was a different dragon, white and gray and silver, blue eyes sparkling gemlike.

Staring at him.

Time froze, stretched. He thought, *Her eyes are the same color as mine.** Only afterward would he realize he'd assumed the dragon's gender. Time snapped forward. The dragon spread her wings wide and pulled her head back. She whipped her head forward as razor-sharp ice shards rushed from her huge mouth in a hurricane-force blast.

He scrambled to shut the opening, but it was a two-person job.

Then Janel stood next to him, grabbing at the door's edge. She lifted the bar and slammed it down into position as the ice shards hit. The barrier shuddered while Janel leaned against it.

"Your sword!" she shouted. "Pierce your sword through the wood! Nothing can withstand Urthaenriel!"

---

* You know, that's a good point. Is there some sort of relationship between the eight original Quuros Royal Houses and the Eight Immortals you haven't told me about?

He unsheathed the dagger at his side, which transformed into a slender white-silver sword.

Urthaenriel screamed in his ears—oh, a siren roar to compete with any storm-tossed tirade. She screamed at him to destroy the woman. Screamed at him to destroy something behind him back in the tavern. Screamed for him to destroy the dragon. Anything magic. Anyone who knew magic. Urthaenriel sang a song of chaos and hated all other voices but her own.

He ignored her.

"Duck!" he shouted at Janel. She did.

He rammed the blade through to the hilt. The wood gave, more like paper than fire-hardened oak. Then something massive slammed against the door. The building shook, and a bellow filled the air.

He pulled Urthaenriel out. Blue-violet blood coated the blade. Ice crystals formed as the liquid dripped to the ground.

"What are we—" Kihrin turned to Janel.

"The dragon's not done!" Janel grabbed his misha and heaved him away from the door. Janel smashed herself against it, rooting her feet against the paving stones. A howling, hissing noise filled the room. Thick ice layers formed around the portal. The foundation rock cracked and groaned.

Finally, the sound of the wind outside faded.

Janel sank to the wet ground, her breath frosting the air. Kihrin sat down before her, Urthaenriel dangling from one hand. Water dripped nearby. The horses made soothing noises to each other as the firebloods edged forward to investigate.

After a long, weighty silence, Kihrin said, "You could've mentioned the dragon was coming to us."

"Yes . . ." She exhaled, rubbing a hand against the side of her head. "I would have, except for one small problem."

"What?"

"That's the wrong dragon."

1: THE OUTLAWS OF BARSINE

Jorat Dominion, Quuros Empire.
Two days since Kihrin D'Mon was sacrificed to Xaltorath

When Kihrin walked back into the tavern, a swell of questions greeted him—or greeted *her*. The guests wanted answers. What was that noise? Had it scared the horses? Were the horses all right? Had the weather worsened? Did anyone check the horses? Did the firebloods want to join them at the bar?*

That last offer had sounded serious.

"The storm is still too severe to travel," Janel projected in a loud voice. "Don't try to leave."

Kihrin raised an eyebrow but didn't contradict her. An ice sheet several feet thick now trapped everyone inside. With an angry dragon waiting for them on the other side.

Just your typical night out at a tavern.

There seemed little point in panicking the crowd over something they couldn't fix. Kihrin doubted *he* could help either, even with Urthaenriel, but he knew one thing: any dragon-slaying debate had become significantly less debatable.

But if the one outside was the wrong dragon, who was the right dragon?

After everyone returned to their drinks and chatter, Janel wandered back to the Vishai priest. She dumped Kihrin's bag onto a chair.

---

* Q: How do you know the person you're talking to isn't Joratese?
A: If they don't start telling you about their horses within fifteen minutes of meeting them, they're not Joratese.

"Aeyan'arric's outside," she whispered to Brother Qown, "and she's iced over the tavern's front door."

Kihrin sat and stared at his bowl. He wondered how many provisions the tavern had stocked, how long the supplies would last. How would the locals accept rationing, or worse, the food running out?

No. Kihrin had no intention of letting a dragon trap him. And Urthaenriel's hateful melodies had revealed the presence of powerful magic. Kihrin couldn't be sure if Urthaenriel was reacting to wizards or to the presence of one or more Cornerstones, but the sword gave him enough of a vague sense of direction to make an educated guess. Urthaenriel wanted Qown dead as much as she wanted to kill the dragon, Janel, or the old woman who kept the horses.

These people weren't as powerless as they seemed.*

"Aeyan'arric's here? Already?" Qown leaned forward, lowering his voice to match Janel's. "That's far too soon after the fight. If she's recovered this fast—"

"Not *if*," Janel said. "She's recovered. It's an unwelcome confirmation of how hard it is to permanently kill a dragon. She didn't even stay dead for *two days*. And we've no way to know if the other dragons recover slower or faster."

Kihrin furrowed his eyebrows. "She was dead two days ago? How did *that* happen?"

Janel sighed. She glanced around to make sure no one was paying attention. "I slew her." She added, "To be fair, I had significant assistance."

"So . . . let me see if I understand. You lured me here using a combination of bribery and logic. You have a hypothetical dragon—Morios—you claim will rip up Atrine any minute now. But Aeyan'arric—a dragon who is *not* hypothetical—has instead

---

* Notice that Kihrin's sheathed Urthaenriel here. By every account I've ever read, he shouldn't be able to hear her if he's not holding her drawn, but he still can.

So that's terrifying. Is there some reason Kihrin can use this sword differently from anyone else?

stalked you here. Because you were rude enough to kill her two days ago." Kihrin grabbed his bowl and a spoon. "There's no point worrying about your first problem until you do something about the second. Did I miss anything?"

Janel frowned at him. "No."

"So answer me this. If this dragon—Morios—is heading for Jorat's capital, why didn't you set up shop in Atrine and have the Gatekeeper send me there? We'd already be in position. I didn't see a Gatekeeper manning this side of the local Gatestone when I arrived. So unless this is your Gatekeeper's day off and he's drinking over at the bar, we can't open a gate from here. Why enlist my help here—assuming I'd even agree—if it takes two months to reach Atrine? How much of that city would be left when we arrived?"*

Janel and Qown shared that look again.

"Okay, you two need to stop that," Kihrin said. "Whatever you think I won't believe or won't accept—just tell me. I've been through and seen a lot. I'm a master at accepting the impossible."

"The way your hands are shaking suggests otherwise," Janel said.

"That's a normal reaction to being attacked by a dragon."

Qown cleared his throat. "Sometimes a particular action sounds bad if one doesn't have the context to interpret it. For example, if somebody told me you had killed Emperor Sandus—"

"Just an example?" Kihrin narrowed his eyes. "I *hypothetically* killed the emperor?"

"Let him finish," Janel said.

"Yes, thank you. As I was saying, I would be upset. But only because I lacked context. After all, Gadrith the Twisted had taken possession of Sandus's body using the Stone of Shackles. You didn't kill the emperor, because he was already dead. You see? If we blurt out certain facts—well, without the right context, you might reach an incorrect conclusion."

---

* Nothing. Nothing will be left at all.

Kihrin stared. "Where are you getting your information about me?"

He found their accuracy distressing. Kihrin checked the man's hands; no intaglio-carved ruby rings. If Qown belonged to the late emperor's secret society, the Gryphon Men, he wasn't wearing his allegiance openly.

Qown cleared his throat. "That's also one of those situations where context is important." He turned to Janel. "We have a lot to explain."

"Yes, you do," Kihrin agreed. "Luckily for you, I don't have anywhere else to be."

Janel scowled. "Our focus must be on Atrine, Qown. Morios could wake at any moment. When he does, Atrine will be defenseless."

"Do you want me to check?" Qown asked. "Sorry. Of course you do." He pulled an egg-sized stone from his robes. Toward the middle, the brown agate seemed to transform to some more expensive gemstone. The colors layered until a flame appeared to burn in the center.

Urthaenriel *screamed* in his mind.

"Is that . . ." Kihrin paused and wet his lips. "That's a Cornerstone, right?"

"Worldhearth," Qown said. "One of the eight god artifacts. Each Cornerstone possesses unique abilities its owner can use—"

"I know what a Cornerstone is. I destroyed one two days ago." *And freed every demon in the world.*

"Right. The Stone of Shackles." Qown fidgeted. "A moment, then."

The priest didn't do anything special or spectacular. He stared into the rock as though admiring its beauty. After a few seconds, he blinked and tucked the stone back into his robes.

"He hasn't attacked yet," Qown said.

"He will soon. We need to be there when he—" She glanced over at Kihrin in time to see him roll his eyes. "You don't believe us."

"I still haven't heard why we're not in Atrine."

"I have my reasons."

"And what might those be?"

"Mine." She narrowed her eyes.

But Kihrin had no interest in placating her. "You won't give me information, and you still expect me to help? Why would I?"

Janel leaned across the table. "Because the man I encountered two days ago wasn't a spoiled brat. Because he didn't hesitate to aid me, even at the risk he'd be trapped in the Afterlife. Because I thought that man—who would risk his soul to save someone he'd never met before—" She curled her lip. "I assumed he'd risk his life to save two hundred and fifty thousand *other* people he'd never met before. Apparently, I was mistaken." Janel stood up while Brother Qown gave the impression he wanted to hide behind his hands.

Kihrin grabbed her wrist. The scathing look she threw at him suggested he was about to lose the hand—followed by his life. "I'm sorry." He stared into her eyes, red with glimmers of orange and yellow—*not* House D'Talus. "I was out of line. But please understand, you're asking a lot. You're expecting me to accept your story on blind faith. Anyone would be skeptical. Give me something to work with."

Janel studied his face before sitting. "I can't return to Atrine because of my status in the eyes of Jorat's ruler. The moment Duke Xun learns I'm not deceased, I'll be treated to my prompt execution. The only way I can visit Atrine is if they're too distracted with other problems to pay any attention. For example—Morios."*

Kihrin stared at her. "Why does Duke Xun want you dead?"

"It's a rather long story."

"We have time," Kihrin said. "I mean . . ." He pointed back toward the front door. "We're not going anywhere until the ice queen outside tires of this game. Or until we kill her."

Brother Qown perked. "That's a wonderful idea."

---

* Funny how she wasn't in a hurry to spell out how defeating Morios benefits her.

"Which part? The tiring or the killing?"

"Qown—" Janel said.

"Don't scold me. He's right; we should tell him." Qown smiled at Kihrin. "Plus, it's important for you to see how you fit into all this and why we need you."

"I know why," Kihrin replied. Urthaenriel. If they'd already killed a dragon, then doing so again wasn't the issue. Apparently, killing a dragon permanently was the problem. They thought they needed Urthaenriel to make it stick.

Qown paused from fishing through a satchel. "Hm, I doubt it."

"Where should I start?" Janel said. "Perhaps with Duke Kaen?"

Qown pulled a small, neatly bound tome from his book bag. "We'd have to go back further than Duke Kaen or it won't make sense. Further than Atrine. All the way to events at Barsine." He tapped his thumb against the book cover. "Fortunately, I've logged the whole story."

"Barsine. Is that a person or a place?" Kihrin asked.

Janel's smile was wan. "It depends on context. Qown, you start. I'll go fetch us all another round. And more upishiarral."*

Kihrin followed her with his eyes as she headed toward the bar. She started talking to the bartender. Whatever Janel said made the other woman throw down her towel and cross her arms. A few seconds later, they slipped through a back door.

Meanwhile, Brother Qown picked up his notebook and read aloud. *"There are many accounts of the rebellion, the reasons for it, the manner of its successes and failures. Brother Qown was certain his account wouldn't match any other histori—"*

"Hold up. I have a question," Kihrin said.

Brother Qown paused. "Just one?"

"I make no promises," Kihrin said dryly. "A rebellion? What rebellion? I thought we were talking about a dragon."

"Context, remember?" Qown said. "Please be patient. It's not

---

* Literally, *rice and vegetables*. Not bad, though. Qown's right: the chili sauce is key.

as though you have any choice, until certain draconic obstacles are removed."

"Fine, fine. Is this recent? Duke Kaen moving against the rest of the empire?" Janel and Qown had mentioned Duke Kaen earlier, and Kihrin's friend Jarith Milligreest had been concerned about the duke's undeclared rebellion. For that matter, Jarith's father, High General Qoran Milligreest, had been concerned about Duke Kaen. Father and son had both watched him, waiting for the man to give them an excuse to send in the army.

Which reminded Kihrin his friend Jarith had been claimed by the Hellmarch two days before in the Capital.

He exhaled.

"My apologies," Kihrin said. "Please continue."

"Right, yes." Qown looked for his place in the journal. *"So . . . Qown would always insist the rebellion began in Jorat.*

"It began with a robbery . . .

"The whole affair had been problematic from the start. The outlaws had proved unwilling to engage in the 'robbing' part of their duties. Brother Qown knew the bandits lurked in the nearby trees; he'd felt eyes on their position for hours. He wondered what they could be waiting–"

Brother Qown looked up, frowning. "Yes?"

"Third person?" Kihrin asked, trying not to laugh. "Really? If you were there . . . why wouldn't you tell this from your point of view?"

"It's a chronicle," Brother Qown protested. "I'm a chronicler. One does not write a chronicle as a first-person diary."

"I never found anyone who'd refer to themselves in third person trustworthy. I knew this mimic–"

Janel set down a tray filled with ciders, local beers, and several more bowls of upishiarral. "Here we are."

"Problems with the barkeep?" Kihrin asked.

"Hm? No problem at all," Janel said. She helped herself to a cider as she sat.

Kihrin glanced over at the bar. The bartender had returned, but now she huddled with the old groom, whispering.

"He keeps interrupting me." Brother Qown looked over at Janel as if pleading for protection. "May I please continue?"

Janel touched Kihrin on the hand. "There'll be no living with him if you don't allow him to read."

Kihrin let the little man read.

Qown's Turn. Barsine Banner, Jorat, Quur.

The previous bandits had never hesitated like this.

In fact, they were taking so long to make their move that Mare Dorna joked about inviting them into the camp to share breakfast.

At last, a lone masked figure wandered into their clearing. Brother Qown hid his surprise; he hadn't expected the brigand to be a woman. Then again, Jorat had defied so many expectations.

"Finally," Dorna muttered. Brother Qown elbowed her to keep quiet. Evidently in *this* part of Jorat, criminals were timid creatures who had to be lured from their warrens.

"Where are your guards?" the bandit asked as she looked around—a sensible question to ask when about to commit a crime.

Mare Dorna snorted as she scraped stale sweet rice from her iron stir pan.*

Their party's third member sat still and poised by the camp-fire. She embodied all the motives the desperate might ever need for banditry. A jeweled ring on a chain hung from her neck. Gold thread stitched her riding tunic. Jade pins decorated her laevos hair.

"Guards? Why?" Janel asked the newcomer while she sipped her tea. "Are you looking for work?"

The bandit rolled her eyes at the jest. She continued examining the clearing as if armed soldiers hid under the bedrolls. Her gaze lingered for a moment on the deer corpse, hanging upside down from one of the trees.

---

* I was surprised to learn that *Mare* is a term of affection, something like calling an older woman *Auntie.*

Brother Qown could guess her thoughts: there were just three of them, and none looked capable of stringing up a deer, let alone defending themselves. Dorna looked older than many mountains. Brother Qown himself was ill-used to strenuous exercise. The noblewoman, Janel, muddied the distinction between woman and child. Their horses foraged in a nearby pasture: harmless by casual observation. No sign, anywhere, of the all-important guards who might protect a Joratese aristocrat from those with less fortunate births.

Easy metal.

"Too simple," the bandit murmured. "You're too well-bred not to have protectors."

That makes her smarter than the last four outlaw leaders, Brother Qown thought.

This trap always reminded Brother Qown of the salos, a snake living in the Manol Jungle. He'd never seen one himself, having never been as far south as to leave Quur's borders, but Father Zajhera had described the creature. The reptile hunted by mimicking a wounded animal with its tail, twitching the tip in distress. Any predator who pounced on this free appetizer discovered they were intended as the main course.

His employer, Janel Theranon, Count of Tolamer, looked just as vulnerable.

His gaze shifted out into the woods as he heard dry leaves crackle, the twigs snapping underfoot. "Count," he said, "this one isn't alone."

"I should hope not, Brother Qown," Count Janel said, setting down her teacup with exaggerated care as she regarded the brigand. "Are your companions seeking employment as well?" She smiled at the woman.

"Depends. What are you paying?" a man shouted from somewhere beyond the tree line. Others, also unseen, laughed in response, revealing the woman had brought all her friends to the party.

The bandit sighed. She was dressed in an ornate leather tunic dyed in contrasting brown and green shades. Two pieces of embroidered green fabric comprised the mask over her face, overlapped to leave a slit for her eyes. Brown skin surrounded one eye, while wine-red skin surrounded the other. She had a bow stowed across her pack and a sickle in her hand.

Probably a farmer gone feral. That quality seemed infectious, given how often brigands had attacked them since Count Janel's canton, Tolamer. However, there was an upside. Most ruling nobles in Jorat offered a bounty on captured bandits.

A fine way to earn a living if one didn't mind the risk.

Brother Qown minded rather a lot, but it wasn't his place to tell his count how to fill her coffers with metal.

The outlaw turned toward the woods. "Shut it!"

Janel's smile broadened to a grin. "Give your men time. No horse is born saddled."

"Ain't that the truth," the bandit admitted, then squared her shoulders as if reminding herself not to be distracted by a friendly victim. "See here. We've been following you and yours ever since you crossed the river, asking ourselves the whole while what a fancy mane like you is doing out here. You expect us to believe you have nothing but an ancient mare and a fat gelding for company?"

Brother Qown straightened. "Now hold on . . ."

"Oh, she don't miss the obvious, do she?" Dorna said as she pulled herself up to her feet, still holding on to the iron fry pan. "I'm old, and you ain't never passed by a second helping of noodles in your life."

Brother Qown frowned. "Dorna, whose side are you on?"

A whistle interrupted them. Brother Qown jumped backward, not from training as much as animal instinct. An arrow hit Dorna's fry pan, sending it flying.

Everyone stopped.

Count Janel's lips thinned. She no longer looked amused.

"Ow! Why'd you do that for? I weren't done cleaning that!" Dorna rubbed her hand and scrunched up her face in protest.

Brother Qown's heart beat so fast he thought it might turn into a rabbit and scamper away. The last bandits they'd encountered had been all pitchforks and long knives—close-combat melee weapons, which played to the count's strength. She looked so helpless; it always brought the wolves near.

Arrows were another matter. She possessed no immunity to arrows.

Neither did Qown nor Dorna.

The bandit tightened her grip on the sickle in her hand. "We're not here to entertain you, crone. Give over your valuables. Now." She pointed to Janel's family sword, sheathed and hanging by its belt from a thick branch. "Whose is that?"

Janel tilted her head. "Mine."

"Horse crap." The woman laughed. "I'll be damned if you could even lift metal so big. Where's your guard? Out in the woods, maybe, relieving himself?"

Brother Qown looked toward the trees. The leaves rustled as the bandit's men shifted position or expressed their impatience. Whoever had fired their bow either knew their business or had been blessed by Taja. But if they had more bows, if their main assault came as a volley of arrows . . .

Brother Qown suspected the count knew the danger, but she had a gleam in her eye, as if enjoying herself.

Brother Qown suspected she *was* enjoying herself.

He made a sign to the morning sun. He wondered what he'd done to upset Father Zajhera. Did this assignment serve as punishment?

"You're so convinced I must have a guard," Janel mused. "There's a saying about judging how fast a horse runs by the color of her coat. It may apply here." She stood then, brushing the remaining breakfast crumbs from her embroidered riding tunic before she bowed. "I offer you a deal."

"You think you're in a position to make deals?"

Brother Qown met Dorna's eyes. The old woman made the smallest gesture toward the large camphor tree near them, one with thick roots perfect for ducking behind. Janel always did well in fights, but Dorna and Qown needed a place to hide.

Count Janel waved the complaint aside. "You're the herd

leader. You're concerned about my guards, and rightly so; you don't want your people injured. So I suggest a compromise. A duel. I'll fight any of your associates—yourself, if you wish—using any weapon *you* choose. If you win, I'll give you everything I have. You have my word."

Brother Qown held his breath and watched to discover if the leader would take the bait and leap at that twitching, vulnerable tail . . .

The bandit said, "You must fancy I'm a fool or a weakling, and I'm neither."

"You *are* a robber." The insult had no sting to it; Janel's smile harkened back to a child at play with her new best friend.

She seemed so pleased to fight another woman. Few women in Jorat turned to robbery. The bands she'd faced so far had been male.*

The bandit put one hand on her hip. "You're getting on my nerves, little girl."

Janel laughed outright. "I might care more if you weren't robbing me."

"Now I'll take the sword too."

"If I'd been polite, would you have left it?"

"And that fancy ring." The woman pointed to the chain around Count Janel's neck.

The Theranon family sword and the Tolamer Canton signet ring. Brother Qown fought to keep from sighing out loud, but at least their would-be robber hadn't yet said no.

"And the deal," Count Janel pressed, "will you take that too?"

The outlaw paced, then gestured toward the sword. "Oh yes. Fine. Fight me, but not with your blade—the branch it hangs from is the weapon I choose for you."

Brother Qown couldn't help but blink. The proffered

---

* After the Lonezh Hellmarch, so many people insisted on moving to larger cities— under the hilariously mistaken impression that they'd be safer—it triggered an economic crash. By the time the fools figured out they had no job skills anyone gave a damn about, a whole bunch had lost their farms.

Result? Bandits.

"weapon"—a horizontal limb—spilled out from the main tree's trunk. The bough was as thick as Count Janel's arm; removing it required an ax.

They hadn't brought an ax.

The bandit saw the look on Qown's face, the raised eyebrows on Janel's. "Now we'll have no more games, little girl. All your valuables in the camp center and consider yourselves lucky we have no use for your horses."

Something moved in the woods behind them. In the distance, hooves galloped.

The woman must have believed the galloping signaled that much-feared guard, returning to protect his noble lady. "Circle out!" she cried. "Make ready!"

As the bandits focused on the imagined reinforcements, Janel Theranon, twenty-fourth Count of Tolamer, reached over and ripped away the tree branch. The crack of splintering wood echoed through the clearing.

"I accept your terms," said Janel. "Now let's begin."

The clearing stilled as the bandit leader realized her mistake. Brother Qown almost felt sorry for her. Who would ever think the count dangerous? Just a girl. So helpless.

The trembling, vulnerable worm wasn't a free meal after all.

The air smelled like green resin and old woodsmoke and the coming day's rain as men and women spilled from the woods. As many women as men, which startled Qown, but they didn't look any friendlier than their male counterparts.

"What are you doing?" the bandit woman asked, shocked from her silence. "By the Eight! Why are you leaving cover? Back into the trees, you lot!"

Brother Qown was at a loss as well. He didn't understand why her band had fled concealment instead of shooting when they had the chance. Mare Dorna and Brother Qown hadn't yet made a break for shelter. They were unshielded, unprotected.

The bandits not only left the woods but put away their weapons, slung their bows over their shoulders.

The biggest, a large man with black-splattered gray skin,

looked askance as he pointed to Janel. "She challenged you. You accepted." His expression suggested the explanation was obvious.

A second man tugged on the big man's sleeve. "Five chances the fancy mane goes down with the first hit."

Dorna straightened. "Ah, now you're running in my pasture. Put me down for ten thrones my count kicks your boss's ass." She tapped Brother Qown on the shoulder. "Priest, I need to borrow ten thrones."

"Dorna, no!" Brother Qown said.

"You have to spend metal to make metal, you know."

"You idiots," their boss snapped, "I wasn't serious!"

"This is *Jorat*." The big outlaw folded his arms.

A woman with a white blaze down the center of her face said, "You don't joke about contests in Jorat."

"Are you lot this *stupid*?" The bandit leader made no effort to hide her exasperation.

Janel laughed and bounced the branch in her hand. "You're not from around here, are you?"

At that moment, Arasgon trotted into the clearing.

In a sense, the bandit leader was right about Janel's guard. If the count ever needed an escort, Arasgon qualified. He'd been her loyal companion from childhood. His mere presence while traveling had proved so intimidating that Janel had ordered Arasgon to stay away from camp lest he ruin her trap. But Arasgon wore no armor, carried no weapons, and wasn't human at all.

The fireblood stood eighteen hands high, black as sable with a crimson mane and tail, what the Joratese call *flame-kissed*. The similarity to his cousin horse breeds ended there; red tiger stripes wrapped around his legs, and his eyes were the same ruby hue as his mistress Janel's. He'd have made a magnificent horse, but firebloods were not horses. As firebloods delighted in reminding anyone foolish enough to call them a "horse" within range of their hooves.*

---

* Please. Qown should consider himself lucky if a fireblood only smacked him with a hoof. They're omnivores: they have *fangs*.

Arasgon voiced a noise that sounded like a cross between a neigh and something far more deliberate and sagacious. Brother Qown knew it was language, proper language, but he couldn't understand a word, much to his endless frustration.

"I'm fine," Janel said, glancing back over her shoulder toward Arasgon. "She'll be no challen—"

Which was when the bandit kicked Janel in the head.

Three times.

The bandits cheered. They'd have broken out tankards and pennants if they could. And why not? Even with the fireblood's presence, revered almost to holiness by the Joratese, the outlaws had them outnumbered four to one. This wasn't a robbery; this was *entertainment.*

Easy enough to forget their leader fought a woman who could tear the limbs off trees.

Janel reeled from the blow, staggering so Brother Qown feared the fight would end right there. The brigand who had bet that outcome cheered.

Instead, Janel shook the fog from her head, her red eyes focusing on her attacker. "Oh, have we started? My mistake." She wiped the blood from her mouth, leaving behind her bright smile.

The bandit leader stopped in her tracks. "How are you still standing? I've knocked him cold with that move." She indicated the large man organizing the betting pool.

"I'm known for my stubbornness," Janel answered. She punctuated the statement by wielding the tree limb, forcing the other woman to jump to the side as the wood hit the ground.

The thief who had bet on an easy win groaned and handed coins over to another bandit.

Janel closed in again. This time, as the bandit leader ducked under the branch's swing, she also swept out with her leg, tripping Janel. The count just missed falling into the breakfast fire. Then the leader pressed her advantage, stomping down with her boot. Janel rolled to the side, putting a hand down into the burning coals as she stood back up again.

The cheering stopped, shocked.

Janel's right glove was on fire. She looked down, sighed, and tucked the tree branch under her arm while she stripped the fabric from her fingers. The pitch-black skin underneath was very different from her face's cinnamon hue. As far as Brother Qown could tell, she hadn't been burned at all.

"That was my favorite pair of gloves," she protested.

"Ah, foal," Dorna said, "'twas your only pair of gloves."

"That's what I said, Mare Dorna," Janel agreed. She steadied herself and swung the bough around her like a baton as she pointed at her adversary. "I underestimated you, thief."

"Oh, likewise." Wary concern tinted the woman's laughter. "You're wicked strong and sturdier than an ox, but you'll never win with a tree branch."

"Be grateful you didn't choose the sword."

The bandit's laughter held a nervous edge. "You'd have to hit me first. I'm faster than anyone else here."

The largest bandit turned to Dorna and confided, "It's true. She's the best fighter we have." He tapped his chest. "And I went professional in the circuit."

Janel smiled at her opponent. "I need only hit you once."

Brother Qown forced himself to stop clenching his fists. Every imperial dominion had their own stereotypes. Khorveshans were great soldiers. Kirpisari prided themselves on their magical aptitude. Yorans were barbarians. The Joratese loved horses . . .

But he wished someone had warned him about the Joratese people's love of *fighting*.

The whole time, Janel and the bandit leader circled each other, looking for another opening. The outlaw never attacked with her sickle, but she didn't discard it either. Whenever Janel swung, the woman twisted aside or deflected the tree limb. Janel always ended up as the one punched or kicked.

Eventually, the thief would wear the count down.

"Not too shabby," the woman said after Janel missed her for the umpteenth occasion, "but it's a shame no one ever trained you."

Janel lunged forward with the tree branch, and the bandit deflected, stepped to the side, and kicked her in the . . .

Her hindquarters, let's say.

Count Janel stopped playing around, or maybe she just lost her temper. When she came in again, she wasn't trying to dodge or avoid blows. She'd transformed into something relentless. The woman struck again, hard, but Janel just grunted, eyes narrowed. The count straightened and tossed the bough up in the air. It spun up and over end to end like a great leafy wheel.

She seemed unarmed.

Vulnerable . . .

The bandit leader didn't waste the opportunity; she attacked.

Janel moved fast, jumping up and to the side. She caught the tree limb as it came down and swatted the sickle away, sending the ersatz weapon flying. Then Janel reversed the branch and slammed it down on her opponent's leg, stretched out to deliver a hammer-like kick.

A loud crack split the air, followed by the bandit's scream.

The woman's leg bent in a way legs aren't supposed to bend. She fell to the ground, sobbing.

Janel threw down the tree branch.

"Oh no," she said. "I didn't mean—" She blinked and stepped back. "Brother Qown! Help us!"

He ran forward. "I'm here, I'm here. Let me get my bag . . ."

The largest bandit took in the scene and frowned, crossing his hands over his chest. "That's not how I figured this would go *at all.*"

Next to him, Mare Dorna held out a hand to gather her winnings.

2: A ROTTED FRUIT

Jorat Dominion, Quuros Empire.
Two days since Xaltorath started a Hellmarch in the Capital

Brother Qown paused, his voice breaking.

"Tea might soothe your throat better than cider," Janel said.

The priest nodded. "You're right. I'll go check the kitchen." He gave Kihrin a polite nod as he passed.

The resulting silence left Kihrin and Janel staring at each other.

Kihrin asked, "Did that really happen?"

"What? Qown checking to see if there's tea?" She rested her chin on a hand, grinned at him when he rolled his eyes. "Oh, you mean bandits attacking us."

Kihrin returned her smile. "No, I meant when you ripped the branch off that tree."

"Yes. I suppose that part *is* hard to believe."

Kihrin set his upishiarral aside. "The way you handled the stable door—I can't do that. My friend Star can't do that. We both tried. But you closed and barred the front door like it was made from sugar floss and compliments."

She raised an eyebrow. "Then perhaps that story is true."

"Why don't you tell this tale instead of Qown? Nice work on having your own chronicler, by the way*—but I doubt his version is unbiased."

---

* He doesn't understand his relationship with Thurvishar D'Lorus at all, does he? Or did Thurvishar forget to mention to Kihrin that he intended to fashion an entire historical account of dubious accuracy out of Kihrin's dialogues with that insane little mimic?

"And telling it from my viewpoint would be different? At least he remembered to document our travels. I was too distracted."

"Maybe I'd just prefer to hear it from you."

Their eyes met again.

Janel's mouth twitched. "Answer a curiosity for me. Stallions or mares?"

Kihrin blinked. "What?"

She leaned forward, mirroring his position at the table. "Do you run with stallions? Or mares?"

"I've never put any thought into my horse's gender—" He stopped. "But you're not talking about horses, are you?"

"Not in the least," she said. "There's a trap in there for people who don't understand our ways."

"How do you mean?"

"There are multiple meanings to how we use the words *stallion* or *mare*." She traced the table wood grain with a finger. "It's important to know the context, or you might end up in trouble."

"And *your* context right now?"

"The preferred sex of your bed partners, naturally." Mischief sparkled in her eyes. "Do you run with stallions? Do you run with mares?" She shrugged. "Some don't like to run at all, but that's not you, is it?"

Kihrin scraped his hand through his hair. "No, that's not me. Mares, then." Kihrin hesitated. "Why is that a trap?"

"Because it's the only time in Jorat where the words *stallion, mare,* and so on indicate the equipment between one's legs. Normally, when one refers to a human as a stallion or mare, we're discussing their gender."

Kihrin stared. "And you weren't talking about gender before? You're a woman. Isn't that what you mean by *mare?*"

Her mouth twisted. "You're conflating gender with sex. My sex—my body—is female, yes. But that's not my gender. I'm a stallion. And *stallion* is how Joratese society defines our *men.* So you're wrong; I'm most certainly not a woman."

Kihrin's eyes widened. "You just said you were female."

She sighed. "Who I am as a man is independent of"—she gestured to herself—"this. It wouldn't matter if I were male, female, or neither; I would still be a stallion."

Kihrin stared harder. "You're . . . a man." His gaze wandered down her tunic, lingered at her legs, then hiked back up to her face. "Obviously."

Janel rolled her eyes. "Again, you're conflating woman and female. I can't blame you; they must be synonyms in the west. But rest assured, they're not here." She looked down at herself, plucked the neck of her tunic. "Normally, when one uses *mare* or *stallion* to describe a person, they're talking about gender. And by that definition, I'm a man. But for sex, the rules change. Because then we're talking about aesthetic preferences, in which case"—she looked down at herself—"I'm most likely to meet the standards of someone who prefers female partners. I am in fact a female man." She smiled. "Do you see the trap now?"

He shook his head. If someone looked like a woman to him—Janel, for example—how was he supposed to act around them if they defined themselves as . . . a man? And how was he supposed to know the difference? He'd always assumed the equipment between one's legs was in fact an important part of figuring out who was a man and who was a woman.

But not according to Janel, and apparently not according to the rest of Jorat either. Oh, he saw the trap. He just wasn't sure he understood how it worked, let alone how to avoid it.

How long did it take Brother Qown to make tea, anyway? "Uh . . . I might need time to adjust to the idea. Do I refer to you as *he* or . . . ?"

"*She,*" Janel said. "We try not to confuse the rest of Quur too much."*

---

* Yeah, right. Luckily, the rest of Quur isn't paying attention to Jorat's rather remarkable social customs, or just how different they are from the rest of the empire. Consider that a good thing.

"I don't think it's working." Kihrin took a moment to collect himself. "So . . . what about you, then?"

"Me? I'm not confused on the matter at all."

"No, I mean, do you run with . . . stallions or mares?"

She raised her eyebrows at him. "Why would I run with just *part* of the herd?"

Kihrin was glad he hadn't been taking a drink. "Aha, why indeed." He smiled back. He liked her forwardness. He liked her unflinching lack of shame. And while Kihrin understood Janel had an agenda, she only had to meet his stare for a few seconds too long before he started to forget why that might be important. Kihrin knew this wasn't smart. Not smart at all.

Kihrin reached for her hand, anyway.

Brother Qown set down a tray laden with a kettle and cups.

Kihrin pulled his hand away. "You found tea. Great."

"Isn't it?" Brother Qown said. "I'm so pleased."

Janel said, "Brother Qown, shall I take a turn? It'll help save your voice."

"Are you sure?" Qown offered his book to her.

"That won't be necessary," Janel said. "I'll tell the story my way."

Kihrin almost laughed at the scandalized stare Qown gave her.

The priest recovered and poured himself a cup of tea. "Would you mind if I recorded your account, then?"

Janel blinked at Qown. "If you did what?"

Qown reached into his satchel and recovered another journal. "It's a spell I learned from"—he cleared his throat—"my old monastery. To document interviews for historical records. It's very subtle. You won't even know it's happening."

"Wait." Kihrin leaned forward. "You know a spell that will record everything we say? Because I'm familiar with that spell." His adoptive father, Surdyeh, had known how to do something very similar.

"Really? Oh, it's a lovely spell, isn't it? I can't even begin to tell you how many times it's saved my fingers from cramping—"

"You don't own a ruby ring, do you?" Kihrin's eyes narrowed.

Qown regarded him strangely. "What an odd question. No, I would never. Vishai priests live modest lives."

Kihrin pulled himself together. "Sorry. Of course."*

"Well," Janel said. "I, for one, don't mind if you record my account, Qown, so why don't I just begin?" Without waiting for his response, she did.

Janel's Turn. Barsine Banner, Jorat, Quur.

After I broke the woman's leg, I threw down the branch and stepped back, so Brother Qown might rush forward. Arasgon nosed around me, making sure I'd taken no serious injury. Not without cause; I already felt the bruises ripening along my jaw and ribs.

That woman kicked like Khorsal himself.

The other bandits dropped their weapons by the campfire, signaling surrender. I paid little attention to them, besides counting their number. Eight total, including their leader. I caught a few names in spite of my best efforts at apathy. The woman with the white stripe was named Kay. Someone else was named Vidan, although I wasn't sure who. Fool that I was, I didn't think them important other than as a method to raise funds.

Luck was with us since Barsine's capital seat, Mereina, was about to start their tournament, which the local baron was obligated to attend. We wouldn't have to wait long for our reward.

Brother Qown had been astonished the first time we had played bait the bandit. He couldn't understand why the other bandits never ran or fought once their leader was beaten. And while I tried to explain . . .

You see, everything in *our* world is divided into two concepts—

---

* Really, Kihrin? If Qown had been a Gryphon Man, did Kihrin honestly think the priest would have just admitted it? I think even Qown is more astute at espionage than *that*.

idorrá, the power and strength possessed by those who protect others, and thudajé, the honor gained from submitting to one who is superior. We hold trials, contests, and duels to determine the difference. This fosters good leadership and good community bonds. There is no dishonor in defeat either. Our bandit prisoners would find sympathy and pardon by showing their thudajé. Naturally, they would surrender. And naturally, they would be treated well.

How could one strong in idorrá do otherwise? Those who use their strength to oppress are nothing more than bullies and tyrants. We have a word for that too in our language: *thorra*.

I knew Qown didn't understand. Things were done otherwise across the mountains, to the west.

Everything, I think, is done otherwise in the west.

But in this particular scenario, one bandit had less thudajé than the others. A man with a laevos, the horse-mane hair we claim to hallmark our noble status. The same man who had bet on my defeat and lost. While all other eyes were on their former leader or Brother Qown, he stared at me.

"I know you," he said. "You're Janel Danorak, the Count of Tolamer's granddaughter."

Oh. How wonderful. He knew who I was.

I raised my chin even as I cursed my luck. "You're mistaken," I said.

Confusion flickered across his handsome face. He had dark gray skin and a white laevos, which must have been lovely once. He struck me as someone used to luxury turned to squatting in the woods, hiding from his enemies.

Much like myself, I suppose.

"I am?" He blinked his surprise.

"Yes. Once, I *was* the Count of Tolamer's granddaughter. Now I'm the Count of Tolamer." I forced my eyes back to his. "How do you know me? It's been many years since I've visited this banner. I expected no one here to recognize me."

His bitter smile mocked himself more than me. "I remember your visits from when we were children. You always convinced

Tamin to play with you and that fireblood. You'd ride back filthy after making castles in the mud or climbing trees. You're she, aren't you? You're Janel Danorak."

"My family name is *Theranon*. You're one of Baron Barsine's pledge men?"

"Was." A pained expression crossed his face. "But you *are* Danorak?"

The bandits had been a noisy gaggle of birds fretting over their leader's injury, but with that question, all talking stopped. Every eye turned to me.

I sighed. "I'm merely someone who ended up in a Hellmarch's path."

He chuckled. "Humble too."

"No, I'm not—" But I bit off the rest of my sentence without finishing. I had been warned my entire life never to tell what really happened at Lonezh Canton when the demons had rampaged through its borders. As a result, I never corrected people when they wove myths from my childhood horrors.

For those unfamiliar with Joratese history, Danorak was a fireblood. He rode Jorat's length and breadth for a week straight— without food, drink, or rest. He warned the human and fireblood herds to reach high ground before Emperor Kandor flooded the Endless Canyon to force our tyrant god-king into the open, where he could be slain.

Once Danorak had saved everyone, he dropped dead from exhaustion.

The Lonezh Hellmarch had started because some witch in Marakor had summoned a demon more powerful than they could control. The results were predictable and only ended after a large swath of Jorat and an entire canton—Lonezh—had been depopulated.

People started calling me *Danorak* afterward. Word spread I'd run for days, a step ahead of the demons, to warn Emperor Sandus about the invasion. They meant it as a badge of honor. Instead, it served as a reminder of how my life, my reputation, was based on a lie.

No one outruns demons, especially not an eight-year-old girl.

I didn't want to talk about the Hellmarch. So I turned my attention to Brother Qown, still patching up their leader. "Will she be able to travel?"

"I'm right here," the woman said, struggling to sit.

"Stop that," Brother Qown chided. "I haven't finished setting your leg."

"You touch my leg again and I'll show you how hard I can kick with the other one."

"I have to—" My priest turned to me for aid. "Count, please, would you explain to her that I'm trying to help?"

"Trying to get a peek at my legs, that's what you're trying to do."

Dorna laughed. "He ain't. Our Qown here is a gelding through and through." Her grin widened. "They are pretty legs, though. I'll look if he don't."

Qown closed his eyes and whispered a prayer.

"What's your name?" I asked the woman I had defeated.

She sniffed and looked away.

I tugged the mask from her face. She batted at my hand, but her strength had fled. Without its concealment, she looked Joratese enough: dark brown with an irregular rose splash across her left cheek and forehead. Her hair was straight and black. I guessed her age at twice my own.

But she wasn't Joratese.

She'd convinced an entire Joratese band to give her their thudajé. Perhaps they hadn't realized her true ethnicity.

Or perhaps she was just that good at kicking.

"She's Ninavis," said the man with the laevos. "We all call her Nina. She worked as a hunter around here before the baron declared this all his forest. His soldiers have moved whole villages out on pain of death. Families who've hunted these lands for generations are now poachers."

"Really, Kalazan?" Ninavis scolded. "Why don't you just go ahead and tell my name to the baron too!"

"It's fine to let *her* know," Kalazan said. "Don't you see, Nina? She's the one we've been waiting for." He turned back to me. "I'm Kalazan. The big man is Dango, and the man with the scarred face is Tanner. That's Kay Hará and Jem Nakijan, and standing next to them is Vidan and Gan—"

"Gan the Miller's Daughter," interrupted the indicated woman. She was young, beautiful, sported a gorgeous laevos, and if she was actually a miller's daughter, I was the Queen of Old Zaibur. "Kal, Nina's right. You shouldn't have said our names."

"It's her, Gan." He became animated, gesturing with his hands. "We've eked out a pitiful existence in these woods for months, while the baron and his damn captain burn down village after village looking for their prophesied threat. The demon-claimed child, remember? But what if *she* is the one they fear? What if it was always Danorak? Nothing in prophecy said it must be someone *local*."

I felt a lump form in my stomach, and a blossoming dread stretched over me from head to heel. I closed my hands in fists at my sides rather than succumb to the urge to pick up Kalazan by the neck and shake him by the scruff until answers spilled forth.

"What are you talking about?" I asked. "And be clear, for I loathe prophecy."

But we never finished the conversation.

Arasgon's senses are better than any human's. The fireblood screamed out, "Count, we're not alone!" just as three dozen armed men on horseback wearing Barsine Banner's gold-and-brown colors rode into the clearing from downwind.

They all had crossbows.

Or more specifically, they all had crossbows pointed at us.

Several bandits ran for their weapons, or the woods, or what little shelter they might find behind a tree root. Ninavis was in no condition to follow. Although Kalazan didn't run, I noticed both he and Gan the Miller's Daughter flipped up the hoods on their cloaks to hide their laevos hair.

"What have we here?" the guard commander said as he rode forward. "Hold your positions; no one move!"

"Ah, good," Arasgon said, trotting over to greet the newcomers. "We captured these strays. Now help us bring them to your herd master."

The guard captain ignored Arasgon. "You have nothing to say? Who's in charge here? Speak up!"

Arasgon blinked and looked back at me. I knew what he thought. No matter if these men looked Joratese; no native son of our fields would dare ignore a fireblood.

Unless they hadn't *understood* the fireblood.

Impossible. In ancient times, the god-king Khorsal had chosen us to care for his favored children—his firebloods. When those same firebloods joined humans in overthrowing Khorsal, our relationship had strengthened. Every Joratese child learns to understand our four-hoofed kindred.

But this soldier hadn't understood Arasgon's speech. Either he was an idiot, or he wasn't any more Joratese than Ninavis.

I'd bet metal on the latter.

I stepped forward. "I'm in charge here. I am Count Tolamer, traveling to Mereina to visit Baron Barsine."

He gave me a critical eye. I didn't look like a peasant—I had a well-groomed laevos, and my clothing was luxurious enough if one ignored the wear. If fashion and grooming could be faked, however, my idorrá was more difficult to counterfeit. I carried myself as a count.

"Oh yeah? Where are your guards?" he asked.

I heard a strained protest from the bandit leader, Ninavis.

I forced a pleasant smile on my face. "I'm accompanied by a fireblood. What more protection would any noble require?"

The man glanced over, finally realizing Arasgon's nature. Arasgon tossed his head up as he walked back to the bandits, gathered together in a dense, awkward cluster.

The soldier's leader dismounted. "I'm Captain Dedreugh. We've been hunting criminals who've been pillaging and burning villages along the river for almost a year. And this lot seems like a good fit for those crimes, so if you'll pardon us"—he motioned his men toward the bandits—"we'll take them off your hands."

Half his troops dismounted, trading crossbows for swords. Their expressions worried me, though. Nothing so simple as anger. This was the stalking predator's naked hunger; I saw one eye Ninavis on the ground and lick his lips.* That look had never known good intentions. A wave of fury filled me with a nasty warmth as I fought to keep my temper reined.

I placed my bare hand against Captain Dedreugh's leather breastplate.

"*I* captured them, Dedreugh," I said. "Defeated them and bound their thudajé to my idorrá. They're under my protection until I tender them to the baron. Directly to the baron."

The irony wasn't lost on me. Doing as Dedreugh asked *was* the original plan, you see. The trap's whole point. The other times I'd hunted bandits, I had turned them over to the local authorities without even learning their names. I never wanted to be responsible for them. I didn't wish to adopt ne'er-do-wells, but fill coffers left empty by my swift departure from my home in Tolamer.

There wasn't a banner, canton, or ward in the entire dominion that didn't offer a bounty for brigands. I had indeed meant to turn them over *easily,* in return for a bit of metal.

But here I was, claiming them under my idorrá, as if they were more important than garbage commoners, criminals, and robbers. Why was this group different? Was it because I'd lost my temper and injured their leader? I didn't know.

Maybe Captain Dedreugh just ran with the wrong gait.

"Captain," one soldier cried out, "that one in the back! It's *him!*"

Dedreugh tried to shove me away and stopped in surprise when he discovered he couldn't. Behind Dedreugh, the mounted

---

* This is the sort of situation where I find a good curse works wonders in convincing men to respect boundaries.

guard leveled their crossbows. The bandits—dear Khored, they were *my* bandits now, weren't they?—would never reach their bows before those soldiers fired.

Captain Dedreugh cut an intimidating figure. He stood at least a foot taller than I, his pale gray skin broken up by darker gray jaguar spots at his hairline. His eyes were ice colored. Although handsome enough, a stink lingered near him I didn't like, something lurking on the edge of rot no bath would cure.

"Out of my way." He sneered at me, and then added *my lord* as an afterthought, without the proper respectful qualifiers. "These criminals are wanted for treason and witchcraft. If you speak for them, I will have to level those charges against you."

"Captain, if these people committed crimes, they'll pay for them. However, they're under my idorrá now. So let's go to Mereina for judgment, as is proper."

"Woman—"

"Woman?" I raised an eyebrow in disbelief.

He frowned. "You have no say in the matter. Be grateful I'm willing to escort you back to the town." He bent down until his face hovered next to mine. "It's been a hard and dangerous winter. Anything might happen on the way back."

I stared at him, unamused and uncowed. "Is that so?"

"If you're real nice to me, I'll make sure you arrive—"

He made a gurgling noise as my hand closed around his throat.

I won't lie; I found myself tempted to tighten my grip until my fingers touched.

"I am the Count of Tolamer," I said. "I'm a stallion, not a mare. I'm not asking your permission; I'm giving you an order."

Despite his advantage in height, I still lifted him a few inches off the ground. He also blocked the line of sight his people might have used to shoot me.

"Uh . . . Count?" Dorna said. "I hate to interrupt your flirting, but you ought to see to the children—"

I glanced over. The soldiers were pointing their weapons at Dorna and Brother Qown and, yes, even Arasgon, although the nervous look in their eyes suggested they were less certain about the wisdom of threatening the enormous fireblood.

"Tell your people to back down," I said to Dedreugh. "Or they can watch as I rip your jaw from your face and choke you with your own tongue.* You don't use that tone with a *count*. Nor do you raise weapons against those under my protection. Do you understand me?" I paused as he made strangling sounds. "Blink if you do."

His fingers plucked at mine, but he blinked, then gasped and sputtered when I released his neck. "Lower your weapons!" he rasped to the men behind him.

When he finished, he turned back in a heated rage. "On your word, you'll help me bring these criminals in, or being a count won't save you."

I raised an eyebrow, wondering how Barsine Banner's ruler had been training his people. I remembered the baron as a hard stallion, fonder of the whip than the carrot. If Dedreugh's attitude proved anything, he'd grown worse over the passing years. "You seem confused, Captain. A baron is *lesser ranked* than a count. And I already offered to bring them in, didn't I?"

He backed away, glaring. He had poor thudajé. I had proved my idorrá over him, but he reacted with resentment, not honorable submission to my will. He was a bully, a thorra, one who thought their physical strength was the only strength that mattered when proving their right to dominate. I could see the threat in his stare: *Watch your back, or when I get my chance, you'll suffer for this humiliation.*

I narrowed my eyes. Our system had functioned for five hundred years. It worked because people understood their place.

He proved himself less by insisting on idorrá over me. Equally intolerable after I'd already forced him to submit. There have always been those who mistook idorrá and thudajé as synonyms for male and female.

Outsiders make this error.

---

* She's growing on me.

I would hardly have the right to call myself a count if I'd let someone of such common status treat me thus.

I whistled for Dorna's horse, Pocket Biter, and Brother Qown's gelding, Cloud, as I began to lower the deer we'd caught earlier from the tree. "Mare Dorna, Brother Qown, help tie up our friends while these men assist us in breaking camp. Ninavis, you'll ride Arasgon. I'll saddle our horses. The rest of you—don't make trouble."

The smile on Kalazan's face surprised me. I remembered his talk of prophecy, of a demon-claimed child. He had no fear. Of course he had no fear—the hero who would deliver them all from Captain Dedreugh and his men had arrived.

I didn't know if I wanted him to be right.

3: THE BARON'S JUSTICE

Jorat Dominion, Quuros Empire.
Two days since the death of Emperor Sandus

"Wait," Kihrin said. "The firebloods talk? Those horses in the stable can *talk*?" He pointed behind him for emphasis.

Kihrin had always spoken to Scandal as though she understood him. When he was a boy, he'd treated a cat named Princess the same way. People liked to regard their pets as family. That didn't mean the animals talked back.

"Oh no," Brother Qown said. "Now you've done it."

"What?"

"They're not horses," Janel insisted. "Firebloods are imperial citizens with full legal rights."

Kihrin's eyes widened. "Has anyone told the empire?"

Janel set her mug down firmly. "When Atrin Kandor liberated Jorat from the god-king Khorsal, he granted citizenship to both races the god-king had enslaved: humans and firebloods. Calling a fireblood a horse is like calling a human an animal. Yes, they talk." She crossed her arms over her chest. "It's not their fault you never learned to understand them."*

"Well, that puts a different slant on Darzin's attempts to breed Scandal." Kihrin made a face. "A rather obscene slant." Not that it would have changed his horrible brother's actions

---

* Khorsal didn't just muck about with centaurs and firebloods. Every horse in the Quuros Empire is descended from Joratese stock. Wouldn't surprise me if gaining control of Khorsal's herds was the real reason Kandor invaded. After all, Joratese horses aren't just stronger, faster, and sturdier; they also don't suffer from colic.

Khorsal *really* loved horses.

at all. In fact, it wouldn't have surprised Kihrin if his brother had known the truth about firebloods and tried, anyway. That sounded like Darzin.

"You call Hamarratus *Scandal?*" The tone in Janel's voice implied Kihrin had flunked a test.

"Is that . . . wait. Why do you think Scandal's name is Hamarratus?" Kihrin remembered Star mentioning the name to the old groom.

"Hamarratus told me in the stable," Janel said. "Remember, they can *talk.*"

Kihrin considered the sounds the horses—rather, the fire-bloods—had produced during the dragon attack. He'd assumed they were normal excited horse noises. Storm. Big dragon. Lots of danger. But speech?

Maybe.

"I realize this is a shock," Brother Qown told him. "Believe me, I sympathize."

"Star says she likes the name Scandal," Kihrin said. "I'll keep calling her that."

"Fine," Janel said. "If that's her choice rather than the pet name you gave a slave."

Kihrin's eyes narrowed. "She's not a slave."

"She'd better not be."

Brother Qown looked back and forth between the two. "Janel, may I take over reading? You can eat."

Janel pulled a bowl to her. "Yes. Please do."

Qown's Turn. The town of Mereina, Barsine Banner, Jorat, Quur.

Turning in the bandits for their reward required traveling to Mereina, Barsine Banner's local seat. It wasn't a happy trip. The guards joked and bantered the whole way, bragging as if they'd done anything more than arrive. In contrast, the outlaws were a dour bunch.

Brother Qown couldn't help but compare them with the

previous criminals they had captured, who had treated their situation like a game.

He'd been surprised. The rest of the Quuros Empire punished banditry with mandatory slavery. Here in Jorat, the men and women they arrested hadn't taken the matter with any solemnity at all. They had been criminals and happy to take metal by force, but they had treated their arrest as a grand lark. They had lost; the count had won. Well played.

Ninavis and her gang behaved differently.

The silence from both the bandits and Count Janel herself was thick and sullen. She gazed around her with narrowed eyes as if she expected an attack at any moment. The whole group's tension pulled tighter with each step toward their destination.

As they left the tree line, Mereina Castle came into view. Qown didn't recognize it at first. He only realized the building wasn't a watchtower or storage depot when the guards headed in that direction.

To be fair, it wasn't much of a castle.

The squat, square structure dated from antiquity, when all these lands dwelt outside the Quuros Empire. The border fortress had been repurposed into the local government seat. Gracing it with the label *castle* was like comparing his native Eamithon's gently rolling hills with the Dragonspires.

The "town" resting in a valley below the castle plateau differed from the clay brick, wood, and stone structures used in western Quur. Instead of houses, private patios and arbors covered the valley. Flags and banners flew from the posts. In a high wind—or even a low wind—the town became a sea of waving cloth. Pretty, but useless for protecting anyone from the storms for which Jorat was so infamous.

Horses and elephants wandered through the streets. Dholes—a dog breed with fox-like features—roamed streets or stayed close to family patios.

But where were the houses?

The only structures resembling buildings nestled on the same plateau as the castle: hundreds of Joratese tents called *azhock*. Formed from fabric and hides stretched over a wooden frame, the azhock were large enough to house men and horses both. These temporary homes sheltered the tournament travelers: merchants, traders, farmers, and those who represented their interests in the event itself.

The captured bandits walked before Brother Qown and Dorna, apart from Ninavis, who rode astride Arasgon. Count Janel journeyed with the outlaws too, refusing to ride with Captain Dedreugh or the guards, although she'd been content enough to let them carry the deer carcass intended as a guest offering for the baron. Brother Qown suspected Janel escorted the prisoners to make sure no one molested them. He recognized his naïveté, but even he noticed the way the male soldiers eyed the female brigands.

The Joratese have a word for this: *thorra*. The word literally means "a stallion who is not safe to leave with other horses."

It is never a compliment.

The road to the castle took them through the fairgrounds. More than one person peeked from otherwise quiet camp flaps and then ducked back.

A black-skinned girl with silver dapples and coarse gray hair dashed from one tent to another, spreading news of their arrival. Seconds later, a larger dappled man, a blacksmith by his apron and thews, stepped outside an azhock and watched the group, wiping his hands off on a towel. His disapproval lingered long after they passed.

The hate wasn't directed at Brother Qown, Dorna, Janel, or the bandits. The smith reserved his anger for the guards. A young man, fur clad, paused while hooding one of the eagles the Joratese often used for hunting. He seemed about to unleash his bird against the escorts, but another hunter held him back with a hand on his arm.

The townspeople recognized the outlaws, but not with malice. They were not the enemy here; the guards were. The whole town eyed them like the baron's men were lions wandering into their meadows. Thorra—bullies—to put it mildly.

Brother Qown felt chilled. Jorat wasn't a dominion he associated with rebellion.* Joratese society rested on the idea each member in it accepted their place. This hatred for the banner's soldiers stood out like a thunderstorm in an otherwise cloudless sky.

As the group continued toward the castle, Kalazan flipped around and walked backward to address his companions. "It's been an honor and a privilege. You're the best of people. Let no one tell you otherwise."

The largest bandit (Brother Qown thought he was Dango) snorted. "Ah, Kalazan. Save your sweet talk. We ain't even married yet."

Kalazan gave Dango a sad smile. "In my next life, perhaps. I think I'll lie on the Pale Lady's wedding bed tonight, not yours." His eyes met another bandit's, the young woman with laevos hair named Gan the Miller's Daughter. His sad smile turned bitter.

Dorna turned back to Count Janel, who watched the exchange with a flat expression. A funny look crossed Dorna's face. "Couldn't we—"

"Keep walking, damn it," Captain Dedreugh ordered.

"No burial speeches just yet, Kalazan," Ninavis said. "We're not done here."

"You will be soon enough," Dedreugh snapped. "Now move, or I'll use my sword."

"Let's continue," Count Janel suggested.

They kept walking.

Brother Qown had assumed Mereina Castle would be comfortable since this banner's rulers called it home. He realized his mistake. The stone walls had been made for security, not comfort, but in this age of modern magical siege-craft, they were long since obsolete. The castle was stuffy, cold, and cramped. He

---

* That's because no one appreciates the Joratese insistence that bad rulers step down or be overthrown. Rebellion is steeped in their blood. Consider: they're the *only* dominion to overthrow their own god-king.

suspected when the summer rainy season arrived it would be stuffy, hot, and cramped. At no point did the fortress seem a pleasant place to live. The azhock tents appeared much more practical.

Qown pined for a House D'Talus Red Man to cast a warming spell, but given the local superstitions about magic, he didn't like his chances of finding one.

Despite its lack of comforts, the castle had beautiful original features: wooden corbels made from cypress and Tung wood, carved with horse motifs. Tapestries, old and faded, hid the crumbling walls. Lanterns—sun patterns burned into their stretched hide covers—cast painted shadows over the tile floors. The fortress hadn't strayed far from its military roots; armed men and women camped in the courtyard, horses left to mill in the mud-churned yard.

The guards paused at the gate while Dedreugh sent a messenger inside for the baron.

"Preparations for the tournament," Captain Dedreugh explained to Janel. Between their first encounter and final destination, Dedreugh had decided to impress the count, transforming from belligerent to obsequious.

"I see," she replied.

He grinned, a gleam in his eyes. "I'll be competing myself."

She looked at him sideways. "How nice for you."

"I'm going to win," he confided.

Her jaw set against her neck in a manner that suggested the grinding of teeth. Brother Qown watched her for any sign she might be rash. Not that he could stop her. He just needed to know which way to jump.

Captain Dedreugh leaned toward her. "I always win."

That time she focused on him. "The baron doesn't consider that a conflict of interest? Don't you oversee who's arrested?"

As Captain Dedreugh pulled himself up to counter the accusation, the double doors leading into the castle were flung open.

The Baron of Barsine marched into the courtyard.

The baron was dressed in sumptuous attire, far more opulent

than Count Janel ever wore. Still, he didn't match the priest's expectations. Golden skinned and fine featured, he was also young.

As young as Count Janel herself.

"Tamin." Janel laughed. She threw out her arms in delight as the baron gave her the traditional Joratese greeting: forehead to forehead, hands placed behind each other's necks. She cradled him like the finest porcelain, her touch so gentle it would be easy to mistake her delicacy for shyness. "I've brought you a gift for your fires and goodwill for your herd."

"And I welcome you as a guest to my fields," he said, finishing the formal greeting. "I'm so sorry about your grandfather," Tamin said when they parted. At Count Janel's surprised blink, he added, "My men told me the Count of Tolamer had arrived. Yet instead of your grandfather, I find you."

"He died in his sleep," Janel said. "His heart failed him." She stepped back. "But you . . . where's *your* father? I expected to see him—?" The words tripped and tangled.

"He didn't die in his sleep, but die he has. Murdered by a vile cabal, including my castle steward. I'm told I have you to thank for bringing me the last of my father's assassins." Tamin looked past her, toward the bandits.

Brother Qown shouldn't have been surprised at what happened next. Tamin, Baron of Barsine, walked past Count Janel to where Dedreugh's soldiers watched the prisoners and stopped before Kalazan.

Tamin slapped the man.

Kalazan grinned. "Nice to see you too, Baron." Shockingly, he dispensed with the Joratese suffixes, the cases showing respect: *my* baron, *my* lord.

Brother Qown wasn't fluent in Karo, the old Joratese language, but he recognized the insult. Kalazan had, with a single word, denied Tamin's status as his liege. He declared Tamin *unworthy* to be his liege.

Baron Tamin would have taken it as a mortal insult even if the words hadn't come from his father's accused murderer.

"Is this the part where I'm supposed to throw you into the dungeon until your little friends can organize a rescue?" Tamin asked. Without waiting for an answer, he waved his hand at Dedreugh. "Kill him."

"No!" cried Gan the Miller's Daughter. She threw herself forward, so suddenly and unexpectedly she caught the soldier off guard. The rope tied to her hands pulled the next person in line, Vidan, off balance too. He yanked Jem Nakijan's rope, who fell. Jem's bonds wrenched Kalazan's.

His ties came undone.

The soldiers may have been caught off guard, but not Kalazan. He stole a sword from a guard's belt, slicing the man's side as he pulled the weapon free. Another guard stood close enough to act, but Ninavis's foot caught the man under the chin before he moved, sending him tumbling backward.

Arasgon reared up on his hind legs, screaming as Ninavis fell to the ground. Her short cry ended in sobbing as she landed on her injured leg.

Kalazan grabbed Count Janel from behind and placed his sword's edge against her throat.

"Stop!" Tamin cried out. "Everyone, stop!"

The courtyard stilled. All present paused as they noticed Kalazan's hostage.

Brother Qown heard Kalazan whisper, "Apologies, my count."

He noticed Kalazan had remembered the correct form this time. *My* count. *My* liege.

"Leave her be," Baron Tamin ordered.

Kalazan smiled as he pressed the sword harder against Janel. He pulled her back toward the gate entrance.

Count Janel didn't speak. She clenched her jaw, her hands tight fists at her sides. Brother Qown recognized the signs well enough. Kalazan had seen Janel fight Ninavis. Didn't he understand what would happen if she defended herself?

"Let her go," Tamin repeated.

"Not yet," Kalazan said. "It's rude, I know, but your reception's been so cold I've little choice but to refuse your hospitality." He backed up toward the archway.

"Very well," Tamin said.

Kalazan smiled.

"Shoot through her," Baron Tamin ordered.

Every eye present stared at him in disbelief.

Every eye but those owned by Dedreugh and his soldiers, who followed orders.

Much happened then.

First, Kalazan pushed Janel forward, away from him. Arasgon shielded Janel with his body. The crossbows fired, or rather *misfired,* as their drawn strings snapped, all at once. Of the crossbows that discharged, one bolt hit Arasgon's saddle, and another missed him by a coin's width. The remaining soldiers didn't waste their ammunition attempting to find a mark. Given his size, Arasgon made an excellent wall.

Kalazan ran.

He skipped the main doors and darted to the side. He then slipped through a door behind a bulwark, even as soldiers found the clear shot they needed.

"After him!" Dedreugh screamed. "After him!"

The soldiers were quick to give chase, although some stayed to keep an eye on the prisoners.

Dedreugh crossed back over to the guard who'd lost his weapon. He grabbed the man by the jerkin and lifted him right off the ground, giving him a violent shake. "Idiot! Take these filth to the jail, and if anything goes wrong, I swear you'll join them."

Brother Qown rushed to Nina's side. The woman was unconscious, which didn't surprise him. Landing on her broken leg must have been excruciating.

Still, she was alive.

While Brother Qown looked over Nina, he heard the others debating another prisoner.

A soldier: "What about this one?"

Tamin answered, "She's saelen, is she not? If she wants to

slum with thieves, so be it. Put 'Lady' Ganar with her own kind."

Saelen.* Brother Qown remembered his Karo lessons. Lost, or a stray. A terrible insult by Joratese standards. Almost as bad as *thorra,* but with the implication the subject is a small child who doesn't understand what's in their own best interest. His heartbeat skipped. For a second, he thought Tamin referred to the count. But no. Tamin meant Gan the Miller's Daughter, gnashing her teeth and straining to reach the baron with fingers hooked into claws. She'd have made his beautiful face much less so if her hands had been free.

Tamin had already turned to Count Janel. "I'm so sorry for this unfortunate incident."

She raised an eyebrow. *"Shoot through her?"*

"My men are the best marksmen in the whole dominion," he assured her. "I had no fear at all for your safety." He gestured toward the main castle entrance. "Shall we? I'll have my men deliver your gift to the kitchen for the evening meal."

Meanwhile, two guards bent down next to Brother Qown and picked up Ninavis.

"She's injured," he told them. "You must be careful. Let me follow, and I'll treat her wounds."

They paid Brother Qown not the slightest attention.

"What happens to the other saelen?" Count Janel sounded bored, the question asked for propriety's sake. When she saw Brother Qown approaching, she made a small motion with her hand as a warning: *I will handle this.*

"Oh, the usual—we'll award them at the tournament," Tamin said. "Kalazan's fate is already sealed. We'll capture him soon enough."

A scream rang out.

Brother Qown might have thought it signaled the promised capture, except Gan the Miller's Daughter laughed outright, and Dango, still bound, smiled.

---

* I loathe this concept. All manner of garbage can be justified by saying they're doing it for someone's "own good."

"This Kalazan," Janel said. "Is he familiar with the castle?"

Tamin's expression soured. "He was the steward's son."

"Ah."

Tamin scowled and gestured to Dedreugh. "Damn it. Find him and kill him. I'll not have him live to see the sunrise, do you hear me? And then figure out which idiot made a mess of tying Kalazan's hands and have him flogged."

Brother Qown made sure his eyes were on the ground, lest his glance betray him. Only when the soldiers had cleared away the prisoners, and Captain Dedreugh had left to oversee the search, did he let himself look up. Qown stared at the person who had tied Kalazan's hands.

Mare Dorna hummed a dirty song to herself, smiling.

Brother Qown followed the guards into the castle, then stopped when one, a hulking fellow with gray skin and black blotches around his eyes, turned back.

"What are you doing?" the guard demanded.

Brother Qown pointed to the trussed prisoners being carried or led farther into the building. "I need to treat them."

"They don't need treating," the same man growled.

Brother Qown smiled, shaking his head. "The count gave explicit orders. I must care for their well-being."

And prove a complication. Brother Qown had seen the looks the guards had passed between themselves the entire ride back to Mereina Castle. The prisoners would be fair game to whatever molestations the soldiers devised, as soon as anyone who might care left.

The fact this behavior was abnormal for Jorat wouldn't stop it from happening here.

"See them in the morning," the guard ordered.

"But what about the blood sickness?" Brother Qown asked.

The whole group, guards and prisoners both, stopped.

"What was that?" said one man.

"The Falesini blood sickness," Brother Qown repeated, elaborating. "It's not very contagious. Nothing requiring a full quarantine or the like, but communicable through blood or other fluids." Qown started over. "I mean, you'll catch it if you touch them with your bare skin. The bandits all showed the symptoms. We were planning to treat them as soon as we settled everyone in, but in all this excitement—"

The first guard blinked, then guffawed. "What nonsense is this? These people aren't sick." He waved a hand as if dismissing the entire tale.

Brother Qown raised a finger and pointed at Dango.

The large man had his hands tied behind his back, and he frowned at Brother Qown. But the brigands didn't object to Brother Qown's story, which had been his worry.

Fresh blood dripped from Dango's nostril.

Dango didn't have to copy panic, because the panic was real. Brother Qown hoped the giant man was smart enough not to let it get the better of him.

Dango wrinkled his nose as if fighting off a sneeze. "It's starting again, priest."

"Yes," Brother Qown said, "but at least we found it before you bled from your eyes."

The guards stepped back.

Brother Qown waved his hands. "Oh, don't worry. There's no danger as long as you avoid any skin-to-skin contact."

A soldier pulled his sword.

"What the hell are you doing?" the leader barked.

"They're sick—" the man pointed.

"Shut up and drag them downstairs. Wear your damn gloves if you must. The captain wants them alive, you understand. They're no good to us dead." The leader turned back to Brother Qown. "This won't kill them, will it?"

"Oh no. It's treatable." He tugged on his satchel. "I need to make a tisane for them. It should clear up in a few days."

"We don't need a few days as long as they're well enough to stand tomorrow." The guard waved to his men, motioning for them to lead the outlaws down some steps. Brother Qown assumed these led to the castle dungeon. The guards who had been giving hungry looks to the prisoners looked a lot less interested now. In fact, most left at once.

Nobody made a fuss this time as Brother Qown followed them down into the prison. To be fair, it was more like a wine cellar, a cool, dark space where one might safely secure the best of the local lord's bottles. If so, the wines had been removed, although a few stray boxes stacked up in rows suggested that using the space for storage was still an option. The basement was clearly not meant to serve for living quarters. He couldn't imagine being imprisoned there for any length of time.

He was unsure if such was a good sign or a terrible one.

The soldiers divided the prisoners. They also traded out the prisoners' ropes for chains, which were fastened to iron rungs set in the walls. There was a bucket for necessities and a well.

Brother Qown pulled up a pail of water while the guards remembered they'd volunteered to find Kalazan. He then set about performing procedures with herbs—ones that might look serious to anyone without medical training.*

A last guard found himself a chair and settled in by the door, which was barred from the outside. Additional guards waited in the hallway.

Brother Qown stopped at each prisoner, offering them the water.

Dango whispered, "How did you—?" He sniffed his nose for emphasis.

Brother Qown wiped the blood from the man's face. "Trade secret. We shouldn't talk about it here."

Dango nodded. "Thank you. Someone was going to try something and end up with their throat ripped out. You could tell."

Brother Qown paused. He suspected Dango wasn't speaking in metaphor. Joratese women had a certain reputation. Qown replied, "The count won't stand for this. We'll be back for you."

Brother Qown walked around the room, handing out drinks

---

* In Jorat, that's very nearly everyone.

to the prisoners and pretending to treat them for a disease they didn't have. Kay Hará seemed so genuinely terrified that Qown thought they were either taking the story at face value or had spent a considerable length of time in theater. Jem Nakijan wouldn't even look at him. Vidan asked the priest to treat Gan instead, and acted put out when Qown insisted on seeing to everyone. Tanner said nothing, but his gaze softened into something less murderous when Brother Qown gave him water. The guards had searched the outlaw, but Qown suspected they hadn't searched him well enough. That might have been his imagination, though. Tanner just struck him as the sort who always had knives.

He stayed the longest with Ninavis because of her injury. Her fall from Arasgon—and the unconsciousness that followed— gave him a chance to set her break. The priest would have liked to have done more, but he sensed the remaining guard's eyes on him as he treated her. Brother Qown didn't wish to risk the guard recognizing magic if he saw it. Anyway, everyone knew Ninavis had a broken leg. He'd be doing her no favors if she'd healed by morning.

After seeing to the others, he left to talk tactics with the count.

4: THE DEMON-CLAIMED CHILD

Jorat Dominion, Quuros Empire.
Two days since the first day of Gadrith
D'Lorus's reign

"Falesini blood sickness? That truly exists?" Janel looked over at Brother Qown.

Behind her, tavern regulars organized an elaborate game throwing shaped rocks at a slanted clay board. A betting pool formed.

The priest coughed into his hand. "Oh yes, very much so. It's a hemorrhagic fever contracted from a desert mouse's dried urine. Just one reason cats are so popular in Khorvesh." He added, "It's never broken out in Jorat. Wrong climate."

"Very sneaky," Kihrin said. "But I'm not surprised, considering."

The other two paused.

"Considering what?" Brother Qown said.

Kihrin waved a hand at Brother Qown's robes. "You're a priest of the Mysteries. I knew a devotee once. You lot are tricky."

"I beg your pardon," Brother Qown said. "I am not 'tricky.' I'm very dedicated to helping others find both physical and spiritual harmony."

"Perhaps he's a touch tricky," Janel said, grinning.

Kihrin continued, "Wasn't your order illegal?"

Brother Qown cleared his throat. "That was politics.* All sorted out now. And our faith has always been accepted in Eamithon." Then he brightened. "But you know someone who follows the Way? That's wonderful! There aren't many of us."

"Sure. He fenced my spoils."

"I'm sorry, what?" Brother Qown's eyes widened.

Janel gave Kihrin a curious look as he chuckled. "You didn't grow up in a palace, did you?" she remarked.

"And you did," he pointed out. "Clearly."

"It wasn't a palace," Janel said. "It was a castle."

"Forgive me. That's *completely* different. Still, I notice you're not using the noble title anymore," Kihrin said. "Why is that? And why call yourself *count* and not *countess*?"

"Isn't *countess* a Quuros title for a male ruler's wife?" Janel shrugged. "If so, I don't qualify."

"It's also used for a female ruler," Kihrin pointed out.

"What a strange thing to label. We don't care if our rulers are male or female. We only insist they're stallions."

Behind her, a large gray-skinned man splashed with black achieved some victory at the rock-tossing game. He shouted and marched around the room, fists in the air. Cheers, claps, and a few boos heralded this win before the noise settled back down again.

"Did you know the Joratese native language, Karo, doesn't even acknowledge gender?" Brother Qown said. "Only positions of authority or obligation. And in practice, I've found at least three distinct genders in use. Well, two genders and a third catch-all term, but still—"

As Kihrin looked wide-eyed, Janel put aside her bowl. "I'd better take a turn or this will transform into a lecture on Jorat social structures. He's done it before."

---

* No, that was one of the religion's core tenets: "Hey, did you know the gods are just wizards who are really good with spells? Maybe you shouldn't worship them." Seriously, I'm amazed the Vishai faith was ever legalized anywhere.

"Uh, right," Kihrin said. "That might be for the best."

Janel nodded. Then sat there.

Just when Kihrin assumed she'd changed her mind, she began speaking.

Janel's Turn. Mereina Castle, Barsine Banner, Jorat, Quur.

No matter who we are or what our background, thief or noble, priest or witch, we always want to be our story's hero.

No, that's not right.

We don't want to be.

We *need* to be our story's hero.

We all imagine we must be. No one ever judges themselves a fool or a knave. I suppose if they do, they invent some plausible fiction to justify their deeds. We all see the world thus. We all interpret our every act as an epic tale's culmination, centered on ourselves. Is it arrogance or our limited ability to perceive the universe through eyes other than our own? If ours is the only perception we can experience, does it not follow that ours is the only perception that matters?

The result is the same. We bend the rules, break them, and ignore them. We put our own needs before others. That's what a hero does, is it not? Are we not entitled to be special exceptions? Just this once? And the next time too?

This time is different. *This* time it's important.

I was reflecting on the bandits, of course. Not myself.

They deemed themselves heroes. And as I was raised to believe myself entrusted with protecting these lands, it followed I must judge them criminals, yes? Robbing strangers on the road doesn't define courageous action.

And yet . . .

Kalazan's words burned at my edges like a curse waiting to flare incandescent.

They were waiting for the demon-claimed child, he'd said.

Damn him.

Worse, how could I miss the way Tamin had stocked his

troops? Soldiers who didn't understand the language of fire-bloods. Soldiers who treated me as a mare despite my stallion attire. The joyful gleam in Tamin's eyes when he'd ordered his men to shoot *through* me.

Baron Tamin's plan to execute Kalazan proved the final point against him. One didn't protect the herd by killing the saelen, the strays. And if Kalazan, his father, and others had conspired to assassinate the former baron, then it meant they had tried Censure. Tried and *failed* to remove an unworthy ruler.

I couldn't believe the old baron so dishonorable that he wouldn't have stepped down before the situation ever became so dire.

Tension stifled dinner. Under normal circumstances, I would have expected the castle to be packed to overflowing with friends and guests eager to partake in the feast. Instead, the main hall seemed nearly empty. While I was the only one who'd brought my own game (only proper by the requirements of idorrá), the baron had bought or hunted a great deal of his own. Unnecessarily, as it turned out. Most of the fresh meat slaughtered for the tournament celebration—prepared in any of the several proscribed tamarane styles—went uneaten.

I knew why.

The guards still hadn't located Kalazan. Tamin was polite enough to me at dinner. After all, was I not an old friend? (Not to mention higher ranked.) But his temper encouraged most guests to avoid the dining hall.

One soldier swore he'd hit Kalazan in the back with a crossbow. They'd even found a blood trail, but no body. No clear proof the "traitor" had journeyed south to the Afterlife for Thaena's final judgment.

Later, I watched, envious, as people drifted away from dinner in twos and threes. I had just come of age when Sir Oreth had shown up on my doorstep with his eviction orders and his threats. There'd been no time for adult celebrations and adult games.

However, this didn't seem the time to make up for that lack.

I rehearsed my excuses in case Tamin, his other guests, or—gods help me—the odious Captain Dedreugh turned chest or hindquarters in my direction. "No, I'm sorry, it's my red moon, but thank you for the compliment." "I'm still in mourning for my grandfather and wouldn't feel it proper to engage in bed sports."

Or my favorite, the one I could never say to Tamin no matter how much I meant it: "No, and don't ask again. I may be nice enough to look upon, but I'm a monster of the first rank. I'd rip you limb from limb—no matter how fondly I remember wintering here when we were children."

Looking back, I don't know why I worried so. As I was the highest-ranked titled noble in attendance, everyone would have waited on me to approach them. Technically speaking, rank and idorrá–thudajé relationships are kept separate from bed play, but I'm skeptical that's ever true.

So no one approached me, and Tamin never asked. For all I knew, Tamin had decided he preferred to run with stallions, anyway.

Tamin assigned us a fine suite of rooms, though. They seemed less fine when I realized the truth. They must have belonged to Kalazan's family and his father, the unnamed steward executed for his part in the late baron's assassination.

I couldn't help but wonder just how many people had been claimed as part of that "cabal." The castle's neglected air suggested more staff, more people, had once walked its halls. But who was I to judge? That was true of my home as well.

The last Hellmarch had been hard on everyone in Jorat.

"Am I making a mistake with the bandits?" I asked Dorna later as she unbraided and combed out my hair.

Dorna tsked under her breath. "We need the metal."

"Not that," I said. "They threw themselves under my idorrá, and I did nothing when those men came to collect them."

"You're young," Dorna said, her most common excuse for many otherwise unforgivable sins. "I bet Ninavis and her people thought they'd sway you better than the son of the man they'd

THE NAME OF ALL THINGS   69

murdered. Nicer odds. Taja's dirty luck for them the soldiers found us, before those bandits delivered the full pitch."

"What if they're right?" I asked. "Something *is* wrong here. And what Kalazan said about the demon-claimed child—"

Dorna grabbed me by the chin, startling me. "Offal and dung, foal! Anyone paying even half-assed attention knows what happened to you at Lonezh Canton—"

I nudged her hand away. "No, they don't. You know that. I'm Janel *Danorak*. No one knows; who else survived? Without witnesses, truth twists into rumor. Rumor distorts into myth. Jorat needed a symbol—so they invented their own."

"Always wondered why that fancy high general never set the record straight."*

I sighed. "He told everyone Xaltorath led the Hellmarch. Which is true." I lowered my head for a moment, closed my eyes, inhaled. "I suppose this 'demon-claimed' label just hits too close to home."

"I still say it's chance. Nothing but chance. Anyhow, we're lucky to lose those outlaws. That lot was trouble, mark my words."

I looked away, certain we were not even slightly rid of them. "Maybe I *should* have married Oreth—"

She scoffed louder. "Oh, that would have worked real well. Both of you stallions, and he's never forgiven you for it. Sir Oreth don't just want to ride you, he wants to break you." She set her hands against her hips. "Can't believe the baron didn't ask you to stay with him tonight. That one wants for a strong rider, mark my words. You'd be perfect for each other."

The blood flowed to my cheeks. "It's not his place to make that suggestion, Dorna. That role is mine."

"He still shoulda turned his quarters. Rude not to."

"Only to hear my refusal? Much less embarrassing for him that he didn't."

She blushed then, her expression showing less chagrin than

* But did you, Dorna? Did you *really*?

guilt. "Aw, foal . . . maybe once we're done here. Atrine might be a better place to find someone—"

I was in no mood to discuss bedchamber politics. "Enough, Dorna."

"Go rest, child. We've a big day tomorrow."

I nodded despite how I dreaded sleep and all it brought. "Yes. Thank you, Dorna."

Of course, I delayed slumber as long as I could.

As long as I ever could.

But Hell always claims me eventually.

I loathed sleeping. I hated it even though it came easily. I never have any trouble drifting off, sleep taking me the moment my eyes close.

Perhaps because what I do isn't, technically, sleep.

We live in a universe divided into two worlds, Life and Death. If I spend my waking hours here among the living, my sleep belongs to the goddess Thaena.*

I die, you see.

Every night, I die.

I shut my eyes and opened them again, no longer in Mereina.

I stood in a clearing in shadowed woods under storm-red skies. My nightclothes were gone. Instead, I wore plate armor, made from metal so dark it absorbed all the light, a silhouette darker than the night.

I arrived with weapon drawn, something other than the Theranon family sword. Nor was the armor the same I had inherited from my grandfather, tucked away inside my traveling valise. In the Afterlife, I had no physical body to wear real armor or weapons. It was all in my mind—or rather, all in my souls.

A ghost village spread out before me. Not ghostlike in some poetic sense, hollow buildings left skeletal in abandonment. The village haunted the air in spectral hues, phosphorescent blues and violets lingering in transparent phantasms.

---

* Oh, well, that's something it would have been helpful to know!

And it wasn't abandoned.

Its residents remained, murdered right alongside their homes. All of them, village and villagers, had died together.

The village's citizens struggled against their ties, nailed to its trellises and arbor posts, trussed up like so much livestock after the slaughter. Demonic runes painted on azhock walls with glowing human blood. I'm not sure if the people had perished from sword strike or when the cellar homes and patios had been set ablaze, but die they had, even though they screamed still. They writhed and begged for someone to cut them down, to release them from their torment.

They wouldn't have to wait long; the demons had come to feast.

Too many demons.

I felt more than heard the first wave, a vibrato bark sending shudders of anticipation trembling over my skin. The hellhounds bayed, their pitch excited as they tracked the sacrifices left for them. They would eat most souls trapped there. They would choose a few for worse.

The demon-hound howls grew sharper as they scented me.

It's my curse, you see. In the Afterlife, I burn hotter than everything around me. I glow from the fire I bring with me. And demons do so love heat. Few have the willpower to divert to other, easier prey once they have caught my scent.

I have wondered if I had reversed cause and effect. Was I this way because of the Hellmarch demons who found me in Lonezh? Or did those demons target Lonezh Canton because they'd been drawn to my fire?

Enough of that.

My point is they always pursue me, assuming me the hind in their hunt, a timid deer to be chased down and savaged.

I had grown content with the arrangement.

I was the trap already baited.

I smiled as I spun around, sword taking the first hellhound through the skull, splattering black ooze across the dead ground as I cleaved it in twain. The second hound leaped, bit at my armor, gnawing against the metal plate. I laughed and slammed the creature against the earth, rewarded with the sweet sound of breaking bones.

More hounds followed. And died.

These were the younglings, the newest infected, the weakest, and the least experienced. These demons were still acclimating to the torture of their new existence, cursed to hold ignoble shapes until they proved their worth. The dogs died easily.

Next came the riders.

Older and craftier, they didn't rush to their deaths the way the hounds had. They'd developed individual personalities, a preference for their appearance. Nothing original: skulls and horns and fangs are always popular. Demons prefer forms mortals find frightening: the rotting dead, monsters from myth, god-king tales.

We find human fear delicious.

I mean, they do.

A demon with a rhinoceros's skeletal head shook a spear at me. "Begone, whore. A feast has been readied for us."

I laughed and bounced the gore-soaked flat of my blade against my palm. "Then come take your due, but you'll work for this supper."

This demon group wasn't stupid enough to attack me one at a time. They wouldn't have survived long in the Afterlife by being unobservant. They must have seen how well that tactic had served the dogs.

It mattered not. All demons take a savage delight in slaughter.

In this, I was no different.

I stepped to the side as a demon on a skeletal steed's back tried to run me through, setting his twisting reptilian ride to cross my path. The lizard-mount cried out as I punched the monster between the eyes. Then I grabbed its spiked ruff and dragged it to the ground, so its rider slid within reach. A human skeleton, crafted from pale blue flame, keened in pain as I ripped through his rib cage with my sword.

His compatriots were not idle as I yanked my weapon free.

I felt a searing agony where a demon's barbed lance pierced my armor. The attacking demon bellowed in gleeful triumph, a cry cut short as I grabbed the weapon and pulled her off balance. An arrow bounced against my breastplate, but the second shot found a weak spot along my arm and hit true. Someone shouted flanking instructions from the rear.

I felt a shiver hovering between dread and desire as the battle turned against me.

I fought on. What else could I do? Surrender was impossible. These were not Joratese. They had no mercy for the defeated.

They had no mercy for anyone.

I had accounted for half their number when I heard the howls of incoming reinforcements.

I screamed in defiant response, laughed in their faces, smashed my sword through another demon. His twin responded with claw strikes, melting through my armor's crumbling edges. I felt her blow as a white-hot blaze across my thigh.

Then the attack shifted. Paused. A gap formed. Demons who had closed all around me fled, running into the woods.

I knew why the demons ran.

Staunching phantom blood with shaking fingers, I turned to face their queen.

She was the most beautiful and horrible monster, skin pale as death, hands slick with fresh-spilled blood. Her gore-dipped hair glowed lurid white; her lips shimmered fungal green. Her breasts and hips held the promise of endless carnal delights, which more than one poor idiot had given their soul to taste.

A demon may look however she wishes, be whatever gender she wishes, but Xaltorath prefers to be female for me.

She knows it hurts me more.

IS SOMEONE BEING TOO HARD ON HER PLAYMATES? THESE TOYS FIGHT BACK.

"I'd say it's nice to see you, but I hate lies." I interposed myself between Xaltorath and the village. Its people would remain trapped in their cellar houses, nailed to their arbors, until Thaena's servants arrived to rescue them. If the demon to whom they'd been sacrificed didn't find them first.

Xaltorath observed my movement, knew what I meant by it.

THOSE ARE MINE.

I glanced behind me. "From the runes, I'd say those are Kasmodeus's."

ALL THE MORE REASON I SHOULD CLAIM THEM, DON'T YOU THINK? I NEVER LIKED KASMODEUS.

I raised my sword against her.

She smiled at me. ***ADORABLE. THIS IS WHY YOU'RE MY FAVORITE DAUGHTER.***

"I'm not your daughter," I spat.

NOW WHO JUST SAID THEY HATE LIES? The demon queen cocked her head to the side and studied me with an expression that always made my laevos stand on end. A brutal, alien look, heralding anything from a lecture on courtship rites to a lesson on torture with myself as the test subject.

She is not my mother.

She'll never be my mother. I remember my mother, vague memories of dark hair and hearth fires. I recall her sweet apple scent, her fingers brushing my laevos, the nights spent counting stars when those distant jewels made themselves clear past Tya's Veil.

No, Xaltorath isn't my mother. But by her cursed race's rules, I am her child. Her adopted child. Her *claimed* child.

Thus why Kalazan's overheard prophecy bothered me so.

Xaltorath turned to face the village. ***YOU HAVE BEEN SUCH A GOOD DAUGHTER, DEAR CHILD. I WONDER: WILL YOU ALLOW COLDWATER TO HAVE DIED IN VAIN?***

My sword wavered. Coldwater village lay a short ride from Barsine's capital, Mereina. I'd been there several times as a child, when my parents visited the baron's family. Coldwater had prospered as a small village of skilled craftsmen. They made a watertight reed basket so fine it resembled cloth. My mother had bought a basket on a visit years before. I still owned it, left behind in Tolamer when I'd been forced to leave.

I didn't recognize this place as Coldwater, but that didn't mean it wasn't.

I have no control over where I wander in my sleep, but the Afterlife mirrors the Living World. It's not exact. The Afterlife might hold a mountain long since whittled to rolling hills in the real world, or plains and chasms now buried under dammed lakes. Cities are usually too new to have ghostly reflections, but villages are sometimes older than countries. A village razed to the ground, with all its inhabitants slaughtered, may last far longer in the Afterlife than it ever did in the Living World.

Her first words stuck in my throat. "Good daughter?" I spat at her. "I strike out at you at every turn. I slay every demon I find. I defy your every desire. I don't want to be your 'good' daughter. I want to be your nemesis."

She smiled proudly. ***AS I HAVE EVER WANTED. YOU HAVE BEEN SO DEFIANT, SO REBELLIOUS IT MAKES ME WONDER AT THESE HUMAN STORIES THAT CLAIM BEING A PARENT IS HARD.*** She put a hand to her heart. ***ALL I HAD TO DO TO RAISE A GLORIOUS CHILD WAS MAKE YOU IMAGINE I WANTED YOU TO BE MY MIRROR. I HAVE UPHELD MY BARGAIN WITH YOUR BIRTH MOTHER.***

"My mother made no bargains with *you*." My rage flared as I buried my doubt. Xaltorath loved to lie and twist truth together in binding chains. I'd long since learned not to trust anything she said.

***OH, YOU'D BE SURPRISED WHAT MOTHERS DO TO PROTECT THEIR CHILDREN. SEND THEIR NEWBORN BABES AWAY WITH A HANDMAIDEN.[†] MAKE BARGAINS WITH DEMONS. IT WASN'T EVEN

---

† Xaltorath's making a snide reference to Kihrin here, right? Just as I recall from Thurvishar D'Lorus's chronicle that when Xaltorath met Kihrin for the first time, the demon made a similar snide reference to Janel.

YOUR MOTHER'S FIRST TIME. WE'RE OLD FRIENDS.***
She grinned and set a crimson tongue against her green lips.
***WILL YOU CONTINUE TO BE CONTRARY, I WON-
DER? KNOWING ALL YOUR BEHAVIOR IS BY MY
DESIGN?***

"And how little you understand me if you think I act this
way from spite. I despise you and I hate everything you represent. I won't rest until your kind is no more."

Xaltorath half blinked, slowly lowering her eyelids like a
house cat. Her green lips curled. Then she leaned forward and
uttered the single word that has haunted me for years since.

GOOD.

5: THE COUNT'S JUSTICE

Jorat Dominion, Quuros Empire.
Two days since the slaying of the dragon Xaloma

Janel broke off her narration and looked away.

Kihrin stared. "Xaltorath is your *mother*?"

She glanced back, her smile black as night. "Much to my regret. But I have it on good authority I'm not a demon. Not fully."

"Oh, that's reassuring. And who told you that, again?"

She twisted her hand in a flourish in his direction. "You did. But others have told me the same." Her bright eyes shone for a moment before pain ambushed her. She exhaled.

"Was it bad, the Hellmarch at Lonezh Canton? I can't imagine—" Kihrin winced and felt a fool. Of course it was. What a demon would do with a child . . .

Then he remembered the Capital's streets years before. Remembered being trapped, still reeling from the same demon's psychic assault, as he listened to General Milligreest trade insults with the monster. Xaltorath had boasted about what they'd done to the general's eight-year-old daughter.

And Janel had already told him she'd been eight years old when the demons overran Lonezh Canton.

Kihrin looked away, feeling like an idiot.

Janel's age matched Kihrin's criteria perfectly. He felt quite certain that her parentage would as well, that it would turn out her father was really High General Qoran Milligreest.

That made Janel the fourth "son." Apparently, the demon-claimed child.

A Devoran prophecy somewhere probably mentioned it.

Kihrin hadn't noticed the table had fallen silent until Janel spoke. "The worst part is it wasn't always awful. Sometimes Xaltorath was . . . nice. I never knew which way it would go as a child. If she'd present herself as the demon or something passing for human." She shrugged and picked at the food she'd been eating earlier. "When I realized she couldn't control me, I left. I started destroying demons, but apparently, that had been her design all along."

Kihrin made a sympathetic noise. Looking back, his child-hood was happy. Full of crime, true, but also full of song. By comparison, he had no idea how Janel could even form coherent sentences.

Their eyes met again.

Kihrin said, "I'd give a lot to understand what Xaltorath's angle in all this is. I always assumed it involved trying to summon more demons, but now I wonder. What's their game?" He pointed his spoon at Janel.

"I don't know," she replied, "but I agree. Why didn't she kill me when I was a child? Why did she attack you? I've never made sense of her motives." Janel shrugged.

"May I tell this next part?" Brother Qown asked.

Kihrin shifted. He'd forgotten their chaperone.

"Please."

Qown's Turn. Mereina Castle, Barsine Banner, Jorat, Quur.

When Brother Qown joined Dorna in the kitchens the next morning, the Vishai priest's eyes were sunken and bloodshot. He groaned as he slid into a chair.

"Didn't sleep well?" Mare Dorna asked him.

"Why must everyone sleep on the floor?" Brother Qown whined. "Haven't you people heard of beds?"

Dorna was taken aback. "We have beds. What were you napping on last night?"

"Pillows," said Brother Qown. "And rushes and cushions.

None of which are an actual bed. And the liveryman I slept next to snored. I'm surprised the noise didn't wake you. He threw elbows too."

"Ah, you have to nudge 'em a little when they do that." She gave him a curious look. "You mean everyone where you come from sleeps in separate rooms? How high and mighty. Here, only noble types do that. Rest of the house sleeps together, the way the gods intended."

"Or don't sleep at all," Brother Qown bemoaned.

"If you find yourself the right partner . . ." Mare Dorna winked at him.

"Oh stars, that's not what I meant." He'd been propositioned the night before too. When he'd refused her, the woman had taken no offense at all. She'd said if Brother Qown preferred to run with stallions, she knew just the man. Indeed, she would've matched Qown up with a male herald before the evening finished, if Qown hadn't told her no. "But at least tell me you look for some privacy for *that*."

"For what?" She was all wide-eyed innocence.

"I should have gone back to the Temple of Light when I had the chance," he said.

"I've always found the best thing for a good night's sleep is finding yourself the right bed warmer. Then the elbows don't matter so much."

"Does *vow of celibacy* mean nothing to you?"

She stared at him, bemused.

Brother Qown reminded himself to stop asking questions to which he knew the answers.

"So you don't run at all, then?"

"No!" He claimed a bowl and set it down more forcefully than proper.

"Then just say so. Ain't no shame in it."

"I belong to a monastic order, Mare Dorna. We take a vow. Physical pleasure is a distraction from our contemplation of divine mysteries."

The staff was largely absent as they busied themselves

preparing the day's tournament feast. This evidently involved a great many different ways of roasting fruits, vegetables, and game—far more methods than Qown found familiar—most of which was conducted outside. No one had really protested Dorna staking out a corner of the kitchen.

Someone in the castle's kitchen had left a large pot of porridge to cook over the fire, but it didn't smell like rice. He scooped what looked like oats into his bowl. Barley? Probably barley.

"Ain't food a pleasure?" Dorna dribbled red chili sauce over her porridge and added pickled vegetables to her serving.

"Food's purpose is to fortify and sustain. But what is that?" Brother Qown pointed.

"This?" She held up the lacy shape. "Lotus. You know, you ain't supposed to eat your porridge plain." She picked up several bowls on the table and started dumping portions into Brother Qown's bowl. "Lotus, ginger, cabbage—"

"That's not cabbage."

"Course it is. Fermented dor beans, fenis root, pepperleaf, and pickled sour apple. Now throw pepper sauce on top—"

"Dorna, please—" Brother Qown tried to interrupt, but she paid no attention to him.

She handed him the bowl. "Now that's a proper breakfast. I don't know what you people cook out west, but it must be boring as dirt."

"No, not at all. Our cuisine is excellent. I would be happy to prepare a dish—"

"You were going to eat your porridge naked. No thanks." She returned to her own meal. "Anyway, your whole 'vow of celery' sounds stupid, if you ask me. If you don't want to run, fine, but people forcing you to promise you won't run? Acting like running's a sin? Ain't right."

Brother Qown inhaled. Losing his temper wouldn't help his cause. "I appreciate you noticing I didn't ask you. Besides, it's not about engaging in carnal relations. We live a simple life to fulfill our spiritual needs and escape the chains of our physical forms."

Dorna stared. "Our count 'escapes the chains of her physical form' every night. I don't think she'd agree it's so wonderful."

"That's not what I mean—" He paused as Count Janel entered the kitchen. She looked grim.

"How did you sleep, Count?" Brother Qown asked.

"Like the dead." She pointed to Dorna's porridge. "Is there any more left?"

"Oh aye, colt." Dorna fetched another dish and filled it from the cauldron.

Count Janel also added vegetables and pepper sauce to her portion.

Brother Qown thought the remaining cook still using the kitchen would faint when she saw the visiting count plunk herself down on a bench and eat. The cook didn't dare tell the noblewoman to leave. She did, however, hover around the count like a wren fretting over a raven too near her nest.

When Count Janel noticed, she stood. "Walk with me," she said to Dorna and Brother Qown. She took the porridge with her.

No one tried to stop the trio from leaving the kitchen or walking out onto the castle walls. Brother Qown suspected people would have objected—soldiers or the like—but Janel was a visiting count. She wasn't Tamin's direct liege, but the title still meant something. She could wander freely as long as she didn't stray into private areas.

"Is anything wrong?" Brother Qown asked. The noblewoman wore a dour expression, extreme even by her own dour standards.

Count Janel leaned against a crenelated wall. "That depends on what my spymaster has discovered." She looked at Dorna.

Mare Dorna ducked her head and put her hand to her face as though covering for a shy blush. "Ah, you're a shameless flatterer, my dearest. I'm just a withered old gossip."*

---

* I could stand to have a few more withered old gossips like that under my command.

Janel scoffed. "A withered old gossip who could convince a pebble to confess the name of the river that birthed it. Get on with it."

Dorna straightened and checked for eavesdroppers. "It's nothing good. News on the wind is Barsine Banner is filthy with witches. Winter came early, cold and hard. Water buffalo froze to death still chewing their cud; jaguars have turned to picking off people because the wild herds all hightailed it to warmer climes; the late spring will mean a later harvest, assuming there's anything left. So witches must have done all that, right?"

"And what about the prophecy?" Count Janel asked. "The demon-claimed child?"

"Nobody said nothing about no prophecy," Dorna admitted. "Demons, though? Word is the local farms harbored demon cults, so the baron stopped all that when he inherited the title. That's why so much land has been declared forest."

"Um, forest?" Qown asked. "There's a huge forest in Kirpis, but it doesn't convey any magical protection from demon cults."

"In Jorat, a forest is off limits," Janel explained, "so it gives the local baron permission to go in and drive off anyone living inside. And yes, that might include any so-called demon cults. Unfortunately, it absolutely will include everyone else as well. No one may live or hunt there. Anyone who does declares themselves saelen, to be arrested on sight."

"Off limits to all but nobles, you mean." Dorna shrugged. "Anyhow, whole villages and towns have been cleared out and burned for this reason."

"Demon cults here?" Janel said. "Where does he think this is, Marakor?"

Brother Qown fought against the impulse to suggest many worthy Marakori had nothing to do with demon cults.

Dorna held up her hands. "I'm just repeating what I overheard. The old baron died in winter. Ever since, the new baron has been tearing up the land trying to put down the witches he insists are attacking his people." She paused. "Don't take much, I hear, to be accused of being a witch. And this baron is a firm believer in using fire to deal with witches."

"What? That's barbaric." Brother Qown couldn't help himself. "Besides, witches aren't vulnerable to fire."

"No more so than any person is vulnerable to fire," Count Janel agreed, "but Tamin isn't wrong. Someone in Barsine *is* a witch and is summoning demons."

"You think there are witches?"

"Yes. And I will find and destroy them." Her tone left little room for argument.

Count Janel left the bowl and began to walk away with purposeful strides. Dorna and Brother Qown shared a look before they followed, with Dorna darting back a moment later to pick up the abandoned bowl.

"Where are we going?" Brother Qown asked when he caught up.

"The dungeons. I need to speak with Ninavis."

Brother Qown assumed the dungeon would be one area where Count Janel's title didn't gain her automatic entry, but he was mistaken. Few people paid them any attention as they walked. Count Janel looked like a queen strolling through her kingdom, servants scrambling behind her.

However, her confidence was unnecessary: no guard stood at the entrance.

"A soldier was here yesterday," Brother Qown said. "They'd barred the door from the outside too."

Indeed, the heavy iron bar lay on the floor. The door appeared open a fractional degree.

Dorna moved beside the door and used her toe to nudge it farther ajar.

A loud clatter greeted the movement; a sword and scabbard resting against the door fell to the floor. They'd just given someone inside in the jail a few seconds' warning.

"Shit!" Someone cursed as punctuation to a strangled scream. "Ow! Bitch!"

Count Janel abandoned subtlety and barged inside. The dungeon looked much the same as the night before, with a single exception: it appeared empty.

Brother Qown saw no sign of guards or prisoners.

Then a guard ran out from behind stacked wine crates, straightening his tunic and brushing his hair to the side.

Dread twisted in the pit of Brother Qown's stomach. They'd surely interrupted something sordid.* If his story about a contagious disease hadn't been believed . . . if someone had called his bluff . . .

"Hey, you're not supposed to be here," the guard protested upon seeing who had interrupted him.

"That makes two of us," Count Janel said.

"Now why are you bleeding, colt?" Mare Dorna cocked her head to the side and pointed to the man's scalp. Even with his hair pulled over, blood trickled down and stained his leather-covered shoulder.

If the guard had been smarter or more creative, he might have had a plausible story ready. Instead, he reached for the sword at his belt and realized he'd left it with his scabbard—leaning against the dungeon door. He picked up a discarded chain and shackle, wielding it like a flail.

Then the guard rushed Janel.

The count sighed. She stepped forward, grabbed the man by his jerkin, and threw him against the stone wall. He collided with a thick thud, headfirst.

The man's eyes rolled up as he slumped to the floor.

"Stars!" Brother Qown hurried to the guard's side, hoping by some miracle Count Janel hadn't killed the jailer outright. Brother Qown saw other signs of violence; someone had bitten the man's ear, and they'd been dedicated to the task. Quick on the heels of that thought, Qown realized he should first

---

* Sordid? Yes. Nonconsensual? No. He was just an idiot who Ninavis convinced to trade "favors" with her—apparently all a ruse so she could pick his pocket and escape.

check on whoever had bitten the man. Count Janel must have had the same worry, because she rushed behind the stacked crates.

When the priest caught up, he saw Ninavis unlocking her shackles with the jailer's key. Scarlet dripped from her lips and chin as she brandished the manacles at them like a weapon.

To Brother Qown's amazement, Count Janel smiled. "Ah, now the blood makes sense."

"I'm *not* staying in this basement." Ninavis tightened her grip on the chain and glared.

"No," Janel agreed. "That would be ill-advised." She appeared to be putting an effort into controlling her laughter. "Let's leave this place."

"Aren't we going to be in trouble for this?" Brother Qown resisted the urge to wring his hands. He failed to see how the baron could ignore a visiting noble—even a count—attacking his guards.

"Oh yes, I should think we'll be in a great deal," Count Janel said, still grinning. She pulled a handkerchief from her sleeve and held it out to Ninavis as the woman hobbled out into the main area. "You have a little something on your chin."

Ninavis blinked as she took the cloth. "You're not turning me in?"

"Oh no. It's not safe here."

"Huh." Mare Dorna stood from where she'd knelt, looking at the guard. She raised a hand so they all saw the gray greasy makeup smearing her fingers. "Methinks the girl ain't the only one with a little something on her chin."

Ninavis rested against the wall for balance while she used her other hand to clean her face. She resembled a flamingo, balanced on her one good leg, doing it with far more skill than Brother Qown could muster. "I'm thirty-five years old. It's been a damn long time since anyone had the right to call me *girl*." She focused on Dorna's hand. "Is that paint?"

Brother Qown knelt next to the guard and rubbed at the gray leopard spots shading the unconscious man's chin.

His fingers also smeared the makeup.

"Why would a guard fake their coloring?" he asked.

"The same reason so many hulking guards around here don't understand a fireblood, I imagine," Mare Dorna said. "'Cause they ain't Joratese." She shut one eye and squinted as she studied his features. "This one's Yoran, or I'm still an acrobat in a traveling tournament show." She patted the soldier's pockets.

Count Janel spared the man a cursory glance before she turned back to Ninavis. "Where are your people?"

"The guards took them to the tourney." A sour, angry look stole over her expression. "I thought those bastards would make all manner of fuss about leaving me behind when they saw I couldn't walk, but they laughed and said the baron wanted even numbers, anyway."

Brother Qown finished examining the prone guard. He had a concussion for sure, but the priest couldn't do much for him with an audience. Qown stood. "Why would they bring prisoners to the tournament? Why wouldn't they just leave them here in the dungeons or send them off to a proper jail before their trial?"

The count looked startled. "What? Oh no. There's no trial. Not in the sense you mean."

"Excuse me?" Brother Qown felt a moment's sharp outrage. Even in the Capital, trials were standard. It might have been a twisted and warped pretense, favoring those with money and connections, but by the Eight, there would *be* a trial.

"We don't keep jails in Jorat. When someone has trespassed our laws, we hold prisoners for long enough to ensure their presence at the next tourney. Prisoners are given to tournament winners under the belief a champion's idorrá will bring saelen back into the fold. I've never heard of a tournament where the number of saelen awarded mattered, however."

"Awarded?" Brother Qown choked. "You mean ever since Tolamer, we've been selling bandits into slavery?"

"Yeah," Ninavis said, "that's just what you've been doing."*

The count's glare would melt glass. "No, it isn't. The awarded men and women aren't slaves or prisoners. They are adopted, brought into a new herd for their rehabilitation. It's not at all the same thing as slavery."

Ninavis snorted. "You say *sword*, I say *blade*."

"Now, now, my foals. There'll be time for philosophizing later," Dorna said. "We need to figure out what's what with that guard. Why's a Yoran trying to disguise himself as Joratese?"

"Plenty of people disguise themselves as Joratese," Ninavis snapped.

"Aye," Dorna agreed, "but letting folks assume a wine-stain birthmark means you're a local girl ain't much of a disguise."

Brother Qown blinked. Ninavis wasn't Joratese? Her accent was perfect. After Dorna had pointed it out, Brother Qown realized the large maroon splash across Ninavis's face didn't resemble Jorat skin marking as much as a regular birthmark.

"He's not the only soldier like this either," Count Janel said, moving the conversation back to the original topic. "Captain Dedreugh should have been able to understand Arasgon. He couldn't."

"Dedreugh's new," Ninavis volunteered. "Most of the soldiers are. They showed up a few months ago, when Tamin took over after his father's death. Tamin said he didn't trust the guards who let his father die."

"What happened to those original guards?" the count asked.

Ninavis spread her hands. "That's a damn fine question." She handed back the handkerchief, now streaked with blood. "Look, I know you and the baron used to be pals, but there's nothing friendly about him now. You want to help us? Pull him out of power. You're the only person who can."

"I'm not his count. I have no authority over him."

"So don't give him an order. *Kill* him. You can get close

---

* I think Ninavis has a point here. Sure, it's not technically slavery, but what happens when someone doesn't want to be "brought back into the fold"?

enough to do it, and you wouldn't even need a weapon. You're Danorak. If you say you had a good reason for doing it, people will believe you."

Janel stared. "That is not how we do things here."

"To Hell with how you do things! Do you think anyone dares Censure him? As far as the baron is concerned, anyone against him is automatically with the witches. That's all the excuse he needs to have his men strike us down. He won't step down from power. If Kalazan's prophecy is right about you—"

"Wait." Janel raised a hand. "What of Kalazan's prophecy? This business with the 'claimed child'?"

"Oh, hell if I know," Ninavis admitted. "Kalazan talks like it's the cure for every problem we have. He overheard Tamin and his teacher talking about it, before the old baron's death. How this prophecy predicted someone called the *demon-claimed child* would ruin everything. They needed to track this person down. That's why Tamin's so obsessed with fighting demons. Tamin thinks the demons are leading him to this 'child'—who will kill Tamin if Tamin doesn't kill him first."

"I won't murder Tamin."

"So you *are* the demon-claimed child? Because that sounded like a confession."

Count Janel ignored her and turned to the other two people in the dungeon. "Brother Qown, Mare Dorna, can you smuggle Ninavis to our quarters?"

"They'll see me." Ninavis pointed to her face. "This is distinctive."

"Ha, found it!" Dorna lifted a small tin from the guard's pockets. She unscrewed the lid, revealing the gray cake makeup the guard must have used to paint his face. "Give me five minutes and your own nana wouldn't recognize you. Then it's just getting you back with a bad leg, but I reckon we can manage."

"What about him?" Ninavis indicated the unconscious guard.

"Drag him behind those crates," Dorna suggested. "That buys us at least a few hours' head start, before the other guards find him. We should have a good solid lead on any pursuit the baron organizes by then."

"We're not leaving."

Dorna sighed at Janel. "Foal—"

"We're not leaving," Janel repeated, looking her true age for a moment, a sullen teenager about to stomp her feet. "I promised these people if they surrendered, they'd be treated fairly. I refuse to flee as long as there is a chance Tamin will trample my word."

Ninavis pursed her lips and looked Janel over. "You might just be worth something after all, little noble."

Brother Qown hid his smile. It wasn't an occasion for smiling even if he felt pleased by this result. "How will you discover Tamin's plans?"

Janel straightened her shoulders. "By the simplest method possible: I shall ask." She gave the three a stern gaze. "Wait in my chambers. I'll return once I have more information."

She left before they could lodge a single protest.

They stared after her. Then Dorna pulled off a split overskirt, a gray wool wrap with indigo thread forming horse head patterns along the hem. She tossed the garment to Ninavis. "Wear it like a cloak. If we don't want folks staring, we best be covering up your sorry excuse for armor. That shabby leather stands out a damn sight more than a bit of parti-color on your face."

"Hey now. Tanner made this. It just needs patching." Ninavis wrestled with the wool fabric, draping it around her.

"Tanner's a tanner?" Dorna guffawed. "What would you lot have called him if he was the village piss farmer?"

"Mare Dorna!" Brother Qown winced and tipped his head to the bandit leader. "Don't let Dorna bother you. She's just upset we're not running."

"Running's the smart move," Dorna said. She waved a hand in Ninavis's direction. "Now come over here where the light's better, dear, while I fix your face. Priest, be a good foal and drag the guard into the back, would you?"

Brother Qown started to protest, but they didn't have much

time before someone realized this guard had been left by himself. He dragged the man backward.

The going was slow.

When Brother Qown had been first given this assignment, he'd thought he'd be posted to Tolamer Canton's castle. A quiet, sedentary duty where he could concentrate on meditation and guiding the count's spiritual development. Something where he didn't have to move around.

He needed to exercise more to keep up, if he intended to keep traveling like this.

Ninavis kept throwing annoyed glances in his direction, as if about to interrupt her painting session with Dorna to drag the guard's body herself, broken leg or not.

He dropped the man behind the crates, using a frayed and tattered blanket to cover him. As long as no one looked too closely, the guard appeared to be napping. Brother Qown checked to see if Dorna or Ninavis were paying him attention.

They weren't.

Brother Qown put a hand to the guard's chest, focusing his energy as his mentor Father Zajhera had taught him. He entered Illumination, a peculiar sensitivity to the tenyé surrounding all things, the universal light playing across cloth and skin and dirt and flesh. Illumination allowed him to see tenyé, the essential nature of every individual object in the world. That energy didn't always coincide with objective appearances. He might well trip and crack his head open while seeing through its filter. But to make up for the inconvenience, a whole universe of possibility opened to him.

The Joratese—or those from Eamithon or Kazivar—might call what Brother Qown did magic. He knew better; he tapped into universal grace, tasted the divine. A holy gift.

No, it was the *holiest* gift.

The angry mottled gash marring the guard's aura suggested concussion, internal swelling, bleeding. If Brother Qown left him there, the man would sleep his way right through the Second Veil and into the Afterlife.

Brother Qown set his hand against the man's head. First, he soothed the brain tissue inflammation, then fortified the cracks in the man's skull before shoring up the bleeding wounds too small to see. The guard would sleep and sleep hard, but if Qown finished his job, the guard wouldn't die.

And if any Joratese discovered what Brother Qown had done, they might well put the priest to death instead.

"Hey, what's taking so long?" Ninavis called out.

"Coming." Brother Qown rushed after them.

6: A JORATESE TOURNAMENT

Jorat Dominion, Quuros Empire.
Two days since Kihrin D'Mon was Returned to life

"I like the way you describe looking past the First Veil," Kihrin said to Qown when the priest paused. "Does everyone who trains with the Vishai Mysteries learn that? I mean, I don't know much about how religion works. I've spent time around religious people, but I wouldn't call them priests. What you did just sounds like sorcery, so what's the difference?" Kihrin looked around, a little embarrassed, as he realized he should have checked for anyone listening before bringing up what might be heresies.

"I don't know how other religions function either," Brother Qown admitted. "I suspect it involves prayer and promised offerings for favors? But the Mysteries aren't like that. You see, our god is dead."

Kihrin coughed. "Your god is dead? Excuse me?" Butterbelly had talked about light and the temple at Rainbow Lake. He'd never mentioned worshipping a *deceased* deity.

Janel started to say something, then stopped herself.

Brother Qown smiled. "We follow Selanol's teachings, try to spread his light to the world, and protect people from the demons he died fighting."

"Selanol? I've never heard of him," Kihrin said.

"He's the eighth of the Eight Immortals. In his memory, we give of ourselves and hope to experience and encourage enlightened lives. But as our god is dead, he cannot answer prayers, so we must make do with our own magical gifts." Qown paused. "My views on sorcery are rather heterodox."

Kihrin sat back, stunned. "Wow." The name was different, but there was only one "vacant" slot among the Eight, only one among them who might be considered "dead", although different regions were always offering up new candidates for the role. Kihrin himself had grown up thinking Grizzst the Mad, who'd bound all the demons, was the eighth god. That had turned out to be just as wrong as all the other stories.

The real Eighth Guardian had been named S'arric, not Selanol. And if that was who Qown meant, Kihrin suspected the priest would be horrified to know what had really happened to the "god" of the sun and stars. Kihrin certainly was. "So that's why your religion was outlawed?"

"Oh no. Our religion was forbidden because we maintain gods are nothing more than mortals who've given themselves great power by exploiting magic, and thus shouldn't be worshipped."

Kihrin stared. "Huh. Yeah, I can see how that might upset folks." Kihrin shifted in his seat, gaze still fixed on Brother Qown. The priest wasn't wrong, of course. The Eight hadn't started out as gods to be worshiped, but as champions tasked with saving everyone else from the invading demons. But S'arric hadn't died fighting such. He'd been murdered, betrayed. Still, Kihrin could see how the narrative might have slipped into saying he'd died that way. Or how, over time, the "god's" name had changed from Solan'arric to Selanol.

Kihrin hoped the Vishai Mysteries didn't have some belief Selanol would return to save everyone, but he wouldn't be surprised if they did. He looked over to see Janel had a blank expression on her face. She looked like someone with her fists balled up under the table to keep her from commenting.

He had a feeling she considered "gods" a sore point.*

So to change the subject, Kihrin said, "I'm curious, Janel:

---

* My goodness, why would that be? Maybe because the Eight have been willfully perpetrating a fraud for millennia? The idea that Kihrin still "worships" Taja boggles my mind. He doesn't seem *that* naïve.

Did Baron Tamin just out and out tell you his plans?"

She smiled ruefully. "You know, he rather did."

Janel's Turn. The tournament grounds in Mereina,
Barsine Banner, Jorat, Quur.

Outsiders seldom understand the tournament's importance in Joratese life. The knights who perform in the contests are heroes. In other dominions, knighthood, if it exists, is a function of noble blood; the aristocracy's sword-wielding arm. In Jorat, we don't attach such trappings to our knights. They are our finest horsemen, athletes, and swordsmen, trained and sponsored to represent their liege's interests on the field of honor. Anyone can aspire to be a knight.

Anyone *but* a ruling noble.

Is it any surprise, therefore, that the knightly class is so beloved here? Knights sit at a pinnacle reachable by anyone daring enough, brave enough, and strong enough to win the field, no matter what their birth. Knights are champions who might represent lords, merchants, towns, but they are risen from commoners. The crowds who come out to watch their displays of prowess are best described as "every mare, stallion, and gelding who can possibly attend."

The tournament is the heart of the Jorat community.

And thus, it didn't take me long to realize how much of Barsine's heart had rotted.

After I left Mare Dorna, Brother Qown, and Ninavis, I found the nobles' box at the head of the stands. A thin crowd filled the seats, a few tired pennants waving from wooden poles. All belonged to Joratese merchant associations, who had arrived with the opening of the morning Gatestone—travelers from other parts of Jorat arrived for trade. All the knights who had milled about in the fortress courtyard the night before were gathered on the sides. Their demoralized, tense postures spoke of people with no real interest in the contests to come; they'd shown up because their wages depended on it. The sullen atmosphere felt more appropriate to a funeral than a tourney.

If the tournament's antipathy troubled me, the twin wooden posts sunk deep into the lawn—facing the nobles' box—made my laevos stand on end. Kindling and branches were piled high at each post's base. Chains pierced holes drilled through the thick timbers, which had glyphs carved along their lengths. The scorched earth underneath those woodpiles testified to previous bonfires.

Next to each would-be pyre rested a large cage, covered with oilcloth. I didn't have to check under them to realize who I would find, to know why the guards had said an even number would be better.

I'd found Ninavis's companions.

"Did I miss anything exciting?" I said, masking my anger as I entered the baron's box. I'd missed the opening invocation, the ceremony that dedicated each tournament to the Eight. I'd likely also missed at least a few of the earliest contests. Hopefully, none of that was important.

Tamin paused mid-drink. "Janel! I worried you had taken ill." He grinned as he crossed to me, setting his hand behind my neck and resting his forehead against mine.

Or at least, he tried.

"Are you well?" He drew back.

I touched his hand, a compromise for the greeting I'd denied him. "It was a trying journey."

He swallowed and, for the first time since I arrived, looked uncertain. He motioned to his side. "Count Janel, may I present Warden Lorat, one of my banners." He introduced an elderly man in his dotage, too weak to stand on his own. Too weak to still be warden, but I held my tongue.

Warden Lorat paused from feeding meat scraps to a small dhole puppy on his lap, which occupied his attention far more than the tournament itself.

"Warden." I inclined my head.

The elderly warden said something unintelligible, and the

serving woman standing near his chair rushed to his side. She pressed her ear to his lips, listening while the old man continued mumbling. The puppy licked his fingers.

The nurse straightened and turned. Her coloring was startling: a gray-eyed milk mare, bleached of all hue save the subtle blue and violet veins marbling her skin. I'd have thought her another ice-cursed Yoran, but her features were wrong. Too long, with thin lips and a straight nose, compared to Yoran small noses and pouting mouths.

"The warden greets you." Her accent betrayed time spent in the west.* "He apologizes he cannot do a better job of addressing you, but red fever has left it difficult for him to speak."

"Of course," I said, speaking to him. "It's a pleasure to meet you." I smiled at the nurse. "Thank you for helping with translation."

Those gray eyes rested on my face. She tilted her head in acknowledgment. Then she returned to waiting on the warden.

I had the feeling I had just been dismissed.

"And this," Tamin said, motioning to the last person present, "is my esteemed teacher, Relos Var. I feared you wouldn't be able to meet him before he left." Tamin sighed at the man. "Is there nothing I can do to convince you to stay?"

I remembered Ninavis's words then; Kalazan had overheard Tamin speaking with his teacher about a prophecy . . .

The man looked unassuming, Quuros by ancestry, dressed in simple clothes appropriate to a servant. Relos Var wore his hair trimmed in a short cut, his face shaved, his boots suited for horsemanship or travel.

The man looked over at me, and our eyes locked.

Relos Var smiled.

I notice when people stare at me with desire. Men and women had been giving me such looks long before it was appropriate to my age. This was something else.

---

* That's because I was *born in the west.*

"Janel Danorak," he said, smiling in pleasure. "The Lonezh Hellmarch's only survivor."

"Janel Theranon, Count of Tolamer," I corrected. "And many souls survived the last Hellmarch, or we wouldn't be having a conversation right now."

Relos Var chuckled and ducked his head in a gesture a forgiving person might interpret as a bow. "Still, your reputation precedes you." Relos Var gave the baron an equally insincere bow. "And my apologies. I'm so very sorry to leave your side, but I received word a relative has fallen into some trouble. I must return at once to see to his proper disposition."

"What sort of trouble?" I asked.

I asked only because he presented a strange addition to an already strange tableau. Too many foreigners, too many mysteries, too many changes from how tournaments are conducted. And there was this talk of prophecy. Was Relos Var the same person Kalazan overheard talking to Tamin, about the "demon-claimed child"?

Something about him . . .

I'm not sure to this day what gave him away. Maybe he wanted me to notice him.

His confidence showed when our eyes met. Tamin hadn't introduced him as being western nobility or royalty. He should have been a being of thudajé, comparable to the serving girl. He was . . . not.

Indeed, his idorrá was so strong, I didn't understand why everyone in the viewing box wasn't on their knees.

Relos Var paused before answering my question. "My younger brother is about to go up on the auction block in Kishna-Farriga." He let out a bitter laugh. "He has a talent for getting himself into trouble. Himself and everyone around him."

"Sold as a slave? That does sound serious. Safe journey, then." Ah, how I wished I might have plied him with the questions his comment provoked. Where was this Kishna-Farriga? Since the baron wasn't sufficiently ranked to have his own Gatekeeper, how did Relos Var intend to depart to rescue his brother? Had he worked out a deal with the Gatekeepers, or was he a Gatekeeper himself?

"Thank you, Count," Relos Var said. He bowed then, a real bow. The warmth in his eyes when he smiled surprised me. "What atrocious timing. I hope we'll meet again in circumstances where I can give you my full attention."

He seemed sincere, his expression kind, and yet his words struck me as a threat. I felt a chill, married to the certainty I wouldn't enjoy Relos Var's "full attention."*

"And you," I said.

He left as the crowd drummed their feet in anticipation. I claimed his now-empty chair and tried to act interested in the outcome for all the normal reasons, but I couldn't stop staring at the pillars. Var had almost distracted me, but my true purpose for being there stood right in front of my eyes.

"Sir Xia Nilos," Tamin said, drawing my attention back to the match. He pointed to a knight in a beautiful sky eagle headdress and a gray-and-white beaded coat, riding a lovely dappled gray mare with matching ribbons in her mane. "She represents the Seven Journeys Trade Consortium. Facing against her is my man, Sir Dedreugh." He didn't need to point out the other knight. Dedreugh dressed in yellow and brown, gold and bronze, his parade dress resplendent with streamers catching the air and sailing behind him. He made his turns along the contest grounds and shouted threats to his opponent.

The crowd's enthusiasm felt forced and unnatural. If Dedreugh's boasts to me hadn't been a fool's bluster, then he was this little wood's tiger king. I expected him to have loyal fans and admirers, waving his flags, dressed in his colors. Instead, the locals clearly cheered for him because they had to cheer for him.

Visitors cheered for Dedreugh for the same reason they cheered for any knight: they'd placed a wager on the outcome.

"Your captain mentioned last night he usually wins the final

---

* You must admit her choice of words here is hilarious.

tournament prize of arrested saelen. Your judges don't feel that's a conflict of interest?"

Tamin's expression soured, but then he laughed. He waved at the old, doddering warden. "There sits my only judge."

My eyes widened.

"I know," Tamin said. His mouth twisted. "But what can I do? My other wardens refuse to attend, claiming hardship from the winter. It would be a scandal if I tried to lead the judges myself, and he's the only one who's bothering to show up these days. The others have deserted me."

"There are no high mares—?"

"Warden Dokmar's daughter Ganar is down there in a cage," he snapped. "She's a murdering whore, who threw her lot in with witches and assassins. Shall I have her be a referee?"

I shuddered. I wondered if Warden Dokmar knew his daughter waited to be executed for treason and witchcraft.

Tamin reached out and grabbed my hand. Had I been any other person, I would say he grabbed far too hard.

"You," Tamin said, "are the only good thing that's happened in months, Janel. Your arrival feels like the coming of spring."

"Tamin," I said, trying to keep my voice calm, "it *is* spring."

He stared at me for a second as if I'd just said something surprising and unbelievable, told him the sky was blue instead of teal, announced magic legal throughout the land.

If I'm being honest with myself, he didn't look sane.

A loud, jarring clash interrupted whatever response he'd have given. We both turned back to the grounds in time to see the two knights complete their initial pass. Xia Nilos, being lower ranked in idorrá, had chosen the form of the bout, in this case, the Contest of Khored. In turn, Dedreugh picked the technique—Sword Crashing style—which favored brute strength over subtlety. I thought it a poor strategy for Xia Nilos, one that resulted in her current predicament: knocked from her horse, struggling to find the weapon she'd dropped. To the side, Nilos's squire grabbed a second blade and ran toward his knight.

Sir Xia Nilos raised her shield in time to intercept a stunning blow from Dedreugh, which pushed her backward. Nilos fumbled her sword, put both hands up to support her shield.

I'm sure under other circumstances, against other opponents, Sir Xia's skills would have seen her through. But not here. Not against an enemy like Dedreugh.

I looked over at the warden. "She's defeated. Call it."

The old man mumbled to himself.

"Let Sir Xia decide when she's conquered," the servant said on Warden Lorat's behalf.

The blows Dedreugh rained down on Xia seemed less appropriate to a contest of skill than to hammering a blade on the forge. Xia's shield dented.

"Do it," Tamin whispered. His eyes brightened.

The woman picked the dhole puppy up from the warden's lap and turned away.

"Do you yield?" I cried out. I didn't think the knights could hear me over the boos of screaming spectators.

The squire ran in with the second sword.

I saw what followed as if time herself had slowed to watch. The reverberating blows from Dedreugh, supernaturally strong and so forceful I thought he could punch through the shield to overwhelm his opponent. Sir Xia's unsteady steps as she tried to find her balance. The shout from the young squire as he put the blade into a position for Nilos to grab it. Time paused.

Dedreugh swung his sword back and took the squire straight through the stomach.

I stood. Everyone stood.

Shock and the naïve belief that the match had finished—it had to be over, didn't it?—lowered Sir Xia's guard. Her gaze fixed on her dying squire.

She stopped paying attention to her enemy.

Dedreugh pulled his weapon from the dead boy's body, spun back to Sir Xia, and used the bloody blade to flip the woman's shield out of line.

Sir Xia screamed as Dedreugh's sword pierced her armor's

neck seam, before punching down into her armpit. Dedreugh yanked the blade up, blood spraying as he opened a major artery and severed her arm.

"Tamin!" I shouted.

Tamin's expression turned ecstatic, his focus lost in victory and bloodlust. His nostrils flared as he heard my admonishing voice, and he turned to me. "You're my friend, not my count. Your tone is unwarranted."

"They'll die," I said. "Both Sir Xia and her squire will die."

Tamin stared at me as if I spoke a foreign language. Why should those deaths bother or concern him? He sat in his chair. "Aren't the tournaments designed to ready us for war? In war, don't people die?" He raised a hand in a benediction to Sir Dedreugh while others came out to collect the bodies.

"Tamin—"

He smiled and waved, but his expression turned cold when he glanced at me. "Don't question my actions, Janel. I have a banner on the brink of catastrophe. I have to take drastic action."*

"Drastic action?" I fought to keep my voice level. "Tamin, Dedreugh is your man. You're responsible for paying the death price for those he slays. If your banner is in such straits, how can you afford that?"

"I won't accept advice from a stallion who fled her own canton, rather than face Censure." Tamin leaned forward, his expression nasty. "You think I don't know the truth behind your visit? Your former betrothed, Sir Oreth, bought out your people even before your grandfather breathed his last. All the while you sat there, oblivious to being made a laughingstock. That's why you didn't come by Gatestone—you had neither Gatestone nor Gatekeeper to use."

His words hurt worse than blows, not least because they were true.

---

* I don't think I'll ever understand what Tamin thought he was accomplishing here.

They were also a deflection, and I wouldn't be turned aside.

"Dedreugh is a monster. As a friend, I caution you not to employ a monster to prove your idorrá."

There have always been people who think idorrá requires violence—that the stick is the most effective enticement to keep the herd in line. That mistaken belief is the reason we have Censure. Nobles may rule in Jorat, but they rule because they have our citizens' trust. And when the nobility becomes a greater hazard to our people than any other danger?

They are removed. Such has always been our way.

"As a friend," Tamin said, "I caution you to manage your own herd, not mine."

I held up my hands in acquiescence. "Tamin, I meant no offense. The winter has been hard for us both."

In my peripheral vision, I saw the tournament's Black Knight enter the contest ground. He'd been sent to distract the crowds from the gore being mopped up behind him. The crowd had been cursing, "Thorra, thorra!" but when Captain Dedreugh turned his attention to them, they fell silent.

Some of the anger left Tamin. "How I envy you, Janel. At least you could outrun your demons."

I felt those words like cuts. "Not all of them." I put my hand on his, choosing what I said carefully. "But we could help each other."

The Black Knight japed and pranced as befitting his role. He dressed in ornate black armor, too small for him in all the wrong places. His large belly flopped exposed while he danced and cantered around the yard on a flame-kissed black fireblood.

Tamin jerked his hand away from mine. "I don't need help. Those witches think they can get the better of me. I'll show them. I will burn them all."

"Is that what you intend to do with the prisoners I brought you?"

"They're witches or in league with witches. What choice do I have?" He gritted his teeth. "I've known Kalazan since we were children, Janel. I can't believe he betrayed me."

The warden paid no attention to our conversation; the serving woman had returned his puppy. She, on the other hand, studied the frame of the nobles' box with such intent concentration she must have hung on every word. The woman only stepped away when a field judge approached with questions.

She didn't consult the warden before giving instructions.

"You must feel much like I did, after what Oreth did to me," I said. "After he turned on me."

"He loves you," Tamin said.

"An obsession with owning something isn't the same as loving it."

He sighed and poured himself more wine. "Have you always been so wise, dear Janel?"

"You flatter me, Tamin. If I were wise, I wouldn't be in this mess."

"You understand, don't you? We both must do what is necessary. I must kill every witch in this banner. Every one. I'll leave none to summon the demons who would destroy us. Relos Var has opened my eyes to the danger."

I turned to him. "What danger?"

"The child," Tamin said. "The demon-claimed child. There's a prophecy: *The demon-claimed child gathers the broken, witches and outlaws, rebels outspoken, to plot conquest and uprising while winter's malice hides her chains in the snow king's palace.*"

I stared at him.

"Don't you see it? It's obvious!"

"I don't—"

"There's another," he persisted. "*The claimed child waits, not dead but sleeping, dreaming of evil and souls for reaping, for when day and night at last are one, the demon king's bars will come undone.* Surely that's clearer. If the demons find the child they seek, they will use him to destroy the world."*

I didn't think it clear at all, but I also didn't volunteer my opinion. "When day and night at last are one . . . an eclipse?"

---

* Not how I'd interpret that one.

He missed the sarcasm that crept into my voice despite my best efforts to tame it. "Yes, I think so. But I can't be sure. It could mean anything."

I resisted the urge to ask him to repeat that last sentence again, more slowly.

I lifted my chin. "So the runes carved on the posts down there? Those are designed to . . . hurt . . . demons?"

"Yes. Every witch who dies is one less witch who can summon demons."

"Ah, how clever," I said. "I understand now."

Which was true. I understood perfectly.

You see, because of Xaltorath's "loving" upbringing, I could read the runes carved on those stakes. I also saw the unnatural strength that gave Dedreugh his victories. I'm not a fool. Tamin's teacher Relos Var, his trusted mentor, had spun a pretty web of lies. Tamin had swallowed every single one. Someone was indeed summoning demons in Barsine Banner.

Unfortunately, despite his own clear belief to the contrary, that someone was Tamin himself.

7: PLANS OF ATTACK

Jorat Dominion, Quuros Empire.
Two days since Urthaenriel was picked
up off the ground

Kihrin sat back in his chair, feeling like all the stone surrounding them was pressing down against his skin. He shuddered. "That was me, you know. I'm the younger brother that was sold as a slave in Kishna-Farriga. And Relos Var did try to buy me."

"Oh," Janel said, "so you're *that* brother."

"Yeah, well, I'm not his brother at all, technically. At least, not in this life."

Janel shrugged. "I don't think he sees the distinction."

"No, no, I suppose he doesn't. He hates me like I'm his real brother, anyway."

She paused, her expression unreadable. "Does he?"

"Yes. Very much so." He looked at her again. "You think he doesn't?"*

She pondered her answer before saying, "Our emotions are rarely simple when it comes to family."

"Easy for you to say. You've never met my older brother Darzin. I'm happy to say you never will."

She looked startled. "I see. Well, it does feel like we know all the same people, so who can say?"

He leaned forward and smirked. "Darzin's dead."

Janel stared at him. "So were you."

---

* Why hate a sword when it's more effective to hate the hand wielding it?

Kihrin felt the smirk fade. Could Darzin—no. The Death Goddess had loathed Darzin. She'd never let him Return.

"What about those prophecies Tamin mentioned? They sound—" Kihrin hesitated. "They sound like Devoran prophecies. I once met a Voice of the Council who was a Devoran priest—he was convinced that every time a bird chirped, it related to one of those damn quatrains."*

"Oh, they *are* Devoran prophecies," Brother Qown interjected. "I checked in case either Tamin or Relos Var had invented them whole cloth as an excuse for their atrocities. But no—the stanzas Tamin quoted are genuine. Of course, that doesn't mean they're any truer than any of the other thousands of quatrains the Devorans have collected over the centuries."

"How reassuring," Kihrin said. "Tamin got it wrong, you know. At least with that first prophecy. That has to be referring to Vol Karoth." He inhaled as he glanced at Qown. "Let's just hope that particular quatrain never comes true."

"You said that name before." Janel's eyebrows drew together. "Who?"

Qown's mouth dropped open. "What? Janel! You don't know who Vol Karoth is? No one's explained who *Vol Karoth* is to you?"

Janel turned up her hands in a helpless gesture. "No? I assume from your scandalized tone that they must be someone important."

Kihrin cleared his throat. "Yeah, you might say that."

Janel narrowed her eyes at him.

"He's the King of Demons—" Qown started to explain.

"No, he's not," Kihrin snapped. "He's what happened to that god you do and don't worship, Qown, the eighth of the Eight Immortals."

Qown just stared at Kihrin, mouth open, expression full of horror.

---

* I always thought it was funny that they're called the Devoran Prophecies when they come from demons rather than the island of Devors.

Kihrin sighed. "A long time ago, a wizard tricked one of the Eight Immortals into participating in a ritual," Kihrin finally said. "I say *tricked,* because the ritual apparently culminated with the Immortal in question being sacrificed. One assumes he didn't volunteer for that. Anyway, something went wrong.

"The rest of the people who were involved in the ritual all became dragons, but that Immortal—I realize you call him *Selanol,* but that's not his real name—became something even worse. He actually died, but what was born out of his corpse was an avatar of annihilation and evil so dangerous that the monster had to be imprisoned or he'd have destroyed the entire world. Maybe the whole universe. And so, they renamed him: *Vol Karoth.* I really don't think he's the King of Demons. He's just as eager to destroy demons as he is to destroy everything else."

"Oh." Janel swallowed. "Then I apologize; I know exactly who that is. The morgage call him something else.* And the Devoran Prophecies I've read never referred to him as Vol Karoth. The King of Demons, though? That name I've heard."

Kihrin exhaled. He didn't explain the rest—that even though S'arric's body had been turned into the vessel to house a corrupted force of darkness, S'arric's *soul* had eventually been freed and returned to the Afterlife.

To eventually be reborn as Kihrin D'Mon.

Janel's gaze locked with Kihrin's. "But I have also heard that this prophesied *Hellwarrior* will be the one to free him, the one to usher in the end of the world."

"That's . . . that's still very much under debate. I don't think that's true at all either." Kihrin said, "We're sure it's not just one person, anyway. Not just a single 'Hellwarrior.' There are four of us."

"*Us?*" Qown repeated.

Kihrin made a face and didn't answer.

---

* Warchild. Obviously, he has a ton of names, though. When you're so scary gods and demons shudder at your mention, I guess you've earned them.

"That makes no sense either," Janel said. "Why not eight? Eight immortals, eight dragons, eight Hellwarriors?"

Before Kihrin could make any comment, Qown interrupted. "Okay, wait. Go back to that part about the dragons. Even if the rest of what you say is true, you said the participants became *dragons*. Are you sure you heard that detail correctly?"

"Emphatically," Kihrin replied without looking at Qown. "That's how all nine dragons were created."

"Eight dragons," Qown corrected.

Kihrin frowned as he glanced over at the priest. "I can see this is going to become a habit. *Nine*. That's what I was about to say to Janel: the numbers don't always match. You see, the man who devised the ritual, performed it—he became a dragon too. You've met him. He runs around calling himself Relos Var these days."

Qown blinked. "Relos Var isn't a dragon!"

"Oh yes, he is. Relos Var just chooses not to look like a dragon most of the time." Kihrin shrugged. "Maybe that's why he's not insane the way the other dragons are? I honestly don't know."

As Qown sat there, eyes wide and shocked, Kihrin turned back to Janel. "The first quatrain *does* sound like it refers to you."

She raised an eyebrow. "Does it really? Am I gathering outlaws and witches while I plot an uprising?"

"You tell me. Are you?"

Brother Qown held up his book. "I'll just keep reading, shall I?"

Neither Kihrin nor Janel protested.

Qown's Turn. Mereina Castle, Barsine Banner, Jorat, Quur.

The castle felt empty, with a skeleton crew and a locked gate left behind. Most residents crowded into the arena on the tournament grounds. But Brother Qown still felt exposed and vulnerable as Mare Dorna and he, supporting a limping Ninavis between them, pretended to be servants returning from some assignment gone awry.

"Is she all right?" A guard pointed at Ninavis.

Mare Dorna waved a hand. "Oh, she's fine, fine. Just a clumsy mare. Tripped on a stair."

"Hey now, what do you mean I'm clumsy?"

"Well, who went and tripped over her own two feet? Wasn't me, I tell you."

The guard chuckled and returned to walking the castle grounds. He never gave Brother Qown so much as a glance.

They headed for the third-floor suite where the old steward's chambers now housed the count.

All three exhaled as they closed the door behind them.

Dorna abandoned Ninavis and started packing.

Brother Qown frowned. "The count said—"

Dorna looked back over her shoulder. "You think I've gone deaf, foal? I know what she said. But I guarantee you we ain't leaving this place slow and leisurely-like. Best be prepared for the quick exit."

Brother Qown started to retort but then stopped himself. Ninavis still leaned against his shoulder. "Let me look at your leg. The splint was a temporary solution. I should try to come up with something more durable."

Ninavis gave Brother Qown a flat stare as she pulled the impromptu cloak off her head and began limping toward the bed. "You sure you're not just hoping for another peek at my calves?"

Brother Qown fought the urge to roll his eyes toward the heavens. "I'm a priest of the Vishai Mysteries."

"And?"

"He can't run with the herd at all, if you know what I mean." Dorna made snipping motions, miming scissors.

With effort, Brother Qown ignored Dorna. He motioned for Ninavis to sit on a nearby chair. "Not *can't*. Won't. We take a vow. I'm not interested in your legs except to make sure they'll heal."

He also ignored Dorna's snort.

He didn't use Illumination on Ninavis for several reasons, not least because she was awake, alert, and damnably Marakori. That last point meant she might even recognize what he was doing. The Marakori didn't share the Joratese distrust of magic.

Indeed, the Marakori were the *reason* for the Joratese distrust of magic.

Fortunately, the broken bones had never pierced skin, which created less chance for infection. She had predictable muscle damage and swelling. Given adequate rest, she'd make a full recovery. He just wasn't sure she'd have the chance.

"Dorna, do you think it might be possible to find wax creeper? I'll make a plaster." Brother Qown started to look around the room for fabric that might be boiled and cut into strips.

Before he'd begun his preparations, however, Count Janel came rushing into the room. "You made it back. Good. Dorna, help me with my armor. Then I need you three to leave here at once. Go north to Visallía. The Markreev there is a distant cousin. She'll give you shelter." She crossed over to where Dorna had packed their belongings and retrieved her family sword.

"Colt? What happened? You can't . . . wait, what are you doing?" Dorna set her hands on her hips.

"I gave my word," the count said. "I will keep it."

"What's going on?" Ninavis tried to stand, then teetered and sat back down again. "What are they planning to do with my people?"

"Wait," Brother Qown said. "Count, you're upset. But please explain what's going on."

The Count of Tolamer crossed over to where a pewter goblet and pitcher rested on the sideboard. Her hand trembled as she poured water into the cup, before draining it dry and tossing it to the side.

She hadn't been as careful as normal. She discarded a crushed finger-dented mass of metal.

Janel pulled her fingers through her laevos. "So before we

left Tolamer Canton, when my grandfather still lived, he kept the services of a House D'Aramarin Gatekeeper named Kovinglass. Kazivarian man. I didn't like him, but I never thought him disloyal. At least, I didn't think that before my grandfather's death. When I began to look through my grandfather's papers, I changed my mind. I don't know if my grandfather paid Kovinglass too little or if Kovinglass had suffered some slight never forgotten. As my grandfather sickened, Kovinglass recommended poor decision after decision, which mired our house further in debt."

"Not all thieves use swords," Brother Qown said. "Some are more successful with brushes and ink."

The count nodded in bitter agreement. "So it seems."

Ninavis scowled. "What does this have to do with Tamin? With my people?"

"Because of my experience with Kovinglass's betrayal," Count Janel explained, "I wanted to believe Baron Barsine had been misled as well. He seemed to be spinning a story about Kalazan's dead father—and his father's attempt at an assassination and coup. Even if Tamin had overreacted to his father's murder, Tamin himself might have been exploited by men like Captain Dedreugh—and perhaps this Relos Var person."

"Who?"

"Relos Var. A foreigner.* Tamin's teacher. After all, I've known Tamin for years. I wanted to give him the benefit of the doubt."

"Of course you did. You nobles stick up for each other, don't you?" Ninavis rolled her eyes. "Always covering up each other's shit."

"Shut it, you," Dorna said. "You don't talk to my count that way!"

"No, Dorna. She's earned the right to scold." Janel sat down. She looked bereft.

---

* Apparently, in Jorat, anyone who comes from the other side of the Dragonspires is a "foreigner."

"Count," Brother Qown said, "what happened?"

"The baron doesn't realize it, but he's the one summoning the demons," she explained. "He thinks he's killing witches. But he's claiming innocent people are witches, having them executed, and then dedicating those deaths to a demon named Kasmodeus. There *is* a witch problem in Barsine—and Tamin is the witch."

"You have to kill him," Ninavis said. "You have to kill the baron. There will never be a better opportunity. You're the only one who can get past his soldiers and do it."

Count Janel stared at the woman in shock. "Haven't you heard a word I said? Tamin is being tricked. We have to show him—"

"And that's supposed to make it all right? The villages swept clean? The men, women, and children sent to the flame?" Ninavis pushed herself upright from where she'd been sitting. "Don't you dare tell me his gullibility excuses what he's done."

The count's jawline whitened as she stared at Ninavis. Dorna stood. Brother Qown stood as well, unsure what he could do.

"There are ways—"

Ninavis thrust out her jaw. "Are you about to start talking about Censure? Because I swear if—" Her voice died, though, trailing into a numb silence as she stared at the Count of Tolamer.

Janel's eyes glowed incandescent. Inhuman.

"Allow me," the count said, "to explain how we do politics here in Jorat." She stepped forward, and Ninavis stepped back. Except Ninavis already stood at the bed's edge, so she sat down.

"If I march in there and murder the baron," Janel explained, "who has no children, who has picked out no heirs—his title and lands don't fall to me but to the strongest stallion in his service. Who might you think that would be, hmm? Dedreugh. *Dedreugh* will be in charge. You didn't see him at the tournament. He's as strong as I am, if not stronger. He'll kill all of us, and nothing will change. In Jorat, you cannot assassinate your way into power.* Maybe, just maybe, allow the possibility I have some idea how to handle this."

The count walked over to a chest, threw open the lid, and began rummaging around inside.

A long, awkward silence wrapped around everyone in the room.

"What *are* you?" Ninavis asked.

The Count of Tolamer turned her head. "Determined."

"That's not what I meant."

"I know. I just don't care."

Ninavis inhaled. "Look—"

"Are you going to help me, or are you going to peck at my every action like a little bird?" Janel dropped the clothes in her arms and turned to face the woman. "I can help you and your people outside. But not if you think I'm an enemy whose purpose is to give you something to rebel against."

Silence.

Dorna and Brother Qown both looked at the two women, not daring to breathe as they waited to see who would move first.

"Might have been a touch out of line back there," Ninavis said.

Brother Qown exhaled.

Janel tilted her head to acknowledge she'd heard, but otherwise said nothing as she began to toss more clothing onto the floor.

"They're my people," Ninavis continued. "And they're about to be sacrificed to demons."

"Maybe . . ." Brother Qown cleared his throat. "Couldn't we send a message to Tamin's liege? Warn them he's a rogue baron? Who is the count here, anyway?"

"Ysinia," Dorna said, "but just how would you plan to do that, young man? It ain't like we have a Gatekeeper, unless you have some talents you ain't advertised yet?"

---

* Of course you can, silly girl. It's just a game based on popularity instead of bloodlines.

Brother Qown smiled wanly, which Dorna took as a negative.

He had no aptitude at all for teleportation magic, assisted by a Gatestone or otherwise. He'd never been much bothered by this. Although the Gatestones connected every corner of the empire, Qown had no real interest in being a glorified toll gate operator.

However, Brother Qown did have a legal House D'Mon license to practice magic. He kept up his membership fees. Unfortunately, in Jorat, unless someone was a priest of the Eight or an official Gatekeeper, they were labeled witches. Brother Qown wasn't at all sure the local Joratese would give him enough time to present his paperwork before they reached for their torches and pitchforks.

"Well, then," Mare Dorna continued, "since Barsine's a banner seat, it's home to a Gatestone. But way I hear from the locals, the baron's too stingy to pay for his own Gatekeeper. He has those House D'Aramarin folks doing nothing but the barest. A Gate opened the day before the tournament. A Gate's gonna open the day after. Anyone wants more, they got to pay it themselves. And like as not, have arranged it in advance."

"That doesn't help us," Ninavis snapped.

"Oh no," Dorna agreed. "Not at all. Which is why I'm still a mighty fan of running." She moved two fingers in imitation. "I'm real sorry about your people, Ninavis. They all seemed like good folk. But I ain't hearing a plan that's going to let us get near enough to free them. We'll have so many crossbows pointed at us one of them's bound to hit. And if this Captain Dedreugh fellow is strong as you, foal, but twice your size? I don't think of your chances in straight-up warfare as all too great. Plus, let's not forget your friend Tamin's got himself some witchy magic at his fingertips. I wouldn't bet all your metal on that absent teacher being the only one casting spells." Dorna squinted at the count through one eye, cocking her head to the side. "So how are you going to handle this?" She raised a finger. "Don't say, 'I'll fight my way out.' You hear me, young stallion? Don't you dare."

"Not at all," the count said as she pulled a thick pile of mail from her valise. "I plan to fight my way *in*."

The dark indigo mail hauberk shimmered with iridescence as if spawned from night and rainbow, fire dancing below the blue-black metal surface. Not brass, iron, or steel but shanathá—the metal for which the Quuros Empire had conquered Kirpis and cast out the vané. Shanathá metal was all but illegal for civilians to own, even if they could afford the cost.

Joratese nobles, technically still Quuros military, were exempt.

"'In'?" Dorna demanded. "What do you mean by fight your way 'in'?"

The count smiled as she picked up more clothing from the ground: a burgundy arming doublet so dark it looked black and a worn cloak that had seen better days, its true color indecipherable. "The timing couldn't be better. The baron is young and inexperienced."

Ninavis snorted. "What are you? Seventeen?"

The count scowled. "Don't be ridiculous."

Brother Qown glanced sideways at Janel and cleared his throat.

She looked abashed. "I mean, I reached my majority three months ago, just before we left Tolamer."

Ninavis's eyes widened. "Oh. Oh, I see. You're right. What was I thinking. You're *sixteen*. Obviously, that's different." She glared at Dorna and Brother Qown as if daring them to correct her.

"Young in years," Janel said, "not in misery."

Ninavis met her eyes. Whatever she saw there made her swallow and look away.

"And what does this have to do with what you have planned, colt?" Dorna had lost her patience.

Count Janel didn't seem to mind her nurse's ill temper. She seemed pleased to see the subject turned from her age, young by anyone's reckoning. "Tamin isn't our target. Dedreugh is.

And unlike the baron, Dedreugh is accessible; he's fighting in the tournament. Although after what I saw, I'd be very surprised if he does much fighting after this. His opponents will withdraw and give him victories by default. Since no one wants to share Sir Xia's fate, he'll win—but make no mistake, for the baron to legally kill Nina's men, Dedreugh *must* win. Those prisoners don't belong to the baron otherwise."

"But . . . the accusations of witchcraft against them?" Brother Qown hated to bring up the point but felt obligated.

Janel shook her head. "Also decided by the tournament. Tamin will combine the normal contest of judgment with the tournament outcome. It's not unprecedented. But again—for the baron to prove them witches, Dedreugh has to win."

"But who's going to fight him?" Ninavis asked. "My leg's broken, and you're a titled noble. You're not allowed to fight in the tournaments."

"No. No, I am not," the count agreed as she shrugged herself into the arming doublet. "As Count Tolamer, I may be represented by a knight in a tournament, but I would never be allowed to participate myself. It's not allowed." Humor hinted her voice. She'd told a joke but hadn't delivered the punch line.

Dorna gave the young noble a stern look. "The Black Knight? That's what you're talking about, isn't it? You're thinking to go in as the Black Knight."

Brother Qown blinked. "I don't understand. Who is the Black Knight?"

Dorna snorted. "Nobody. Anybody. Anyone who wants to can take on the knight's identity. The Black Knight is anoy-amony—"

"Anonymous," Ninavis said.

"Right. That. The Black Knight's a fool, a jape. Heaven's jester. They're unknowable—black's the color of mystery and danger, you see—and living proof no matter how fine the barding on your horse, there's always going to be some jack's ass who can piss on your riding boots. The knight's the pisser. It's a lark job, a retirement prize, given out to some drunkard who gets to spend all day mooning the crowds, guzzling free ale, and squeezing cute boys on the bum. Lots of fun."

"I still don't understand. How does that help us?"

The count finished fastening the doublet. She wore several thick layers. Since she always wore a corset bound tight across her bosom, the net effect hid her curves. "If the Black Knight's identity is never known," the count said, "then anyone can play the part—even a ruling noble. No one talks about it, but the worst-kept secret in the dominion is that the person wearing the black armor at any given tournament might well be a titled noble having fun. Which means I can fight—and Dedreugh's chances in the tournament aren't as certain as he's been led to believe." Her mouth quirked.

"The Black Knight is always picked out before the tournament," Ninavis said. "I think folks might notice if a second one shows up."

But the count's smile hadn't faltered with this declaration. "Indeed," she agreed as she shook the shanathá mail down over her body, "so I suppose it would be rude not to pay Baron Tamin's Black Knight a visit in advance."*

---

* In hindsight, I really should have checked the backgrounds of *all* the baron's people.

8: THE FOOL

Jorat Dominion, Quuros Empire.
Two days since the Stone of Shackles was destroyed

"You *are* the Black Knight. I knew it." Kihrin leaned back in his chair, pleased with himself. His theory about Janel looked increasingly probable.

"I'm sorry to disappoint you, but no."

"What? But you just said—"

"I *was* the Black Knight," Janel corrected. "At any time, there are as many Black Knights as there are active tournaments."

Kihrin paused. "You're not the one Duke Kaen is offering a bounty to kill?"

Janel looked toward the bar, then returned her attention to Kihrin.

"No," Janel said.

"Oh."

"You sound disappointed."

"I am. I came here to find that person. Duke Kaen of Yor has a significant bounty out on their head. More metal than most people will see in their whole lives. I figured that anyone Kaen wants dead so badly is someone I want as an ally."

But even as he made his proclamation, Janel and Qown gave him a very odd look.

"If you tell me Kaen's standing right behind me—"

Janel snickered. "No, he's not."

"So why are you both looking at me like that?"

Janel exhaled. "Let's just say I don't think Kaen's going to be a problem."

"But don't worry!" Qown tapped the table with his knuckles for emphasis. "We'll have whole new problems to replace him. And they're just as bad, if not much, much worse."

"If you were trying to be comforting—"

"Not really."

"Oh good. Fantastic job, then."

More cheers from the people playing their strange throwing game distracted Kihrin.* The large man tried enticing others into a new round, but no one proved interested.

Brother Qown laughed into his tea. "What a shocking conclusion," he said. "He wins every game, and then is surprised no one else wants to play."

Janel grinned. "Wait for it."

"Will no one dare challenge me?" the man boasted, throwing out his hands. Groans and laughter met his question, with a few people throwing cloth napkins at him. "Come on, people, this is just for fun!"

Then the bartender leaped over the counter, using one hand as balance, and plucked a throwing stone from the winner's hand. The wiry woman reminded Kihrin of the female members of his old criminal band, the Shadowdancers, who specialized in burglaries and knives. She had dark red-brown skin and shoulder-length maroon hair shaved to the scalp along one side. The rest of her hair fell forward to cover half her face.

The crowd made an *ooooh* noise, followed by shouted encouragements.

Kihrin had no idea how the game's scoring worked, but the game itself involved bouncing rocks to hit a target. The woman skipped the rock against the stone floor. It made a birdlike chirp before landing in a perfect bull's-eye at the board's center.

She bowed to the crowd and made a rude gesture to the gray-skinned man on her way back behind the bar.

---

* The game's called *pacer* Popular in taverns all over Jorat, but a problem whenever bar fights break out.

Kihrin chuckled as he turned back around. "I feel like I should be betting metal on this."

"Why not? Everyone else is," Janel agreed.

"Something to think about later, when the dice come out. In the meantime, tell me more about this Black Knight," Kihrin said.

Janel's Turn. The tournament grounds in Mereina, Barsine Banner, Jorat, Quur.

By the time I led Brother Qown and Dorna back down to the tournament grounds, the sun had peaked overhead. The festival contests paused for the midday meal while everyone behind the scenes regrouped. As I suspected would happen, Captain Dedreugh hadn't been involved in any more matches; his opponents forfeited their challenges, walking away embarrassed but living losers. Only an idiot could fail to notice how the crowd's mood had turned nastier.

While Tamin's Black Knight had been on the field of honor just after Sir Xia's death, trying to distract the crowd from Dedreugh's actions, he was absent when we returned. I suspect his exit had been a fast one, as the angry crowd had begun expressing their displeasure with thrown vegetables and spoiled wine. If he had retreated, his shelter options were limited to the azhocks behind the grounds.

The tentlike azhocks formed a temporary, traveling encampment that moved from city to city with each tournament. Despite its roaming nature, it maintained a pattern of streets and addresses as constant as visiting taxmen just after the harvest.

Dorna guessed the secret of just who we were visiting when we passed a band of horses—stallions—being kept well away from any mares. The single fireblood stallion in their number stood out like a giant redwood among dwarf pines.

She saw the fireblood and snorted. "Oh, so that's how it is."

"Be nice," I warned her, and then walked inside a tent marked with red spiderwebs.

"Hello, Sir Baramon," I said as I flipped back my sallí cloak's hood.

The man who looked up from his Eamithonian plum wine looked well past his prime, by the kindest definitions. He possessed blue roan skin and a magnificent black mustache whose ends trailed past his chin. He still wore his Black Knight armor; the helmet rested on a small portable table next to the man's rope bed and more liquor bottles.

The man looked up, surprised at our entrance. "You're not supposed to be in here—"

"Well, look at you." Dorna walked into the tent behind me. "Fatter than I remember you being, last I saw you."

"And you've grown no prettier in your dotage, you old sow. I haven't—" But then all the color fled from his face as he shifted his attention from Dorna back to me.

He'd recognized me.

The knight didn't even look as Brother Qown slipped into the tent. He ignored Dorna even though they had just traded barbs. I had his full attention.

"From your reaction, I'll assume I don't need an introduction."

Sir Baramon barked out a laugh and wiped his mouth. "Oh no, lord. You don't. Frena would be proud, to see how you've grown."

He poured himself another drink.

I grabbed his arm. "We don't have time for that."

He tried to snatch his arm away, but he'd have had an easier time bending an iron statue. He scowled, his gaze flicking from his trapped arm back to my face. He might have been old and out of shape, but he was still a stallion. "What do you want?" he sputtered.

"Do you remember when last you saw me?"

"Of course." A sick look stole over his features. "You were . . ." His gaze dropped down to his arm. "Let me go."

I did. "Lonezh Canton," I said, "with the demons at our gates. And you ran."

"That's not what happened—"

"Ran," I continued, "with Talaras, in the middle of the night. You deserted your post and lied to the guards at the postern gate. You told them you had a mission from my father and they should let you out. So they did."

"I remember what happened." Sir Baramon's stare hardened as he sat the bottle down and leaned back in his chair, which creaked in protest.

Sir Baramon's silence drowned in emotions. He worked his jaw for a moment before leaning forward again. "I tried to take you with me. Do you remember?"

My throat tightened. "And I yelled and kicked and wouldn't let you."

"So that's why you're here?" His gaze landed on Dorna. "Come to mock the coward?"

I pulled a second chair away from the azhock tent wall and sat down on it, facing him. I smiled at the old, fat knight. "Now why would I mock you, Sir Baramon? You alone had any sense."

Baramon's head jerked as he stared back at me. Whatever he'd thought I would say to him, I rather doubt it had sounded anything like my actual words. "What?"

"They were *fools.*"

Baramon blinked. I rather think Dorna and Qown might have too.

"Fools," I said again. "I love my father, but he was an idiot. I haven't the slightest clue why he decided to stand and fight. If I *had* gone with you?" My voice cracked on the last word. I swallowed and turned my head to the side, fighting what-might-have-been's emotional storms. I inhaled deeply. "You escaped the massacre. No one else did."

"I wouldn't say that," he mumbled, bowing his head.

Brother Qown sat down on the rope bed's edge. The ropes creaked. The sound broke the spell. As soon as Sir Baramon looked up to see who had caused the noise, he turned back to me with a hard expression on his face.

"What is it you want?"

"A boon," I explained. "I'm going to take over your role as Black Knight for the day."

Sir Baramon laughed outright in surprise, but his expression sobered as he realized I hadn't shared his laughter. "Are you—? What? You're not—" He cleared his throat and started over. "We're not the same size, my lord."

"You and a rhinoceros ain't the same size either," Dorna said, "but I don't see it stopping you from trying to impersonate one."

"Dorna," I chided. "Stop it." I turned back to the knight. "In all fairness, the armor is a bit, hmm, small for you. It doesn't need to be a perfect fit. I have a shanathá mail shirt I'll wear under it." I opened my sallí cloak, revealing the blue mail underneath.

Sir Baramon stared at the metal. His look wasn't lascivious—he didn't run with my sex—but rather one of shocked recognition. "That's your grandfather's mail."

"*Was* my grandfather's mail."

His expression clouded. "I'm sorry. How did he die?"

"His heart gave out." I fought to keep my expression placid. Just because he'd died in his sleep didn't mean my wounds had healed. I'd been given no time to mourn.

"You have my sympathies. He was a good man."

"Thank you." I picked up the helmet left on the table and gazed at the black painted metal. Most of the core armor pieces used in tournament fighting are every bit as sturdy as any armor soldiers might wear on the battlefield. Tournaments aren't without risk, even in bouts less calculated than Captain Dedreugh's demonstration. Sir Baramon might have been a drunkard on his last legs, but he hadn't shaken his training; the helmet was well maintained and practical. It would serve.

I set it down. "Do you think Talaras would let me ride him? Arasgon is willing, but someone might notice he's not the same fireblood."

"Arasgon's here?" He sighed and pinched the bridge of his nose. "Silly of me. He never leaves your side."

"He did once."

Sir Baramon didn't take the bait. He picked up his wine bottle and jammed the stopper back in. "Why would you want to play the Black Knight? It's an ugly crowd out there. And with the way this tournament is going, leaving while you can sounds like a better use of your time."

"It's a matter of idorrá. Besides, if I don't do this, you'll have to face the choices you made at Lonezh Canton a second time."

Dorna's face went gray. "What?"

Sir Baramon stood and snatched the helmet back, which I let go rather than fight over. "What foolery is this? You shouldn't try to scare people with ghost stories."

"Oh, don't claim you're a skeptic. How often have you listened to the new Baron Barsine claim his banner is overrun with witches and their summoned demons?" I crossed my arms over my chest. "Just how do you think a Hellmarch starts?"

"This witchcraft business is just the paranoid delusions of a child still mourning his father."

"Oh no," I said, narrowing my eyes. "It's much worse." I'd admit I hoped it would be easier to sell Sir Baramon on this idea. I suppose I'd hoped he'd jump at the chance to regain his honor. But . . .

Demons. Could I blame him for flinching?

It meant I would have to play a harder game.

"Don't make me take what I need, knight. I won't be denied this."

"You're a little girl," Sir Baramon chided. "A little girl who needs to go home."

"You abandoned my mother to die."

He flinched. "That was uncalled for."

"If my father were alive, he'd disagree. My grandfather would disagree. You failed the Theranons. When we needed you, you deserted, thinking of yourself—"

"No!" Sir Baramon's eyes were wet. "That's not true. Frena ordered me to go. Your mother begged me to take you and get you to safety. She said the gods demanded it. The demons couldn't be allowed to have you under any circumstances. You were the hope of the world. I—" His voice broke off in a choking sob.

Dorna handed the man a handkerchief and patted him on the shoulder, her expression unreadable.

I blinked and stepped back, not saying another word. My mother had ordered Baramon to take me to safety? If true, then on some level, she'd known fending off the demons was hopeless. She never would've sent me outside the castle's walls if she thought we'd repel the demonic onslaught. It implied something terrifying . . .

I'd grappled with this guilt for years, you understand; the suspicion that my capture by the demons, my possession by Xaltorath, wasn't coincidence. That Xaltorath had *searched* for me, rather than picking out a little girl at random. I know, I know—we all want to think we're special. But this sort of "special" would have given me nightmares, if I dreamed. I found the idea as horrible as it was arrogant: that half of Jorat and Marakor combined had fallen to the Hellmarch as demons searched for one girl. And only ended when Xaltorath decided she was done playing.

I didn't outrun the demons, you see. Not even close.

But I couldn't let myself be distracted.

"Now I need your help," I said. "You were my grandfather's best knight, and now? You're my grandfather's last knight. I need your aid. I call you back to serve the House of Theranon. I call you back to repay your debts."

He wiped at his eyes with the handkerchief and scowled. "I serve—"

I shook my head. "No. You don't. Not anymore. Tamin isn't worthy of you. You're my man now, as you always should have been."

His jaw tightened, and he stared at me until I started to wonder if I'd made a mistake.

Sir Baramon held out the helmet. "The strap's a little loose."

Dorna intercepted it. "Well, now. Just you let me take care of that."

9: The Contest

Jorat Dominion, Quuros Empire.
Two days since the last day of Gadrith
D'Lorus's reign

Kihrin said nothing at first when Janel paused her story and motioned for Brother Qown to continue. He chewed on his lip for a moment. "You know, I hate to say this, but I think . . . I think you're right. I think Xaltorath was looking for you. Specifically, you. Just like I think he . . . she . . . was looking for me back in the Capital. It *was* intentional."

"While it's a distressing idea, I concur," Brother Qown said.

Janel swallowed and then nodded. "I know now. I hate it. I hate it with everything in me, this idea—that people have died just because I exist. It's so senseless. I do feel guilty." She raised a hand. "I know it's not my fault, but it doesn't change my feelings."

Kihrin met Janel's eyes. "A good friend told me we volunteered for this. Four of us. From the Afterlife, we volunteered to return and help fight the war. I think you're one of us."

"Let me guess—my name was Elana."

Kihrin blinked at her. "What? Why would you think—"

"When we met in the Afterlife, you called me Elana." She paused. "Repeatedly."

"Oh. Odd. I don't know an Elana. Hell, the only time I've heard that name—" He frowned. "Huh."

Janel raised both eyebrows and waited.

"I've been told that in my past life, a woman named Elana

saved me from something, uh, terrible. In fact, I wouldn't be sitting here without her."

"Oh?" Janel rested her chin on her knuckles. "And however do you plan to say thank you?"

For a second, Kihrin thought she was talking about Atrine, but then he realized that no, she really wasn't. He slowly smiled. "I have a few ideas."

"I cannot wait to hear them."

Qown cleared his throat.

Kihrin startled. He kept forgetting the priest was still sitting at the same table.

Janel looked vaguely embarrassed. "Anything else I should know?"

Kihrin gave her a sour smile. "There's a prophecy."

She rolled her eyes and laughed as she looked up toward the ceiling. "Gods."

"Pretty much. So I think Xaltorath—as a demon—would have every reason to look for us. To track us down."

"But then why hasn't she killed us?" Janel questioned. "It makes no sense."*

"I think to understand whether or not it makes sense, we'd have to understand Xaltorath."

"Good luck with that," Janel said.

"The demons want to live," Brother Qown said, speaking up at last. "What does anyone want? They want to survive. The question we must ask ourselves is: Can they *only* survive at *our* expense? Is this a Zaibur game where a single side wins, or is this ravens and doves?"

Kihrin and Janel looked at each other. "Uh . . ."

Kihrin said, "Ravens and doves? I don't know that game."

---

* Oh, nonsense. It makes perfect sense. One doesn't destroy a tool that might still prove useful. We're not the only group playing this little game of "who controls the prophecies." Let's face it—*everyone* wants to make those four their special little puppets.

"Oh," Brother Qown looked abashed. "I grew up with it in Eamithon. It's a children's game, where it's possible to have multiple simultaneous victories, and in fact, the most prestigious victory involves all the players winning."

Kihrin made a face. "Eamithon sounds nice. Doesn't Eamithon sound nice? I was going to open a bar there for my father." He sighed, stared into his glass, and motioned to the bartender for another refill.

Kihrin turned back to Qown. "It's your turn."

Qown's Turn. The tournament grounds at Mereina, Barsine Banner, Jorat, Quur.

Plans were made, tasks allocated—which, in Brother Qown and Dorna's case, meant finding seats at the tournament. That ended up being a more complicated endeavor than Qown ever expected. While the stands were underpopulated, attendees crowded toward the front. A great many spectators had huddled together to talk in hushed tones about the day's strange events, who else might be killed, and just how upset they should be over the whole matter.

"How long do you think it will take Sir Baramon to break down his tent?" Brother Qown leaned over and whispered to Dorna. If, or rather when, things started to go wrong, time would be at a premium. Someone would need to retrieve Ninavis too—a danger-fraught endeavor—so Qown wanted everything else readied first.

Dorna examined an engraved leather purse in her hands. "What was that?" She tucked the purse away into her skirts.

"How long do you think it will take Sir Baramon to break down his tent?" he asked again.

"It's called an azhock," Dorna said.

"That's not the point."

"Well, if you're going to learn our ways, priest, you'd best start with the important words, doncha think?" The old woman winked at him before turning back to the tournament.

Dorna leaned over to tug on the sleeve of a woman sitting in a box seat. She wore a merchant family's square crest on her sleeves. An embroidery hoop rested on her lap. "Morning there, Mare," Dorna said. "Who's the knight in the blue and yellow?" She pointed to the field, where two new knights approached.

The woman eyed Dorna's lack of team colors before answering. "Gozen. Works for the Sifen family." She sniffed. "Farmers. They grow mangoes."

"Ooooh," Dorna said. "He any good?"

The woman snorted this time. She started to return to her embroidery. "Wait, my purse! What happened to my purse?"

Dorna ignored Brother Qown's accusing look. "Did you drop it? When did you last see it? Did you buy something? Maybe it's still there."

The woman gave Dorna a panicked look, grabbed her embroidery bag, and bolted back between the stands. Dorna took the woman's place and motioned for the Vishai priest to join her.

"Dorna!"

She pulled him over beside her. "Don't make a fuss. People will notice."

"But you . . . *you* . . ." Brother Qown all but pointed a finger at her. "That seat doesn't belong to you. Neither does that purse."

"We're saving a spot for Her Highness, if she comes back. You agreed." Dorna took a sip of the weak tea she'd bought from a vendor earlier, made a face, and traded up for the cider flagon the woman had left behind. "Much better. Now shush. Gozen's up, and he's my favorite."

"A minute ago, you'd never heard of Gozen!"

"Don't be silly, priest. Gozen works for the Sifen family. They grow mangoes." She returned to watching the sport.

"You're a terrible person," Brother Qown muttered.

The old woman looked proud.

Two knights entered the grounds. The one in yellow and

blue, Gozen, looked like he'd just purchased the basic knight starter kit. Too new or unsuccessful at the contests to have yet gained himself full armor and barding for his horse. He faced an older knight in full red regalia. The older knight's colors and banners identified him as a Red Spear, a mercenary company who sold their skills to the highest bidder.

The two knights entered the yard and made their customary first circuit around the field, complete with hurled invectives. Brother Qown saw Count Janel, or rather, the Black Knight, enter the grounds.

No one noticed. No one had paid much attention to the Black Knight earlier in the day, and the new Black Knight still wore black armor and rode a flame-kissed ebony fireblood. The differences seemed obvious to Brother Qown. The knight rode a flame-kissed ebony fireblood, but since Talaras had not agreed to let Janel ride him, it wasn't the *same* flame-kissed ebony fireblood. The tiger striping on his legs was an easy giveaway. The Black Knight's armor suddenly appeared oversized, strapped down to a slimmer body.

Still no one paid any attention.

All energy focused on the two men, now before the warden and a table filled with eight different statues.* Gozen bent down from his saddle and picked up the small statue of a pregnant woman sitting cross-legged on a tortoise's back: Galava, the Mother. Gozen held the statue aloft so the crowds in the stands might see his selection.

"Ah," Dorna said. She chewed on a wrapped porie leaf, another item Brother Qown hadn't seen her buy. "The Fourth Contest. Interesting choice."

"What's the Fourth Contest?"

"Shhh. It's starting."

The priest gritted his teeth and returned his attention to the

---

* There are eight contests, with two forms each contest can take, so sixteen different styles in total, which is why your richer Joratese nobles have a stable of athletes who specialize in particular fields.

combatants and their contest, whatever form it would take. The Red Spear rode up to the table as squires ran to them with ropes. They carried two kinds—small, thin ropes, such as one might use to tie bundles, and a single large rope thick as a strong man's wrist. Since Gozen had picked the contest, the Red Spear now had the right to pick which sort of "weapon" they'd use.

The Red Spear reached down, put his hand on the smaller ropes, then paused. He changed his mind and picked up the thick rope.

The crowd cheered or booed, depending on preferences and where they'd bet their metal.

The count rode over to Gozen, just as he picked up the other end of the rope. A murmur swept over the crowd; the group surrounding them stood. Brother Qown found himself feeling both guilty and grateful Dorna had found them such a nice spot.

Then the Black Knight pulled the rope from Gozen's hand and motioned for the young knight to move to the side. He wouldn't be the one fighting this bout. She would.

"Can she do that?" Brother Qown whispered to Dorna.

"Aye," Dorna replied. "There ain't much a Black Knight can't do, truth be told. Taking over one side of a contest is the least of it. If she wins, it's her victory, but it'll still count for the Sifen family."

"And if she loses?"

Mare Dorna slapped his chest. "Shut your mouth, priest. My count don't lose."

The Black Knight rode to the field's center. The Red Spear rode after her, holding the other end of the rope, just long enough to allow both riders to sit on their horses several lengths apart.

"Are they—?" Brother Qown frowned and leaned forward. "That's a children's game."

"The rules are simple enough for that, aye. Each rider holds one end of the rope and don't let go. The one who does, loses. If they're pulled off their horse, they'll let go."

"But this single contest won't decide anything, will it?"

Dorna glanced back at him. "I reckon it will decide how much the Sifen family charges for their mangoes."

"What? But—" Brother Qown raised his chin in the direction of the prisoners' cages. "I meant about that."

Dorna studied the cages, her expression sullen. She looked around in case anyone eavesdropped. "Problem with that is—"

The crowd roared.

Dorna broke off whatever she'd been about to say and jumped to her feet. Brother Qown craned his neck to see what had happened in the ring while he'd been distracted.

The match had ended.

The Red Spear clambered to regain his footing after he'd fallen off his horse, who stood at the side pawing the ground and looking surprised. A referee ran over to talk to the warden, or rather, to the warden's nurse, but the outcome seemed clear. The referees hoisted the Sifen family's flag, a yellow-and-blue field affixed with a trade group's square mark.

Winner.

Dorna slapped Qown on the shoulder. "Told you."

Count Janel, or rather, the Black Knight, now had everyone's attention.

Arasgon pranced back to the center, facing the box where the baron sat. Captain Dedreugh lounged in a chair a short distance from the box, enjoying a drink. He lingered there in case someone foolishly tried for a match.

As the baron raised his arm and leaned forward to give some command or judgment, a shout rang out in the distance. Several people began to point.

Qown looked around to spot the cause. Surprised and dismayed cries rang out from the crowd.

Finally, the priest realized people were pointing back at the castle, toward the thick black smoke snaking up from inside the walls.

Something inside Mereina Castle was burning.

Dorna and Brother Qown shared a look.

"You don't think . . . ?" Dorna worried at her lower lip.

"Ninavis," he said.

Brother Qown didn't know what could've happened, but he'd splinted and cast her leg. How much harm could she do . . .

No. It was she. Possibly she and Kalazan, but he knew in his bones she'd done *something*.

Baron Tamin ordered his soldiers back to the castle, his wild gesticulations communicating his anger as clearly as if Brother Qown stood right next to him.

It might have been the priest's imagination, but he thought he heard the name *Kalazan* floating by on the breeze.

Tamin didn't himself leave. Instead, the baron returned to his seat, casting angry scowls back to the fortress.

While the baron dealt with his new problem, Count Janel drew her sword and pointed it at Dedreugh. Arasgon screamed out something to call attention to the challenge.

Dorna whistled. "Oh, I wondered how she was going to do this without fighting her way through a dozen knights. This works much better."

Baron Tamin walked to the edge of the box. Although Brother Qown couldn't hear his words, his consternation and confusion were evident. Tamin must have realized this wasn't *his* Black Knight, wasn't Sir Baramon. He likely recognized the fireblood too—in which case, he had to realize Janel's identity.

The crowd surged, wild and shouting. The tournament had turned into something unexpected; it excited their fancy. Tamin raised his hand until they subsided. He motioned for the Black Knight to leave the field.

Arasgon shifted his weight and strutted. Count Janel again pointed her sword at Dedreugh.

Brother Qown saw the baron bend down and listen to something the warden's nurse had to say, saw him shake his head in refusal. The baron motioned for the soldiers who hadn't left for the castle to remove the Black Knight from the field. As he did, the crowd in the stands began to stomp their feet and shout.

Black Knight! Black Knight! Black Knight!

The crowd came alive, chanting the title in unison.

Brother Qown realized he hadn't actually understood what role the Black Knight played in these tournaments—in Joratese society.

Yes, a jester figure. A fool on horseback, providing entertainment to the crowds during breaks in the show. But if one looked at this figure and saw only the mountebank, then one missed the whole point.

The Black Knight might be a fool, but this fool served the gods. The Black Knight was a holy idiot, destiny's joking hand, the mischievous herald of divine fate.

The people of Barsine Banner hated Dedreugh. And now the Black Knight was calling him out. Nothing would come of this. Surely, this was the baron's attempt to defuse the morning atrocities. This couldn't be the Eight's judgment. It was a prank and a lark and nothing more.

But what if?

What if?

The baron gave the crowds a sour look and nodded to where his man Dedreugh sat. The guard captain drained his drink and stood. He called his horse over and vaulted into the saddle, directing the stallion around the ring.

"Who dares think they can take me?" he screamed out. "Do you think I fear the unknown? That I will quake at the dark? *I am the dark! I am the unknown all men fear!* I will tear this impostor limb from limb." He pulled out his sword and waved it in the air. He continued in this vein for several more circles around the yard, each time elaborating on the many ways he'd grind into dust the poor fool stupid enough to challenge him.

Dedreugh's bluster didn't seem unusual. For reasons defying Brother Qown's understanding, every knight at the tournament indulged in this cock's parade of insults. Maybe they did it to intimidate their opponents, give the crowds a chance to place their bets, or impress their loyal fans. Some traditions start without anyone knowing why.

The Black Knight waited in the ring. She didn't make a sound.

When the time came to ride to the contest table, Arasgon strolled over with head and tail held high.

Neither side moved to pick a statue.

Of course. The one with the least idorrá picked first in these contests, and neither side would make that admission.

"It's my lord's banner," Dedreugh growled. "You pick first."

Janel didn't respond at first. Then she tilted her head—as close as she could come to a nod wearing that helmet—and reached out a black-gauntleted hand. She swept up a statue of an upright man with an eagle's head and wings: Khored the Destroyer. Brother Qown wasn't sure what the contest indicated, but given the god chosen, it seemed safe to assume it would be violent.

The count held the statue over her head for the crowd to see. Everyone roared their approval.

Instead of picking a variation, Dedreugh immediately attacked.*

Dedreugh launched himself from his horse and tackled Count Janel, which Brother Qown wouldn't have thought possible had he not seen it. Dedreugh moved so quickly even Arasgon must have been taken by surprise; before the fireblood could take action, Count Janel hit the ground with a thud.

The crowds pressed behind Mare Dorna and Brother Qown until the priest found himself wedged against the fence. The audience seemed aware they were witnessing a singular moment, something they might never see again. The Black Knight existed as a faux knight, a paper knight: at best a symbol, and at worst a crass lampoon. The Black Knight didn't behave this way.

Then again, if the Black Knight embodied divine mystery, perhaps this change fitted the role.

Baron Tamin stood still against the edge of his box. The warden's white nurse had also come forward, leaning her hands

---

* It's not like he really cared about rules or anything.

against the wooden railing while she watched the match. Neither seemed happy.

The two knights rolled around in the dirt. Both stood as quickly. If their plate armor was supposed to make their movements clumsy or hampered, no one had bothered to tell them. They both shared an animal grace.

Dorna reached over and grabbed Brother Qown's agolé, twisting the fabric into a ball in her fist. He felt the same nervous dread.

Dedreugh unsheathed his sword, while Arasgon rode up to Janel so she might draw the blade still attached to his saddle. She barely had time to pull the weapon in line before Dedreugh rained down blows. She stepped backward, even at risk of pinning herself against the stands.

Dedreugh swung at her; Janel ducked under the blow. As she did, Dedreugh swung his sword so hard he embedded it in the wooden fencing. He covered his arm with his shield to buy himself the seconds he needed to extricate his weapon. Janel used the opportunity to pierce the weaker mail at his hip, drawing blood.

Brother Qown had told himself this fight didn't need to be to the death. She only needed to embarrass Dedreugh after all, force him to acknowledge her as superior, bow to her idorrá.

As Dedreugh roared with fury, Brother Qown realized he'd been naïve. Dedreugh tore his sword free and swung back again at his enemy. Janel blocked the attack with her own shield, darting in with her blade to take advantage of the opening.

Brother Qown thought Janel took quicker advantage of opportunities, not to mention moving faster on her feet. Dedreugh proved to be a hulking brute on the battlefield, all fury and no strategy. Against an enemy who equaled him in strength, it wasn't enough.

Dedreugh came in with another massive, cleaving blow. Count Janel danced away, slamming up his shield with her own, pulling her sword down hard against his elbow. A strip of his mail came loose, little rings falling on the sand like a rich man emptying his purse into a beggar's hands.

The Count of Tolamer laughed.

Dedreugh came in again, furious, and Janel danced back. Brother Qown realized with startled shock she was copying Ninavis's strategy: goading her enemy into attack after attack, exploiting the openings as he weakened. Then she stumbled, and he roared his pleasure.

It was a trap.

Her sword slash found the weak spot again, the same place she'd cut his armor previously. The sword sank deep, shearing steel and leather this time, sending sparks down into the sands and the smell of burning metal into the air. Her blade bit true into skin, muscle, and bone.

Dedreugh's sword fell to the churned earth, followed a second later by his arm.

The whole crowd erupted in a deafening roar.

Brother Qown felt instinct kick in, beyond his control or desire to rein in. He yanked his agolé from Dorna's hands as he climbed over the yard's low wooden railing. If he could reach Dedreugh fast enough, before the blood loss killed him, Brother Qown might be able to save his life.

But the crowd fell silent.

The crowd fell silent, and Dedreugh didn't fall.

Instead, Dedreugh stood there and gazed fondly at Janel. Dedreugh began to laugh, a sound that made all the skin along Qown's arms prickle. No human could make such a noise.

The blood dripping from Dedreugh's severed arm wasn't red. It was black—the thick black ooze of old clotted blood seeping from a corpse.

An old corpse.

Dedreugh hadn't fallen because Dedreugh was already dead.

He'd been dead the whole time, animated by the diabolical spirit possessing him. Such a spirit wouldn't care if it pushed the body it possessed past all normal endurance. Such a spirit wouldn't care if the body it wore took further injury. Easy to mistake such carelessness for supernatural strength. Easy to mistake it for the same curse that gave the count her infernal strength.

They had made a terrible mistake.

AH, I KNEW IT WAS TOO GOOD TO LAST.

No noise issued from Dedreugh's throat. He hadn't used anything as prosaic as his voice.

Every single person in the crowd, Brother Qown included, felt the demon scream those words straight into their minds.

"Oh, Selanol," Brother Qown said, not caring who might hear him. "He's not Dedreugh. That's not Dedreugh at all." Brother Qown reached over the railing and grabbed Dorna by the shoulder. "Dedreugh isn't tainted by demons. His body is being possessed. Do you hear me? He *is* a demon."

Brother Qown didn't think Dorna could hear him. The old woman shook off his arm and mumbled something under her breath, her attention focused on Janel and the demon.

I ALMOST FORGOT. WHAT WAS IT YOU SAID YOU'D DO TO ME, LITTLE GIRL?

Dedreugh grinned. He dropped his shield and put his remaining hand's gauntleted fingers into his mouth.

He yanked downward. Bone and muscle broke away with a sickening crunch.

Dedreugh ripped his own jaw off.[†]

People screamed, fainted, fled.

I WON'T NEED THAT ANYMORE.

Popping sounds filled the air as the straps holding his armor in place broke under the stress of his expanding form. Thick black blood oozed down the cracks in his flesh. The severed arm began regenerating, tumorous warping flesh flowing from light to dark blue at his fingertips, which ended in wicked black claws.

"Kasmodeus, I presume? Did you think that would frighten

† Demons are so melodramatic.

me? Because the next thing I'm going to do is rip your entire head off and—"

YOU KNOW ME?

"Oh, I know the name. We haven't met, but you know what gossips demons are."

His tongue licked his cheekbones. **I WILL FEAST ON YOUR SOUL.**

"Aren't you the flatterer." The count laughed and raised her shield. "You're going to have to use more than honeyed words if you want to impress me."

He screamed and leapt at her. They rolled together. A terrible growling sound filled the air.

The crowd panicked. Half the audience didn't know if they should run or nudge closer for a better look. No one was doing anything helpful.

Brother Qown began going over any possible action he might be able to take to help the count.

She'd given him the demon's name. Brother Qown struggled to remember the names and qualities Father Zajhera had demanded he memorize.

Kasmodeus. A mid-level demon, associated with brutality and the desperation of those so starved by winter they turned to cannibalism. He preferred using a male form and liked sacrifices given to him as burnt offerings. His weaknesses included the first year's snow melt and clean water blessed by holy men.

Clean water . . .

Nothing in the stands would be water. Plum wine or green tea or pepperleaf beer, but not pure water. Brother Qown reached inside the railing and grabbed Dorna's stolen flagon and then sprinted for the horse troughs near the nobles' box.

Behind him, Brother Qown heard screams. People ran, trying to escape the demon's growling laughter. Qown dumped the cider as he ran.

Baron Tamin gestured to guards who seemed to have gone quite deaf. The old warden leaned forward and blinked in dumb shock, attention drawn to the tournament. The warden's nurse, whom Janel had described as Yoran-like in coloring, leaned against the box's rails. Her hands rested on the carved wood, all her attention focused on Dedreugh and Count Janel. As Brother Qown saw her, he knew why Count Janel had mistaken her race.

Not only wasn't she from Jorat, but she wasn't even Quuros. She was Doltari, a race from far south of the empire's borders, usually only seen in Quur as slaves.

A shocked roar from the crowd made him stumble, and he turned back to the fight to see Janel's family sword spinning in a lazy end-over-end arc through the air. The sword embedded itself a scant few feet away from the covered cages by the execution stakes.

The count was unarmed.

Dedreugh/Kasmodeus grinned and swung back to finish the job. Arasgon started to move forward, but Janel shouted for him to stay back.

She ducked Dedreugh's swing and began running for the stakes.

Brother Qown forced himself to focus on the task at hand. In any other imperial dominion, he wouldn't trust the water in a horse trough, but the Joratese elevated horse care to religion. The horses were given cleaner water than the people.

He pulled a copper sun medallion from under his robes and began praying over the trough water. As he did, Qown saw the Doltari slave withdraw a smooth stone slab from under her bodice, where it must have nestled against her bosom. Then she removed a small blue-gray glass bottle from her basket and a hair stick from her white hair.

No, Brother Qown thought, not a hair stick. A calligraphy brush with a barrel sharpened to a point.

Another roar. Brother Qown tried to ignore it, but keeping his focus proved difficult when he felt the blast of heat.

He blinked. *Heat?*

He finished his blessing and looked over. Count Janel had

ripped a post from the ground, using the thing like a mallet. The demon was . . .

Kasmodeus was on fire.

Demons were great fans of fire. They set fires whenever possible, basking in the glow, absorbing the heat. They fed on fire.

Setting fire around a demon who had been summoned by a wizard was a terrible idea, but this was something else: a demon possessing a corpse. Kasmodeus *needed* Dedreugh's corpse. He needed that link to the physical world. Destroying his body might well sever the demon's ties to the physical world and send him back to Hell.

But what had set him on fire?

A mystery for later. Qown scooped his flagon full of the now blessed water and started to run.

"There you are."*

Brother Qown turned. The Doltari nurse pulled her attention away from the fight for long enough to jab the sharpened point of her calligraphy brush into the back of her hand. Then she flipped the brush over to load the bristles with her own blood.

She drew a single glyph on her forehead. That same glyph immediately appeared on the foreheads of every guard.

A terrible foreboding came over Brother Qown.

He possessed a different definition of witchcraft from the Joratese, but he knew a spell being cast when he saw one.

"What are you doing?" Brother Qown yelled. "Stop her! Stop her. Baron! *You must stop her!*"

The white-skinned woman looked at him and smiled.

All of winter couldn't have been as cold.

She tipped the glass bottle over. It tumbled off the railing's edge and shattered against the ground, a tiny tinkling overlooked in the tumult raging in the tournament grounds.

Thick blue smoke poured from the shattered bottle. The smoke curled around the Doltari woman's face without touching

---

* I was so sick of Mereina by that point.

it. The old warden, however, was less fortunate. The smoke poured up his nostrils and pushed into his mouth. He began screaming, choking. The warden dislodged the dhole puppy, who whimpered and snapped at the curling smoke.

The Doltari woman picked up the puppy, drew the same mark on its forehead too, and turned to leave.*

"Senera, what have you done?" Tamin demanded.

"My job," she snapped. "Follow me, boys. We're finished here."

The soldiers, who in theory worked for the baron, obeyed her command.

The baron started to protest, but the smoke hadn't stopped its spread. It snaked tendrils up his nose, down into his mouth. The smoke billowed out.

Another roar sounded behind Brother Qown. The priest turned to see Janel standing. Dedreugh's body lay on the ground, burning to ash. The count had raised an arm to hold Dedreugh's head by his hair, black blood dripping down from the neck and spine. It looked for all the world as if she'd ripped the corpse's dead head from its body.

Probably, she had.

The flesh burned fast, even without fuel. Brother Qown had no doubt nothing would be left behind for Kasmodeus to animate.

But they'd run out of time.

The blue smoke flowed over Brother Qown as well.

---

* Of course, I saved the puppy. I'm not a *monster*.

10: THE CHOKING OF MEREINA

Jorat Dominion, Quuros Empire.
Two days since the Breaking of Gaeshe

Brother Qown closed his journal and set it aside.

Kihrin waited a moment.

Brother Qown picked up his teacup and took a long, luxurious sip.

"So what happened?" Kihrin said. He pointed at the priest. "What happened with the smoke?"

Brother Qown cleared his throat. "I just, uh . . . perhaps if you might give me a moment. I find this next section emotionally draining."

"Would you like me to continue?" Janel asked.

Brother Qown breathed in obvious relief. "Would you?"

"Of course."

Janel's Turn. Mereina, Barsine Banner, Jorat, Quur.

I often fight demons, but rarely in the living world. Would it be wrong to admit I enjoyed fighting Kasmodeus? I mean, we're supposed to seek battle only from necessity. A stallion protects the herd, and to enjoy the fight too much is . . . hmm . . . it's a bit thorra, isn't it? It's crass to admit I might have relished leading that beast on a chase, tripping him, tricking him, ripping his head from his shoulders.

Would it be wrong to admit I felt hollow disappointment Kasmodeus had been alone? That I didn't wish to stop with his slaughter, that I wanted to turn to the next enemy, and the next, and the next after that?

Even though I knew Kasmodeus's banishment would be temporary, even though I knew no right-thinking person could enjoy such barbarity, I couldn't stop myself from smiling at the end.

Yes, it would be wrong to say such things.*

Forget I mentioned it.

At the end, I remember hearing Brother Qown shouting my name. I turned toward him, intending to lash him for breaking cover. My words died as I saw rolling blue smoke spread out from the baron's box. The smoke moved as fast as a strong man walked. Nothing about it seemed natural.

Inside the box, the death-pale nurse who had attended the warden gathered up her embroidery basket and a puppy. She directed Tamin's soldiers to follow her, but I didn't see Tamin himself.

Neither nurse nor soldiers seemed bothered by the smoke. Each had a strange symbol marking their foreheads. Whatever it meant, it hadn't been there when I had visited earlier.

Then I saw the blue smoke surround a servant, tendrils invading the man's nostrils, forcing entry into his mouth. He dropped his drink tray and began choking, hands closing around his throat.

I turned back to the crowds.

"Run!" I roared, but the spectators were already galloping to safer fields. I hurried to the two cages containing bandits and rebels.

There would be no running for them.

"Arasgon, help me!"

He screamed back to let me know he'd heard.

Brother Qown stumbled from the smoke. A yellow glyph shone on his forehead, but otherwise he gave no sign of distress. He saw me, pointed, yelled as he ran forward. His fingertip *glowed*.

Helmet. He was shouting, "Helmet!"

---

* Cute. Didn't stop her, though, did it?

The screams around me changed in tenor and tone, mixed now with coughing, choking, sobs. I decided the time and place for anonymity was over and pulled the helmet from my head. Brother Qown ran to me and traced his fingertip against my forehead. The air quality changed. I no longer smelled ash or smoke, the rotten scent of stale blood, burning flesh, or the warm-grass scent of horse manure. This air smelled pure, so fresh and sharp it was like being back home, after a day riding in the mountains.

"Hurry," Qown said, "we have to mark this rune on as many people as possible."

"Where's Dorna?" I asked.

"I'm here! I'm here!" My old nurse ran out toward us, tripping once on the churned, muddy ground. She already had a glyph on her forehead, although hers had been inscribed with something wet and red, too dark to be fresh blood.

"Is that . . . is that chili sauce?" Brother Qown's tone was incredulous.

"No time," I said. "I'll free the others. Mark Arasgon, then Ninavis's crew."

Arasgon had already pulled the tarp from a cage, revealing Tanner, Kay Hará, and Vidan. They stood, yelling for attention, but I had none to spare. I broke the lock on the cage door.

"Let Qown draw on your foreheads," I told them. "His blessing will protect you from the witchcraft." I moved on to the next cage. I had no time to talk them through explanations I didn't possess myself. What Qown had done, or its ramifications for our souls, seemed unimportant if we didn't survive.*

I tore the lock off the second cage, the one holding Gan the Miller's Daughter, Jem Nakijan, and Dango. Screams grew louder in the distance. I had expected to fight Baron Tamin's soldiers, but those same soldiers had no interest in the tournament stands or the citizens trapped there. The soldiers had vanished, retreating

---

* I should think the ramifications to their souls would be especially important if they didn't survive.

even as everyone else made their bids to outrun the animate witch-smoke.

Next to me, Arasgon tossed his head. "Look to the castle!"

I did and froze.

The blue smoke rolled out in all directions from its initial starting point. Toward us, toward the town, toward the rest of the fairgrounds. And in a maneuver that would have been impossible, had the phrase *black magic* not been involved, it moved against the wind toward Mereina Castle.

"Snap out of it." Arasgon slammed his head against my shoulder.

I shook my head and motioned to Dango. "Find everyone you can. Dorna will show you what to draw on their foreheads." I assumed she would, anyway. If it had just been Brother Qown, I would have suspected he'd countered the smoke with a spell, but Dorna had no such power. She'd kept herself alive somehow through the clever use of condiments, so there was no reason to think she couldn't do it again. True, Dango might have to hold people down, before they willingly let a strange old lady draw on their faces with pepper sauce, but I was confident he was the man for the task.

I pulled myself onto Arasgon's back and offered a hand down to Brother Qown. "Come. We must ride fast if we've any chance of reaching the castle in time."

To his credit, he didn't shy away. I'd always suspected he was made from harder metal than he pretended.

One didn't train to exorcise demons without possessing a mighty will.

I didn't pull him up so much as let him use my arm as a brace. Arasgon tilted himself downward to make it easier for Brother Qown to slide into the saddle behind me. I didn't have time to teach him how to ride Arasgon; one couldn't ride a giant fireblood the same way one rode a smaller steed.

"Hold on!" Arasgon yelled.

We galloped toward the castle then, trying to outrace the cloud.

Even though the runes created sweet air around our heads, the blue smoke was worse than the densest fog, obstructing all sight.

"If I trip and break a leg," Arasgon said, "I'm going to find whoever is responsible for this and bite out their tongue."

"You have my permission!" I yelled.

"What did he say?" Brother Qown asked. I was surprised he could hear Arasgon over the galloping, over the screams from the town.

"He said he's not happy!"

"Oh. I'm not either. But don't talk unless you must!"

I turned in the saddle. "What? Why?"

"I don't know if this makes the air clean or if we have a limited supply, like breathing from a bag."*

I took a deep breath on instinct, unable to stop myself. Was my air bubble smaller than it had been before? I couldn't tell.

In any event, neither Arasgon nor I said another word while we raced toward the castle.

We broke free from the smoke a hundred feet from the gate. The blue tendrils clutched after us like a predator lamenting its prey's escape, but the fighting ahead was an equal concern. A different sort of smoke ruled the castle, billowing thick and black from the fires burning across multiple fortress sections: the stables, the storerooms, part of the tower.

Sabotage. I'd have bet Ninavis was responsible—if I hadn't known Kalazan was still loose, with his expert knowledge of the castle's servant passages.

From the look of things, the guards had tried to close the castle gate against the rolling smoke advancing from the fairgrounds. This happened as several knights—Sir Baramon included—arrived on horseback, hoping to gain entry and safety inside the castle walls. The desperate skirmish that followed was still raging as the witch-smoke arrived on our tails, to end

---

* They'd have run out of air in minutes if that were true . . . ah well. I suppose they figured it out.

all debates. Sir Baramon fought on the far side, holding off two soldiers, but looking weaker with every step. The other soldiers, though . . .

"Janel!"

"I see them," I said.

They were raising the drawbridge.

It wouldn't help them against the smoke, but it would stop our progress.

"Come on, Arasgon!" I shouted to him.

We galloped.

We jumped.

I reached back and grabbed Brother Qown's agolé midair, but he held on to me so tightly I imagined I felt his fingernails through my armor. Mid-leap, I saw Sir Baramon take advantage of the defending soldiers' wide-eyed awe to stab one through the leg before ripping his sword free to hack at a second's soldier's thigh. He might have gained some weight, but he hadn't lost his skill.

We hung in the air forever, time slowing to a crawl. Then the seconds sped up again as Arasgon landed hard on the wooden planking, the impact jolting through his body and reverberating through my bones. Qown let out a surprised yelp.

Then we were galloping again. The soldiers scattered. I didn't see anyone with the glyph marked on their foreheads. These poor fools had just been trying to protect themselves with wood and stone. And failing, because they had no idea what they faced.

Neither did I, but I knew more than they did.

Arasgon pulled into a trot, calling out a greeting to his brother Talaras.

"Let my man give you his blessing," I ordered Sir Baramon. "It will protect you when the witch-smoke comes."

"It's already here, Count," Sir Baramon called out.

Which was true. The closed drawbridge bought us a few seconds, but the blue smoke shimmied through cracks and leaked around the edges like a living thing seeking warm bodies and blood.

Brother Qown half fell, half slid off Arasgon's back and ran forward to mark the rune on Sir Baramon and Talaras. It looked for all the world like he traced their skin with a glowing fingertip, leaving behind a mark the same glowing color.

"We have to find Ninavis!" I shouted.

"Her leg's still broken," Brother Qown responded. "I told her to stay in her room and rest."

"I doubt she listened," Arasgon said as he pointed his nose across the courtyard. "Someone had to start the fires."

Across the way, I saw someone in a hooded sallí cloak leading another person with a limp up a staircase from the basement. I couldn't see their faces, but I recognized Dorna's second-best riding skirt.

"Ninavis!" I yelled out. "Ninavis, wait!"

The second person looked up.

Ninavis hesitated. Kalazan stiffened, with his arm still around her. I suspected both were thinking about how much simpler their lives might be if they just ran. Of course, they didn't yet know about the blue smoke. They didn't understand what horror had just overtaken Barsine Banner. They didn't understand that all that lay between their freedom and an ugly death was a foreign Blood of Joras they barely knew.

Ninavis pulled back her hood. "Do you have my people?"

Kalazan asked at the same moment, "What happened to Baron Tamin? Did you kill him?"

I ran to her, aware Brother Qown was running too. "Never mind Tamin. Your people are safe. Possibly they are the only ones who are."

"I don't understand—"

"I have to mark this blessing on your forehead," Brother Qown gasped as he caught up with us. "Quickly. The blue smoke kills anyone not wearing this sign."

Ninavis looked over Qown's shoulder toward the front gate. She blanched. The witch-smoke was inside now, spreading fast.

Already, the sound of choking echoed as the cursed air found new victims. Ironically, the vapor smothered the fires meant as a distraction while Kalazan rescued Ninavis; the flames died as soon as the witch-smoke rushed in and replaced all the air.

"What—?"

"No time," I said. "Lower your hood, my Kalazan." I used a possessive I had no right to use. *My* Kalazan, *my* loyal man. I had just declared him my vassal, taking up the offer Kalazan had made the night before, when he called me his lord.

He inhaled, but then, perhaps because he saw the smoke rushing at us from across the courtyard, he did as I ordered.

Brother Qown finished the glyph on Ninavis and moved on to Kalazan.

The smoke enveloped us. Kalazan closed his mouth, shut his eyes, pinched closed his nostrils. The smoke tried to force its way inside, but Brother Qown finished the line, connected the last points, completed the glyph. The tendrils snapped back, pushed out by the pocket of clean air around Kalazan's head.

"Find as many—" I started to order Brother Qown, but he needed no orders to do what came as instinct. He'd already gone to a serving maid on the ground, wide-eyed, choking, gasping for breath. He painted the glyph on her forehead.

But the witch-smoke was in her lungs. She died while we watched, powerless to help her.

They all died.

Kalazan gained his voice first.

And lost his wits first too.

"What just happened? What is this?" He looked at us wide-eyed, crazed. He had the hostile anger of someone who didn't understand what they'd just witnessed but damn well intended to find someone to blame.

I almost felt sorry for him, but this wasn't the time for sentimentality.

"You mustn't use up your air." I turned to Ninavis. "Calm him. We have much to do and little time in which to do it."

She looked a bit wide-eyed herself, but she squared her shoulders and put both her hands on Kalazan's arms. "We've come this far. Just come with me a little further."

"*What happened?*" He didn't want to be quiet.

"Witchcraft," I snapped. "The real kind, and not the stories people use as an excuse to kill old mares with too many warts on their chins. We need to leave, Kalazan. Sooner, not later. Now. I swear to you I will explain all once we're away from here."

His face paled from fear or anger or some combination. "The baron did this?"

"No," Brother Qown said. "I saw the woman who cast this spell. She wouldn't have left Baron Tamin to die if they were partners."*

That stopped Kalazan. "He's dead. Tamin's dead?"

My heart broke at the hope in his voice, the dread, the . . . regret. I'd just dropped by Barsine Banner on special occasions, with the periodic tournament as excuse. Kalazan had grown up with Tamin. They had played together, gone exploring together, whispered stories, and dreamed of becoming knights.

"We have no time for that right now. Dorna, I need—" I grimaced as I remembered I'd left Dorna back at the tournament grounds. "Never mind. I'll gather our belongings. Everyone do the same, but take no more than five minutes. Grab what you can and follow me."

"I don't mean to spoil a good plan, but the smoke seems to be killing horses as well as people," Ninavis said, looking across the courtyard toward the stables.

I cursed. She was right. Our animals weren't immune.

Sir Baramon raised his head from where he'd been bending over a fallen knight. He'd been holding the dead man's hand, and just before he stood, he kissed the man on the lips. Tears fell from Sir Baramon's face as he pulled a striped scarf from the man's body.

---

* True, I wouldn't have. Probably.

I ground my teeth and looked away. The last thing I needed was a reminder the dead had been people with lives, loved ones, *importance*. I couldn't deal with that crushing loss and still function, so I pushed the reminders away and hardened my heart as best I could.

I suspected it was easier for me than the others.

I'd had more practice.

I found myself thankful the blue vapor made it hard to see. The witch-smoke hung in swirling eddies in the air, on the ground, which made it difficult to discern all the dead bodies hidden under the diaphanous fog. I only wished the smoke might have done something to mask the awful stench of that many dead.

Sir Baramon tied the scarf around his arm. "Talaras and Arasgon can do the heavy lifting for a while, if they're up for it. At least until we establish how large an area the smoke fills. Maybe it didn't reach the town."

"Will of the Eight," I agreed. "Gather what you need. Arasgon, would you be so kind as to let Ninavis use your saddle once more? We'll meet back at the fairgrounds, and find the others."

"Gan? Dango? You said they're all right?" Ninavis asked.

"Unless something else has happened in my absence. But let's not wait to find out."

I ran upstairs. We carried all our possessions in a single valise and a few extra packs. There were advantages to being forced to travel light, even if it meant I rarely had anything nice to wear when attending a local noble's gala soiree.

Parties were the least of my worries at the moment.

Afterward, I lowered the drawbridge so we could leave.

Ninavis rode on Arasgon's back to take the weight off her leg. Arasgon and I walked together, helping each other navigate through the impenetrable smoke.

I wondered if this resembled traveling through the sandstorms of Khorvesh or the blizzards farther north in Yor. If not for the air pockets around our heads—

Well. I suppose I wouldn't be in any condition to puzzle over the smoke if not for the fresh air around our heads.

Halfway back to the fairgrounds, I spotted something moving on the main road. Not walking, as one bearing the glyph might, but crawling. Injured. Maybe dying.

"Brother Qown, someone's over there—" I couldn't believe someone had survived the cursed smoke for so long. From the way they convulsed and stumbled on their knees, they seemed in pain. Perhaps someone wearing the glyph had also been injured.

I approached and bent down to see the person better. My stomach flipped over while I tasted bile.

"By the Eight," I whispered.

It was Tamin.

He didn't have a glyph on his forehead, nor anywhere else as far as I could tell. The white-skinned witch had left him to die. Somehow, he hadn't.

But he was trying.

Tamin's face had turned an ugly purple. Blue smoke danced through his open mouth and nostrils. His mouth gaped open as he failed to draw breath, but despite all this, he somehow still lived.

I once heard of a child who had drowned in the river near Tolamer Castle. She fell through thin ice in winter and then found herself unable to surface. By the time the local farmers cracked the ice and brought her to a priest, she'd been without air for ten minutes—and lived. Everyone had agreed, however, that such had been the grace of the Eight and the cold water acting to preserve her.

Tamin had no such benefits, and I was damn sure the Eight were not on his side.

Brother Qown knelt next to me. He didn't hesitate, as he never hesitated when someone's life was at risk. He drew the glyph across Tamin's forehead.

I shook my head. "The smoke is already inside him."

"I'll find a way to draw it out," he said. "Some force is

keeping this man alive. His case isn't like the others. Even an injury healed by magic can't work if no one draws the sword from the wound."

I heard Ninavis behind me. "Kalazan, no!"

I had that much warning.

I stood and whirled about in time to see Kalazan running toward me, sword out. I wasn't his intended target. Kalazan reserved his anger for the baron, who'd ordered Kalazan's father executed, made Kalazan an outlaw, who would have killed Kalazan and all his companions. For the man who had betrayed their friendship.

Kalazan saw me and checked his progress.

"Get out of my way, my lord."

"Am I your lord?"

His mouth twisted. Even with the smoke between us, his eyes were bright. "So it would seem."

"Then lower your sword."

"But he—" Kalazan pointed. "He was your friend before you ever met me. He betrayed you too."

"He was *our* friend," I corrected. "But our friend is gone. I don't know what happened to him. Something terrible, I suspect. This creature writhing on the ground behind me? I don't know him. If you worry I'm going to protect Tamin, rather than see justice done, rest easy."

"Then let me by—" He started to move and stopped as I held out a hand.

"He's the one person here who may be able to tell me why today's events occurred, as well as the identities of those responsible. As a Count of Jorat, I'm obligated by oath to protect this dominion. I have a duty to discover who did this and ensure they will never be in a position to do it again. I care not what happens to the Baron of Barsine—but I need *this witness* to live until I can ascertain the truth of what transpired here. Do you understand?"

Kalazan licked his lips, his face sullen as a dog denied water.

"Do you understand?" I repeated.

He sheathed his blade. "I'll carry the feet if you take the head."

I could carry Tamin by myself, but this allowed Brother Qown a chance to do what he could for the man while we walked. I nodded and lifted Tamin up by the shoulders.

We continued to the fairgrounds. Along the way, I refused to look at the obvious bodies littering the ground. The smoke made this easier, even as it lashed back and forth in anger at our escape.

I didn't think that was hyperbole. Perhaps the mist was angry. The smoke had acted almost with intelligence. I hoped it was my imagination.*

When we reached the contest grounds, I saw Dango and Tanner, along with a dozen or so others whom we'd saved. They were busy piling bodies next to the large wood pyres. Dorna was helping.

I tried not to lose my temper, not to start screaming at them for being idiots, the worst fools.

They didn't know as much about demons as I did.

Besides, I couldn't scream; I didn't know how long the air would last.

I set down Tamin's shoulders, motioned for Kalazan to lower the man's feet. Tamin had quieted some, a product of whatever ministering Brother Qown had provided, but his color remained ghastly. He might live but never be whole or right again.

"What are you about?" I asked Dorna. Calm, I reminded myself. I must stay calm.

"Oh, Dango said we should start a pyre. You know, because—" Dorna made a significant gesture.

"This isn't the time for funerary rights," Brother Qown said.

I sighed and resisted the urge to pinch the bridge of my nose or punch someone, anyone, in the face. "We don't burn our dead in Jorat for religious reasons, Brother Qown. We do

---

* It's drawn to sentient minds within a certain range of its initial dispersal point, which might *seem* intelligent behavior if one didn't know better. Nasty stuff.

it to make sure demons have nothing to possess. You saw what happened to Dedreugh. That potential exists anytime a body's left to rot."*

Brother Qown blinked at me. "What?"

I frowned. "Your order are experts on fighting demons. How has Father Zajhera never told you this?"

Brother Qown stared at me. *"What?"*

I raised an eyebrow at him.

He sputtered. "I saw Dedreugh was possessed, but I assumed black magic summoned the demon . . ." His voice trailed off as he turned to Ninavis. "Is she serious?"

Ninavis understood our customs. "As metal. Demons have to take possession of a living person to summon more of their kind, but they can possess the dead too. Make 'em walk. Make 'em kill. That's not how it works where you're from?"

He started mumbling something under his breath.

My attention focused back on Dango and Dorna. "This leaves me with two questions. First, since the witch-smoke smothers fire, how did you intend to light the wood? Second, are you really planning to burn those bodies using ritually enchanted burning stakes, designed to send souls straight to waiting demons?"

"Oh, dear," Dorna said.

Dango's eyes widened with horror. "But . . . ?"

I pointed to the stakes. "You can't use this wood. You can't use this wood, and you can't burn the dead here. You'll be doing the witch's work for her."

Tanner threw down the flint and steel he'd been trying to use to light kindling. "Damn it all, we have to burn the bodies!"

"No," I corrected. "We *want* to burn the bodies. But as it happens, we can't. So stop wasting my time."

He straightened, glaring at me. "If we don't burn these, the dead won't stay dead for long."

---

* I have a theory on why this happens on the eastern side of the Dragonspires but not the western side, but I need to work out some of the details.

"If we don't leave here soon, we won't stay living for long. We don't know when the smoke will dissipate. Maybe it will still be here when the demons start playing dress-up using our slain. We cannot wait. Do you understand? We cannot stop this."

"Is that the baron?" A voice I didn't recognize asked the question. I groaned inside. People might well be eager to blame him for the day's events.

And they might be right.

A dozen voices raised at once.

Kalazan—*Kalazan,* of all people—silenced them. "Whoever did this made no effort to protect Tamin. He was a target as much as any of us."

"Who's to say *you* ain't the one responsible?" someone shouted. "He said you was helping witches. Was this your doing?"

"No!" Kalazan scowled. "Of course not."

"Be quiet," I ordered.

They ignored me.

I sighed and inhaled deep. Just before I raised my voice, Arasgon raised his.

"My lord said *be quiet.* You're alive because she saved you. Be silent!"

The voices paused.

"Thank you, Arasgon," I said. "Everyone, grab what you can. We will meet in the town if the smoke hasn't yet reached it. If it has, keep moving until you find an area free from smoke and wait there."

"But my husband—"

I raised my voice, despite all my intentions not to. "If he isn't here, if he hasn't been blessed by my people, then it is too late to save him. Today, we leave the dead where they fall. Now *go!*"

"How do we know we can trust you?"

I whirled back to the crowd. They were so few compared to how many there had been just a short time earlier. "Because

I'm still here. Trust me or not as your conscience demands. But if you stay here and do nothing, or stay here to burn your dead, you will soon join them. You will only add your corpses to these others. So make your choice. We leave now."

The gathered crowd scrambled to find their azhocks and possessions. Ninavis and her people had already been parted from their meager possessions some time ago.

Ninavis's group had gained in size. I recognized the smith who'd left his azhock to stare at us the previous night, as well as the black-skinned, silver-haired girl who had fetched him.

Dorna had done well, rescuing all these plus her own horse, Pocket Biter, and Brother Qown's sweet gelding, Cloud. Only a few dozen people, in addition to the ones Brother Qown had saved. Thousands had attended the fair.

No. I couldn't dwell on that.

"Which way to town?" I asked Arasgon.

He tossed his head, pointing into the smoke. For all I could tell, he might as well have been pointing to the castle, but I knew his sense of direction was superior to my own.

I helped Kalazan pick up Tamin, and we walked.

11: EIGHT GATES

Jorat Dominion, Quuros Empire.
Two days since the Devoran Prophecies stopped
being so hypothetical

"That smoke wiped out a whole town?" Kihrin didn't try to hide the horror in his voice. "How many people died?"

Janel scowled. "I didn't count."

"Just over three thousand," Brother Qown said.* "We were lucky. Mereina's normal population was closer to fifteen thousand, but a large percentage of the population had already left to avoid the baron's overzealous witch hunt."

"Still that's—" Kihrin found himself at a loss to express how hollow he felt at the news.

She gave him a shrewd glance. "You should know what you're up against. That bottle of blue smoke wasn't unique."

"Anyone who would use a weapon like this is a monster."

"You'll hear no argument from me," Janel said, her voice soft.

Kihrin leaned forward in his seat and scrubbed at his eyes with his palms. "It's not right. I still don't know how many died in the Capital. I don't know if you've heard—"

"I heard," she said. "What happened in the Capital wasn't your fault."

"If I hadn't come back—" He stared into the fireplace and left the sentence hanging.

"If you hadn't come back, Gadrith would still be 'alive'—or

---

* Three thousand seven hundred eighty-five. I always count.

whatever you want to call his particular exemption from decomposition."

Kihrin frowned. "That almost sounds like you knew him."

"Maybe I did, but we'd be jumping ahead of the story, wouldn't we? Let's let Brother Qown continue." She smiled. "He loves this part."

"I don't," Brother Qown protested. "It's very sad."

But he was quick to start reading.

Qown's Turn. Mereina, Barsine Banner, Jorat, Quur.

Brother Qown fought the temptation to fall to the ground and pray to Selanol when he saw sunlight. It meant the smoke hadn't reached the town. There would be survivors.

At least, there would be a few survivors.

A small crowd waited at the town's edges. Not more than a few dozen people who, for various reasons, hadn't been near the fairgrounds when disaster struck. Not all those had survived either. At least a few townsfolk had braved the cloud seeking friends and family. Their bodies just inside the witch-smoke border told their fate.

Besides the few human survivors, animals fared better, some innate instinct encouraging an earlier flight. Dholes wandered the main street in packs, upset and ill-tempered. All six elephants used at the fairgrounds had escaped, wandering up to familiar townsfolk for reassurances or making calls to one another. Some horses made it out too, although many more died in fenced corrals.

Brother Qown watched Janel work, feeling numb, not ready to deal with what had just happened. If he didn't know her, Qown wouldn't have guessed her true age. The count seemed immune to the deaths they had just witnessed, immune to the horror, immune to the shock. Whereas Brother Qown fought not to break down, the count ordered survivors to separate into groups. She instructed them to search the town for others: those who hadn't attended, or those who had fled when the demon revealed himself. These might have taken refuge in their homes, praying the horror would pass them by. Janel ordered people to gather supplies, confiscate wagons, prepare the evacuation.

She's been trained for this, he thought. Trained her whole life to be the voice anyone would follow in an emergency. She assumed she was in charge, and thus, it was true.*

Brother Qown watched as people vanished into patio areas, until what he saw registered: ramps. In every private area, ramps led underground or back into hillsides, as if Mereina had forgotten to build houses over their basements. The circular brick stacks he'd taken for firepits were chimneys.

Brother Qown snapped from his reverie when he heard shouting; Dango yelling for the survivors to be quiet. Count Janel had covered herself with a long red cloak she must have picked up from the tournament grounds. It was obvious she wore armor, but her temporary disguise as the Black Knight was hidden. She took Ninavis's place on Arasgon, using the height this gave her to speak to the crowd.

"Mereina was attacked today," Janel declared. "Foul black magic has been used against her people. The blue smoke you see behind us is that witchcraft manifested; it will kill anyone who lingers near it without protection. We don't know how long the smoke will last, but it's not possible to burn the dead while it remains. For this reason, it isn't safe to stay here past sundown."

"What about the Gatestone?" someone in the back shouted.

"What of it?" Sir Baramon replied. "It's back at the castle! Might as well be at the bottom of Lake Jorat."

Ninavis scowled. "What happens when the Gatekeeper opens the portal tomorrow morning?"

Janel's expression flattened as she hesitated.

"Depends on whether that Gatekeeper is fool enough to step through, doncha think?" Dorna wiped her chili-stained fingers on her skirts. "He's supposed to step through. That way, he

* Wait until she ends up in the Capital City. Trust me, it won't be true then.

can open the gates all them tournament folk and travelers need to go home. If he's watching his step, though, he'll stay right where he is. He'll see the smoke and go tell his people in House D'Aramarin something's gone screwy. But if he ain't paying attention?" Dorna shrugged. "Figure he'll either die from the witch-smoke, or he'll meet the local hell spawn when they start ambling about—and then he'll die from *that*."

"But even that's good, though, right? When the Gatekeepers realize one of theirs didn't come back, they'll send the army," Dango said. "They'll send the army through the gate."

"No," Kalazan said, "that's the last thing they'd do."

Janel tilted her head to Kalazan in acknowledgment. "He's right. If the Gatekeeper steps through tomorrow to open return portals for the tournament visitors, he'll either be overcome by smoke or by the demon-possessed dead. Either way, no new portal will be opened afterward. And if he's smart enough *not* to step through? No new portal will be opened either. A protocol is followed in such circumstances. There will be no deviation."

"A protocol?" Someone new asked the question—Gozen, who had been forced to give up his place to Janel in the lists.

"The gate system is Quur's greatest strength," Janel explained. "It is also our greatest weakness.* If an enemy force gains control of a single Gatestone location, they could move an army to any point in the empire in seconds. Every titled noble in every dominion is trained in invasion protocols, mortal or demonic. This Gatestone will be presumed lost and in enemy hands. At that point, the Quuros army will open a gate—but not here. Never to this location. They'll try to open a gate to the Gatestone nearest us. If that gate can be opened safely? Only then will an army march back here to discover what has happened to this Gatestone. That will take a week, minimum."

"A week?" Ninavis gaped. "Every dead body here will be risen as hell spawn in a week!"

---

* Why yes, yes, it is. That might be a problem someday. Wouldn't that just be a shame?

"I'm aware."

"But what can we—"

"There are eight locations the army may use, based on proximity to Mereina," Janel explained. "The gate they open will be picked at random from those locales, to ensure any enemy forces cannot predict where the army will arrive and lie in ambush. If we plan to meet the army and make sure they understand what's happened here, we'll need to split up. Nine groups. Eight of those will travel to the possible gate sites and meet the approaching army before they arrive in Mereina."

"What happens to the ninth group?" someone asked.

Janel looked at Ninavis. "Not all of us can travel quickly. There are children here, the injured, the ill, and the elderly. Those will need to shelter at a secure location. By tonight, this town won't be safe for any living being. Since this isn't my banner, I direct the question back to you: Where can we take refuge?"

The crowd murmured and looked at each other. "The old mill—"

"Oh sure, that will fit two of us, and rotted through besides."

"What about Coldwater? Ain't no one there now."

"Ain't no Coldwater there now either."

"What? What happened—?"

"Dedreugh happened."

Ninavis sighed. "I have a place."

Janel hadn't looked at anyone else. She must have suspected Ninavis knew a location but gave the woman a chance to offer it herself.

Once Ninavis had spoken, it seemed to free up the others. Jem Nakijan nodded, as did Tanner, Vidan, and Gan Not-Actually-the-Miller's-Daughter-After-All.

"Aye," Dango agreed. "It's big enough to fit us all too."

"Good." Janel pointed to the crowd. "Now I want our eight strongest riders and every available horse. Volunteers, step up."

While Janel and the others fretted over team distributions, Brother Qown focused his attention on Baron Tamin. He'd had little success in pulling the smoke from Tamin's lungs, but removing the baron from the smoke's borders had helped. The blind panic behind his eyes haunted Brother Qown most—the look of a man awake and conscious, feeling every desperate failed pull from his lungs.

"That glyph thing ain't working?" Dorna knelt next to Tamin and checked his eyes, his nose, his mouth. Tamin still choked, although never quite to death.

"It makes the air around his head clean, but I don't think it's doing anything about what's already in his lungs. New air can't get inside." Brother Qown shook his head. "This glyph . . . I've never seen anything like it, Dorna."

The old woman frowned. "What are you on about? You're the one who was using it. I just copied what I saw you doing."

"But it shouldn't have worked! The only reason—" He caught himself. "I'll explain later. I have to figure out how I'm going to clean his lungs."

Dorna stared at him as if he were missing something very obvious.

Brother Qown glanced up. "Why are you looking at me like that?"

She leaned in. "Ain't you supposed to be proper educated? Got your shiny Blue House magic license and all that?"

"I never told you—" Brother Qown lowered his voice to a whisper. "I never told you I owned a Physickers Guild license." He didn't talk about such things while in Jorat. The local beliefs didn't mesh well with the knowledge he held formal training and licensed permission to practice magic. The Joratese only put up with the Gatekeepers because the Quuros military and their economic stability demanded it. Everyone ignored a little heathen magic if it meant they could cross the realm to see their favorite knights perform on a regular basis.

"Ah, well. Heard the old count talking about you people before he passed on. You have book training. That's my point."

"I don't need your mockery right now, Dorna—"

She visibly rolled her eyes and indicated Tamin. "So answer

me this, priest: Does like not call to like? You and your fancy education learned that much, didn't you?"

"What are you–?" Brother Qown stopped.

He stared at her, dumbfounded, not understanding her meaning for a smattering of long, pregnant seconds. He couldn't do anything about the witch-smoke in the baron's lungs. However, yes, if he tied the cursed fumes to something close enough to their basic nature—say, normal non-magical smoke— he could encourage a sympathetic link. Then what happened to one, happened to the other. Brother Qown scuttled to his pack and began running his hands through his pockets. "A candle," he muttered. "I need a candle."

"Mmm-hmm." Dorna held out a small beeswax candle, then snatched it back as he reached for it. "Not here," she said. "Are you daft, colt? This ain't something we should share with the whole town and any who might feel like watching. Best bring him behind the farrier's banners."

Brother Qown felt blood flow to his face, but he couldn't deny her logic. If the locals saw him using magic on Baron Tamin, they wouldn't stop to clarify he was a priest.

They would just reach for the clubs and the knives.

On the heels of that, he realized Dorna somehow understood the rules of sympathetic magic, but this wasn't the time to challenge her on that.

"You take the head." Dorna picked up the baron's feet.

Brother Qown picked up Tamin by the shoulders. Together, they made an awkward shambling trio as they ducked behind several large banners concealing a patio complete with large sturdy forge and work area.

Of course, he thought. The horses wouldn't want to go downstairs into the building if they didn't have to, even with a ramp.

Everyone else seemed too distracted by Janel's instructions to pay them much attention. Brother Qown hoped they'd managed to bring Tamin over to the forge without anyone noticing.

He grabbed a cloth and opened the door to the brick forge itself. They didn't shoe horses often in this part of Quur. He assumed they just used the forge for spot repairs on tournament armor and the like. The banked fire was enough to light the small wooden taper, which Brother Qown used in turn to light Dorna's candle.

The candle was poorly made and smoky. Normal smoke, thick and gray. Perfect.

He sat down cross-legged on the straw-strewn brick patio floor, with the candle in one hand. He made sure he could see the smoke spiraling out from its small orange flame and Tamin's hacking, coughing body. Brother Qown breathed deeply and tried to enter Illumination.

It wasn't easy. He'd seen too much horror. What he'd witnessed flashed through his mind like haunting ghosts. He finally calmed himself enough to *see,* although he didn't use normal sight at all.

A dark, twisting blue mass spiraled inside Tamin, warring against the golden aura flashing over his body. Each light wave fought back the twisting blue mass; when the golden light retreated, the darkness returned.

The blue energy was slick with malice. Brother Qown forced his conscious will against it and found it responded like a living being. It twisted away from him, slid away from his grasp.

Smoke, Brother Qown thought. *You're nothing but smoke.*

Sweat ran paths through the dust and ash on his forehead, but he refused to relent, refused to stop. His win happened so suddenly he reeled as if the ground shifted under his feet.

Tamin's coughing changed from the timbre of a man choking on a bone to a man choking up phlegm after a long illness. Then he rolled to one side and vomited. Smoke escaped from his nose, from his mouth.

Normal smoke.

The baron fell back, gasping. He closed his eyes and drew in deep, shuddering breaths. His face took on a more regular color too.

Dorna slapped Brother Qown on the shoulder. "Nicely done, foal."

Brother Qown rocked back on his heels and looked up toward Dorna. "How long have you known about me?"

The old woman shrugged and looked at her fingernails. "You think I wouldn't notice when a guard who's had his skull bashed in don't die? I'm old; I ain't blind." She lifted a metal hoof-pick from a workbench, examined the tip, and then casually put it in a pocket. "Nobody's explained what being Blood of Joras means to you, have they?"

"I need—" Tamin's rough voice only faintly resembled speech.

"What you need is a good swift kick to your ass," Dorna said. She reached down and grabbed the noble by his collar, dragging him behind her. Normally, this would have been a pointless exercise, but Tamin's strength was gone. He shuffled after her, almost on his knees but managing at last to stand. He shouted out something incoherent at the end as he tumbled out onto the street.

Brother Qown followed, not sure if he wanted to see what would happen next.

"My count!" Dorna shouted.

Janel looked over. As soon as she saw Tamin, she broke away from the townsfolk and joined Dorna and Brother Qown.

"You cured him."

Brother Qown couldn't tell if the news made her happy. Perhaps she didn't know herself.

"He ain't gonna die from the smoke, anyway. Plenty still wrong with him."

"Janel—" Tamin gasped.

The count's jaw tightened. She stared at Tamin with flared nostrils. Slowly, she tucked her fingers into fists at her sides. "Who was the woman, Tamin? The warden's nurse. The foreigner."

"I didn't—" His voice sounded granite rough. "I didn't know. I didn't know . . . what she would . . . what she'd do."

"I didn't ask you if you knew what she'd do. I asked you who she is."

A crowd began to gather. Ninavis and Kalazan held back the others, explaining the need for patience. Janel ignored them all.

"She was . . ." Tamin licked his lips. "She was a slave. A Doltari slave. Senera. Her name was Senera."

Janel's frown tightened. "She commanded those soldiers. Slaves don't command soldiers."*

"Relos said . . . said she was a slave. He brought her—" Tamin winced. "Water?"

Janel bent down next to Tamin while Brother Qown reached for his waterskin. "Who is Relos Var? Tell me about him."

Brother Qown handed Tamin the waterskin. The baron drank in desperate gulps. Evidently, he'd needed the water, because he sounded much better after. "What have I *done?*"

"Too much and not enough. But right now, I need your focus, Tamin. Who is Relos Var?"

Tamin struggled to sit, while Brother Qown supported him. "A teacher. My father hired him to—" He hesitated.

"To what?"

Tamin's eyes shone glassy bright. He took a deep breath. "To cure me of being a witch."

Someone in the crowd gasped. Another person cursed. Dorna turned around, hands on hips, and faced the crowd. "Be quiet, you lot. You let the man speak or you'll be answering to me, understand?"

Janel cocked her head, narrowed her eyes. "Witchcraft isn't something one cures like red fever or pox."

"I didn't want to be a witch," Tamin said, "but I couldn't . . . I couldn't help it. It's what I am." He tilted his head up to stare at Janel's face. "You know what it's like."

Janel scowled, glanced skyward as if addressing her gods, then refocused her attention on her childhood friend. "I'm quite sure I don't. Tell me, then. Tell me how you can be a witch against your will."

---

* Yes, thank you. I'm glad someone noticed.

"By being cursed. I've always been cursed," Tamin said, "since I was a child. I would cure animals, cure cuts and bruises. I didn't realize I was doing anything wrong. Not at first. Then I—" He scowled. "A hunting accident injured my father. I loved my father, so I . . . I saved him."

"You poor man," Brother Qown murmured. "If you'd been born anywhere else, such a gift would have won you a scholarship to the Academy *and* a sponsorship by the Guild of Physickers. You're not a witch. You're a sorcerer."

Tamin gave the priest a confused, sick look. "I can do magic. That's witchcraft."

"I take it," Janel said, sounding very less than pleased with the entire conversation, "your father didn't tolerate your gift?"

"He—" Tamin's jaw tightened. He looked away. "No, he didn't."

"Strange, then, for you to be so friendly with the man your father hired as punishment."

"No, it wasn't like that. Relos Var is a great man. He showed me I didn't have to be ashamed. I didn't have to hide what I am." His voice dropped, and his eyes flickered toward the fairgrounds. "And when my father—" He didn't finish.

"What happened to your father?"

Tamin closed his eyes.

"Oh, I think I know, right enough," Dorna volunteered. "His father hated witchcraft. And Tamin here was learning to use his 'witch' abilities right under his father's nose. Just a matter of time 'fore the old man caught him at it, right?"

Janel's expression had seemed grim before, but as Dorna spoke, her whole face froze into something harder than stone. "What did you do, Tamin?"

"It wasn't my fault."

"You're the Baron of Barsine. Everything that happens in your banner is, *by definition,* your fault."*

He flinched at the anger in her voice. "Relos Var said witches

* Technically, Tamin wasn't baron at the time.

cursed me. You should know what it's like. You've been cursed too."

Janel's nostrils flared. "Who told you that?"

"Relos Var. He's right, isn't he? You're cursed."

"Not by witches."

"It's the same thing."

Brother Qown tightened his grip on the man's shoulders. "No, it isn't," he protested, but he didn't think Tamin was paying any attention.

"Did you kill your father, Tamin?"

The man cast his gaze around him, but the crowd had surrounded them. Everyone from town listened, watching, waiting on his answer.

"I didn't kill him," Tamin said, "but I . . . I removed my healing. Took it all back. He'd have died the first time, so the second time . . . he did."

Brother Qown blinked. "That's not how it works." He turned to the count and whispered, "That's not how healing works. You can't do that."

Janel nodded to him to indicate she'd heard and put up a hand for Brother Qown to be quiet. Then she continued talking to Tamin. "Was it your idea, or Relos Var's, to execute the castle steward for your father's death?"

"It was . . ." Tamin's voice trailed off as something haunted and dark entered his eyes. He looked like a man waking up from a nightmare.

A little girl's voice broke the silence as she set a small basket on the ground next to Tamin. "Mare Xala made you steamed buns for dinner." The tiny girl was maybe six years old, with dark red skin and white fingertips. She sniffled and wiped her nose with her hand before turning back to an older woman. "Did I say that right?"

The old woman nodded. "You did, foal." She tossed a green wool bundle at Tamin's feet. "You'll need a cloak too, so's to keep you warm."

Dorna straightened and put her arm on Janel's.

The count's eyes widened.

Brother Qown felt the crowd's mood shift, but he didn't understand its cause or meaning. Tamin looked puzzled before his expression changed to panic.

"No." Tamin shook his head. "No, I don't need your charity—"

"You will take what we give you," Kalazan said with the softest voice. He pulled a dagger and sheath from his belt and set them down by Tamin's feet. "Here's a blade to keep you safe."

"I have a pair of saddlebags for you," Dango offered. "It's a long road."

Brother Qown tugged on Dorna's sleeve. "I don't understand. He just admitted he killed his own father and framed Kalazan's father for it. Why are they giving him presents?"

Dorna crossed her arms as she watched the townspeople hunt for trinkets: a sack, rope, dried apples.

"They ain't presents, exactly—" She scowled, having trouble finding the words in Guarem. She gestured to the crowd. "More like, uh, 'mustering out' pay."*

"What? I don't understand."

The crowd bustled. The gifts were impromptu, pulled from supplies they'd grabbed while running from the smoke. Brother Qown didn't think they could afford to do without them. Yet they did, but without any warmth. They gave the baron their gifts with all the malice of offered poison, each present a dagger's stroke.

Tamin began crying.

Tears marked streaks down his face as he stood. "Please, Janel. Please don't let them do this—"

"Don't let them do this?" Janel's expression was incredulous. "This is their right."

Old anger flared hot in his eyes. "You hypocrite! The only

---

* Used to be literally that, as I understand it. This practice is a variant left over from the days when the "nobles" of Jorat were Quuros army officers—who'd been awarded lands in exchange for service.

reason you're here right now is to avoid your *own* Censure! How dare you chide me for not wanting to give up my birthright when you're running from the same fate!"

Janel's breath caught. For a moment, Brother Qown thought she might hit Tamin, but she clenched her fists instead. "I'm not running from justice. I'm running from a bastard who thought he could buy Tolamer Canton and bribe its people—*my people*—to Censure me if I refused to keep his bed. Sir Oreth didn't even wait for my grandfather's body to cool before he showed up with his troops, his ultimatums, and his eviction notice," Janel corrected. "I didn't let witches, Yoran spies, and *demons* have free rein to send the souls of my people straight to Hell."

"I didn't know I was doing that!" Tamin screamed.

"That only proves you're too young and too naïve to keep others from manipulating you into doing it for them."

His laughter was a choked-off sob. "Too young? Janel, I'm a year older than you."

"And yet so much younger in all the ways that matter."

Tamin scrambled to his feet, ignoring the blankets and the backpack and the cloth-wrapped food. "So you'll do nothing, then? You're a count!"

"I'm not your count!" Janel shouted.

All talking stopped. Everyone who had been preparing for departure paused as she raised her voice.

"Be thankful," she continued in a softer tone, "because I'd order your execution for what you've done here. I'd hold the sword myself. Do you understand me, Tamin? I watched you order a man's death, whom you just admitted you knew was innocent. You killed your own steward for a crime *you* committed. You laughed while a demon you'd empowered slaughtered a knight and her squire, turning the field of honor into a mockery. You burned innocent people at the stake for the crime of witchcraft. You would have killed more, and all for this Relos Var's approval and a prophecy he probably invented. Don't ask me to interfere, Tamin. You would not like how I'd rule in your case."

Brother Qown realized he hadn't heard the count refer to Tamin as *Baron* since her fight with Dedreugh.

Silence lingered, a few tense, quiet moments. Then Gan the Miller's Daughter—or rather Ganar Venos, Warden Dokmar's daughter—came forward leading an old horse. She smiled at Tamin, although it looked like an effort. "I've saddled you a horse. They tell me her name is Orchid. She doesn't see very well at night, so you'll want to get some distance from the town before sundown."

"Gan—" Tamin's expression was stricken.

"Don't," Gan said. "Don't you dare. You need to leave, Tam, now." Gan regarded the man she'd once planned to wed. "I wouldn't stop Kalazan from taking your head. I'd cheer him on while he struck the blow."

Tamin swallowed. Then he picked up the offerings, shoved them into the backpack, and mounted the horse.

He rode south. The survivors watched him go in silence. And then, once he'd turned past the last pergola's flag-covered patio, every eye turned back to Count Janel.

She paused, wary, and then shook her head in denial. "Oh no. Not I. I'm already the Count of Tolamer. I cannot also be the Baron of Barsine."

"Well, who, then?" Dango said. "Not me. I ain't doing it."

Brother Qown frowned. "You can't just—" He turned to Dorna. "Are they going to just . . . pick . . . the next baron? Like that's something you can just *choose*? Doesn't whoever Tamin owed fealty to . . ." He bit his lip. "Won't the count he owes fealty to object to commoners just deciding Baron Tamin isn't in charge anymore?"

Dorna stared at him.

"That's not how it works, colt. I don't know how you lot do things in Kaziwatsis—"

"I'm from *Eamithon*."

"Whatever. In Jorat, a stallion who can't protect their herd sure as hell don't get to lead it. What you protect is what you rule here."

"Stallions don't actually lead horse herds, though. Mares do." That detail had been bothering him to distraction ever since he'd first arrived.

She rolled her eyes. "Stop talking real horses when we're talking politics. In Jorat, the human herds are led by stallions. Always stallions. Anyway, if an old stallion gets kicked out because he can't do his job, who decides who replaces him? Some other herd's leader who won't ever be around? No, foal. It's the herd itself what chooses its leader." She cocked her head. "'S why I didn't put a gift in the pile. He ain't my leader. I didn't give him any thudajé."

The heresy of the notion made Brother Qown feel dizzy.* And Dorna had presented it so matter-of-factly. Of course, the people would decide on their ruler. Of course, the herd would choose. How could it be any other way? And if a leader did a poor job, the herd simply . . . asked them to leave . . . didn't even ask. Tamin had just understood he should go.

Gan put her hand on Kalazan's arm. "It should be you."

"Me? But I—" He stopped himself and turned to Ninavis. "No, it should be you. You recognized the danger before anyone else. You led the fight against him."

Ninavis shook her head. "Oh no, kid. I don't know the first thing about ruling a banner, and I don't want to know. I'm a thief, not a lord. It's all yours. I wish you Taja's own luck."

He swallowed, looked around at the crowd. "If everyone agrees, then of course I'll take the responsibility."

The crowd murmured in assent, this coming loudest from Ninavis and her crew.

"Good," Janel said, "you're a fine choice. But for now—" She tilted her head, making the gesture seem almost apologetic. "You'll need your eight best riders and all the horses we have left so you'll all be able to change mounts when they tire."

---

* Oh, but I love this heresy. Think how close the Joratese are to rejecting the idea of nobility! Why, if they keep going like this, they might even decide that someone shouldn't automatically be in charge just because their parents were.

"All the horses?" Dorna asked. "Not my Pocket Biter too? What about Cloud?"

Janel's expression turned rueful. "There are none to spare, Dorna. So yes, they'll need our horses as well. The eight will ride for the gates to pass the word—or catch the army and warn them. The rest of us will travel to Ninavis's stronghold."

"The rest of us? You're coming with me?" Ninavis sounded surprised.

"Of course. I almost allowed you to come to harm before. It won't happen again."

Ninavis frowned. "So Arasgon is coming with us too? But your horse—" She stopped to clear her throat. "I mean to say, the firebloods are the fastest runners here."

"He also makes his own decisions."

Arasgon tossed his head and said something. So did the other fireblood, Talaras. Brother Qown didn't understand their language, but their manner suggested they didn't agree about their next course of action.

"I'd ride," Sir Baramon said, "but I'm out of practice."

"And a lot out of shape," Dorna said.

The knight ignored her. "But Talaras can run without me. He's done it before."

Janel considered the matter. She turned to the fireblood. "Is that your wish?"

Talaras tossed his head and stamped a foot, and it seemed obvious that it was.

She nodded. "Fine. If Arasgon is to come with—"

Talaras snapped at Arasgon, who replied with obvious anger. Talaras stood his ground but looked ready to start a fight.

"We'll be fine without you," Janel told Arasgon. "We're taking the elephants with us. Besides, someone will need to lead Pocket Biter and Cloud to Atrine when you're finished. We'll meet you there, when we know the townsfolk are safe."

Arasgon didn't look like he believed her, but he pranced a few steps, blew air out his nose, and turned to join his brother.

Janel picked up a bag from the ground. "Come, then. The

same advice Gan gave Tamin applies to us as well. Let us put as much distance as possible between us and this town by nightfall." She turned to Ninavis. "If you would be so kind as to show us the way."

"Should have made that bastard Tamin heal my leg before he left," Ninavis mused. Then she turned to the elephant keeper. "Sana, think one of your girls will let me ride up top?"

A middle-aged woman looked up. "A wee slip like you? Tishar won't even notice." She smiled, a forced expression that didn't hide her tears.

"Let's get this herd moving," Count Janel said. "We've a lot of ground to cover before it grows dark."

The red-orange sun set as they headed toward the tree line, where they planned to stop for the night and make camp. Twilight turned the blue-green skies a burnt vermilion.

Adrenaline carried the townsfolk through the first few hours, but the horrors they had witnessed and the people they had lost began to sink in. The refugees had fallen into silence. A few were in tears. They stared at the camphor and cedar as if the forest were a lake after an eternity crossing a desert.

If they made it to the trees, they would be safe.

Ninavis and her crew were in their element. They directed the elephants, made sure able adults carried children on their shoulders, and patrolled the small convoy's edges to prevent unexpected surprises from sneaking up on them. They did it all with smiles and jokes, singing songs about their wonderful adventure, kidding the elderly about misspent youths. They made it almost possible to forget the horrors they left behind.

Almost.

During this, Brother Qown noticed Count Janel had wandered off to the far side of the group. She walked by herself, maintaining a steady distance from the others. Dorna, who was helping the children, hadn't noticed.

But then Dorna's responsibilities didn't include seeing to the count's emotional and physical healing. Qown's did.

Brother Qown had almost reached the count when she wiped her face.

She was crying. Her tears were silent, wet paths rolling down her red cheeks.

"Count . . . ," Brother Qown began.

Janel looked away. "Don't. The others can't see me like this."

"No one would blame you for being upset by what happened, Count. It was . . ." Brother Qown fought for words and failed. "It was horrifying."

She sniffed again, tossed her head back, swallowing a short laugh. "I'm a stallion. They need to think me strong. When this is over and they're safe—then they may realize how they've misplaced their trust a second time."

"Count Janel, you're making no sense," Brother Qown said. "If not for you—"

"If not for me," she said, "all those people in Mereina would still be alive."

"Not true."*

"Ninavis was right; I should have struck down Tamin when I had the chance. Am I not Janel Danorak? I was the one who insisted on my way. My way led straight to a town full of dead."

"Tamin's murder would have stopped nothing! Tamin didn't unleash the witch-smoke, and you had no reason to think Senera a threat."

"No," Janel agreed. "But she did it in response to what happened with Dedreugh. Because I revealed his true nature as Kasmodeus. She did this to cover up the real crimes, and she's proven how far she'll go to erase their tracks." Janel grimaced. "A long way, as it happens."

Brother Qown bit his lip. He believed the count had misjudged the Doltari witch's motives. For some reason, Senera had been . . . satisfied . . . when Janel triumphed over Kasmodeus, as if the Doltari woman had just finished a task.

---

* A little true? I'm sure you would have ordered me to target Mereina sooner or later . . .

Nothing in Senera's attitude suggested she considered what followed a setback.

"You can't blame yourself," Brother Qown said. "Besides, you weren't wrong. You said it yourself. If you had killed Tamin at that point, his men would have shot you. Do you think Dedreugh would have canceled the tournament? Do you think the warden's 'voice' Senera would have done so? No. All of Ninavis's people would have ended up burned at the stake."

"Do you think the citizens of Mereina would consider that trade fair?" Janel countered. "All those people dead, in exchange for fewer than a dozen lives?"

"That spell wasn't your doing. You cannot take responsibility."

"Taking responsibility *is* my job. I caused this by revealing Dedreugh's true nature as a demon."

"Then you must try to make it right as best you can. I think Relos Var and Senera would be quite amused to see you shouldering the guilt for their crimes."*

Janel stopped walking.

"Aren't I right, though?" he pressed.

"I just . . . I hadn't . . ." She shook herself, and her eyes regained their focus. "Thank you."

"You're welcome. Anyway, we have other matters to discuss."

She began walking again. "We do?"

"The manner of our survival." Brother Qown looked back toward the refugees in case anyone was close enough to eavesdrop.

"That's not so mysterious. You saved us from the smoke."

Brother Qown blinked, left open-mouthed for a moment. "I—uh . . ." He found himself near to blushing. "Yes. Well. I'm going to assume you know nothing about magic."

She gave him a sideways look that might have set the forest on fire.

---

* Well, it did make me smile.

"That's what I thought." Brother Qown cleared his throat. "Without boring you, let me say this: the symbol I drew saved our lives, but I don't understand why it worked."

The count blinked. "I don't either, but I admit I assumed you would be more knowledgeable."

"All objects have . . . energy . . . in them, which people call *tenyé*. It's the vital essence of you, me, that tree over there. There isn't any difference between a god's tenyé and a sorcerer's tenyé except in quantity—"

"Brother Qown, talk like that is why your order is heretical in half the empire."

He coughed. "The problem with heresies is they are named so because they touch on uncomfortable truths. My point is this: art has no tenyé."

Janel blinked. "I don't understand."

"A superlative drawing only has as much tenyé as the materials used to make it.* Paper, paint, ink. There is no difference in tenyé between a doodle and a masterpiece. Symbols in a book convey information, but they don't contain extra tenyé. And magic is only possible with tenyé to fuel it." Brother Qown gestured behind him, toward Mereina. "What I did back there. What Dorna did. That shouldn't have worked. I only did it in the first place because I hoped to link the symbol I'd copied from that woman—Senera—to her spell. If it worked, I hoped to insert myself into the same category as those soldiers under its protection. It was a desperate, impossible long shot."

"And yet you hit the target. It worked."

"No, no, it didn't. That might explain why it worked on me, but what about Dorna, who used the glyph while I was absent, with no idea what spell I had tried to cast? It shouldn't have worked for her. And if I grab Ninavis or Dango or Tanner and have them draw the glyph, it *still* works. This symbol is inherently magical—which is impossible."

---

* I want to argue this because it isn't always the case, but fine, the point stands.

The count thought over the matter as they walked. "But what of demon summoning? That requires specific symbols. Aren't those symbols inherently magical?"

Brother Qown blinked. "That's . . . very astute."

"But am I not right?"

"No. No, you're wrong, but it's an easy mistake to make," Brother Qown said. "The symbols used to summon demons have no intrinsic magical nature either, but we—humans and demons both—have agreed to give them significance. They symbolize the treaty between our races."

Janel stopped again. "*Treaty*? We have a treaty? Xaltorath never—"

She continued walking, looking ahead.

"We have a treaty," Brother Qown confirmed gently. "More specifically, we have gaeshe. What we call the binding of the demons is in fact the gaeshing of the demons—all of them. The demons were given gaesh commands they must follow. For example, they are forbidden from manifesting in the physical world unless summoned. And they have to follow their summoner's orders."

Count Janel shuddered.

"Why would the demons agree to that?"

Brother Qown frowned. "I don't think they did. I think it was imposed upon them."

"They must have agreed. Anyone who is powerful enough to *force* the demons into such a pact would be powerful enough to destroy them. Which means they must have agreed to it. But why? What did they get out of it?"

"I always assumed they lost the original war between the Four Races and the demons. So the gods forced this on them."

Janel laughed. "No. No, demons don't work that way. They must have gotten something. They would never, ever have agreed to such a deal otherwise."

"You may be right, but that's not my point. You see how the demonic symbol has no intrinsic magical properties, yes? It's powerful because we've agreed these symbols represent a specific result."*

"Couldn't that be true here? A symbol agreed to have a desired, specific effect?"

Brother Qown wrinkled his nose. That was a very good question. A very good, very troubling question. He searched around the edges until he found a flaw. "Agreed upon by whom, my count? The gods? It would take divine power to create such an effect, but no priest of the Eight uses this power. Father Zajhera knows more about magic than any other person I have ever known. He'd have mentioned if this existed."

Count Janel frowned. "What are you saying, then?"

"This Doltari woman, Senera, probably does traffic in demons, given what we saw, and thus qualifies as a 'witch.' Besides that, though? She has access to a magic I've never seen before and don't understand. The only good side I've discovered is the air glyph doesn't run out. The firebloods would have suffocated otherwise."

She sighed. "I wonder which of them was the leader."

"Which of whom . . . ?"

"Senera or Relos Var."

"We shouldn't assume they're connected."

"Tamin said Relos Var brought her. I only met the man once, but he didn't strike me as the sort to be someone else's tool. I'd think him a mare because he's a teacher, but . . ." She smiled ruefully. "I don't think Relos Var views such matters the way a Joratese would. The real question: Did he leave because of an emergency or so he wouldn't be present for what followed?"

"That logic suggests they could've planned the smoke from the beginning, rather than using it as contingency."

"What if they did?" Count Janel asked. "We don't have

---

* Qown dear, *all* language is nothing but a set of symbols we're agreed represent a specific result.

enough information. And none of this explains the Yorans disguised as Joratese. Neither Senera nor Relos Var are Yoran, although I thought Senera was at first." She picked three blades of tall field grass as they walked, braiding the strands. "Doltari, you say?"

"They're more common in the west," Brother Qown admitted. "They have a reputation for being a somewhat primitive folk."

"Or at least not very good at eluding slavers."*

He coughed. "Yes. That as well."

She squared her shoulders. "Fine. So all these are questions to which I must discover answers."

"You must?" Brother Qown raised an eyebrow. "Haven't you done your part? Shouldn't the rest be the army's job?"

"Perhaps." She snorted. "Probably. But I won't spill all this onto someone else's lap and let it be their problem. Whoever these people are, they used Tamin. They killed . . . I don't even know how many people. I won't ignore that." She added, "Did you notice the prophecy too?"

Brother Qown paused, hoping she hadn't grown better at reading him. "Prophecy?"

"Don't pretend you didn't spot it. Relos Var told Tamin the demon-claimed child would be his undoing. Which it was." Janel stopped walking. She stood there, looking puzzled.

"Did you just think of something?"

"No, there's something wrong—"

An elephant's trumpet shook the ground, followed by a chorus of her herd mates. Her call sounded panicked. Then the whole herd started running, paying no heed to their human partners. Screams echoed across the grass plains.

Brother Qown recognized one of those cries: Ninavis.

"What's going on?" Qown scanned the plain to see what might have upset the elephants.

The sky darkened.

---

* I wouldn't know. I was born in Quur.

An enormous shadow blanketed the forest, sailed out over the fields, slid back toward Mereina. The refugees ran.

Brother Qown looked up.

A gigantic form undulated across the sky, wings spread out like an enormous bird. The setting sun lit fire across the monster's edge but couldn't hide its shimmering white color. That opal shine reflected blue-and-purple depths as though it were formed from ice. Its head resembled a serpent, but no snake ever grew so large or soared on massive wings.

The dragon banked.

People screamed and dropped to the ground as the beast extended its wings, dropping down to swoop over the grassland.

The elephants, Brother Qown realized. The dragon was hunting elephants.

"Ninavis!" Janel screamed. She sprinted back toward the main group.

"Count! Wait!" he called out after her, but Brother Qown had as much chance of catching her as a dhole does of chasing down a falcon.

The dragon dove and snatched up an elephant in each front claw before pulling up, mighty wings driving it back into the heavens.

Everyone ran. Most ran away from the scene, but not all; Janel, Brother Qown, and Ninavis's band ran forward. The remaining elephants rampaged, stampeding back and forth as they vainly attempted to regain their stolen sisters.

A half dozen arrows loosed from somewhere in the tall grass impacted the dragon as the beast continued her flight. Unfortunately, even as the arrows hit, they did no damage at all. Indeed, the dragon gave no hint she even noticed herself under attack. When Brother Qown reached Janel, she was standing over Ninavis, who was sitting up in the grass. The bandit leader had strung her bow and fired at the retreating dragon. Seeing the results, Ninavis had resorted to ineffective shouted curses.

"Bastard!" Ninavis screamed. "Bastard, you come back here!"

"I don't think it can hear you." Janel crossed her arms over her chest. "And I don't think we want it to. At least you didn't catch its attention by firing arrows at it. How foolish would that have been?"

Ninavis responded with a string of blistering expletives.

"Brother Qown," Count Janel said, "might you see to Ninavis's wounds? She seems to have injured herself. Again."

"Only my pride," Ninavis groused.

"Oh? I could've sworn you must have fallen on your head."

Ninavis scowled and unstrung her bow. "What was that monster?"

"A dragon," Brother Qown volunteered. "I've never seen one in person before." Brother Qown would have liked to go on about how beautiful he'd found the beast, but he didn't think the sentiment would have been appreciated.

"Come on, then." Count Janel held out her hand to Ninavis. "Lean on me. We need to get these elephants calmed down and move fast." She pointed up at the sky.

In the wake of the dragon's passing, the sky began turning black, not from nightfall, but storm clouds.

"What . . . ?"

"A bad storm is coming," the count said, "so wherever your hiding place is, I hope it's close."

12: The Feast of Demons

Jorat Dominion, Quuros Empire.
Two days since Queen Khaeriel lost her
patience with House D'Mon

Kihrin said, "So what was Aeyan'arric doing—?"

The room quaked, a single jarring tremble. The cause seemed obvious enough; something massive had just landed on the hillside above the tavern.

Something as heavy as a giant dragon, perhaps.

Conversation throughout the tavern stopped. Everyone looked up at the ceiling and waited to see if it would repeat.

In the silence, Kihrin had no trouble hearing the old woman at the bar say, "You don't figure she can dig down here, do you?"

At that moment, Kihrin realized the tavern customers weren't ignorant about what was happening outside. They hadn't responded with panic or screams or frantic questions about what made that noise. They hadn't looked around, trying to pinpoint the threat's direction. They'd all stared up at the ceiling.

They already knew.

Kihrin met Janel's eyes. She hadn't been looking around the room. She'd been watching him.

"Did you think I wasn't going to tell them?" she said.

"I assumed that, yes."

She stood up from her chair and trailed her fingers over Kihrin's hand as she walked past him to the center of the room. "All right, everyone! Pay attention."

Everyone did. Immediately.

"I'm sure by now you have all heard about the little problem we have waiting for us outside," Janel said.

"Yeah, what are we going to do?" a large man said. "We lost fifteen people in Ferra because of that damn dragon."*

The bartender snapped, "We lost fifteen people in Ferra because they didn't follow orders." She absently moved her hair from her face as she spoke.

A wine-stain birthmark covered part of her face.

Maybe it was just coincidence . . . no. Kihrin didn't think so. Ninavis.

"What the—" Kihrin looked around the room again. Too many stallions, now that he knew what to look for. That made no sense for a small town, but worked perfectly for a military group. Kihrin glanced at Brother Qown; he didn't seem surprised either.

"I have a theory about what's going on here," Janel said. "I hope I'm wrong, but in the meantime, there's nothing we can do but wait. And yes, Dorna, if she wanted to dig her way down here, she could. Aeyan'arric isn't trying to kill us. At least not yet."

"But how did she find us—?" a large roan man with an impressive mustache started to ask. Sir Baramon.

Janel cut him off. "I don't know, but this changes nothing. Make yourselves comfortable. Look like you belong."

Janel returned to the table.

"Don't give me that look," Janel told Kihrin. "Or do you mean to tell me you have never arranged a tricky meeting, in a neutral location, and replaced everyone with your own people? Not once?"

"Yes, but it ended with me on the auction block, so I don't recommend it."

"I'd have avoided this option if I had any alternatives."

Kihrin gestured to the room. "These are all those people from Mereina, aren't they?"

---

* We almost had them too. It was so close.

"There's a few faces I don't recognize," Brother Qown said. "But it has been a while."

"We gained some, we lost some," Janel said. "And I'd have told you earlier, Kihrin, but you seemed suspicious enough."

He had to admit there was some truth to that. Still . . .

"You said you have a theory about our dragon friend. Do you? Or did you just say that to calm them down?"

Janel started to shake her head. "Unlike you, I'm not impossible to track with magic, so Relos Var must have told Aeyan'arric where to find me."

Kihrin stared. She didn't seem to be joking. Not that he could think of any circumstances where bringing up Relos Var would be funny.

"You don't know he did that," Brother Qown said. "We have no evidence at all."

"True," Janel said. "And I hope I'm wrong. I suppose I'll just have to ask him when next we meet. Shall I continue with the story?"

Kihrin exhaled. "Sure. We're already at the party. Might as well sing along."

Janel's Turn. The ruins of an estava, Barsine Banner, Jorat, Quur.

By the time we reached the shelter, we desperately needed it. A light drizzle had begun to fall soon after the dragon's passing, and it became a torrential downpour within minutes. Strong winds whipped icy rain, joined by hail, which fell with increasing frequency as time wore on. Fortunately, not much rain made its way past the tree canopy once we entered the forest proper, but what did fell hard and wet upon us. The wind strengthened; the trees creaked as they bent and sometimes cracked under the strain. Lightning lit the air in snapping flashes, some bolts so close the whole ground shook from the thundering boom which followed.

"It's up ahead!" Ninavis yelled. "Just at the base of that hill!"

She pointed at the spot in question through a break in the trees, a green tree-lined hill decorated with old stone blocks and crumbling ruins. Halfway up, a rough stone ramp led to a yawning black opening. The cave mouth might have been taken as natural if the entrance hadn't been so symmetrical. Relief washed over me as I realized what I saw.

"What is this place?" Brother Qown asked.

"An estava,"* I answered. "Thank the Eight."

"A what?" He looked bewildered.

"Shelters built by Khorsal and his centaurs." Dorna scrunched up her face as if tasting something foul.

"Since it's going to save our lives, I don't give a pile of horse crap who built it," Ninavis said. "Everyone inside, right now. Go, go, go!"

Sana the elephant minder shook her head. "Them places are cursed!"

I turned to the woman. "Mare, if by *cursed* you mean 'a place where Ninavis and her people hid from Captain Dedreugh for months,' then perhaps so, but we have no time to find anything better. So please, follow Ninavis inside." I tried to make it clear from my tone I wasn't making a request.

Sana wanted to argue, but Ninavis's people were already moving. A lightning crack and thunder clap far too close at its heels decided the issue. She started leading the remaining elephants.

Brother Qown asked, "What does *estava* mean?"

Dorna answered first. "Storm shelter." A nasty grin cracked her face. "You ain't seen a Joratese tornado yet, have you, foal?"

His eyes widened.

I fought not to laugh while Dorna grabbed him by the robe. "Come on, then," she said. "It's going to be a bad time to be outside tonight."

---

* In hindsight, if I'd known these places existed, I'd have tracked down their locations. I didn't know to ask.

While not all Joratese houses are underground cellar homes—indeed, many aren't—we have never forgotten we're host to the most vicious storms to be found in the empire. Joratese architecture derives from the estava, not so different from cellar houses today except in scale. They were not fortresses; they acted as shelters for times when, for whatever reasons, the Horse Lords hadn't wanted to move their herds away from approaching storms.

Ninavis's people had lit a few lamps as we entered the shelter. Too few for the place's size. Presumably, lamp oil was a rare treat for bandits on the run.

The tunnel opened into a gigantic stone hall supported by massive granite columns, so large the lamps didn't illuminate the far walls. The estava showed signs of great age—cracks in the floor, places where rubble had fallen from the ceiling. Running water echoed beyond the torchlight, but I didn't know if I heard runoff from the storm or if the shelter had permanent access to fresh water.

Ninavis and her crew would know.

The hall's current owners had left their mark. Crates rested against a stone wall, opened to reveal foodstuffs and cloth bundles, supplies and rations stolen from across the banner. I even recognized the merchant groups. There, tea from Eight Coins Trade Consortium, and over there, dried mango donated courtesy of none other than the Sifen family. A grand pile of pillows and rugs marked the main bedding location, and someone had taken time to craft an earthen oven.

The refugees needed no instructions; they spread out, set down their possessions, and began making camp.

Brother Qown waited for me to help Ninavis take a seat on a piece of fallen masonry before he bent down next to the woman. "Let me look at your leg."

I saw her about to protest. "Ninavis, I bear the responsibility for your injury. Let Brother Qown heal your leg. Vishai priests are without equal in the healing arts." I sat down on a wooden box, stretching as I began removing the black enameled armor I'd borrowed from Sir Baramon. Sir Baramon had been right about the poor fit. My muscles were not happy.

"The Physickers Guild wouldn't appreciate you telling folks that," Ninavis said.

"The Physickers Guild is more concerned with lining their coffers than helping people,"* I replied. "And they hardly bother doing even that much in Jorat."

"Maybe if you stopped burning them as witches," Ninavis suggested, "they'd be keener to take your metal."

I was about to protest, but I realized she was baiting me. I didn't have the patience for it. I was about to respond, anyway, when Sir Baramon joined us. His red face suggested both the rigors of a hard march and the tears he'd shed along the way. I reminded myself he'd lost someone very close just a few hours prior.

I didn't even know his lover's name.

Sir Baramon sat down next to me. "That was . . ." He pressed his lips together and tried again. "I'm not imagining things, am I? A dragon attacked us? I thought they were myths . . ."

"Oh no," Brother Qown said as he unpacked his satchel, looking for whatever supplies he needed to treat Ninavis. "That was Aeyan'arric."

Everyone stopped.

Ninavis blinked. "You know its name?"

"*Her* name," Brother Qown corrected. "And yes, I know her name. There are eight dragons.† Based on the descriptions I've read, that's Aeyan'arric, the Ice Bringer, Lady of Storms." He hesitated as he saw the expression on our faces. "Father Zajhera taught me their names."

"Eight of them," I repeated. "Like the gods?"

Brother Qown gave me a shocked look, the one he wore whenever I asked a question he'd rather I hadn't. "No! I mean, there are more than eight gods, anyway . . ."

---

* What do you know? Janel and I do agree on something.
† Fine. *Nine* dragons. Kihrin *is* right, after all.

"Only eight gods who matter."

He cleared his throat. "Yes. Well. Dragons are the living antithesis of the natural order the gods personify, so you can't compare them." He held out his hands. "Sometimes a number is just a number."*

I stared at him and felt in my bones my priest had just lied to my face.

"So eight in all the world," I said, "and yet one shows its face—her face—here. Now." I finished pulling the plates from my arms. "Even if we call ourselves fortunate that the dragon was only interested in our elephants, I find myself discomfited. She flew toward Mereina . . ."

"It may be coincidence," Qown said.

"Oh aye. And when vultures circle in the sky after a battle, that's just coincidence too." Dorna began picking up discarded armor and placing the pieces in neat, organized rows next to Sir Baramon. "I'd see about helping the group fix supper, but I'd say they've had enough catastrophes for one day. I can help with the ritual of parting, though."

Embarrassment washed over me. Of course, the townsfolk would still have a funeral. Even if they didn't have bodies to burn, ashes to scatter over fields, they would still honor those they'd lost. We wouldn't have enough rations for the funeral feast, but . . .

But. They had to do something.

I couldn't blame them.

"Do you think they'd mind if I said a few words?" Brother Qown asked.

"Well, you ain't a priest of the Eight, colt—" Dorna began to protest.

Qown frowned with disappointment. "Dorna, I am. My lord Selanol is one of the Eight. I'm as much a priest of the Eight as anyone who follows Khored or Galava."

"Oh." She shrugged. "Sorry. Guess I didn't think of it that way."

---

* But not in this case.

I touched Brother Qown's hand. "I'm sure they would be grateful for someone to speak for the dead. Please."

Dorna gave me an odd look. "What? You ain't doing that?"

"I cannot. I'm going to sleep now."

Dorna's hands froze on the armor.

"Early for that, isn't it?" Sir Baramon asked.

"Quite the opposite. I'd hoped we might make camp earlier. Now I fear I'm too late." I stood and gathered up the cloak I'd picked up from the Red Spear's body. I saw where everyone put their blankets together for sleep and headed to the other side, where I would be alone.

I would have liked it better if Arasgon had been with me, but I would have liked it better if none of this had happened too. I bundled my cloak into an impromptu pillow and lay down, curling myself into a ball.

Death's touch came immediately, as it always does.

Janel's Turn. The Afterlife.

In sleep, I walk the lands of the dead.

Even within the Afterlife, I often wake to find I have been drawn to some death scene. Some spot where the crossing of souls has made the barrier between the land of the living and the land of the dead easier to pass. Demons seem drawn to these places too, hungering for a return to the land of the living—which is otherwise so difficult for them to reach.

Or was it?

(A treaty was the only thing preventing them from attacking us at will, Brother Qown claimed.)

I found myself back in Mereina.

A great many lives had crossed over in the old fortress's history, so it was easily recognizable. And each death had created echoes through the Veils, giving its castle more strength. The newer town itself might have been invisible here, under other circumstances. Previously, the town had been too young

and too peaceful for its structures to have left a memory reson-
ating into the Afterlife.

Now?

Town and castle both stood in grim relief, solid and firm.
Glowing phosphorescence lingered along battlements or
outlined the patios, the tournament stands, the azhock. Ghosts
wandered the grounds, addled and frightened. Their appearances mirrored their deaths. The poor warder stood in the
nobles' box, blue-faced, freed from his illness but perplexed by
his current predicament.

Sadly, I didn't have time to take these poor souls aside and
clarify their situation, guide them to Thaena's Land of Peace,
offer them advice. I didn't have time to explain they could die
twice, the second death more permanent than the first. The
demons would use those deaths to gain what they wanted most
in the whole world.

Namely, the whole world.

Oh yes, the demons had come to Mereina. They would start
a Hellmarch here if they could, would puppet these dead across
Jorat slaughtering village after town after city until they had
gathered enough souls to call a demon prince's attention.*

And then the killing would never stop.

The demons had arrived to ravage the souls of the dead.

I had come looking for more challenging prey.

I wasted no time. Sword drawn, I laughed as my first swing
took a demon's head from his shoulders and—blocking a hellhound's lunge with my shield—I stepped to the side. I began
the slaughter, letting my hate and my rage fill me with a fire-like
warmth. The first demon's blood was black, the second a
glowing purple; there were no rules for how a demon's gore
might appear.

I was impaling a demon tiger's jaw with my sword when I

---

* Kasmodeus thought if he just gathered enough souls, he could make himself
another Xaltorath, but I'm definitely starting to think that was never going to
work.

heard a shout. I looked up in time to see a massive hammer smash into my face, throwing me backward.

Awake, such a blow would have slain me, but the rules are different when one's existence is metaphorical.

I slammed my hand down into the ground for leverage and pushed myself upward. A massive skinless demon stood before me, muscles glistening red between white divisions of connective tissue and yellow fat.

He was still missing his lower jaw, though.

"Kasmodeus?" I spat blood to the side. "You recovered quicker than I thought you would, given how easily you died the first time."

The muscles of his cheekbones pulled. A grin, or as close as he could manage.

OTHER DEMONS WILL SCREAM AND HIDE THEIR FACES WHEN THEY SEE WHAT I DO TO YOU.

I laughed. "Plan you, then, to save a few drowning puppies? Make soup for an old sick mare?" I smiled. "Roses. You shouldn't have."

His eyes glowed. **DIE, WHORE!** He swung his maul, letting momentum send it crashing down.

I barely dodged it. He was more powerful than before, but then again, he'd stolen at least a few poor souls who'd died too close to those damn stakes. Who knew how many souls he'd taken from dire sacrifices burned at previous tournaments?

He gave me no time to collect myself. No sooner did his first swing send dirt flying in all directions than he swung again and again. One devastating blow followed by another. I lifted my shield to block a strike, buying myself a chance at a closer swing. His blow drove me to my knees. I ground my teeth as I lashed out with my sword. The edge hit true, shearing through chest muscle and rib cage.

He didn't notice. Or perhaps he didn't care.

I screamed as his hammer caught me in the ribs in turn. Bones cracked. As it had in the tournament, I felt a great spreading warmth overcome me.

Fire sprouted from the ground under my fingertips, spread out in a spiral around me on the grass. It looked unreal in this place, a red-and-orange pattern against the Afterlife's blues and purples. I had no time to question it, but I pulled strength from the heat.

What remained of his face grinned. **I WILL USE YOU AS A FOOTREST. I WILL MAKE MY CHALICE OF VICTORY FROM YOUR SKULL.**

He raised his hammer.

"Why don't you stick with the practical? Clearly, you need a jaw—"

In the distance, an elephant's trumpet split the air.

I raised my head.

He paused.

More elephants called to each other, their sound like thunder. In the living world, this would have been no great occasion. Elephants were not so uncommon there. In the Afterlife, however?

Elephants in the Afterlife have only one mistress.

I started to laugh.

"Well, then," I said. "It seems Death has found us both."

13: WAITING OUT THE STORM

Jorat Dominion, Quuros Empire.
Two days since the House D'Mon royal family massacre

Janel smiled as she stopped talking and reached for her drink.

Kihrin sighed and tried not to look at Brother Qown while he mulled over the messy, ugly complications of Qown's religion. He couldn't think of anything more awkward than realizing the priest sitting across the table worshipped . . . Kihrin.*

Or at least, who Kihrin had been in his past life.

He broke his reverie as he realized Janel hadn't started talking again. Kihrin looked over at her. "Wait, you didn't finish."

"Is anyone hungry?" she asked. "I think I might see what they have in the kitchen."

"No, no, no," Kihrin protested. "You can't just leave it there. *Did* Thaena appear? I mean, what happened?"

"Oh, I thought we might take a break." Janel's feral grin couldn't be described as evil, but only by the thinnest of margins. "Maybe skip ahead."

She was teasing him.

Brother Qown opened his book up. "Are we really skipping?" He didn't sound happy at all.

"No, never fear, Brother Qown. Do you have anything you want to add before I finish my part?"

---

* Oh . . . I honestly hadn't thought of it that way. Kihrin's right: that *is* awkward. This is why I don't like religion.

Well. One of many reasons.

"Just a bit. If I may?"

She waved a hand. "Go right ahead."

Qown's Turn. The ruins of an estava, Barsine Banner, Jorat, Quur.

Ninavis scowled as Count Janel walked away. "Hey, we're not done talking."

The count ignored her and curled up to sleep.

Ninavis started to hobble over to her, but cursed in pain and stopped.

Brother Qown sighed. "You're so stubborn." He offered Ninavis his arm. "Would it kill you to stay off your leg for a few days?"

"Given what we just left behind us, I'd say the answer is yes." Ninavis limped over to Janel.

"Save your strength," Dorna said. "She's asleep. You ain't waking her now."

"Hey," Ninavis said. When Janel didn't respond, she screamed it.

A few people at the main camp looked over. "You need something, boss?" Dango shouted back.

Ninavis balanced on her good leg and bent down to shake Janel's shoulder. The young noble gave no response.

"Dorna's right," Brother Qown said. "You won't wake her. She'll stay sleeping until the morning, and I've never seen anything hasten the process."

Ninavis drew back, startled. "Priest, she's not breathing."

"Oh, she is," he said. "Just slowly. And please, call me *Brother Qown*. I hate being called *priest*."

"She's not, priest. I can see she's not breathing."

Sir Baramon drew closer, listening to the conversation with growing alarm. "What magic is this?"

Dorna shrugged as she smoothed out her riding skirts. "She's cursed. Ain't nobody spreading those damn stories about 'Danorak' ever mention the curse?"

"What? But—"

Dorna gestured toward Janel's sleeping form. "She's asleep. The priest here says she ain't dead right now, but you couldn't tell it by my sight. She don't breathe. Her body grows cold. Dead to the world, and that's not just a figure of speech. Dead to the Living World. This estava could fall around our ears and she'd wake as much as any corpse would. Except when dawn comes, she'll be right on her feet again, like she'd had a solid night of sleeping sound."

Ninavis's grip on Janel's shoulder tightened. "I just assumed she was a witch."

"Excuse me?" Dorna raised an eyebrow.

"Because she's so strong. I thought she was a witch."

"My foal don't summon no demons!" Dorna looked ready to start her own fight.

"I mean—" Ninavis sighed. "I mean she uses magic. That makes her a witch, doesn't it?" She waved a hand toward a crate on the ground. "Help me over there, would you, priest?"

She ignored his sigh as Brother Qown helped her over to the impromptu seat.

"The Count of Tolamer does *not* use magic," Sir Baramon retorted.

Dorna and Brother Qown shared a look.

Dorna cocked her head. "Course she don't. No one's suggesting otherwise. Now why don't you go check on our fine new friends from town—see how soon they'll be ready for the funeral dinner? From the smell, I'd say somebody put some stew on or I'm still the Count of Leanan Pass."*

He narrowed his eyes. "I don't owe you thudajé, you old crone."

Dorna grinned. "Oh, my sweet Baramon. You're under the count's idorrá now, and I'm her lead mare. Close enough, eh? Now git. This ain't for your tender ears."

Sir Baramon huffed and retreated to the impromptu kitchen.

---

* Honestly, it wouldn't surprise me if this were true. I'm almost tempted to check.

"You don't like him, do you?" Ninavis asked.

"Sir Baramon? I love him to bits. I've known him since we were both colts, and if I ran with stallions and he ran with mares, we'd have married years ago." She made a face. "Should have, anyway. We'd have made great herd parents."

Ninavis looked down at the sleeping girl. "She looks her age when she's asleep." The bandit leader eased down onto the box, sitting full upon it once it proved sturdy enough to hold her weight. "My Hava would be as old."

Brother Qown grimaced. "I'm sorry."

"Don't be sorry. Wasn't your fault." She stared down at her lap for a long moment. "She was a sweet girl. A heart as pure as spring. You ever have children, Dorna?"

The old woman smiled and gestured toward Janel. "Don't that one count? I love her like she were my own."

Brother Qown wasn't sure if he dared ask what had happened to Ninavis's daughter.* The woman's pain ached tangibly, dark and private.

Ninavis preempted the priest and pointed to the sleeping count. "My husband died in the Hellmarch she stopped. My daughter, after that."

Dorna and Brother Qown both grew still.

Ninavis waited for them to say something, say anything, but what could they say?

"I saw what demons do to people," Ninavis continued. "They do horrible things, but they don't . . . they don't 'curse' them. So why don't you two stop lying and tell me what's going on?"

"We're not lying," Brother Qown said. "Janel is a special case."

"Is she a witch or not?"

Brother Qown cleared his throat. "If your definition is someone who makes bargains with demons, then the answer

---

* I checked. Hava was killed for being a witch. Ninavis probably would have been too if she'd been a normal soldier's wife. And no, her daughter wasn't a witch by anyone's definition.

is no." Brother Qown was skating around the question, qualifying it with technicalities, but what choice did he have? "Tamin isn't a witch either. You people confuse being able to use magic with witchcraft, when it's not the same thing at all."

"Not my people," Ninavis reminded him. "Anyway, just tell me what happened to her. Tell me why she's like this."

"Oh, he don't know," Dorna said. She had an angry look on her face. "Qown only joined up with us a few months ago because his church ordered it. I'm sure that Father Zajhera told him what he was getting into, but hearing it secondhand ain't the same as being there."

Ninavis scowled. "And if I ask you for her story, are you going to tell me it's none of my business?"

"Well, it ain't, is it?"

"You're wrong," Ninavis said. "It is my business. I may not have been born here in Jorat, but my husband and daughter were both Joratese. I know enough about the customs here to understand that little girl just strolled into my backyard and stole my people right out from under me. Kalazan's loyalty is to her now. He may be this banner's new baron, but I guarantee you she's his new count." She cocked her head. "Not real sure how the old count's going to feel about that."

Dorna rolled her eyes. "Don't much care. Old bastard should have put a stop to Tamin's foolishness before it ever got this far."

Ninavis raised her hand. "That's not my point. My little band of thieves are horse folk just like you. And if there's one thing I know about Joratese, it's that you're too damn trusting. I'm not. I need to know what kind of person I'm following, especially when you tell me she's cursed."

Dorna sighed. "I weren't there when they went to Lonezh, when she was a child. I'd gone to the Festival of the Turning Leaves that year and—" She shook her head. "They was just visiting her father's cousins. Nothing special. Going to see a tournament. I don't know what happened either . . ."

"But the stories say—" Ninavis started to protest.

Dorna raised her hand. "Except the legends ain't true, what they say about Danorak. She didn't outrun the demons to get warning out to the emperor. She was caught up in it same as everyone else, but the demons didn't kill Janel. Instead, their leader, this demon prince, well, he decides to possess her body so he can summon more demons. Wore her like a riding dress. So there's this demon army on a trek of death and destruction from one side of Jorat to the other, commanded by an eight-year-old girl. Even after the emperor went and stopped the march, he couldn't get that bastard to give up his pretty new body."

"Father Zajhera believes the demon wanted to force the emperor to kill a child," Brother Qown offered.

"And who's he again?"

"Father Zajhera. He's the leader of my faith." Brother Qown put a hand to his chest. "When Xaltorath possessed Janel, no one could make the demon *leave*. The emperor hoped Father Zajhera might have better luck.* Which he did. Father Zajhera cured Janel's possession and then watched over her and made sure—"

"Made sure what?" Ninavis said.

"Possession has a disastrous impact on the mind. Most people are never sane again. Father Zajhera made certain Janel recovered. She needed mental and spiritual healing, not physical."

"Yeah, yeah," Dorna said. "The father's all right, I suppose. Janel stayed with him in his fancy temple for six months while he fished that demon out. When she came back to Tolamer, the father came with her. Stayed another three or so years, making sure she was right in the head. And she was . . . but that don't mean she was ever the same. I guess those six months must have seemed like years. She came back strong as an elephant and with that curse sending her back to Hell every night, like Xaltorath still has a hold on her soul."

---

* Emperor Sandus couldn't banish a demon? Oh, now that *is* interesting. That should be impossible because of the gaeshe binding all demons. Huh.

"I've told you, it's not Hell," Brother Qown protested.

Ninavis stared down at the girl. "So what is she?"

"Ain't you been listening?" Dorna settled back down and shook her head. "That's what I've been trying to tell you: I ain't got a clue."

14: THE NIGHT HUNT

Jorat Dominion, Quuros Empire.
Two days since the last sighting of
High Lord Therin D'Mon

"Okay, *now* it's your turn," Kihrin said.

"Are you sure you wouldn't rather have a break?" Janel smiled, even as she clearly still teased him. "Obviously, it doesn't have so unhappy an ending—for me, anyway. I'm still here."

He shook his head. "Just tell me the story."

"All right, all right. You come up again in this next part, you know. I didn't know your name at the time, but still . . ." She shrugged. "I do think we know all the same people."

Janel's Turn. The Afterlife.

Something large thundered through the Afterlife's forests. Several large somethings. I heard toppling trees crash as beasts moved through the dark woods, ravens scattering at their approach.

Kasmodeus paused, lowered his hammer to the side, stared in shock.

I couldn't blame him. The Hunt's arrival boded ill.

And not just for him.

I rolled to the side and hefted my shield as high as my broken ribs allowed.

He glanced back at me. ****WE COULD TAKE THEM TOGETHER. LET US PUT THIS PETTY SQUABBLE BEHIND US AND JOIN FORCES. THEY'LL KILL YOU AS SURE AS ME WHEN THEY ARRIVE.****

I brushed blood from my face with my gauntlet, although I suspect I just spread the muck about.

"Interesting idea," I said. The approaching elephants grew closer, and Mereina's ghosts emptied out as demons took the opportunity to run for their lives.

There are few things demons fear. They are the ones others fear, the ones who feed off fear, the creatures who make mothers scream and old men wet themselves. The Eight Gods, though, are among the entities who garner a demon's respect.

Demons run when gods take the field.

And what approached us was, at the very least, a servant of those Eight. If we were lucky, only that.

If we were not lucky, it would be Thaena herself. I brooked no illusion about whether I would survive such an encounter. I trespassed here as much as any demon. Kasmodeus knew that; it's why he'd made the offer.

I smiled. "Alas, I have one issue with it."

The demon cocked his head to the side. **WHAT'S THAT?**

I slammed my sword into him.

"The gods aren't my enemies. You are."

Kasmodeus's hammer was a heavy, staggering weapon, but that didn't always work in his favor. The demon had difficulty blocking with the weapon, while I had speed on my side.

Also, I had nothing to lose. I was dead either way.

I reminded myself the pain was all in my mind. Literally so, in this place. I wrenched my sword free and then stabbed him a second time. I didn't think I could win, but I thought I might prevent him from leaving before Death's forces arrived to finish him.

Kasmodeus had absorbed many souls. I wanted to ensure he had no chance to profit from his feeding frenzy. The death I provided would be temporary, a momentary weakening while he returned to Hell to regain his strength.

But what Thaena could do to him? She could restore all the souls he'd slain, undoing the damage so those who had died might be reborn. Demons broke the cycle of reincarnation; that is what makes them abominations. I could do nothing to restore the proper balance.

Thaena could.

I managed to cut a deep slice into his arm, severing the muscles and tendons allowing him to swing his oversized meat tenderizer. Even so, he remained dangerous and lethal and twice my size. I regretted Xaltorath had never taught me shape-changing. Then again, I would have rejected her lessons if she'd tried.

Kasmodeus bellowed and struck out with his arm, staggering me as the hammer crashed into my shield. It threw me out of line, but the unwieldy hammer prevented him from following up with a finishing stroke. I screamed and head-butted him as he leaned forward, thinking to do the same. When the blow made him pause, I kicked his side. I slashed my sword between his legs as a distraction and then slashed back across his stomach.

An elephant's bellow—close now—made Kasmodeus look to the side. A whistling filled the air. I paused myself, trying to place why I knew that sound. *Ninavis,* I thought.

Oh. Arrows.

I dropped under my shield as white arrows rained down from the storm-dark skies. Any demons who hadn't fled the field screamed, as white-feathered shafts found their marks. Kasmodeus roared, but his cry was no armor. A white arrow pierced his chest, another his left arm, several more striking his stomach and legs. A radiant light spread out from the arrow wounds, while Kasmodeus lurched back in surprised dismay.

Several arrows thunked against my shield.

Then an arrow hit true, spearing me through the leg.

The pain was beyond anything I had ever experienced, and I had thought myself jaded to agony. Searing fire spread out from the injury; I had to grind my teeth to keep from crying out. It felt as though fire was burning my leg from the inside out, blazing beneath my skin.

But I couldn't lower my shield. The rain of arrows hadn't slackened.

I saw Kasmodeus take an arrow through the neck, another through his right eye. His whole body pulsed with light from a dozen sources.

His muscles began to flake away, glowing fragments floating away on the wind.

I looked down at my leg and saw flakes of light there too, smaller but still excruciating. More arrows impacted my shield. One managed to pierce the wood, stopping just a scant hairsbreadth from my face.

I started laughing.*

I was going to die there. Truly die.

I didn't embrace the idea. There was so much I hadn't done with my life. On some level, I had the childish thought dying would be allowing the man who'd pushed me from my home to win. That I'd be letting Sir Oreth do as he wished with my canton and people.

Yet . . .

And yet. I'd stopped a Hellmarch here. Thousands would live because of that.

Not so bad a way to end one's days.

I lowered my shield then, because I wanted to see the faces of my slayers.

Unlike the normal gray elephants who lifted timber or helped around villages and towns throughout the empire, these elephants glowed white and stood twice their size. Their eyes sparked as red as my own.

This was appropriate. White and red, Thaena's sacred colors. Of course her elephants were white and red. They were dressed in the most beautiful and ornate silver armor too, intricately engraved with roses, entwined branches, their goddess's sharp-edged thorns.

Men and women rode their backs like hidden shadows,

---

* I know Qown insists she's sane, but reactions like this make me wonder.

overwhelmed by their mounts' glowing brilliance. They dressed in dark colors, armed with bows and arrows—shadows raining down death's justice on those who deserved it.

One last arrow pierced my chest. I didn't scream; rather, I let out a soft whimper. A glory of icy fire spread over me, something so far beyond understanding my soul stopped trying to communicate the damage. The whole world darkened. The woods fell silent.

The arrow fall stopped.

I knew Kasmodeus had died; he'd stopped screaming.

Dead was the wrong word. What did *dead* mean in the Afterlife? Discorporated, disintegrated, unmade.

A fate I would share soon enough.

I had wondered if I remained human on many occasions since Xaltorath first tricked me into accepting her help. If so, perhaps there would be a next life for me.

If I was a demon, quite a different fate awaited.

An elephant slowed, then crouched with an impact that shook the woods. Her rider swung down from her back.

He wore strange clothing, green and gold, the pattern looking something like snake scales. He wore no shirt at all, but fabric hung about his torso like long fringe, a knight's parade dress—if the knight in question had foolishly forgotten to wear armor.

His black skin made his features difficult to pick out in the dim light, but I thought he was exceedingly handsome.

His eyes shone like clear, bright jade.

He held two daggers in his hands, a bow slung across his back—not an idle passenger but one of Thaena's warriors, out hunting demons.

I found myself coughing and felt liquid touching my lips—blood, or whatever played that role here.

"You're still alive," he told me. He seemed surprised by the revelation.

I felt like laughing, but the pain stopped me. I smiled at him instead, or at least I tried to. It's more likely the expression on my face resembled a rictus. "Not for much longer, I think."

I winced and tried not to let agony overwhelm me. "Come closer. I would ask you a boon."

"A boon?" He tilted his head and shifted his grip on his weapons.

"Yes, my beautiful killer. A boon. A favor before you take my head."

He stepped closer.

"Well?" He bent down next to me on one knee, but I noticed he kept his weapons ready, his eyes wary and alert. He hadn't lowered his guard.

Good. I liked him already.

"They were trying to start a Hellmarch," I told him. "In Jorat. They were trying to create a prince instead of summoning one. They would have kept killing people, offering all those souls to a single demon. The demon would become more powerful with each death. Every soul fed to him would make him strong, until finally he'd be as strong as a prince. Strong enough to open gates to Hell on his own. Set demons loose. You have to warn them. This time, it failed, but they'll try again."*

He met my eyes. "What makes you think I give a damn what happens to Quur?"

That stopped me.

I blinked and looked at him again. It hadn't occurred to me to question his tall height, his perfect features, the fine angles of his jaw and cheekbones. He wasn't Quuros. He wasn't even human. He could only be a vané, the immortals who dwelt in the Manol Jungle to the south. The vané, who remained unconquered after orchestrating Quur's only defeat.

A Manol vané would indeed not give a damn what happened to the empire.

"You're not . . ." I gritted my teeth, stopping myself from letting out a toxic laugh. "Of course. You're Manol vané."

He smiled. "Someone paid attention to their teachers."

---

* Interesting theory. Completely wrong, of course, but really quite plausible. You know, I think I'm glad she's not on the demons' side.

"It would have been hard not to; I trace my lineage back to Emperor Kandor." Normally, I'd have said that with more pride in my voice, but this man belonged to the race who slew Kandor.

He laughed, flashing teeth as white as the elephants behind him. I didn't think the news funny. I'm not sure he did either; his laugh rang with more gallows humor than joyful mirth. I'd told him the punch line to a joke I didn't understand myself.

I wondered if he'd been *the* vané who'd slain my ancestor during Kandor's flawed attempt to invade the Manol. I supposed it would be a fine jest, then, if this vané killed me as well.

But I needed the help of Thaena's servants; I had to give him a reason to care.

"They were starting a Hellmarch," I told him a second time. "I don't know why. A woman named Senera and a man named Relos Var plotted it. Evil sorcerers who still live, who will try again. Even if you care nothing for Quur, Thaena must care for all the souls who will never reach the Land of Peace."

I felt I'd achieved something by making that speech without dying . . . or at the very least without passing out.

"Relos Var? You've met Relos Var?" Surprise and recognition tinted his voice. He stopped grinning.

He tried to lift my shoulder but pulled his hand back as I stifled a scream.

"Yes," I said, "but he left before it all began. Went to fetch his brother."

His stare sharpened. "His . . . brother. *His brother?* Are you sure?"

"I'm certain that's what he said. He had to leave because his brother had ended up on the auction block. About to be sold as a slave someplace called uh . . . Kesha-Farigona. Wait, was that it?"

"Kishna-Farriga."*

"Yes. That." I coughed and told myself I had to stay alive for just a bit longer. "He left before the trouble started, but I

---

* So that's how the Black Brotherhood knew Kihrin would be for sale that day.

don't think him innocent. They killed everyone. Do you understand? Everyone. Please. Don't let me have died in vain. You must warn them."

He put his hand to the arrow piercing me through the leg. His hand glowed for a moment. The arrow vanished amid a painful flash making me clench my teeth. His hand on my leg felt intimate, even through the armor.

"You misunderstood what I meant before," he said. "I said you're still alive. You still have a body. Your connection to the Living World is faint, but it exists. You're not dead, and you're not a demon. You won't die here tonight."

"I'm a demon, though. I—"

He leaned close to me. His eyes were jewels. I found myself distracted from the pain, which faded into the background as unimportant.

"You're not a demon. You'd have ripped out my throat by now."

My throat felt rather dry. And his throat . . . well, his throat was quite beautiful, the velvet line of tendon from ear to collarbone possessing a carnal elegance. I raised a hand to his face. He didn't move to stop me. I touched his lips, not quite trusting myself to do more. I didn't know if my strength in this realm would sabotage me here too, where I had never done more nor less than hunt and slaughter demons.

"It's not my fault you're too pretty to kill," I told him.

He smiled at my jest. Then he put his hand on the arrow through my chest, the one still spreading its brilliant light but not yet disintegrating me into nothingness. Perhaps he was right about my nature; the arrows had worked faster on Kasmodeus.

"This will hurt," he warned me.

I placed my hand on his. "Not as much as not knowing your name."

He laughed outright. "Ask me again the next time we meet."

He dissolved the arrow. I remember screaming, but nothing more after.

15: WHERE THE HERD WANDERS

Jorat Dominion, Quuros Empire.
Two days since demons were freed to rampage
through the Living World

When Janel stopped talking, Kihrin stood up and left the room.

He couldn't help himself. Also, he knew losing his temper in front of Janel wouldn't make a good first impression.

Or second impression, since they'd apparently met before.

Kihrin walked past the main group. What were they now? Military? Mercenaries? They seemed a little too well organized for bandits. They'd gone quiet, debating among themselves in low whispers. Star sat at the end of the bar, ignoring him or rather still in deep conversation with Dorna. At some point, Kihrin needed to find out what their connection was. Between Star and Dorna, they'd managed to kill a bottle of something that looked far stronger than cider.

Kihrin took a deep breath, slid into a seat at the long, high wood counter, and promised himself slitting throats wouldn't help his current situation.

Besides, the person he wanted to kill wasn't there.

The bartender looked up as he sat down. She pulled a towel from her belt and wiped down the counter. "What can I do you for?"

"Ninavis, right?"

She smiled. "Yeah, that's right. But shh." She flipped the hair back down. "I'm in disguise."

Kihrin laughed. "Right. I'd never recognize you. What are they having?" He pointed to Star and Dorna.

She chuckled, reached under the bar, and pulled out an amber bottle. "Here you go."

Kihrin reached for the bottle, sniffed at the open top, and blinked as his eyes started to water.

"Try not to breathe while you're drinking it. You'll cough less," the bartender advised him.

He gulped it back and, despite her warning, started coughing. It tasted like an ash fire and burned all the way down, as though someone had taken sassabim brandy and skimmed off all the smoothness. "What the hell is this?"

"Aris," she said, sounding rather proud.* "Local distillery makes it from barley, then ages it in wooden barrels for a few years until it's mellow."

"Until it's *mellow?* Does he set the barrels on *fire?*"

"Gives it a nice flavor, don't you think?"

He decided it would be better to be diplomatic. "I suppose I could get used to it. What do I owe you?"

She smiled. "Nothing. Tonight, a kind benefactor is picking up the tab."

"When I was a kid, when someone said 'a kind benefactor is picking up the tab,' they meant they'd just robbed someone down to their undergarments."

She grinned.

"Understood." Kihrin set down the glass. "I'll have another."

Ninavis leaned forward on her elbows. "You've been talking with Janel awhile. Seemed like you were making friends there until the end. Or do you run with stallions?"

Kihrin thought over Janel's earlier lessons in Joratese courtship rituals. Whether someone was a stallion or a mare had nothing to do with biology, unless the discussion involved sex— and then it did. "I'm pretty sure I run with mares."

The woman chuckled. "Only pretty sure?"

---

* A thoroughly nasty concoction the Joratese make, by letting various plants decay and then distilling the sludge. Kind of like sassabim, but it tastes like moss.

"Very sure," he corrected firmly. "This frankness takes getting used to."

"Yeah, the Joratese are funny like that." She grinned. "I like it. There's no guessing with them, and it's rare you meet anyone who has a problem hearing you say no. Their old god-king may have been an asshole, but Khorsal never got around to telling his people to be hung up about sex."*

Ninavis filled his glass and then stared past him. "Hey, Janel."

"Hello, Nina." Janel sat down next to Kihrin at the bar and turned her attention to him. "Was it something I said?"

Kihrin looked at her sideways. "It's complicated."

Janel snorted and waved at Ninavis. "A cider, if you wouldn't mind, Nina. And a cup of kulma tea."

"Anything else, Your Holiness?"

Janel smiled. "Put a pot of coffee on the fire?"

Ninavis rolled her eyes. She came back a moment later with a cup of cold tea she'd poured from a large glass jar.†

Janel took the mug and held it in both hands. It began steaming. "Anyway, let's talk about what I said to upset you. It wasn't me flirting with that Manol vané, was it?"

He debated gulping the second glass of aris. "Yes." Kihrin turned in his seat toward her. "But not because of the flirting. I'm upset because he wasn't any Manol vané; that was Thaena's son, Teraeth. Who happens to be my *best* friend."

"Oh. Is that all?" Janel drank the entire cup of tea in one long swallow.

"When Teraeth bought me in Kishna-Farriga—" He paused. "Apparently, I have you to thank for that rescue, so—thank you. Anyway, afterward, Teraeth and I became friends. But I had people who needed me back in Quur, and I wanted to leave.

---

* I will miss that about Jorat. Whenever I told people I didn't like to run with anyone, stallion or mare, they actually believed me and stopped making overtures. It was nice.

† In case you ever wondered how a sexually uninhibited population isn't crammed mountain to mountain with babies, they have a wildflower called kulma, which provides effective birth control. Yes, kulma as in the swamp. Guess where it grows?

He didn't want me to. We fought over it. He convinced me to stay by bringing you into it."

"Me?"

"Yeah. I won't go into details. I asked him how he even knew what you looked like, and he—" Kihrin laughed. "He didn't lie. He just let me believe a lie. He couldn't just come out and say you two had met. He knew I would have definitely left to find you, if I'd known."

He drummed his fingers against the countertop.

Ninavis brought over a cider and sat it before Janel. Ninavis started to say something, then shook her head and went back into the kitchen.

Janel traded her tea for the cider.

The room felt quiet for a place where so many people had been laughing and singing just a few hours before.

Kihrin looked at Janel sideways. "'It doesn't hurt as much as not knowing your name?'" he quoted her words and raised an eyebrow. "*Really?* That pickup line was the worst."

She wrapped her dignity around her. "I was delirious and in pain. Shut up."

He laughed outright, great guffaws, and after a few seconds, she joined him.

"It's not my fault," she muttered. "Have you seen him? He's beautiful."

"Oh, he's handsome. No argument there. I just wouldn't have the wherewithal to make an amorous play at someone while I lay dying in their arms in the Afterlife."

She turned to face him and blinked at him several times, smiling. "Are you so sure?"

That gave him pause.

Kihrin stared at Janel. "Wait, what did I say in the Afterlife? What did I do?"

She chuckled. "Quite a lot, although nothing I'd hold a grudge over. I'm sorry. I didn't mean to upset you."

"Oh no," Kihrin said, "I'm the one who should apologize for storming off."

"I'm glad. Do you want to join us again?"

"Yeah, I should."

She stood up from her stool and started to walk back to their table, but then turned back. "Kihrin?"

"Yes?"

"When we were in the Afterlife together, I told you I was insulted—" She paused for a moment, still finding her words. "That I was insulted Xaltorath had assumed you and I would have a relationship—as long as you consented. That my interest had been taken as already granted."

Kihrin felt like he'd eaten rocks. "Oh."

"You should know I wouldn't reject you just to spite Xaltorath. If I'm interested in a relationship, I'll tell you." She grimaced and held up a finger. "That didn't come out right. What I mean to say is this: Xaltorath was right. I *am* interested."

The rocks in his stomach changed into butterflies, a much more pleasant feeling. Still . . . "What about Teraeth?"

"Oh, I'd ask *him* about his attraction to you. It's not my place to say." The corner of her mouth turned up.

"Very funny," he said.

"I thought so." She smiled at him. "One more story. Then we'll stop for dinner."

Kihrin picked up his drink and headed back. It was Qown's turn.

Qown's Turn. The ruins of an estava, Barsine Banner, Jorat, Quur.

The rain poured down.

It stopped being rain by the second day, turning into slushy, dank snow. Mereina's survivors huddled for warmth. Brother Qown felt grateful for being underground; the huge stone cavern provided insulation from the weather, but everyone still clumped together and shared their blankets.

They had no way to judge morning, but Janel opened her eyes at what Brother Qown suspected was the moment the sun crested the horizon to the west. She sat up and pulled away her blankets, stretching and examining her limbs as if amazed they were still attached.

Then she wandered over to the hearth in search of breakfast.

"They were clever," she said later as Dorna, Sir Baramon, and Dango gathered together to play dice.

"Clever?" Brother Qown kept his voice neutral.

"Yes," she agreed. "They knew the smoke would kill everyone in the town. The demons would then eat their souls and animate—kill still more people for their brethren to possess. Then the dragon comes through and buries the local countryside in storms and snow"—she waved a finger toward the ceiling to the storm still raging above them—"so when the army comes through, they are slowed by the weather."*

"Oh, I see," Brother Qown said. He bit his lip. "I hate clever. I would much rather we were dealing with stupid."

She sighed. "Alas. That would have been preferable." She brightened then. "But at least they didn't succeed. The weather may be grim, but it will have all been in vain. There will be no Hellmarch."

"You're sure?"

She smiled. "I am."

"We can't stay here." Ninavis limped over in their direction. "We don't have enough supplies for all these people. Folks didn't grab near enough before they left. Nobody is prepared for snow. It never snows here."

Janel leaned back on one arm. She nursed a strong cup of tea from Dorna's stores, but in general, everyone had agreed to half rations. No one thought it wise to assume when the unnatural storm would end.

"When the storm passes, you should return to Mereina," Janel said.

"Mereina?" Ninavis looked appalled. "Where the demons are?"

"Where the demons *were*," Janel corrected. "Not anymore.

---

* Again, it's a good theory. Just completely wrong.

And you know the army is traveling there next. You can't just abandon the place, Ninavis. It's your home now. Where else would you go?"

"You keep saying 'you,'" Ninavis said. "I'm noticing a distinct lack of 'us.'"

Janel sighed. "I'm not your baron. When Kalazan returns . . ."

"*If* Kalazan returns," Ninavis snapped. "We don't know—"

Janel looked over toward where Ganar Venos (who no longer had to pretend to be Gan the Miller's Daughter) helped with the cooking. "Keep your voice down, please."

Ninavis's expression softened. "Fine. But you're just leaving?"

"Someone has to try to warn the others. I'm not just talking about the army either. Someone has to make sure people know what happened here. My people and I will go to Atrine and speak with Duke Xun."

Dorna looked up from her dice. "Atrine? Oh, foal. We can't! I know you told Arasgon to meet us there, but it's a terrible risk . . ." She didn't look behind as she slapped at Sir Baramon's hand. "Don't be changing those dice. I'll cut you. See if I don't."

"I would never!" Sir Baramon protested, while moving his hand away from the dice. "Um, why would going to the dominion's capital be a risk?"

Dango nodded. "I was gonna ask that."

Brother Qown studied his hands as tension played over Janel's and Dorna's expressions.

"Is there something you haven't told me?" Sir Baramon squinted. "Tamin said something about you outrunning Censure. That true?"

Janel sighed. "It's true. It's not . . ." She shook her head. "It's not earned, you understand. My grandfather wasn't even cold when Sir Oreth showed up on my doorstep with a small army."

"Sir Oreth? The Markreev of Stavira's second son?"

Dorna rolled her eyes.

"The same. Our parents arranged the match when we were children, but it . . . it didn't work out."

"Naturally, it didn't work out," Dorna agreed. "You're a lovely young noble, and he's a horse's ass. Cross-species relations are frowned on in these parts." She grinned, her expression impish. "Ain't that what you said in that last letter just before we left?"

Janel couldn't quite stop herself from smiling. "You know, I think it may have been."

Sir Baramon's eyes went quite wide. "Well, then. I see why he's so upset with you."

"No, I suspect he harbors a grudge—because just after our engagement, he behaved like a thorra, and I gave him a lesson in manners." Janel frowned. "He wanted me to bow to him, and I refused. So he tried to force me."

"Oh aye," Dorna chortled. She leaned over to Sir Baramon and said, "I hear she broke both Oreth's arms and dragged him by his feet into his father's bedroom. Oh, I wish I could've been there." She made a face. "But I ain't welcome around the Stavira estate."

"My point is that he thinks I should owe him thudajé," Janel explained, waving a hand disdainfully. "When he returned after my grandfather died, he gave me a choice: marry him, agree to accept my place as a mare, and make him count, or . . . or the alternative was paying off the people he'd already bribed to declare Censure on me. Since I had no way to do that, I left."

"What was your plan? Keep moving until he grew tired of the chase?" Sir Baramon frowned at the young woman.

"No!" Janel paused. "All right . . . yes. But Sir Oreth cannot sustain this forever. Oreth thought he could march in with his soldiers and keep me prisoner until the Censure finished. He thought it would take a week. The longer I drag this out, the more bribes Oreth must maintain, and the more his father's patience erodes. Markreev Aroth may have vaults of metal to spend, but that does not mean he'd do so willingly."

"Aroth's always been shrewd with the finances." Dorna rolled the dice. "I win again."

"Damn it, Mare!" Sir Baramon scowled.

Dango shook his head. "Nobody's that lucky."

"I don't like it," Dorna said. "Going to Atrine is too risky. Best if you stay away from the capital altogether." She paused. "You know your letters. Send a note. *Hello, Duke Xun, I hope this letter finds you well. Sorry I couldn't visit. By the way, evil plots are being hatched in Barsine. You should do something about that. Love, Janel.*"

Janel shook her head. "Letters can be ignored, mislaid, fall into the wrong hands. And if we travel by foot—which we will have to do since we sent all our four-legged friends away—we will reach Atrine around the same time as the Great Tournament. Attending *that* tournament is mandatory for all nobles ranked warden or greater. I might avoid Oreth, only to have Duke Xun strip me of rank for failing to pay my respects. I have no choice."

"That just means Oreth is counting on you attending," Dorna insisted.

"It's not so much a risk as you might think. Even if Sir Oreth should be in Atrine, it would still take time for him to locate all the people he needs to call Censure against me. It's a much larger number than Tamin required—who, after all, had lost so much of his banner's population. As long as I don't linger, I can slip in to see the duke and be gone before Oreth has a chance to confront me."

"She has a point," Sir Baramon said.

Dorna pressed her lips together into a thin line. "Still don't like it."

Janel smiled. "Noted, dear Dorna." She turned to Ninavis. "Does this satisfy you? I know it must seem like I'm deserting you, but I'm doing the opposite. I must find out who this Relos Var is, who Senera is, and most of all, what they are attempting to accomplish. It's the best chance we have to stop them."

Ninavis looked sullen and still not placated, but she nodded and ducked her head in agreement. "Fine. You lot go to Atrine. We'll stay here and rebuild." She paused. "We'll have a hard time of it. There's not many able bodies left."

"Do what you have to do," Janel said, "although I would recommend trying to convince the army to leave a segment here, as a precautionary measure. It may be the whole goal was to weaken this region of Jorat's defenses."

Ninavis stared at her. "This region of Jorat? We're in the *middle* of Jorat. Right smack in the middle. If someone invaded, they'd have to cross a half dozen cantons and thirty or so banners to get to this point. It's not exactly a choke point for military invasion."

"It is if you have an undefended Gatestone, with no Gatekeeper," Janel said. "Then it becomes an excellent way to flank and sneak Yorans into our dominion."*

"I suppose, but still, I would think there are better places to gain a foothold. I don't know . . ." Ninavis waved her hand.

"Tolamer," Sir Baramon offered. "Count Janel's canton would be perfect."

"Right. Tolamer," Ninavis agreed. Then she paused and looked back at Janel.

"Yes," Janel said, "even more reason I want the issue with Sir Oreth cleared up, but I doubt he's in league with invading Yorans."

"*Can* Yorans invade?" Brother Qown asked. "I mean, they're part of the empire. Seems a little odd for one section of the empire to try to take over another, doesn't it?"

The other three people looked at each other as if sharing a silent communication—and reminding each other Brother Qown wasn't from the eastern side of the Dragonspire Mountains.

"Yor was the last dominion added to the empire," Dorna explained.

"I *know* that," Brother Qown said.

"Well . . . ," Dorna said, shrugging. "They's raw about it. I mean, us Joratese have been Quuros for five hundred years or so. We're comfortable with the idea. Proud of it. Plus, here in Jorat, we threw over to Quur so as to get Emperor Kandor's help tossing out our old god-king. We wanted Quur here. But there's Yorans whose grandparents remember being ruled by

---

* Okay, she was wrong about the demons. But this? Yes, exactly right.

their god-king, Cherthog, and his nasty god-queen, Suless. Nobody had Urthaenriel, so killing god-kings was slow and messy. A real bloodbath. Door-to-door slaughter, putting anybody with an ounce of magical power to the torch. Proper Yorans still ain't allowed any power. Ain't allowed to practice their beliefs or speak their old tongue. They aren't so keen as us to think themselves loyal to the empire, is what I'm saying."

"Still a better deal than Marakor got," Ninavis complained. "At least Yorans are allowed to own weapons."

"That's because Yorans don't keep revolting," Sir Baramon retorted. He shrugged. "Or maybe they're just being a lot more patient about the idea. Would you live in a place as miserable as Yor if you didn't have to?"

Ninavis rolled her eyes. "No."

Sir Baramon raised his hands. "Well, there you go. Motive aplenty to try to expand their territory into lands sunnier and more fertile than their native snow-packed, frozen, personal Hells."

"Relos Var," Janel murmured.

The others looked at her.

"What about him?" Dorna said.

She shook her head. "Never mind. I will find out who he is, how he's involved in all this, and how he ties in with that witch, Senera."

"And then?" Ninavis asked.

Janel tilted her head. "And then I shall kill them. What else?"*

---

* Two words: *bring it.*

PART II

THE SILVER SWORD

They took a break for dinner.

The evening meal entailed a spicy tomato stew with peppers and oxtail meat over long noodles. Kihrin ate most meals with sag bread, but he accepted the two-pronged forks the locals used for the noodles.

As he finished eating, he realized the smell of burning wood had grown more intense. His eyes watered. Right around the same time people started to cough.

Himself included.

Kihrin looked up from the stew in time to see smoke pour from the fireplace next to him. Also, from the larger fireplace across the room. A man he hadn't seen before came running out of a room he assumed led to the kitchen, gasping. A gray smoke cloud followed him, pouring from the room beyond.

Janel stood. "Everyone on the ground! Stay low."

"What's going on?" Someone said.

"Glyphs, people. Right now!" That sounded like Ninavis.

Kihrin crouched. As he did so, Qown dropped down next to him. "Pull your hair back," Brother Qown said.

"Why, what are . . . ?" He didn't finish the sentence, remembering how Brother Qown had dealt with the witch-smoke back in Mereina. This smoke was the normal variety, but that didn't mean he couldn't choke to death on it. He pulled back his hair.

Brother Qown hesitated. "Wait, the sword—" He looked toward Kihrin's waist, where Urthaenriel rested.

"Should still work," Kihrin said. "As long as I don't try to dispel it or Urthaenriel thinks it's a threat to me. You're affecting the air, not my body or tenyé, right?"

"Right." Qown touched Kihrin's forehead with a finger and drew something. Qown then moved on to the next person. Immediately, the air tasted sweet and fresh. Kihrin couldn't smell smoke anymore. He stood up and watched as the smoke parted around his head as if there were an invisible barrier there. Kihrin couldn't see very far into the smoke beyond, but at least he could stand. And breathe.

"Horses first," Janel ordered to the room at large. "They'll end up on the ground fast."

"Somebody put those hearth fires out."

Kihrin almost volunteered before he remembered he carried Urthaenriel. No magic for him. As much as he'd have liked to help, he wouldn't set her down.

He wasn't sure Urthaenriel would *let* him set her down.

"What can I do to help?" Kihrin shouted.*

"Check the back rooms," a man answered. "Make sure there's nobody sleeping or . . . whatever."

Kihrin couldn't see far enough to find the back rooms, but he had a rough idea. He stumbled his way over to them and started opening doors. "Anyone back here?"

The inn offered rooms for overnight guests.

The last of which was occupied.

Kihrin turned away. "Okay, people. Put your clothes on and hurry out here. Stay low—the fireplaces are blocked." He left as soon as he heard the trio yell back their agreement.

When he returned, the smoke had thinned. Given Urthaenriel's grousing, he had to assume someone had used magic to dissipate it. Janel came back from the stables with Arasgon, Talaras, and Hamarratus. No one seemed to think that strange.

"Attention, everyone!" Ninavis shouted. "Let's settle down.

---

* Did grabbing a bucket and putting out the hearth fires with water not occur to him? I swear, stop someone from using a little magic, and suddenly, that's all they can think about . . .

It'll be a while before any cold seeps its way down here. We'll clean up the smoke. Maybe even see if we can heat these stones up for warmth."

"Did Aeyan'arric do this on purpose?" someone asked.*

"I don't think so," Janel answered. "All the accumulated snow and ice must have finally blocked up the chimneys. This doesn't change a thing, so everyone relax."

The crowd didn't disperse, but they settled down. People pushed chairs and tables to the side. Since most felt it too early for bed, this seemed like less a sleeping arrangement than a lounging arrangement. Everyone sported glyphs on their foreheads, some drawn in ash or chalk, but most formed from elegant glowing yellow lines. Clearly magical in a land that notoriously hated magic.

Kihrin hoped they had enough warning to remove the marks before the last person Janel expected arrived.

If not . . . they wouldn't be fooling anyone at all.

* No, no. Aeyan'arric accidentally stumbled out of Yor, tripped over the tavern, and then breathed all over it. Purely coincidental.

16: BLACK LOTUS

Jorat Dominion, Quuros Empire.
Three days since a woman finally *became emperor*

When everyone had finished cleaning or dealing with various minor emergencies, Kihrin settled down on a seat at the bar next to Star. "Hey there. My name is Kihrin. What's your name? And would you mind introducing me to the lovely woman who's been monopolizing your attention all evening?"

Star stared at him for a second before making a face. "Keep calling me Star. I don't mind."

"I'm Dorna," the old woman said. She looked Kihrin up and down. "Huh."

Kihrin had no idea what that meant.

Janel sat down next to Kihrin, so close their thighs touched. He was ridiculously aware of their thighs touching. Every nerve of that leg felt alive. Every time he came anywhere near Janel, the air between them felt charged.

A second later, Ninavis walked behind the bar, grabbed a bottle of aris, and began pouring a glass for everyone.

"Water for me. We've all been drinking fit for a wedding or a wake tonight." Dorna pointed to the group. "You all should start drinking water too, you hear me?"

"Yes, Mother," Star said.

"So this absent friend of yours—" Kihrin said.

Janel kneaded her knuckles into her temples. "We're waiting on a wizard who knows how to open gates. I don't expect him to use the front door."

"And he was supposed to be here by now?"

"Yes, but—" Janel paused as Brother Qown arrived, taking a seat next to Dorna.

Brother Qown pushed away the aris. "Do you have tea?"

"I've a pot of coffee in the back."

"Even better," Brother Qown said.

"Qown, any word from Thurvishar?" Janel asked.

"Thurvishar?" Kihrin blinked in surprise. "You're expecting Thurvishar D'Lorus?"* He had mixed feelings about the Lord Heir of House D'Lorus. Thurvishar had worked for the evil necromancer Gadrith D'Lorus, but only because he'd been gaeshed as a child. With the gaesh removed, Thurvishar had proved himself more willing to help Kihrin than assist Gadrith's other associates—including Relos Var.† Plus, Thurvishar was indeed a damn powerful wizard. Powerful enough to be able to open a gate on his own, no Gatestone required.

"I told you we know all the same people, didn't I?"

"Who's Thurvishar D'Lorus?" Dorna asked. "Besides no-good royalty scum." She glanced over at Kihrin. "No offense."

Kihrin shrugged. "Oh no. I'm with you."

"I've been leaving messages," Qown said. "Nothing yet. Oh, thank you, Ninavis." He reached for the coffee.

"Wait, you can communicate with Thurvishar? How?" Kihrin looked past Star and Dorna to address him.

Brother Qown bit his lip. "It's—"

"Do *not* say it's complicated," Kihrin said.

Brother Qown swallowed. "My Cornerstone, Worldhearth, allows me to see through heat sources at a great distance. That's one way we know Morios hasn't started attacking Atrine yet— I've been checking through a lantern in the city. I can also, uh . . . I can also cast spells through to any location I see, which is how I leave messages."

---

* A little presumptuous of Kihrin to assume that the only Thurvishar in the world just happens to be the one he knows. The fact he happens to be right is just going to make him even more insufferable.

† Ha. You're an *associate*.

Kihrin whistled. Any Royal House in the Capital would give a dozen favorite sons and daughters to have that ability.* Hell, Teraeth would be a very happy little assassin to have that ability too. Kihrin almost felt jealous—the Stone of Shackles had been an artifact you hoped to never use. Brother Qown's Cornerstone seemed a lot more helpful on a day-to-day level.

"Have you checked on Atrine recently?" Janel asked.

The priest nodded. "Just before dinner. Still nothing."

"Let's hope it stays that way. The three of us were just—" Janel looked around the bar. "We were in the middle of something earlier. Dorna, Ninavis—" She looked at Star. "Uh—"

"Star," he replied.

"Right. I know I'm being rude, but could you let us have a bit of space—"

"Oh no you don't," Dorna said. "I haven't seen either you or Qown here since the Great Tournament, and you know how that went. It's been years. We've got some catching up to do. I'm staying right here." She crossed her arms over her chest for emphasis.

"Same," Ninavis said.

Kihrin chuckled. "I guess that makes it your turn to narrate, Janel."

Janel's Turn. The Afterlife.

There's a part of this story that none of you—not even Brother Qown—have heard before.

Let me tell what happened after we left Mereina and our shelter.

The storms passed. Mare Dorna, Brother Qown, and I were now joined by Sir Baramon (who had insisted a journey would be good for his constitution). We'd started out for the capital of Jorat, Atrine. I'd insisted. I knew the army marched to Mereina,

---

* Let's be realistic here: any Royal House in the capital would give a dozen daughters for a handful of rusty, used nails.

but I felt obligated to report on the disaster to Duke Xun. Ninavis and the townsfolk had agreed to go back and keep watch over Mereina—and see if the witch-smoke had dissipated.

Tempers were frayed by the time we made camp. We'd given most of the food to Ninavis and the townsfolk. The unseasonal ice and snow had played havoc with the native wildlife, for whom this should have been spring. Dorna foraged for herbs and plants, edible if flash-frozen. I found myself pining for someone with a bow and a keen hunting sense. Dorna's efforts hadn't provided us with more than a few handfuls of roots and berries.

Yet going to bed hungry never made it any harder for me to cross the Second Veil, when I closed my eyes.*

I opened them again to find myself on a small hillock overlooking a town. My heart wailed at its resemblance to Coldwater—more azhocks, perhaps, but still the same communal cooking areas, the same horse yards and cellar homes.

The same dead trapped inside.

Demons roared in the distance. I unsheathed my sword, knowing what the night's work would be.

Then Thaena's elephants filled the air with trumpet sounds once more.

I grinned and changed tactics. Instead of wading into battle, I herded the demons straight toward the Death Goddess's glowing war elephants. I stayed away from the arrow fire this time, cutting down any stragglers who assumed I posed less of a threat than the Hunt.

I looked for him. The whole time, I scanned the tree line, examining the elephants to catch a glimpse of the Manol vané man in green and gold. The one I'd warned about Relos Var.† The one who'd saved my life.

---

* No, seriously, I'm bringing this up again. Did we know she could do this? And by *we*, I mean *you*.

† I'm not loving the fact they have a means to communicate over vast differences. That's supposed to be our trick.

But he wasn't there.

Disappointed, I funneled my anger into its natural outlet: killing demons.

These demons—all young, foolish, green—didn't understand the Afterlife forest had become their charnel house. They had been promised power and their slaughtered victims' fear. No one had warned they could still be prey themselves.

As the last demon fell, I flicked violet gore off my sword and watched the elephants trumpet their victory. They hadn't acknowledged my presence. Considering the alternative—becoming their victim—that pleased me enough.

No sign of my nameless Manol vané, though.

"Who are you looking for?"

I spun around.

He stood behind me, leaning against a dead tree trunk. He wore the same outfit I'd seen on him last and had his arms crossed over his chest. This time, his daggers stayed at his belt.

He'd suffered a chest wound, as though he'd been stabbed, but he didn't seem to notice the injury.

"It's you . . . ?" I said intelligently as I walked toward him. I hadn't heard or felt his approach, and for a moment, I felt suspicion. Could this be Xaltorath? Was it possible she'd known about our previous meeting? Did she impersonate him even now?

No, I told myself. She didn't know. And if she did, she wouldn't have dared approach me so close to where Thaena herself might appear. This was real. Or at least, as real as the Afterlife could be. His green eyes held me, and he smelled of blood and musk and the deep, wide sea.

"Who else would I be?"

"Never mind," I said and I . . .

Well, no sense being coy about it. I kissed him.

It was stupid. I'm aware just how stupid. I hadn't asked his leave; I still held my sword. If he'd decided to take my movement as an impending attack, the fault would have been my own. Even if he hadn't, it's uncouth to make such an overture without certain discussions. I had let my desire override my sense.

I felt him flinch. He'd started to reach for his weapons, his instinct to assume a trap. I had no excuse at all. He stopped himself.

"You remember me?" He looked at me as if I were a miracle.

"Of course I remember you. You saved my life."

He stepped back, looking strangely disappointed.*

Then someone cleared their throat behind us.

He inhaled. I turned around and saw . . .

Thaena.

Thaena, Goddess of Death, stood right behind us.

Like her statues, she was dark-skinned, clad in white silk. Roses and skulls circled her hips, crowned her shimmering hair. Her identity was clear. It's not just how she looked: beauty personified in obsidian, bone, and crimson. Her aura, her dread demeanor, her aspect proclaiming she endured as the absolute and the inevitable. In her eyes, all found their final judgment, their sins and graces laid bare before her quicksilver gaze.

I went down to my knees and lowered my head, prostrating myself before her. Behind me, I heard the Manol vané man step away. His movements smacked of guilt—the manner of a man caught red-handed—and I found myself wondering if Thaena herself held this man's thudajé. I'd heard many a joke about Thaena's marriage bed as a euphemism for dying. It had never occurred to me there might be some reality behind the humor. Had I just been caught taking liberties with Thaena's lover?

Then I heard a scuff of shoe, a swish of fabric, the hiss of metal slicing through air.

What? *No!*

A lifetime spent surviving Xaltorath's unsubtle and abrupt "lessons" had made certain instincts irrevocable.

---

* He's disappointed that the woman he saved is so happy to see him she starts kissing him? I know I'm hardly an expert on romance, but I don't think it's supposed to work like that.

I rolled to the side as Thaena's sword slammed down into the ground where I had been.

"Mother, no!" the Manol vané screamed.

"Not a lover, then," I said as I rolled to the side.

Son wasn't necessarily an improvement.

She carried a blade in each hand and moved them with blurring speed. She approached steadily, relentlessly—a tiger walking, slow and sure, toward a prey too wounded to escape. And though she never ran, she closed on me in an instant, arriving in eye blinks without ever seeming to rush or hurry.

"Please! Stop!" I shouted as I tried to dodge away. I felt the blow as her sword connected with my shield, vibrating up the metal. "I'm not your enemy!"

My arm felt numb from the strike.

"No?" Thaena stepped toward me. "Then why did Xaltorath spare you? Why did she choose *you* to survive the Lonezh Canton's Hellmarch?* What reason other than you have pledged yourself to her?"

My protest froze in my throat. Tears sprang to my eyes. "I don't know why she spared me."

"Yes, you do."

She kept swinging.

I saw her son scramble away, and I ducked under her swings. Then she opened a thin, shallow gash along my thigh, cutting straight through the armor.

My strength did me no favors here. My ability to strike an enemy's weapon away, or even break it, meant nothing against a god. The utter futility manifested in every swing, every dodge, every near miss or not-so-near miss. Cuts crisscrossed my armor, razor marks made by an enemy with no need to hurry an inevitable outcome.

I never landed a single blow on her.

I never came close.

---

* I wonder if Thaena actually used female pronouns for Xaltorath here or if this was just a modification Janel made when she told the story?

I tossed my sword and shield aside and went back down to my knees.

I felt cold metal across my neck as the two blades came to a stop against my skin.

"I don't know why," I repeated. "She asked me if I wanted her protection. She didn't look like a demon. She looked like a beautiful woman. So I said yes. But I never submitted to her. She once—" I didn't quite dare swallow, aware of Thaena's stare the whole time, a single motion capable of ending my existence. "She once claimed my mother—my real mother—made a deal with her to protect me. I didn't believe her then, and I don't believe her now; Xaltorath loves to lie."

"Yes. Yes, she does. Look at me." The blades nudged my chin upward.

I felt her voice in my bones as much as heard it. I dared not deny the order.

I looked up. Our eyes met.

Looking into Thaena's eyes meant staring into the mirror of every past sin I'd ever committed, every wrong, every hurt. Those eyes saw all. Every shameful deed or deed of which I *should* have been ashamed. Those eyes said, *I have seen all you've done. You can hide your sins from all others, even from yourself, but not from me. Never from me.*

I found a kind of comfort to it.

I know that sounds odd, but there can be comfort in ripping the scab off a wound. Pain, yes, but relief. Finally, this is out in the open. Finally, I have confessed my sins. Finally, *someone knows.*

I didn't see her drop the swords or put them away, but they vanished. She took my face in her hands as she continued looking into my eyes, examining my features.

"Who is your lord?" she asked me. "Who owns your thudajé?"

"The Markreev of Stav—" I began to answer.

"No," she corrected.

I shuddered as I realized the truth in that single, simple word. Supposedly, I owed my thudajé to the Markreev of Stavira,

Aroth Malkoessian. Supposedly, I knew my place, gave him my loyalty. Yet in truth, I'd had none for him since the day he'd decided to place his son's ambitions over my house's honor. So who was left? Xun, Duke of Jorat? Possibly Duke Xun. But I hadn't seen the man in years; it's difficult to be loyal to someone who is only a name.

Then I realized the obvious answer.

"You," I said. "The Eight. You have always had my thudajé."

Her gaze continued to trap mine, judging and righteous, but her hands shifted their position until they cradled my cheeks. She bent over and kissed me on the forehead before letting me go. "I was wrong about you."

"Wrong?" Was that good or bad? Did she mean she shouldn't have spared my life?

She turned away, releasing me from her gaze. I felt like I had been held up on strings, freed to slump against the ground and regain my breath. I sought out the vané man for some explanation, but he stared at me as if he'd never seen me before.

"I have a bad habit of writing off people as lost causes too soon," Thaena explained. "I assumed that once Xaltorath had her claws in you, you would be lost to us."

"I don't understand."

"Mother didn't believe me," the Manol vané interjected at last, "when I told her you aren't a demon yet."

Thaena spread her hands. "In my defense, it is unprecedented. Demons devour or demons infect. Demons do not show *mercy*."

I raised my head. "I wouldn't call it mercy."

That stare again from those mirror eyes. "No, I can see why you wouldn't." She held out her hands, benediction or apology. "I was wrong about you," she said again, "and therefore, you haven't received aid that might have served you. So now I owe you a boon. What do you want? Ask me a favor, and if it is in my power to grant, I will do so."

My heart beat so fast I could hear nothing else but its rushing in my ears. A boon from the Goddess of Death. I could've asked for enough metal to restore my family seat, to buy back the liens owed to the Markreev of Stavira, to regain my vassals' loyalty in Tolamer. I could've asked for the death of Oreth, the man who had forced me from my own home, or for Thaena to Return my grandfather. I could've asked to see my parents again . . .

I shut my eyes in pain. No. I couldn't. "If it is in my power to grant" didn't include Returning my parents or even seeing them. My parents' souls lay beyond the reach of gods.

It's not easy, in our dual and intertwined worlds, for someone to truly die, but it can be done. Demons most easily bring this true death to others.*

But in any case, I could only make one request and still live with myself after.

"Then I ask this: put a stop to Relos Var."

Thaena blinked at me. Then she chuckled and turned to her son. "What have you been telling her?"

"It's not me," he protested. "She found out about the wizard all on her own."

"Please," I said, standing to my feet. "I know Relos Var is plotting ill in Jorat. He has a witch and a dragon giving him aid, and I don't know his goals, but they cannot be good."

"Oh, you don't need to convince me," Thaena said. "I know better than anyone just what he's capable of doing. Unfortunately, you have named a boon not in my power to grant."†

I felt faint.

I had assumed Relos Var to be strong. Strong enough, anyway. But strong enough to dwell beyond the gods' judgment? I stared in shock.

---

* And Gadrith could do this too. I think I shall refer to him as Nomed from now on, since he was basically a backward demon.

† I considered omitting this passage for fear of what it would do to your ego. In the end, I left it in, both for completeness and also because it's nice to occasionally hear what the enemy says about you behind your back. You deserve a treat now and again.

"Indeed, stopping Relos Var is a topic that much preoccupies myself and my brethren in the Eight," Thaena admitted. "So instead of helping you, it will be the reverse."

I frowned. "I don't understand." She did something with her hands. Nothing flowery, but one second her hands were empty, and the next she held a spear. A golden spear, beautiful and shining. She offered it to me.

Mind you, spears aren't my preferred weapon.

I couldn't remember any occasion where I'd ever used one. I'd practiced with swords or maces for the greater part, which isn't the same thing at all.

However, when a god hands you a weapon, you take it. You don't ask for a different style.

The metal felt warm in my hands. The long, barbed spear was decorated along the shaft with sun symbols. It was light and well balanced. Without being told, I knew every inch was magical.

"Her name is Khoreval," Thaena explained. "An old friend owned her. If I'm correct, then she's one of the few weapons in the whole world that may be able to slay a dragon. I regret I cannot give you the weapon itself."

I looked up at the goddess, meeting her smile with my own. "Is that so?" Then her words sank in. "What do you mean, you cannot give me the weapon? It's right here."

"No child, this is but a seeming. The real Khoreval is kept hidden behind many locks in the palace of Azhen Kaen, Duke of Yor, who is Relos Var's champion."

"That does complicate matters."*

"So it seems I'm giving you a quest rather than granting you a boon. Recover this spear in the Living World. If the spear is capable of slaying dragons, then you have an opportunity to remove one of Relos Var's greatest weapons—Aeyan'arric."

---

* She didn't even blink when told Kaen works for you and not the other way around. She's either much smarter or much stupider than we've been giving her credit for, and other instances prove she's not stupid. Be careful.

"Mother, that's reckless. Even the Brotherhood have never been able to infiltrate the Ice Demesne—"

She raised a hand. He fell silent.

I smiled at him, flattered at his concern for my safety. "Your son isn't wrong, you know. I haven't the slightest idea how I would infiltrate such a camp. I'm not a thief or a spy."

Thaena tilted her head in my direction. "When you reach Atrine, look for a man named Mithros. He runs a mercenary company of free riders. He'll be only too glad to counsel you in how to best tackle this problem."

"Mother, you can't ask her to do this."

Thaena gave him a look to make a thousand elephants stampede.

"It's too dangerous," he insisted. "Relos Var will destroy her, assuming Duke Kaen doesn't do it first. There's no way Relos Var won't know who she is. There's no disguising her. No pretending she's someone else."

"Yes," Thaena agreed, her voice soft and dangerous. "I'm counting on that. I'm counting on that very thing. I know he won't hurt her. He loves to turn our families against us. She'll be irresistible to him."*

"It's not your decision," I scolded the vané, who seemed rather surprised at my interruption. "It's mine."

"You don't know the risks—"

"What risks would matter? That he controls people and forces capable of killing thousands? I already know. That he has magic and power beyond my ability to fathom? I knew that when Thaena herself told me she can't defeat him. I know it's dangerous. Does that matter when so many lives are at stake?"

He scowled. "Why must you be so stubborn?"

"Why must you think I can't decide my own path?"

He drew himself up. "I didn't say that."

"Just who do you think I am?" I gestured to the Death

* Oh, good tip. Thanks, Thaena.

Goddess, his mother. "*She* has my thudajé, but don't think I have handed you my reins. I have *not*."

"Teraeth, she has made up her mind."

I paused. "His name is Teraeth?"

"Yes."

I chewed on my lower lip while regarding Teraeth. He seemed young enough. Not much older than myself.

I turned back to Thaena. "Is he claimed yet? He's lovely."

She blinked again, looking once more surprised, while Teraeth stared at me in mute shock. Then Thaena smiled. "Why . . . what are you offering for him?"

"Well, you do still owe me a boon."

"A very good point."

"Mother!" Teraeth's scandalized tone banished any possible doubts I might have had about their relationship. He was mortified. His mother was embarrassing him.

Perfect. Adorable.

Oh, I wanted him.

I spun the illusionary Khoreval in my hands. "I think I will be fetching a great many souls for you before I'm done, great lord, and I shall begin tonight." I had no idea what courtship rites existed for gods, or the offspring of gods, but by my people's customs, I had stated my intentions. I didn't worry about his father—Thaena's idorrá rose greater than anyone she might have taken to her bed. My bargaining for her son would be with her.

"Mother, you cannot mean to *sell* me." His tone teased, but something sharper than laughter laced the edges. Something darker. Doubt. A question lurked in that statement, an ugly question.

"Am I not Justice?" Thaena answered. "Would you not deserve it if I did?"

And suddenly she didn't laugh or smile. This had become serious, and I didn't understand why.

Teraeth glanced at me, and those beautiful green eyes filled to overflowing with regret and guilt.

"What's going on here? What do I need to understand to make this clear to me?"

Thaena and Teraeth stared at each other for another heartbeat before he shuddered and looked away. Then Thaena turned to me. "We don't always escape the sins of past lifetimes. But if you like my son and you win his heart, then he's yours and you'll find no protest from me. In the meantime, good hunting, my child."

"Teraeth?"

He looked up from where he'd been staring at the ground. "Yes?"

I tipped my head to him. "We'll see each other again."

Teraeth's smile turned wry. "Don't I have a say in that?"

"Always. Until then—" I saluted Thaena and strode into the woods, searching for demons.

17: TIGA PASS

Jorat Dominion, Quuros Empire.
Three days since two women became the
de facto heads of House D'Mon

"Please tell me you're not married to Teraeth," Kihrin said.

"Technically—" Brother Qown started to say as Ninavis handed him a cup of coffee.

"I'm not married to Teraeth," Janel said. She reached over to flick thumb and forefinger against the priest's shoulder. "Don't give him a heart attack."

Qown sipped his cup, smiling.

"Who's this stallion you're talking about?" Dorna demanded. "Teraeth? How come I ain't met this man?"

Dorna hadn't demanded any such introduction to Kihrin. But he suspected everyone in the tavern knew his identity.

"Dorna, I've never met him in the Living World," Janel said, "but if I ever do, I promise I'll bring him around to meet you." She paused. "Assuming he ever figures out he's not in charge."

"Oh, you have got to stop falling for stallions who think you have to be the mare," Ninavis said, shaking her head. "Anyway, you don't even know if he's alive."

"Oh, Teraeth's alive," Kihrin said, feeling much better about the entire conversation. Teraeth hadn't won Janel over? Perfect.* "I spent a few years training with him. He is, however, an assassin and would-be revolutionary."

---

* Yes, I think so too. I wonder if Teraeth's the jealous type. I'll just write a note to myself for later, in case that proves useful . . .

Ninavis grinned. "Oh, now you're talking. Sounds like my kind of man."

Dorna held up a finger. "But is he reins or saddle? That's the question."

Kihrin frowned. "What does—gods, you're not talking about horses again, are you? Stop that."

Everyone, save perhaps Brother Qown, had a good laugh.

"Now keep going," Dorna said, waving. "I want to hear what happened to my foal."

"Oh, we've been switching back and forth, Mare Dorna," Brother Qown explained, "so our voices don't wear out." He pulled out his journal and started to read.

Qown's Turn. Just outside the Tiga Pass, Jorat, Quur.

They traveled from Mereina to Atrine in the most miserable fashion. The weather continued to be execrable since leaving the estava. Brother Qown resorted to using magic to keep them from losing fingers and toes to the cold, and not even Sir Baramon protested. They were only able to forage after several days, when the weather finally turned in their favor. Later, they stopped at a small village to buy supplies.

Brother Qown chose not to point out the count never seemed to need healing. Her skin stayed warm no matter how cold the ice or snow, as if she kept a real fire behind her red eyes.

By the second week, they had moved to areas of Jorat beyond the reach of Aeyan'arric's cold snap. The land bloomed with flowers. Smiling was easier. The count woke one morning as if she'd never known pain nor suffering, a broad smile on her face, which made even Dorna stop and stare.

"Were you any other, foal, I'd say you must have had sweet dreams."

"Sweet enough," the count agreed. She looked to her side, blinked, and then shook her head. "I keep expecting to see Arasgon."

"He'll find us soon enough," Sir Baramon said. The man

stretched, groaning. "Every part of me is sore. Even my toenails ache."

"Oh, do I need to take a look—" Brother Qown started to offer.

"I'm fine," Sir Baramon snapped.

The count stopped smiling.

"Qown's Blood of Joras, you know,"* Dorna said. "Don't treat the boy like he's a local mare. Let him help you."

"Blood of what?" Brother Qown said. "Wait, what am I?"

But Dorna had stopped paying attention to him. Her stare focused on Janel. "Foal? What's wrong?"

"The Tiga Pass." Janel pointed. "Look at it."

Brother Qown turned toward the north. They had almost reached the switchbacked trails and bridges leading from the Grazings of southern Jorat, to the Great Steppes, where both Tolamer and Jorat's capital, Atrine, were located. They'd come this way to reach Barsine the first time. While Qown preferred the trails to climbing the sharp steppe cliffs, it was still a narrow, unpleasant, vertigo-inducing experience.

But what made his gut clench was the pass's color.

White as snow.

No one spoke, but they rushed to break camp. The count's urgency infected everyone. Brother Qown found himself missing Cloud, the gelding Janel had given him when she'd first learned Qown didn't own a horse. He'd never considered himself a horseman (and Dorna would be quick to point out this was still true), but Cloud had made himself easy to love.

"We could always take the Great Lift," Dorna pointed out.

"That's another hundred miles," Janel snapped.

"Look at the snow. It don't ever snow in Tiga Pass. If that dragon's up there, we should be someplace else."

---

* A quaint Joratese cultural artifact. If you're perceived to have descended from Joras (as anyone from west of the Dragonspires would be), your magic is somehow acceptable. It allows them to ignore the dichotomy of hating magic, while still enjoying all the benefits of House D'Aramarin's Gatekeepers. The hypocrisy is so blatant I'm almost not angry.

"I have to be sure," the count said, and kept walking.

Dorna cursed under her breath and exchanged a parental look with Sir Baramon, but he shrugged as if to say, *What can we do?* and followed Janel.

They all did.

As soon as they crested the pass, Brother Qown knew the count's worst suspicions had borne bitter fruit. The Tiga Pass was the busiest and best way to travel from the plateau to the lower grazing fields. As such, the pass saw all the traffic too poor or stubborn to use the Quuros gate system. When they had come this way themselves they had stayed just outside town, too poor to afford to pay for hospitality and too proud to beg.

The experience had, in fact, been what inspired Janel to start hunting bounties in the first place.

Now the pass and the town lay under a glacial layer, frozen solid.

The count didn't wait for them to catch up. She walked, then ran.

"Don't you go leave us—" Dorna choked off her scold as something moved near the town's far side.

Aeyan'arric, the Lady of Storms, raised her head from where she'd been napping.

The count skidded to a stop. They all did, barely believing they'd been so caught out in the open. They couldn't hide without shelter or nearby buildings, even trees. They were exposed.

And the dragon saw them.

Brother Qown knew they were about to die.

Aeyan'arric could've killed them in an instant. Qown didn't possess nearly enough skill in battle magic to fend off a dragon. They carried no weapons that might affect such a creature. Aeyan'arric was larger than the town.

Count Janel stood still. The dragon and the girl stared at each other.

Then Aeyan'arric launched herself into the air and flew away, sweeping north.

Silence lingered over the frozen town.

Brother Qown couldn't be certain what had saved them, but he had his suspicions. He didn't think it was mercy. Rather, Brother Qown suspected Aeyan'arric hadn't killed them for the same reason he wouldn't kill a beetle if he saw one in the woods—what care did he have for the fate of beetles?

As Aeyan'arric took to the air, Janel ran toward the town for all the good it would serve. Every resident was dead.

Brother Qown couldn't help but wonder just how closely the tragedy here had followed the pattern of Mereina. Had a white-skinned Doltari witch released a cloud of magic blue smoke here too? Or was this the dragon's random attack?

It had been a very long time since Quur had seen a rampaging dragon.

When they caught up with the count, she'd fallen to her knees in the middle of town. Her eyes were bright and wet.

The temperature near her felt warmer than it should, given the surrounding ice. And that temperature grew less tolerable by the second. The ice under Janel's knees began to melt, uncovering spring grass.

Sir Baramon drew his sword, looking around as if expecting some new attack.

"Foal, you mustn't," Dorna whispered. "Stop this."

A choking sob came from the Count of Tolamer.

Dorna put a hand on Janel's shoulder. "Please child. Stop."

The thawed grass near Janel's feet burst into flame. Dorna removed her hand and backed away.

"We should find shelter," Brother Qown offered, not certain what else he could say. The sky grew darker with every passing minute. The storms Aeyan'arric's passing summoned were on their way.

"There's no time," Sir Baramon said.

"Count, I know—" Brother Qown cleared his throat, feeling the panic rise. He was speaking just to speak, with no goal. He had no idea how to persuade Janel to stop using a spell-gift—one she may not have consciously been aware she possessed. Did she even realize she was thawing the ice? That she was setting nearby objects on fire?

"If we heat an empty azhock," Qown continued, "then we might be safe enough here, at least until the storm clears." He didn't mention food. They didn't have enough.

No one said a word, not even Sir Baramon. They all held their breath. The count's affinity with flame proved to be one of those terrible truths everyone accepted, as long as no one ever acknowledged it aloud.

Brother Qown wondered if he could take credit for the fire, claim the spell work as his own. Dorna's reminder that Qown was a "Blood of Joras" (whatever that meant) seemed to have given the priest immunity from the crime of practicing magic. As such, Sir Baramon would have an easier time accepting Qown as the flames' source, rather than his count.

Janel wiped her eyes with her hands. "I can't control it," she whispered.*

"You can learn," Brother Qown suggested. "You're not a witch."

She flinched. "You mean the way Tamin isn't a witch?"

"What does it mean, to be Blood of Joras?" he asked. He'd been willing to let the question slide before. Not now.

She sighed.

Dorna answered in her stead. "When Emperor Kandor freed us from the horse god, Khorsal, he asked for all our mage folk in return—because our mages were the strongest in the whole world. Mostly that meant the great wizard Joras, who had led the rebellion against Khorsal. Important man, that Joras—Kandor named our dominion after him, you know. Anyway—Joras gathered up his family and all his blood kin. He took his whole clan, and they all went back west to teach and intermarry among all you Quuros—"

---

* Since she didn't burn all her friends to a crisp, I suspect this isn't true.

"Jorat is part of the Quuros Empire. We're all Quuros."

"No," Dorna corrected. "You're Quuros. We're Joratese. Anyhow, his kin went back there so you folks would have powerful mages too. And that's why you all know magic so good. *Blood of Joras* means Joras's blood runs in your veins, giving you his powers. Anyone else who can do magic must have made deals with demons or been tainted by Marakori blood. And *they* sure make deals with demons, don't they?"

Brother Qown blinked. "Are you . . . are you saying using magic is okay if you're descended from a particular lineage?" He looked to the other two, but neither one seemed to think anything Dorna said was shocking or a surprise.

She humphed. "I didn't say I believed it. I think it's the stupidest thing I've ever heard, but you asked."

Brother Qown turned back to Janel. "Your eyes are red. Anywhere else in the empire and they would just assume you're an Ogenra bastard, of House D'Talus. Their wizards specialize in *fire*. So maybe you're Blood of Joras too and not a witch by anyone's standards." He left out the part where the rest of Quur would still consider her a witch because she was unlicensed—as all women were unlicensed. He'd leave that talk for another day.

"Are you implying she's of tainted blood?" Sir Baramon had been pulled back into the conversation.

Dorna punched him hard in the shoulder. "Shut it, you. Janel's mother was a commoner. Maybe Frena was one of them 'oginrays.' You don't know."

"Ogenra," Brother Qown corrected.

"Oh, go soak it," Dorna snapped. "I don't give a ripe plum how you say the damn word."

Janel rose to her feet. "All of you. Stay back."

Dorna took Sir Baramon's arm and began pulling him away from the town—as if Baramon was a child who didn't understand not to stray under a merchant cart's wheels. He looked anguished.

Brother Qown heard water trickling from the ice near Janel as it thawed in a growing circle and rapidly uncovered bodies.

Bodies that animated.

"Oh, Selanol," Brother Qown prayed. "Count, look!"

Dorna drew back in frightened shock.

"Behind me," Sir Baramon called out, drawing his sword.

Brother Qown forced himself to remember that Baramon's sword skills were impressive, whatever his weight.

The count stood her ground. She unsheathed her sword and waited for the demon-possessed dead to find her.

Brother Qown tried to think of anything he could do to help. A blessing might make the demons pause, but not much more. These demons were not physically present. Instead, they were exploiting the halfway state of corpses, worming their way into a puppetlike presence in the land of the living. These demons must have possessed the dead, only to find themselves trapped in the ice.

Qown frowned. The dragon had *thwarted* the demons' ability to start a Hellmarch.*

Janel swung her sword. A village woman's head rolled away from its shoulders. A dead man swung at her, and Count Janel ducked to the side and punched it hard enough to dislocate its jaw and stagger it. She then made a mighty overhand cut with her sword, cleaving the corpse from shoulder to groin.

These dead were too frozen to bleed.

"Don't thaw any more out!" Dorna cried out.

If the count heard her, she didn't acknowledge it. She stepped forward and swung at another demon.

Then a little girl stepped forward.

The count hesitated.

A flash of motion to Brother Qown's side caught his attention. He turned to look and realized a chestnut-haired corpse in tattered homespun hadn't gone to attack Count Janel but had instead moved to flank them.

He yelped and jumped backward, tangled his foot on his agolé's train, and tripped.

* Yes, I *know*. That was the whole damn point.

Sir Baramon came to Qown's defense immediately. The knight struck out with his sword, but he didn't have the count's demonic strength. He opened a long, shallow cut in the demon's frozen flesh. The demon ignored the blow and swung at Brother Qown.

Brother Qown screamed.

The demon lashed out with curled fingers, and Sir Baramon pulled Brother Qown to the side. The knight struck again, this time hewing off an arm.

The corpse kept fighting, anyway. Of course.

Then its head rolled away from its shoulders. Count Janel stood behind the falling body, eyes looking like twin suns.

"That was the last," she said. "Are you two all right?"

"Damn thing nicked my arm," Sir Baramon said. "No worse than I've taken in a bout. I'm fine."

"Let me look," Brother Qown said.

"That can wait." Sir Baramon told Brother Qown. "We have to make sure there's no more."

"Oh, I reckon there's one for every frozen person," Dorna said, brushing her hands against each other. "But they're all trapped under ice, so as long as we don't go and melt that, we're safe as foals." She stopped and gave Janel a hard look. "Now tell me. Tell me you ain't gonna insist we unfreeze them."

Janel's expression was ugly. Behind her on the ground lay a rumple of homespun covering multiple corpses. Janel pointed to an azhock that stood far enough from the main town that it hadn't been frozen and from which no dead had emerged. "Shelter there. Don't come out until I return."

"And then what?" Dorna didn't tell her not to do it. She knew how well Janel would have listened.

"And then we keep going to Atrine. We'll melt the snow the whole way there if we have to."

Janel waited until the rest of them had taken shelter.

Then she began her deadly work.

18: Demon Falls

Jorat Dominion, Quuros Empire.
Three days since Jarith Milligreest was
killed by Xaltorath

Brother Qown shut his book and gestured to Janel. "Your turn."

The trip to our dominion's capital was a dark one for many reasons, not least because of what we'd seen in Tiga Pass.

Ninavis leaned forward. "Wait, what happened next?"

Janel stared at her hands. "Nothing surprising. I thawed the village, dealt with the possessed, then we sheltered in that same azhock while I handled the demons in the Afterlife." Heartbreak lurked in the matter-of-fact tone she used to describe the day's events.

"I'm sorry," Kihrin said. He'd had his own problems at the same age, of course—that business about being gaeshed and sold as a slave came to mind. Yet he couldn't help but notice Janel had a familiarity with the battlefield many soldiers in the Quuros army couldn't hope to match. Jarith Milligreest had once offered him a military commission, just because he'd been willing to fight one demon. What would he say to a woman who'd fought hundreds?

What would Jarith *have* said, Kihrin corrected. Past tense.

"You're sorry? You had nothing to do with it," Janel replied.

He hoped that was true.

Janel's Turn. The road to Atrine, Barsine Banner, Jorat, Quur.

Why slaughter a whole town and then freeze it? Demons could've hunted those slain souls in the Afterlife. But demons never passed up an opportunity to travel to the Living World, even if only by proxy. Except those demons had then been trapped by the ice. What did that accomplish?

That upsetting question lurked over a deeper chaos within me.

The flames I'd summoned.

I kept hearing Tamin's words. We were both *witches.*

Preoccupied with my thoughts, I almost didn't notice when we arrived at the falls.

"What's that noise?" asked Brother Qown as we rode our horses down the main road.

Oh yes. We'd found horses again.

When Tiga Township had been attacked, the town's work-horses had run. Not all of them. I'd been forced to put down demon-possessed horses as well as people, but we Joratese have never locked away our horses unless we're sheltering from storms. Once the town lost its icy layer, we'd picked up tack and harness before coaxing some of those horses to return.

Sir Baramon looked surprised at Brother Qown's question and clapped the Vishai priest on the shoulder. "Haven't you ever seen Demon Falls before?"

"Demon—" The priest blinked. "I thought we were still a day away."

"A few hours at most," I corrected.

"But should we be able to hear it even now?" He seemed flummoxed by the implications.

I clicked my tongue and coaxed my horse forward. I'd decided to call her Ash Flower. While she was never meant to be more than a farm horse, I found her sweet, if a bit anxious. She deserved someone who would feed her carrots, call her beautiful, and take her out for gentle rides. Not me, but I promised myself I'd find her a worthy companion in Atrine.*

We crested the rise. I halted Ash Flower while I waited for Brother Qown to catch up.

He did, questions still sharp on his face. I pointed.

He followed my arm with his eyes, and then his jaw dropped.

"Demon Falls," I said.

I'd been to Atrine many times, but since I'd always arrived by Gatestone, I'd never seen it from this vantage. I'd never seen the Great Steppe curve into the distance as Lake Jorat spilled over its side to form a giant waterfall, miles across.

Atrine, the flower of Jorat, sat on that waterfall's summit, in the center of the dam holding back Lake Jorat's waters. The city soared upward, a mountain of white quartz and blue granite, its palace and temples a series of high spires scratching a storm cloud sky. The city spread out in an enormous circle, protected by thick white stone walls looking delicate and dainty as porcelain from this distance.

Two bridges connected Atrine to the outside world, graceful lanes of stone lacework stretching from city to shore. In reality, the bridges spanned hundreds of feet wide and miles long, large enough to ride an army of horses across. From this distance, the scale distorted. Everything looked tiny and fragile: eggshell thin.

I frowned as I studied the scene. Something about the bridge looked wrong.

"What's that smudge on the bridge?"

Sir Baramon blinked. "Smudge, Count?"

Dorna scrunched up her nose. "Ah, my sight ain't what it used to be." She shielded her eyes with a hand and squinted hard. "Are those . . ." She paused. "Are those buildings out on the causeway?"

"Who would build on the bridge?" I asked. "That's bizarre."

---

* I wonder what happened to Ash Flower? Did she make it out of the city, maybe in the company of some nice farmer or little girl?

Shut up.

To my surprise, Brother Qown responded with indignation. "Cities are like rivers, Count. They overflow their banks, spread outside their borders. It happens everywhere."

"Other cities," I said with a dismissive snort. "The Capital, I've heard, overflows on a regular basis with human detritus, but there's nowhere for anyone to go beyond the walls of Atrine. The city is an island."

"That's true, foal," said Dorna, "but you're forgetting how wide those bridges are. And anyway, the city's empty most of the year. Plenty of room."

Brother Qown said, "I don't understand. Why would a city this size be empty?"

"Because it's a trap," I said.

At Qown's astonished look, I shrugged and gave him what I hoped would pass for a sincere smile. "It's not a trap now, mind you, but Atrine wasn't built to be a city. It was built to be . . . a taunt. You see, Emperor Kandor had infantry and he fought the god-king of *horses*. Khorsal's vast cavalry included thousands of centaurs, not even counting firebloods and all the other horse beasts in his service. Quur couldn't win the war by engaging Khorsal on his own terms, so Kandor dammed all the plateau rivers, flooded the Endless Canyon, and built this city as a lure. Emperor Kandor designed Atrine to be a place Khorsal's ego would *demand* he attack. He built Atrine to kill a god—occupying it afterward was incidental." I pressed my lips into a thin, disapproving line. "There shouldn't be so many people here their numbers would overflow onto the bridge."

Sir Baramon gave a half-hearted, apologetic shrug. "Have you visited lately, Count?"

My jaw tightened. "We came here right before . . ." I paused. Before Lonezh Canton. Before Xaltorath. "It's been a few years," I admitted.

"Well, Count." He scratched at the growing beard on his chin. "Things do change."

I sighed. "Some things." I edged Ash Flower back toward

the main road. "Come on, then. The sooner we reach the city, the sooner I can warn Duke Xun about the danger to Jorat. This threatens his entire dominion. He'll have to do something."

"I ain't in no hurry," Dorna said. "You know Oreth's waiting for you."

"It changes nothing," I said. "I have a duty, Dorna. The duke must be warned."

"Fine," she said in a sullen voice that made it clear she thought little about the situation fine at all.

We continued riding.

Atrine's scale became apparent as one crossed the Merat Bridge connecting land to island. The city looked small in comparison to Lake Jorat, a vast inland sea terminating in an endless line of demon-mouthed spillways, spraying plumes of water. Scale made Atrine seem like a quaint pastoral castle, a god-king tale come to life. Then you saw people and realized the city's true size.

It was as I'd remembered it from childhood.

Well, almost as I remembered it.

I didn't remember the ramshackle shantytown squatting on the bridge leading to the city proper. Someone had built the shacks from wood and cob mud pulled from the lakeshore. I saw a dozen different styles of architecture, from western Quuros plaster to some sort of coiled mud structure resembling a beehive. Not one resembled a Joratese azhock.

"Marakori," I said. I noted the sullen stares from the windows, the curtains pulled aside and then quickly shut. Glimpses of even skin, light brown to dark chestnut, dark hair, red or black. "What are *Marakori* doing here?"

A narrow, twisting passage ran through the shantytown, large enough to take the horses single file. We decided it safer to walk them than ride. With every step, I felt the squatters' reproachful stares.

"Refugees and runaways. Admittedly it has . . . uh . . . grown a bit worse in the last few years," Sir Baramon said.

"You mean it's been like this for years?" I blinked at him. "Who holds their thudajé?"

"No one," he said, surprised. "I mean, they *are* Marakori."

A shout ahead drew our attention. Soldiers dragged a woman out onto the bridge and cuffed her to the ground, while a second band ransacked the cob house where they'd found her. After a few seconds, they exited, shouting and dragging a Marakori man out with them. The woman screamed and reached for him, but the soldiers struck her down.

Brother Qown tensed next to me. "Aren't we going to do something?"

I hesitated. "It's not our business," I said. "Besides, those men wear the duke's colors."

My heart hammered in my chest. I *wanted* to do something. I should have taken the whole incident in stride, trusting the duke's men to enforce the laws, but Barsine's corruption still tasted sharp and bitter on my tongue. I could no longer—

Even as I debated my options, a guard pulled a dagger across the Marakori man's throat.

The woman's scream filled the air.

I grabbed Brother Qown by his robe before he could run over and try to save the Marakori man's life.

"No, I can help!"

"You're wrong."

The soldiers left. They tossed the man's body to the side, ignored the woman, and marched toward the gates. Whatever their objective, they had either accomplished it or didn't think it worth the effort.

I let Brother Qown go. He ran over to the woman, who sobbed over the slain man. He might have been anything to her: brother, father, friend, husband. She ignored Brother Qown until he tried to comfort her, and then she lashed out at him, screaming.

"Come on, then," Sir Baramon said as he pulled Brother Qown back. "I promise there's not a thing you can do here."

I felt Qown's stare. Although he didn't say the words, I knew what he was thinking.

You could have stopped this.

"Enough," I snapped at him. "This isn't our business. Anyone who lives here does so at the duke's sufferance. We don't know the circumstances."

"You said the Joratese didn't just kill criminals! What about saelen? Where was his trial by combat? His tournament? Who was going to win *his* thudajé?"

"Brother Qown—"

"How was this justice?" Tears spilled down his face, tears of furious anger.

"Ah, you sweet colt," Dorna said, patting the priest on the shoulder. "You know that only applies to Joratese."

I walked Ash Flower past the scene, refusing to look back behind to make sure the others would follow. I refused to look back and see the dead Marakori man.

I didn't know the circumstances. I didn't know the man's crimes. Perhaps he'd deserved it. Perhaps he hadn't. But I knew one thing for certain.

In Jorat, what you protect is what you rule.

Brother Qown didn't understand. He didn't understand how standing up for some random Marakori refugee might be perceived as an act of rebellion.

I pulled the hood up over my head as I approached the gate, which always struck me as an underwhelming, tiny little door— because Kandor had designed it to be difficult, bordering on impossible, for horses to use.

What had Emperor Kandor cared for horses? He hadn't come to save horses but to slaughter them.

If the front gate was small, the archery platforms were not.

"My count," Sir Baramon said, "let me do the talking."

I nodded, relieved, still not trusting my own voice. Brother Qown's words had hurt like razors against my soul.

I had hoped for a subtle, quiet entrance to the city, but it wasn't to be. All this business with refugees and improvised buildings parked on the bridge like a besieging army ensured the guards not only checked each entrant but wrote down particulars as well. Those reports would be compiled later. Entering the city unnoticed became complicated if I ended up in a file reported to my enemies.

Damn it all, but I do have such enemies.

"Name and reason for visiting?" the guard asked when we reached the front.

Sir Baramon laughed. "Reason for visiting? Tell me, my good man, does anyone answer with aught but *tournament* with the thing itself two weeks away? As well to say one is interested in moistening one's brow, while swimming in the Zaibur!"

The guard cleared his throat and gave Sir Baramon a calculating look. "Watching or participating?"

"Starring!" Sir Baramon barked out. He then leaned in toward the man and lowered his voice. "Not me, you understand. It's been a few years"—he patted his stomach for emphasis—"since I've been the star of a tournament. Still, surely you've heard of the great Sir Kavisarion of Dalrissia?" He lowered his voice again until he was whispering. "This year, I bring my newest protégé, Ember—it's her first show, but you'll be seeing her at the games, I promise you that—as well as our trainer, Bitsy, and her personal servant, Featherbottom."*

Brother Qown blinked in surprise. Dorna, on the other hand, grinned from ear to ear and puffed out her chest.

The guard looked us over, settling on my red cloak before returning his attention to Sir Baramon. He sighed and rolled his eyes. "Why didn't you say you were with the Red Spears?" He scribbled something on his paper. "Your people are in the usual place: the Green next to the Temple of Khored. Tell Captain Desrok I said hello."

"Desrok?" Baramon raised an eyebrow. "Don't you mean Captain Mithros?"

I fought to keep my expression bored and still. Mithros was the name Thaena had given me, the man who would help me find a way inside Duke Kaen's palace.

---

* Oh, I'm going to remember that one. Let me make a note.

The guard smiled. "Oh, right. My mistake. Enjoy the games." He motioned for us to bring our horses inside.

I realized just how odd we must have seemed. Tournament performers would come in through the Gatestone. We'd walked up on foot, with inferior horses too poor to ever be used in the ring.

So he'd tested us.

Fortunately, Sir Baramon passed.

I heard a yelp and looked back to see Sir Baramon hopping on one leg. "Damnable woman! What was that for?"

Dorna put her hands to her hips. "As if you don't know. Bitsy?"

"Well, it's not like you're growing larger in your old age, is it?"

Mare Dorna poked a finger at Sir Baramon's stomach. "Unlike some!"

"Count." Brother Qown said a single word, low and warning. He stared up.

I followed his stare with my own and saw he was looking at one of the city's many bridges, stretching from rooftop to rooftop. A crow's cage hung on the bridge closest to the entrance, meant to be viewed by all who passed by. A fire had twisted and blackened the metal. The same fire had surely killed the person inside, now nothing more than a charred skeleton.

A wooden sign hung from the cage, proclaiming the criminal's deeds.

Witch.

Behind me, the whole group fell silent. Dorna and Baramon ceased their bickering.

No runes marked the cage, unlike what I'd seen in Barsine. It seemed this was more of a routine burning. Given the Marakori slums close by and the Marakori reputation for demon worship and black magic, I felt I could reliably predict this witch's ethnicity.

The last Hellmarch had started in Marakor, after all. Started in Marakor but ended in Jorat.

We have never forgotten.

I felt a hand on my shoulder. Sir Baramon said, "We shouldn't linger here."

I nodded and led us to the duke's palace.

Atrine is the most beautiful of cities,* and after our entrance, I saw none of it.

Every corner held dangers. Every shadow hid a knife's edge. It took all my will to stay calm and steady, to smile and act like I had no enemies and no reason to hide.

I raised my borrowed cloak's hood, anyway.

The city itself was laid out in a circular maze pattern, but the narrow, twisting roads and alleys of the ground level had one purpose: killing horses.

The streets had been meant to trap Khorsal's invaders, funneling centaurs and horses both into canyons where boiling oil, heavy stones, or barbed arrows might be rained down on them from above.

The city's livable areas started on the second floor or higher, all accessed through narrow stairs—twisting and curving in ways impossible for horses to navigate. Brother Qown had asked why we spent so little time in a usable city, but that answer should have been obvious. How could any Joratese worth her mane stand to spend so long removed from our herds?

The city's center played host to several notable buildings: the duke's palace, a cathedral dedicated to the Eight, and a much larger cathedral dedicated to Khored, Emperor Kandor's patron deity. A grass ocean lapped in front of those buildings, the only land large enough to support horses, firebloods, and even elephants. Thus, it was the only spot where the Great Tournament of Challenges could be held.

The Green swarmed with activity as carpenters finished buildings and raised azhocks. Tournament participants set about

---

* Clearly, she's never been to Tara-Moatassa in east Doltar. (Neither have I, but I've heard stories.)

last-minute practice sessions, while they still had the opportunity. Despite the Green's size, most of it fell under someone's watchful eye. Dorna had every reason to be concerned.

But I thought this might work to our advantage. The crowded field was also a chaotic, distracting field.

So I'd believed.

We'd traveled all the way to the palace's shadow before Arasgon's scream set me straight.

"It's intolerable!" Arasgon shouted. When I realized who he shouted at, I put a warning hand before Dorna and Qown. Sir Baramon had already stopped in place, looking like he'd just come around the corner to see lions feasting.

"Janel Danorak isn't chattel to be sold at whim! Her lineage goes back five hundred years!" Arasgon's jaws snapped forward as he choked out the words; I felt his anger in every tensed muscle. He hadn't yet raised up on his hind legs, but the moment was coming.

"That's the Markreev Stavira," Sir Baramon said. "Aroth Malkoessian."

"Yes," I agreed, feeling the bowels in my gut twist.

Next to me, Dorna cursed under her breath.

Although an older man, the Markreev still looked in his prime. Like his sons Ilvar and Oreth, he was golden-maned and dark-skinned. I had never in my life seen the man smile. And I hadn't seen him in person since the day I'd marched into the Markreev's bedroom and presented him with his youngest son's crimes.

Of all my enemies, I considered him the worst; he was *my* Markreev. I owed him my thudajé.

But I didn't give it to him. Arasgon hadn't been wrong; the Markreev of Stavira had treated me like chattel. I would never forgive him.

"I never sold her," the Markreev said. He crossed his arms over his chest, his back straight. No angry fireblood would intimidate him, although his men looked more nervous about the situation. "And where is your master?"

"I haven't seen her in months," Arasgon said—possibly true if he hadn't noticed me yet. "I am—"

The Markreev said, "We have been through this twice already. I will speak to my son on the matter, but what is done is done. You try my patience. Begone before I decide you're out of line."

Arasgon snorted and tossed his head before he trotted away from the palace's front door.

Aroth Malkoessian, the Markreev Stavira, walked inside, and his men followed behind.

Or rather, most of his men. Not everyone fell in line behind the Markreev. I watched as a guard exchanged looks and a significant nod with a gardener who pretended to be busy pruning flowers. I recognized a fireblood lurking near the Green as Sominias, a beautiful mare who had long been friend and companion to the Markreev's wife, Shiniah.

So the Markreev watched the palace entrance. Easy enough to guess why.

In theory, I served the Markreev. If he ordered me to accompany him, then his son Oreth could organize my Censure at his leisure. It wouldn't matter Oreth had used bribery to buy the will of Tolamer's citizens. The protocols would have been observed. And once I'd been cast out? Those same bribes might well convince my people to make Oreth my replacement.

"Well, if that ain't a fine pack of troubles," Dorna muttered, next to me. "Do you think Arasgon saw us?"

"Yes," I said. "Now let's walk away."

"Where are we going?" Brother Qown asked.

I sighed. "Home."

19: Oreth the Snake

Jorat Dominion, Quuros Empire.
Three days since Thurvishar D'Lorus retreated to
Shadrag Gor to work on his notes

"So you were engaged to marry this Oreth person?" Kihrin asked.

"The Markreev's second son, yes," Janel answered. "But Oreth and I had very different ideas about my place in the relationship. I'm not a mare. I'm never going to be a mare."

"And mare doesn't mean . . . female?" Kihrin wanted to make sure he understood.

Nina laughed. "Not even a little. Mares stay at home and see to the house, yes, but they're also farmers, teachers, caretakers, organizers. And stallions are the preening, prancing warriors circling the herd in case lions show up. Ask most stallions and they'll tell you they're in charge too while the mare who's making sure everything gets done just laughs."

"It's not so simple," Janel chided. "And not everyone is so labeled."

"No," Dorna agreed, "but you ain't ever going to stay at home and raise the foals while your stallion mate goes off to war, and that's a fact." Dorna wagged a finger at Kihrin. "Something for you to remember."

"Oh, not a problem," Kihrin said, raising his hands. "As an old friend used to say, I only become romantically involved with those who can beat the pants off me in a fight."

Ninavis turned to Janel. "This one might be okay."

"Oh, thank you. Now that I have a stamp of approval from the *grandmothers*—"* Janel rolled her eyes at Dorna and Ninavis before she turned to Qown. "It's your turn."

Qown cleared his throat and began to read.

Qown's Turn. Atrine, Jorat, Quur.

Brother Qown felt lost by the time they reached the apartment granted to the Count of Tolamer and family. The city's twisting passages and switchbacks formed a maze that confused anyone not familiar with the turns.

Plus, no one used the roads.

People never traveled down to the ground level unless absolutely necessary. These occasions included entering the city through the main gates or crossing over to the Green—the giant parklike space in the city's center. Otherwise, everyone used the stairs, climbing the spiraling steps until they reached the bridges and thoroughfares on the third story (which would be the fourth story if anyone counted the ground level). These constituted Atrine's true roads.

Count Janel stopped before a wooden door, identical to all the other wooden doors they had passed. While Dorna paused to light an old brass lamp, Janel pulled an ancient-looking key from her sallí cloak and unlocked the door.

She waited.

No one cried out. No one came to the door. No movement echoed from inside.

Janel opened the door and ushered everyone inside. They passed a reception hall and sitting area, the kitchen on the right, before heading down a main staircase.

Brother Qown bumped his shin on a low side table as soon as he left the stairwell. He fought the temptation to curse. Mare Dorna raised the lantern, illuminating spacious rooms. Brother Qown felt a small thrill to think the Theranon family had used

* If I were Ninavis, I'd have given her my stamp of approval with my boot.

these quarters for almost half a millennium, in an unbroken line since Atrine's creation by Emperor Kandor himself.

Count Janel stood there and scanned the lower hall as if trying to determine if there had been intruders by studying patterns left in the dust. But finally, she shrugged and walked over to the built-in wardrobes along one wall of the main sitting room—delicate stone doors cut with patterned grilles. She opened each in turn, rummaged around, and then piled boxes before the cabinets.

"I'll look downstairs soon as I'm done here." Dorna started lighting the lanterns in the room.

Sir Baramon sat on a low stone bench. "This brings back memories."

"Well, keep 'em to yourself," Dorna snapped. "Now stop your sitting and help me out—"

Janel lifted a small metal box from a closet and held it close. "It's fine, Dorna. I've found what we need." She set the chest down on a table and opened the lid.

The box contained jewelry. Precious metal chains, a carved shell cameo, a jade brooch with matching hairpins, a carnelian pendant carved with a lion, a fire opal necklace, and a string of perfect dark pearls.

Janel sighed with relief. "I'm so glad they're still here. I worried my grandfather had already sold them."

"Why didn't he?" Dorna asked. "Might have helped with the liens." She'd stopped bickering with Sir Baramon when Janel announced her discovery; the jewels had distracted her from her errand downstairs.

"Because it would have been theft. These belonged to my mother. Now they belong to me." She closed the box back up again and offered it to Dorna. "Would you and Sir Baramon sell these?"

Dorna blinked. "But you just said they belonged to your mother."

"Jewelry isn't what I need to remember about her."

Dorna stared at her with bright eyes. Then she ducked her

head and snapped her fingers at Sir Baramon. "Well, come on, then. Let's go see if Gerios still buys as well as sells baubles from that shop of his." She took the box and began to walk back up the stairs leading to the entrance.

"Don't you snap your fingers at me, woman. Stop talking to me like I'm your lackey."

"Oh, you should be so lucky." Dorna snapped her fingers again. She turned to Janel and rapped her knuckles against the door in a pattern. "When we come back, we'll make this sound. So's you know it's us."

"Thank you, Dorna." Janel turned back to sorting. She returned the boxes, shut the doors, and went to the next closet.

"Is there anything I might do to help?" Brother Qown asked.

Janel paused. She pointed to a desk pushed up against a wall. "There may be letters in there. Correspondence. Even a record of my grandfather's liens would be more than I have now." She smiled. "My creditors could say I owe any sum. I have no way to deny their claims."

Brother Qown nodded and began to search through the drawers until he could stand it no longer.

"What happened on the bridge—"

Silence greeted his outburst. Brother Qown had just decided Janel wasn't going to pick up his dropped sentence when she said, "You're disappointed in me."

"I just don't understand. You interfered in Barsine . . ."

"I shouldn't have. Barsine isn't one of my banners. Someone would argue I had no right. They wouldn't be wrong."

"I just don't—" His throat felt thick. "I don't understand."

"Is it so difficult?" She turned to face him. "You see children at play, being supervised by a parent. One child is being picked on by the others and has started to cry. What do you do?"

Brother Qown blinked. "I tell the other children to stop picking on them."

"And what are you saying?"

He frowned. "I don't . . . what do you mean? I'm saying children shouldn't be allowed to bully each other."

"No, you're saying the child needs someone to protect them, and you're also saying the parent isn't doing their job."

Brother Qown swallowed his exasperation. "Count, that comparison falls apart when the parent clearly *isn't* doing their job."

"Are they not? How do you know? Maybe your hypothetical child is the bully and the parent has encouraged a role reversal as a lesson on empathy. Maybe the child is prone to crying because they like the sweets their parents give them to make them stop. Maybe the child needs to learn to push back against bullying, because it's not like bullying stops once we reach adulthood. You've come into the middle of a situation and made a snap decision and, further, made a snap judgment on how to fix matters. All you've done is prove your arrogance."

"Arrogance? Me?"

She didn't back down. "Is there not an arrogance in humility? An arrogance in healing and good deeds? Don't you know—know in your heart—your pacifism and good works make you a better person than someone like Dedreugh, someone like me?"

"Dedreugh was a demon!"

"I'm a demon. What's in a name? Maybe we shouldn't be so quick to presume the automatic evil of monsters."

Brother Qown choked on the heresy. "Count—"

"I agree a terrible event happened on the bridge. But if I had interfered, I would have proclaimed I knew better than the person in charge—Duke Xun."

Brother Qown sighed and shook his head. "That analogy only works when you're talking about Joratese. The duke isn't affording the Marakori the same rights your people take for granted."

Janel sighed and sat down on a box. Her gaze turned distant.

He paused his search to look at her. "Am I wrong, my count?"

"No, but—"

A noise from upstairs interrupted her. A noise which sounded like someone putting a key into a lock.

And there had been no knock, patterned or otherwise.

Janel stood, grabbed Brother Qown by the arm, and, before he could say anything in protest, pulled them both inside a closet. They crouched down behind the stacked boxes.

As the front door opened, Qown remembered they had left the lanterns lit, the containers open with their contents strewn. Anyone would notice someone had been searching for something. They would be discovered right away, betrayed by the priest's heartbeat if nothing else.

"What—? By Khored, who's been here?"

Brother Qown winced as he heard the voice. He hadn't been in Count Janel's service for long. However, he recognized the voice of Sir Oreth Malkoessian, the Markreev of Stavira's youngest son. Also, formerly the count's sworn fiancé.

"One moment, sir. Let me check." The second voice sounded unfamiliar.

Brother Qown ducked lower as swift footsteps approached, followed by a closet door being slammed. Not, thank Selanol, the one where the count and he hid. He heard boxes being tossed about. If the newcomer searched both closets, he'd find them.

"I'm sorry, sir. They took the jewelry box."

"Are you sure they kept it in that closet?" Oreth growled, his anger obvious.

"Yes, sir. I'm quite certain. It seems we have been robbed, although I can't imagine who'd think anything was worth stealing in here."

"You can't, Kovinglass?" Oreth snapped. "Do you think perhaps your former liege's granddaughter might have known about her own mother's jewelry box?"

"She can't be so stupid as to show her face here, sir," Kovinglass said.

"I need that jewelry to pay my father's interest rates!"

"Perhaps you can convince him to give you an extension?"

Sir Oreth scoffed. "I doubt it. He thinks it's character building."

"Yes, sir." Kovinglass kept his tone neutral.

"He wants me to fail. He'd love nothing better than to see me crawl back to him." Sir Oreth's voice dripped with hatred. "Let the servants clean all this. Perhaps we can salvage something of value."

"Am I interrupting?" A third voice spoke, a pleasant tenor with a western accent.

Metal plate and chain clanked. "Who are you? What are you doing here?"

"Pardon my rudeness. I seek the Count of Tolamer."

"Again, I ask: Who are you?"

"Oh? My name is Relos Var."

Silence. Brother Qown imagined the two men looking at each other in surprise. He could only guess at Janel's reaction. This must be the man she'd met at Mereina.

"*I* am the Count of Tolamer," Oreth said.

Relos Var chuckled. "Are you now? Have you done something with your hair? I didn't recognize you. Probably because you're male and look nothing like Janel Danorak—"

"Her name is Janel Theranon."

"Yes, that too. Lovely young lady. What do you call her coloring? Night-kissed? Fitting."

"Janel is my betrothed," Oreth corrected. "I'll be Count of Tolamer soon enough."

"No doubt she's counting the minutes until *that* happy day."*

"She's not here," Kovinglass said, "so perhaps you should leave."

"Ah yes. I'm sure you're right." Footsteps walked to the stairs and then stopped. "But my pardon. I couldn't help but overhear your conversation. I believe we have a situation that may be mutually beneficial. I'd be remiss not to mention the opportunity."

"Speak plainly," Sir Oreth said. "What do you mean?"

The footsteps returned as Relos Var walked back. "Clearly,

* Ha. I like this Relos Var fellow's sarcasm. We should recruit him.

you're a man who isn't shackling himself to these quaint Joratese customs. Idorrá and thudajé are fascinating concepts, but a wise man uses all the resources at his disposal."

"Choose your words carefully, old man."

"If I'm wrong, then I apologize. I tried to reach a trade agreement with the old count, but he wasn't interested. I can't understand why; it would have solved all his financial woes. I thought his granddaughter might have been willing to consider my offer, but on hearing your own predicament . . ." Relos Var paused. "I'm sorry to waste your time. Good evening, gentlemen."

The footsteps retreated once more.

"Wait," Sir Oreth said. "What offer?"

"Oh, did you want to hear it?" Relos Var's tone of voice made it obvious he was smiling.

"What—yes. That's why I asked." Sir Oreth might well have been grinding his teeth.

"I have a few friends who are looking to establish a mercantile route into Jorat and need a . . . let's call it a safe harbor. Metaphorical, not literal.* Tolamer Canton is well positioned. In exchange for preferential Gatestone access and your discretion, my associates are willing to provide a generous stipend to compensate you for your trouble."

"A stipend?" Kovinglass spoke up. "When you're asking us to break Gatekeeper bylaws? You're going to make a fortune by avoiding royal tariffs."

"I'm sure we can come to a suitable arrangement," Relos Var replied. "If the late count had been willing to hear me out, all his financial problems would have been avoided."

"I don't remember the count ever mentioning you," Kovinglass said. He sounded suspicious.

"Oh, I didn't approach him when you were around. You're a Gatekeeper, after all. Why would I make such an offer, only to see you run off to House D'Aramarin with my plans?"

---

* Normally, I'd make a comment about not needing to spell out the obvious, but I've met Sir Oreth, so . . . carry on.

"And it doesn't bother you to tell me now?"

Relos Var chuckled. "Now I know you're for sale."

"How dare you—"

Qown heard scuffling and gurgling. He held his breath. He'd never met Kovinglass in person, but he knew the name; Kovinglass had been Tolamer Canton's Gatekeeper. And also the man whose poor advice had put Janel's grandfather in such dire financial straits.

Brother Qown thought this Relos Var person had picked the wrong target for his insults.

Then he realized he'd had it backward.

"Uh . . . ," Sir Oreth said. "Would you mind not killing my man? I need him."

Something heavy fell to the ground.

"Thanks," said Sir Oreth.

"Think nothing of it. But are you sure you need him? In my experience, a man whose loyalty may be purchased once with your metal may find it purchased a second time with someone else's."

Sir Oreth laughed. "Oh? And how do you buy loyalty?"

"Purpose, meaning, and appreciation," Relos Var answered without hesitation. "My people aren't loyal because of my coffers; they are loyal because of my cause." He paused. "The coffers don't hurt, though."

Brother Qown started to understand why Count Janel thought this man the real threat.

The answer seemed to take Sir Oreth aback. "Where did you say you were from?"

"Most recently? Kazivar."

A box creaked as Sir Oreth stood. "Let me extend my hospitality so we might discuss this further over dinner. I—" He paused. "The servants need to clean, put a fire in the oven. Might I suggest we retire to the Green? I know a fantastic tavern."

"Nothing would please me more. Wake." An impatient snap of fingers accompanied the last command.

Kovinglass said, "Whah, what? What happened? What just—"

"Relos Var and I are going to dinner. Clean up here while we're gone."

A long pause followed. Gatekeepers were not, after all, servants. They often acted as advisers, simply because their level of education made them well suited for that role. But first and foremost, they were mages who paid their dues to House D'Aramarin.

Kovinglass eventually snarled, "Yes, sir."

Brother Qown prayed his thanks. As he did, Relos Var and Sir Oreth left. The room fell quiet. Brother Qown started to wonder if Kovinglass had departed with them, after all.

Then the Gatekeeper walked over to the closet where Janel and Brother Qown hid and threw open the doors.

Brother Qown almost shrieked but managed to stay silent as Kovinglass opened the top chest in a stack. The Gatekeeper rummaged through what might have been cloth. He stopped as someone opened the front door upstairs.

Brother Qown held his breath, hoping against hope Dorna and Sir Baramon hadn't returned. Luck smiled on him.

"What kept you?" Kovinglass snapped. "We need fresh linens on the beds, and someone needs to clean the kitchen. It hasn't been used in years. Get started!"

A chorus of "Yes, Master Kovinglass" rewarded his scolding; the house servants had arrived.

A woman said, "Would you care for tea, Master Kovinglass? I brought a pot from the castle along with steamed sesame buns. Sinon is setting up in the kitchen."

"Yes. Oh yes." Kovinglass's annoyance seemed to melt at the suggestion of tea and fresh food. His volume lowered as he moved away from the closet. "Siva, what would I do without you?"

She laughed. "Go hungry and without tea, Master Kovinglass. Now get you gone. You Blood of Joras types are too important to be left with the sweeping. I'll take over down here."

Brother Qown frowned. The woman's voice sounded familiar.

Kovinglass's footsteps faded from the room, and a second later, Janel stood up.

"Ninavis, what are you doing here?" she hissed.

Brother Qown blinked and peeked over the chest.

Ninavis stood there, dressed in a Joratese serving mare's dull brown split skirts and tunic. She had one hand frozen as if reaching for a weapon no longer by her side.

"By the Eight!" Ninavis whispered. "Don't do that! What in the hell are you doing here?"

"I asked you first."

Brother Qown stood up and fled the closet. "Never mind all that. We need to leave before anyone returns."

Janel looked up toward the kitchen areas, then grabbed Ninavis's hand and pulled her into the hallway and down a second set of stairs. Brother Qown followed, feeling naked and vulnerable and like they would be discovered at any turn. Had the servants gone downstairs? Would they stay quiet? It all made his stomach ache.

The staircase down to the first floor ended in a long hallway, already lit as the serving staff had moved through the house. Chatter echoed through the apartment as the staff cleaned and uncovered furniture, preparing the house for occupation. The count ignored this noise and motioned for everyone to follow her into a dark storeroom.

Once in the room, Janel grabbed a lantern from the wall and handed it to Brother Qown. "Light this." She moved over to a thick iron grating in the floor, fastened shut with a chain.

"What are you—" Ninavis started to ask.

Janel broke the metal chain with her bare hands. "Follow me."

She yanked up the grate and set it to the side.

Brother Qown lit the lantern and held it over the trap door while the count lowered Ninavis. Janel then did the same with Brother Qown.

"What the—"

A Marakori family sat up from their bedrolls, blinking at the intruders. From the way boxes had been pushed to the side to form a mini-fort, it seemed obvious they had disturbed squatters. They were taking advantage of the fact ground-floor basements were seldom used or visited.

For several heartbeats, no one said anything.

"Excuse us," Count Janel declared. "I apologize for the interruption. I recommend you all leave. Our pursuers will eventually search down here." She stepped over an old man as she headed for the door.

"Sorry," Brother Qown said to the family. "Is there anything I can do for—"*

Ninavis grabbed him by the arm and dragged him with her.

The basement exited to Atrine's ground level. The count unbarred the door and opened it, revealing the city's garbage-strewn streets. From the smell, Brother Qown surmised refugees had been using the streets for sewage disposal.

Count Janel turned around to face Ninavis.

"What are you doing in Kovinglass's employ? Talk," Janel whispered, her face stony.

Brother Qown understood the count well enough to realize she wore this expression when she was furious.

Ninavis rolled her eyes. "Nice to see you too."

Janel's nostrils flared.

"Nina, please," Brother Qown said.

The bandit leader shrugged. "It was the baron's idea. Kalazan, I mean. We figured since you lot were on foot, the hike to Atrine would take you some time. In the meantime, once the army had cleared matters up back in Mereina, their Gatekeeper opened that stone for anyone who wanted to leave. I asked to go to Tolamer. Figured I could find work at the castle, keep an eye on Sir Oreth, and give you warning if I ever saw him move forward with that whole Censure business."

"Khorsal's droppings," Janel muttered as she pinched the bridge of her nose. "I don't need your help."

Given their most recent conversation on protection, Brother Qown understood why she'd say that, even though—from his

---

* This man makes my teeth ache.

perspective—she lied. Count Janel did need help. She needed as much help as she could get.

Ninavis raised an eyebrow. "I don't hold to your idorrá ways, Count. I'll help who I damn well like, and I don't expect any hand-holding or oath swearing in return."

"I just meant . . ." Janel inhaled. "You didn't have to do this. Kalazan didn't have to do this."

"Beg your pardon, but we damn well think we do. Kalazan owes you thudajé and don't you try to deny it. He's baron because of you. You think he's just going to forget?"

"And you? Didn't you just say you don't believe in this idorrá or thudajé business? Why are you doing this?"

"My reasons—"

Brother Qown cleared his throat. "I hate to interrupt, but how are we going to find Dorna and Sir Baramon? If we don't, there's a very good chance they'll run into Kovinglass when they return. Or worse, Sir Oreth or Relos Var."

Ninavis startled. "Relos Var? He's here?"

"Yes," Janel said, "and just as much a villain as when last I saw him."

Brother Qown turned to her. "*Did* he offer your grandfather the opportunity—?"

"No," Janel said. "I'd never met the man before Mereina, nor seen his name mentioned in my grandfather's papers. He told lies to Oreth, and whispered honey, and because Oreth is twice a damn fool he never thought to look for poison." She slapped her hands against her hips. "The moment I learn Oreth is where I want him—on the verge of being too broke to continue with his schemes—Relos Var comes along. And with gifts and a cure for all Oreth's problems. I was wrong. Oreth *is* in league with Yor. At least he is now. Damn the man to Hell."

Brother Qown wasn't sure which man she wished demonic vacations upon. Both, probably.

"But why approach Oreth?" Brother Qown asked. "What does Relos Var hope to gain from such a partnership? Revenge?"

"It's not revenge," Janel said. "We cost Relos Var his unwatched

Gatestone in Mereina. He's replacing it with a better one. Mine."
She paused. "Maybe it's a little revenge."

"We can talk about this later," Ninavis said. "Come on. It
can't be safe to linger here, never mind what sickness we might
catch from breathing in the fumes."

The count nodded and took the lantern from Brother Qown,
casting her gaze around the dirty streets with distaste. "If I
remember, there's a stairway at the end of the street."

"Here," Ninavis said before pulling a wrought iron key from
her apron. "The key to Barsine's apartment here. Kalazan wants
you to use it. Unless the situation's changed since I left, he'll
be in Atrine just long enough to swear fealty—but won't stay
for the Challenges. There's too much work to be done in
Barsine."

"Wait, you're not coming with us?" Janel didn't reach for
the key.

Ninavis shook her head at Janel's question. "I can't spy for
you unless I stay."

"I didn't ask you to spy for me," Janel protested. Then she
added, "Also, I don't know the way to the Barsine House. Did
Kalazan give you directions?"

Ninavis ground her teeth. "Intolerable girl."

The count grinned—a rare moment where she looked her
age. "It's what you love about me."

"Oh, blessings of the sun, you two." Brother Qown sighed
and shook his head. "Can we please discuss this elsewhere?"

Ninavis scowled and put the key back in her pocket. "Fine!
Follow me. And watch your step."

20: BANDITS, AGAIN

Jorat Dominion, Quuros Empire.
Three days since Thurvishar D'Lorus committed
crimes against historical accuracy

"In hindsight, I think Relos Var told the truth. He may have approached my grandfather," Janel admitted. "In some ways, Oreth interfered with Relos Var's plans, which I find ironic."

Dorna blinked. "Your grandfather would have never taken metal from an outsider."

"Oh, I know," Janel said. "But *I* would have."

"Janel!"

"No, Dorna. I absolutely would have. The canton needed aid. If Relos Var—or his people—had arrived in Tolamer offering that aid in exchange for 'minor favors,' I would have accepted. Except Oreth made his move to confiscate my lands and castle the moment he heard my grandfather had passed, before anyone else reacted."

"But why would Relos Var care?" Kihrin asked.

"There aren't many passes through the mountains between Yor and Jorat," Janel explained, "but one is in Tolamer. Indeed, we have a mountain pass and a sea route, besides the Gatestone itself. Since I'd dismissed Kovinglass, there was no Gatekeeper on staff to warn anyone about unauthorized Gatestone usage. Just as no one in Mereina would have warned House D'Aramarin or the imperial army about unauthorized Gatestone usage there. If you're going to invade a place, wouldn't you desire as many approaches open to your forces as possible?"

"That's not the only reason Relos Var would have chosen

Tolamer," Qown said. "Duke Kaen wanted your canton for that, but I doubt it was Relos Var's only motivation."

"That's true," Janel agreed. She met Kihrin's eyes. "It's what you said about Xaltorath seeking me out. Relos Var was hunting the 'volunteers,' the people who'd agreed to help the Eight. He was looking for me." She smiled. "I should thank Taja you ended up on that auction block in Kishna-Farriga. It meant Relos Var had no time to deal with me in Barsine."

"Hmm. That's an unexpected blessing I hadn't considered," Kihrin agreed.

"Anyway, I should finish this next part," Janel continued. "It's not my favorite."

Janel's Turn. Atrine, Barsine Banner, Jorat, Quur.

I have never been comfortable in cities.

I admit this is due to unfamiliarity; Tolamer is a rural canton. The closest equivalent to a city I had ever known were the tournaments. A city as western Quuros sees it—a large concentration of permanent residents—lay outside my understanding or notions of comfort.

Still, it turned out cities are like forests in one important regard; they both come stocked with thieves.

We hadn't walked for more than a few minutes before we ran into them.

"All right, then," the lead man said as he stepped from an alley. "Lovely evening for a walk, ain't it?"

The man had hidden in ambush, his intentions anything but pleasant. He wore a patchwork mask over his face and a dark gray cloak over beaten, worn leathers. I couldn't tell if he was Joratese, Marakori, or some other more exotic fare. I recognized the loaded crossbow easily enough.

As well as the crossbows of his friends.

I sighed as I stepped forward.

"It is indeed a lovely evening. We don't wish for trouble, so let us pass."

I thought the odds he'd take my offer slim; he didn't disappoint.

"That ain't up to you, girlie," the man said, "and there's a toll to pay to come this way. Figure you owe us five thrones each for the lot of ya, and that ought to do it."

He was Marakori. A Joratese would not have called me "girlie."

I looked back at Brother Qown and Ninavis, both without weapons. At least Brother Qown was; I hadn't forgotten how Ninavis kicked. I had my sword, but it would be awkward to wield in quarters this tight. I wore no armor, no other protection. Arasgon didn't graze nearby to sweep in for a dashing flank attack. They outnumbered us, and they had range.

Most importantly, we carried no metal to pay them.

"That won't be possible," I said, "but since what you're asking is illegal, why don't we call it even and both be on our way?"

The bandit chuckled. "Ah now, you're a small thing to be talking so large. I like the look of you, though, so I'll make you a deal. You leave your fancy sword with us, and if you want it back, why, you can just come back here with our metal." He aimed the crossbow at my head. "Not that I'm giving you a choice."

I clenched my jaw. His demands would have never been agreeable, but this was less agreeable than most. My family had owned that sword for five hundred years, since Jorat's founding.

Ninavis must have seen the look on my face. She stepped up next to me. "Are you lot this stupid? You know our kind can't own swords by law. You walk into any shop in the city and they'll know you stole it."

"That's why it's ransom, not theft. I'll melt the damn thing down before I—" The man tilted his head and raised an eyebrow in Ninavis's direction. "Wait a minute. 'Our kind,' you say? What clan are you, woman?"

"It doesn't matter."

"Oh, I say it does."

She gave the men a critical eye. "What are you lot? Leumites?" She scoffed. "Be off. You don't want the trouble I bring with me, let alone her. She'll make you scream for your old god-queen." Ninavis removed her apron and began twisting it.

I didn't think it was a nervous gesture.

"Look at her face." A bandit pointed to Ninavis's wine-stain birthmark. "She's Diraxon, I bet."

I kept my face blank. Diraxon. Leumites. These names meant nothing to me. Were they Marakori regions? The way I hailed from Tolamer, a canton of Stavira?

The bandits seemed more familiar with Ninavis's clan name. The crossbows wavered. One man went so far as to clutch crossbow and bolt to his chest. "Diraxon, but . . ." He took a step back.

Their leader proved more immune to intimidation. "I could call myself the high general of Quur and it would mean as much. Now strip off your valuables and drop 'em on the ground."

"What happened to just taking the sword?" I asked as I unsheathed my weapon and held it with the blade pointed downward.

"That was before I found out your bitch is Diraxon." He pointed at Ninavis with a combination of chin and elbow, still holding the crossbow aimed at me. "Count yourself lucky I'm not slitting her throat. Most good folk would consider it their duty to kill any Diraxon they met, after they caused the Hellmarch."

After they . . .

My muscles tensed. I looked over at Ninavis for an explanation, but she paid no attention to me. She didn't deny his accusation, but only because she wasn't listening.

Ninavis was preparing for a fight.

"Don't do this," I said, not quite sure if I spoke to the man or to Ninavis. I lowered my arm, still holding the sword. It wouldn't do much against crossbows, but at least I had freed it from its sheath.

"You know what? Never mind. I changed my mind," he said. He raised a hand to give an order I was sure I would neither like nor enjoy.

"Don't do this," I said again, but he paid no attention either. "It doesn't have to be this way."

No one gave me the slightest mind; all their focus was locked on Ninavis.

"I'm a count! Harm me or mine and the duke will never stop hunting you."

The bandit sneered. "The duke can go freeze."

"Brother Qown, hide."

"Count, please—"

"To Hell with you," the bandit leader spat. He pulled the trigger.

I twisted to the side. The bolt's feathers whistled as it passed, ripping through my tunic and cloak, and tearing open a gash on my left arm. It sailed on to slam against an apartment's dirty white marble wall.

Pain made me hiss.

"Damn it," Ninavis cursed. She swung the rolled-up apron at one man's crossbow while she lashed out with multiple swift kicks to another bandit's head. He collapsed.

Others remained, however, each a heartbeat from loosing a barrage at us. They all thought Ninavis the greater threat.

I needed to change their opinion.

I ran at the bandit crew's leader. He had time to consider his mistakes in life before my fist, wrapped around my family sword's pommel, smashed through his skull. A shocking spray of blood splattered against a wall, but I paid little mind. Instead, I grabbed the corpse by its tunic and held it up as a shield—to block two bolts otherwise headed for Ninavis. I threw the corpse at another bandit to distract him while I sliced him open from groin to gullet. Someone called my name in warning.

I turned and for a moment . . .

Ah, but for a moment.

I didn't recognize Ninavis. I didn't see her as a friend. She stared at me with wide eyes. She must have realized I stood a hairsbreadth from turning my sword on her.

The same bandits trying to kill her saved her life.

A crossbow bolt hit me in the back.

I felt the pain as a hot wash of flame across my spine. I screamed in rage and twisted around, ignoring Ninavis to concentrate on my attacker.

I didn't bother with the sword.

I tore out his windpipe with my nails, tossing it to the ground as I moved to impale another bandit through the stomach, ripping up and out until he spilled his intestines in a great steaming pile on the ground. A fecal stench, sharper than the road's sewage, joined the aroma of spilled blood and wet metal.

I don't know what happened to Ninavis or Brother Qown. I didn't see them, for which I will be forever grateful. The two remaining men backed away with their empty hands raised. I think they begged, but I had no ears for human tongues.

I killed them too.

It's just as well for everyone I don't go into details.*

I don't think I stood there for long before I returned to my senses. At some point, I realized I stood in the middle of a half dozen Marakori corpses, no more recognizable as humans than slaughtered livestock. Blood covered me, some of which was my own.

And I didn't know if Ninavis or Brother Qown were alive or dead.

"Nina? Qown?"

I heard whispering to the side. Brother Qown stood up from behind a broken, overturned cart despite Ninavis's best efforts to pull him back. He scanned the scene, horrified. I wouldn't have begrudged him for throwing up, but sometimes I forget he doesn't faint at the sight of blood.

I wanted to say something, but my vision began darkening.

"On second thought, I'm also kind of glad you didn't prove

---

* Too late. Remind me not to read Janel's parts of this story right after eating.

you could use that sword when you and I first met," Ninavis said. Her joke fell flat as she stared at me. "Janel? Janel!"

The world slid out from under my feet, and I plummeted into an abyss.

21: A DIFFICULT HEALING

Jorat Dominion, Quuros Empire.
Three days since Kihrin D'Mon, Hamarratus, and
Star left the Capital in search of a Gatestone

Kihrin frowned.

"I told you that wasn't my favorite part," Janel said.

"No, I just had the oddest mental image of watching you kill a demon using someone else's severed arm." Kihrin studied her. "But you didn't describe that. Also, remind me to stay far away from you in a fight."

"I hardly ever lose control anymore."

Kihrin shook his head. "Now see, it's that 'hardly ever' part I find so disconcerting."

"Welcome to the party," Ninavis said. "At least the beer's free."

Janel cleared her throat and looked away for a second. "Your memory of the arm happened. In the Afterlife when we last met."

"Huh." Kihrin wasn't sure how he felt about the idea he was remembering the Afterlife or, by implication, his past life. Unsettling.

Dorna reached over and slapped Qown's shoulder. "Go on, priest. I wasn't there for this part. Tell us what happened next."

Qown's Turn. Barsine apartment, Atrine, Jorat, Quur.

As Ninavis and Brother Qown carried Count Janel away from the ambush, Qown pondered how much lighter she was than he expected. She took up so much space in a room when awake it was easy to forget her true size.

They had climbed several flights and made their way several buildings over from the ambush site, when they heard shouts and a scream behind them.

Ninavis looked over her shoulder. "Sounds like someone just found the bodies."

"Stop."

"We can't," Ninavis said. "They'll chase soon."

Brother Qown stopped, anyway, and with him, Janel. Ninavis began speaking in a language Brother Qown didn't understand. He assumed Ninavis was engaging in a graphic description of his ancestry.

"What are you doing?"

"I can't see," Brother Qown said. "We left the lantern behind us. I'm worried we're going to trip over a bench and fall twenty feet. Aren't you?"

"There's spill light—"

Brother Qown summoned up a small ball of yellow light. From a distance, it looked like a candle, bright enough to light their passage.

She shook her head. "Hell of a risk. If people notice, they're not going to stop to make sure you're Blood of Joras first." She took the opportunity to reposition her grip on the belt and scabbard holding the giant sheathed Theranon family sword.* She ended up slinging the whole belt and scabbard over one shoulder, cross-body. "Let's go." Her face looked pale, her expression grim. With the fighting over, the shakes were setting in.

She stooped to pick Janel up by the shoulders, while Brother Qown grabbed Janel's feet. Ninavis and Brother Qown ignored the blood covering them both—Janel's blood, mostly.

The apartment proved close, although Brother Qown would have missed it without Ninavis's navigation. To the priest, one

---

* Nice of them to have retrieved that for her. Personally, I'd have left it.

windowless corridor looked much the same as any other. But when they reached one—the right one—Ninavis whispered for them to set down their wounded charge. She pulled an iron key from her pocket, unlocked the rooftop gate, and let them inside. Together, they carried the Count of Tolamer into the apartment that had been set aside for the Baron of Barsine.

Brother Qown paid no attention to the decorations or furnishings, except to look for what he needed. That table there. Yes. "Help me put her down on this. On her stomach."

"Do you need hot water? I can start a fire—"

"Do it. We don't have much time." Brother Qown gestured, and the small magical candlelight became a dozen candles, enough to illuminate the room.

Ninavis gaped, mouth open.

"Set a fire," Brother Qown snapped. "Boil water. Who knows what poison these men used on their bolts?"

"Leumites don't use poison."

Brother Qown exhaled, relieved.

"But they do like to dip their arrowheads into dung."

Something inside him tightened. He bowed his head. "Selanol grant me light." Brother Qown tried to reach Illumination.

Ninavis stared at him.

He straightened as he pulled a small knife from his belt. "Well? Help me or find Dorna so she can help, but I don't have time for you to get over your superstitions."

Ninavis flushed. Her jaw worked, and then she turned, storming to the hearth. She began piling logs from the wood box into the fireplace.

Brother Qown began cutting Janel's clothing away from the wound. It would have been easier—alas, so many things would have been easier—in the west, where most women wore midriff-baring rasigi. The Joratese preferred full tunics, and those with bosoms tight-laced a reed-strengthened bodice over their chests. It made cutting the fabric away difficult. Frustrated, Qown sliced open the bodice ties and ripped the garment open.

Brother Qown grimaced at the revealed wound.

Ninavis had snapped off the bolt shaft so the injury wouldn't tear open as they ran, but now he had little choice. The moment he removed the rest of the bolt, the clotted black blood would rip loose, and the bleeding would resume.

Ninavis made a loud noise with something. Something metallic. A cook pot. He looked up.

"So was that because of the curse too?" she asked.

Brother Qown ground his teeth. "I'm trying to concentrate."

"It was never just her using magic, was it—"

Brother Qown slammed his hand down against the table. "I don't have time for this! *She* doesn't have time for this. Be quiet!"

He didn't wait on her response. He returned his attention to Janel and once more attempted to shift his vision. He could do this. He had to do this.

This time, Ninavis didn't interrupt.

Count Janel's aura appeared unlike any Qown had ever seen before. It twisted and blurred, folding in on itself like smoke buffeted by swirling zephyrs.

An aura that scoffed at his attempts to twist her body back into health.

Brother Qown tried again.

Again, he failed.

He couldn't heal her. Panic twisted his heart.

Janel had paled from blood loss and shock. If Brother Qown couldn't find a way to heal her . . .

If he did nothing, she'd die. The bolt had missed her spine but not her liver. She'd die from that alone, assuming infection and sepsis didn't claim her.

Brother Qown fished in his robe and pulled out a small metal box.

"What's that?" Ninavis asked. She must have been watching him the whole time.

"Desperation," he said. The priest opened the box. Inside rested a nest of small twigs and feather down. A perfect blue robin's egg sat in the middle.

Well, it looked like a robin's egg.

The thin clay had been painted to look like the real thing, as beautiful and fragile.

Brother Qown smashed it to the tile floor, shattering it into countless pieces. "Father Zajhera, I need your help!"

The second stretched out into an eternity. A thousand worries gave birth to a thousand more.

Had the magic failed? Had something happened to Father Zajhera? Was he too busy?

Then the wall began to glow. Its luminance condensed, flowed into shapes and fractals circling each other while the center fell back into nothingness.

"What the—" Ninavis started to say.

Brother Qown remembered to breathe.

"Thank Selanol."

He'd known Father Zajhera since he was a boy. Father Zajhera, tall and thin and wise. The man who had offered his parents another option besides House D'Lorus, when their son's mage gift first manifested. He wore his white cloud-curl hair matted into thick strands, held back by bamboo clips, and dressed in robes the same as Qown's. He looked like a simple monk rather than the leader of an entire religion.

Zajhera read the situation with a glance, dismissed Ninavis as unimportant, and rushed to Brother Qown's side. "How long ago did this happen?"

"A half hour, perhaps? She's lost so much blood, and yet she rebuffs my efforts to heal her."

"I'm not at all surprised." Father Zajhera pulled the agolé from his shoulders and set it aside. "Let us begin."

Such a simple thing reminded Brother Qown the Joratese lived in a city they hadn't built:

Atrine possessed working plumbing.

Even by western Quuros standards, the bathing rooms amazed: beautiful tile work, efficient sewage disposal, sunken wading pools—heated, of course.

He wondered if the Joratese took it for granted. Did they think about it at all? Did the citizens ever stop to marvel at the sorcery that brought fresh water to their apartments, which also bore away their waste? Did some forgotten branch of House D'Evelin maintain the sewer system—or was Atrin Kandor's enchantment on this city so great it continued to function after centuries? Did the sewage dump into Lake Jorat or the Zaibur River, or did someone do a roaring business selling fertilizer back to the Royal Houses?

Trivial matters such as these filled Brother Qown's thoughts as he washed his hands.

"She'll be fine, dear boy. I can see from the look on your face you're still worried about her." Father Zajhera stepped through the door behind Qown and presented the priest with a cup of hot tea; Nina's hot water had served a different purpose.

"I'm worried for her. It's not just her injury." Qown took the cup of blue-glazed Kazivar porcelain from his leader's hands. Qown wondered if the cup had come with the house or if Zajhera had brought it with him. Focus. "I don't think—" Brother Qown fumbled, started again. "I don't think I'm the right person to help her, Father. I know how much she means to you. I think sending me to her was a mistake."

Father Zajhera stared at Brother Qown, who in turn tried not to cringe. Zajhera had a way of looking at people that channeled every parental disappointment ever to sting tears in a child's eyes. Seeing dissatisfaction in Zajhera's eyes hurt worse than a dagger's edge.

"Tell me what happened. Something more, I think, than her injury by brigands."

Brother Qown motioned for Father Zajhera to follow him, since this wasn't an appropriate conversation for bathing rooms. They walked downstairs, where a small sitting room offered comfortable chairs and tables upon which to rest their tea.

Ninavis had left to track down Mare Dorna and Sir Baramon. No one else occupied the apartment save for a sleeping count, who would continue her deathlike slumber throughout the night.

"I have followed your suggestions," Brother Qown said as they both sat down, "and I have avoided discussing the source of her abilities. She has, since I first met her, maintained her strength is due to Xaltorath's curse. But in recent weeks . . ." Brother Qown paused to sip his tea. "Well. It's become difficult to ignore abilities that cannot be described this way."

Father Zajhera looked surprised. "She's developed a second spell-gift?" Neither would call it a *witch-gift*. Witches were not just sorcerers who'd forgotten to pay their license fees.

"With all respect, Father, I believe she has developed a third. You've long contended her strength is her own doing, a defense mechanism after the trauma she experienced at Lonezh. I believe the 'curse' that sends her to the Afterlife every night is also a spell-gift. And I think she's beginning to show signs of a third ability involving fire."

Father Zajhera chuckled. "Impressive. It's such a shame her grandfather would never let me train her."

"Of course he wouldn't. She's not 'Blood of Joras.'" Brother Qown gave the other priest a scolding look. "A concept that you never mentioned to me."

"Hmm? Oh yes. I'd forgotten about that."

"Well, I'm never going to forget that label. I'm wondering if I can find someone to embroider it on my robes. Maybe Dorna . . ." Brother Qown sighed and stretched. "That's not all. That's not even half." Without waiting for a response, he continued, "We were in Mereina when it was attacked. A sophisticated attack organized by genuine witches, who wiped out almost the entire town and everyone gathered for the tournament. Thousands dead."

Father Zajhera didn't seem surprised. Brother Qown supposed he should have expected that. Father Zajhera knew a great many people and a great many things.

"The people responsible for the attack included a Doltari woman named Senera. She released magical smoke that choked its victims—it's how almost everyone died. However, I also saw what she did, so she wouldn't be overcome by the smoke herself."

Brother Qown reached out and drew a line in the air, tracing out the sigil. It glowed but didn't do much else—although Qown assumed the air around the glyph was clean and pure. The demonstration would have been more obvious if he'd drawn the glyph near smoke.

Father Zajhera's expression shifted fast through several emotions, including anger, before settling on unhappy concern. He stared long and hard at the rune, before sighing and leaning back in his chair.

Brother Qown had known Father Zajhera for his whole life. He knew how to read the man's moods.

"You know what this is, don't you?"

"It's a sigil," the elder priest said, then shook his head. "No, I apologize. That makes it sound like a toy one might paint on a child's nursery for luck. What you have just drawn is a symbolic and equivalent representation of tenyé, an object's true essence. Tell me, this woman, Senera, did she keep a small stone on her person? A necklace or jewelry? Perhaps this large? A crystal?" He held thumb and forefinger a few inches apart.

"No, nothing like—" Brother Qown paused. "No. No wait. Not jewelry, no, but she had an inkstone. A small one. She kept it tucked into her bodice, pulling it out when she cut herself. She used her blood to draw that sigil on her forehead. I thought it was ritual magic." He frowned. "I still think so. That brush must have been made from hairs pulled from all her Yoran soldiers. Sympathetic magic would have ensured her 'sigil' ended up on everyone's forehead simultaneously."

"Yes," Father Zajhera agreed. "Astute. Even more astute to notice the sigil itself and use it to your advantage.* I'm proud of you."

Brother Qown blushed. "Father, I—thank you, but that glyph is what worries me. What is its nature? Where does it come from? I put no tenyé into its creation. It should have no power,

* To think how this all might have turned out if he'd been just a little less observant.

yet every time this sigil is drawn, its magical effect is the same."

For a long time, Father Zajhera said nothing. He sipped his tea as he contemplated his response. Finally, he said, "This woman, Senera. If that is her real name.*" He nodded to Brother Qown. "The stone she used is no river rock. It is the most dangerous of all Cornerstones: the Name of All Things."

Brother Qown felt a shiver sweep through him. The priest knew very little about the Cornerstones. Father Zajhera seldom spoke of them, but Brother Qown remembered enough to know they were eight artifacts with different and significant magical abilities.

"You once told me the Cornerstones are gods trapped in stone," Brother Qown whispered.

Zajhera waved a hand, irritated. "I was being poetic. That description gives the stones more credit for sentience than they deserve. The Cornerstones are eight gems, tied to universal concepts. They contain godlike power, but not a divine being's will and intelligence. Such direction must be supplied by another. Anyone who holds them in fact." His smile turned sardonic. "Even an escaped slave from Doltar."

"What . . ." Brother Qown's throat felt dry and thick. "What does the Name of All Things do? What are its powers?"

Zajhera shrugged. "Who can say with any certainty? It provides information. Its power is subtle. Its sphere is knowledge. It seems the stone can be used to answer questions. Even perhaps questions as esoteric as, what tenyé sigil might turn the air sweet and pure?"

"*Any* questions?" Brother Qown felt a panicked flutter in his chest. Could its owner predict the future, research their enemies' weaknesses? What couldn't someone do with such answers at their fingertips?

"I cannot say." Father Zajhera set his tea aside. "But it is a mystery you must unravel."

"But I—"

* I'll never tell.

Zajhera raised two fingers. "She needs you, my son.* She needs someone to light her path, for the dark is all around her. Xaltorath has been a terrible influence, and you have seen what she becomes when she loses control."

"She should be trained. I have never known anyone with so much potential. Three spell-gifts, Father! She maintains her strength at all times and doesn't even realize she's doing it."

"Trained by whom?" Father Zajhera said. "She's a woman. The empire does not grant women licenses to use or learn magic. A woman who knows even a single spell-gift, no matter how much potential she may have, is a witch. And witchcraft is a crime the empire punishes with death, not slavery."

"You know Quuros laws are vile. However, I'm not even sure they'd be applied here, because of the Joratese treatment of gender. For example, Joratese law makes it clear only men may hold a noble title, yes?"

Father Zajhera's brows drew together. "Yes."

"No." Qown held up a finger as emphasis. "Only *stallions* can hold a noble title. But the rest of the empire assumes that means men. For example: What's the Guarem translation for the root of the word *idorrá*?"

"Why, *male*—" Father Zajhera paused. "Male, but that isn't actually what *idorrá* means."

"No, it isn't. Idorrá is a gender-neutral concept. But because we western Quuros can't imagine power, or leadership, tied to anything but masculinity, we assumed the word must mean *man*. It doesn't."

"But it's just a mistranslation, then; the Joratese clearly do understand the difference between male and female."

"Do they? They know the difference between stallions and mares. But if you tell them only a man may inherit a noble title in Quur, they'll nod and agree that's how they do things here too. And if you pointed out someone like Janel has inher-

* I do not! Oh, he meant Janel.

ited a title, they would still agree they do things the same way. Because they don't understand how that's a contradiction."

Father Zajhera looked confused. "But she's female . . . ?"

"Physically," Brother Qown agreed. "But do you remember when you first told me about her? How you said there had been all those false reports about the Count of Tolamer having a grandson? You assumed people saw her dressed up in boy's clothes and jumped to the wrong conclusions. I don't think they did. Because the Joratese don't see it the way you or I would. She's not a mare; she's a stallion. To the Joratese, Count Janel—and note how it's *Count* and not *Countess*—is a *man* to the Joratese, by all the standards we'd use in the west. Except for one thing: she's female."

"But she was engaged to marry that boy—"

"It's no scandal for two stallions to marry—and notice how those labels have nothing to do with biological sex. And they have three, you'll note."

"Three what?"

"Three genders. Gelding is also allowed. It has nothing to do with whether you like sex or are even capable of sex. *Gelding* is a catch-all term for anyone who doesn't quite fit into the stallion and mare definitions or who doesn't *want* to fit into those definitions. Anyway, there's no reason two stallions can't work as a match. But I gather Sir Oreth decided she should be a mare and tried to force the issue. She disagreed." He paused. "Violently."

"Huh." Father Zajhera shook his head. "Well, there can be no doubt it's a strange land. But even if they think she's a man—or stallion—they'll still burn her as a witch."

"They'll burn anyone who's from this side of the mountains as a witch. Magical aptitude or not, apparently. It's only us lucky few from the west who're given a pass." Brother Qown sighed. "I should mention the prophecy . . ."

Father Zajhera's eyes regarded his, bright as gemstones.

"You knew about that too," Brother Qown said.

"It is always hard to see where prophecies will lead," Father

Zajhera agreed. "I suppose I'd have an advantage if I had that Cornerstone, the Name of All Things, for example.* Still, I have known for a long time that Janel is wrapped up in such matters. Why else would demons single her out? Keep doing as you have, keep your head down, report back on everything, try to help Janel without putting yourself at risk. Remember a dead physicker heals no patients. As for Count Janel . . ." He picked up his tea again.

"Yes?"

Father Zajhera smiled. "Being cursed by a demon breaks no laws, my son, and makes no distinctions between genders. So. I say any powers she may manifest are because of a curse. And you shall say so as well. Do we understand each other?"

Brother Qown nodded. "Yes. Of course, Father. I understand perfectly."

---

* Yeah, let's make sure that never happens.

22: THE COST OF IDORRÁ

Jorat Dominion, Quuros Empire.
Three days since the fires started in the
Capital City

Janel studied Qown for a moment. "So you've always known."

Qown shifted under the scrutiny, his gaze lighting upon the other people in the tavern before settling on his hands. "Known?"

"About the source of my strength."

"I didn't know *for certain*," he admitted, squirming, "but we suspected. Trauma often sparks spell-gifts, and, well, your talent manifested immediately following a rather terrifying amount of trauma, didn't it?"

Mare Dorna tsked and shook her head. "My poor foal."

"Are you still in contact with this Father Zajhera?" Kihrin frowned.

Janel and Qown looked at each other.

"I suppose we could be if we wanted, but why?" Janel asked.

"Look, I realize you both like this man a lot, but something about that story bothers me, though I can't put my finger on it." Kihrin snapped his fingers. "Wait. I've got it. Qown, you never told Father Zajhera that Senera was an escaped Doltari slave."*

Brother Qown blinked. "I . . . what?"

"You never told Father Zajhera she was a slave, escaped or otherwise. So why did he say she was?"

---

* I wondered if anyone was going to catch that.

"Oh." Qown's brows drew together. "I never noticed that."

"He wasn't wrong," Janel said slowly, "but we didn't know that about Senera until later. Qown, are you sure that's what he said?"

Qown winced. "I'm sure."

"And what does that mean?" Mare Dorna asked. "Maybe he assumed. I hear that's how most of those people end up in Quur, ain't it?"

Kihrin shrugged and leaned back in his chair. "I don't know. It struck me as off, but maybe Dorna's right and he just assumed she must have been a slave."

"No." Qown shut his eyes for a second. "No, he made a mistake—or he was testing me. Either way, I should have noticed."

Janel looked at Qown oddly. "What are you talking about?"

"We haven't reached that part of the story yet," Brother Qown said, "but it's your turn."

Janel's Turn. Barsine apartment, Atrine, Jorat, Quur.

I have wondered if it would be better if I couldn't remember what occurred that night. Would it be cleaner, happier, if I had woken the next morning, unsure what I had done, innocent through ignorance? Could I pretend I had committed no wrong, or would I wallow in doubt? Which would be worse, to wake hoping I hadn't killed someone or to know with absolute conviction I had?

No matter. I knew. I remembered.

I threw off the bedcovers and reached for a robe.

"Ah, foal!" Dorna scolded as soon as I moved. "You shouldn't be out of bed." Dorna sat at a small table by the hearth, darning the tears in my bloody tunic. She'd be the first to admit she's a terrible cook, but amazing with needle and thread; by the time she finished, I wouldn't be able to tell the fabric had ever been ripped. She'd dye the whole thing a new color to hide the stains.

"I'm fine, Dorna." Which was true. I wasn't in any pain, and touching my lower back, I felt no injury.

I picked up the bodice from the table next to her. "Who healed me? Qown?" I poked my finger through the hole in the back. The bodice could be salvaged. Not so long ago, I'd have thrown the garment out and ordered a servant to make me a replacement.

Now I would have to make do.

Dorna hadn't answered. When I looked at her, she focused so hard on her embroidery I wondered just what had happened to me while unconscious. "Dorna? Did Qown heal my wounds?"

Dorna ignored the question as she laid her embroidery to the side. "Was it a bad one? To be fair, last time you weren't shot through the middle, but still . . ."

I set the bodice back down on the table. "Where are we? Is this the Barsine apartment?"

"Aye, foal," she said, smiling. "We're even here legally. Kalazan granted us permission."

"I know. Did you meet up with Arasgon and Talaras?"

Dorna gave me a hard look, started to say something, then pressed her lips together. "Foal—"

"What about my mother's jewelry? Did you sell it?"

Dorna sighed. "No. Aroth's always been a crafty bastard. He's got the pawnshops watched too. But I'm wise to his tricks." She saw the look on my face. "We'll figure something out. I still have a little metal saved up. We're not turning out our pockets yet. And the firebloods are fine. Romping over on the Green and catching up with old friends. Flirting with the mares like the shameless stallions they are." The old woman stood. "Ninavis told me what happened. Don't be hard on yourself. They were bad men."

"They were desperate men," I corrected. "I know nothing else about their character."*

"They would have killed you."

---

* I'm reading this thirdhand, and even I know something about that lead bandit's character. Janel needs to get over herself.

"I don't know that. Neither do you. Unless I meet their souls the next time I'm in the Afterlife, their true intentions remain unknown to me." I rubbed my fingertips together. Dorna or someone—Qown, maybe—must have washed my hands while I slept. They hadn't done a very good job, though; a sticky crust of blood lingered under my nails.

"All I know for certain is I massacred them."*

Dorna had nothing to say to that, either because she agreed or because she thought arguing with me was pointless. "Let me fetch you some breakfast."

"No. Let's go back to the original question. Did . . . Qown . . . heal . . . my . . . wounds?" I asked. Dorna's refusal to answer had turned an idle question into an important one.

"Oh. I imagine he did, with Zajhera's help—"

Zajhera? My eyes widened.

"You should rest!" she called after me as I walked out into the main room.

Most apartments in Atrine have a sameness to them. There isn't much variety to the floor plans, although since a baron is lower ranked than a count, the Barsine apartment is smaller in scale than the Tolamer apartment. Same fireplace in the same position, same ornamental corbels, same carved ceiling, same main hall. A hundred generations had burnished the plaster walls into a soft smoothness you'd be forgiven for mistaking for marble.

A pot cooking on the hearth smelled like something spicier than normal for Joratese breakfast porridge. A large and prominent altar to the Eight held pride of place in the main hall, but only a few paintings or tapestries decorated the apartment. No sculptures, no books. That fit what I remembered of Tamin's father, a grim man who had associated everything from art to poetry as a potential entry point for demonic corruption.

Sir Baramon, Brother Qown, and Ninavis all sat in the main hall, talking to a fourth person. He was leaning toward them

---

* My personal rule of thumb: when people are shooting you with crossbows, they mean to kill you. But then, I'm pedantic that way.

in earnest enthusiasm, ignoring the spiced porridge cooling on the table beside his elbow. A white beard and plaited cloud-curl hair marked the newcomer, vivid against his Quuros brown skin. He had wise eyes and a cheerful smile.

Without him, I would never have made it to adulthood at all. Father Zajhera had saved me in a thousand ways. He'd made it possible for me to ignore the screaming in my mind, to believe I could be better than Xaltorath's daughter.

"Have you seen her when she's like this? It's terrifying—" Ninavis shut up as soon as Sir Baramon nudged her with his boot. An awkward silence fell over the group as they realized I'd entered.

All except for one.

"My dearest Janel!" The old Vishai priest rose to his feet and walked toward me with arms outstretched. "My dear child, it has been too long. I'm so sorry to hear about your grandfather. His light shone to the furthest reaches of our souls."

"Father Zajhera," I said, trying with everything in me to keep my voice level. I had to fight the urge to run into his arms, to collapse crying with my head against his chest. Instead, I set my hand against the back of his neck, rested my forehead against his. He returned the greeting. He probably hadn't been subject to a proper Jorat greeting since the last time he'd seen me, years before. "I thought you were across the Dragonspires."

Brother Qown rose to his feet. "Oh, he was, Count. I sent a message for him." He paused, and a shadow crossed over his face. "I thought it would be best."

I stepped away from the Vishai faith's leader, lowered my hands. "I see. Thank you, Brother Qown." I examined them, and my heart broke. Brother Qown looked anxious, Sir Baramon shame-faced, but Ninavis—

Ninavis wouldn't look at me at all.*

---

* If Ninavis is Diraxon (which would explain some things), this is a little pot-and-kettle of her. According to rumors I've heard, they've killed people in *considerably* more . . . creative ways.

"I need the room," I said. "Father Zajhera and I have matters to discuss."

Silence lingered, and then everyone shuffled out.

"Ninavis?"

She paused at the doorway, turned to face me.

"I'll speak with you when we're done here."

Ninavis started to say something, frowned, and nodded an affirmative before following the others.

I stared after her a moment before turning my attention back to Father Zajhera. "Your Luminance, you know I owe you everything, but you shouldn't have come."

The old man smiled. "Sit with me. Tell me how things have been."

"Why? Am I to believe Brother Qown hasn't already given you a full report?"

He tsked under his breath and patted the chair cushion across from him. "Don't be so hard on him, child. Brother Qown called me in because he found out what I've known for some time: you're not an easy person to heal. You fight it. You fight it the way a sorcerer fights a rival's curse."* His kind gaze turned stern. "Now sit."

Some ancient tone all parents learn from their children had me following his orders—I sat down by the fire across from him. "How much did he tell you?"

"Something about an evil sorcerer, an evil witch, you needing to find a way to see the duke. Continuing troubles with the Malkoessian family that have never gone away." He leaned forward. "Nothing you can't solve, my dear. I have all possible faith in you."

I breathed deeply and once more fought the desire to collapse into his arms, a little girl finding comfort in the priest who had

---

* In my limited interactions with Janel, I've noticed she's internalized her talismans. That makes her the third person I've met who can do that, and the other two are you and Gadrith (and Gadrith cheated by literally sewing them inside his body).

Just something to think about.

always been there for me. At least, the priest who had been there for me since I was eight years old.

Instead, I said, "I murdered six people last night. Did Brother Qown tell you?"

"Murder," Father Zajhera answered, "requires premeditation. And if I understand the legalities, you had every right to defend yourself against those men or indeed to take their lives for their affront." He held up a finger as I started to retort. "They didn't belong to your herd. They were not saelen. These were dangerous men committing illegal acts. But that's not the real problem, is it?"

I sighed and stared down at my black fingers. "No, the real issue is that I lost control."

"So it would seem. Was it possession? Did Xaltorath return?"

"No, I . . ." I turned away and stared at the dancing flames. "I became so angry. Furious. It just welled up inside me like a fire I could only quench with blood. I fear . . . I fear I'm becoming the very thing I hate."

"Hmm."

I glanced back at him, blinking. "Hmm? That's all you have to say? Hmm?"

He shrugged, leaned back in his chair, and began to eat his porridge. "This is delicious. Dorna's cooking?"

"You said it's delicious, so no."

"You're blessed to have her by your side, my child. It's not rice, is it?"

"I haven't the faintest. Barley? You're changing the subject."

He chuckled and ate more while I waited. Finally, after I dearly wanted to shout at him, he set the bowl down on a side table. "I think the young are so . . . dramatic."

"Dramatic?" I stared. "I killed—"

"Yes, yes. You're a young woman in a difficult situation, forced into making difficult choices, with extraordinary pressure on your shoulders, and an even more extraordinary weapon at your disposal—yourself. Is a demon necessary to explain why you might have lost control? Even if your perceived experience is older than your age, your body is still transitioning from child to adult. It's not a mystery as to why you might be having a hard time." He folded his hands over his lap. "I'm much more concerned about this business with the Baron of Barsine. What were you thinking?"

I gaped. That hadn't even been on the list of things I had expected him to scold me over.

"I have no idea what you mean."

The old priest sighed. "These aren't my people, but I know enough about Joratese ways to understand the ramifications."

I narrowed my eyes. "The ramifications? I stopped a Hellmarch, Father Zajhera. Remember how the last one went, when I was a child? They were creating a demon prince from the souls sacrificed to Kasmodeus. They were going to open up Jorat like a rotted plum."

"Yes, and you Censured the baron, installed your own man as the new ruler—"

"I didn't Censure anyone, and Kalazan isn't my man—"

Father Zajhera waved a hand. "I know how idorrá and thudajé work, my dear. Kalazan is your man. You rule Tolamer—"

"Oreth would disagree."

"Until Sir Oreth finds a way to strip your title, you're the Count of Tolamer. And what happens, my sweet girl, when you walk into the duke's palace, explain the danger to him, and he . . . dismisses the threat?"

"He won't do that," I protested.

"Oh, but he will. Because barring the last Hellmarch, Jorat has known peace for almost a hundred years. Your young Duke Xun cannot even begin to imagine how quickly that can change. He'll think you're trying to live up to your sobriquet, Janel *Danorak,* riding out to warn the dominion. He'll decide you're overwrought, upset about your grandfather's death, looking for an angle in your feud against Oreth Malkoessian. He'll dismiss your concerns as nothing but a young girl who thinks she's a stallion, when she should have accepted her place as a mare. And what will you do then?"

I froze in horror as his words sank into my soul. No. No, that couldn't be . . .

I shuddered. "I need to stop Relos Var. *I must stop Relos Var!* The town at Tiga Pass is *gone,* Father. Coldwater is *gone.* How many more towns will vanish as Mereina has? How many more will die?"*

He leaned forward, elbows resting on his knees. "And have you given any thought to what it will mean when *you* are the one saving these towns, banners, and cantons? When you save them, even as their rulers dismiss the threat? How will Duke Xun react when his people owe you more thudajé than they owe him?"

The blood fled from my face as I finally understood his meaning. In my eagerness to do the right thing, to stop these demons and these madmen, I had forgotten the most fundamental rule in Joratese politics.

What you protect is what you *rule.*

"I would—" I swallowed. "I would do it in the duke's name. He'd take credit for any defense I offered."

He nodded. "A commendable plan, assuming Duke Xun is smart enough to recognize your loyalty. We shall see, won't we?" He extended his arm around me. "I have always known how special you are, Janel. Once, you led an army across Jorat—"

I made a noise, half protest, half whimper. "No, I didn't. Xaltorath—"

"She didn't pick you by chance.† Oreth's mistake—the same mistake his father, Aroth, is making, the same mistake Duke Xun will make—is to see you as inferior, someone over whom they hold idorrá. Bride, vassal, supplicant, submissive. And it's not true. Mark my words, my daughter—before this is done,

---

* One of the few times I agree with her. If there were any other way . . .

† Are Darzin, Kihrin, and I the only people who view Xaltorath as male aspected? (And yes, I know, energy beings don't have gender, but demons almost always present themselves with a gender. It's almost as if they view themselves as gendered . . . which, now that I write this down, seems strange. I need to do some research.)

you will lead an army across Jorat again. Your idorrá will cover this whole empire, and Quur will bow before you."

His words struck me like blows. I stared at him, mouth dry and throat tight. "I have always valued your counsel. You helped me when no one else could. But this . . . you're wrong, Father. You're wrong." I paused to collect myself. "This is a test, isn't it? Like the games you used to play with me to make sure I'd escaped Xaltorath's corruption. You're trying to ensure I'm not losing myself to pride and ambition."

He smiled. "You see through me so easily."

"I know I'm willful," I said, "but I'm not thorra. I know my place. When it comes time for me to submit to Duke Xun's idorrá, I will."

Father Zajhera clasped me on the shoulder. As he started to speak, however, steps echoed on the stairs, quick and loud. Ninavis burst into the main room.

"Janel! You said that witch back in Mereina was a white-skinned Doltari, right?" She didn't look panicked, but her urgency proved impossible to ignore.

"Yes. Why, what's happened?"

"Well, I hate to interrupt you, but she's here."*

Because Emperor Kandor built Atrine to be a slaughterhouse rather than a capital, towers sat on many rooftops. Towers where one might sit and watch several twisting, winding streets at once, better to raise the alarm and organize a defense. Sir Baramon had been sitting in one when he saw a snow-white woman† leading armed soldiers toward us, and sent Ninavis to find me.

"I'm not wrong, am I?" Sir Baramon squinted his eyes to make out the figures. The soldiers had stopped in a cul-de-sac, arguing over the right direction to go.

"No," I said. "You're not wrong. That's Senera." I recognized

---

* Cue the dramatic minstrel music.
† Oh, come on, I'm not that pale.

her even at this distance; the way she stood, the way she tilted her hips, had left as indelible an impression on me as her skin color. I felt dread shiver through me. She'd wiped out an entire town using magic.

Now she'd arrived in Atrine. And was on her way to the Barsine apartment.

It took no great genius to realize why this was. Only someone who knew Baron Tamin was dead or Censured would think to lodge in his empty apartments. Someone who had survived the attack on Mereina. So either Senera had the same idea we did and looked for a place to sequester herself and her men . . .

. . . or she was looking for us.*

"There." Ninavis tugged on my arm. "The skyways." She pointed across the roofs. I saw more men crossing over, heading toward us.

Maybe it was coincidence. More people in Atrine traveled by the skyways than traveled by the labyrinthine streets, after all.

But I couldn't help but notice such travel cut off our escape routes. And these men roaming the skyways carried themselves like soldiers.

"They're here for us," I murmured. "They must be. Quickly, gather our things."

"Perhaps I can help?" Father Zajhera suggested.

Sir Baramon frowned at him. "I'm not sure what you could do, priest, although it's a nice offer . . ."

Father Zajhera took no offense at the dismissal. Indeed, his eyes twinkled with warm amusement. "Where would you like to go? Still in Atrine, I assume?"

I blinked at him, but Brother Qown stammered. "Father! This is Jorat. Are you sure such a display is wise?"

"Don't fret. No one's going to come after me for being a witch. That silly god-king tale about Joras and his descendants must have some advantages. Although don't tell House

---

* I'm not telling. It makes me look smarter.

D'Aramarin. I've never paid a lick of dues to them."* Father Zajhera adjusted his agolé and raised his hands, positioning his fingers just so—his body posed like a dancer before a performance. He whispered something, low and gentle and velvety, a voice to drift a thousand restless babies into slumber's arms. Energy strands floated from his fingertips, fractal shapes coalescing in the air into mathematical skeins. There was an order to it, a pattern. It tugged at me, daring me to comprehend its meaning. The energy circle brightened, then cooled, leaving a mirror finish at its center.

A mirror finish that didn't reflect the rooftops behind us.

"Witchcraft," Sir Baramon sputtered.

"Blood of Joras, you oaf. He can't be a witch. Not by anyone's definition." Mare Dorna crested the steps with several bags slung over her shoulders. "Now grab our things and go. There's a saying about gifts and horses that applies right about now, so quit your whining."

Sir Baramon started to protest.

"Follow me," I ordered him, and I ducked back inside. I didn't need Sir Baramon's Joratese sensibilities about magic clashing with our need for an escape route. I hefted my travel valise and let him grab his own bags, reflecting I should be glad I'd habitually kept my possessions packed and ready to go since Tolamer. I had no idea what trinkets from the Barsine apartments had slipped and fallen into Dorna's pockets, but I would send my apologies and replacements to Kalazan at the first available opportunity.

Back on the roof, traveling supplies now in hand, I saw the soldiers lurked just a few rooftops away. Close enough to see their faces, pale and almost certainly Yoran under makeup and disguises.

Banging echoed from the door downstairs.

"Go!" I shouted. I saluted the soldiers, then walked through the gate myself.

---

* What a daring rebel he is.

23: THE GREEN

"So let me see if I've got this straight," Kihrin said, "you're saying that in Jorat, being a hero is seen as an act of . . . *conquest?*"

"Not necessarily," Janel said. "If centaurs appeared in Tolamer and I fought them off, then I'm doing my duty as count. Both heroic and acceptable. It's the job of a stallion to protect the herd from threats. If I can't, what good am I?"

"And if you can't, but someone else comes along who can . . . what then? Do people expect you to step down and let this new person take over?" Kihrin couldn't believe anyone would be so naïve. People who had power didn't just give it up. That wasn't how power worked.

Kihrin remembered Father Zajhera's words. *That* man understood power. He'd understood Janel's need to save her homeland would inevitably force her into conflict. She'd clash with people who would see her aid only as a threat to their own authority. And that would lead to . . . to what?

Overthrowing Duke Xun? Janel had said he wanted her dead. Rebelling against the entire empire? Quite possibly, yes. On a fundamental level, the Quuros Empire couldn't allow a woman—a witch at that—to wield genuine authority. They'd squash her for that alone. Kihrin thought of prophecies describing how the Hellwarrior would shatter Quur and remake it. He also reminded himself that the Hellwarrior wasn't one person but four.

Which meant when the armies marched across Quur, he wouldn't have to be the commander leading them. That honor might be Janel's.

"It's how it's *supposed* to work," Janel said, head down. "But it seems our leaders have forgotten why they have power in the first place."

Ninavis shrugged one shoulder and smiled. "Eh. We'll just have to remind them. Your turn, right, Qown?"

Brother Qown nodded.

Qown's Turn. Atrine, Jorat, Quur.

Few people in the whole empire are strong enough in the magical arts to open a gate by themselves. Brother Qown wasn't one; his skills had always centered around healing. In fact, even most Gatekeepers beholden to House D'Aramarin couldn't open a gate without assistance. That's why they needed Gatestones.

House D'Aramarin closely guarded their monopoly. They'd therefore be horrified if they ever learned of someone strong enough to open a gate, single-handedly, who didn't take orders from their guild at all. Worse, that he led a fringe religion many viewed as little better than a cult.

Watching Father Zajhera touch the divine always filled Qown with joy; Zajhera made spellcasting seem as easy as writing out a prayer with brush and ink. His movements shaped the universal tenyé with a skill Brother Qown envied.*

Father Zajhera blessed them with his presence. Qown knew everything would be better now.

"Father Zajh—" As they crossed through the portal, Brother Qown saw the old priest give his pupil a warm smile.

He raised his right hand and moved his fingers in a twisting motion.

"No, wait—" Brother Qown knew in that instant Zajhera had never planned to follow them. "Father!"

---

* Well it *is* nice to watch a professional work.

And the gate vanished.

Count Janel set down the large traveling valise holding her belongings. She'd raised her cloak's hood over her hair and face. "He didn't stay behind, did he? Senera—"

"Oh no," Brother Qown reassured her. "I'm sure he just went back to Eamithon. He's a busy man, after all. He only stayed to heal your injuries."*

She put a hand to her back, to where the crossbow bolt had run her through. "Yes, of course. I'm sure Father Zajhera is quite able to see to his own protection. Which we should do as well. That's the second hiding place we've been forced to flee."

"To be fair, foal, they weren't clever hiding spots, were they?" Mare Dorna squinted and looked around. "So let's see if we can do better in the middle of the herd."

Brother Qown chewed on his lower lip. The priest hadn't yet had a chance to tell Janel about the Name of All Things. He hadn't had a chance to tell her Senera might well track them—no matter where they went to ground.

She only had to ask the Cornerstone.†

Then Dorna's last comment struck home, and Brother Qown realized she hadn't, in fact, been speaking metaphorically. He'd been so wrapped up in Father Zajhera's departure, he'd paid no attention to their circumstances.

Horses surrounded them.

Hundreds at least. Horses nickered, shifted weight, blew air through their noses. Grass and musk scented the air, mixing with the more odoriferous but still green scent of horse

---

* And chat. And help her *escape* me. I'm not bitter, though.
† Oh, I wish it were that easy.
  "Where is Janel Theranon right now?"
  "At the corner of Valiant Boulevard and Triumph Street."
  "Great. Where's that?"
  "Where's what?"
  "Where is the corner of Valiant Boulevard and Triumph Street?"
  "In the city of Atrine."
  Some questions just aren't worth asking.

droppings. The horses roamed over an enormous parklike space, Atrine's buildings encircling them like a giant wall. The shining pinnacles of the duke's palace and the sword-point towers of Khored's Temple formed an axis pointing to the sky.

This was the Green, which they had seen in their first futile attempt to meet the duke. Most of a large city might have fit inside that ocean of grass, the only place inside Atrine large enough to hold all the horses needed for the Great Tournament. Colorful azhocks and waving banners, galloping horses, and practicing knights overwhelmed the senses. Hiding in such a space seemed impossible, except so many people and so many horses milled in the area, identifying any one single person became an exercise in frustration.

Somewhere in the Green, the firebloods—Arasgon and Talaras—met with family and caught up with important news and gossip. Somewhere here, the horses they had brought with them from the Tiga Pass grazed. Their own horses too, brought all the way from Barsine by Arasgon. Brother Qown looked forward to seeing Cloud again. He had grown fond of that sweet little gray, even if the horse loathed moving faster than a walk.

Probably *because* of that reason.

"Sir Baramon," Janel said, "help me with this trunk. Also, where does Captain Mithros keep his training camp?" She plucked at the red cloak resting on her shoulders. "It seems I have something to return."

"Oh, smart thinking, foal. Some mercenary work would be just about what we need right now. Hired knights are always coming and going. Nobody pays them no mind." Dorna put her hands to her hips and grinned. "'Sides, the captain's an old friend."

"The Markreev of Stavira's your 'old friend' too," Sir Baramon said. "Please note how Dorna's old friends never seem to want to have anything to do with her."

Dorna snorted. "The Markreev's still sore about his wife, that's all."

Sir Baramon rolled his eyes as he picked up the case. "Really? That's *all*, is it?" Without waiting for an answer, he turned back to the count. "We do need to find you something else to wear. The Red Spears will take offense at you wearing that, even if you mean to return it."

Janel hesitated before nodding her agreement. She'd been wearing the red cloak since Mereina, although Brother Qown wasn't sure why. She ducked her head and pulled it off, folding the fabric over her arm. Dorna handed her a plain brown sallí—Brother Qown didn't ask where she'd found it—and Janel wore that instead.

"This way." Sir Baramon jerked his head back toward Khored's Temple. Their destination veered from the temple itself as they headed to a roped-off area in the temple's shadow. Red-hued azhocks adorned with bright pennants and crisp streamers populated the rear grounds. A second roped-off area, tourney combat yard-sized, provided an area where knights practiced. Other training grounds surrounded it, their purpose obtuse but with one common quality: they all catered to contests fought on horseback. Women trained as well as men, and almost everyone wore some variation of red cloak, or at least a red arm band. Only one figure didn't wear red: a knight on horseback practicing to be the Black Knight. He wore the appropriate hue.

If they wanted to enter the grounds, they would either need to duck under the rope or deal with the guards at the solitary entrance.

"I'm here to speak with Captain—" Before she finished the sentence, the guard snatched the cloak from her grasp.

"Thanks for returning the cloak. Only Spears inside the practice yard. No exceptions. Have a nice day."* He went back to talking to the other guards, clearly expecting the count and her retinue to move on.

The count stared at him, open mouthed.

Brother Qown realized Janel didn't resemble a noble or even

---

* That was abrupt. I'm offended on Janel's behalf.

a stallion. Her stained and patched clothing, combined with an unbrushed laevos and no jewelry, left little doubt as to her gender. Who would look at her and think her anything other than a mare?

"Hey now! Do you have any idea who this—?" Dorna stopped as Janel put her hand on the old woman's shoulders.

"I'm here to audition," Janel said.

"Auditions ended two weeks ago," the guard replied. "We're good now, thanks."

Ninavis chuckled and pulled her bow off her arm, stringing it. The guards didn't notice.

"I just need to speak with Captain Mithros."

He grinned at her. "Funny how all the pretty mares do."

She inhaled.

Brother Qown winced and reached out to her before she did something foolish. "Count—"

The guard waved a hand. "Go on, get off with you. He'll be out to say hello to his fans later. Right now, he's busy."

Ninavis snapped an arrow to her bow and fired.

The blasted arrow moved so fast Brother Qown didn't see much more than a blur, but he thought the arrow passed right before the guard's face, parted the raven feathers decorating the Black Knight's helmet, and then embedded itself, still quivering, in the central archery target on the far side of the compound.

Brother Qown later discovered it had been a perfect bull's-eye.

Then all hell broke loose.

Both Count Janel and Sir Baramon stopped, turned, and gave Ninavis an incredulous look.

Ninavis shrugged at them even as she lowered the bow and gave the guard a smug smile. "You're good here, huh?"

Janel's expression suggested she was struggling not to laugh.

"Are you out of your mind? Why, I'm going to—" But galloping interrupted whatever punishment the guard had in mind.

The Black Knight rode over.

This Black Knight didn't dress the fool, the way Sir Baramon had during the Mereina tournament. His ornate armor was embossed with scenes of ravens and screaming demons; he wore a black feather cloak. Still more feathers formed a crest that mimicked a horse's mane over his helmet—a feather version of a laevos. His black horse wasn't a fireblood, but still proved an impressive specimen.

Then the man removed his helmet, and Brother Qown saw the black went all the way down to the skin. His eyes were light green, but his skin and hair looked blacker than the raven feathers.

Brother Qown had grown so used to seeing Joratese parti-color flesh he didn't understand what he was seeing for a moment. Then he noticed the man's features weren't Quuros. Any Quuros, from either side of the Dragonspires.

He was vané. A Manol vané, to be specific, and that idea so startled Brother Qown, he could only stare in shock.

What was a Manol vané doing in Jorat?*

"Who shot that arrow?" The vané leaped off his horse and stalked in their direction.

"Captain, I'm sorry. I didn't think anyone would be stupid enough to—"

But Captain Mithros paid him no attention. His gaze raked over the group, paused a second to linger on Janel's face longer than anyone else's, and stopped cold at their wine-stain marked archer.

Ninavis waved her fingers at him.

He grinned then, a wide stretch of white teeth breaking the ebony dark of his face.

"Can you do that while riding a horse?"

As it happened, Ninavis could.

The whole camp stopped their training to watch. The Red Spears captain, Mithros, set up a series of targets along a

---

* Playing the Black Knight, obviously.

winding path so Ninavis would have to aim and fire even as she steered the horse he'd provided her.

Most importantly, Captain Mithros let the entire group inside the roped area to watch.

"Warning, ready, *go*!" Mithros waved a hand.

Ninavis urged her horse into a gallop.

Brother Qown hadn't seen this demonstrated at the Mereina tournament, although he had to assume it could've been included among the games. And Ninavis wasn't a native Joratese, but he couldn't tell by the way she rode; her control of the horse seemed effortless. She began pulling arrows from her quiver and loosing them at the targets. She made the bull's-eyes seem easy.

She rode past the end of the track, slowed, and turned the horse around to trot back to the group.

Applause filled the air. Metal changed between more than a few hands, proving yet again Joratese would take any excuse to wager, even on a complete unknown.*

Mithros laughed and then bowed as Ninavis dismounted. "I haven't seen shooting like that since the last time I was home. Marry me, beautiful woman. Our children will save the world."

Ninavis stared at him, blinking, looking more than a bit nonplussed as one of the Red Spears reclaimed his borrowed horse. She scowled and unstrung her bow. "You're a bit young for my taste.† Anyway, the count wants to talk to you." She nodded in Janel's direction. "If you're so keen to have me fighting under your banner for the tournament, you'll want to talk to her as well."

The man didn't seem much taken aback by her refusal, grinning all the wider. He didn't so much as glance at the rest, not even at Janel. "But where did you learn to shoot like that?"

---

* I must go back to Jorat once the dust settles. All I need is an accomplice, a bushel of peony seeds, and a black goat.

† Thus proving Ninavis has never paid any attention to god-king tales about the vané.

Ninavis narrowed her eyes. "My husband served in the army."

His expression turned thoughtful. "Quuros archers must have improved their skills since the last time I visited their training camps."

Janel walked over to Ninavis. "I cannot imagine Quuros training camps allowing a Manol vané to visit."

Brother Qown blinked. He'd have sworn the count would have no idea what a Manol vané looked like. He chided himself. Father Zajhera had spent three years treating her. Of course she wasn't ignorant.

For the first time, Janel caught Captain Mithros's attention. "You're assuming I ever ask permission—"

Count Janel crossed her arms over her chest and frowned at him.

"Mithros, you horny old ass, stop baiting the children and get yourself over here. You still owe me a hundred thrones from the last card game we played, and I mean to take it from your shiny black hair." Dorna grinned and wrinkled her face. "Plus, we need to talk somewhere private."

Mithros looked surprised. He tilted his head and stared at Dorna, then his eyes widened. "When did you become a woman?"

Dorna rolled her eyes. "Years ago, you clueless oaf. I told you I was visiting the Festival of the Turning—ack!"

Mithros ran over to Dorna, picked her up, and spun her around while giving her a hug. "I didn't recognize you! What happened?"

"Put me down, you sod, before I kick you so hard you never ride a horse again. What happened? I just told you—"

"No, I don't mean *that*. You're old!"

"Oh, you big fool," Dorna said, "it's been thirty years. Humans grow old."

Mithros took a step back, looking embarrassed. "So long as that? How the time passes." He smiled at her, gentle and sad. That smile implied a closer relationship than friends. But in all the time he'd known Dorna, she'd consistently maintained her preference ran for mares and mares alone. Except . . .

Brother Qown leaned over to the count. "Uh . . . did I hear her correctly?"

Janel paused, distracted, and looked over at him. "What part?"

"Dorna used to be a man? How's that possible?"

Janel blinked. "The Festival of the Turning Leaves. They hold it every year in Nivulmir, and Galava grants the suppli- cants' prayers. It's the reason Dorna wasn't at Lonezh Canton." She paused. "Do you do it differently in the west?"

Brother Qown blinked. "No! No, we don't do it at all. Ever."

Janel frowned. "Really? That's odd."

Sir Baramon cleared his throat and gave the Manol vané a half bow. "Sir Baramon, Captain. We met four years ago, at the tournament here in Atrine."

"Ah yes! Good to see you again. Where's your charming—" He paused while clasping Sir Baramon's shoulder. "I'm sorry. Was it recent?"

Sir Baramon nodded. "But thank you."

"Of course. It never stops hurting, to lose the ones we love." They shared a look.

Captain Mithros squeezed the man's arm once before letting go. "All right, everyone. Back to practice!" he bellowed, waving a hand at the archers. He then motioned for the entire group to follow him. "All right, you lot. You've convinced me. We do need to talk somewhere more private." He began heading toward the temple, his long strides forcing everyone into a trot to keep up.

"You're planning to talk to us inside a temple to one of the Eight?" Janel's tone sounded scandalized.

To be fair, Brother Qown felt a bit scandalized himself.

Mithros snorted. "It's not just a temple to one of the Eight; it's a temple to Khored." Mithros flashed Janel a smile. "Don't worry. I have permission to lurk about as much as I like."

Brother Qown felt a chill he couldn't quite explain.

They all followed the man into the God of Destruction's temple.

24: THE BLACK KNIGHT

Jorat Dominion, Quuros Empire.
Three days since property values in the harbor
district of the Capital City dropped precipitously

"Mithros," Kihrin said. "Huh." Then he grinned at Ninavis. "Did you take him up on his proposal?"

"No!" Ninavis said. "Don't be ridiculous. I'm not a brood mare who's going to spit out children for some ageless vané who likes to slum with mortals. Me? Married? I'm not doing that again." She leaned an elbow on the counter and grinned. "I mean, sure, I did have sex with him. I'm not *stupid*."

Kihrin stifled a laugh. "Oh no, I never thought you were."

Ninavis pursed her lips, her gaze far off for moment. "Oh yes. I recommend that, by the way. Find yourself a vané. Apparently, when you're a couple of thousand years old, you *learn* some stuff."

"If only he were female," Dorna said.

Janel started laughing. She laughed so hard she put her head down on the table.

"It's not that funny," Ninavis protested.

Janel raised her head, still grinning. "Oh, Nina, you have no idea."

Janel's Turn. The Green, Barsine Banner, Jorat, Quur.

I found it difficult to keep my expression placid. I hadn't taken Dorna's boast about knowing Captain Mithros seriously. Captain Mithros must have known my mother, Frena, who had started in tournaments under Dorna's tutelage. My parents had met during the tournaments.

Captain Mithros posed a different problem. His resemblance to Death's green-eyed son Teraeth seemed too close to be co-incidence. They clearly weren't the same person, but the similar-ity . . . Unlike Teraeth, Mithros favored broad grins and flirty winks. Yet when he waved a hand or rested his wrist against sword pommel the resemblance to Teraeth's lethal elegance shone. I felt a further familiarity too, as though Mithros reminded me of someone else besides.

Since I only knew one other Manol vané, I found the feeling disconcerting.

"Hells and ice. Keep your hood up." Dorna tugged the replacement cloak's hood farther over my eyes.

I blinked at her but ducked down my head.

No sooner had I done so than I saw red and gold. Looking from the corner of my eye, I saw an honor guard dressed in the Stavira March's colors.

The Markreev of Stavira's colors. My liege lord Aroth Malkoessian's colors.

Everyone in Atrine stopped by Khored's Temple at some point to pay their respects and pray for good favor in the tour-nament. The temple always echoed with the susurrus of worshippers.

I know dedicated gods of games and sport are worshipped in other dominions, but those were all once Marakori god-kings. Any Joratese would rather smear hot lead onto their feet than honor them. Some might say Taja—Goddess of Luck—would be more appropriate in such contests. But in Jorat we don't believe tournaments are won by luck. Thus, it is the custom to look to Khored as the patron of challenge, conflict, and contests.

Also, Khored was Emperor Kandor's patron god. Now he's ours as well.

Khored's Temple is awful. Awe-filled. Horse statues stand guard around the perimeter, while a red marble carving of swarming crows ascends or descends from the battlefield altar at its center. Incense smelling of blood and cinnamon filled the cathedral with fog. Light, red and violet, filtered through the stained-glass windows above.*

And Aroth Malkoessian, Markreev of Stavira, prayed at the main altar.

Dorna tugged at my elbow. "No, don't slow down. Don't stare."

I forced myself to keep walking and muttered a prayer under my breath to the Eight. I pushed down panic when I remembered Brother Qown wore a Vishai priest's distinctive robes. I reminded myself Aroth had never met Qown. The Markreev likely had no idea what a Vishai priest even looked like.

Regardless of one's destination inside the temple, everyone stopped at the altar first. No rule said I had to stop right next to Aroth. So I found a pillow farther back and went down on my knees as I offered the ritual prayers. Dorna picked a spot several seats away, and the others spread out farther so as not to draw any attention. Qown, I noticed, sat quite far away as if to distance himself from me in case his presence might betray my own. As I prayed, I saw Aroth stand from the front row, gather his soldiers to him, and turn to leave.

I breathed a sigh of relief.

A few seconds later, Dorna made a small, strangled sound as Aroth Malkoessian sat down on the cushion to my left.

All the air in the cathedral turned heavy and weighted, a thick morass allowing me to neither move nor breathe. My skin burned, and I didn't have to look to know Aroth's men surrounded us. Even here, they would be armed.

I didn't look at him. He didn't look at me. We gave each other no formal greeting.

"I wasn't convinced you would appear for the tournament."

"It's my duty."

"Given the circumstances surrounding your departure from Tolamer, your feeling toward duty has been in question."

"It's an odd situation," I said, trying hard not to grind my

---

* Blood and cinnamon? Yuck. That's not how you convince people to attend church.

teeth, "to be a canton's ruler yet own no land within it, not even one's ancestral castle."

"You have my condolences on your grandfather's passing," he murmured next to me. "He was a good man."

"And far too trusting," I agreed.

"He knew his place." His rebuke was unmistakable.

Clearly, I didn't know my place. Then again, Aroth had always felt my "place" was married to his son Oreth.

I would rather eat dung.

My fists clenched. "Perhaps because you never tried to force him into an unwanted marriage."

"Insolence is unbecoming."

"So is foreclosing on the liens of someone under your idorrá."

"Oreth would have returned those debts paid as a wedding gift."

"Was that supposed to be a comfort or a threat?"

He sucked in his breath, exhaled it as a low growl. "I've protected you in ways you can't understand."

I bit back on the impulse to say something rash. I wanted to say a great deal to the man. I wanted to ask how he'd managed to sire a creature as vile as his son Oreth. His older son, Ilvar, was as different from Oreth as night from day. I wanted to know why Aroth had betrayed my grandfather's trust.

I didn't ask. I'd already pushed further than decorum allowed. He'd be well within his rights to tether me right then.

I tilted my head, looking at him as much as I could without turning my face from the altar. "Oreth believes his right to command me is the natural order. He thinks he's the stallion and I should be the mare. That is not and never will be who I am."

He gave a hard look to the side, past me to where Dorna sat, not moving and barely breathing. "You should have gone to the Festival of the Turning Leaves, then."

Anger spilled into me, anger with Oreth, anger with his father, anger with my own grandfather for putting me in this situation. The Markreev's suggestion burned. Not because I had any problem with those who spent their year in the nature goddess Galava's service, in exchange for the gift that followed. If Dorna lived happier as a woman than as her birth sex, who was anyone to question it? If the Markreev had chosen to become male, that was his right too.

But I wished to remain female.

Whereas the Markreev seemed to think I could only be a stallion if my sex and gender matched. Suddenly, I understood where Oreth had acquired his vile opinions.

The pillow underneath my fingers started to feel warm.

No . . . no, no. Not here. Not now.

I inhaled and tried to calm myself. I prayed to Khored, chanting the Litany of Challenges under my breath.

I inhaled and closed my eyes, feeling a deep bitterness welling inside me. "How little you know your son, if you think changing my sex would change his need to control me."

"Oreth is very fond of you."

"And Oreth thinks his choice is the only choice that matters."

I heard Aroth stand. "That does not excuse your failure to meet your obligations—excuse me?"

I opened my eyes and looked up.

Mithros stood there, offering Dorna a hand up to her feet. "Apologies for losing you back there. Let me show you the way." As soon as Dorna steadied, he extended his hand to me.

Aroth Malkoessian narrowed his eyes. "I don't think you know who you're—"

Mithros met his eyes.

All the color fled the Markreev's face. "I—" His speech trailed off. He blinked several times.

Mithros stepped toward the Markreev. The mercenary captain seemed larger than he had been outside. Now he took up an enormous amount of space. A few feet separated the two men, but Aroth stepped back, as if Mithros stood far too close.

No one watched except for my people and Aroth's. Everyone else was lighting incense, saying prayers, or leaving flower wreaths around the necks of horse saints.

A soldier put a hand to his sword. The Markreev shook his head, and the man lowered his hand, sword undrawn.

Aroth paid me no attention. All his energy focused on Mithros. I had no idea what the Markreev was thinking or feeling, but his eyes were wide and fearful.

Mithros raised his hand. Aroth flinched but didn't move, and Mithros lowered it to the back of Aroth's neck, touching his forehead to Aroth's own. Mithros somehow turned the traditional greeting into something aggressive. Adversarial. A salutation between equals became an act of dominance. Aroth made a sound, but I couldn't tell what emotion lay behind it.

"Go," Mithros said as he released Aroth. The Markreev of Stavira stumbled back a few steps and uttered a swift apology as he stumbled over another penitent at prayer. He turned around. Motioning for his soldiers to follow him, he and his entire retinue left.

Aroth never looked at me.

Mithros turned back to me, smiling. "Sorry about that."

"Khored?" The word slipped out before I could stop myself, at once question, prayer, and statement. I had already met a god once that week. It didn't seem so impossible an idea I might meet another. I'd grown up on a thousand divine stories. Not one featured Khored as a black-skinned Manol vané.

But not one said he didn't look like such either.

The smile slipped a little from his face, but then returned and shone all the brighter for the lapse. "Please, call me Mithros. Come now. This way."

The others waited when Mithros led us to a back room, where a stairway stretched down under the temple. Priests of Khored also used the well-traveled passage, but they paid no attention to us. A few nodded or waved to Mithros as he passed.

When we left the main cathedral vault, Sir Baramon turned to me. "Was that Aroth Malkoessian? What happened? Are you all right?"

"I'm fine. He came to pray."

"But what—"

I shook my head. "We'll talk later."

The group fell into silence. Ninavis gave me several odd looks. She knew something had happened but hadn't been close enough to hear. Qown wore the air of a child ignoring his parents arguing.

And Mithros felt no need to provide any explanations at all.

He led us through a long underground complex used for housing and meditation chambers for the temple priests. Like the others, they paid us little mind.

By the time we reached the second staircase, I felt like a fool. How could I have let my overactive imagination get the better of me? I had witnessed an impressive demonstration of idorrá upstairs, but Mithros's race was immortal. Cowing Aroth hadn't required a god, just a man who was a thousand years old.

Plus, the priests didn't treat Mithros with any reverence. They all but rolled their eyes at him, like he was an old uncle who embarrassed everyone by telling lewd jokes at dinner. He was family, taken for granted.

Not how one treated a member of the Eight.

The second staircase debouched into a space so large its edges vanished into darkness. The air felt cold and moist. In the distance, I heard running water. This would have been quite normal for an estava, but Atrine had been built by a Quuros emperor. He wouldn't have made estavas or cellar homes. Indeed, as far as I knew, Atrine had no cellars. Not one. The stairs weren't designed for horses; even a fireblood would have balked at descending them.

Old stone blocks, massive but fitted, lined the floor. Small glowing lanterns illuminated the area, glowing whiter than candlelight or oil lanterns. Couches and tables filled an area similar to a tavern, manned by Red Spears, to judge by the armbands. They waved at Mithros and looked at us with interest before returning to more important activities: eating, drinking, gambling.

"Most people think this is a little oppressive, even for a people who prefer to build their homes underground," Mithros explained, "so the priests let us use the space. I find it helpful for talking in private. Now do you want to continue pretending I'm only interested in hiring your archer's services"—he motioned to Ninavis—"or do you want to explain what this is about?" He paused and smiled at Ninavis. "I should add the marriage offer is sincere."

Ninavis rolled her eyes.

"We need to talk in private." I cleared my throat and looked around. "At least, as privately as this allows."

"Everyone, show my guests a good time." Mithros pointed to the men and women at the bar. "Don't take too much metal from them at dice."

"Dice?" Dorna perked up. "Oh, I just couldn't. I'm terrible at dice."

"Oh hell," Mithros muttered. "She's going to rob them for every throne, chance, and chalice they have." He gestured toward another stairway leading even farther down into the darkness. "Shall we?"

My companions all wore bemused expressions, because I hadn't told them about my conversation with Thaena. They all thought I wanted to speak to Mithros about Ninavis, to gain a new place for us to stay—so why wouldn't I be willing to talk about it publicly?

I ignored the questions I saw in their faces and followed Mithros down the stairs.

The darkness didn't last long; he called up mage-lights to brighten our path. The stairs disgorged us onto a porch, lined with carved stone railings to keep people from going over the side. Rushing water sounded louder now, the air filled with fine, cold mist. The space felt homely; someone had set up bamboo mats and chairs and strung lights. A Zaibur board sat on a carved wooden table, pieces aligned on each side.*

---

* I need to visit this place. Given the number of stairs they descended, this has to be under Lake Jorat. I want to see how he's keeping back the water. Besides the obvious.

"How close are we to the falls?"

He gestured into the darkness. "Still another mile farther up. We wouldn't be able to hear each other talk if we sat closer. Would you like something to drink?"

"No, I—" I looked around. I didn't see any drinks to offer but stopped myself from asking. He may not have been a god, but I assumed he was a sorcerer.

I realized we had nothing in our legends to deal with vané magic. The Blood of Joras label didn't apply, but they could hardly be called tainted by Marakori blood either.

"I'm here because a mutual friend recommended you to me."

He sat down behind the Zaibur board and picked up the two starting stones, one wood and the other metal. "No one can hear us, so you might as well say what you mean. Thaena sent you to me because she wants something done, can't figure out how to do it herself, and thus wants me to solve the problem. Do you know how to play?" He held a stone in each hand before putting his hands behind his back.

"My grandfather taught me," I admitted. When he showed his hands, each clenched into a fist, I tapped the one on the left. "As for Thaena, I can't speak to the motives of gods."

He opened his hands. I'd picked the wooden token, which meant he went first. A lucky break for him. "I've known her a long time." His tone implied he wasn't a fan.

"Is Teraeth your son?" The question flew out of my mouth before I could stop it.

He blinked at me, mouth open. He abandoned whatever he'd been about to say. "You've met Teraeth?" He turned the board athwart so we'd be playing along the long edge.

I looked over the game pieces. Different sets used different pieces. This set included Khorsal, naturally, and anyone might assume a Joratese stallion would start there. So after a moment's hesitation, I picked the witch-queen Suless. "He must be related to you. I mean no offense when I say you resemble him. A son? A brother?"

He smiled as he made his selection, giving the matter no thought at all. He picked the god-king Nemesan, always a strong opener with a good offense. "Technically, he's my grandson."

"Technically? I would think he's either related to you or he's not."

He laughed with surprise. "I suppose so! Please don't misunderstand. I'm not ashamed of Teraeth. Just the opposite. In his last life, I favored him a great deal."

I felt a chill twine its fingers around my spine. "You knew who he was in his last life? How? I thought people lost all memories from prior lives when they're reborn?" I picked a dragon piece, pausing as I did.

I counted a total of eight dragon pieces. How had I never noticed? I wondered if they had once been named and if one of those names was Aeyan'arric.

"I wasn't reborn. He was." He pointed at me. "Just as you, also once part of Teraeth's life, were reborn." Seeing the look on my face, he grinned cruelly in a way that ruined all his normal prettiness. "Come now. Haven't you ever met someone with whom you shared a connection, even though it made no sense, even though you couldn't understand why? Someone you immediately distrusted or knew would run into a fire for you? Or you for them? It's not so hard to believe souls from one lifespan seek each other out in the next." He shrugged. "Or that the Eight might track certain souls from one life to the next."

I cleared my throat and looked away. I'd felt it with Teraeth, that immediate connection.

I'd also felt it with Relos Var, if not in so positive a manner.

"So what is it Thaena can't figure out on her own?"

"I need to steal a spear named Khoreval."

He stared at me like I'd just told him ice was hot. "Why?"

"Thaena thinks the spear is capable of killing Aeyan'arric." I felt the words come in a rush, almost a confession. "Relos Var has been sending the dragon into Jorat, having her attack towns. And while I know I can't go after Relos Var directly, I can attack his allies, tear down his supports. Without Aeyan'arric, it will be harder for him to—" I faltered. "Do whatever he's doing.* Thaena says that you can help me."

"Thaena lied."

I faltered, knocking a piece over. "What?"

The Manol vané man sighed. "You want me to help you infiltrate Duke Kaen's palace, yes?"

I blinked. I hadn't explained who had the spear. "Thaena said you would know how to do that."

"Technically true. But if she claimed I would help you, she lied. I won't."

"What? But—"

"It would be strategic and literal suicide for you. Perhaps a woman who controls the powers of death itself doesn't understand what that really means anymore." He began placing his pieces down on the board.

I narrowed my eyes at him. "Has Teraeth spoken to you about this?"

"He told you not to do it? I like this incarnation already. You might want to place your pieces on the board."

"What? Damn—" I blushed as I realized I'd been too busy debating him to play the game. I hurried to try to keep up.

Mithros gave me a wry grin. "You're young and gifted, and very much your mother's daughter, but don't make the same mistake Thaena's making. The same mistake she *keeps* making: don't underestimate Relos Var."

"I'm not. I know he's dangerous."

"Oh. You know he's dangerous. Good start." He moved his piece first, immediately pinning my piece against the adamant. "To infiltrate Duke Kaen's palace, you'll need Relos Var's approval. He'll have to believe he's recruiting you—that you've

---

* Ah, the mind-set of the so-called Destined Hero. We need to stop so-and-so. Why? Because he's . . . he's . . . I mean, he's a bad guy! Why? Because I don't like him, that's why.

Save me from fools and would-be "heroes."

switched sides. But he'll never accept your defection at face value. He'd be a fool to do so, and we've already established Relos Var is no fool. So what prevents him from just gaeshing you?"

I stopped dead.

Again, I felt a chill.

"He'll chain your soul," Mithros said. "Why not? There's zero reason for him to assume your loyalty. But he can make it impossible for you to disobey him. For you to convince Relos Var he doesn't need to gaesh you would require a truly vile demonstration of loyalty. One so awful you wouldn't be able to live with yourself afterward. He'd accept nothing less. Maybe those who serve him don't start out as monsters, but they all end up that way."*

I fought down panic and the desire to lash back, to scream he was wrong, that I could somehow stop Relos Var from gaeshing me.

What if he wasn't wrong?† The true foolishness would be to go into the situation without considering Mithros might be right.‡

"You may have a point," I said. I captured a piece, but it felt like a small and insignificant win.

"Then I can't help you, and you shouldn't want me to." He leaned back in his chair. "Now if you want to join the Red Spears, I'm happy to have you. Oh, and that Marakori woman too. She shoots well enough to be Diraxon."

I cleared my throat and let the comment pass. "I said you may have a point. But I know Relos Var doesn't believe in the same rules we Joratese do. He's been using that against us. You think I should leave him alone, but I don't think he's going to leave *me* alone. He's already recruited someone to his side for no other reason than their animosity to me. I've captured his interest."

* Now that's just rude.
† He is.
‡ He's not.

His lips thinned. "Regrettable."

"Thaena thinks he won't hurt me."

"Thaena won't be the one dead or gaeshed if she's wrong. And while I agree he'd recruit you if he thought your loyalty sincere—"

"Then this could work—"

"Don't underestimate his ability to discern the truth.* Lying to him is seldom successful, and once he catches you out, he'd twist you until you're unrecognizable."

I swallowed and looked away. "I saw what he did to Tamin."

"And Tamin didn't lie to him."

"Relos Var's arrogant," I said, turning back. "Arrogant enough to think he can corrupt me. He thinks he's smarter than everyone else."

"He *is* smarter than everyone else."†

"Fine. Even if that's true, sooner or later, our strengths always become our weaknesses. This can be used against him. I know how dangerous this is, but I refuse to back down just because it's hard."

He started to say something and then stopped.

"Please. I need your help."

"Name some other boon."‡

I stood and began pacing, feeling the despair like a heavy weight around my middle. I had assumed this man would serve Thaena or some other member of the Eight, that he would be cooperative.

He was anything but cooperative.

Still, I had been granted another boon. I would be foolish not to use it.

I turned back to him. "Can you sneak me into the tournament? I would at least wish to warn the duke. Someone has to."

* Good thing Qown hadn't had a chance to tell her about the Name of All Things yet.

† It's nice to be recognized, isn't it?

‡ "Name a boon . . . no, not *that* one. Nor that one. Nope, not that one either. Okay, fine, I'll tell you what boon I'm going to give you."

He made a face. "That won't work the way you think either."

"Can you gain me admission or not?" I felt my temper starting to slip.

Mithros sighed. "Oh, I can sneak you in. I'm just a little worried about how you're going to get yourself out."

I lifted my chin. "That's my problem."

25: The Marakori Slums

Jorat Dominion, Quuros Empire.
Three days since the Crown and Scepter totally failed to
protect not one but two Quuros emperors

Ninavis turned to Janel. "Did I sleep with Khored or not?"

Janel held up her hands. "You don't want me to spoil the surprise, do you?"

"Oh gods," Ninavis growled. "You *are* a demon."

Dorna chortled. "I bet you said that to Khored too."

Then the old woman ducked as Ninavis swung at her.

Kihrin poured a glass of aris and handed it to Ninavis.

"Thank you," Nina said. She looked over at Brother Qown and stage-whispered, "Save me."

Brother Qown smiled as he picked up his journal. Then the smile faded as he looked at it for a moment before closing it again. "I'm going to skip ahead a bit, if you don't mind. I mean the interesting stuff happens at the tournament."

"Oh no," Janel said. "I never did hear about what happened to you while we were training."

The priest cleared his throat and opened his book again. "Very well."

Qown's Turn. Marakori slums, Atrine, Jorat, Quur.

Count Janel, Sir Baramon, and Ninavis spent the next two weeks learning to blend in with the Red Spears and training to pass in the tournaments. Easy enough. Ninavis possessed an undeniable talent for archery, mounted on horseback or otherwise. Sir Baramon, while too old to excel in the tournament itself, proved an excellent coach. Dorna too offered advice to performers. She also managed to unearth every single game of chance to be found anywhere in the camps, walking away with a tidy sum.

But Brother Qown's services were unneeded.

The priest began visiting the Marakori slums.

Some social mixing occurred between the Joratese and Marakori, but not nearly enough to soften relations between the two groups. The Joratese considered their southern neighbors to be an intruding herd. They also seemed convinced every single Marakori practiced witchcraft in secret, stole babies, summoned demons. The Joratese treated the Marakori accordingly.

Now if the Marakori had banded together for their mutual defense . . . but the Marakori didn't even consider themselves Marakori, let alone united.

Most of them lived in hovels built on the bridge, using materials they'd brought with them. Or they purchased materials from whatever enterprising merchant had brought building supplies by the wagonload and traded them for family heirlooms. Most Marakori wouldn't talk about why they'd left Marakor. When they did, they cursed the Royal Houses and spat to the side.

No one talked about going back home.

"How did you break the arm?" Brother Qown asked a teenage boy as he applied an herb plaster. The boy's coloring was typical: dark brown skin with dark auburn hair.

The boy didn't say a thing. He just stared at Brother Qown.

"Damn Agari bastards did it," his mother spat. "His father's gone out with my brothers to make it right."

Brother Qown hesitated. "You mean break their bones too?"

The flat stare she gave the priest suggested he was being naïve. But she just said, "Thank you. We have a hard time finding help these days. Too many people claiming they can cure anything when they're just peddling grass and river water."

"Yes, I would imagine that's a problem."

"Demons take them. It's not right. Anyway, I—" She paused, hearing something.

A pot of burning oil crashed through the open window.

The wood caught. The mother started screaming. Brother Qown grabbed the boy by his good arm and started to lead him outside, but as he did, two arrows slammed into the wooden lintel.

They couldn't go that way.

Fortunately (if it could be called that), the hovel proved less a house than a balanced hill of rubble. The mother (Brother Qown had never learned her name) kicked a hole through the planking, and they all crawled out. Mother and son took off running.

Brother Qown started to follow them.

Started.

He heard a shoe scuff behind him. A sharp pain exploded at the back of his head.

He didn't remember anything else.

Brother Qown heard voices, shouting.

He kept his eyes closed and pretended to be unconscious.

Really, just one voice. "Have you lost your little mind? You can't just kill a priest! Do you have any idea what the duke's men will do when they find out?"

A second voice. "Oh, quit your complaining. He ain't dead, just knocked around a bit. Tell him how he can't be going around cutting into our business, and then we'll send him on his way."

"No, you idiot. We don't have any choice now. We're going to have to—"

Qown heard a rattle, followed by two more. Then a sound like someone dropping a large book.

A second thud followed.

Brother Qown tried to reach Illumination. If he could, he'd be able to see without opening his eyes, without revealing he'd woken. He needed all his concentration. He needed—

A hand tapped Brother Qown on the shoulder.

"Come on, priest," Ninavis said. "Let's go."

Brother Qown opened his eyes.

Ninavis crouched over him. She wore a cloth wrapped around her hair and face—very similar to the bandit mask she'd worn the first day they'd met. A hanging oil lamp cast shadows against the walls of a rough-hewn shack, while the Three Sisters' light streamed in through the window. Two tough-looking men lay on the ground holding their heads or privates while they moaned.

Brother Qown took her hand and let her pull him to his feet.

"How did you find—"

"Later, holy man. This isn't safe." She pushed him out the front door, where the priest saw several more people, two men and a woman, in similar moaning states. Ninavis and Brother Qown made their way back out to the main street, lit by celestial light or the occasional lamp too near a window.

Ninavis led. She wasn't armed; her bow and arrows had been left behind. Of course, she didn't need such weapons.

"I don't understand why those people—"

"Classic scam, priest," Ninavis said. "They come through selling healing spells to the Marakori, because none of these poor bastards can afford the prices the House D'Mon Blue Houses charge. Which means you were undercutting their profit margins."

"Were they really physickers—" Brother Qown looked behind him, but Ninavis tugged on his sleeve to keep him focused.

"Don't be stupid." She sighed and led him down a back alley. Someone had piled up some boxes and nailed together wood to look like rubbish. Instead, it acted as a ladder. She showed him the way up, which scraps supported weight and which to avoid. Finally, they emerged on a ragged shanty roof. Brother Qown swooned as he realized how close they stood to the edge of the bridge, with an endless drop below them as water poured over Demon Falls.

"Careful now," she said, taking his arm.

"Where are we going?"

"Just sit here awhile." She made herself comfortable on the roof, leaning against what might very well have been an impromptu chimney.

Even as she said the words, Brother Qown heard a commotion down on the streets below. A large crowd with torches began to surge through the streets. Conversations drifted their way, including words like *healer* and *he can't have gone far.*

A search party was looking for him.

"Would you like to know the secret of the Diraxon?" Ninavis asked softly.

Qown blinked in surprise. "I . . . what?"

She must have taken that as a yes, because she continued speaking, her voice so soft that if Qown had been a foot farther away, he'd have heard nothing. "The secret of the Diraxon is that we don't exist. Not really. We are a clan made up of the rejects and outcasts of every clan. The Diraxon take in the people no one else wants. The babies with cleft palates or ill-omened birthmarks, too many fingers or not enough, club legs or bent spines. Marakori know if they don't want to keep a babe, they can leave it by the edge of the Kulma Swamp and that child will just . . . vanish. Claimed by the Diraxon, the ghosts of the Kulma, who raise their foundlings on a steady diet of darkness, death, and vengeance."

"Oh," Qown said. He felt a mixture of sadness and revulsion. Sadness for the abandoned children; revulsion for the people who had left them to die. "And then you're trained to be killers."

"Yes. Hated, feared, and always, always in high demand." Ninavis's gaze was far away. "I left before the Lonezh Hellmarch. I was done with killing. I lost my taste for it. Unfortunately"—she waved a finger at the slums—"these people haven't figured out what I did: that the rest of the world wants us feuding and fighting. And the Hellmarch just made it worse."

"I don't understand, though. The Hellmarch has been over for years."

"The Hellmarch was just an excuse to target us." She shrugged. "The perfect opportunity. After all, we started it, didn't we? So House D'Aramarin opened the gates and then House D'Erinwa swept through entire towns. They snapped up anyone they could find, put them to Murad's shackles—made them slaves—whether they'd committed crimes or not. Stocking the House D'Knofra plantations with slave labor is a whole lot cheaper than paying farmers for their crops. Profits galore and no sign of it stopping. I bet you metal within twenty years any Marakori born to slave parents will be a slave from the start."

"Slavery isn't inherited." Brother Qown felt sick to his stomach just thinking about the idea.

"Aren't you adorable? It's not hard to force the issue. Lots of ways to do it. And it's so profitable for the Royal Houses. House D'Erinwa sells the slaves. House D'Knofra runs the farms and harvests the crops. That brings in supplies for House D'Kard to turn into useful trade goods. And since House D'Aramarin specializes in transport, they make metal for every shipment that passes through one of their gates. So clans who ran from the Hellmarch start hearing what's waiting for them if they come back. They go farther north until they're in Jorat, but Jorat doesn't want anything to do with them. Then they hear that rumor. You know the one; there's a whole city at the top of Demon Falls sitting vacant most of the year. So they drag their asses over here and find out it's not quite as empty as they'd been led to believe. And the Joratese don't like Marakori, do they? Being invaded by all these refugees, who start fighting each other as soon as they put down roots, just convinces the fine citizens of Atrine their prejudices are justified."

Brother Qown caught his breath as men walked down the alley where they'd taken shelter. They had torches and clubs, but nothing edged or bladed.

Ninavis put her hand on his shoulder and squeezed.

As the people looked around, Brother Qown realized the torches made them blind. If Brother Qown and Ninavis didn't move, the crowd couldn't see them.

Assuming no one found the ladder.

A man saw it and started to climb, but as he did, Qown heard shouts and hoofbeats. The whole group scattered, racing back out to the main streets as soldiers wearing the duke's colors raced by, shouting.

"I saw how upset you were," Ninavis whispered as she watched the men go, "when you saw the duke's people kill that man on the bridge. I don't know whether he had it coming, but I know my people deserve better than to be run down like dogs. I shouldn't have to pretend to be Joratese to be treated right. I don't think Janel really understands. You do. At least, you're trying."

"There must be something we can do. Some way we can convince them to stop fighting each other."

"Yeah, I've been wondering about that," Ninavis mused. "I used to think it would be impossible. That we Marakori would never give up our feuds, but I'm not so sure anymore. Symbols can be so powerful. All the clans have always known that, but we all had our own special symbols, our own god-kings, to wrap around ourselves and use to feel special. We flocked to those. Hell. The Joratese are really just another Zaibur Basin god-king clan, when you think about it. What we really need is a symbol we can all rally to. Something more than Joratese, Diraxon, Agari, or any of the rest."

"But what?"

Ninavis shrugged and grinned. "Not sure yet. If you figure anything out, let me know." She hopped to her feet. "Come on. The mob should be down the street by now. Let's get you back to the pasture."

26: THE GREAT TOURNAMENT OF CHALLENGES

Jorat Dominion, Quuros Empire.
Three days since Teraeth failed to kill a mimic

Janel looked Ninavis in the eyes. "I really am trying to understand, you know."

The older woman shrugged. "Yeah, I know. But at the time . . ."

"I had no idea what the Royal Houses were doing in Marakor," Kihrin said.

"Why would you?" Ninavis traded out her liquor for more water. "It's not like the Royal Houses are going to walk around saying, 'Hey, did you know we're trying our damnedest to enslave an entire dominion? *So* much profit to be made. It's working out really well for us.'"

Dorna chuckled. "At least, it *was*."

Janel nodded. "There's that. Pity people keep disappearing off the plantations. So unfortunate."

Kihrin stopped and looked at the three women. "Wait. What are you . . . what are you saying?"

"That depends," Ninavis said. "How loyal are you to House D'Mon?"

"I'm not," Kihrin said. "Believe me, there's no love lost there." He paused a minute, frowning. "Although it occurs to me I should at some point check to see if I'm Lord Heir or if Galen is . . ." Kihrin shrugged. "Doesn't matter. I'm not returning."

"Okay, so what we're doing is—" Nina paused as Janel put her hand on the other woman's.

"Not so fast. I think our new friend needs to hear about my meeting with Duke Xun first." Janel threw Kihrin a smile that flirted with apology but made no firm commitments.

Kihrin leaned back and crossed his arms over his chest. "Be my guest."

Janel's Turn. The Green, Atrine, Jorat, Quur.

"Did you find Brother Qown?" I said as Ninavis entered the tent. I put a hand down to my waist, fighting down nausea. "Please tell me he's well."

Ninavis threw herself down into a chair, cocking her head to the side to look at me as Dorna continued fussing over the feathered cloak and headdress. "He's fine. Got himself into a spot of trouble with charlatans, who didn't like him cutting into their profits. So Mithros is letting you take his place as the Black Knight?"

"This is the easiest way to gain access to the palace. Dorna, this cloak is too heavy. I feel like I'm suffocating."

"Ain't the cloak, foal. That's nerves." Dorna gave me a knowing look. "Your mother used to be the same way. Threw up before every show, she did."

I felt queasy. Of course. The last time, I'd been focused on fighting, on Dedreugh. This was so much worse.

"Your mother used to perform in the shows?" Ninavis looked intrigued.

"Yes," I said, still hoping to keep the meager porridge I'd been able to force down. "That's how she—" I paused and cleared my throat.

"That's how her parents, Frena and Jarak, met," Dorna said, "and how Janel's mother met me." She thumped her chest. "I helped train her."

Ninavis eyed me. "So you're upholding a family tradition."

I sat down and concentrated on my breathing. "It's only for today. When the duke leaves his box to go to dinner, I'll be waiting for him."

"Be careful," Ninavis said, all levity gone.

I stood up again, aware my cloak flapped around me like a giant crow as I let my restless energy get the better of me. Still, the thick worry in Ninavis's voice stopped me with a sudden insight.

I looked at her and wondered just when Ninavis had become my woman. Any promises to Kalazan had been kept weeks ago. She bore no onus to look after my people, to help with my quests, to care about my safety. And she wasn't Joratese, which meant any lingering herd instinct to stay—because she'd nowhere else to go—didn't motivate her.

She stayed because she wanted to.

I wondered if Ninavis realized she'd switched her loyalties, but had she ever had any? Kalazan had been her man, not the reverse. Her loyalty to him had been idorrá loyalty, not thudajé.

She squinted at me. "Now don't look at me like I just cursed your favorite horse. I just think you're walking into a jaguar's den, for all he's your duke. *Be careful.*"

I shook myself and grabbed the feather-plumed helmet from the tent-side table. "I will. Don't worry—" My eyes widened as a thought occurred to me. "Dorna, they'll recognize Arasgon—"

Dorna waved a hand. "Nothing about this will kick back to you. I dyed his legs; Mithros spelled his eyes. He's a handsome black stallion right now. Beautiful and larger than most, but nothing special. Borrowed the saddle and kit from the Red Spears. As long as Arasgon keeps his mouth shut and doesn't go shouting his name to anyone who will listen, he'll be fine."

I breathed deep and tried to calm myself. "Thank you."

Dorna put a hand on my back and shoved me toward the tent opening. "Now be off with you. You've a crowd to entertain."*

*

---

* Oh yes, that's how to combat stage fright: remind them exactly how many people are about to watch them fall on their face. Whose side is Dorna on, anyway?

The day passed quickly.

The tournament started with grand spectacle: knights, contestants, and entertainers all parading through the city before entering the tournament grounds. Joratese filled every stand and rooftop with enough height to see the contests. Enterprising souls rented spaces on sky bridges to those unfortunates who hadn't managed to find themselves seats in the stands.

The tournament contestants wore riotous colors to proclaim the hues of their sponsors, their homes, and any businesses whose interests they'd been paid to represent. The next week of fighting would decide a great deal: business contracts and commodity prices and even the guilt or innocence of accused criminals. No one in Jorat would do any significant business without first establishing the respective idorrá and thudajé for all involved parties. The most civilized way to establish those parameters was through the contests.*

Everyone watched and cheered and drank. Fights broke out both inside and outside the tournament grounds. Jorat's finest artists had sculpted the lacquered armor worn by the knights into fantastic shapes—jaguars and elephants, monkeys and parrots. Such armor gave way more easily than its metal equivalent, so broken bones often took knights out of the competition.

I had a hard time watching the tournament without remembering Sir Xia Nilos and her squire, dead by Dedreugh's blade. Or Mereina's people, choked to death on blue smoke.

But no, that wasn't relevant here. Atrine was Jorat's capital. Even if Jorat frowned on magic, every noble had brought their Gatekeepers. Every priest of the Eight attended. No witch could try Senera's trick without being caught.†

So Arasgon and I played with the crowd and pretended to be black-clad jesters while we passed the time. Finally, the

---

* And the Joratese wonder why the rest of the empire considers them barely more civilized than Yorans.
† I could. I totally could.
  Just saying.

evening sun set behind the eastern mountain, and the duke waved his goodbyes to the crowds as his court rose to go inside.

I knew they would be headed to the parties: eight evenings of dancing, drinking, and merriment to match the daytime festivities.*

I quelled my envy and disappointment. This would have been my first Great Tournament after coming of age. My first opportunity to show myself in splendor as Count of Tolamer, to parade before my peers and revel in dancing and accolades.

No one stopped me as I made my way to the corridor I had chosen for my ambush. I had once used it as a child to lie in wait for the duke—the current duke's father—who rewarded such ambushes with sugar candies. I stood there, acting like a bored knight awaiting orders.

All my plans would be for naught if the duke took another passage.

Footsteps told me I had guessed correctly. And as they drew close, I pulled the helmet off my head. I tucked it under an arm and stepped out from around the corner.

Foran Xun, Duke of Jorat, had gained his title young—like me he'd lost his father in the Lonezh Hellmarch. His mother, Pyna, walked just after her son, dressed in rich brown robes, only technically obeying mare propriety. Foran himself was a beautiful mahogany color, with a white laevos and light-kissed hands.

His brown eyes widened in surprise as he saw me ahead in the hallway. His soldiers, armed and armored in real metal rather than lacquered leather or reed, seemed no less surprised . . . but a great deal less pleased.

"My duke." I crouched down to the floor even as guards drew their weapons. "Please hear my plea."

Footsteps toward me.

How he reacted to this would tell me if he had been poisoned against me. I tensed, even made ready to run.

* Sounds exhausting.

"Wait. Janel Danorak? From Tolamer? I haven't seen you in years." He sounded surprised. Then he began to laugh. "No, no, she's fine. Leave her be."

They did not leave me be, but the guards respectfully helped me to my feet.

"Look how she's grown," Pyna Xun murmured to her son. "So lovely, but we must get her in a different color. She looks like a Black Knight dressed so." She laughed at the ridiculous idea.

I breathed deeply and kept my eyes to the ground. "My duke, I would speak with you about Barsine Banner."

"Barsine? Barsine . . . Mother, why does that sound familiar?"

"The witches, dear."

"Right! Yes, the witches." Duke Xun snapped his fingers. "And you attended, didn't you? By the Eight, that must have been hideous. Walk with us. You're coming to the party tonight? I'm told the chefs have made a life-sized stallion from rice flour and corn silk. I'm so excited."

I glanced up at the duke in surprise, unable to stop myself. While his knowledge of the disaster reassured me, he'd given far more importance to the party.

"Sorry to hear about your grandfather," the duke continued, "although I can't say I'm surprised. He was so old. Wasn't he, Mother?"

"Oh, quite so. But very loyal."

"I suppose. He always made me feel like I had food caught in my teeth," the duke admitted. "I bet he makes Thaena straighten her dress in the Afterlife. Was he very strict with you?" He didn't look back at me, so it took a second to realize I'd been addressed.

"Uh . . . I admit I didn't find him so, my duke."

"Of course. You were all the family he had left, after all. Probably let you get away with all manner of things. You did bring a different outfit, I hope? That armor's just fantastic for the tournaments, but it's not going to work at all for the feast. People are going to think you're a mare if you don't wear any jewelry."

"I hoped I might speak to you about Barsine first—"

"Oh, of course. I mean, someone shows up and wipes out an entire town, during a tournament no less . . . I have to pay attention, don't I? We can't have that happening again."

I exhaled and felt tension leave me as we walked down the hallways. "Yes, my duke. I quite agree."

"Fortunately, I have been briefed on the situation and have everything under control. It won't be a problem."

"That's wonderful, my duke. The baron told you what happened?"

"No, no. I have a letter from the new baron, but I haven't had the pleasure of meeting him in person yet. No, a survivor made it here to the city and explained everything. Wonderful fellow. I'm thinking I might keep him around, even if he isn't Joratese."

We came to the hallway's end, where soldiers waited before ornate double doors. They saluted at the duke's approach and then opened the doors for him.

"He isn't Joratese?" I had a moment's puzzlement. Even as the doors swung open, I realized the only person he could be describing. The bottom dropped from my stomach.

"My duke," said Relos Var, sweeping into a deep bow. "I'm so pleased to see you."*

* And Father Zajhera said it's young people who are dramatic. Ha!

27: Hunting the White Hind

Jorat Dominion, Quuros Empire.
Three days since Darzin D'Mon got what he deserved

"Seriously?" Kihrin threw Janel a flat glare. "You're stopping there? Nina's right; you *are* a monster."

Janel just laughed as she reached for her water. "But I'm so parched." She saluted him with the glass. "Anyway, at least I can laugh about it now. I didn't find it funny at the time."

"Wait," Ninavis said. "I thought—" She shook her head in pure wonderment. "Is there any noble this side of the Dragonspires whose ear that bastard wasn't whispering in?"

Qown shook his head. "Not really."

"The Duke of Marakor?" Kihrin offered.

"There hasn't been a Duke of Marakor since the Lonezh Hellmarch," Janel said. "And no one on Quur's High Council—you know, the one owned by the Royal Houses?—seems to be in a real rush to replace him *for some reason.*"

Kihrin shook his head. "So that's what Mithros meant when he said he didn't think you'd have much success warning Duke Xun. Because of Relos Var."

"Maybe," Janel said. "But there is another possible explanation."

"Oh?"

Janel shrugged. "Duke Xun's a fool, without the wisdom to realize standing outside during a storm results in getting wet?"

"Ah," Kihrin said. "So no thudajé for him, then?"

"It's hard to hold thudajé for someone when you think a

horse would do a better job." Janel raised a finger. "Not a fireblood. A horse."

"Now I really want to hear how your meeting went."

Qown cleared his throat. "Except it's my turn."

Kihrin leaned against the counter. "Right. Sorry."

Qown's Turn. The Green, Atrine, Jorat, Quur.

"Ah, now that's some nice metal," Mare Dorna said as she counted out the coins into her hand.

Brother Qown blinked at her. She'd been counting a different coin purse earlier. This purse matched the bodice of a woman with whom Dorna had left earlier.

"That's not—" Brother Qown paused and cleared his throat. "She gave you a gift?"

Dorna's grin was best described as lascivious. "She appreciated my lesson."

"What lesson would she have paid—?" Brother Qown held up a hand. "Never mind. Please forget I asked. I'm quite sure I don't want to know."*

She cackled at him.

Ninavis left the priest in Dorna's care like a stray puppy returned home, before returning to help the Red Spears with their contests. Sir Baramon had vanished to renew his own contacts within the tournament circuit, and Janel continued to prance as the Black Knight. That left Brother Qown alone with Dorna, who roamed the tournament, treating it as a movable feast, a banquet of larceny, liquor, and lust to feed her considerable appetites.

Brother Qown sometimes thought she performed her antics to shock him.

A low, appreciative whistle from Dorna drew his attention back to her. Brother Qown followed her stare. Predictably, she was ogling a woman passing on a sky bridge.

---

* You and me both, friend.

If the Joratese liked to compare themselves to horses, then the subject of Dorna's attention was a white stallion. Not that coloring called "gray," which looks white only when full grown, but true white. The sort of white where the foal usually dies. This woman displayed a whiteness of skin and hair anathema to sunlight, stretched thin to translucence over a ripe body. She dressed like royalty, not following the Jorat fashions but dressing as men do in the Capital. She sported a tight, high-necked, gray silk misha over silvery velvet kef pants, tucked into high boots. Diamonds sparkled against her lustrous agolé like snowflakes falling at winter's twilight. The soldiers who walked with her, as an honor guard, seemed more than capable of ensuring no one could do more than look and envy.*

Then she turned her head, and Brother Qown saw her face.

"Dorna!" Brother Qown grabbed the old woman by the arm. "Dorna, it's the Doltari woman from Mereina. That's Senera!"

"Oh? Well, nobody told me she was smuggling *all* the damn melons in the garden under her bodice."† Dorna finished tucking her purse away. "I never got a good look at her last time."

"She dressed less scandalously last time."

"She's dressed like a stallion, but I wouldn't call it a scandal."

Brother Qown craned his neck to stare after the witch. "We have to follow her."

"You don't have to tell me twice." Dorna handed her mug to a man next to her. "Hold this, would you?" She grabbed Brother Qown's arm and dragged him from the stands.

Brother Qown would have never been able to follow Senera on his own. He had no idea how to get from the tournament stands to those labyrinthine skyways where they'd seen the woman pass. Fortunately, Dorna knew Atrine as if she were born here (which, for all Brother Qown knew, might have been the case) with all its shortcuts and back-alley skypaths.

---

* That was uncomfortable to read. Flattering? But really, I wouldn't have thought Qown ran with mares.

† Melons? What is she talking about—oh. Never mind.

Senera, for her part, proved easy to track. Her white hair glowed like a beacon in the distance. Just when Brother Qown thought they'd lost her, they would catch a glimpse of agolé or her soldier escorts and be on the trail once more.

Brother Qown yelped as Dorna pulled him back behind a corner. He realized the problem right away: he'd been so intent on following Senera he'd stopped paying attention to where she'd led them.

The Markreev of Stavira's compound.

He swallowed as he saw Stavira soldiers in red and gold patrolling the grounds. Nobody looked alert. The soldiers seemed more interested in the cheering crowds, jealous of a tournament they couldn't attend. But Brother Qown felt certain they would become vigilant immediately should the need arise.

Dorna tugged on Brother Qown's sleeve. Senera was approaching the main azhock. To Qown's surprise, a Malkoessian noble waited to greet her: Sir Oreth, no less.

Sir Oreth greeted Senera warmly. Brother Qown suspected Relos Var had wasted little time putting Sir Oreth in touch with Senera; they had clearly met before.

"There's no guards around back," Dorna whispered.

"Dorna, it's not safe. We should go back and tell Count Janel."

"Wait for it . . ."

Across the compound, a Stavira knight returned from his turn at the lists. His armor looked disheveled. A giant faux bird wing at his shoulder had broken, dragging across his fireblood's back.

Then the saddle's girth strap broke.

The knight, already top-heavy, did what one might expect in these circumstances: he fell. Brother Qown assumed the fireblood cried for help from those nearby. The guards came running.

Mare Dorna moved.

Brother Qown didn't dare protest lest he draw the guard's attention.

In the confusion, Dorna found a spot for them behind the main azhock Senera and Sir Oreth had entered, behind haystacks and rice wine barrels. She leaned in toward the tent, intending to eavesdrop, and waved for Brother Qown to do likewise. He did, praying to Selanol they wouldn't be discovered.

"I can't hear anything," Mare Dorna whispered. "Can you?"

Brother Qown listened. The knight who'd lost his saddle (how had Dorna accomplished that?) didn't seem worse for wear, judging by the quality and heat of his cursing. The guards began returning to their posts. He heard nothing from inside the azhock itself.

"Maybe they're, uh, you know—" He blushed.

"That makes noise too, priest," Mare Dorna admonished.

"Maybe they're sneaking up on the eavesdroppers," Senera suggested from behind them.

Brother Qown turned.

Senera and Sir Oreth both stood there. Sir Oreth had his sword drawn, as did the half dozen soldiers behind them. Sir Oreth was staring at Mare Dorna with a murderous expression.

Senera smiled. "We have a lot to talk about. Won't you both come inside?"

28: Accusations of Witchcraft

Jorat Dominion, Quuros Empire.
Three days since Thaena found a loophole in the
Quuros emperor selection process

"Not you too," Kihrin told Brother Qown as the man paused to take a drink.

Qown smiled. "I'm parched."

Janel laughed and reached over to bump her forearm against Qown's.

"Oh yeah, I see how it is," Kihrin said. He turned to Ninavis. "So what have you been up to, then?"

"Oh, rebelling against the empire. Working to tear down the Royal Houses." Ninavis smiled. "You know, the usual."

Kihrin realized she wasn't joking. "How's that going?"

"Honestly? Not bad, but the moment the empire decides to take us seriously, we're going to be in for a rough time. They don't play nice." Ninavis turned to Janel and slapped her hand on the wood bar. "Come on. I want to hear what happened next too."

"Right," Janel said, taking a deep breath. She stopped smiling and began to talk.

Janel's Turn. The duke's palace, Atrine, Jorat, Quur.

My focus on Relos Var meant I didn't notice the other person in the room, at first. The other person was kneeling at Relos Var's feet, head bowed and on all fours. They were covered by a hooded cloak, so I couldn't see details.

"Had any luck with the questioning?" the duke asked Var as he stepped forward. He showed no fear at all, no hint he stood before someone dangerous.

Someone whom Thaena herself had said she couldn't stop.

"Oh yes, very much so," Relos Var answered, but he barely glanced at Duke Xun. His eyes slid right past him and settled on me. "Janel Danorak. How my heart sings at your presence. I never doubted you'd survive."

"Yes, isn't it wonderful?" The duke clapped his hands together. "I met her out in the hall. She's just as worried as we are about the witches, Var. I thought she might appreciate seeing all the work you've done to ferret out their coven."

"I'm sure she's thinking of nothing else," Relos Var agreed. He put a hand on the man kneeling next to him and met my stare.

His idorrá hadn't lessened in the slightest since the day I'd met him in Mereina. I still found myself tempted to flinch, to look away, to bow. And the look in his eyes . . .

I find it difficult to explain. The smile on his face shone through in his eyes too, but it was a secret smile: Relos Var sharing a fine joke whose punch line Duke Xun would never be able to interpret.

In that instant, I knew. Relos Var knew *I* knew. He understood that I had come there to point the finger at him. That smile acknowledged the truth between us. We both recognized our true nature: enemies.

It pleased him.

"Duke, whatever he has told you—"

"Janel? Janel, is that you?" A querulous voice rose up, reedy and broken. The man kneeling on the floor looked at me. The hood fell back from his gold laevos.

Tamin.

His cheekbones sported multiple bruises, purple and swollen. Both his eyes had been blackened. He was missing teeth. A sudden and immediate sense of wrongness washed over me.

He should have been able to heal himself. He hadn't.

"Tell the duke about the witches, Tamin. There's a good boy." Relos Var's hand stroked Tamin's laevos as though petting a hound.

Tamin started to say something, then a visible shudder moved over him. "There was a whole coven of them. They made me . . . they made me do things. Had me under their spells."

"And their leader? Who was she?" Relos Var asked with softest malice, while his eyes never left mine.

I felt like time stood still and pregnant even as Tamin spoke, even as I knew the duke and his mother, his soldiers, hung on every word.

"I never knew her name, but her skin was white"—Var's hand tightened on Tamin's laevos—"splattered with black. White splattered with black. I'm sorry, Janel. I'm so sorry. She was an old woman with black-splattered skin. Please forgive me."

"You—" I knew the game. Having described Dorna, Tamin would go on describing people. Perhaps Brother Qown next. Ninavis. Myself.

"That description sounds very familiar. Count, don't you have a woman in your service like that?" The duke circled around us both, so focused on Tamin he seemed to miss the battle of gazes happening before him.

"Oh no, Duke," I answered, keeping my voice light and sweet. "My nurse has black skin, not white."

"Oh, right. I remember now."

Relos Var's mouth quirked. The bastard was trying not to *laugh*.*

"My duke," I said, still not able to break eye contact with Var. "I very much wish to attend the festivities tonight, but I'm afraid with the attack on Barsine, my formal wear and jewelry

---

* Only because that's hilarious. I'm not sure what's funnier, that Janel was trying to semantic her way out of the situation or that Duke Xun was such a fool that it was *working*.

didn't survive the journey. May I throw myself on your mercy and the generosity of your wardrobe?"

I didn't plan to attend the festivities, you understand. I just didn't know if Var would try anything here, if this would turn deadly. I wanted Lady Xun out of the way.

"Oh, my poor dear! Yes, I'm sure I can find something appropriate." Lady Xun sniffed. "And you all have a great deal to discuss. With your pardon, my dear?"

"Did you want to leave now? It's just getting exciting. Tamin's naming the witches."

"Oh, I'm sure you can handle that without me." I heard her cloak fabric swirl as she left us.

Relos Var lifted his head. The bastard still smiled. "Shall I ask Tamin to continue with his accounting?"

Before the duke could speak, I did. "He's been through enough. Besides, I would think the duke would like to hear my account."

"Oh, that's true, I would. By the gods, is there something wrong? You two are staring at each other like you're about to draw swords or elope."

So he had noticed after all.

Relos Var broke eye contact, as the duke's words made him laugh outright, a deep pleasant laugh. "Oh no, my duke. I'm afraid the count is a bit young for my tastes. No offense."

"None taken," I murmured. "Although maybe that younger brother of yours is closer to my age. Did you bring him with you?"

Oh, so his brilliant control had a flaw. The glare he gave me was spite itself. I assumed then the situation with his "brother" hadn't gone the way he'd have liked. I didn't know if I should be happy or sad about that.

I walked in a slow circle around Relos Var, forcing him to turn to keep an eye on me. "I did see the witch at Mereina. White-skinned and foreign. She'd enchanted a warden, pretended to be his serving girl."

"Ah, so you see, Duke, that matches the former baron's description." Relos Var's smile had returned, the armor back in place. "But she must have been working with others. Witches always have a coven, after all."

"And you would know, being their leader." I said the accusation as simple fact. I couldn't let Var continue to control the conversation. I couldn't let him lead the duke to myself and my friends.

"What? Janel! Relos Var's our guest." Duke Xun's look suggested he was scandalized.

"Choose your next words carefully," Relos Var said.

"Oh, I have. You see, Your Grace, this seems harmless enough, and this Relos Var's all smiles and wise eyes. But the white witch who choked Mereina owes Relos Var her thudajé, just as Tamin did, and does still. He uses honeyed words to twist the truth. He'd have you think that my people or I are witches, to stop us from revealing the truth: he summoned those demons. His will caused all those deaths."

Relos Var's expression turned ugly. "I'm disappointed in you. This is the desperate and ill-fated allegation of a woman who knows her guilt is about to be uncovered."

I laughed out loud, even though I found nothing about this funny. I'd always thought someone might one day make such an accusation against me. My grandfather had known too—so had demanded I never correct anyone's beliefs about the Lonezh Hellmarch.

"You're a foreigner. You don't understand us. You don't understand our ways. You hear him, Your Grace. You hear his words. And you hear mine. You know there is only one way this can be decided."

The duke nodded. "Oh, quite. How exciting. But . . . Janel. Please tell me you're not a witch?" His expression was better suited to finding out whether his favorite horses had snuck inside the palace to have an attack of diarrhea.

"I'm not, Your Grace. I swear I'm not." I had long ago decided Brother Qown's definition of witch—one who summons demons—rang truer. The so-called crime of possessing a talent for sorcery didn't deserve a death sentence.

"Now who lies?" Relos Var snapped.

The duke didn't seem to have heard Var's words, or if he did, he took it all in stride. "Well, then . . . it is decided."

I exhaled in relief. "Here? Or in the main yard?"

"Oh, the main yard," the duke said. "It is the tournament, after all. No reason not to share."

Only then did Var look uncertain. "Wait. What's been decided?"

The duke and I looked at each other.

"He's a foreigner, my duke," I said, letting my voice drip with condescension.*

Relos Var schooled his expression into one less angry. "I don't deny this. But I think I have a right to know what you both mean."

The duke waved a hand. "Oh, well, you have each accused each other of serious crimes. There is one way to settle the matter: in combat."

I smiled at Relos Var. "That means we're going to have a duel. And if you refuse, everyone will know you for the fraud you are."

He stared at me. He looked a little shocked or, at the very least, a little appalled. Then he started to chuckle.

"My dear girl, you must know you cannot win against me."

"You mean I can't win against a sorcerer of your caliber?" I rested one hand at my belt, near my weapons but not on them. "Yes, I know."

He made a face. "That's your game? You think you can put me in a position where I would have to use magic to defend myself? A fool's plan. I expected better."†

"We'll see," I murmured.

The duke said, "I hate to interrupt, but it is traditional to

---

* Pfft. Joratese.

† Especially given that whole "Blood of Joras" thing they're so fond of, but I suppose those people are expected to stay out of politics. I mean sports. Business? Whatever the hell tournaments are.

separate the two sides. Relos, why don't you accompany me? We must find someone to fight in your place."

"I'll fight my own battles."

"What?" The duke seemed taken aback, but then shrugged. "Well, if you wish. Then we must find you armor and a weapon. Come with me . . ."

I smiled. Relos Var's stare never left mine until he allowed the duke to lead both him and Tamin out. As soon as he exited, I felt like all the air returned to the room, and my heart remembered how to beat again.

"What have I done?" I muttered to the quiet.

But no one answered.

29: An Ill-Advised Duel

Jorat Dominion, Quuros Empire.
Three days since Kihrin littered the Capital City
with unwanted talismans

"You didn't," Kihrin said.

"Oh, I did," Janel admitted.

"But you didn't fight him." Kihrin raised an eyebrow. "I mean, I'm not kidding when I say I've seen Relos Var face down gods. Not just god-kings. The Three Sisters themselves: Luck, Death, and Magic. At the same time."*

"Oh, she fought him," Dorna said. She looked up at Star. "I can't reach her from here. Do you mind, dear?"

"No problem," Star said. He leaned over and slapped the back of Janel's head.

"Hey!" Janel glared at Star. "Watch it!"

"And you deserve a thousand more, colt," Dorna said. "I raised you better." She stabbed her finger at the bar top. "Don't pick a fight with someone who scares gods. Words to live by."

"I knew exactly what I was doing," Janel protested. "Mostly."

Qown opened his book. "I *really* hate this part."

---

* In Janel's defense, that was a magic situation. She must have thought she'd caught you out in a clever loophole: swordplay. Moderately clever of her to try to control the battlefield.

I almost feel bad for her.

*Qown's Turn. The Malkoessian compound, the Green,
Atrine, Jorat, Quur.*

The guards pulled Brother Qown and Mare Dorna into the
tent. Flame motifs stitched in red and glittering gold decorated
its interior. The Stavira jaguar grinned at them from every
surface, as if to mock their foolhardy trespassing.

Brother Qown had met Sir Oreth once, when he arrived at
Tolamer Castle months ago with soldiers and malice. Sir Oreth
had grown no less handsome in his absence. The Joratese called
his coloring sun-kissed—a golden-white laevos and bronze-brown
skin paired with darker brown socks on his hands. A white
blaze surrounded one eye, which gleamed a lighter brown than
its twin.

His temper hadn't improved either. When they returned to
the tent, Sir Oreth raised his sword to Mare Dorna.

"No, Sir Oreth," Senera admonished. Her accent placed her
origin in the Quuros Capital.* "Bodies lead to investigations.
We don't wish to draw attention. Lord Var would be very
disappointed."

"This bitch knows me," Sir Oreth said. "If she tells my father,
he'll call due on his loans, and then your people won't have a
Gatestone in Tolamer to use."

"She's an old woman. She can't hurt you." Senera looked at
Mare Dorna, then at the guards. "Someone remove her gag."

Brother Qown had expected expletives to rain from Mare
Dorna's mouth as soon as the guard ungagged her. But perhaps
because Dorna understood their situation, they didn't.

"What happens now?" Mare Dorna asked, chin held high.

"Oh, the usual," Senera said. "We talk, I ask questions, you
try to give me some story—truth or lie, whichever you prefer—
to convince me not to let the charming Sir Oreth here slit your
throat."†

---

* I do *not* have an accent.
† That was sarcasm, in case it wasn't obvious.

Brother Qown swallowed. "It's not done here, you know. Trespassing isn't seen as a capital crime in this dominion. It would seem very odd to put us to death. No one is going to believe we're assassins caught in the act. If Sir Oreth kills us, there will be repercussions."

Senera turned and looked at him for the first time. Her warm gray eyes were not god-touched, not one of the Royal Houses' divine colors.

She winked at him.

"The priest has a point," she said to Sir Oreth.

"The old woman is an evil hag with a wicked tongue," Sir Oreth said.

"Ay, that's just what your mother used to say," said Mare Dorna.

He drew his sword again and took a step in her direction.

A guard stepped in the way.

"Dorna!" Brother Qown said. "You're not *helping*."

"Sorry," she muttered. "Couldn't stop myself."

Senera watched the group with an expression bordering on disbelief. She crossed over to a table and poured several cups of tea. "I stand corrected. The old woman can hurt your *feelings*." She held up a cup. "Would anyone like tea?"

"Oh, I would," Mare Dorna said. "If you'd just untie me . . .?" She wriggled her arms behind her to emphasize her restraints.

Senera studied her and held out the cup. "Untie yourself. We both know those bonds might as well be made from pulled sugar floss to someone like you."

"What are we doing?" Sir Oreth gestured toward the azhock's front. "My family will be back any minute. We have no time for socializing with peasants. You're sweet enough to look upon, Senera, but you're not fooling anyone into thinking you're a stallion.* Leave this to people who know what they're doing."

---

* So pretty and so stupid. Somehow, he managed to miss the fact the guards all followed my orders. If that's not the definition of a "stallion" in Joratese culture, I don't know what is.

He motioned to the guards. "Take them both. We'll move them to the south barn and figure out what to do with them later."

"Still charming as ever," Dorna muttered.

Senera's expression tightened, and she closed her eyes for a second. She set down the tea. "Sir Oreth, what's that noise?"

The knight turned back to her. "What?"

Brother Qown realized Senera wasn't making idle chatter. A dull roar had risen in the distance, as if they'd found themselves too close to Demon Falls.

Cheering. The tournament crowds were cheering.

A runner in red and gold came into the tent, panting. "Noble lords," he said between gasping breaths. "There's a late contest added to the schedule. The Count of Tolamer is to fight Relos Var."

"Oh, that bloody idiot," Mare Dorna said.

Brother Qown knew Dorna wasn't referring to Relos Var.

"Damn it to Hell," Sir Oreth said. "She's going to kill him."*

Senera stared at Sir Oreth. "You *are* new here, aren't you?"

"Janel's strong as ten men," Sir Oreth said. "Your master talks a good game, but in a duel, Janel's going to rip him apart."

Senera rolled her eyes. She looked inconvenienced, not worried.

"Come on, then." Senera motioned to the guards. "Let's get these two over to the stands. The least we can do is allow them to witness their beloved count's death."

"How could she be this stupid?" Mare Dorna uttered under her breath as they walked along, sometimes shoved from behind by an impatient guard. "She said she'd talk to the bloody duke, not challenge some sorcerer to a duel. What the icy hell was she thinking?"

"I don't know," Brother Qown said. "What did Senera mean about the ropes?"

---

* So, so pretty. So, so stupid. Having met the rest of his family, I assume Oreth was dropped on his head as a baby. Repeatedly.

"Never you mind, priest."

"I'm thinking of the fireblood whose girth snapped," he said. "And Kalazan's ropes. For that matter, remember all those crossbows aimed at Count Janel back in Mereina? Where the strings just snapped?"

"Stop talking," the guard behind them said. His accent sounded Joratese, but something else lingered around the edges.

Brother Qown sighed, but he followed the guard's orders. They couldn't stop him from thinking, though. Brother Qown wondered if Count Janel had any idea Mare Dorna also qualified for the Joratese definition of a witch. He remembered all the people who'd lost their purses around the old woman, although he'd never seen a knife in her hands. He thought of how well she darned fabrics, making stitches so small he'd never been able to pick them out with the naked eye. She probably knew just a single spell—binding and unbinding—but she wielded it with brilliant expertise.

"What was she thinking?" Dorna muttered again.

Senera walked like a queen. Nothing about her attitude suggested she thought anyone would call her to justice for the deaths in Mereina. Sir Oreth, on the other hand, fidgeted and kept looking around to see if anyone was watching.

He was probably looking for his father.

Senera led the group to a higher, private area in the stands, where everyone had their own servants and guards.

"You have a *box*?" Dorna sounded scandalized.

Senera laughed as she sat down. As soon as she did, a small dhole, perhaps eight months or so old, woke up from a velvet cushion and bounded over to the woman, hopeful for scraps and attention. Senera rubbed the dog's ears and let it sit down next to her, so its head lay in her lap.

Brother Qown blinked as he recognized the dog. The warden's puppy from Mereina, the one Senera had taken with her when she abandoned the town to choking gas.

"I'm going to check in with my father," Sir Oreth said. "If

I find him first, he won't come looking for me. I assume you have this well in hand." He left, motioning for his soldiers to follow.

"There goes a very handsome idiot," Senera said, shaking her head. "I'm glad we don't need him for anything *important.*"

Brother Qown started to respond when another roar sounded, and Count Janel rode into the ring. She waved her sword and shouted to the crowd.

Brother Qown realized she was shouting her accusations. That Relos Var, a sorcerer, had ordered demon and dragon attacks within the province, with a white witch from the south aiding him.

Next to him, Senera paused while petting the dhole.

"That may prove inconvenient." Senera turned to Dorna. "Don't your people have laws protecting against slander?"

"Yeah. You're watching it."

Relos Var came next, and although he didn't have the same panache as Janel riding Arasgon, he still looked at home enough on a horse not to embarrass himself.

Relos Var's speech was damning.

"This woman is no proper Joratese!" he cried out. "I know I'm a stranger here, but at least I don't lie. She made her pacts with demons as a child, at Lonezh Canton. She did not outrun the demons. She led them! She led a demon army against you! And now she seeks to twist the truth when we would stop her and her machinations. Did she not visit Mereina just before its destruction? Did she not abandon her ancestral canton of Tolamer? She attacked her betrothed when he discovered her treachery. And now she points fingers at *me* because I know what she is and I'm brave enough to say so."

The crowd went silent, and then they roared.

They didn't take Relos Var's side. He was a foreigner, and she was Janel Danorak. They would give her the benefit of the doubt.

Unless Janel lost. His words had an ugly quality to them, in no small part because he'd twisted her story into a damning slice of hell. Brother Qown felt sick. If Relos Var won, this fight would be all the evidence anyone needed to put Janel to death. The duel would be followed by a burning.

Senera smiled and resumed petting her dog.*

When Relos Var finished his ride, he surprised everyone by dismounting his horse, leaving it to the side. After a moment's consideration, Count Janel did likewise, sending Arasgon back to the stables despite the fireblood's strenuous objections.

The combatants closed with each other, each armed with a sword and shield. Janel used her family sword, which gave her reach. She wielded it, as always, as though it were a one-handed sword. Anyone else would have required both hands to control the weapon.†

Relos Var looked like a librarian someone had forced into a gladiator match.

But his appearance didn't match his skill. Relos Var dodged her swings, while Janel was being pushed back by his attacks. Her strength proved no advantage at all.

If any conversation occurred between them, it wasn't obvious.

The entire stadium began chanting.

"Danorak, Danorak, Danorak!"

Then something happened. Brother Qown didn't see the mistake. Maybe Janel didn't make one. Janel raised her sword, Var swung his across hers . . .

And Janel's sword shattered as though made of glass.

Everyone jumped to their feet. Everyone, from the duke to the humblest child sitting at her parents' feet on the rooftops across the Green.

A moment later, Janel fell to her knees, defeated.

She surrendered to Relos Var.

"Well, damn," Mare Dorna said. "Your man won fair enough—"

---

* Who's a good puppy? Rebel is! Yes, she is!

   Don't judge me, damn it. She's adorable.

† Almost anyone.

Relos Var ran Janel through with his sword.

Time stopped. Brother Qown stared in shock. Even from that distance, Brother Qown saw Janel's shocked expression. Relos Var yanked free his sword, and Janel fell. A pool of blood spread out under her, seeping into the ground.

She didn't move again.

The crowd fell silent. Senera sighed and stood. "So that's done. Let's go fetch the body."

30: A WALK IN THE WOODS

Jorat Dominion, Quuros Empire.
Three days since Kihrin saw the Jade Gate
closed for the first time in his life

Kihrin pointed a finger at Janel. "Wait, what? Did Thaena Return you? What happened? How—"

"Shhh," Janel said. "I'm about to tell you."

Janel's Turn. The Afterlife.

The problem with dying every time you close your eyes is never knowing if this time is the last time. If this time it's for real.

Was I dead or just unconscious?

I couldn't tell.

I stood on a hillside in the Afterlife, clad in black armor only subtly different from what I'd worn just a few moments before.

The Chasm stood before me.

Everyone called it the Chasm, even Xaltorath. A giant crack in the earth, a mighty canyon marking the boundary where the Afterlife gives way to the Land of Peace. Giant chunks of rock and earth sailed upward in a continuous stream, like a waterfall running in reverse.

The demons were attacking the Chasm, but demons were always attacking the Chasm. Few places in the entire Afterlife were more likely to be visited by the Eight Immortals. I'd always avoided this region. I'd be attacked by both sides if I showed myself. Even if Thaena had told her people to leave me alone, the other gods and their forces wouldn't automatically feel the same. Attack first and ask questions later remained a rule here, and they didn't know me.

So I retreated.

I wondered how people in the Living World would react if they knew the truth about the Afterlife. Most souls never reached the Land of Peace. No religion I knew spelled out that the reward for a life well lived would be another eternity on the front lines—in the Afterlife, fighting demons.

But who knew? Maybe the ghostly soldiers had volunteered. It's not like I knew what it was like to truly die.

Although given how the duel with Relos Var had gone, maybe I shouldn't assume.

As I fell back, I heard movement in the trees behind me, and I turned, ready to fight whatever came.

What came was a god.

Khored the Destroyer wore red armor and a matching helmet, with a raven-feather cloak. In his hands, he held a red glass sword I knew would annihilate anything it touched.

Then he sheathed his sword and removed his helmet.

"Walk with me," Mithros said.

The battle continued to rage behind us, but no one seemed interested in capturing this area. We walked alone.

"I'd convinced myself you couldn't be Khored," I said. "Your priests . . . they don't know?"

He ignored the question, and as we walked, I felt his ire. Any joy I might have felt at seeing him faded.

I had disobeyed him, had I not? If not his specific instructions, certainly his intent. I grimaced to myself.

This wasn't going to go well.

"When you challenged Relos Var to a duel," Mithros said, "I'm curious . . . what was your brain doing?"

"That's not fair," I protested.

"Isn't it? Because I want to know what minuscule amount of logic could've played into the decision to challenge *Relos Var* to a duel.* Please tell me you weren't so stupid as to think he couldn't swing a sword just because he's a wizard?"

I raised my chin. "I played a Nemesan gambit: a battle he couldn't win."

"Must I point out the flaw in your plan? He won. Decisively."

I fought the temptation to cross my arms over my chest. "If I won, well, then I would have proved my case against him. Given what Thaena and you both said about this man, I didn't think that outcome likely. But I could turn losing to my advantage. To my people, there is prestige to be gained by losing *well.*"

Mithros stared at me for a second, trying to figure out the riddle. Then he threw his head back and scoffed. "Of course. You surrendered to him. Bowed your head and gave him a proper Joratese demonstration of thudajé."

"The only way he could've 'won' would have been if he had accepted my surrender gracefully. He didn't," I said, "which makes him thorra. He's tolerated in Jorat because he portrays himself as a wise mare who wants to serve, profoundly humble, worthy of trust even though he's not Joratese. No one will believe him now. The whole dominion saw him strike down a young stallion who had acknowledged his idorrá. It won't matter that he proved me a witch by winning—*he* didn't have the right to put me to death, even after he proved his idorrá over me. By doing so, he told everyone watching he thought himself better than Markreev Stavira, better than *Duke Xun.* Relos Var overstepped his authority. He won. And by winning, he lost."

The God of Destruction stared hard.

I swallowed and returned the stare. He was easier to look at than Thaena, but that didn't make it *easy.* "You asked what I was thinking."

Mithros tipped his head. "And I admit, your answer surprised

---

* Ah, come on. I'm with Janel on this one. You "looked like a librarian someone had forced into a gladiator match." I would have thought I could take you in a sword fight too.

me. I apologize. I assumed you'd given the matter no real thought at all."

I raised my chin. "Believe me, I had."

"And did you think about the price you'll pay for this very minor victory?"

The price I'll pay . . . "So I'm not dead, then?" I felt my heart—or the illusion of my heart—pounding inside me. I had assumed . . . when I'd seen Relos Var's sword coming at me . . .

I'd survived?

"No. You're not dead. Did you think—?" He put his hand under my chin. "Does the idea of your own death mean so little to you?"

Warm rage filled me as I jerked my chin from his grip. "*The idea of death?* Look around you. Where do you think I spend my evenings? Every evening? Why would I fear the playground I've known *every single night* since the Lonezh Hellmarch?"

"But what comes next—"

"I wake up or I don't, but either way, I know what comes next. Back here again, another night, fighting the same battles I've always fought. Death isn't an end; it's a change of venue."

He scowled, pacing like a frustrated tiger locked in a cage. "You think you have nothing to lose. You're wrong."

I looked away. "I know what I have to lose. What I *will* lose. I'll be stripped of my title, forced to go into hiding. I'm prepared—"

"No." His voice was soft. "Relos Var's going to give you what you wanted."

I didn't understand. Not right away. I stared at him, uncomprehending. "What I wanted?"

And then I realized. He didn't mean wanting Tolamer Canton back, or clearing my name, or even the part about stopping Relos Var.

He meant my quest to infiltrate Duke Kaen's stronghold.

"Relos Var isn't leaving you behind in Jorat," Mithros said. "He's going to take you with him back to Yor."

I'd given up on this outcome. Dismissed it as untenable when

Mithros had first pointed out that Relos Var would almost certainly gaesh me. And now . . . I felt dread shudder through me as I turned to face Mithros. "Why? Why would he not leave me? I'm the duke's problem now. Why would Duke Xun let Relos Var take me?" I grappled with motives I scarcely understood. Had I been wrong about Relos Var? Would he want revenge? Want to make me suffer for defying him? Would he—

Saelen.

Relos Var could claim me as saelen, as a stray. He supposedly cured witches, didn't he? If he convinced the Markreev of Stavira or Duke Xun I could be rehabilitated, if he appealed to the Joratese desire to keep the herd strong . . .

All my work to make Relos Var claim idorrá over me only helped his cause.

Mithros held out a hand as he saw my horrified expression. "It's not what you think. Var is many things, but he wouldn't kidnap and defile a young woman. Not even someone who interfered with his plans."

I blinked. "You're right. That's not what I thought. Indeed . . . that option never occurred to me."

He cleared his throat, looking embarrassed for a moment. "Just as well." Mithros continued, "But now we need to worry about gaeshing."

I felt sick. "Yes. We do." I'd never seen anyone gaeshed, but Xaltorath had always loved to talk shop about technique. The right way to pull out just a sliver of someone's soul. How to bind it with a talisman that could be used to give the victim commands. The victim either obeyed . . . or they died in agony.

I wasn't immune. No one was.*

Mithros nodded. "If he cannot be sure he owns you, he'll gaesh you. And a gaesh will destroy any chance you'll have of stealing the spear Khoreval from Duke Kaen. The first command any gaesh victim receives is an order not to attempt escape. He must *not* gaesh you."

---

* And yet . . . Again, I'm not *bitter.*

"And how am I supposed to stop him?"

"You can't. Myself, on the other hand . . . I'm going to take steps."

Then I swallowed. "What steps?"

"It's better you don't know," Mithros said. "He'll try to mold you, turn you to his side. He's good at that.* He'll ferret out secrets you didn't know you possessed, reveal truths you never knew existed. He's had millennia of experience, and you are—much as you may not wish to admit it—hardly more than a child." Mithros raised an eyebrow. "If you want to triumph, you'll first need to fail. Relos Var will try to break you. You must let him succeed."

---

* I both laugh and weep that the Eight never seem to stop and consider why you're so good at that.

31: SAELEN

Jorat Dominion, Quuros Empire.
Three days since Darzin D'Mon made a bad bet

Ninavis slammed her hand on the bar. "Damn it!"

Dorna rolled her eyes. "Oh, quit your whining. So you sexed up the God of Destruction. So what? At least you had fun." She pointed a bony finger at the woman. "Seems to me you got off light compared to the rest of us."

Ninavis's expression turned to a scowl. "Right." She grimaced. "Right."

Kihrin looked at the group. "It's about to get worse, isn't it?"

"Oh yes," Qown said and began to read.

Qown's Turn. The tournament grounds, the Green, Atrine, Jorat, Yor.

Brother Qown gripped the wood railing so hard he drove splinters under his fingernails. Everything seemed to slow down. He heard Mare Dorna's shuddering gasps and, a long way away, Arasgon's furious screaming. The crowd booed their displeasure at the outcome, but no one stopped Relos Var from leaving. No one rushed forward to pick up the count, whose blood made a small, neat pool on the ground.

He'd won; she'd lost.

He was strong; she was weak.

Winners were right; losers were wrong.

Innocent; guilty.

Brother Qown felt hands on his shoulders as the guards stopped him from leaping down into the tournament ring.

"No," Brother Qown said, "I can help her!"

"Patience, priest," Senera said. "She doesn't need your help."

Her calm, pleasant tone stopped him. Brother Qown turned back to Senera. "She's dying down there, but you don't care, do you?"

"I care a great deal," she said. "And don't worry. Hurting you and Dorna isn't part of the plan, no matter what that idiot Oreth thinks."

"Why not? Why would you treat us any differently here from how you did at Mereina?"

Her gaze tightened. "Be grateful I'm treating you differently."

"Ah, foal. How long have you known you're on the wrong side?"

Senera whipped her head around and stared at Mare Dorna. The old woman's expression looked grim as tears slipped down her face, but she held her chin up, defiant. She met the younger woman's eyes without flinching.

Seconds passed.

"I'm not on the wrong side,"* Senera said. She motioned, and the guards pulled Mare Dorna and Brother Qown to their feet. "There's no point waiting around."

The guards escorted them back to the staging grounds.

"There has to be something—"

Mare Dorna shook her head. "Shush."

Brother Qown shut his eyes and tried to slow his racing heart. The whole way back from the tournament grounds he'd tried to plan any kind of escape. But he couldn't think past the numb pain. Had Janel challenged Relos Var to a duel? The reverse? Had Duke Xun forced this, to determine who was guilty?

Count Janel was dead.

---

* I'm not on the wrong side. I just wish we had a different way to . . .
  Well. You know my feelings on this. No need to waste ink repeating them.

Wasn't she?

A guard nudged him as Brother Qown slowed, forcing his thoughts toward more immediate concerns. His own safety, for one thing. They needed to escape; he couldn't imagine how they were more useful to Senera and Sir Oreth alive than dead.

Unfortunately, his own magical talents had always been subtle. He'd never had much talent for the destructive arts.*

Instead of returning to the Stavira azhock, the guards took them behind the main stands, to the "backstage" areas of the tournament not meant for the public.

Of course. Senera had said she wished to collect Janel's body.

The guards asked a few questions. Directions were given. Brother Qown saw a pair of grooms carrying a body wrapped in tournament flags.

Senera burst into tears and began waving for the grooms to wait.

As she did, Brother Qown felt a guard pull him close, pressing a dagger against his ribs. The message seemed clear enough: *Don't make trouble.* The grim expression on Mare Dorna's face suggested a similar experience.

A groom paused. "Uh . . . can I help you?"

"My count!" Senera wailed.

Brother Qown couldn't help but notice she knew enough Karo to use the correct pronouns.

"We, uh—" The two grooms looked at each other. "We're taking the body to the Blue House."

She sniffled and wiped her eyes. "Her fiancé, Sir Oreth, asked me to collect her. I can't believe this has happened." She pulled herself up, gathering her dignity around her. "We'll take her."

He had hoped the grooms would be suspicious. But rather than question her unorthodox request, they seemed glad to pass along responsibility. They gave each other a significant glance and then motioned for Senera's guards to take the body.

---

* Given how Darzin D'Mon turned out, I'm glad Qown has "no talent" for the destructive side of healing magic. If he ever figures it out, it might just break him.

The guards assigned to Brother Qown and Mare Dorna kept them under the knife, while others collected the stretcher.

Brother Qown almost didn't notice the archers at the sidelines. They'd all quieted as the procession passed.

One of those archers was Ninavis. She made eye contact with Brother Qown and gave him a single nod before continuing her low conversation with the other archers.

Brother Qown forced himself not to make a sign of thanks to his god.

"What are you going to do with us?" Brother Qown asked Senera. "We're no threat to you."

"Oh, now let's not be liars to each other," Senera said, looking back. "But don't worry. I have no plans to hurt you. We're just taking a little trip. Someplace far from here where I don't have to worry about you talking to the wrong people."

"And why do I get the feeling I ain't dressed near warm enough for this little getaway?" Dorna muttered under her breath.

Senera's smile broadened for a moment.*

Brother Qown kept an eye open for any sign of the others—Sir Baramon, Ninavis, the Red Spears. If they were near, they hid very well.

For her part, Senera didn't try to hide. Like Janel, she'd mastered the art of being a queen in her own kingdom. Her posture screamed idorrá,† suggested everyone should stay out of her way.

Mostly, they did.

Brother Qown found himself back in the Stavira compound, in the azhock where Senera had met with Sir Oreth. Guards pushed Brother Qown and Mare Dorna into chairs, while the other guards placed Count Janel's body on a large table.

Senera removed the tournament flag covering the count's body.

* I like Dorna. She's smarter than she looks.
† Thank you! "Never believe you're a stallion" indeed.

Mare Dorna made a strangled sound and looked away.

Brother Qown almost did likewise, but his professional training took over. Janel had suffered a nasty penetrating injury, running through her torso just underneath the sternum. On anyone else, Qown would have assumed the wound fatal.

But this was Janel. Qown knew her metabolism slowed when she "slept" to the point where she seemed dead to the uninitiated. Could she still be alive?

The tent flap flew back as Sir Oreth entered. He took one step inside and stopped, staring at Janel's body with an unreadable expression.

Senera frowned at the Joratese knight. "Don't tell me you loved her."

"Is she dead?"

"That question doesn't mean what you think it does," Senera replied. "In any event, we need to leave, before the wrong people ask the right questions."

Sir Oreth scowled. "My father will take this personally."

"Of course he will. What happened today was an insult to his honor. What you can't protect, you forfeit the right to rule. Isn't that how it works here?" She smiled at Sir Oreth.

Sir Oreth's expression turned ugly. "She wasn't supposed to die."

"Life is unfair."

Another man entered the tent then, looking harried. The plump, well-dressed man looked more Kirpisari than Joratese.

"Kovinglass, what is it?"

"Your father is coming this way," Kovinglass said. "And the duke with him."

"That didn't take long," Senera said. She looked at Kovinglass with pursed lips. "I'll need you to provide us with an exit."

"Absolutely not. I can't just—" Something made him gasp, and the air seemed to catch in Kovinglass's throat. He grimaced in pain.

"Hurry, sorcerer," Senera said. She'd her hand raised toward him, and although Brother Qown couldn't see any obvious spellcasting, he knew magic must be involved. "We haven't much time."

She lowered her hand, and Kovinglass seemed to deflate. He caught himself before he fell and, gasping, nodded.

Sir Oreth's gaze shifted to Brother Qown and then to Mare Dorna. A hateful expression settled there.

Mare Dorna winked at him.

"I'm never going to be able to explain this to my father," Sir Oreth said.

"If we leave now, you won't have to," Senera said. She gave Kovinglass a significant and menacing look. "Do you not understand what *hurry* means?"

"You don't tell me what to do, woman," Kovinglass snapped. Perhaps he had convinced himself whatever spell Senera had cast, just moments before, had been a fluke. Or perhaps his pride wouldn't let him admit he *couldn't* open a gate without a Gatestone.

The soldiers stepped toward him.

As they did, Sir Oreth drew his sword. Instead of moving toward the soldiers, Oreth did something else.

He stabbed Dorna.

The old woman looked at him with dull-eyed shock before sliding off his sword in an untidy little heap on the floor. Brother Qown cried out, but no one paid attention to him, and his outrage had little impact on the outcome. He tried to run to Mare Dorna, but his guards held him back.

Senera's expression tightened. *"Why?"* she asked Sir Oreth.

"She knew my father," he spat out. "Had some leverage on him. I think blackmail, but I could never be sure. In any event, he'd believe whatever lies she fed him."

Brother Qown tried to center his feelings, tried to slide his vision past the Veil. Impossible. He barely stopped himself from sobbing. He saw the light fade from Dorna's stare, and unlike Janel, he had no reason to assume Mare Dorna faked her death.

Senera stared a moment at Dorna's body, her expression unreadable, then she snapped her fingers. "Negrach, Molash, carry the count's body. Pragaos, take the priest. Kovinglass, why isn't that gate open?"

Even as Kovinglass attempted to open a magical portal, a quick slicing sound filled the air. A long panel of tent fabric fluttered down.

A split second later, an arrow took Kovinglass through the throat.

The soldiers spread out. Some had shields, but they didn't know who had fired the shot.

Brother Qown, familiar with Ninavis's archery skills, had a better idea, but he saw no reason to educate them. As a soldier grabbed him by the elbow, Qown faked a stumble and fell, using his weight to throw both himself and the guard off balance.

Arrows penetrated both azhock and Yoran bodies in equal proportions. Qown heard shouts and the sound of fighting.

"If you want to do something *right* . . . ," Senera muttered.

Brother Qown had the terrified thought Senera might have more blue smoke.

But no. She'd opened her own gate to replace Kovinglass's failed portal. Several azhock walls had fallen by this point, so she'd also done it in full view of a great many Joratese. Whether she'd be considered Blood of Joras or not, she'd just given a lot of credence to Janel's story.

As Brother Qown stood, a soldier saw him and swung his sword. A passing swing, much like swatting a bug. Qown heard his agolé rip; the sword edge parted skin. He fell backward, in agonizing pain, bleeding.

Another soldier grabbed him. He felt himself hoisted up onto a shoulder.

Senera ushered her men through the portal, including the ones carrying Janel's body. "Well?" she said to Sir Oreth. "Are you coming or not?"

Sir Oreth scowled at her, but a shout from outside the tent made him leap through the portal. The soldiers followed with Brother Qown. Finally, Senera retreated with her puppy, closing the gate behind her.

By the time the Markreev, the duke, and a band that included Ninavis and Sir Baramon entered the tent, it was empty.

Or rather, it was empty, save for the corpses of several guards, one Gatekeeper, and a single old woman.*

* You have no idea how tempted I was to leave Oreth there. Fucking idiot.

PART III

WINTER'S CHILDREN

32: BY THE SEASIDE

Jorat Dominion, Quuros Empire.
Three days since Kihrin wondered if he could
take Gadrith by himself (answer: no)

Kihrin just stared at Dorna.

"What?" she said. "Oh, like you've never been dead before?" She raised her eyebrows while reaching for her drink.

Kihrin paused. "That . . . is a fair point." And his own death had only happened a few days previously, no matter how long ago it seemed. "I forget sometimes how easy it is to pull off if you know the right people."

"Everything is easier to pull off if you know the right people," Dorna said gently.

"I'm just curious," Kihrin said, "what *do* you have over the Markreev of Stavira?"

"I have wondered that myself," Janel said.

"Nothing as sinister as what that brat Oreth seems to think," Dorna said. "I played the tournament circuit in my youth. Aroth was a fan . . . and one thing led to another."* She put an arm around Star and ruffled his hair.

"Momma," Star said. "Stop that."

Dorna did, grinning. "No regrets. Got Palomarn out of the deal, didn't I? The whole thing fell apart after a few years, though. Later on, I decided I'd be happier female, and Aroth decided he'd be happier male. Fine by me, except I still run with mares

---

* Oh, I didn't know they'd had a child. Hmm. Aroth's oldest too. That could prove interesting.

and he ain't one anymore." She shrugged. "It was never gonna work out."

Kihrin raised an eyebrow at Star. "Palomarn? Your real name is Palomarn?"

The large man shrugged. "I like Star."

Janel gave Dorna a long, slow blink. "You had a *child* with Aroth Malkoessian?"

"Hey," Star said. "Not a child."

"So your son . . ." Kihrin had a hard time imagining Star as having been born at all. He seemed more like something spawned into existence. Star as a child? Star as a baby? No. "How did I just happen to stumble across your son for sale in the Octagon slave pits?"

Dorna gave Star a disapproving look. "What's this? A slave?"

"Not my fault," Star said. "People who mistreat horses don't deserve to keep 'em."

Dorna slapped Star's shoulder. "No, I mean you letting them *catch* you. Raised you better than that."

Star grinned as he turned to Kihrin. "I didn't plan on you buying me. Luck, I suppose."

"Right. Luck." Kihrin couldn't even discount the possibility. The Goddess of Luck sometimes did him favors. She rarely asked permission first.*

Janel said, "Would you mind taking a second turn, Qown? I've never heard what happened right after we were kidnapped."

Qown gave her a long look.

"What?"

The priest sighed. "You'll see." He opened his book.

Qown's Turn. Senera's cottage, location unknown.

The guard carried Brother Qown through the gate and set him down on a wooden bench. "Colonel, this one's injured."

---

* I suppose we should expect Taja would be very good at orchestrating events to ensure certain people would meet.

Brother Qown ground his teeth together as he tore at his wet robes, stained red. The wound still bled freely.

It also hurt. He'd been warned it often proved difficult to heal oneself, because pain sapped concentration, but he'd never experienced the phenomenon. If he was being honest, he'd always assumed he'd be the exception, able to ignore the agony through force of will.

"Put the count's body on this table. On her back, please. Molash, go bring my bag. It's the red leather one hanging next to the door." Senera set down the eight-month-old dhole and untied her collar. The puppy made an immediate beeline for a velvet pillow by the fireplace, her bed, turning around three times before lying down, tail thumping her approval.*

Sir Oreth looked around for a moment, blinking, then crossed over to Senera. "Take me back. I must speak with my father."

She ignored him and bent down next to Brother Qown. "How bad does it look?"

Qown winced. "Could've been worse. Skin and muscle tissue. The rib cage did its job and saved my internal organs. Mostly blood loss. If I could just . . . concentrate . . . I could . . ."

"Has anyone said you talk too much?" Senera smiled at him. "It's no wonder you can't reach Illumination."

He blinked at her. "What did you say?"

Brother Qown felt his heart grow heavy. *Please don't let her be a follower of the Way of Vishai. Please don't let her be someone who claims to share my faith.*† She didn't answer his question but continued uncovering the wound on his chest.

"Are you listening to me, woman? I said I need to go back, right now." Oreth's anger bordered on panic. His hands started to shake.

Senera put her hand on Brother Qown's chest. "Pragaos, watch Sir Oreth. If he makes any threatening moves, kill him."

---

* Rebel has very strong opinions about her pillow.
† Like I would *ever* worship his god.

"Yes, Colonel." Pragaos pulled his sword and moved to stand next to Sir Oreth.

"What?" Sir Oreth grimaced at the man. "Stand down this instant. You take orders from me."

The soldier's mouth quirked. "You may find you're mistaken about that."

"Why don't you pour yourself a drink, Oreth," Senera said. "You're shaking like a—" She paused at the edge of a metaphor and narrowed her eyes at Sir Oreth. "You've never killed anyone before."

Sir Oreth crossed his arms over his chest, looking more than a little wide-eyed. "What? Don't be ridiculous. Of course I have. I just didn't think—" He went over to the bench and sat down. "I didn't think—"

A soldier poured a glass of brandy at the bar. He crossed back to Sir Oreth and handed it to him.

"I have to talk to my father," Sir Oreth whispered as he took the brandy and drank it, too quickly. "I need my father."

"Why are you helping me?" Brother Qown tore his gaze away from Sir Oreth to look at Senera.

"Seems a shame to waste a perfectly good healer," Senera said. "You never know when you'll need one. Now stop talking; I need to concentrate."

Brother Qown understood that last part all too well. He leaned back and tried not to think about the pain, although the wound hurt less with every passing second. The physical pain, anyway.

Dorna. Damn it all, Dorna. It had happened so fast . . .

To keep himself from repeating that scene in his mind, he concentrated on gathering information. Brother Qown looked around the room. It was still night, but by the time the sun set in Jorat, it had already been night for several hours on the west coast of Quur. Mage-lights set into glass lanterns lit the room. Herbs hung from the rafters in neat bundles. Occult formulas had been burned into the wooden joists. A fire blazed in a hearth large enough for cooking or cremations. Racks of bottles framed an apothecary cabinet of medicinal powders and supplies. Windows were set into two walls, two doors led from a third—and an impressive accumulation of books, piled floor to ceiling, took up the entirety of the last. The whole room existed as a messy and cluttered altar to the arcane.

The windows provided no clues; the view outside was black.

He could make guesses, though. The cottage sat above ground, so it couldn't be a cellar home. It clearly wasn't an azhock either, eliminating Jorat's two main styles of housing. The temperature felt moderate, removing Yor as an option. With cob construction, straight plumb lines, and a stone floor, it didn't match Marakori stilt-house styles.

The room, despite its large size, felt cozy. Books and shelves filled with odd knickknacks filled all the gaps in the walls not taken up by windows or doors. Also, drawings were pinned to the beams: anatomical renderings, landscapes, architectural drawings. All of it seemed drawn by the same hand.

In the distance, Brother Qown heard crashing waves. Since Senera could open gates, they could be nearly anywhere, but he suspected Kazivar—possibly even Eamithon.

Assuming she'd bothered to stay on the same continent.*

A cool energy spread over his skin. He looked down to see Senera closing the wound and sealing it.

"Thank you," he said, because it would have been rude to do otherwise. "I'll heal the rest." He hoped by volunteering she'd forget to tie him up. He'd have an easier time acting on an opportunity to escape if he wasn't bound.

"Good." She stood up and crossed back over to her men. "How many did we lose?"

"Four," one answered. "Two killed during the fighting, and the other two were about to be captured."

A look of consternation came over Senera's face. "Thank you."

* And I'm not telling. I realize you already know, but there's always a chance this might fall into the wrong hands.

The soldier nodded and stepped back, his expression unreadable.

Sir Oreth slammed his drink against the table and stood up. "Order your men to leave the room, right now. You and I are going to talk in private."

The lead soldier raised an eyebrow. The other men straightened and stood at attention. Several hands drifted toward sword hilts.

"If it pleases you," Senera said.

"Colonel—" The soldier didn't agree.

Brother Qown struggled to sit. He found himself agreeing with the soldiers, even though every person in the room made him regret his vows of nonviolence.

She waved a hand. "It's fine. I assume the priest can stay? He shouldn't be moved right now."

Sir Oreth glanced at Brother Qown. "I don't care about him."

You should, Brother Qown thought to himself. *Because if you come a step too close to me, I'll gladly—*

No. He stopped himself. *No. This isn't what I believe.*

He concentrated on healing any damage Senera might have missed.

The soldiers hesitated.

"Go," Senera said.

The lead man bowed before he walked from the room. The other men followed, giving Sir Oreth dirty looks on the way.

The moment they left, Sir Oreth slapped Senera across the face.

She rocked back from the blow almost without reaction. Just a hand to her cheek as her eyes went to the floor.*

But Brother Qown knew her meek response was a ruse. *Are you this stupid, Oreth? Female wizards, holding the rank of colonel in someone or other's army, do not obey just because you hit them.*

"You forget your place, woman. I don't know what lies you've

---

* You see how well behaved I was here? I didn't even turn his bones into acid. It's not like they know about talismans in Jorat . . . it would have been *so easy.*

told those men, but Relos Var sent you to help *me*, not pine over some damn mare who wants to paint herself a stallion. And I know Janel isn't dead, so you can stop pretending; Xaltorath's curse just makes her look dead when she sleeps, so heal her. I need her alive so she can give her title to me."

The white-skinned woman blinked once when Sir Oreth mentioned Xaltorath's name, then her gray eyes shifted upward. "Interesting," she murmured. "There can't be many Joratese who've ever heard of Xaltorath. Where did you?"

"I don't have time to answer your nonsense." He drew his sword. "Heal her and open that gate back up for me."

"Senera—" Brother Qown warned.

The puppy by the fireplace crouched, looking toward Sir Oreth and growling.

"Enough." Senera gestured toward Sir Oreth with two hooked fingers. His sword twisted and warped in his hand, the hilt reforming around his fingers like manacles. The blade itself drew back, hovering point first like a snake rearing back to strike.

Sir Oreth tried to drop the sword and found he couldn't. "Stop it! What are you—" The blade edge came to a stop just a hair from his throat. Sir Oreth stopped moving.

"What am I doing?" Senera chuckled. "I should think that's obvious; I'm dealing with you. And you're not playing the backwater circuits anymore, my pretty idiot. These contests involve enemies of such scope and prowess you haven't even begun to comprehend the odds. That's why Relos Var ordered us not to kill anyone. Brought with us, the old woman could've been kept from spilling secrets. But dead? Oh, being dead plays to our enemies' strengths."

"You're not making sense . . ." Sir Oreth didn't look at her. He didn't take his eyes off the sword.

Senera narrowed her eyes. "Who do you think you are?" She walked over to the fireplace and bent over to pet the dhole puppy, whose tail thumped against the hearth in response.

"What do you mean? I'm Sir Oreth Malkoessian—"

She rolled her eyes. "Meaningless. Ephemeral. Titles and quirks of birth order can be stripped from you in an instant. Who are *you*?" Without waiting for him to answer, she turned to Brother Qown. "Let's try this again. Who are you?"

"I—" Qown made a face. "I'm a priest of—"

Senera cut him off with an angry gesture. "I expected better. That's a *job*. If I slay you now, priest, do you cease to exist?" She turned back to Sir Oreth. "Do you think you're nothing more than your physical form? Pretty and quick? Young and stupid?"

"Hey!" Sir Oreth flinched as the sword reminded him not to move.

"Our souls," Brother Qown said. "We are our souls."

"Right," Sir Oreth agreed. "When I die, my soul will go to the Land of Peace."

"Don't assume Thaena likes you that much. I'll allow you'll at least travel to the Afterlife." She walked over to Janel's body. "This body you wear isn't who you are. It's not your identity. In fact, it's your prison. Your body keeps you pinned to this side of the twin worlds, locked away, controllable. While we had that old woman in her physical body, healthy and alive, her soul was under our control. But now that you've killed her?" She tsked. "Dorna's telling Thaena everything she knows even as we speak. And Thaena will tell her people. The Goddess of Death will then tell your father, the Markreev, the first time he makes a funerary offering at one of Thaena's shrines. Tell me, what sort of man is the Markreev of Stavira? Will he lie to protect you? Or will he tell the duke the truth: that his son is a traitor gone so very saelen? What a disappointment you must be . . ."

Sir Oreth seemed so horrified by the question, he stopped paying attention to the hovering sword.*

"Wait," Brother Qown said. "You're talking about this like Thaena is the enemy. Thaena herself."

---

* Oh, save me from beautiful, spoiled little boys with daddy issues.

Senera shrugged. "Thaena *is* the enemy. They all are. Khored, Taja, Galava—all of them. You've been sold lies all your life. The Eight Immortals aren't our guardians. They're our jailers, our rulers. They sit at the pinnacle of a system that benefits from humanity's enslavement. Why would they ever set us free?" She picked up scissors and began to cut away the leather straps holding Janel's ornamental black armor to her body.

"That's not—" But before Brother Qown could even begin to protest, light blazed brightly before a bookcase, solidifying into a familiar fractal swirl—which circled while the center turned mirrorlike.

Relos Var stepped through.

The wizard closed the gate behind him and raised an eyebrow at the silver sword-snake wrapped around Sir Oreth. "At least someone's been having a good time."

He ignored Brother Qown and Janel's body on the table and walked over to the side table to pour himself a drink. "I'd ask how things went, but I just spent the last ten minutes talking to a thoroughly hysterical Duke Xun about the Markreev of Stavira's youngest son. Apparently, our young knight just murdered the Markreev's ex-wife. Or is it ex-husband? I'm not sure it makes a difference."

Sir Oreth started to choke, but neither Relos Var nor Senera paid any attention.

Brother Qown had never seen Relos Var close-up before. He couldn't shake an unmistakable sense of familiarity. He frowned, trying to imagine what had triggered the feeling.

Relos Var threw Senera an apologetic look. "Unfortunately, I had to reassure the duke that you and I are unconnected. My sincerest apologies."

She waved a hand as she continued to work. "It's fine. The tournaments have grown boring, anyway. "

"My father—" Sir Oreth's voice broke.

Relos Var gave Sir Oreth an annoyed look. "What are we going to do about this one? He's useless to us in terms of Tolamer. The Markreev of Stavira will now call due his loans.

Since young Oreth here can't repay them, the canton will default back to his father. I doubt we'll convince Aroth to work with us instead."

"Relos, we had a deal. I was helping you!" Sir Oreth interrupted. "I can explain everything. I didn't—I didn't mean to kill Dorna. I just—I lost my temper."

"Not your temper," Brother Qown spat, "your courage. You didn't murder her until you knew your father was about to arrive."

"Oh, well, that was one bad decision after another then, wasn't it? Added bonus: Dorna's not dead," Relos Var said as he returned with his drink and sat down in a chair. "You didn't even accomplish that much. Honestly, Oreth, what good are you?"

"But I saw her—" Brother Qown blinked.

Sir Oreth seemed just as surprised. "You just said I murdered her."

Relos Var shrugged. "Oh, she died. Absolutely. Stayed dead? Not a chance." He gave Senera a significant look. "She's an angel. I'm sure Thaena's sending Dorna's soul back to her body as we speak."

Senera raised an eyebrow. "An angel? Are you serious? One of Thaena's? I suspected that old woman had depths, but she never struck me as one of Thaena's chosen helpers."

"Oh no. She's one of Tya's servitors."

Senera turned back to Janel. "That makes much more sense."

Brother Qown leaned forward. "Wait. Dorna serves the Goddess of Magic?"

Relos Var gave him a split-second glance before returning his focus to Senera. "What *are* we going do with our handsome Joratese knight here? Gaesh him?"

Sir Oreth's eyes widened.

"I suppose," Senera said. "But for what purpose? He'd get himself killed in a gaesh loop the first time we send him to collect firewood." She pulled her small inkstone from her misha and began mixing up a small batch of ink.

Brother Qown wouldn't have found the grinding sound of the ink stick moving against the stone quite so sinister if he hadn't known she was using a Cornerstone. Using such an artifact as if it were a scribe's tool seemed sacrilegious.

"You can't gaesh me!" Sir Oreth protested.

"Be quiet," Senera said, "or I'll make you be quiet, and you won't enjoy how." She resumed her conversation with Relos Var. "He'd make a nice peace offering to Gadrith?"*

Relos Var wrinkled his nose. "I'd rather not. Gadrith prefers sorcerers, anyway." He tilted his head and looked over at Sir Oreth. "How's your singing voice?"

"What?" Sir Oreth looked bemused. "I . . . uh . . . I'm sorry. I can't carry a tune. I could try to learn . . . ?"

Senera shuddered. "Oh, and I thought my suggestion was cruel. Relos, you're the worst."

Relos Var shrugged. "I don't know where Sharanakal is sleeping these days, anyway."

"Shall we make him Duke Kaen's problem, then?" Senera's wide eyes personified innocence.†

Relos Var started laughing. "Yes, fine. Kaen's problem. The look on Kaen's face alone should be worth it. The last thing he wants is another puppy added to his collection." He finished his drink and stood. "I'm going to take a walk along the beach. I'll be back in a bit."

Senera smiled. "Going to say hello to your vané friend?"

Relos Var's eyes widened. "I have no idea what you might mean."

"Uh-huh." Senera wrinkled her nose. "Hug her for me."

He chuckled. "She's not a hugger. But I'll give Her Majesty your regards."

"Mind if I gaesh Danorak while you're gone?" Senera asked.

* Honestly, I'm glad he's gone. I know Gadrith had his uses, but he was more trouble than he was worth.
† What? *I* didn't write that. Qown did. I'm quite sure I don't have an innocent drop of blood in my whole body.

She might as well have been asking if he minded her making more tea.

"Go right ahead."

As soon as Relos Var left, Senera returned to her ink preparation.

Sir Oreth licked his lips, then said, "Colonel?"

Senera looked up, annoyed.

He moved carefully to keep from impaling himself on the still-animate sword. "I, uh . . . I wanted to apologize."

Senera set down the inkstone and turned to look at him, both eyebrows raised.

"I'm sorry," Sir Oreth said. "It was wrong of me to mistreat you. I was in the wrong, and I want to emphasize how sorry I am. Could I please . . ." He glanced at the sword. "I can be very helpful. I promise."

Senera's mouth quirked. "I should use animated swords on men more often."

"If you're not idorrá, you're thudajé," Brother Qown said.

Senera must have heard him, because she chuckled.

She leaned forward and studied Sir Oreth. "I wonder if you're sincere. Well, I suppose we'll find out. Just realize that if you're not being sincere, I can fashion up such fates for you as would make demons hide their eyes."

"I believe you."

"Good." Senera waved her hand and the sword in Sir Oreth's hand straightened. The hilt returned to its former shape.

He dropped the weapon to the ground.

"So is there anything I can do to help?" Sir Oreth asked, the embodiment of solicitous care and attention.

"I'm sure Brother Qown would appreciate some tea," Senera said. "I would too, but I'm going to be a bit too preoccupied." She gestured toward Janel's body.

"Gaeshing Count Janel is a horrid idea," Brother Qown said. "Is there any chance I can talk you out of it?"

She smiled. "No."

"I thought as much." He felt sick.

Brother Qown had never seen anyone gaeshed, but he'd heard about it from Father Zajhera. He knew enough to understand the ritual's blasphemy. For someone like Janel—

It would kill her. He rather doubted she'd play along with gaesh commands, even at the cost of her own life.

As Sir Oreth went to the fire to put a kettle on, the puppy growled at him and seemed disinclined to let him approach.

"Rebel, down," Senera said. "Go to your pillow."

The dhole gave Sir Oreth a reproachful look and circled back over to the velvet pillow.

"The dog's name is Rebel?" Sir Oreth asked.

"Hmm. Shush. This is quiet time," Senera said, staring at Janel's body. She frowned.

Brother Qown shifted his position, wincing at the wounds he hadn't yet fixed. He had a good idea what Senera attempted: healing Janel's body before the gaeshing ritual. He also had a good idea why it wasn't working. The same reason it hadn't worked when he had tried it several weeks before.

If he did nothing—

Janel seemed stable, but Brother Qown didn't know if that was due to some spell cast by Relos Var or Janel's own magic. In either case, at some point, the spell would end and Janel would finish dying.

If Senera healed her, she'd suffer a worse fate. Being kidnapped and taken to Yor was bad enough; the dominion didn't have a sterling reputation for its treatment of women. But if Relos Var and Senera planned to take Janel there under gaesh . . .

Qown thought about Senera's statement, that death would be an escape. Thaena would bring Janel back, wouldn't she? Maybe, maybe. But there was always the risk that it wouldn't be Thaena who received Janel's soul, but Xaltorath. Indeed, Qown was willing to bet Xaltorath had rigged things to obtain exactly that result. Which fate would be worse?

It wasn't exactly a hard choice.

"You're going to need help," Brother Qown suggested.

Senera looked up.

"Her magical defenses are indiscriminate. It makes her hard to heal," he elaborated. "You'll need someone helping you."

"If you try anything—"

"I know, I know. If I try anything, you'll make me wish I was never born."

"With a few variations, but yes, basically." Senera motioned him over. "Pull up a stool, and let's get to work."

The work itself took about thirty minutes, and by the end, they had two cups of tea and a healthy, whole Joratese count.

Brother Qown wished he felt better about it. Saving Janel's life had felt like a betrayal.

"Go sit back down. I won't need you for the next part," Senera said. "Also, this is the part where you're likely to try something stupid from sheer moral fortitude, so it might be best to remove the temptation. Sir Oreth, if you'd like to prove yourself useful, keep an eye on the priest here. You shouldn't need to resort to violence, but I'd keep the sword close, just in case. Oh, and it should go without saying, but *don't kill him.* Yes?"

The Joratese man nodded and bent over to retrieve his fallen blade. He held the sword gingerly, as if it had just come fresh from the oven.

Brother Qown sat down again on his original bench, moving his fingers over himself to check for lingering hematomas. However, professional curiosity overcame him, and he started watching Senera paint markings on Janel's hands, her face, and her chest.

"You're not—" He frowned. "Who does that summon?"

Senera chuckled. "No one."

"But I don't understand."

"I'm not surprised."

Sir Oreth looked back between the two other people. "Wait, why are we summoning a demon?"

Brother Qown blinked at him. "Because you have to. You have to summon a demon if you want to gaesh someone."

"Oh." Sir Oreth hesitated. "So . . . I mean, I've always

wondered. What is a gaesh? I know it's a thing you do to slaves . . . ?"

"Adorable," Senera said. "But as it happens, Brother Qown is wrong. You don't have to summon a demon to gaesh someone. It's just easier to have a demon do it."

"And a gaesh?" Sir Oreth insisted.

Senera rolled her eyes. "It's what you've heard. It keeps someone under your control. Not always successfully."

"You rip away a piece of someone's soul," Brother Qown said. "You rip out a piece of their soul and use it to put them in unbearable pain if they disobey you. So unbearable it often kills." He gave Sir Oreth a significant look. "If you recall, it's what they debated doing to you."

Sir Oreth looked uneasy, but he shrugged it off. "So we're summoning a demon, then?"

Brother Qown would have expected him to fear such a pronouncement or at the very least be disgusted.

Yet Sir Oreth sounded excited.*

Senera shook her head. "I said we *weren't* summoning a demon. We're using a Cornerstone."

Brother Qown straightened. "Which one?"

"The Stone of Shackles."

"You have the Stone of Shackles?"

"No, but it's irrelevant." Senera continued talking as she sketched on Janel's body. Brother Qown couldn't tell what purpose the markings served, but perhaps calling on the Cornerstone's powers required them.

Finally, she stepped back, tilted her head, and examined her work. Senera had drawn a spiraling design that covered the unconscious woman's vital energy points.

"Now I need you both to be very quiet," Senera said as she picked up a lion medallion from a shelf, "and I'm not joking when I say that if you defy me in this, you will spend your remaining days screaming." She looked up at them. "Understood?"

---

* Pretty. Idiot.

The two men nodded.

Senera tucked her brush back into her hair and gestured toward Janel's body. The body levitated and then tilted so Janel seemed to stand, her body vertical.

Holding the medallion in one hand, Senera touched the other to Janel's hands, her neck, her forehead, and held her fingers in a claw shape over the woman's heart.

Brother Qown couldn't help but think that last gesture must be symbolic or even performative. *There's no special dwelling place for spiritual energy in the heart muscle.*

He kept the thought to himself.

As Senera pulled her fingers back, thin energy strands flowed from Janel's body to the woman's hand. The motion reminded Qown of spinning thread: tiny strands of floss pulling from ball to spindle. As soul stuff pooled in Senera's hand, she shaped and stretched the thread before feeding it into the medallion.

When Senera finished, anyone who held Janel's medallion could give her any command they desired. Janel would disobey those commands at the cost of her own life.

Janel didn't move or make a sound. She still walked the Afterlife. She'd have no idea what had happened until she woke, and then it would be the start of horrors lasting all her days.

He searched the room for anything he might use to distract Senera, anything he might use against Sir Oreth. He found nothing. He'd just get himself killed. *A dead physicker heals no patients.*

Finally, Senera stopped pulling filaments and closed her fist around the medallion, which glowed for a moment before fading into junk-worthy jewelry.

"All right," Senera said, "the hard part's done—"

The necklace disintegrated to dust.

The glowing soul matter flowed back into Janel's body.

Senera stared.

"Is it supposed to do that?" Sir Oreth asked.

Even Brother Qown couldn't help but lean forward.

"No . . . no, it's not." Senera looked appalled. "Stay back." She collected a different necklace, this time a hunting cat's tooth.

Senera performed the ritual again, going through the same motions with the diligence of a student who'd memorized rote lines a thousand times. She executed the steps more slowly this time to make sure she hadn't skipped a step.

The hunting cat's tooth also turned to ash when she'd finished.

"How the hell—" Senera muttered.

"I've never seen anything like that," Brother Qown said, which overlooked the fact he'd never seen a gaesh performed in person before either.

"Pragaos, Molash, get in here!" Senera shouted.

The guards came through the door, swords drawn and ready for violence, but they relaxed their stances when they saw there was no need. A soldier glanced at the topless count, but otherwise, the men focused their attention on Senera. "Yes, Colonel?"

"Go find Var," Senera said. "He needs to see this."

When Relos Var returned, he cleared the room of everyone but himself, Senera, Janel, and Brother Qown. Sir Oreth seemed positively giddy to be out of Senera's sight. After the others left, Relos Var and Senera conducted the ritual together for a third time. And for a third time, it failed.

Then Relos Var did it by himself, with Senera watching. He broke down the ritual, explained each step, and went over it in such explicit detail Qown believed *he* could've gaeshed someone by the end. Brother Qown realized this wasn't a spell, any more than the sigil he'd copied from Senera qualified as a spell. If one followed the ritual, step by perfect step, a dependable, predictable response resulted. Spellcasting ability made no difference. Anyone could do this if they followed the directions.

But still it failed.

Relos Var then cast other magics, pulling in power and reweaving connections. At one point, he opened a gate to another location, after they'd exhausted their supply of gaesh trinkets. As Relos Var worked, something about him again pulled at Brother Qown's attention. That sense of familiarity. That sense of recognition. Var wasn't a stranger. Qown *knew* him.

Since Brother Qown had been quiet and hadn't moved from his position, he'd been easy to ignore. No one stopped him from letting his focus drift into Illumination.

So he saw why Relos Var seemed so familiar.

He cast magic the same way as Father Zajhera.

Now Brother Qown had received a more in-depth education on the magical arts than most Academy graduates. Father Zajhera had been a thorough instructor, one who believed in teaching fundamentals and theory. So Brother Qown knew magical instruction could only inspire and advise. Magic was personal. No two people approached spellcasting the same way. Even twins would have different approaches to how they cast spells.

But Relos Var cast spells the same way as Father Zajhera. *Exactly the same.*

Qown saw no difference at all.*

And his eyes widened in horror as he stood up from the bench.

"Zajhera," he whispered.

Relos Var looked up.

Their eyes met across the room.

Relos Var frowned. For that split second, Var looked bereft. Heartbroken.

Relos Var broke eye contact and tossed down the crystal he'd been using as a focusing device. He chuckled. "I'm not surprised you failed, student. Someone's beaten us to it."

Senera blinked at him. "What?"

"You can't gaesh her because she's already gaeshed. Someone has preempted us. Her soul already belongs to another."

"Who?"

Relos Var seemed to give the matter some thought. "I don't know." He laughed. "Oh, now, that's a sentence I haven't said in centuries. Unfortunately . . ." He gestured toward Janel. "We don't have time to answer it to our satisfaction. If gaeshing isn't possible, we'll need to find a different way."

---

* Oh. So this is what happened. I always wondered.

"What are you thinking?" Senera asked.

"Declaw our little lion," Relos Var answered. "Let's at least limit her ability to toss soldiers about like mice. I don't relish taking her back to Duke Kaen only to see her rip his head off." He paused. "Don't tell Duke Kaen about her gaesh. He has enough problems with paranoia."

They didn't seem to be paying attention to him. Brother Qown thought Relos Var must not have heard what he'd said. Qown felt the metaphorical hand around his throat loosen. He exhaled.

"Let's turn her over," Senera suggested. "This will be better on her back." She added a bit more water to thin her black ink, while Relos Var gently flipped Janel over on the table.

Brother Qown looked toward the door. How far could he run before the guards caught him? He didn't know any good spells for invisibility either—he only knew how to hide words. Maybe if something distracted the guards . . .

Yet when he looked back, Senera was drawing on Janel's back. He couldn't help but pause.

She was drawing a sigil.

Not the same one he'd seen her use to clean the air, but it shared a similar style. As Senera swirled the brush over Janel's skin, the ink sank in and dried, permanent and dark as Janel's fingers.

Senera stood back and admired her work.

"That should do it," she said. "Declawed as ordered." She paused, and her expression took on a sad, bitter note. "Why are we doing this?"

Var raised an eyebrow.

"Why are we bringing her with us? What do you mean to accomplish?"

Relos Var looked surprised. "Are you questioning me?"

"You've stripped a woman—" She stopped. "No, not a woman. You've stripped a *girl's* power, and now you're throwing her to the wolves. That's not like you."

He chuckled. "But we haven't stripped her power. Only her

crutch. She never needed to develop her gifts any further before. Call this motivation. As for what I have planned . . ." Var glanced back at Qown before returning his attention to Senera. "What do I always have planned, dear child? I'm making sure the prophecies are fulfilled. The demon-claimed child, remember?"

"*The demon-claimed child gathers the broken, witches and outlaws, rebels outspoken, to plot conquest and uprising while winter's malice hides her chains in the snow king's palace.* The Devoran Prophecies, book 3, quatrain 17." Senera's mouth twisted. "Fine. I'll allow the snow king's palace is in Yor, but I don't see how she's going to plot a rebellion while a prisoner there. Anyway, isn't Duke Kaen the demon-claimed child?"

"He *might* be." Relos Var grinned. "But between you and me, I've always felt that interpretation was a bit forced." He looked down at Janel's body and stopped smiling. "My metal's on her. But you know what I say. If you want to win a horse race—"

"—bet on every horse," Senera finished. "Shall we go, then?"

"Not quite." Relos looked remorseful. "I'm afraid we have one more gaesh to perform first."

He turned around and stared straight at Brother Qown.

And Brother Qown knew he hadn't fooled Relos Var after all.

33: A FRIENDLY REUNION

Jorat Dominion, Quuros Empire.
Three days since Kihrin discovered who
controlled the Gryphon Men

"Did Relos Var gaesh you, then?" Kihrin asked.

Qown shuddered. "What do you think?" Then he grimaced. "My apologies. I'm being rude. After three years of not being allowed to talk about it . . ."

Janel shoved her chair back and walked out of the room, toward the stable.

Qown stood. "Oh. She—"

"Did she know who Father Zajhera really was?" Kihrin stood as well.

Qown looked helpless. "No."

Kihrin remembered how she'd spoken of Father Zajhera, how the Vishai priest had helped her recover from Xaltorath's possession. Dorna's words: *When Janel came back to Tolamer, the father came with her . . .*

A noise rang out. It sounded like something had just slammed into the front door. Everyone in the tavern paused.

Dorna stood. "I'd best go—"

"No." Kihrin raised his hands to the group. "Let me."

Not that he waited on their permission. He followed Janel.

He arrived in time to see her slam herself against the ice-trapped door. The sound of breaking ice filled the massive stone room. Chunks of the fire-hardened door split off and fell to the ground, but despite that, the giant frozen wall stood firm.

"No more games!" she screamed. "Where's your uncle,

Aeyan'arric? Tell that arrogant horse's ass to come out and face me!"

Behind Janel, Arasgon whinnied and pawed the ground near her, angrily tossing his black mane. Whatever the fireblood said to Janel, the words fell on deaf ears.

She set both hands against the door.

It exploded into flame.

Kihrin thought Janel intended to melt her way out, but he was less certain what she thought she could do against the dragon outside.*

In any event, he couldn't reach her with a screaming, parental fireblood standing in the way.

"Hey, Arasgon. Let me try."

Arasgon spun to face him. Kihrin remembered . . . something. A flash of fire and hooves, the feeling Arasgon had blocked his path before, somewhere else. Kihrin thought the fireblood might strike out at him, but instead, Arasgon retreated toward Scandal and Talaras.

Janel's fingers clenched around charring wood as she continued to burn her way through. "I won't be Relos Var's game piece! *Do you hear me?*"

Kihrin put his hand on Janel's shoulder.

The fire died.

She spun around, swung at him, but she was suddenly no stronger than any woman her size and weight. Urthaenriel wouldn't allow her magically increased strength to affect him.

Kihrin caught her wrist. "Janel," he said, "stop. Please stop."

Fury and tears filled Janel's eyes. Her breath was ragged as she leaned back against the charred door, forcing a quiet sob from her throat.

"Father Zajhera used to tell me stories," she whispered. "He'd sing me to sleep at night."

Kihrin's throat tightened, but he tried for lighthearted, anyway. "Wait. He can sing?"

---

* Give her indigestion? Get caught in her teeth?

Janel stared at him in despair. "No," she said. "He really can't."*

She burst into tears.

He put his arms around her, drew her to him, and let her cry into his misha. He knew this wasn't easy for her—crying was embarrassing, messy, a sign of stallion weakness. Kihrin was beginning to understand Jorat put the same expectations on its men that the Capital did; they just allowed some of those men to be female.

He held her as if none of that mattered, because it didn't.

Janel made fists against his chest and sobbed with all the anger of someone betrayed by a loved one. Which is what Relos Var had almost certainly been.

After a while, the crying slowed, and Janel pulled away enough to wipe her nose and look embarrassed. She seemed seconds from excusing herself and retreating to a more private location.

Kihrin didn't let go.

Instead, he touched her cheek. "I know what it's like. Okay, sure, the person I trusted didn't turn out to be *Relos Var,* but even so . . . I know how this must hurt."

"He was *grooming* me." Janel's face twisted. "That ass . . ."

"He healed you after Xaltorath possessed you. I can't hate Relos Var for that. Is Xaltorath the one who gaeshed you?"

"I don't know—" Janel looked away. "If she was, she never exploited it.† Anyway, Relos Var only healed me because he can't use a broken tool."

"His motives can go jump off a cliff. I don't care why he did it, only that you're here."

They stared at each other. Then Janel walked her fingers up his misha until they reached his jaw, resting there with the

---

* Um . . . really? I mean, I've never heard you sing, but . . . you know what, just forget I said anything.

† That really doesn't make any sense. But I checked with the Name of All Things out of an excess of curiosity. Xaltorath did indeed gaesh Janel. To what purpose? Your guess is as good as mine.

lightest of touches. Kihrin wondered who'd started playing drums in the room and then realized that was his heart.

"I'd like to kiss you," Janel whispered.

"Oh, good. I'd like that too." He lowered his head to meet hers.

Their kiss started soft and slow and gentle, the touch of their lips against each other almost shy. That didn't last long. He couldn't even be sure which of them escalated, but suddenly their kiss graduated into something needful and fierce, a dance of lips and tongues that left them both gasping. She dug her fingers into his back and yanked him closer, until he felt every curve of Janel's body pressed against him. He smelled the woodsmoke lingering in her laevos hair, heard their hearts beating in time. What had Khored called it? An immediate connection? That. A thousand times that.*

He pushed his hands up under her tunic and felt metal instead of skin. Kihrin blinked and looked down. "Are you wearing mail?"

Janel paused, embarrassed. "I want to be ready the moment Morios shows up."

"Ah. Right. Makes sense." Kihrin started kissing the side of her neck when several loud horse snorts interrupted them.

Janel looked over at the firebloods and rolled her eyes.

"Did they just tell us to find a room?"

"Worse. They're critiquing." Janel smoothed his misha over his chest. "We could always use a few straw bales in the back." Her eyes were bloodshot from tears, but her smile told Kihrin she was serious.

Kihrin felt sure she was. As much as that idea excited him—and oh, did it excite him—he knew what this was. Another way of drowning the pain, using slick flesh and motion instead of aris and beer.

Kihrin kissed her forehead. "That sounds itchy and quick."

---

* I thought you'd want the nuance of their . . . encounter. Trust me when I say it was as uncomfortable for me to write as it likely was for you to read.

He whispered, "I don't want our first time to be either of those things."

Janel shuddered against him. The good kind of shudder. She gazed up at him with lidded eyes as her hands traced a path lower down his back. Then she pulled him flush against her again and ground her hips. Kihrin groaned and decided he could live with being used as pain relief.

But Janel pushed him away, panting. She exhaled slowly as she leaned back against the door. She didn't seem to care that it was covered with melting ice. "Right. If you don't want that, then we should stop."

"Don't . . ." Kihrin ran his fingers over the links in her chain armor. "Don't think I'm not willing."

Janel laughed. "I can feel how willing you are." She closed her eyes and leaned back against the door. "But . . . no, you're right. This is bad timing. And there's something I need to tell you first."

"As long as you're not going to tell me that you're running outside to become a frozen Hellwarrior as soon as I turn my back, I can take it. Neither Aeyan'arric or her uncle are—" Kihrin paused as he realized what he'd just said. What Janel had said, earlier. "Hold on. *Uncle?*"

Janel cleared her throat. "Yes, uncle. Relos Var is Aeyan'arric's uncle."

Kihrin blinked and took a step backward. "Aeyan . . . arric."

Janel straightened and adjusted her tunic.

Kihrin hadn't made the connection. Relos Var's real name was Rev'arric, just as his own past life's name had also ended with *arric*. Evidently, that was the family name.

"Does Relos Var have any . . . other . . . siblings?"

Janel shook her head. "No."

"So that dragon out there is Relos Var's niece and my—" He pressed his lips together.

"Your daughter." She quickly amended the statement. "Your past life's daughter. Not *your* daughter, obviously."

"That doesn't make me feel better." Kihrin felt a temporary

rush of anger. Had Aeyan'arric participated in his past life's murder willingly, the same way Sharanakal and the other dragons had? Had she thought to become a goddess, been tempted by all that glittering power, only to be turned into a terrible monster instead?

Had Relos Var whispered in her ears too?

Kihrin took her hand. "Let's go back. We stay here any longer and they're going to think we really did go behind the straw bales. And much as I'd enjoy that, I need to hear the rest of this story."

Janel gave him a worried look. "Yes, I really think you do."

"You all right, foal?" Dorna asked when they returned.

Janel sat down in her seat. "Yes, thank you. I'm sorry about that. It was just a shock."

Qown nodded, looking sympathetic. "We'll get through this."

Janel started talking.

Janel's Turn. The Ice Demesne, Yor, Quur.

I woke the next morning in a bed, healed.

It wasn't my bed. I wasn't wearing my clothes. Multiple things felt wrong. Very wrong.

The most obvious: I had never felt so weak in all my life. All the strength had been drained from me. It was all I could do to push the furs off my body.

"Count?" Brother Qown had fallen asleep on a small couch near me, and he yawned as he sat up.

"What—?" I winced as I stood.

It's hard to describe what felt different, except I've been preternaturally strong since childhood. After the Hellmarch, I had to learn how to safely hold everyday objects. You have no idea how easy it is to crush a cup while holding it or to rip one's boots while trying to put them on. To find myself no stronger than any person my age and fitness felt like illness.

"How are you doing?" Brother Qown rubbed his eyes.

White fur blankets had covered us. Thick slabs of smooth, polished black stone made up the windowless walls. Several lanterns hung from hooks, and a fire burned in a hearth across the chamber. The room felt more like a tomb or mausoleum than a place for living beings to dwell. A large door pierced one wall, with two smaller doors in the adjacent one. Thick, sturdy furniture adorned with curious geometric patterns and lattices decorated the room.

Nothing about the décor felt Joratese.

I inhaled and winced. "I feel . . ." I rubbed my chest where I'd been stabbed. Not even a bruise remained to commemorate the event. "I don't feel well, to be honest. Does Relos Var have us prisoner?"

Brother Qown hesitated, but then nodded.

The priest didn't look well either. The dark circles under his eyes suggested he hadn't slept much. Plus, he had added a flinch, the sort to convince a village to take a child from their parents back in Jorat.

"Brother Qown, we're going to get through this. Now when they come back, they're going to try to gaesh—"

Brother Qown interrupted me. "No, they're not."

I hesitated. "What?"

"They already did."

My heart nearly stopped. I stared at him and felt like an idiot. Of course they'd done it while I slept. Much easier when I couldn't protest. Khored had said he'd protect me, but I still didn't know how . . .

"I mean—they tried." Qown seemed to choose his next words carefully. "But they failed. You can't be gaeshed."

I blinked. "I can't be gaeshed? But that's impossible. Anyone can be gaeshed. Anything with a soul can be gaeshed. *Demons* can be gaeshed—"

"I saw them try. I saw them try four times. Every time, it failed."

I sat back down again. Khored had done it. Somehow, he'd done it.

"Did they capture the others?" I asked.

He hesitated. "Dorna . . . Sir Oreth stabbed Dorna—"

I inhaled, made fists with my hands, before I remembered Sir Oreth wasn't there. And I felt too weak to do anything if he had been.

He added, "Relos Var seemed confident she'd be Returned. I don't know what happened to the others, though."

Could I trust anything Relos Var said? But why would he lie? If Dorna had died, why not just admit it and blame me? On the other hand, if anyone could steal their way back from the Afterlife, my metal would be on Dorna. She knew more tricks than Taja herself.*

If no one else had died, then it had all gone well.

Except for the part where my reputation lay in shambles. Except for the part where Duke Xun had almost certainly stripped away my title. Except for the part where I had meant to take this mission alone.

Get in, find the spear, get out. I'd thought this would be the easy part, eclipsed by using Khoreval to kill Relos Var's ice dragon pet. Except, now it was anything but easy.

I walked over to him. "Oh, Qown, I'm so sorry," I said. "I didn't mean to get you wrapped up in this. Var was just supposed to take me."

"Just supposed to—" He blinked at me, then held up a hand. "Please don't say another word. I can't be trusted anymore. I said you proved immune to gaesh. I didn't."

My mouth dropped open. Horror stole over me even as the truth squeezed my heart.

I had never meant to put my friends at risk. Certainly not like this.

"Who has it? Who has your gaesh? I'll make—" My body reminded me once more that I felt weak as a new foal. Gangly, not possessing even a tenth my normal strength.

I put my hands to my knees and breathed deeply. I hadn't

---

* I almost . . . *almost* . . . believe that. And no, Dorna isn't Taja. I checked.

planned on it going like this at all. I had just assumed every-thing would go my way.

I always won, didn't I?

Mithros would laugh at me, and not in a friendly fashion. Teraeth wouldn't laugh, but his "I told you so" anger would be worse. They had both said the risk was too great and I had ignored them. Overconfident, arrogant, certain of my success.

And so very, very wrong.

"What did they do to me?" I asked.

"There's a tattoo on your back," he answered. "Similar in style to the sigil we saw in Mereina. I don't know what it does, but Relos Var said it would 'declaw' you."

I nodded, fighting down nausea and despair in equal measure. Taking my strength would indeed declaw me, but they were mistaken if they thought their sigil would turn me from a stallion to a mare.

I placed my hand against the surface of a wall and felt the dark stone's smooth texture. How many walls separated me from freedom? Had they put us in a room without windows to keep us from escaping—or because in a dominion bound by perpetual winter, only a fool would ever build windows at all?

"So we're in Yor," I said.

"We're in Yor," Brother Qown agreed.

Senera entered, holding a tray. Unlike Brother Qown and me, she looked lovely and in her element, wearing a fur jerkin and a long, flowing gray tunic. "I'd ask how you're both feeling this morning, but I already know the answer. I hope you're comfortable. I asked them to put you in a warm room. Yorans sometimes forget not everyone tolerates cold as well as they do."

Senera set down the tray. "I brought you lunch. We're going to have a feast soon, but you should eat beforehand. The Yoran diet is almost exclusively meat. You'll need time to adjust."

I found myself wondering if she'd gone back to Jorat just to fetch us the meal. I saw several bowls of coconut-and-jasmine-scented rice, fragrant vegetable stew, fried duck eggs, a jar of chili sauce, and all the normal side vegetables and fermented snacks. She'd even brought tea.

I frowned. She was treating us like saelen. Not like prisoners, not like enemies—like new family members. As if it could be taken for granted we'd come around. The strays always did.

Then I realized this wasn't generosity, trust, or a desire to bring us into the fold; this was a safety measure. Meat required knives. This meal did not.

"I don't eat meat," Brother Qown said.

"Bad luck, I'm afraid. You're about to start." Senera went over to a smaller door, which proved to be a closet. She pulled out a shirt, pants, and a long, dark red dress. "I brought clothing over while you slept so you have something to wear to meet the Hon."

"Hon?"

"What you will call the duke." She smiled. "The Yorans reject Quur's titles."

I narrowed my eyes. "The duke *is* Quuros."

"I wouldn't mention that in front of him."

"Why not just kill me? Why bring me back here?"

She stopped smiling. "Relos Var thinks you're more useful to him alive. At least for now. You should try to behave accordingly."

She tossed the clothes on the bed and gestured to a dresser. "You'll find jewelry and hair combs in there: enough to satisfy stallion pride. Eat lunch and make yourselves ready. I'll be back in an hour to take you to the duke."

"And if we say no?" I crossed my arms over my chest.

She scoffed. "Don't be stupid. Just because we don't want to hurt you doesn't mean we won't. And you're nothing special now. Just a normal girl. And him?" Her gray eyes flickered over to Brother Qown. "Hurting him is easy."

"Don't you dare—" I moved toward her, making her flinch.

Just for a moment, though. Then she grabbed my wrist and twisted, and I cried out because it hurt. I found myself too weak to push back. She forced me against the table's edge.

"Any. Time. We. Want," she whispered.

Senera walked out the door.

When I turned to Brother Qown, he began helping himself to breakfast.

"Eat," he told me. "We'll need our strength."

The clothes Senera had brought were heavy, thick, and woolen. They included wool pants and a shirt trimmed with animal fur for Qown, and a long, red woolen dress for me. I stared at the dress with distaste.

"I wouldn't want to fight in that," I said.

"I suspect Yorans believe women shouldn't fight," Qown said.

"I'm not—" I paused and sighed. "I'm not going to be able to convince them to treat me as one of the men, am I?"

"I don't . . . I don't think so. No."

I growled something unintelligible as I stripped off the night-gown. Paint flaked off my skin underneath.

"I need a bath," I said. "But I very much doubt I'll get one in Yor—wait." I didn't see a chamber pot anywhere. Either Senera had forgotten—which didn't seem like her—or she was being cruel—which didn't match her behavior.

I examined the walls. Black stone perfectly fitted without mortar. If I had a knife, I wouldn't have been able to fit the blade between the blocks. The level of workmanship rivaled anything I'd ever seen in Jorat—except Atrine.

Which suggested . . .

I walked to a smaller door and discovered a bathroom, one with hot running water. I remembered some royal guild or another who handled such matters. The duke (or Hon) wasn't afraid to hire magical services.

That's the one thing I miss about Atrine every time I leave; running water on demand is glorious.

"You need to escape," Brother Qown said, his voice echoing from the main room. "You can't stay here. I've heard stories about how the women are treated."

I paused while wiping the ink stains off my face. "I've heard those stories too. Anyone who tries anything with me is in for a rude surprise."

"I don't just mean that," Brother Qown said. "Well, I do mean that, but also . . . I mean . . . I've never heard of an unmarried woman in Yor. Never. If you're not married, they marry you. Women don't have a choice."

"Again, I'd like to see them try."

But I knew I'd have to deal with this. As much as I wanted to believe my sex shouldn't be an issue, Yorans didn't see gender as role expression. To them, it was nothing more than a person's physical form. The vessel's shape, never the contents within. So I was a woman to them, and they thought women were . . . only.

Only wives. Only mothers. Only chattel.

I ground my teeth.

I heard the main door open. "Are you two ready?"

Senera's voice.

"One moment." I sighed and tossed the chemise and red dress over my body. The dress fit tightly around the bodice and flowed below the waist. I thought I'd trip on the damn thing, coming and going, if I ever had to use stairs. Despite the wool, the fabric provided no protection if I ever had to go into the cold, which was probably deliberate.

Winter is a fantastic cage if all you're wearing is a summer dress.

"I brought shoes. I hope they'll fit. Qown, why don't you try those on?"

I entered the room. Senera had switched to a silver dress that made her look like a marble statue enchanted into life. It had the same flaring shape as mine, although the dress had been cut looser at the top. She wore tiny silver pins in her hair and rings on her fingers, but nothing I could take away from her and use as a weapon.

For some reason, she wore a small slate inkstone. The undecorated gray stone rested in a silver cradle hanging around her neck. I thought it must have been a guild symbol or perhaps a scribe symbol.

"You look lovely," she said to me.

"I don't feel it." I walked over to the dresser and opened it. Arrayed in neat rows, I found gold rings and necklaces and a long sweeping metal belt meant to be worn low around the hips. I took it, thinking I could use it as an improvised flail. The jewelry looked to be very fine quality: gold with gems like fire. Rubies, jacinths, topazes, and carnelians. I didn't recognize the style except to note it wasn't Joratese.

Halfway through, I realized the signals this would send in Jorat—a powerful, proud, successful stallion—might not have the same meaning in Yor.

I paused.

"Whose jewelry am I wearing?"

"Relos Var's," she replied.

I began removing the jewelry.

"No, no," she said, holding up her hands. "Look, I understand how you must be feeling."

"No, I don't think you do."

"This is for your protection."

"In what possible way is that true?"

The witch sighed. "Look, Yor is . . . provincial in its views about women. Even compared to the Capital, which is saying something. Women of a certain age are expected to be married. It's a matter of religion, believe it or not. We've had to work around these quaint local customs. You're going to need to adapt too."

"Are you suggesting I need to be married? Who did you have in mind as this partner?" I gestured toward Brother Qown. "Him?"

She grimaced. "No. Definitely not. Here it's acceptable to murder a man for his wife. Well, not acceptable . . . the Hon has outlawed the practice. But it happens. Our dear Brother Qown wouldn't last long if we told everyone you two are husband and wife. It needs to be someone no one dares try to kill."

"If you say Sir Oreth—"

"Hmm, not a bad idea," Senera agreed, "but I'm not supposed to let him die either."

I crossed my arms, remembering the conversation where Khored promised me Relos Var wouldn't kidnap a woman and take her by force. "So you mean Relos Var, then."

Senera shrugged. "I've been 'married' to Relos Var for five years. All for show. You won't even suffer the indignity of a ceremony."

"How considerate." I rolled my eyes.

"I wanted to warn you," Senera continued, "so when Relos Var introduces you to the Hon as his wife, you don't do something rash. Polygyny is legal here, so no one will question Relos Var taking another bride."

"What are you going to do with Brother Qown?" I asked.

"Relos Var's new assistant," Senera said. "No one needs to know what he really is: our hostage for your good behavior."

"You don't need to do that," I protested. "I'll behave. Let him go."

She tapped me on the cheek. "Finish dressing. It's time you meet the rest of the rebellion."

But Brother Qown had his own plans. We both turned as we heard the Vishai priest retching all over the floor, just before he collapsed.

34: THE ONLY WAY OUT

Jorat Dominion, Quuros Empire.
Three days (sort of) since Talon gave
Thurvishar a magic rock

Brother Qown cleared his throat, looking uncomfortable. "I, uh . . . I don't have good notes for the next part."

Janel seemed surprised. "What? But you—" Then she stopped herself. "Oh."

Kihrin raised an eyebrow. "I'm missing something, aren't I?"

"I didn't write down much of what happened next," Brother Qown admitted. He opened his book. "I'll read what I have, but then you should take back over, Janel."

She nodded. "Of course. Whatever you need."

Qown's Turn. The Ice Demesne, Yor, Quur.

Brother Qown spent the first few hours after his gaeshing giving serious consideration to the benefits of killing himself.

What could they do to stop him, after all? If he disobeyed the gaesh, the pain would kill him. So to commit suicide, all he had to do was disobey. His free soul would travel to the Land of Peace and his next reincarnation. Or be plucked up by demons, but he might escape.

He'd be free. That meant Janel would be free. If he guaranteed Janel's good behavior, then removing that guarantee was as simple as removing himself.

The gaesh meant he always held a weapon he could use upon himself. They could never take away his power to say no—or that refusal's consequences. They could make him follow every order except one—the order not to kill himself.

But he didn't do it.

He didn't commit suicide because of a single word: *too*. Janel hadn't planned on him ending up in Yor *too*.

Which meant she'd planned to end up there herself.

He couldn't put such a thing past her. Challenging Relos Var to a duel had been foolish behavior for a young woman not normally foolish—even if she did possess a distressing tendency to reach for violent solutions to her problems. Janel had to have known that using Joratese idorrá/thudajé concepts would be meaningless against an outsider. But if she'd intended to lose from the start . . .

Maybe. Just maybe.

But Janel didn't know the truth about Relos Var's identity. She also didn't know someone out there possessed a slice of her soul.

She didn't know the truth, and he couldn't tell her.

He had never in his life felt as powerless as he felt right then.

Brother Qown ignored the conversation between the two women and concentrated instead on the sun medallion he always kept on his person. They hadn't taken it from him, and neither Relos Var nor Senera had been so sadistic as to make it the vessel for his gaesh. He still had the symbol, and he habitually polished it with his thumb. Father Zajhera was a fraud, but was the religion as well?

Was Selanol's grace, Illumination's truth, forever tainted by lies? Could truth still be found there? Was that truth too important to discard, even when its outcome had been twisted to serve an evil man?

He must have put on the clothing Senera had brought, but he didn't remember doing it. One minute he wore his night-clothes, and the next, furs. It seemed an instant thing. Ever since he'd woken, he'd found himself flashing through moments of time, skipping over sections to land on new horrors.

He was in shock. He knew enough to diagnose his own condition. Zajhera's betrayal, his gaeshing, had proved too traumatic.

Zajhera had been like a father to him. Qown had trusted him with his life.

Janel's grandfather, the previous Count of Tolamer, had trusted the man too, trusted Zajhera with his granddaughter's life. Zajhera had been the one who'd exorcised Xaltorath when the demon prince had proved immune to all the normal methods, including a direct order from the emperor. Zajhera had been the one who put Janel together again afterward, who had guided her back to sanity—and kept her from devolving into a festering ball of hate and malice.

Zajhera was a good man. The best of men.

Zajhera couldn't be Relos Var.

Except he was.

Everything was too much. The betrayal was too much, the pain was too much, existence was too much.

But if he disobeyed, the pain would end.*

He remembered vomiting and then nothing else.

* I should probably make some sort of joke here, but I just can't bring myself to do it.

35: THE CASTLE OF ICE

Jorat Dominion, Quuros Empire.
Three days since Talon failed to kill a Manol vané

No one spoke as Brother Qown finished.

"That must have been a hard choice," Kihrin said. He'd known that choice himself, back when he'd been gaeshed, but had never seriously considered it.

"I'm glad you decided to stay," Janel said. She leaned over and kissed the top of Qown's head.

Dorna reached over and patted the priest's hand.

"Me too," Qown said. "I want to help make things better. I thought that ability would have been limited in the Afterlife." To Dorna, he said, "And I didn't know the right people to guarantee my Return."*

"I'll pick up from here," Janel said.

Janel's Turn. The Ice Demesne, Yor, Quur.

Senera and I rushed over to Brother Qown. He had pulled his legs to his chest, rocking back and forth, crying into his robes.

"Is this because of the gaesh?" I asked her.

"No." Senera felt Brother Qown's wrists, the skin under his jaw, then looked at both eyes, lifting his eyelids with her thumbs. "He's not experiencing a gaesh loop."

"A loop?"

"Contradictory gaesh commands. The conflict usually proves

---

* Well, he darn well does now, doesn't he?

lethal. That said, something's put him into shock. Help me get him over to the bed."

I went to lift him and cried out as I felt like my arms might jerk from their sockets. I'd forgotten my lack of strength.

"Together," Senera said.

"I see." I lifted with her this time, and we managed to carry Brother Qown to the bed. I saw what she meant—he hadn't lost consciousness, nor was he having a seizure. He stared straight ahead, eyes unfocused.

And I knew that look. I knew it in my bones.

I'd lived in that state where you're too numb to be sad or unhappy or angry. That place where nothing has meaning and everything hurts.

"It may not be a . . . what did you call it? A gaesh loop? But I do think it's in response to the gaesh. He's gone into a stupor due to what's happened to him." I paused. "Or he's been possessed by a demon, but I don't think so."

Senera sighed. "Fine. Leave him."

I threw her a look filled with venom.

"We don't have time," she explained. "His attendance isn't mandatory at the banquet. Yours is. We'll deal with him later."

I hopped up on the bed and put my arm around Brother Qown. "I'm not leaving him alone like this. He could snap out of it and hurt himself. And if someone tries to hurt him, he's defenseless. I'm staying."

Senera's nostrils flared. "You're not."

"I am."

Before I could do anything else, she touched Brother Qown's forehead. His eyes closed and his chin fell to his collarbone, and he settled as dead weight in my arms. "There. He's sleeping and won't be a danger to anyone, himself included. I'll lock the door when we leave. Now you can come with me on your own two feet, or I can summon guards to drag you, but either way, you're going to the feast, now. I'll let you choose."

I slid my arm back out from behind Brother Qown, eased him back onto the bed, and pulled the furs up over him.

I tried to be as dignified as possible walking to the door. I had always planned to accompany her. I'd come here with a single job: find the spear Khoreval and steal it. Now I had two: find the spear Khoreval *and* Brother Qown's gaesh and steal both. Doing either job would require being treated like something other than a prisoner. I had to convince Relos Var that he'd turned me to his cause. But I had to sell it. I had to make it believable.

Nobody values the prize they win without an effort.*

So we left Brother Qown to sleep, and Senera locked the door behind us.

No guards stood in the halls, no soldiers hovered over us. There was no need.

The building's décor looked like nothing I'd seen before; all perfect black rock and geometric crystal insets and sparkling silver lines. Everything felt clean and crisp and cold, conjuring up an impression of endless glaciers and frozen icicles.

"How old is this palace?"

"Older than the empire," Senera admitted. "Built by the god-king Cherthog and the god-queen Suless."

"I'm surprised it survived the Quuros invasion."

"Technically, it didn't. They rebuilt it."

I didn't even pretend not to be impressed. This construction rivaled Atrine, and Kandor himself had built that.

We climbed stairs, and I decided my earlier assessment of this palace's beauty and complexity had been premature.

At first, I thought the stairs had led us outside, to an enormous marble square set on a mountaintop. All around us, *below* us, jagged mountain ranges wrestled with silken teal skies. White clouds danced at our feet. The father of a thousand storms lurked in valleys below us but left our position untouched, so we might enjoy lightning play in clouds miles away.

Then I realized I felt no wind, no cold. The air didn't swirl

---

* We seriously underestimated her. Or at least I did. I rather suspect you didn't. You helped make her this way, after all.

around me. The sunlight glinted off a silver lattice leading up above our heads. When I reached out as if to touch the sky, my fingertips rested against invisible cold crystal walls. Perfect, transparent walls.

We were still inside.

In a fallen age, the god-king of winter had fashioned himself a great hall to showcase his domain. And by some miracle, his Quuros destroyers had salvaged it, even as they ruined everything else.

The snow king's palace . . .

The view struck me as so miraculous, I nearly forgot to breathe.

"Beautiful, isn't it?" Senera said. "The first time I came here, I must have stood here for hours."

I placed my hand against the clear wall again, watching as my fingers' warmth left condensation trails against the cold, clear substance. "What are the walls made from?"

"Not a clue."*

The walls were angled. I thought they must meet above our heads, a truncated pyramid flattened to form a small square ceiling—the only opaque section. Here, geometric crystal and silver glittered, crafted to suggest a vast and mighty empire of cold and ice. Crystal shards framed in metals jutted up or crouched down at precision angles, fitted together to form patterns like icicles or snowflakes—or cold and distant stars. The ceiling floated at least a hundred feet high, refracting mage-light so it glittered violet and blue through the crystals.

And like Senera, I might have spent hours just taking in this scene, but voices reminded me we weren't alone.

In the room's center, a massive firepit provided the lion's share of warmth for the great hall. A large iron ring, scorched black by the heat, surrounded the pit and provided a barrier against stray sparks. Tables also circled the firepit, each home

---

* Still don't have a clue. Not going to ask the Name of All Things either. Sometimes one should leave a mystery alone.

to courtiers and nobles—who were all watching us. Most of the dinner guests looked Yoran compared to the "normal" Quuros coloring. Yoran complexions were often white, but also pale blue, violet, or gray. These guests wore their pale hair long but braided up into tall topknots. The men wore beards, braided and decorated with jewelry. And they all preferred to dress in light colors. By comparison, Senera had given me a dress guaranteeing I stood out like a flame burning its way across paper.

If I had hoped to blend in, I put those hopes behind me. Clearly, Senera meant for me to draw attention.

An old woman, who made Dorna look like a callow youth, tended the firepit in the room's center, next to a pack of—no. Not wolves. They were hyenas, but white-furred and blue-eyed. The old woman whipped around to stare at me as soon as I stepped foot in the hall. She narrowed her eyes and gave me a scowl, suggesting she'd be tempted to hurl burning logs if I wandered too close. Then she threw me a toothy grin that resembled a dog baring its fangs more than a smile.

I'd never seen her before in my life.

"The god-king's throne sat up above," Senera said, pointing toward a staircase that echoed the angles of the wall and continued through a small door in the far-off ceiling. At the staircase's base, several dozen women sat together at a single, long table.

"Who—?" I started to ask.

"The Hon's wives," she said. "Don't worry. We won't have to sit with them."

"His wives?" I blinked. Senera had mentioned the Yorans had no problem with polygyny. Indeed, neither do the Joratese, but our partnerships consist of smaller groups, fully polygamous. Three people. On rare occasions, four. "Just how many wives does he have?"

"One from each of the forty-eight tribes." She gestured toward the main tables. "Let's go meet the others, shall we?"

Senera led us around the tables until I saw brighter colors than Yoran pastels, worn by men and women with Quuros skin tones. These people wore vivid colors in homogeneous hues. Colors denoting royals, I realized, feeling startled and disturbed. In theory, these people shaped the empire. So why would they share a table with the man so notorious for his hatred of the same?

Then I heard a familiar laugh: Sir Oreth.

He seemed to be fitting in just fine.

Guests had started drinking in advance of meal service. Servants made steady and regular passes around the tables in an unending quest to keep the glasses full.

Sir Oreth saw me staring and grinned nastily. He nudged the next man over, who wore head-to-toe blue. The other man grinned back and made a salacious gesture with his hands.

I looked away and wished I had my weapons.*

Relos Var walked over. He'd been sharing a table with two more royals—although these wore black instead of bright colors. They couldn't have looked less similar otherwise; one looked sick and pale by Quuros standards, while the second man reminded me of Dango, if the muscled bandit had decided to shave off all his hair.

Relos Var took Senera's hands and kissed her on the forehead. "The Hon is on his way. How are our guests behaving?"

"Janel's been good, but I'm worried about the Vishai priest. We had to leave him in the room. There's something wrong with him."

I returned my attention to Relos Var, determined to have some input in the conversation. I never had the chance.

"Well, well, what bit of spice have you brought us today, Icicle?" A man jeered behind us. "I'd love a handful of that with dinner."

And someone grabbed my rear.

I had meant to behave. Don't forget I still felt weak after Senera had drawn her mark on me. The last thing I wanted was a fight. But I still had my pride. In my dominion, certain

---

* I probably wouldn't have stopped her if she had.

behaviors earned an immediate reaction. And this person hadn't just given me a cute pat on the butt—he'd dug in, fingers curled in to touch places where they were not invited.

So I turned around and punched the man behind me as hard as I could.

In hindsight, I overcompensated. I no longer possessed supernatural strength, but I could throw a punch. Unfortunately, I hadn't a clue how to do so safely.

I felt the cartilage in the man's nose give way, and at the same time, something in my hand snapped. The pain was excruciating.

The man I'd hit had light brown skin, ice-blue eyes, and dark, curly hair. He'd just started to grow a Yoran-style beard, still too short for braiding or jewelry. And he hadn't been expecting me to hit him.

I'd knocked him back into the lap of the man next to him, who I would later realize had been the man who'd actually spoken. A too-vain, too-egotistical creature with a handsome face, whose bright blue eyes managed to outshine his embroidered blue silks.

Even though we stood in a room full of warriors and wizards with hardened battle reflexes, nobody seemed to know quite how to respond. Everyone stopped talking. Even the musicians stopped playing.

I cradled my broken hand to my chest, tears in my eyes.

Silver flashed as Senera returned to my side. She grabbed my arm, trying to draw me behind her.

The young man I'd punched stood back up, mouth gaping, his hand going to his bleeding nose. "How dare—!" I think he'd have said more, but his broken nose affected his speech. He must have realized he sounded ridiculous.

Then he reached for his sword.

"Exidhar, what's going on?"

The young man's eyes widened in horror, while everyone else—even the royals—stood. And I recognized his expression: a guilty boy about to be dressed down by a parent before all his friends. The way those friends suddenly found the mountain view fascinating, the way they'd all jumped to their feet, told me said "parent" wasn't a random guest.

Which meant I was in trouble.

I blinked the tears from my eyes, tried to focus past the pain, and took my first good look at Azhen Kaen, Duke of Yor.

Azhen Kaen was the most perfect example of everything a Yoran man should be I've ever seen, before or since. He stood tall, with broad shoulders and skin so white he made Senera look tan. Diamonds sparkled in his gray beard braids like ice crystals, the same color as his eyes. He was an older man, but still handsome, still powerful.

He also had a laevos.

That unnerved me to no end. His gray laevos had been coaxed into a standing position, either by magic or glue. I reminded myself that just as Quur had conquered Jorat using soldiers pulled from Khorvesh, Yor had been conquered by Quur using soldiers from Jorat.

The first governor of Yor, later the first Duke of Yor, would have been Joratese. A footnote that would have occurred less than a hundred years ago. He'd have been Duke Kaen's grandfather or great-grandfather at most.

Exidhar Kaen looked like he planned to crawl under the table. "I was, uh . . . I mean, I—" He pointed at me with one hand, still clutching his bleeding nose with the other. "She hit me!"

Of course, it came out more like "She hith may!"

Duke Kaen raised an eyebrow at him, glanced at me, and then turned to Relos Var. "Am I correct in assuming my son just grabbed your newest wife's ass?"

Behind Exidhar, the royal in blue cleared his throat and started paying attention to his wine. I ground my teeth, wondering if I had in fact punched the wrong man.*

---

* Of course it was Darzin. I'm glad he's dead too.

Mind you, I wanted to punch them all, but that wouldn't help me in the long run.

Relos Var seemed unconcerned. "I believe she's already satisfied any demands of honor."

"Two minutes," Senera muttered. "We've been here less than two minutes."

The royals sitting at the same table as Exidhar started laughing, clearly considering the whole encounter delightful. From the way Exidhar Kaen blushed, he didn't think it was quite as entertaining.

Relos Var acknowledged the laughter with a chuckle. "My apologies, Your Grace, for the excitement. Let me present you with Janel Danorak, my newest wife."

I managed not to roll my eyes. The pain helped. I didn't even correct Relos Var about my name.

Duke Kaen smiled at me. "I'm charmed, of course." A frown crossed his face as he stared at me. "Are you all right?"

I suppose he had noticed the tears.

"I'm fine," I said.

"Is that so?" He reached out and grabbed my hand.

I gritted my teeth and kept from screaming. Barely.

"You seem to have broken your hand," the duke said.

"Have I? I hadn't noticed."

He stared at me in wry disbelief. Then he started laughing too.

Turning to Relos Var, Duke Kaen said, "I *am* charmed. Tell me you're leaving her here."

"With your permission, of course." Relos Var rubbed his nose with a knuckle. "I should warn you she's rarely on her best behavior."

"The good ones never are."

I closed my eyes and concentrated on the pain to distract me from saying something rash. I hadn't been prepared to be treated like I wasn't even in the room, someone who could be talked around rather than talked to. Someone who would stay politely silent while the adults discussed important matters.*

I didn't have a hard time understanding why Relos Var had insisted on removing my strength. I'd have torn out every heart in the hall otherwise.

"Please, let's eat. I don't know about you, but I could eat a horse," Duke Kaen said, still laughing. He gave me a quick glance, just to make sure I'd appreciated the joke.

I started to pull out an empty seat when I felt Senera's hand on my shoulder. "Not that one."

"Please," said the blue-eyed man. "Sit with me. I'd be delighted to look at you during dinner."

As soon as he made the offer, I recognized his voice. He had been the one who'd said he wanted me "with dinner"—not Duke Kaen's son.

"Darzin—" Senera warned.

"Yes, 'Lady Var'? I just want to heal the young lady's injury. Is that a problem?" He blinked at Senera, daring her to object.

I studied his blue clothing. I only knew that color's significance because of Brother Qown's license fees. House D'Mon, the royal family who controlled the Blue Houses and the Physickers Guild.

"Truly, your house is renowned for your healing skills," I said, smiling as sweetly as I could manage around the pain. "So any succor you might give me, I beg you instead direct to the duke's son. He did, after all, take the blow that belonged to you."

Darzin laughed and confirmed who'd really grabbed me.

Senera's hand pulled on my elbow, and we sat down opposite Darzin and Oreth, in between Relos Var and the two black-clad royals. Duke Kaen sat next to Var, and the seat I had tried to take next to his remained empty. Duke Kaen's son, Exidhar,

---

* Yes, Janel, welcome to the fun world of being a woman, where it's always like this and where we're all quietly seething.

left his table for long enough to find the old woman by the fire; she healed his nose, not Darzin. All the while, she cast venom in my direction.

I wondered if she was Exidhar's grandmother, but she dressed in little better than rags. Not the costume I expected for a duke's mother. A bundle twitched in a fur-lined basket next to her, revealing itself to be—not snow hyena cubs—a mewling white bear cub.

"Let me see your hand," Senera whispered as the servants came around with the first course.

I let her take it and tried to pretend I didn't notice everyone staring. The servants were bringing out the food drip by drip, rather than putting all the dishes out at once and letting people choose what they liked. I also saw no sign of condiments: no pepper sauce, no pickles, no dried spices.

A servant set a bowl of blood before me. I found myself thankful Senera had insisted I eat earlier.

"I know it's hard," Senera whispered as she examined my hand, "but try to just smile and enjoy it."

I met her eyes. "I'd rather stab myself with my hand's broken bones a hundred times." I leaned toward her. "Don't even pretend you don't feel the same."*

A warm glow suffused my hand. "Everything about you is difficult," she muttered. When Senera set my hand back down, I noticed she looked quite tired. She'd been sweating too.

Sir Oreth dripped his soup off the back of his spoon. "This . . . what is this?"

"Narwhal blood," Darzin said. "Try it. It took a little getting used to, but it's good."† He waggled his eyebrows. "Spicy. It's a very special dish in Yor, reserved for the nobility. Reminds me of our new friend here."

I couldn't stop myself from rolling my eyes.

Sir Oreth laughed and dropped his spoon back in the soup,

---

* Yes, yes, she was right. You know how I feel about the matter.
† It actually is good, which is incredibly annoying.

so it splattered blood all over the white table linen. "Oh, don't let her appearance fool you. Janel's not noble blood."

Senera moved quicker that time. Her hand closed on my arm before I could stand.

But Exidhar Kaen, returning from having his nose fixed, had no interest in keeping matters quiet, and considering what had just occurred, he had every motive to delight in gossip. "She's not? I thought she was a Kolas? I mean, sorry, a countess? It's *countess* in Jorat, right? How could that be true if she's not nobility?"

"Sir Oreth, your recent experiences have done something to your mind," I snapped. "You know my lineage."

He gave me an evil smile. "Oh, I do. Better than you do, I'd wager. I even have proof. I was going to present this to Duke Xun at the tournament, but—" He shrugged even as he produced a sheet of paper from his coat. The paper looked old, folded and creased in a way that suggested it had been opened and read many times. "Anyway. If no one minds?"

"I mind," I said. "I mind very much."

"Your opinion doesn't matter."

Relos Var leaned over. "I don't think this is the time or place."

But Exidhar waved him off. "Oh no, Relos. I want to hear this."

Still grinning, Sir Oreth snapped open the paper and began to read, *"To my Markreev, Aroth Malkoessian, from your loyal herdsman, Jarin Theranon."*

I stiffened. Jarin Theranon was my grandfather.

"Dear Aroth, I beseech your help, for I'm distraught. With my son's death I now face the unpleasant truth that my lineage is dead. I must therefore confess a secret I had thought to take to my grave: my grand-daughter, Janel, is not my blood."

I shook my head. "That's a lie. You're making this up—"

He turned the paper around so I saw the writing on the page and, worse, saw it matched Jarin's handwriting. "I'm not. I found this among my father's papers years ago. It's a fascinating read."

"Oh, I just love a good family scandal," Darzin said, leaning back in his chair. "Please, keep going. I want all the details. Actually, let's do one better—" He grabbed the paper from Sir Oreth.

"Hey!"

"Since I don't know the names involved, it would be much harder to claim I'm making it all up, wouldn't it?"

"Darzin, you ass," Senera muttered under her breath.

Darzin just grinned. *"I had always suspected. I loved my daughter-in-law, but I'm not a fool. After she tried for so long to bear a child without success, how could I ignore when she returned from their district tour with a babe Frena had never carried? She never produced milk for Janel. She never lost her maidenly figure. I knew my son had had difficulties giving Frena a child. I knew of their longing. So I didn't question too much such a miraculous birth. They loved her, as did I."*

I felt dizzy and faint. The entire table had stopped talking to each other; they were all listening to Darzin's reading. "Please stop."

But Darzin didn't stop. *"But there can be no denying the child is not Joratese. I have been forced to go to House D'Mon—"* Darzin paused. "Oh, hey, that's me. Anyway, *House D'Mon, accepting their outrageous fees—*it's true, we *are* expensive—*to make sure the girl has proper horse markings. The cost left us in poor sorts when the Hellmarch came, and little in our coffers to help with the recovery after. Thus, I throw myself on your mercy and offer a possible solution. Though she's of common blood, Janel is comely. She'd make your youngest son a fine wife. Thus, would Tolamer continue to be ruled by noble blood, as is right and proper. Signed with greatest respect, Jarin Theranon."*

"No," I said. I felt a flustered sense of panic. Yes, I knew my grandfather had arranged the marriage with Sir Oreth. Yet he hadn't protested when I'd announced I'd wanted nothing more to do with the idea. My grandfather had never treated me as anything other than his grandchild. He had never treated me as *less*.

It couldn't be true.

"You should have just accepted destiny and let me marry

you," Sir Oreth said. "Instead, here we are." He gestured around him and then paused. "I mean, no offense."

"Oh, the look on your face, little girl," Darzin said to me. "Your whole world just fell to pieces, right before my eyes." He looked over to Relos Var. "Seriously, name your price for her. What do you want?"

"I want *you* to be smarter," Relos Var snapped. "But it's not a sum you'll ever raise."

Next to him, the bald man in black began laughing.*

I paid attention to their banter just in case Relos Var tried to sell me, but my attention was focused on Oreth. He'd started out laughing and sneering at my humiliation, but the longer Darzin read that damning letter, the more Oreth's mockery turned to anger. An anger that, after all these years, I finally understood.

His actions had always been a mystery to me. We had danced around each other with the tender curiosity of two foals at play, knowing from an early age we were betrothed. But as the stories of Janel Danorak spread, it became clear I would grow up a stallion. His whole demeanor changed. He never showed me thudajé. He must have known about my parentage all along and thought it proof that he was better than I was. My common blood meant I was destined to be the mare to his stallion and never the reverse.

I had refused, for all these years, to know my place.

"Huh, well, that's surprising," Darzin said. "Here I assumed you just wanted a new flavor of young and innocent to corrupt, but I guess you might have feelings for her. Then again, Var, you do like marrying throwaways, don't you?"

Next to me, I felt Senera tense.

"Enough," warned Duke Kaen.

Relos Var raised an eyebrow. "Yes, yes. Janel's real mother was a dancing girl, and her father was a Khorveshan soldier."

---

* I may not like royals, but at least Thurvishar and I will always be united in our mutual loathing of Darzin D'Mon.

He leaned forward to look at Darzin. "Are you implying having a Khorveshan parent is an embarrassment? Wasn't *your* mother Khorveshan?"*

I couldn't help but notice that the eyes of those not focused on Darzin or Relos Var now looked toward Duke Kaen's son. His clearly mixed-race Yoran son. Exidhar's brown skin and black hair clearly suggested his mother hadn't come from Yor.

Exidhar Kaen shifted in his seat, an embarrassed blush on his face. He saw me looking at him and schooled his expression into something haughty and malicious.

I hadn't made a friend there.

Darzin seemed to realize his blunder. "Of course, I didn't mean *that.* The Khorveshan bloodlines are the most honored in the empire. Anyway, despite young Oreth's opinion here, your new bride's not a commoner, not with those god-touched ruby eyes. Her mother must have been an Ogenra of House D'Talus, obviously."

Relos Var reached for his drink. "Obviously."

Beside me, Senera relaxed. People moved on to other conversational topics. Politics. Gossip. What might be done to undermine the empire's control. I should have been paying better attention, but I couldn't focus.

I felt sick. They had to be lying. I had grown up under Xaltorath's tender care. I knew the sorts of lies that could be wielded like daggers to nick and cut and bleed. I also knew the truth could be used to rip open the same veins. And truth was a far easier blade to sharpen.

"Don't let them see it bother you," someone whispered.

I looked over. One of the black-clad royals had spoken. The bald one.

"They thrive on the pain they cause," he said. "It feeds them. Don't give them the satisfaction."†

---

* Wasn't his mother High General Milligreest's sister-in-law?
† I was sitting right there, and I never saw Thurvishar's lips move. I have to assume he was using magic.

"*They?* Aren't you one of them?"

His mouth quirked. "I'm nothing like them." He wasn't looking at me. The voices around us created a din. Yet somehow, I still heard his whisper. "My name is Thurvishar D'Lorus. I'll try to help if I can, but don't rely on it. My hands are tied in many ways."

"Which house is D'Lorus—"

"Books. We run the Academy."

"Thank you." I didn't say anything more. The Academy. A school, yes, but I'd been able to hear the capital letter. The wizard's school in Kirpis.

I glanced at him sideways. I couldn't tell his age. He had the sort of chiseled face that looks old when young and young when old. When he glanced in Relos Var's direction, I saw his eyes matched his dress. Black, the color of mystery. Outside of Jorat, also the color of magic.

Whatever his Royal House colors, he probably just wanted to share the thrill of humiliating the newest addition to court. Thurvishar D'Lorus was just cleverer about it than Darzin D'Mon.

When Senera and I left, the men stayed to share drinks and swap outrageous stories. I didn't notice the nasty old woman had vanished from her place at the fire.

But it wouldn't have meant anything to me even if I had.

"It's a little like eating with a pack of wolves, isn't it?" Senera said later as we returned to the room. "They snap and wrestle and try to push themselves in each other's way. They all want to be favorites when Kaen overthrows the empire, each with their own dominion to rule. Idiots."

I didn't respond. We kept walking.

She stopped in the hallway and turned to face me. "I've studied Joratese culture enough to understand 'noble blood' isn't a requirement for ruling. Don't your people always say the proof of blood is in deeds? Even if you're adopted, it doesn't change anything."

I rubbed my lower lip, reminded myself temper tantrums wouldn't help my cause—no matter how good they might feel in the short term. "You don't understand."

"I think I do."

"If Oreth is right—if Relos Var is right—I'm not even Joratese. And *that* matters a great deal." I paused. "How did Relos Var know who my parents were? My grandfather didn't know."

Senera pulled up the inkstone she wore around her neck and then tucked it back under her gown's neckline. "It's this. If you ask it a question and use the stone, what you write will answer your question."

I stared at her. What a useful toy. Such a useful tool that I felt like a naked baby trying to fight off lions.

Did they already know my motives? Had they known the whole time I was only here to steal a magic spear and kill their pet dragon? To undermine their invasion efforts?

She smirked. "It's not foolproof. Ask a bad question, get a bad answer. And it won't answer opinions. It won't tell you events that haven't happened yet. And my personal favorite: once you start writing, the stone won't let you stop until you've finished answering the question. So it's rather important to ask unambiguous questions. It didn't end well for the last person Relos Var let use the stone. He asked a question so sufficiently vague he was still writing out the answer when he dropped dead from exhaustion."

"So you're the one who asked about my parents."

Senera nodded. "Yes."

"Who are they? Are they still alive? I want names."

She chuckled as we neared the doorway she'd locked earlier. "Maybe if you're good, I'll let you know. Right now, I think it should just be my little—" She frowned. "What?"

I turned to see what she was staring at.

The door stood ajar.

I rushed inside. Brother Qown was missing.

36: An Insufficient Apology

Jorat Dominion, Quuros Empire.
Three days since Tishar D'Mon made a
lovely blue tsali stone

"So you *have* met my brother Darzin," Kihrin said to Janel. "And hard as it may be to believe, Darzin was behaving himself."

"If that's his definition of 'behaving himself,' I have an arrow that'll fix his problem," Ninavis offered.

"Generous of you," Kihrin said, "but I killed Darzin three days ago."

Janel smiled. "I knew I liked you."

"Did you ever find out who your real parents are—" Kihrin started to ask.

"I did," Janel said quickly. "Eventually. And Dorna knew *the entire time.*" She gave the old woman a look.

"Oh, foal, it weren't like that."

Janel raised a hand to stop Dorna from saying more.

"But you do know now?" Qown asked Janel again. "Because I don't want to read this next part unless you do."

"Don't worry. It won't be a shock." Janel's gaze returned to Kihrin, and her head tilted to the side as she watched him. "You know who they are too, don't you?"

Kihrin hesitated, then said, "I have a strong suspicion. I think I've met your mother." He drilled his fingers against the bar top. "And your father doesn't like me. Not after—" He made a vague gesture toward Urthaenriel.

Janel's smile tightened. "I cannot even begin to tell you how little my father's opinion matters to me."

"He's a good man," Kihrin said.

"He supports the rule of the greedy, the oppressive, and the degenerate. How good can he be?"*

Ninavis leaned forward. "Who are we talking about here?"

"That's what I was about to ask," Dorna said. "I don't know who your father is, foal. Never mattered to me."

Janel made a face. "We'll get to that part." She gestured to Qown. "Do you feel ready to take over?"

Qown nodded. "Yes, I believe so."

Qown's Turn. The Ice Demesne, Yor, Quur.

Brother Qown woke in a library. He knew before he opened his eyes, smelling leather and the rich vanilla scent of old paper mixed with the scent of his favorite cinnamon tea. He woke smiling before he remembered why the tea seemed so comforting.

He sat up from the low, backless couch upon which he'd been sleeping. His clothes had been changed. He felt clean. He had no stubble on his chin. His book satchel sat next to the couch and his sun symbol hung from his neck. Brother Qown felt in perfect health, but a metaphoric black chasm of despair lurked off to the side—so wide and yawning he could've almost seen it with his naked eyes, if he'd just turned his head.

But his despair's physical embodiment was present too. Relos Var sat at a nearby table, writing with a Kirpis-style quill. A large blue Kazivar-glazed teapot sat on the table next to matching teacups. The same teapot Father Zajhera used.

Brother Qown knew he should do something, say something, but he just stared, feeling numb.

"Have some tea," Relos Var offered. "It's your favorite."

Qown hesitated a second, but he felt no pain, no suggestion he'd die bent over in misery if he disobeyed. He didn't know if that meant Relos Var didn't have his gaesh or had simply chosen not to *use* his gaesh.

---

* Is it possible that we're actually influencing her?

Tea sounded nice.

Var poured two cups, placing the second one before the opposite chair. "I realize apologies are quite insufficient to the turmoil you've experienced. I would never have sent you to help Janel if I'd intended this outcome. You're one of my favorite students. Curious, intelligent, compassionate toward others. Fine qualities, worthy of better than this."

Brother Qown picked up his tea, fighting back nausea. Apologies were insufficient. Relos Var had torn out a piece of his soul. Qown didn't even know who held the piece now. "Apologies were quite insufficient" didn't *exactly* cover how he felt about the situation.

"You lied to me," Qown said after sifting through a hundred insults and childlike protests.

"No."

Qown couldn't help himself; his mouth dropped open. "No? Did you just say *no*?"

"Qown, I have lived a very long time," Relos Var said. "Was it lying to show myself to you as an identity I've worn since before you were born? Zajhera isn't a throwaway disguise some assassin mimic might wear and discard. Zajhera is a good man who wants to help people find their better selves. He's no less real than Relos Var, although Relos Var's views are more confrontational. And if neither one is who I really am, their existence is no less sincere."

Brother Qown narrowed his eyes at the wizard. In his days with the Way of Vishai, he'd encountered people who had been so traumatized, they'd separated their minds, like crystal shards, to try to protect themselves from trauma. He didn't think Relos Var was so afflicted.

He hoped.

Finally, he snorted and looked away. "That's an excuse. You lied to me. You lied to everyone."

"Let's have this talk again in a few thousand years, when you've had to reinvent yourself a hundred times and have seen your loved ones come and go like leaves falling in a forest."

Brother Qown let that pass. "So who are you? Who are you really? If this"—he waved his hand at Relos Var's body—"is a lie, and Father Zajhera is too, what do you look like? What's your real name?"

"Rev'arric," Relos Var answered. "As for what I look like . . ." He grimaced. "I'd rather not. A ritual gone wrong has left me in a state not fit for polite company. Best not to demonstrate. Kaen would be upset if I destroyed his palace."

Brother Qown looked away, crossed his arms across his chest, and rubbed his arms as if cold.

"You're a monster," he whispered.

"No," said Relos Var. "*Monster* is such an easily digestible idea. Horrible, evil to its core, irredeemable. If I'm a monster, then anyone who opposes me is by logical deduction a hero, yes?" He leaned over. "It's not that simple. Sometimes everyone is wrong and you must decide whose wrongness is more acceptable."

Brother Qown wouldn't look at the tea. It sat there, steaming, smelling wonderful, reminding him of comfortable lies. Father Zajhera hadn't ever been Father Zajhera. Monster.

Relos Var sighed and picked up his quill again. He dipped it in ink and continued writing. "You're being dramatic, Qown."

"I just feel stupid not to have realized the truth."

"Why would you have? And you're not an idiot, Qown. I don't train idiots."

"Baron Tamin back in Barsine Banner suggests otherwise."

Relos coughed. "I'll admit I'd hoped for . . . more . . . from Tamin." He set his tea aside, put down his quill. "Qown, I never meant to betray you."

His wording brought Qown's head up. "So you admit you have?"

Var looked sad. "Of course. How could any sane person interpret what happened otherwise? The fact I never meant to hurt you doesn't change that I had you gaeshed. A fact that gives me no joy. Gaeshing is a nasty business, but I couldn't take the risk you would tell Janel about me."

The fact Relos Var was right—Brother Qown would have told Janel about Father Zajhera—gave little comfort. "And now? What are you going to do with me? Sacrifice me to a demon? Sell me to some Yoran nobleman who wants a healer? Maybe the duke would put some extra metal in your pocket . . ."

Relos Var smiled. "I thought I'd tell you anything you wanted to know. Explain the whole plan. Answer every question you might have."

Brother Qown froze. "What?"

"You must have questions, concerns. And you—" Var looked at him. "Well, you're my punishment for insisting on bright students. Someone with a slower wit wouldn't have made the connection between Relos Var's magical signature and Father Zajhera's." He chuckled. "Senera or Irisia would have caught it, but again, see the point about insisting on smart students."

Brother Qown stared. He knew Relos Var flattered his ego—a lure meant to turn Qown to his cause. Then again, even if Qown's gaesh kept him silent, could he afford to turn away from an opportunity to find out Relos Var's plans?

He didn't think he could. What question to ask, when he had so many? In the end, one question stood out to him above all others.

"Why are you doing all of this? To take over Quur?"

Relos Var didn't laugh or scoff. He nodded, sipped his tea, and pondered the inquiry. "Unlike Kaen or the Royal Houses, I don't care about ruling Quur. It's a means to an end." Var paused. "I'm trying to save humanity. It's harder than you would think."

Qown stared at him. "Save humanity? You wiped out an entire village. That *wasn't* you?"

"No, it was me," Relos Var admitted. "And it's been more than one village. Far more. I don't enjoy killing, but in my quest to save our people, I would soak the ground with the blood of a million newborns if I must."

Qown leaned back in his chair, wide-eyed. The word Relos Var had already dismissed repeated itself: *monster*.

"Qown . . ." Relos Var shook his head. "I don't expect you to approve. I would be horrified if you did. But I would hope, after all the years we've known each other, that you'd take my word this is necessary."

"But I don't know you at all. And you *can't* justify that. There's no excuse that makes it acceptable."

Relos Var nodded. "I understand. War—the very concept of war—is against everything the Vishai believe in. I created the faith to be better than I am. That I succeeded is a comfort, even as it's a current frustration. I won't say you're naïve or you just don't understand. I only hope I can make a world one day where people like you won't fall victim to . . ." His smile was bitter. "Well, to people like me."

Brother Qown wanted to cry. He wanted to scream. "This isn't war."

"But it is. A rare case where the Eight and I agree—the war never stopped."

Brother Qown drew a deep, shuddering breath and set his tea aside. His feelings—his outrage and anger and deep, deep pain—couldn't be allowed to gain control. This was an opportunity. He had to look at it as an opportunity. A chance to find out more information in the hope, no matter how faint or impossible, he could one day share his knowledge with others.

"What about Janel?"

Relos Var raised an eyebrow. "Excuse me?"

"What about Janel? You healed her. You helped her. And you sent me to help her. She must be important to your plans. How does she fit into all this?"

Relos Var smiled. "Would you believe me if I told you there's a prophecy?"

"The quatrain Senera recited back at her cottage."

"Not only that one. I know you're familiar with the prophecies. I lent you several books on the subject, when you were going through that phase as a teenager. I believe a distressing percentage of those quatrains concern Janel. Specifically, Janel."

"They're demonic ramblings."

"Demons, my son, don't perceive time the same way we do. Terrifyingly, they may not *experience* time the same way we do. They speak even less of the universal language than we ever did and are bound by fewer rules. We cannot discount their predictions. I'd love to think there's nothing more to the prophecies than demons pulling our collective legs. Over the millennia, I have come to believe a far worse possibility is likely: the prophecies are *genuine*. And I'm not alone in that belief. The Eight Immortals are just as committed to fulfilling the prophecies—to their benefit, naturally. And they control reincarnation in a way quite beyond my abilities. Janel is one of their 'entries into the race'—bespoke tailored to fit a thousand demons' predictions. I must hand it to Tya—another student too smart for my own good—I almost didn't find Janel. If Xaltorath hadn't tracked Janel down first, I wouldn't have."

"Tya, Goddess of Magic? What does she have to do with Janel?"

Relos Var quirked an eyebrow. "She's Janel's mother. Her real, biological mother. And let me tell you, Tya doesn't have children often."

"Her mother? But that's—"

"True," Relos Var said. "It's true. Tell Janel if you like. I won't stop you. You're smart enough, however, to see how that single piece of news would bring her whole sandcastle crumbling down, aren't you?"

Brother Qown inhaled. He was. Because even if, by some miracle or curse, Janel was the daughter of the Goddess of Magic—rather than the noble family of Theranon—the truth would be anything but a blessing. Where was Tya during the Lonezh Hellmarch? Where was Tya when Xaltorath possessed Janel? Where was Tya when Janel's grandfather lay dying and Oreth evicted Janel from her ancestral home? Where was Tya, a goddess, one of the Eight, in all the painful hours and days and months since her daughter had needed her?

It would break Janel's heart. It would turn her against everything the Eight represented.

And Relos Var would *love* nothing more.

Just as Relos Var would love Brother Qown knowing the secret and keeping it from Janel. The wizard would be able to drive a wedge between Janel and Qown whenever he felt the need. Relos Var could simply reveal Qown had known the truth and said nothing when he could've.

Brother Qown had always tried to be respectful to the Eight. Even so, if Tya had appeared before him, he'd have slapped her. Tya had played right into Relos Var's hands by keeping the truth from her own daughter.

Relos Var left the table and returned a moment later with a carved wooden box. "Knowing you can't help Janel by sharing these secrets, I have a proposal, dear Qown. If you like, I'll send you home."

Brother Qown blinked. "What?"

"I'll send you home. Back to Eamithon. Back to the Temple of Light. You'll still be gaeshed, and you won't be able to reveal any secrets, but you'll be safe and comfortable. You'll be back at the temple, back with your friends, spending your days in meditation and healing the supplicants who travel to Rainbow Lake." Relos Var brought the box over to the table and set it down before Brother Qown. "Or you can help me save humanity. I leave the choice to you."

"What's in the box?" Brother Qown asked.

"A gift if you decide to help me. Open it."

Brother Qown did. A large chunk of agate rested on a bed of black velvet inside. The stone's heart sparkled and shifted like flame.

37: THE DUKE'S WIVES

Jorat Dominion, Quuros Empire.
Three days since Miya's hatred of Darzin
ceased not being personal

Kihrin stared at Qown with wide eyes. "Damn."

Qown nodded. "Oh, indeed. I, uh . . . he seems so reasonable. That's the hardest part. You find yourself wondering if you're the one who's being unfair."

Ninavis looked over at Dorna. "You know, it never occurred to me how deep under I am. Just underwater. Here I'm worried about how we're going to convince the Adoreli to stop warring with the Gadurans." She paused as she saw the confusion on people's faces. "Those are Marakori clans we're recruiting. It's not important. Anyway, you people are on a whole different level . . ." She leaned over toward Janel. "*Tya?* Are you fucking kidding me?"

Janel shook her head and shrugged. "It wasn't *my* choice." She paused. "At least I'm fairly sure it wasn't my choice . . . I'd hate to think it was."*

"Teraeth's got Janel beat, though," Kihrin offered. "Besides apparently being an angel—my new favorite definition of irony—he's Thaena's son and Khored's grandson." Then he held up his hand. "But I don't know if his parentage means anything. Divinity doesn't seem to be a thing you can inherit."

"No," Qown agreed. "It wouldn't be."

---

* Quite sure it wasn't. That's some comfort, I suppose.

Kihrin looked over at Janel. "Your turn?"
She nodded. "My turn."

Janel's Turn. The Ice Demesne, Yor, Quur.

"Where could he have gone?" I rushed into the room, checked the water closet, the wardrobe, any place he might hide.

Brother Qown's satchel was missing.

Senera didn't answer me. She took the stone from around her neck, rubbed her index finger against it, and drew a phantom line against the marble wall. She read the fading warmth against the glossy surface and looked relieved. "It's fine. Relos Var sent Pragaos for him."

"By what definition is that fine?" I snapped. I knew having Brother Qown as a hostage against my good behavior meant nothing if they harmed him. But if Qown had managed to wake and commit suicide in my absence, the sensible response would have been to lie.

She looked up, surprised by my venom, and then smiled. "Oh, darling, you really do think Relos Var's the villain here, don't you? Are you the hero?"

"At least I haven't wiped out *whole villages*."

"No, but you support a government that does," Senera said. "Did you think I invented Lysian gas?"

"What is Lysian—?"

Senera waved her fingers. "The blue smoke. That's a present straight from your Academy of Magic in Kirpis. Quur used it against the Yorans during the invasion. Against, oh yes, *whole villages*."

"T-that was a war," I stammered to hide my shock. I dismissed her claims as fabrication. They had to be.

"Pay attention. *This* is a war. Do you think Quur sat down with the Yoran rulers and said, 'Oh yes, very good. Now we shall accept your formal surrender, whenever you're ready, to bring a lasting peace'? No, the Quuros stomped until blood turned all the ice red. When they concluded they'd well and truly broken the Yoran spirit, that's when they moved in." She laughed. "I suppose subjugation worked in Jorat. All that thudajé business. You people know how to accept you've been beaten."

The casual way she spoke the words belied their razor edge. I felt it even though—if Relos Var had told the truth—my lineage was Khorveshan rather than Joratese.

And what did that mean, anyway? I knew little about Khorvesh except that they have a reputation for being good soldiers, at the forefront of every Quuros military push. I knew they lived in a land opposite from Jorat in almost all respects: dry, hot, and arid. I knew the army that had helped us—helped the Joratese—defeat Khorsal had been Khorveshan.

Well, so much for my pride at being descended from Atrin Kandor.*

"We weren't *beaten* by Quur," I said. "We joined forces with Quur and accepted their aid in destroying the tyrant who enslaved us. And no matter what the Quuros did to Yor, you can't expect me to shrug and say, 'Oh, well, that's okay, then. Go ahead and use a horrible weapon against unsuspecting, innocent people since Quur did it first.'"

"No, but I do get to say Quur made the rules. We're just playing by them."

I didn't answer. There seemed no point. We wouldn't convince each other.

I reminded myself I needed to start pretending she *was* convincing me.

Senera walked over to the couch and sat down. "I know you think he's a terrible person, but maybe you should take a moment to rethink your assumptions. He's the finest man I've ever known."

"If the group we met at lunch is any measure, you should meet a better class of men."

She chuckled. "You may have a point. I wasn't much older than you when I first met Relos Var. Except unlike you, I was

---

* Funny coincidence there. She still is.

a sex slave owned by the High Lord of House D'Jorax. Believe me when I say that compared to royalty, Relos Var looks very good indeed."

I felt a shudder pass through me. "I'm sorry."

"I'd say it was worse than you can imagine, but you've known Xaltorath, so I doubt that's true. In any event, you see why I'm biased in Relos Var's favor."

Looking at her, I understood too. After all, what could ever compete? Var had rescued her from horrors. Why would she ever turn against the man who freed her from that?

But he'd done more than rescue Senera: he'd educated her, trained her, given her a cause. Senera didn't believe she was an evil person. She might do terrible things, yes, but she clearly felt the wrongs she committed were for the greater good, justified by a greater and better future. She wasn't a demon but an angel, fighting a holy war against the monsters who had put her through more pain than any man, woman, or child should ever endure.*

I couldn't look at her and tell myself I'd never fall into the same trap. How easy is it to convince ourselves we're infallible, that our way and point of view are the only ones that matter. Oh, it is the easiest trap, and it always comes loaded with the most effective bait, our own desperate need for self-worth.

"Look, would you mind . . . leaving me be? I need time."

Senera started to say something, paused, and nodded. "Of course."

She walked out the door.

As soon as she left, I drew a deep breath and then let myself succumb to what I'd been holding back for as long as I remembered. Holding back because I had been raised to believe my duty required me to be a symbol of strength for others.

But I no longer existed as a symbol of strength for anyone. No one was counting on me to be the one in control.

I was anything but in control.

---

* Yes, but that's because we're *right*.

I wanted my grandfather. I wanted my parents. I wanted my mother.

Except they weren't my real family. She wasn't my real mother. She never had been.

I collapsed into tears and didn't stop crying until at some point my sobs rolled over into my own parody of sleep.

I woke to find myself back in the Afterlife.

And about to be attacked by demons. Of course.

I didn't hesitate. I waded into the battle, screaming.

In the middle of fighting demons, ankle deep in blood, I realized I wasn't alone. I hadn't heard the elephants this time. I'd seen no arrows from Thaena's troops.

And yet, Teraeth was fighting alongside me, destroying demons too, slicing knives across throats and slipping blades under armor with the most elegant precision. He gave me no sign but a nod, and then we both fell back to killing.

I wasn't done crying. I sobbed even as I discarded the sword as inadequate to my rage and began using my bare hands to rip and maim and slaughter.

Even though I had always acted as though my strength was a curse, this time I reveled in the power denied me in the Living World. I let my savage delight show in every skull crushed in my bare hands or throat ripped out by curled fingers.

And finally, we were the only ones left.

"Janel . . ." He sheathed his knives, his eyes on me filled with concern as he rushed over to me. "What happened? I heard—"

I almost sat on a demon's corpse, but chose a rock instead, knowing the body would fade in minutes. I took a deep, shuddering breath and wrestled my emotions under control.

"Teraeth, I've made a terrible mistake."

He knelt next to me, touched my cheek as delicately as I had once touched his. "I'll organize a rescue party. Mother told me what happened. It's not worth staying there."

"They gaeshed Qown." I winced. "Relos Var gaeshed Qown."

He bit his lip. As he did, I realized he had no idea who Qown was. I'd never mentioned the priest to him before. But even without knowing Qown's identity, Teraeth must have understood my guilt.

"Okay," he said. "My mother can help. We can pull you out."

"No, No. I—" I took a deep breath. "I still have to find the spear. Who knows how many more people across Jorat are going to die until I do?"

His expression tightened. "Thaena said the spear may be able to kill a dragon. *May.* She doesn't know for sure. It's never been done. It's not worth putting you in jeopardy."

I almost felt flattered at the concern in his voice. Almost. Except for the healthy dose of "I know better than you do" condescension that also lurked there.

I wasn't in the mood.

"No," I repeated. "I refuse to retreat when I've come this far. I need to find a way to recover Qown's gaesh and the spear, and in the meantime, I'm learning invaluable information. For example, they have in their possession a Cornerstone called the Name of All Things, which can be used to answer any question. If it has seemed like your enemies know too much, it's not your imagination."*

Teraeth's eyes widened. *"What?"*

"You see? Now you know something new. You're welcome."

"So you mean the only thing keeping them from finding out you're a spy is they haven't *asked*?" His voice rose. "No. Absolutely not. I'm coming after you right now. I'll go to Mithros. He's been worried sick about you—"

"Mithros knows where I am, Teraeth."

He stopped, flustered. "No, he doesn't. I spoke to him yesterday. He said he hadn't spoken to you since the morning of the tournament."

I stared at him. "No, that's not—" I stood up from the rock and paced several times, casting my gaze toward the Chasm.

---

* Yes, because of course she told them everything. Lovely.

"When I saw him here in the Afterlife, he wouldn't go to the Chasm. In fact, he led me away from the Chasm."

"So?"

"You're never more likely to encounter a god than at the Chasm." I looked at Teraeth. "I thought I was speaking with Khored—to Mithros. You do know who Mithros really is—?"

He waved a hand. "I know. But go on."

"What if I've been speaking with someone else? Xaltorath? But why would she—" I resisted the urge to wring my hands. "Teraeth, if it was her . . . she did something to me that stopped Relos Var from gaeshing me. Why would Xaltorath do that?"

"Stopped you from being gaeshed?" Teraeth blinked. "I don't understand."

"Khored—or Xaltorath, or whoever it was—did something that would protect me from being gaeshed. Which, since I'm not gaeshed right now, must have worked."

Teraeth shook his head. "That's impossible."

"Clearly not."

He frowned. "What if Xaltorath gaeshed you? As far as I know, you can't be gaeshed twice."

"I think I'd know if I'd been gaeshed."

"Would you?" Teraeth raised an eyebrow. "Do you sleep without dreams? Do you feel weakened?"

He already knew the answer to one of those questions: I possessed no dreams except for my journeys through the Afterlife. And I did indeed feel weakened—because of Senera.

So if I had been gaeshed, would I notice the difference?

I paced. "You think it was Xaltorath?"

"Who else? It couldn't have been Khored. That would make no sense."*

"Why would Xaltorath help me? That makes no sense either."

"No more sense than demons ever make."

I sat back down again. "Xaltorath breaks many rules for a

---

* I personally don't think we should assume, but it does seem out of character for the man.

demon. She ignored the emperor when he ordered her to leave
me. You should have seen his mouth drop open." I blinked at
Teraeth, who stared at me with a shocked expression. "Rather
like that."

Teraeth rubbed his hand over his face. "Do you realize what
you just said? When all the demons were bound, they were
gaeshed. Who do you think controls those gaeshe? The *emperor*
does. That's what the Crown and Scepter were created to do.
You're telling me a demon just laughed off a gaesh command?"
He exhaled. "That would only be possible if Xaltorath isn't a
demon, which is obviously not true."*

I found myself standing again. "Are you suggesting I'm
'mistaken' about the single most traumatic experience of my
entire life?"

"Janel, it *was* traumatic! It's not unreasonable to think the
horror of what you experienced distorted your memory."

"The high general was there. Emperor Sandus was there.
Do you think Sandus forgot to order a demon to leave a
possessed child?"

"Damn it, Janel, I've *worn* the things. I'm telling you that's
not how this works!"

I paused, whatever defense I'd planned on shouting back at
him dying on my lips. Instead, in a normal tone, I asked, "How
has a Manol vané ever worn a human crown—never mind the
Crown and Scepter of Quur?"

He froze.

"Teraeth . . . ," I started again. "How has a Manol vané—?"

"I heard you the first time." He inhaled deeply. "Fuck."

"Then answer the question, please."

He didn't, not for a long time. Then he walked away from
me and sat down on a rock overlooking the cliff. The Afterlife's
broken, twisted trees spread out ahead. In the distance, yellow

---

* I'm as concerned about this as Teraeth here, so I asked. Do you know what the
stone told me? When I asked why Xaltorath wasn't gaeshed by Grizzst? It said:
You cannot gaesh something that does not exist. I have no idea what that means.

mist floated fingers over a lake's surface, more creepy than romantic.

I walked toward him.

"The cycle," he said, "is that we die and we're reborn and we're not supposed to know what happened to us from one life to the next. Except I remember perfectly. And in my last life, I ended up as emperor of Quur."

"Which one?"

He grimaced. "Janel, that's not important—"

"Which one?"

"Atrin Kandor."

I stared at him in shock. *"What?"**

He rolled his eyes. "I was Atrin Kandor. You remember, the man who—"

"I know who Atrin Kandor is! *Everyone* knows who Atrin Kandor is! Most of Quur wouldn't exist without Atrin Kandor. The man who built Atrine in a single night and slew the god-king Khorsal and kicked the Kirpis vané out of their homeland. That was *you*?"

"You forgot the part where I ordered a goodly chunk of the Quuros army to their deaths, trying to invade the Manol."

"Did you . . . lose a bet with your mother Thaena? Because the idea that Atrin Kandor would be reincarnated as—as *you*—is the punch line to a *joke*. You were the single greatest threat to the vané to ever walk the earth, and she reincarnates you *as* a vané?"†

"She does love her poetic justice." He raised a finger. "But for the record, I've been saddled with sins I never committed. For example, I did *not* wipe out the dreth. They're still around. Just underground. Literally."

"I see," I said. I did too, since as Janel "Danorak" I knew

---

* Huh. You used to have that thing with Kandor, didn't you? Do you think that's why Thaena chose him in particular?

† I have to wonder who Thaena was punishing here—Emperor Kandor or the vané king Terindel? But I'm very curious why Teraeth remembers his past life. That's not normal.

all about the power of distorted myth. "Are there any other confessions you feel like making while we linger here?"

He didn't answer. Teraeth sat there, drumming his fingers against the rock.

"Teraeth—"

"When I was Atrin Kandor, you were my wife."

I waited, just in case he felt like revealing that last part was a joke.

He didn't.

I couldn't fault him for his honesty, but the confession felt awkward. Intimate and also ugly. Like finding out you'd been so drunk, you'd done something you didn't remember. Even if I had been willing at the time, the idea I couldn't remember the choices I'd made or the reasoning behind them left me with a blank, heavy feeling in my stomach.

"I suppose it was a romance for the ages," I said at last, because I didn't know what else to say.

"No," he said, his voice ragged. "No, not in the least. I treated you horribly, I didn't deserve you, and by the time I realized, I couldn't make it right." His voice was smooth and dark and dripped, dripped, dripped with the deepest regret. "When I met you—"

"Don't," I said.

"I just want you to know—"

I put my hand to his mouth. "Shut up."

He stared at me.

"I don't care," I said, which I tried to make myself believe was true. "Some other woman who shares my soul married some other man who shared yours." I lifted my hand away from his mouth. "Are you still Atrin Kandor?"

He laughed. "No."

"And I'm not her. How could I be? What was she? A princess? Some duke's daughter?"

"No," he said. "No. She was nobody." He winced. "I mean, a musician. Played the harp—" His eyes went wide. "Oh gods. I have a type."

"See, if that's your type, then I don't qualify. I don't know how to play any instrument but slaughter. I don't even know how to sing. I like to dance and dress up for parties, although not quite as much as I love to win. I'm no man's wife, although I cannot promise someone won't be my wife or husband or both. I may not limit myself to just one."

He gave me a stunned look, but he didn't seem upset. "Will you marry me?"

"Given our history, I don't think we should ask that question until we know each other much better. I would wager you had no clue of your wife's favorite color or food or what personal goals she carried in her heart. I doubt marrying you capped her life's ambitions."*

Teraeth pulled me into his arms. "That is all very true, but I still think you're amazing."

"That's a good start." I tucked myself against his side and waited.

He waited too.

I whispered into his ear. "This is the part where you ask me what goals I carry in my heart."

"Oh! Uh, I—" He didn't let me go, but the awkwardness returned.

I leaned back to look at him. "Let's start with something easy. My favorite color is turquoise."

He raised an eyebrow. "Turquoise? Really?"

"The color of a cloudless sky in summer. Really. Now what's yours?"

"If I say red, you'll think I'm flattering you."

"Not if it's true."

"It's true." Teraeth's eyes went far away. "There's this red, a shifting crimson, which results from using copper to glaze porcelain. It's very difficult to create it on purpose. Most people use copper to create green glazes. But if you know what you're doing, you can make red and shade it anywhere from Khorveshan

---

* I would damn well hope not.

sandstone to the freshest arterial blood. My father used to make—" He stopped himself. "I mean, my father in my last life. Not this life. I don't really know my father in this life."

"I'm beginning to think it's not an advantage to remember one's past lives."

"No, I suppose it isn't. But then—" He smiled an acid and self-deprecating smile. "Sooner or later, one's blessings are always one's curses."

"Yes." I leaned up to him and . . .

Well.

Let's just say we proceeded to make a start on the "getting to know each other a lot better" part of our relationship and leave it there.*

I woke the next morning in a good mood.

For about two seconds.

And I can't even blame waking in Yor for my ill humor.

I can, however, blame the strange woman leaning over my bed.

She was old. Not a well-aged, graceful old. Dorna is old, but she has a face anyone would love in a grandmother, all warm eyes and sweet smiles.† This old woman looked like she'd be a danger to any child. Her wrinkled skin looked lizard-like, if an albino lizard with watery brown eyes. Her hair evoked rat kings and knotted string.

Her grin made my skin crawl. "I made you breakfast, dearie." On the nightstand beside the bed, she set a platter loaded with cooked oats and apples, crusty bread, and red meat stew.

I was reaching for the bread when Senera walked through the door, took one look at the old woman, and snapped, "Don't eat anything she gives you!" She upended the tray, splattering stew and oatmeal all over the floor.

---

* I'm so glad she edited that out so I wouldn't have to.
† And grabby fingers and wicked tongue . . . the Eight sure do know how to pick their angels, don't they?

I blinked, even as the old woman snarled. "Bitch! I was trying to be nice!"

Senera hit her across the face.

"Hey, now hold on—"

"What meat did you use, Wyrga? Kitten? Puppy? Or did a local woman leave another baby out in the cold?"*

I stopped protesting, and sat there, horrified, more horrified still by the gleeful look that stole over the old woman's face. "Aw, you spoil all my games. I found a stillborn foal last night."

I leaned away, fighting back bile.

"Damn it all, Wyrga. How many times do we have to tell you to stop doing this?"

"Forever," the old woman snarled. "Let me have my fun."

Senera grimaced. "Come on, Janel. We're leaving, anyway. Wyrga, clean this up."

"I'm not your maid," the old woman said. "Clean it up yourself." She turned her attention back to me as I stood. "I know you. I knew your mother too, back in the day. She was a whore. Are you a whore too?"

"By the Eight, what could've happened to turn you into such a nasty piece of work?" Even as I said the words, I remembered how I knew her. She'd tended the fire at the banquet, the woman who'd stared hate at me like a spear's throw.

She cackled. "Ha! Ha ha! Oh, now that's a story! Best question anyone's asked me around here in years." She pointed a bony finger at me. "You come around sometime and I'll show you, just see if I don't."

"Wyrga, don't you dare," Senera snapped. She tugged again on my chemise. "Come on. Let's leave before I do something I'll regret. Wyrga's one of the duke's favorites, for reasons that escape me."

The old crone grinned toothily. She wasn't missing any. On the contrary, she seemed to have too many, all sharp. "He likes what I can do with my mouth."

---

* Seriously, don't ever eat anything Wyrga gives you. Rules to live by.

"Oh, I doubt that very much. Also, you're disgusting."

I didn't hesitate to go, even though technically speaking I hadn't dressed. I didn't care about leaving behind clothing that wasn't mine, for a start.

"Where are we going?" I asked when we were out of earshot.

"I'm going back to work, which I doubt you'll want to have anything to do with. And since I don't dare leave you here alone, I'm putting you with the duke's wives. It's the most guarded area in the entire palace. You'll be safe there."

"Wait, what? I don't want to be—"

Senera stopped and turned back to me. "Two minutes. You got into trouble less than two minutes after being left alone with the men here. I have no reason to think it would be any different this time. And neither I, Brother Qown, nor Lord Var will be around to heal your hand when you break it on someone's face again. So I'd prefer to put you someplace secure."

"Fine."

"You might like it. A few wives are under the laughable impression the duke will impregnate them, but most women are just enjoying not being forced to have anything to do with the men. They even have books."

"Sounds fantastic. I don't suppose they have a stable . . . ?"

"In this climate? No. Honestly, I shudder to think where Wyrga found a horse. She might have lied. The closest thing you'll find to a mount around here are the snow hyenas that pull the sleighs, and the occasional mammoth."

I nodded and reminded myself I needed to find the spear, discover who had Brother Qown's gaesh (and for that matter, Brother Qown), and escape.

The sooner the better.

I had yet to gain a real sense of what the palace looked like from the outside. The walls had all been made from the same windowless black stone. It seemed like an endless and twisting maze, lit by mage-light lamps. The air seemed fresh, though,

I assumed because of magic. Indeed, it wouldn't have surprised me to learn a team of servants patrolled the halls, painting damn air sigils under every chair and behind every painting.

The single guarded entrance to the wives' quarters led to a massive hall. One wall derived from the same transparent crystal I had seen in the main dining room. Several balconies interrupted its near-invisible expanse, jutting out into teal skies. Reflecting pools and blooming flowers lined the hall. The room looked like the personification of winter made fluffy and comfortable. Pillows and furs and all the silks anyone might desire had been tossed about.

Even though cold never bothered me, I still felt the chill. The wives didn't seem to notice.

Their ages ranged from a little older than I to the same age as Ninavis, but no one older. They were all Yoran, pale-skinned and ice-colored, not necessarily attractive.

"No males?" I whispered to Senera.

She gave me an odd look that I couldn't quite interpret, then shook her head. "No, no men allowed. The guards outside are the closest any man besides Duke Kaen ever gets, and even they aren't allowed inside when the duke is in attendance. Duke Kaen insists he should be his wives' only pleasure."

I had to stop myself from choking. "Um, but . . . uh . . ."

Senera stopped fighting her smile. "Yes?"

"Has no one told Kaen we don't need males for that?"

Her eyes turned bright. "Don't spoil their fun. There's more than a few long-term romances tolerated here, but only because their husband doesn't seem to realize it's a possibility."

"Oh, I wouldn't dream of saying anything."

A woman noticed us and drifted over. "Bringing us the Khorveshan girl?" She pursed her lips. "You don't look Khorveshan."

"Thank you," I said and meant it. "I don't feel Khorveshan."

"Bikeinoh, this is Janel." Senera nudged me forward. "I'd appreciate it if you could keep an eye on her while I'm gone."

The woman raised an eyebrow and pursed her lips. "Of

course. We don't have anything better to do, do we?" The bite in her words hinted at previous unpleasantness.

"Just do it. And get her something to wear. Wyrga broke into her room this morning, so I didn't dare leave her there."

I would bet metal the sign the woman made warded against evil spirits.

Senera turned to me. "I'll be back in a few days."

"Don't hurry on my account."

She rolled her eyes and left.

"Who is Wyrga?" I asked as soon as Senera left.

Bikeinoh looked around before answering. "Kaen's monster. And the trainer of Kaen's monsters. She deals with the animals. Polar bears and snow hyenas. She's been here for longer than I have, and she's horrible. Not everyone here feels that way about her, though, so I wouldn't be too loud about criticizing her."

"Someone likes her? That's hard to believe."

Bikeinoh looked around again. "Wyrga claims she's the last witch-mother."

I blinked. "Witch-mother? What's a witch-mother?"

"So this is the wizard's new Khorveshan wife, huh?" Another woman approached. She looked near to me in age, and she didn't walk so much as strut. This woman intended to make sure I didn't entertain any fallacies about the pecking order and my place in it.

I looked at her sideways. "Is that a problem?"

The woman shrugged. "No. As long as you stay away from Azhen."

"Who?"

"From my husband," she elaborated. "Azhen Kaen."

"Oh, Veixizhau, please. You're wife number twenty-eight. Do you think he'd even notice if you went missing?"*

"Well, he wouldn't care if you went missing. How many years have you been married to the man and no child yet?"

"You keep assuming I care."

* I don't.

"You should. He keeps taking me to bed like this and I'll be first wife soon." Veixizhau rolled her eyes and sauntered away, shaking her hips with extra rigor. They were beautiful hips, mind you. But her personality made them easy to ignore.

I stood there, blinking. "She seems nice."

"Don't worry about her. She's just upset because she's not pregnant yet." Bikeinoh laughed and then lowered her voice to a whisper. "As if we'll ever conceive. Kaen wants Exidhar to inherit. It's his insurance against being assassinated by the clans."

"How do you mean?"

"Have you met the Hon's son?"

I thought back to our very unfortunate meeting. "I have, yes." I paused. "They don't wish Exidhar to inherit because he's half-Khorveshan?"

With the unwelcome news that I was at least half-Khorveshan, I found myself interested in the answer. Would I be forced to contend with some deeper prejudice besides my sex?

"Yes. It was a terrible scandal when the Hon married his Khorveshan wife. So much so the clans felt they had to *do something* about it. They say her ghost still haunts the tunnels underneath the palace. If you go down to the storerooms and listen, you can still hear her screams." She chuckled. "Not that we're allowed to go down to the storerooms."

"Why kill the wife? Wouldn't it make more sense to assassinate the duke and his son?"

"The Hon," Bikeinoh corrected.

"Fine. The Hon."

"Yes, they tried to assassinate him. When Azhen Kaen started outlawing the old ways, started talking about education and rights, the clan leaders thought it was their chance. Azhen and Exidhar survived. His wife Xivan didn't." Bikeinoh made a face. "All my life, my father used to say the Kaen family was soft. Too much Quuros blood.* Well, the clans did nice work

---

* I'll buy that Quuros are decadent, greedy, and amoral, sure, but soft? Oh, you poor children.

there. Killing the Hon's wife hardened Azhen Kaen up just fine. And by Cherthog did he ever make us regret it. Tracked down the Simoshgra and wiped out the entire clan. Every single last one. As soon as we heard the news, I told my father we'd better give Kaen assurances. We'd better demonstrate just how sorry we were about what happened, or he wouldn't stop with the Simoshgra. So that's what I am. What all these women are. Assurance. Been here ever since."

"I'm sorry."

"It's not so bad. Never had a reason to complain to Suless about it, anyway."

"No, I suppose not." I looked around the room. This all seemed very pampered and even more boring. "With all these wives, I assume he must keep busy."

"Oh no," Bikeinoh said, laughing. "I think he'd prefer to forget we existed, but occasionally, he remembers and does his duty. But I think if we ever gave him the excuse, he'd be all too happy to send us all packing back to our families again."

"Wouldn't that be better?"

Her eyes widened. "No."

I didn't understand. Back in Jorat, arranged marriages rarely occurred but could be successful if the families had done a good job with the matchmaking. Forced marriages with multiple partners? Unheard of. The likelihood of a partner feeling saelen and just . . . wandering . . . into other relationships made such an option unpopular and unwise. And if a spouse kept their mates imprisoned to ensure they didn't leave, they'd label themselves as thorra. Nobody wanted that.

Of course, these women might not be interested in wandering at all. Bikeinoh seemed quite comfortable in her situation. That told me a lot about how women in the rest of Yor could expect to be treated.

"You haven't broken fast yet, have you?" Bikeinoh continued. "Why don't we go—"

But as Bikeinoh spoke, another wife jogged up, out of breath. Her parti-color skin suggested an ancestry that included at least one or two of the many Joratese who'd served with the Quuros army when they occupied the region, decades before. "You're the new girl, right?"

It wasn't worth correcting her. "May I help you?"

"Not me," she said. "The Hon wants to see you. Right now."

38: THE EYE OF FIRE

Jorat Dominion, Quuros Empire.
Three days since Jarith Milligreest chose option two

"So . . . are those wives still locked away?" Dorna asked. "Someone should go free them."

"Don't be lecherous," Janel said. "I know it's hard, but *try*. Also, trust me when I say they don't need to be rescued."

"And your third meeting with Teraeth confirms who Elana is," Kihrin said, shaking his head. When Janel looked at him, he said, "Remember you said I kept calling you Elana in the Afterlife? That was the only Elana I could recall. Atrin Kandor's wife: Elana Milligreest."

"Milligreest?" Janel looked quite surprised.

"Yeah, after Kandor died, she went back to using her maiden name." Kihrin paused, blinked, and then started rubbing his thumbs into his temples.

Apparently, the Goddess of Death had a mean streak so vicious it left Kihrin open-mouthed in awe. Thaena had taken two infamously mortal enemies—Atrin Kandor and Terindel the Black—and had reincarnated one of them as the other's *son*.

That was just . . . *mean*.

And it didn't even begin to explore the part where Atrin's widow—Elana—had later married Terindel.

Yes, the same Terindel.

Kihrin found himself grateful he could watch that tangled knot from a safe distance. Well, mostly. Given his feelings about Janel, he couldn't claim impartiality.

"Are you . . . all right?" Qown asked.

Kihrin looked up. "Sorry. I just, uh . . . I was just thinking about how Janel also has a 'type.'" Teraeth and his father, Terindel, both possessed a certain resemblance, after all. Just like Terindel probably resembled *his* father—Mithros.

"Oh, that's true," Dorna said. "I never really noticed before, but you're a damn close match to Oreth's coloring, aren't you? I mean, not the eyes, but . . . everything else."

"No," Kihrin said. "That's not what I—" He pressed his lips together and looked over at Janel. "Seriously?"

Janel raised her hands helplessly. "Similar, yes, but I like you a lot better than him." She shifted uncomfortably before she turned to Qown. "Would you mind? Please?"

"Not even slightly," Qown said.

Qown's Turn. The Ice Demesne, Yor, Quur.

Brother Qown waited in the library, staring at the agate sitting in its box. Its raw edges glittered, light flickering over them as though he held the stone before a fire.

Relos Var walked back inside the room. He carried a stack of books, ink, brushes, and probably an inkstone—which he dumped on the table.

Qown frowned. "Why will I need this?"

"You'll see." Relos Var pulled up a chair next to him and sat down. "Pick up the stone and concentrate on it. It may help to close your eyes."

Brother Qown hesitated.

Relos Var just raised an eyebrow. "Second thoughts?"

Qown grimaced and picked up the stone.

And . . . it didn't feel special. His arm didn't burst into flame. He felt no strange energy flow through him. Nothing about it felt special at all. He held a normal, if exquisite, rock.

He closed his eyes and concentrated.

"Now I want you to picture a fire. There's one burning in the fireplace in this room."

Brother Qown did.

He felt a rushing sensation and found himself standing near the end of the table, looking at Relos Var sitting next to . . . himself. All the colors looked wrong. Brother Qown appeared warm red, the table looked colder, and Relos Var shone with a great white-hot fire.

He gasped, dropped the stone, and opened his eyes.

"What—"

"Worldhearth, as you may have just surmised," said Relos Var, "allows you to see clairvoyantly, using fire as the focus point. It takes time to master the ability and longer still to learn how to use it to spy on others. Yet since there is no fire in existence immune to divination, anyone—mortal or god—who is standing next to flame is vulnerable. The trick is finding them."

"I thought you could use the Name of All Things to spy on people."

"You'd think that, wouldn't you? But the Name of All Things just answers questions. A powerful ability, but you must know the specific question to ask. The answers too will be literal. If I asked if you had eaten this morning, it would provide a yes-or-no answer. That isn't helpful if what I should have asked is who ate breakfast with you. This is much more flexible in its use, or at least, has different restrictions."

Brother Qown reached for the stone. "I see. And I assume you want me to write down what the people I spy on say to each other."

"As well as any other details you think are pertinent. I know you're more than up for the task. You have always had a keen eye for detail."

Brother Qown nodded. It's not like he had a choice, if he hoped to throw off the gaesh and help Janel. He looked at the stone again. "Do you have a list of 'targets'?"

"Let's not jump ahead. What I want you to do right now is concentrate on learning to use the stone. It can be tricky to find the person you're looking for and difficult to find a person who is thousands of miles away. The stone will allow you to hop from one fire to the next, but it takes practice to master.

Best you start now." Relos Var paused. "I'll have someone bring in some food for you and hot tea. You'll also want to make yourself take regular breaks. It's easy to become so caught up in the stone you forget what's happening to your physical body."

"Is that what happened to the last person who used this?" Brother Qown asked.

"In a sense," Relos Var answered. "He used the stone while walking and stepped off a balcony. Took the duchess two weeks to find the stone in all the snow drifts." He stood up from his seat and walked to the door. "That should be enough to get you started."

"Wait, that's it?" Brother Qown fought panic. "That's all the instruction you're going to give me?"

Relos Var paused at the door. "I've known you since you were a boy, Qown. You've always learned best when I let you figure things out for yourself. I'll check in on you later to see how you're coming along."

Var had been clever not to explain how the stone worked. By forcing Qown to research the stone's abilities for himself, Relos Var had ensured Qown wouldn't have time to think about his situation. Qown latched onto that life raft with the enthusiasm of a man who had never been able to resist solving a mystery.

Worldhearth did indeed focus on fire, as Relos Var had explained. Clairvoyance played a part too, since Brother Qown could focus the stone on a fire he had seen before, say, a hanging brazier in the Temple of Khored in Atrine. But he couldn't start with the hearth fires inside the Atrine palace, which he had never seen. However, once he had the hanging brazier in his sights, he could goat-leap to a nearby fire, and then the next, and the next, shifting directions as appropriate. He managed to find a candelabra in the dining room and from there make his way to an oven in the duke's palace in Atrine.

Doing so, however, took him almost an entire day. When he tore himself away from the stone, his body was in total rebellion: hungry, thirsty, and in desperate need of a bathroom. Which he had known on some level; he'd just been too caught up in solving the problem to care.

The challenge proved to be discerning his scrying location quickly enough to jump to the next fire. He had no idea how, but if he wanted to find people within a reasonable time, he needed to become efficient at scanning for them.

When he next returned to practicing his scrying with World-hearth, however, he saw something that made him stop cold.

Ninavis.

The former bandit leader sat next to a small coal brazier inside an azhock, warming her hands. She wore a hooded cloak and kept glancing over her shoulder at the soldiers.

Not just the Markreev's people but also the duke's men, all spread out in a search formation. They were moving from azhock to azhock as they hunted. Hoods were pulled back, hair swept away from eyes. They inspected each person, one by one. Eventually, they'd find the tent where Ninavis waited. Every few minutes, she put a hand on her bow, as if to remind herself it was strung and ready. She wasn't going down without a fight.

The air smelled like fire from more than just the cooking pit, and the sky above the city looked like a dirty smudge.

Brother Qown didn't recognize the other people inside the azhock, but they all wore red, presumably members of Mithros's Red Spears. They held themselves with the tense air of soldiers waiting for the fight to start.

Then the ground began to shake.

Brother Qown didn't know what the sound meant, but everyone reacted immediately. "Stampede!" someone shouted. People began running. Indeed, a large horse herd, gathered on the Green for the tournament, now ran in panic.

The azhock's back panel moved, and Dorna stepped inside, holding a large bag hoisted over her shoulder. "There you are. Been looking for you."

Brother Qown exhaled—she was alive. So Relos Var hadn't been lying about Dorna at least.

"What are you doing here?" Ninavis snapped. "The Markreev promised he'd get you out of town."

"I ain't leaving without the rest of you. Besides, Mithros has a plan." The old woman tossed a large bag down next to the fire. "Put that on right fast. Arasgon and Talaras can only keep the horses riled up for so long before another fireblood settles 'em back down again."

"They're arresting any Marakori they find, Dorna, and they have my description. What can you do about—" But she stopped talking as she finished opening the bag and pulled out Mithros's black enameled helmet, armor, and raven feather cloak.

The Black Knight's costume.

"Mithros swears it will fit you. He changed it up special. Now hurry."

Brother Qown turned away as Ninavis stripped off her clothing. He instead watched Dorna wander about the tent. The old woman seemed healthy enough. She nodded to the Red Spears who hadn't left to watch the stampede. While she walked, a variety of small, valuable items disappeared into her skirts, but never when anyone but Brother Qown was paying attention.

"Help me with this cloak, please," Ninavis said.

The black armor hid her general size and gender, with sinister-looking pauldrons and a chest plate whose ornate design obscured her bosom.

A horse whinnied from outside; Brother Qown saw Arasgon's red tiger-striped legs at the entrance to the tent.

"We're almost done!" Dorna shouted. She lifted the raven-feather cloak over Ninavis's shoulders. "Arasgon's ready for you. You head to Khored's Temple. The others are already there. Mithros will smuggle you out of the city."

"What about you? The duke's not going to just let you stroll away . . ."

The old woman waved a hand. "Oh sure. Rise from the dead before a couple of nobles and they label you *witch* before you can fill your lungs. Don't you worry about me. I'll meet up with you in the caves." Noises interrupted them: soldiers returning, horses trotting back to their corrals. "Hurry now. They're expecting you."

"Who are?" Ninavis asked.

"Your army." Dorna wagged a finger. "Best not keep them waiting."

39: HANDED THE CROWN

Jorat Dominion, Quuros Empire.
Three days since Tyentso wasn't even
a little bit ready for this

Ninavis picked up a dishrag and threw it at Qown.

"I'm sorry!" he said, throwing up his hands. "I was gaeshed!"

"Yeah, yeah," she groused. "That's what they all say."

Janel laughed and launched into her turn.

Janel's Turn. The Ice Demesne, Yor, Quur.

Bikeinoh found me a dress and ushered me from the women's quarters. The entire way, I felt the wives' angry stares, who seemed to think me a threat—siphoning the attention that should have been theirs.

I wanted to laugh, call them fools, and mock the very idea. But I didn't know Duke Kaen. Maybe, despite Relos Var's opinion, Kaen wouldn't respect the "territory" of our sham marriage. Maybe he'd want what he couldn't have.

Maybe they had a point.

I didn't feel reassured when Bikeinoh brought me to the duke's private parlor. Like the wives' quarters, this room faced an outside wall, giving one a mind-numbing view of mountain vistas. As soon as she left, another door opened, and Wyrga stepped through. The hunched old woman carried an armful of clothing, including the red dress I'd been given to wear and Relos Var's jewelry. Which also made me uneasy. As she'd pointed out to Senera, Wyrga wasn't a maid.

"Ah, it's the little whore," Wyrga said, chuckling.

"Tell me, do you spend time gossiping with demons? Because you have a similar originality to your insults. I don't think you're trying hard enough to hurt my feelings. Come now. Do better."

She laughed in delight as she dumped all the clothing in a chair. "I knew your mother, you know."

"You've mentioned. And what, by chance, was my mother's name?"

"Irisia, although people don't call her that now. They all came back, after Vol Karoth had finished with them, to find the world had given them new names to replace their old ones." The old woman walked up to me, and leaned close, sniffing me. "I knew your mother, watched the Veils flash. You're just like her. But don't let them turn you into a cute little pet. Irisia made that mistake. Lions should never love their cages."

I paused. "Is that so?"

"You think I can't recognize my own kind? We're both wild monsters, you and I." She grinned again. "So Rev'arric thinks he can tame you. Foolish man. My husband thought he'd tamed me too, but I never learned to love my leash. Oh, I made him pay. Isn't it the prerogative of all unjustly imprisoned, to revenge themselves on their jailers?"

I found myself becoming intrigued, against my better judgment. "Who's Rev'arric?"

"Did I say *Rev'arric*? I meant *Relos Var*." Her breath smelled like raw meat.

"Who . . . who are you? Who are you really?"

She leaned back, looking as scandalized as if I'd just asked her to play bed sports. "I can't tell you that." She started cackling again. "But I know why you're here. I know all about you, little lioness."

I ignored how uncomfortable the entire conversation made me. She seemed quite insane, but that didn't mean she was lying. Quite the opposite.

"And what do you know?"

"In the stone city of three roads, the lion cub singed with great

catastrophe, as the terrible march of death takes the land of plenty. The cub alone lives, cursed with great strength, to be raised by horses." She backed up and pointed at me. "That's you, darling." Wyrga whispered, almost an exhale. "Hellwarrior."

Before I could respond, the door opened, and Duke Kaen appeared. "Wyrga, what are you doing here? Go back to your animals."

"Yes, yes, Your Grace," She gave the man a bow that seemed no more sincere than a hyena's grin and shuffled out of the room.

"Count Tolamer," the duke said. "Please, join me. We have much to discuss."

"Who is that woman? She can't be—" And then my mouth dropped open as I saw his parlor.

A large bookcase covered the wall I'd entered through, but that hadn't drawn my attention. No. The Joratese tournament regalia covering the opposite wall had that pleasure. Flags and banners enough to please half a fairground's worth of screaming, riotous fans.

He hadn't restricted himself to one team either, although he liked Ferra's knights, underdogs in so many tournaments. A map of eastern Quur covered the opposite wall. I noticed a pin stuck into Jorat at Barsine Banner's capital, Mereina. Another at Tiga Pass.

I looked away.

A burning fireplace and comfortable chairs made the room cozy and warm. The black stone walls had been hidden under hardwoods, so this room looked personal and inviting.

"You're a fan?" I couldn't keep the disbelief from my voice. "You watch the tournaments?"

He chuckled as he sat down next to the fireplace. On the table before him sat a large tray of meats and stews, including a fried roll I hoped contained vegetables. I also saw a silver carafe, wafting steam. Next to the tray someone had placed a Zaibur board without pieces.

"Oh yes," he said. "I'm a huge fan. Not just of the contests themselves. It's the basic premise of the tournaments. The greatest question rulers have asked themselves for centuries has been: What does one do with a standing army? Kandor solved the issue by always searching for the next war to fight, but what happens when you run out of lands to conquer?" He waved a hand. "Khorvesh has to contend with the Blight, and I suppose the Manol, but Jorat? Jorat is sandwiched between three other Quuros dominions, with no outside borders save a coastline so storm-ridden no navy would dare attack it. What is Jorat to do with all those raised to believe the flower of adult measure is found on the field of battle?"

Of course, I'd grown up knowing the answer to that question. "We turned it into a sport."

"You turned it into a sport," he agreed. "An important sport, an economically vital endeavor, one with which your population is deeply involved. All the heroic valor of the battlefield, but far fewer casualties. Genius." The duke paused. "At least, until a real threat shows up again. Perhaps not so genius now, when your 'knights' don't know how to cope with a real emergency."

"Yes, who would have predicted you'd set upon them with sorcerers, demons, and a *dragon.*" I didn't bother to hide my scorn.

"Who indeed?" He grinned. "Have you had a chance to eat?" He gestured toward the food. "I'd be honored if you'd share a meal with me."

"Thank you. I'm famished."

I sat down and began helping myself to food. He seemed surprised. I realized either he was supposed to eat first as duke or eat first as male. Whatever the rule, he didn't think I qualified. If I'd known, I'd have *insisted* on being the first to reach for a plate.

I split the roll with my knife and saw a gelatinous white substance inside. "What is this?" I asked.

"Whale fat," he answered. "You should try it. It's delicious."

I looked down at the tray. "Is there anything here besides meat?"

"The tea doesn't have meat in it," he answered. "I'm sorry. No one told me you didn't eat meat."

"I do eat meat," I answered. "Most Joratese do. But it's not something we eat every day. This would make me sick to my stomach." I reached for the tea, since at least that was safe.

It wasn't. A thick head of butter floated on the actual liquid. I didn't have any moral qualms about drinking it, but I almost gagged at the unexpected taste.

He watched me with pursed lips. "It's very cold here in Yor," he explained. "So we eat meat and fat. We used to eat more plants, before the Quuros invaded and destroyed the Spring Caves."

"You could import vegetables," I pointed out.

"Yes," he agreed. "We *could*."

"If you refuse to work with the Royal Houses, why did you have so many eating in your great hall yesterday?"

"You didn't see House D'Aramarin there yesterday, did you? Not a hint of green to be found anywhere. Nor House D'Knofra or D'Kard, House D'Erinwa? They're quite content with the status quo. But the other houses? They're more open to change."

"You're not concerned they'll betray you?"

"I know they'll betray me—if they think I'm going to fail."

I set down the tea. "Your Grace, why am I still alive?"

He laughed and leaned back in his chair. "You don't pull punches, do you?"

"I appreciate being alive, but I'd feel better if I understood the motives involved. And I don't." I folded my fingers in my lap. "You have been attacking villages and towns across Jorat. Attacking them in a way Duke Xun is ill-equipped to recognize, let alone counter. And what is going to happen in Jorat, when the people realize their duke can't protect them from a threat recent enough to still give children nightmares? Another Hellmarch. What happens when you come along and do what our duke cannot—save them from this crisis?" I shrugged. "You're going to have access to all the good farmland you want. It might even be considered a bloodless takeover—if one didn't know you organized the original attacks. You won't have to conquer Jorat. We'll hand you the crown and demand the Quuros High Council put you in charge."

Kaen looked delighted. "You *are* a joy, aren't you?"

I rolled my eyes. "The fact I can see your strategy just makes it all the more perplexing to me why you brought me here. Why not let Relos Var kill me?" I stopped. "Or was keeping me alive all his idea?"

"A little of both. Can you guess why?"

I scowled. "I wouldn't have asked if I—" I hesitated. "Something to do with my parents. My real parents."

Thaena had said so, hadn't she? Relos Var liked striking out at his enemies through their families. For that reason, Relos Var would find me irresistible.

But in theory, I had no living family. At least, I'd thought so before Darzin D'Mon read my grandfather's letter. Now I faced the possibility that I not only had living parents but Relos Var considered them enemies.

If Thaena was right, then I was bait being used against someone *else*.

"Yes," Kaen said. "Not your mother. I'm sure she was a delightful woman. A dancing girl, I think Var said? Something like that. But your father . . ." He smiled. "A Khorveshan soldier, indeed. But higher ranked than a mere officer. High General Qoran Milligreest, the High Council's leader, most powerful man in the empire."

"The emperor—"

"—is a puppet who won a magical free-for-all and takes his orders from the council, which your father commands."

I didn't respond. I think I was still in shock. *The high general?*

"I see the look on your face. Qoran is a fine man. I've met him on several occasions. Sadly, he can't keep his trousers buttoned. His wife deserves so much better."

"Says the man with several dozen wives."

"That's politics," he responded. "I would be faithful in his position. Of course, we're graced by your presence due to his lack of self-control, so it's just as well. His missteps are to our benefit."

I found myself glad I was already sitting, because I felt faint. "I've met him."

"After Lonezh, I imagine."

"I thought—" I reached for the tea and drank it, not tasting the butter this time.

"You thought the high general paid attention to you because he wanted to know why Xaltorath picked you as his host, why Xaltorath wouldn't leave. But no. High General Milligreest picked you out earlier, before the Hellmarch finished. Someone— probably Emperor Sandus—looked at your aura and recognized who you are: a Milligreest. A Khorveshan. And Milligreest never admitted the truth. He left you with the Vishai and returned home, after pretending you were no relation at all. It almost worked."

"And from this, you assume he'll care what happens to me?" I said.

"Oh, I don't have to assume, because he should have unleashed the Quuros army's full magical might on that Hellmarch, if he didn't give a damn what happened to the eight-year-old girl guiding it. Yet he didn't. There's no good excuse for your survival. When the time comes for him to consider unleashing those forces once more, I want him to hesitate like that again. And he will, because he cares."

Words cannot describe how numb I felt. This was so much worse than I had thought. Even worse than the sham of being labeled Danorak and hailed a great hero.

I'd lived because some father I'd never met had placed more importance on my survival than the dominion's. Why? Because I was born of his seed, presumably in bed play that meant very little to him at the time. Jorat could go to Hell as long as his *spawn* survived.

The arrogance burned in my throat.

They will try to break you, Khored had said. No, wait. That was wrong. That hadn't been Khored, had it?

Relos Var will try to break you, Xaltorath had said. *You must let him succeed.*

Why, Xaltorath? Why did you single me out? What did you hope to accomplish? I saw the wheels turning inside wheels, but devoid of context, ignorant of motives, the movements made no sense. I saw the game, but I had no idea what forces shaped the rules.

But in that moment, I knew a great many forces were playing this game, and they all intended to claim me as their piece.

While I sat there and stared out at nothing, Duke Kaen stood up, picked up the tray, and carried it over to a different table. He went to the door and I heard him speaking low words to someone outside.

I turned around and studied the map.

When he returned, I faced him. "I'm sorry," he said. "I've upset you."

"Nothing you say can upset me," I whispered, although even a five-year-old wouldn't have been fooled by so feeble a lie.

"It's not all a threat I've invented, I should add. There are dangers to Jorat your people don't even know about, dangers that would destroy your people if they're not combated."

I raised an eyebrow. "Oh, and I suppose you're the only one who can save us? That sounds very convenient for you."

"Oh, if only. Aeyan'arric—that's the ice dragon you encountered—is well-behaved and mostly in possession of her faculties. Relos Var gives her tasks, and she carries them out. The other dragons, though." He shook his head. "Dragons are insane. They aren't controllable. They aren't tamable. Relos Var can make Aeyan'arric behave, but I'll never trust her. And the largest and the most dangerous—Morios—sleeps under Lake Jorat. When he wakes—and it will be *when,* not *if*—he'll destroy half the dominion before he's subdued. There's even a prophecy about him. Would you like to hear it?"

"A prophecy." I stared at him. "I don't like prophecies."

"They can be useful." He pulled a book from his shelves and opened it to a bookmarked page. "Especially this one. *In the twentieth year of the hawk and the lion, beneath the silver sword, the sleeping beast's chains shatter. The dragon of swords devours demon falls as night takes the land.*" Kaen offered me the book. "A Devoran quatrain."

The leather-bound book in question seemed old. Looking at it, I realized half the bookcase held its twins. "How many . . ." I glanced back at him. "How many Devoran prophecies are there?"

"Many more than this. But I'm an enthusiastic reader."

"The twentieth year of the hawk and the lion. By what calendar?"

"If Relos Var is right—" Azhen Kaen reached out and flicked a finger off the tip of my nose before I could dodge away. "*You* are the lion. Which means we only have a few more years to go before Morios wakes. We're running out of time. And I for one don't intend to let Morios—the dragon of swords—destroy Atrine before I can conquer it. *Atrine,* you realize, means—"

"The Silver Blade." I leaned back in case he felt like any more nose-touching. "I know. Every Joratese child knows what Atrin Kandor's name means. And so, what are you going to do about it?"

"Not a thing."

I waited for the further explanation, but none presented itself. "What?"

"I'm not going to do a thing," Kaen said, "because Var doesn't think I'm ready. And since he doesn't think I'm ready, he's under no obligation to open a gate to a location I don't know. Despite its name, 'Lake' Jorat is an inland sea. Even for a dragon as monstrous as Morios, finding him on my own would be impossible. Never mind how Duke Xun would misinterpret my search as something more sinister. Say, an invasion."

"Relos Var's your . . ." I flailed. "He works for you, doesn't he?"

"He supports me. I can't force his apprentice, Senera, to tell me where to find Morios. Relos Var has so far refused to help too; the time isn't right, whatever that means." He saluted me with his tea. "I'm starting to think the real problem is that I'd assumed I would be the one to slay a dragon, and Relos Var has someone else in mind." He gave me a pointed look. "It doesn't have to be me, after all."

I felt a weight settle down through my core. "What do you mean?"

"I don't have to march in and save Jorat. The High Council won't lightly hand over one dominion's governing to another dominion's ruler. They want to keep the dominions separated. Never mind the Joratese distrust of Yor. But if a Joratese saved the day and slew Morios, if—for example—the famous hero Janel Danorak did it . . . I have a funny feeling the high general wouldn't contest your claim."

I cast about for excuses. "But *apparently* I'm not Joratese."

He dismissed the excuse. "The Joratese think you're one of them. You'll be hailed as a hero."

"And all I'd have to do is betray my people." I knew I'd been stripped of my title, likely branded a witch. If I came back and defeated a dragon as dangerous as Duke Kaen said? I was as good as staking my claim to replace Duke Xun.

What you protect is what you rule.

I was tempted. After all, with my expertise and experience, how difficult would it be to arrange for a much less violent revolution in Jorat? Duke Kaen didn't understand the Joratese the way I did. He didn't understand how to sway their loyalty. I did—without dragons, without demons.

All those deaths would stop if I agreed to his plan. And not after I'd found a spear and killed a dragon. Not after I'd figured out how to defeat Relos Var. *Immediately.*

How many lives would I save if I pledged my loyalty to Duke Kaen? I could gain everything I desired. Kaen would have no reason to send Aeyan'arric after Joratese villages.* If Kaen's story about Morios proved true, I'd help save hundreds of thousands of lives by defeating him.

---

* Ah, sweet girl. If only Duke Kaen's ambitions were the only reason that was necessary.

All I had to do was say yes.

Kaen said, "Would it be a betrayal, though? Is it not justice, when they wronged you first? Relos Var told me about your situation. Your Markreev didn't protect you when he should have. He exploited his power over you to force you into an unworthy match. Your grandfather betrayed you by assuming you would submit to another man's rule and by allowing his lamentably racist leanings to overcome his sense of your true value."

"Yet those people didn't frame me for witchcraft, kill me in a duel, kidnap me, and hold me against my will in another country."

"If your enthusiasm to rescue someone who has done you wrong is proportional to the crime, we've made a fine start at convincing you Yor is worth saving." He smiled, no doubt thinking himself hilarious.

"Oh?" I laughed, because I found it just the opposite. "And why does Yor need saving?"

"Because our land is dying," Azhen Kaen said, all humor vanishing. "Quur has murdered it."

The young wife who'd questioned me when I first arrived, Veixizhau, was waiting for me when I returned to the wives' quarters. I couldn't tell if she'd decided to impress or one-up me, but she wore a samite gown and a blinding diamond necklace.

I was distracted, thinking of honor and whether I placed more importance on my pride than my people. Wasn't the whole reason I'd come here to gain Relos Var's and Duke Kaen's trust by whatever means necessary? So why did I balk at Kaen's deal? I didn't have to *keep* my promise to them, after all.

But I wanted to.

Oh, that was an ugly realization. I *wanted* someone better than Duke Xun to rule Jorat. I wanted the Markreev of Stavira to acknowledge my idorrá. I wanted—

"That took a long time," Veixizhau said, interrupting my thoughts. If she intended to sound nice, she didn't try hard.

"Did it? I lost track. Where is the kitchen? I'm starving."

"Segra, go fetch our guest something from the kitchen, would you?"

"Yes, thank you," I said. "No meat, please. I'll take bread. Porridge if you have any."

Segra, a young woman with large violet eyes, gave me an awkward, nervous smile before leaving.

Veixizhau offered me a chair. "Please, sit. Tell me all about your conversation. I so seldom have a chance to hear about what's going on outside our halls."

Her sweet tone made me pause. "The duke—sorry, the Hon— doesn't give you any access to outside information?"

"Books. Old books. It's nothing current."

That drew another wife's attention. "I rather like the books, mind you, but it's not the same as fresh news."

"Where's Bikeinoh?" I looked around, but I didn't see the Hon's oldest wife.

"Gone off on some chore, I suppose. I don't keep track. What did the Hon say?" Veixizhau leaned forward.

I realized she didn't think we'd talked. She hoped to catch me out by forcing me to fabricate a conversation.

"He wants my help conquering Jorat," I told her.

She blinked, surprised. "What?"

I sighed. I wasn't in the mood. My temper had soured from talking to the duke, and given the way my lower back was aching, I was about to start my flow. I had no patience for a jealous wife who thought I'd made a play for her husband.

"Your husband wants me to help him conquer Jorat. We spoke about it at length." I pulled out a different chair from the one Veixizhau offered and flopped into it. "Something about killing a dragon, which strikes me as a task a smart ruler would delegate to someone else. Oh, and he wants to use me to pressure my father into leaving Yor alone. Also lovely."

I'd closed my eyes so I couldn't see her expression, but she made a surprised sound. "Oh, my poor girl. I'm so sorry! Believe me, I know what it's like to be taken from your family against your will."

I raised my head, opened my eyes, and looked up at her. "Nothing about what you said sounds the least bit sincere. Except the part about being taken from your family."

"You've misjudged me." Her expression was innocence personified.

"I doubt that. I'm going to spell this out: I have no interest in your husband. I have no ambitions toward being the Hon's seventy-third or however many wives he has plus one. If he forces himself on me, I will kill him or die trying."

"You're that dedicated to this wizard Relos Var? You must love him a great deal."

I scoffed under my breath. "Hardly."

She gave me an inscrutable look just as Segra returned with bland porridge, handing the bowl to Veixizhau. My heart sank as I smelled the stuff. Not porridge. Gruel. Gruel made from meat stock.

Veixizhau set the bowl on the table. I stared at the mess for a moment before I proceeded to eat it, anyway. It tasted weird, and I wondered what meat they'd used. Probably nothing I'd recognize. Or would want to.

I looked up at Veixizhau. "Well? Have I reassured you?"

She raised an eyebrow at me and smirked. "Yes, you have. Honestly, you've never even been with a man, have you?"

I paused. In Jorat, we placed no particular virtue on the idea of being "untouched," but I knew that it wasn't like that everywhere in the empire. I certainly didn't like the glee in her eye. "I'm married."

"Are you really, though? I don't think that's true." She laughed. "Don't worry, I won't tell. Honestly, I'm delighted."

I felt uneasy. "Why?"

"Unmarried women have a very . . . special . . . place among our people. You're so rare and so valuable. And an unmarried woman who's as gullible as you is like a shiny diamond."

"What?" I looked down at the gruel. It didn't seem sinister, but then the first wave of dizziness hit.

She was still smiling at me as I slid to the ground.

40: THE EMPEROR'S SON

Jorat Dominion, Quuros Empire.
Three days since I was reminded of how glad I am
Khaeriel's on our side

"Virgins are 'valuable'?" Kihrin's expression darkened. "I don't like the sound of that."

Janel shrugged. "It's not what you're thinking." She paused. "Assuming what you're thinking is sexual."

"Well . . . I . . ." Kihrin cleared his throat. "Glad to hear it."

Ninavis winked at him.

"So you think Kaen's right about Morios and the prophecy?" Kihrin asked, ignoring the previous conversation.

"I do, yes. And you and I are both twenty," Janel said. "And since I'm the lion . . ."

"I'm the hawk. Because House D'Mon's symbol is a hawk. Right." Kihrin laughed. "And given that timing, the prophecies say Morios is about to wake up and go for a stroll."

"I hate prophecies," Janel said. "Have I mentioned how I truly hate prophecies?"

"Ah, and even worse when they come true," Dorna said. "Dark times ahead for all."

They all lapsed into a long, pregnant silence.

"I'll just, uh . . ." Qown pointed down at his book.

"Oh, right. Yes, please," Kihrin said.

Qown's Turn. The Ice Demesne, Yor, Quur.

When Brother Qown woke up the next morning, he found he had gone to sleep still sitting at the library table, drooling onto his hand. He rubbed his eyes and blinked several times, then remembered what he'd spent the previous night doing. His rumbling stomach reminded him that he hadn't eaten in over twenty-four hours.

Qown was beginning to see how someone might kill themselves using that artifact.

"You've been hard at work," a deep voice said.

Brother Qown blinked and looked over to see a tall, broad-shouldered man searching the book stacks. The dark-skinned, bald man dressed in a pure deep black that failed to match the darkness of his eyes.

"You're a D'Lorus royal," Brother Qown said, quite without thinking.

"And you're a Vishai priest. If we can track down a morgage and a fancy bar, we'll have the beginnings of a joke." He tilted his head. "I'm Thurvishar. I don't think you should leave that just sitting around, although I hear they're hard to steal."

Brother Qown blinked and realized Worldhearth sat openly on the table, a few breaths away from his fingers. He snatched up the rock and told himself he needed to find some better way of carrying it. A necklace like Senera had, perhaps.

"Do you, uh . . ." Brother Qown cleared his throat. "You don't know where I might be able to find some food, do you?"

"I'll assume by *food* you mean something a priest of Vishai from Eamithon might find palatable, which won't be anything here in Yor."

"I can cook. I'd be happy to make my own food if I just had the ingredients . . ."

"You'll also find those hard to gather. But follow me. I happen to know the location of a seldom-used kitchen." He paused. "Don't worry about your gaesh. This isn't an escape attempt. I'll make sure Relos Var knows where you're going."

"Oh good." Then Brother Qown paused. "Where are we going?"

"Shadrag Gor."

It didn't occur to Brother Qown until he'd almost finished baking a batch of sag bread and had an eggplant curry simmering away that he should have been suspicious of Thurvishar D'Lorus's hospitality. Worse, since Thurvishar D'Lorus had remained in the room with him, the wizard seemed to recognize the very moment when Qown realized his mistake.

"No one would call you paranoid," Thurvishar commented. "Honestly, it's a bit refreshing."

"Oh, I didn't . . . I mean . . ."

"No nefarious tricks," Thurvishar promised. "On occasion, I like talking to people whose primary interests don't include new and interesting ways to conquer the world."

Brother Qown chuckled. "I thought you might be trying to . . . I don't know. I mean, your family does have a certain reputation."

"Do we?" said a man at the doorway. "I hadn't noticed."

The newcomer also wore black, but his pale skin suggested a long illness, and his was a thinner build than Thurvishar's. His black eyes still looked like holes through the world.

Something about him made Brother Qown's skin crawl.

"Is dinner almost ready? I'm so very hungry." The newcomer looked over Brother Qown the way a starving man looks at dessert.

"He's Relos Var's," Thurvishar protested.

"Var won't notice."

"I rather think he would with this one."

The other man sighed. "Yes, you're right. One day, I'm going to have to do something about him. In the meantime, I'll be in my study. Don't disturb me."

As the other man left the room, Thurvishar exhaled.

Brother Qown also felt relief steal over him, although he didn't know what fate he'd avoided.

"I take it this isn't quite as safe a place as you led me to believe," Qown said at last.

"He never comes into the kitchen, usually. I thought this was the last place he'd look." Thurvishar looked chagrined.

"Who was that?"

"Better you don't know. Else I would have to ask Relos Var to add it to your list of subjects not to be discussed, and neither of us want that."

The two men stared at each other for a long minute.

Brother Qown turned back to the stove. "Well, thank you for bringing me here. I'm sure the house servants back in Yor wouldn't have let me anywhere near the kitchen stoves, and even if they did, they wouldn't have any good vegetables."

"Plus, there are other advantages," Thurvishar added.

Brother Qown paused. "What do you mean?"

"We're both educated men. You must know where we are."

Brother Qown swallowed. "I've heard stories, but sometimes stories are just . . . stories."

"Not here. Shadrag Gor doesn't sit in time correctly. Something happened here. Something that damaged the way this place exists in the universe. So time moves very fast here. It suits my master, since it allows him time to do his research without interruption. You can spend months, weeks, days here, which appear to others as minutes or seconds. And if one sought a way to better study a Cornerstone, this might be a very good place to start."

"I don't know—" But Brother Qown paused. If time moved so quickly here, it meant his attempts to scry the outside world would be like watching still paintings. Convenient, since his largest problem had been how quickly the world proceeded at its own pace. "Huh."

"The offer is open," Thurvishar said. "You'd have to be in my company at all times, though. It wouldn't be safe for you to come here by yourself."

"Well, that doesn't sound so terrible." He mentally slapped himself. That hadn't come out at all the way he'd meant it to.

"I mean, if Relos Var approves, of course. It would be a way to learn much quicker, so I can't see why he'd object. I would ask you a favor, though."

"Name it."

"Find a way to check on Janel? I worry about her. This . . . this can't be easy on her."

"Possibly not, but she's made of metal." Thurvishar nodded. "Still, I'd be happy to look in on her."

"Thank you." With that, Brother Qown set about finishing the meal.

Thurvishar had been right; studying the artifact proved much easier when he didn't have to worry about everything moving. He could even take a break, go make himself tea, and return to his observations while his subject only moved the most minute amount.

Thurvishar proved to be an excellent study partner too. He was quiet, kept to himself, and rarely interrupted, usually because he'd returned from the kitchen with tea or that thick black coffee so popular in Khorvesh. The lighthouse proved livable and secure, and although Brother Qown knew he'd have to return to Yor for baths and sleeping, it felt very much like being back at the library at the Temple of Light.

He quickly learned Relos Var had been wrong about the stone being drawn to fire. In fact, Worldhearth focused on heat, and it didn't matter if the object in question burned at all. The difficulty lay in the fact objects only stood out by temperature in comparison to their surroundings. Two objects of the same temperature appeared as mingled, inseparable. So although he could target people by their body heat, it meant hopping from person to person, one by one. Finding the right person could take weeks.

But not everyone existed at the same temperature.

He fine-tuned the control, which allowed him to search for people who ran hotter than those around them. This included Janel, at that very moment eating breakfast, and Relos Var, who ran much hotter, so much so Qown suspected he could locate the man anywhere. Indeed, Relos Var ran so hot either he existed in a state of permanent spontaneous combustion or . . . he wasn't human at all.

Qown had no idea what it meant.

Several others in the palace emitted similar heat spikes. The old woman who trained the bears ran hotter than anyone but Relos Var, as did, curiously, a polar bear cub.

Brother Qown had no explanation for the heat differences, but he noted them all down for later usage. If nothing else, knowing this made it easier to find those people later—important information indeed.

But in using the stone to hone his abilities, he made two more surprising discoveries. He first discovered that Worldhearth allowed him to cast spells through whatever heat source he scried.

Brother Qown learned this when he attempted to divine Senera's house. He'd used a lucky guess, based on what he'd deduced about the cottage's location. If nothing else, he thought her likely to keep a few warm coals in the fireplace. Except when he scried the location, it proved too dark to see. Without thinking, he waved his hand to cast a light spell.

Which showed up inside Senera's cottage.

As a consequence of that first discovery, Qown made his second: Relos Var was using Senera's cottage to meet with his vané friend, because at that very second they were paused, frozen in the act of walking through the front door.

Brother Qown shut off the light and ripped his mind away from the divination, back to the lighthouse. He leaned back in his chair, rapid-pulsed from fear. Would they have seen the light? If they did see it, would they know what it meant?

"Are you all right?" Thurvishar asked him.

Brother Qown started to tell him and then shut his mouth, afraid his confession might violate the gaesh. "How much do you know about the vané?" he asked instead.

"Uh . . . powerful? Immortal? Only, do you mean the Kirpis

vané or the Manol vané? The Kirpis vané were ignobly defeated by us, and the Manol vané returned the favor tenfold. Neither likes Quur very much, and who can blame them?"

"They all look very different from one another, don't they? I mean, you can tell who someone is just through their appearance, yes? They have cloud-curl hair in every possible color?"

"Mostly. But I think we can assume there is some repetition in their aspects. Did you see someone in particular?"

"I don't know," Brother Qown admitted. "Does the vané queen have blue hair?"

"Does the vané queen . . . ? You do ask the most interesting questions. One moment, I think I have the answer." Thurvishar approached a bookshelf in the study, coming back a moment later with a very thin book labeled *Royalty of the High Races*. "Let's see . . . the current queen is Miyane, and yes, she does indeed have blue hair. Cloud curl, but that's hardly a surprise, since she's half–Kirpis vané." He raised an eyebrow. "Why?"

Qown winced. "I can't tell you."

"Understood. Well, if you've found Queen Miyane, I'm sure someone will want to know, if only because of her husband, King Kelanis. He's new, so no one knows much about him."

Brother Qown bit his lip. "Would you mind taking me back to the palace? I should, uh . . . check on a few things."

If he hurried, he might even make it back in time to hear Relos Var and the vané queen's discussion.

"Did you notice a flash?" the woman's voice asked.

Relos Var frowned as he entered the cottage, gesturing to light various candles around the room. "I did, but I'm not sure . . ." He paused, looking around as he studied the area. "No one's here. I suppose it might have been cloud lightning in the distance."

"I think this may have been an unfortunate idea," the woman said and turned to leave.

"It's fine," he reassured. "You're not breaking any laws. Or even any rules."

"If I were," she answered, "please be assured you and I would not be having any kind of conversation at all." She gestured. "What is this place?"

"One of my students uses it as a retreat. She's away on business, so this is very safe from prying eyes."*

The vané woman swallowed and looked away, her expression unhappy. She appeared to be a young woman—except the tension around her eyes and mouth made her seem older. "Have you found him?"

"Please, sit down. Would you prefer coffee, tea? There's brandy, if you'd rather."

She pulled out a chair and sat down. "Have you found him?"

He hesitated as he sat down himself. "Yes."

She exhaled in relief.

"I can't retrieve him from his current location. But rest assured he's safe and with people who will treat him well."

Her eyes flashed open again, hot with building rage.

Relos Var lifted a hand. "This may work out in our favor. This way we avoid the shuffling required to keep my various 'friends' from running into each other. I should send Khaemezra a thank-you gift."

"Khaemezra!" The woman's expression could've murdered gods.

"Yes." He smiled. "Aren't the betrayals we suffer from family just the worst?"

Her angry expression broke, and she chuckled. "That would be one way of putting it. So she has my—" She paused and winced, pressing her lips together.

Brother Qown felt himself startle. He wondered if she hesitated from caution or if she'd been prevented from voicing her thoughts. He'd become sensitive to such nuances.

Relos Var's expression turned sympathetic. "I'm so sorry. I never wanted it to turn out this way for you."

"I blame myself for thinking the gods were even interested

---

* Yes, I would have thought so too . . .

in finding a different solution. But no . . . Every other race has suffered. Why stop now with the job unfinished?" She inhaled to calm herself. "Speaking of unfinished business, do you have Valathea?"

Relos smiled and ducked his head. "I do. Although it wasn't easy to get her away from the Devoran priests, let me tell you."

She shook her head. "I don't understand what they thought they'd accomplish by kidnapping her."

"To be fair, I don't think they understood either. They only knew she was important. Anyway, that's the other reason I wanted us to meet here." He walked over to a storage cupboard and pulled out a cloth-wrapped triangle, which he set on the main table and unwrapped.

Qown blinked in surprise. It was a *harp*.

The style looked old but elegant, double-strung, made from fine and beautiful old woods. The blue-haired woman stood as Relos Var brought it over and raised a hand to stroke the harp's neck.

"Valathea," she murmured. "It is good to see you again, my queen."

"If I may be so bold, Your Majesty, why didn't you just take her before? I mean, you had her right there with you for months."

"Relos . . . I'm not allowed to steal from the family. However, no one told me I was obligated to return what someone else had already stolen."

"What will you do with her?" Relos Var asked.

"For the moment, leave her with you," she answered. "There's no place I could put her where I would be assured of her safety. When they took her I almost . . . well . . . it turned out I could be hurt worse than I already had been, but it took some effort." She reached down and took his hands. "Promise you won't hurt him, Relos."

"Your Majesty, please believe me when I say hurting your son isn't part of my plans. He's far too important." Relos Var smiled. "He's going to help us destroy Quur. We need him."

She took the assurance like a drowning person reaching for

land, inhaled, and nodded. She leaned down and kissed Relos Var on the cheek. "Thank you."

With that, she stood and inscribed a gate—carving runes in the air, using them to return to wherever she spent her days. The Manol, Brother Qown supposed.

But because he had stayed a moment longer, he was also there when Relos Var leaned back in his chair, snarling silently as he looked off into the distance. The wizard crushed the metal goblet in his hand into a small, dense ball before tossing the whole thing in the fire.

41: A MOTHER'S LOVE

Jorat Dominion, Quuros Empire.
Three days since Kihrin failed to bluff Gadrith

"Kihrin, are you all right?" Janel asked.

Kihrin slumped back in his chair and closed his eyes. "It's like you said—we know all the same people. Hey, at least I know what happened to my harp."

Janel stared at him. "You play the harp?"

"Yes, I play the harp. And Valathea was *my*—" Kihrin trailed off as Janel's eyebrows rose. Then he remembered what Teraeth had said about having a type. He cleared his throat. "It's not like that. Teraeth and I are friends."

"Oh, of course," Janel agreed. "How could it be? You only run with *mares*."*

"Wait, I don't understand," Qown said. "The person you both know is a *harp*? I apologize. I thought you were talking about Queen Miyane."

Kihrin winced and raised his head, turning to Brother Qown. "That wasn't Queen Miyane. Blue hair, yes, and they're probably related, given the first syllable of their names, but not the same person."

"Then who is she?"

Kihrin knocked his head against his chair several times. "No, it's like you said, Relos Var loves to attack people through their families. That was my *mother*. And I'd go through all the weird genealogies involved, but the Stone of Shackles came into play.

---

* I take it back. I think *Janel* might be the jealous one.

If we're only trapped in here for a few weeks, I don't know if we have the time."

"She sounded worried about you," Janel said.

"Yeah. I suppose she went to Relos Var for help after I was kidnapped, when my father's search failed to produce any results. And Relos Var told her what she wanted to hear. I wonder what she'd say if she knew he sent a kraken to kill me.[†] He does *not* want me healthy and in one piece." He shook his head. "I should have known. I should have fucking known. Of course."

Janel and Brother Qown exchanged a look.

"Right," Janel said. "Well, I suppose I should tell the part about *my* mother."

Janel's Turn. The Afterlife.

I knew what had happened just as soon as I woke up in the Afterlife.

"Son of a mule," I muttered under my breath and wondered if I had really died this time. Had I been given drugs or poison? I wouldn't know until I woke up again.

Or didn't.

NOW WHAT HAVE WE TOLD YOU ABOUT BEING TOO TRUSTING?

I drew my sword as I turned to face Xaltorath. Xaltorath's tone didn't indicate she planned a mother-daughter chat about the polite way to eat shellfish.

"You might have had a point this time."

YOUR DEATH ISN'T PART OF MY PLAN. DO YOU UNDERSTAND ME? I WILL NOT HAVE YOU TAKEN OUT BY SOME SPOILED LITTLE YORAN WHOSE AMBITIONS REVOLVE AROUND PUTTING HER BRAT ON A THRONE.

---

† What? I know you could summon a kraken if you wanted to, but honestly . . . *why*? That doesn't sound like you at all.

"Look, I didn't think—"

She backhanded me. That makes it sound like something a noblewoman might do to a courtier who displeased her. But Xaltorath's backhand threw me twenty feet and would have slain me in the living world. And then she rushed toward me wielding a glaive, which hadn't been there a second ago.

I raked my sword across her stomach, but the wound healed immediately. I stabbed her, but she grabbed the sword, grinning as the edges cut her hands. She broke the sword in half and threw the pieces to the ground behind me.

I'M GOING TO HAVE TO TEACH YOU A LESSON.

She reached for me.

"Let's . . . not," someone said.

I cried out as Xaltorath's hand closed around my neck. She dragged me as she turned around. A woman stood before us.

I stared.

She had brown-red skin and black hair, and her eyes looked like mine. No laevos, no horse markings, but those details seemed like minor differences. Unlike me, however, she was swathed head to toe in a beautiful gown of shifting colors: green, red, and violet.

I knew at once who it was. Who it had to be.

Tya, Goddess of Magic.

"Our arrangement is over, Xaltorath," she said, "for you promised to keep her safe, and you have done anything but, haven't you?"

Xaltorath laughed and lifted me up, ignoring my struggling. ***SHOULD I KILL HER NOW THEN, TYA?***

"You won't," Tya said as she walked forward, "or you'd have done it years ago. So shall we have a fight? A battle until your pride is satisfied?"

Xaltorath opened her fingers and let me fall from them. ***NOT LONG NOW. THE PROPHECIES WILL BE FULFILLED.***

"So you claim," Tya said. "We'll see, won't we?"

YES, WE WILL.

I winced and rubbed my neck, then looked around for the sword shards. When I looked up, Xaltorath had vanished, and only the other woman remained.

Tya.

I sat on the ground and folded my legs under me.

The woman turned around. "Janel—"

"'Our arrangement is over'?" I said. "And what arrangement would that be? How do you know me?"

"Janel, please let me explain."

"That's what I'm asking you to do."

"I'm your mother," Tya said. "Your real mother."

I fought to keep calm. The furious rage didn't help. "All my life, I've been told my mother's name was Frena. Or more recently that my mother was a dancing girl. You don't strike me as either."

"Who would have said your mother was—oh. Let me guess. Relos Var?"* She sighed and walked over to me. "I suppose that description held some accuracy once. It's been a long time, however." She sat down across from me, ignoring how her beautiful dress trailed through the muck.

I stared at her. "Do you have any idea what Xaltorath's done to me, over the years?"

My mother looked away, her expression pained. "I . . . have some idea. None of this was supposed to happen."

"What a comfort that is."

She winced at my bitter tone. "I chose your parents carefully. They were good people who wanted a child and would have raised you well."

"I loved them," I admitted, feeling my throat tighten.

"And I thought myself so clever," she said, "because even though I followed the prophecies, the 'recipes,' with your father, I also made you hard to find. I didn't try to keep you. I didn't leave you with anyone who had any connection to me. Except

---

* I do kind of want to know how a dancer ends up as the Goddess of Magic. Really.

somehow Xaltorath *knew*. A fact she made clear when she attacked Lonezh. So I had a choice: agree to her terms or watch as she killed you."

"You're a goddess, aren't you?" I stopped studying my hands for long enough to glare at her. "I mean, you're here, you drove away Xaltorath. She called you Tya. You're one of the Eight. Yet you couldn't dismiss a single demon?"

"She's not a single demon. She's Xaltorath. A million screaming souls make up her identity, and some of those souls belong to god-kings.* I risked your annihilation in such a fight. When a demon kills, it eats its victims, absorbs their souls. It's never certain a soul can be recovered, and when it's *Xaltorath* . . ." Tya shook her head. "Xaltorath wouldn't have gone down easily. So we came to terms."

"And what was it she wanted?"

"You. Access to you. And my noninterference."

I closed my eyes. "Do you know why?"

"No, but Taja assures me we should look at it as a good sign. I don't expect you to forgive me—"

"Good."

Tya sighed. "I had my reasons."

I found myself incapable of dealing with my tumult of emotions. I have no idea why the whole field didn't spontaneously combust. I felt so angry at her, so angry at Qoran Milligreest. And both had proven they would have sacrificed thousands for me. But why? For what?

Why was I so important? Because I fit some demonic prophecy's requirements? Because I'd "volunteered" for this in a life I didn't remember? I wanted to scream at them both. I wanted to call them out as fools. The prophecies were a lie. I knew because demons had created them.

---

* Do we know who? This is just wild speculation on my part, but is it possible Xaltorath started *out* as a god-king? Maybe that's the reason they didn't "exist" when Grizzst gaeshed all the other demons? That said, I thought Grizzt's original deal effectively gaeshed demons and their subsequent offspring in perpetuity, so I'm not sure how that would even be possible.

If there was one lesson I'd learned on Xaltorath's knee, it was this: demons lie.

Demons *always* lie.

I opened my eyes again. "So my father is the reason Duke Kaen didn't have me killed. And *you're* the reason Relos Var didn't have me killed. Because he likes to strike at his enemies through family members."

"Yes."

"Is your real name Irisia?"

Tya frowned. "Where did you hear that name?"

"An old woman named Wyrga."

"There aren't many who would remember my real name. Whoever she is, I imagine she's quite a bit older than she appears."

"And she appears quite old." I sighed. "Fine. I know you're my mother now. You may leave."

Tya looked both surprised and saddened. "Janel, I had thought—"

"Thought what? Thought we'd have a happy reunion? I would hold out my arms and welcome you into them as the mother I always wished I had? The mother I always wished I had died when I was eight, slaughtered by demons. *You* abandoned me. You may have thought your reasons sound, but it doesn't change the result. And when you gave me up, you gave me up for good. You don't get to pretend all is well and forgiven. It isn't. It never will be."

Her expression hardened.

She vanished.

I screamed into the void left by her absence.

"My count?"

My eyes widened, and I scrambled to my feet, turning to see Arasgon standing there. "What? No, what happened? You shouldn't be here . . ."

I only knew one reason Arasgon would be in the Afterlife: his death. But even as the panicked thought rampaged across my mind, I realized Arasgon's appearance had changed.

Fire burned from his eyes and hooves. Instead of tiger stripes along his legs, his mane was a mass of flame and sparks. I'd have thought him demonic if the flames were blue instead of red. And yet, I would have known Arasgon anywhere. The curve of his flanks, the arch of his neck, the gentle bend of his nose. This wasn't Xaltorath.

He walked up to me and bent his head to nuzzle my shoulder.

I threw my arms around him and started to cry.

"Did . . . how?" I lacked any coherence.

"Your mother," he answered. "She thought you might like my company and so showed me how to join you here."*

I hadn't even suspected such a thing might be possible or how Tya might have accomplished it. And yet I could assume the Goddess of Magic knew one or two more things than I did.

"If she thinks I'm going to forgive her just because she—" But the words choked in my throat.

Because as gestures went, this was a good start.

I sobbed into his hide, until Arasgon had enough and butted me with his head. "Come on, then. I want to run."

"You always want to run." Laughter and tears fought with each other, and I wiped at my eyes.

He gave me a silent laugh and shook his head in agreement. "Running is one of life's great joys. You two-legs always want to complicate the matter with duties and obligations and punishments. Just run. Remember how you used to love to run?"

"Just run?" I echoed. "I'm not running anymore, Arasgon."

"Of course you are. You're just not running *away*."

I felt laughter shudder through my chest as I petted his nose, always the softest velvet. No, I wasn't running away anymore. I felt a moment's regret, though, for my canton, Tolamer. I had abandoned it, even as I'd promised myself this was necessary to save it.

And I thought of what my mother had done with me.

---

* He's a mage. *That means he's a mage.* Why didn't anyone tell me the damn fire-bloods could become wizards?

So I was a hypocrite. Aren't we all?

But then I had a different thought. "Wait, are you with Dorna? I mean, in the Living World?"

Arasgon nodded. "And with Talaras, Sir Baramon, and Ninavis. We're in hiding now, because we have prices on our heads." He drew back his lips. "Foolish two-legs."

"Foolish two-legs indeed," I murmured. "Do you think you'll be able to come back here again? Since Tya has shown you the trick?"

"It isn't a trick. She has told me I will know when you're sleeping and will have the choice to join you. That may not be possible every night, depending on the timing."

My eyes widened. I had a way to communicate with Ninavis and Dorna. I had a way to pass messages, to pass along the information I'd gleaned from the duke's invasion map plans on his parlor wall. Even if I didn't help the duke, I could move forward with his plans myself. And if they thought I was helping him . . .

Well. I had to find a way to examine his plans and maps, didn't I?

Wasn't I Janel *Danorak*? Time to make that work to my favor.

I grinned. "Perfect. Then we have a lot of work ahead of us. We're going to steal a rebellion."

I didn't stay in the Afterlife for as long as I normally do, because I had been rendered unconscious rather than sleeping. I felt relief when I woke; I wasn't dead.

That relief lasted five seconds, at which point I realized white surrounded me.

Snow. Snow swirling around me and ice underneath me. I tried to stand, a fact made more difficult because I lay in a puddle, making the ice below slippery.

Veixizhau had dumped me outside the castle, straight into the arctic weather surrounding the Ice Demesne. Ice water soaked through my wool dress, worse than no protection at all.

No sooner did I realize this than I noticed an additional fact:

I didn't feel cold. Senera had stolen my strength, but not my magic.

I started laughing, the sound caught and tangled in the storm winds surrounding me. I'd realized that with my Khorveshan father and my immortal mother, I was as Blood of Joras as they came. So not a witch to my own people.

Only to the rest of Quur, who only cared that I was female.

The snow made it difficult to see any distance, but a series of loud whoops echoed from nearby. I recognized the sound from the plains of my home: hyenas. I'd seen white hyenas in the duke's hall too, thicker-furred and larger than their southern counterparts.

Hyenas could prove a problem, depending on their clan size. I thought I could fight off a couple easily enough, but if they were anything like their southern cousins, I might easily find myself facing thirty or forty of the cursed creatures. I began seeing shapes in the snow as they closed in.

A whoop cut off abruptly.

Thunder cracked the sky, and the ground rumbled. The sky's gray blanket rolled back, and steady snowfall lifted around me. A razor of teal sky sliced the gray clouds from apex to horizon, like the curtains drawn back on the start of the world.

And into that gap in the cloud cover flew the ice dragon, Aeyan'arric, heading straight for me.

42: THE WOLF CUBS

Jorat Dominion, Quuros Empire.
Three days since Xaloma, the Dragon of the Afterlife,
tried to swallow the wrong damned soul

"Don't you think you might have been a bit harsh on your mother?" Dorna said.

Janel threw her a look. "No, I don't."

"But still—"

Janel held up a finger. "You know I love you, Dorna, so please don't remind me you have been working for Tya all this time and never told me the truth."

Dorna sighed and looked mournfully into her cup while Star put his arm around her. Across the bar, Ninavis reached over and nudged Qown.

"Right," he said, returning to his spot in his journal.

Qown's Turn. The Ice Demesne, Yor, Quur.

When not studying in Shadrag Gor, Brother Qown returned to the library at the Ice Demesne. But his studies were interrupted.

The door to the library opened, and several men entered. He didn't look up from his writing at first, being engrossed in describing clairvoyance using thermal variance.

Then someone grabbed his book.

"What's this?" The offending man—tall, handsome, and Quuros—paged through the book. "Are you seriously writing about crop yields?"

Brother Qown stood up, slipping Worldhearth into his agolé as he did. His heart sank as he recognized Sir Oreth. He didn't know the other men, but he knew enough to recognize royalty—except for one pale-skinned young man who looked part Yoran.

"My pardon," Brother Qown said, bowing. "But I'm working on research at Relos Var's request." He hadn't been writing about crop yields at all, but one of his earliest spells involved hiding his writing behind an illusion of tedious drivel. He used it often.

"Oh, look how tame he is, Darzin," Sir Oreth cackled. "This is Janel Theranon's lackey priest, the one Relos Var gaeshed. Kept hostage against Janel's good behavior."

"He doesn't need to worry about that anymore," the Yoran young man said. "What a sad joke, being gaeshed for nothing."

Darzin rolled his eyes. "Exidhar, we must work on your subtlety."

Brother Qown felt cold. "I'm sorry, lords, but I don't understand your meaning."

"Oh, nothing," Sir Oreth said, still smirking. Then he crossed his arms over his chest and mimed a shiver. "Brrr."

The other men laughed.

Brother Qown's sense of dread threatened to turn into a full-blown panic. "Are you implying something has happened to Count Tolamer?"

Sir Oreth said, "She's not a count anymore. She's not even Joratese." He smiled. "She's not anything."

"Give us the room," Darzin commanded. "We came here looking for privacy."

Brother Qown bent down to pick up his supplies.

Darzin slapped his hand down on the brushes. "Just go."

Brother Qown straightened and then held out his hand. "Of course, my lord. But I'll need that. Relos Var is waiting on it."

Darzin glanced down at the book and then cast his gaze at the fire.

"No, please."

Darzin grinned as he threw the book into the fireplace.

Brother Qown darted after it, but the D'Mon royal grabbed him by the shoulders and held him back. "Relos Var is waiting on it, hmm? You'll have to tell him you tripped and it landed in the fire, won't you? How clumsy."

Brother Qown stopped struggling. The royal wanted to see him struggle. Qown stopped resisting, straightened up, and bowed to Darzin D'Mon. "Thank you, my lord."

Darzin blinked, taken aback. "What? Uh . . . didn't you need that?"

"Oh yes, my lord. Very much. And when I tell Relos Var what happened, he'll know I'm telling the truth. But you have given me a valuable lesson in the importance of detachment from material things, even books. There is nothing in those pages that cannot be re-created. So thank you for reminding me." He bowed again.*

Darzin looked bemused. Finally, the man rolled his eyes. "Whatever. Get out of here."

Brother Qown went searching for Thurvishar.

"I think they've done something with Janel," Brother Qown said as soon as Thurvishar answered the door to his suite. He then rushed inside without giving the larger man a chance to answer.

"Hold on. What are you talking about?"

Brother Qown tried to recover his calm. For all he knew, Janel was already dead. But if Relos Var was right . . .

If Relos Var was right, Janel needed to be alive. They all needed her to be alive.

He shook his head. "I was writing my notes in the south library when one of the D'Mon royals interrupted me. Darzin and his companions. Including Sir Oreth, I'm sad to say . . ."

"The Wolf Cubs."

Brother Qown paused. "What?"

---

* I think turning Darzin to sludge would have been more emotionally satisfying, but I suppose just confusing the hell out of him has its merits too.

"We call Exidhar's friends the Wolf Cubs. The fact Darzin has landed among them doesn't surprise me in the least. He's never grown up either." Thurvishar raised an eyebrow. "What did they do?"

"Exidhar and Sir Oreth both made nasty comments hinting Janel is in jeopardy somewhere very cold."

"I understand she's been left with the wives." Thurvishar laughed. "I suppose that's cold enough."

"No, you don't understand. I used Worldhearth to search every fire in the palace. She's not here. I can't find her."

Thurvishar stopped smiling.

After a moment, he said, "Is it possible she's escaped?"

Brother Qown blinked. That thought hadn't occurred to him. Yes, it was possible. She might have escaped. Janel could leave at any time. *She* wasn't gaeshed.

He shook his head. "No. She wouldn't . . . she wouldn't leave me."

"Are you so sure?"

Brother Qown nodded. "I'm sure. And they wouldn't have been so smug if that was it. Something bad has happened, and those men were part of it."

"Let's find the Hon."

43: The Fire Caves

Jorat Dominion, Quuros Empire.
Three days since Kihrin D'Mon discovered that it's possible
to make talismans for other people . . . against their will

"Darzin was always so charming, wasn't he?" Kihrin said, shaking his head.

"Thorra," Janel said.

"Yes," he agreed. "Definitely thorra." He chuckled.

"He sounds like a real winner." Ninavis yawned as she examined her cup. "I think I'll boil up another pot of coffee." She left for the kitchen.

Janel watched her leave, frowning. Kihrin couldn't tell if she was upset with Ninavis or upset in general.

"Are you all right?" he asked, anyway, squeezing her hand.

"Thurvishar isn't the wizard we're waiting on," Janel said suddenly. "Relos Var is."

The whole table fell quiet for a stunned second.

Kihrin pulled back his hand.

"Janel!" Brother Qown stood. "We were explaining the context—"

Dorna added, "Now maybe I wouldn't have—"

"Silence!" Janel snapped. She turned to Kihrin. "We don't have Khoreval anymore. I possessed it briefly, but Relos Var reclaimed it. So we made a deal: if I convince you to help us kill Morios, he'll hand over Khoreval. We need both weapons to finish the job." She added quietly, "That's what I needed to tell you."

Kihrin didn't know what to think, but the expression on

Janel's face left little doubt that she was serious. She had, in fact, been planning to betray him.

Or at least it would have felt like betrayal.

He stood from his chair, not sure what he'd do, only that he had to do something.

"Kihrin, please—"

He whirled back to her and pointed to the ceiling. "If you and Var are working together, why is my angry daughter from another lifetime hovering around outside? Or is that just to keep me from leaving?"

"Var must have realized I would tell Janel about Father Zajhera," Brother Qown mused. "With the gaeshe broken, nothing prevented me from telling the truth."

"Which would lead to me confessing the truth as well. But Relos Var doesn't know Thurvishar is working with us," Janel explained. "We left him in Atrine as insurance.* And the moment Thurvishar sees any sign of Morios, he'll open a portal back to us."

"So . . . I could have left here at any time, with Thurvishar's help?"

"Wait, we could've left at any time?" Dorna seemed just as surprised.

Kihrin ignored the old woman and continued glaring at Janel. "Tell me you didn't know Relos Var was going to send over Aeyan'arric to keep us trapped."

"I swear I didn't," Janel said. "I didn't even realize Aeyan'arric had returned to life. Relos Var had claimed she would, but I had no idea how little time it would take."

Kihrin ground his teeth, wrestling with his anger. "And I'm supposed to trust you? You've handed Relos Var my location. He's not my friend, Janel. He doesn't have a single good intention regarding me."

Janel looked about to protest, but then inhaled instead. "It wouldn't matter if he did. He's a farmer raising livestock. A farmer

* In hindsight, we really should have assumed they'd be working together.

may like a pig—name it, pet it, feed it treats—but it will still see the ax come autumn. Even if he loved you, even if he loved *me*, it wouldn't stop him from killing us if he felt it was needed."

"Sure, and what pig cares that he was loved, when it's time for the slaughter."

"But," Qown said, "I've come to know him well enough to say with certainty that he doesn't kill unnecessarily. The prophecies strongly imply Morios will be defeated—there's no reason to think Relos Var wouldn't want to help us accomplish that goal."

"That makes me feel so much better," Kihrin snapped. "Oh wait, no, it doesn't."

"Qown, send a message to Thurvishar. Tell him to open a gate here so Kihrin may leave." Janel rubbed her temples and made a study of the bar counter.

"But—" Qown's eyes widened. "The . . . dragon. There's a quarter million people in Atrine right now . . ."

"Tricking Kihrin to help us under false pretenses was always a mistake. I don't know why I ever thought otherwise."

"Because of a quarter million people, foal," Dorna said.

Star raised an eyebrow. "You're running?"

"Oh, don't you start," Kihrin said. He sat back down and waved at Qown when the priest pulled Worldhearth from his agolé. "Put that away. I'm staying."

Janel blinked. "You are?"

"I have four reasons," he said as he drank the last of his cold coffee. "First, I came here to find you, and while I'm not happy about the way this is going, I'm not leaving without you. Second, because the hell if I'm running from Relos Var, when *I'm* the one carrying Godslayer. He should be running from me. Third, because I'll feel like a real ass if Morios is real, and I just left all those people to die."

"And fourth?" Janel asked.

He grimaced. "You can't just end the story there. I need to know what happens next."

Janel didn't laugh, but she did take her turn.

Janel's Turn. Outside the Ice Demesne, Yor, Quur.

"This is my place!" Aeyan'arric screamed as she flew toward me. **"You aren't welcome here, trespasser!"**

She loomed even larger than she had in my memories. White and bright with eyes so very blue, a color echoed by her serpentine belly's aquas and greens, flickering pastel hues like overlapping ice blocks. Aeyan'arric blinded in her brilliance, and yet cast a dark shadow all around her. The waning storm revealed the castle above, glimmering. When Cherthog had built his palace, he had lopped off a mountaintop, building a giant crystal and marble pyramid to sparkle in the sunlight.

Somewhere up there, Veixizhau had tossed me out a balcony, to slide down the side like so much unwanted garbage, to die in the frozen cold.

And somehow, I had survived the fall and the cold, although I suspected I now knew exactly how.

But a tolerance for cold didn't mean I would survive being ripped apart by claws half my size.

"I'm sorry!" I shouted, because I didn't know what else to say. "Is there a path back up to the castle? I'll leave right now."

She looked at me with those mad azure eyes, her lips pulling back as she opened her mouth. In mere moments, she'd do something I would deeply regret.

I dove to the side, scrambling to find cover. Even as I did, cold air and snow blasted from her direction. I shuddered as I barely escaped being encased in ice. I felt cold. For the first time since waking, I actually felt cold, a trembling I felt down to my bones.

The ice before me shuddered and cracked as her claws slammed into it, ripping huge grooves into the glacier.

Fire, I thought. I needed fire.

Unfortunately, I had nothing to burn except a soaking-wet dress. Veixizhau had taken all my jewelry, from my belt to my jeweled hairpins. We stood on a mountain of frozen water, useless as fuel.

So I'd have one chance, and even then, I could only hope to distract her.

I pulled the dress off my body and tossed it up into the air. It froze solid the moment it left contact with my skin, but that mattered not at all; I made it burn.

The dragon jerked back in surprise, startled.

And during her shocked blink, I ran.

Really, I tripped and slid as the glacier rolled down beneath me in a rather sharp slope. I'm sure I made a ridiculous sight, naked and without weapons. I couldn't have been more vulnerable.

Which is why running seemed like such a fine idea.

Arasgon would have been proud. Dorna too.

Toward the base of the mountain, the glacier ramped down toward a crevasse. I hoped it would be too narrow for the dragon to follow, although I was still in trouble if she decided to breathe another blizzard in my direction.

But what did I have to lose?

As I listened to Aeyan'arric's screams, I realized Xaltorath might have had good reason to be upset. I could easily die here while accomplishing nothing. That I'd somehow survived for this long was a miracle.

I ran into the crevasse as Aeyan'arric's shadow covered me. She was just seconds behind. I tripped and cried out as a sharp ice shard ripped open my shin, proving I possessed no great immunity to normal damage.

Aeyan'arric attempted to claw at me through the opening, but the crevasse indeed proved too narrow. Her efforts gouged huge ice chunks from the opening, until sparks flew as she hit granite. I shuffled backward, leaving a blood trail behind me on the ice to mix with the meltwater left by my passing.

Then the attack stopped. I heard wings beat as she flew away.

I waited.

I didn't go back to the opening to make sure she'd left. I'm not a fool. But I sat there in the cave for several minutes, listening, naked and shivering from cold that would have slain most people.

Then I heard footsteps. Footsteps from behind me as a warm light cast shadows on the cave wall before me.

I pulled myself up into a crouch.

A woman entered the cave, holding a lantern in one hand and a long, curving sword in the other. Her dark skin had a blue-gray cast, and her black hair was matted into thick, felted wool plaits. She dressed in chain, under a coat of interlocking metal plates. She looked Khorveshan, but more notably, she appeared frozen, with ice rimming her face and snowflakes sparkling on her dark lashes.

She also looked very dead, but that status didn't seem to be proving an inconvenience.

"Well, then," the woman said. "What has little Aeyan brought me today? This isn't a safe place for you, young lady." She smiled. "Although you living this long is an accomplishment. Especially dressed like that."*

"Who—" My teeth chattered to speak. "Wh-who are you?"

The dead woman motioned me to follow her. "I'm Xivan Kaen. Now why don't we find you something to wear."

"I thought—" I cleared my throat as I followed the woman deeper into the crevasse, which had in fact turned into a fine cave mouth, no longer ice, but solid rock. "My apologies. I thought—"

"Let me guess. Someone told you Duchess Xivan Kaen had died." Xivan shrugged. "They didn't lie to you, now did they? And who are you?" She pulled a scarf from her belt. "For your leg."

"Janel Theranon," I said, rubbing my arms. "And thank you." I bent down to clean the shallow wound and then tied the scarf around my leg. I needed to dress it properly, but this didn't seem the time.

---

* Or not dressed at all, apparently.

"And what are you doing here? I'll admit I don't mind having visitors, it's just never happened from this side of the caverns before. You're lucky sound echoes through the tunnels."

"I'm afraid one of the duke's wi—um." I coughed.

"One of the duke's wives. I'm aware he's married others." She didn't look amused about the idea.

"Right. I honestly have no idea why she did this. Because she found out—" I paused, unsure if I might reveal too much.

Xivan raised an eyebrow. "You really must learn to finish sentences. She found out what?"

I stared at her. She was Khorveshan. A dead Khorveshan murdered by Yorans, in fact. I therefore didn't think she'd feel the same way as Yorans about my "unmarried" status. "She found out that I'm not really married. And then she drugged and dumped me outside to freeze to death. I don't really understand why."

"Interesting," Xivan said, "and who are you not really married to?"

I cleared my throat. "Relos Var."

She chuckled. "Ah yes. Relos Var. I know him of old. In fact, I owe him for this." Xivan gestured down at herself.

"I thought the Yorans—"

"Oh no. Var didn't kill me. He brought me back to life, or close enough. And bought himself a duke in the bargain." She frowned. "I know why you were left outside." She stopped walking. "It seems one of my husband's wives is a devotee of the witch-queen Suless."

"I don't understand."

She leaned in close. "Are you doing that on purpose? You're very . . . warm."

I made a helpless gesture. "I'm not doing anything."

"Also interesting." Xivan looked at the lantern light sparkling against the cave wall. "In the old days, before we Quuros arrived, the witch-queen Suless had an understanding with her worshippers. She'd grant any wish her female devotees asked, but only if they sacrificed an unmarried girl to her. Usually a woman would sacrifice a daughter, but technically speaking, the sacrifice didn't have to be a relative."

"I don't feel sacrificed," I said.

But I also remembered hearing the whooping laughs of the hyenas closing in and wondered. What would have happened if Aeyan'arric hadn't arrived?

"Aren't you glad Suless is dead?" Her gaze was thoughtful. "But it's hard to stamp out a religion. People still practice the old ways, hold hyenas and bears as sacred because Suless and Cherthog claimed those animals as their symbols. Men still marry off their daughters as soon as they can too. They probably don't even remember that once the practice derived from a desire to keep girls from being offered to the witch-queen—and being sacrificed and used against them."

"That's barbaric. Let me guess—the sacrifices were left out in the cold."

"Yes, to be claimed by the snow hyenas or worse. Suless ate babies. Ask anyone. I have my doubts that's really true. The old stories never said where the witch-mothers came from. You see, Suless used to have these priestesses—witches, naturally—whom she crafted from snow and would send to marry chieftains who pleased her."

I scoffed. "Crafted from snow?"

"Now I think she was taking all those sacrificed girls and raising them herself, before sending them back among the clans as her own personal enforcers and secret police. After all, if Suless really had been able to create witches out of frozen water, Yor wouldn't have lost the war."

"What happened to the witch-mothers then?" I thought of Bikeinoh's claim that Wyrga was the last.

"Quur killed them all, of course." She waved a hand. "Decades ago, long before you were born."

"Yet if the witch-mothers have been gone for decades, someone had to show Veixizhau how to sacrifice me to Suless."

"Is that who did it?" She smiled. "Now I could be wrong. Maybe you were just dumped outside to freeze to death because

Veixizhau was jealous, but you said she found your maiden status interesting. Her reasons for that interest wouldn't be the same as a man's, so I'm jumping to conclusions. Hug the wall to the left. Whatever you do, avoid wandering too close to the cave mouth on the right."

"Why, what's in there?" The rays of the lantern cast long shadows into the opening.

"Death." She pointed to a place where the cave opened into a medium-sized room. Blue smoke hovered on the ground to the opening's right.

I straightened. "I've seen that smoke before."

"Then you know how dangerous it is." She pointed down the left passage. "This way is safe."

I stepped to the left. I didn't need any explanation to know to avoid the right-hand passage. I'd recognized the witch-smoke we'd encountered in Mereina.

As she walked, the cave path smoothed out and became something more finished and navigable.

"Stay left. We're passing another dangerous cavern."

We walked on a slim ledge with a precipitous drop to our right, revealing a yawning darkness. Normally, I wouldn't have been able to see far into those depths, but something was creating light down there. I saw the blue smoke lurking on the ground, twining through abandoned ruins.

Then the light source itself held my attention.

It was a spear.

A golden spear rested on a stand in the cave's center.

"What is that?" I realized I had stopped to look.

I pretended at ignorance, but I recognized the spear Thaena had shown me. And once I'd found a way to steal Khoreval, I'd be finished with the easiest part of my mission.

I had no false illusions about how difficult it would be to slay a dragon.*

---

* And sometimes not even possible at all. I'm not convinced certain dragons can be killed, period.

"A slower death than the last cave," Xivan said, either ignoring my question or misunderstanding it. "I'm the only one who can walk there without dropping dead, since I already have. If the smoke doesn't kill you, the stone will."

I looked back at her. "The stone? What do you mean?"

"It's a curse the Academy came up with when it proved too hard to dig the Yorans from their caves. They changed the caves themselves, turned them toxic. Rather like setting a castle on fire to force everyone out in a siege, except the castle is still burning a century later."

My throat felt dry. "How many people lived here?"

"Thousands," she answered. "And this is just one cave system. Hundreds were rendered unlivable in pockets all over Yor."

I stared for another minute, feeling dread. As in Mereina, the blue smoke obscured a floor littered with the dead.

She put a cold hand on my shoulder. "We shouldn't linger. Not here."

I let her lead me farther on. The passage looked old, sturdy, and almost comfortable to me, given the Joratese love of cellar homes. We walked rather deep into the mountain, at least another half hour beyond the poison caves where the Yorans had once lived. By the time the tunnel opened into a cavern again, the temperature had turned warm.

The large cavern floor had been polished smooth and divided into sections. Living areas, I realized, although I didn't know how useful or necessary they were for Xivan. Did she need to sleep? Did she need to eat?

If she did need to eat, *what* did she eat?

Also, the cavern was occupied. In one section, someone had drawn rings on the ground and set up wooden mannequins. A beautiful young woman was whacking a wooden practice sword against these pretend enemies, stopping to adjust her footing. She dressed in practical trousers and a loose-fitting shirt, and like Xivan, she looked Khorveshan.

But unlike Xivan, she looked alive.

"Here we are," Xivan said. "Home sweet home, such as it is."

As Xivan's voice echoed, the woman who had been practicing stopped and looked back toward us. Her liquid brown eyes widened as she spotted me, and I flushed. For the first time since entering the caves, I felt embarrassed at my nudity.

"Talea," Xivan said, "we have a guest. Let's find her something to wear before we stir up trouble upstairs. This should be fun."

44: THE COURT OF TRUTH

Jorat Dominion, Quuros Empire.
Three days since Kihrin realized he was homesick

Ninavis came back from the kitchen with a pot of coffee. "What did I miss?"

"This is all a trap set up by Relos Var, I'm going to kill him, anyway, and Duke Kaen's wife is dead but still walking." Kihrin stole the coffee from her and helped himself to a cup.

"You told him about Relos Var?" Ninavis turned to him. "And you're still here?"

"Are you kidding? And miss the chance to know exactly where he's going to be next?"* Kihrin turned to Janel. "So is Xivan Kaen a vampire like Gadrith?"

"Similar," Janel admitted. "At least I think so. Less into sorcery, though."

"That's something," Kihrin said.

"I don't know," Janel said. "She's amazing with a sword."

"Plus, do you need to know sorcery when you can devour someone's soul?" Qown asked. He skipped to the next part and began to read.

Qown's Turn. The Ice Demesne, Yor, Quur.

Brother Qown fell to his knees as the guards pushed him into the great hall.

---

* That's honestly not a bad way to look at it. Still foolish, though.

"Is that necessary?" Thurvishar D'Lorus said.

Qown wiped the blood from his lip and tried to stand. The guard, who liked Qown's prone position better, set his spear butt against Qown's back and shoved him prostrate again.

Brother Qown should have realized the first person who would fall under suspicion for Janel's disappearance would be himself.

Qown wasn't in much of a position to take in the geometric perfection of the palace's grand hall. The air smelled cold and sharp. Qown felt like he was outside on a clear winter's day, standing in a cathedral to winter and snow.

Except for the Yoran crowd gathered to see to his disposition.

Except for the duke, standing near the giant central hearth. Qown's heart sank as he realized neither Relos Var nor Senera were present.

He had been counting on their presence—and Senera's use of the Name of All Things—to establish his innocence. They would have been able to easily ferret out the truth.

"We checked all the rooms, Your Grace," the guard said. "She's not in the palace."

The duke scowled. "Who last saw Janel?" He cast his questions toward the several dozen women standing to the side.

A woman the same age as the duke himself stepped forward. "Veixizhau welcomed Janel back upon her return."

A younger woman—presumably Veixizhau—whipped her head round to glare at the woman who'd spoken. She stepped forward. "I left after Segra delivered her food, my husband, but I must say Janel seemed unhappy. Is it possible she didn't want to be here? The young man is a sorcerer, is he not? Could he not have helped her escape?"

It took Brother Qown several seconds before he realized *young man* meant him.

"I haven't seen—"

The guard hit him.

Brother Qown put his hand to his face. His jaw ached with a dull throb.

"Let him answer," the duke said.

Brother Qown tried to stand a second time. He felt a hand on his arm; Thurvishar had stepped forward to help him. "Thank you," he murmured.

"You're welcome."

Brother Qown wiped the blood on his mouth against his agolé. "With all respect, Your Grace, I haven't seen the count for at least . . ." And then his mind blanked. Had a day passed? Two? How many? He'd lost track. "And I'm quite unable to even contemplate, uh . . ." He paused. "Escape is impossible."

"For you," said Duke Kaen, "but perhaps not for her."

"Maybe she climbed out the window," Veixizhau suggested.

"And what?" Thurvishar asked. "Slid down a castle wall in the middle of a blizzard while wearing nothing but a slip? I doubt she'd be strong enough for such a climb in winter gear."

"You're both wizards," she snapped. "What did *you* do with her?"

"*We* aren't allowed in your apartments."

"Enough!"

Everyone fell quiet at the duke's voice. He walked forward, boots echoing against the marble floor. He stopped before several men—all of whom had been present when Darzin D'Mon burned Brother Qown's journal. Darzin himself was evidently back in the Capital.

"Son," the duke said to Exidhar, "do you have anything to do with this? I understand the woman embarrassed you, but she's important to my plans."

"The priest's probably lying," Sir Oreth interrupted. "He's always protecting her—" The knight went silent as the duke met his eyes.

Kaen returned his attention to his son.

Brother Qown found himself holding his breath. If Exidhar or any of his friends had been involved in Janel's disappearance, Exidhar seemed the most likely to confess. If he convinced his father that Brother Qown possessed an overactive imagination, or worse, was covering for Janel's escape, he was in trouble.

Oh, it made Qown shake just to consider how this might end for him, never mind how it might have already ended for Janel.

"Well?"

Exidhar blinked, then gave a panicked glance at his friends.

"Father, I—" He licked his lips. "I wasn't involved, I swear. I didn't know—" He glanced over at the wives.

The duke sighed. "What you mean is, you didn't know, but your friends did." With no warning, he turned and grabbed Sir Oreth by his laevos.

The knight went for his sword. In turn, Oreth found a half dozen soldiers pointing swords at him.

"It will be no great inconvenience to me, horse man," the duke said, "to throw you out into the storm. And you're new here, so my son won't claim any loss if I kill you. So tell me everything."

Sir Oreth didn't hesitate. "It was Darzin D'Mon's idea, my lord. A prank and nothing more. He said the winter snow wouldn't bother her because she's an Ogenra of House D'Talus."

At this confession, the entire congregation broke out into murmured outrage. Brother Qown felt his own anger, but for different reasons. Janel *was* resistant to cold, but Darzin D'Mon had no way to know that. Indeed, Darzin would have assumed the opposite—because the Royal Houses didn't teach their women magic.

Which meant Darzin D'Mon had tried to murder Janel as a lark. Assuming Sir Oreth wasn't lying. It might well have been the knight's idea all along.

"And how did you gain entry to the wives' quarters?" The duke demanded. "Be specific."

Before he could answer, a woman screamed and everyone turned toward the main doorway.

A dead woman walked into the hall.

She might have been beautiful, except for being so clearly lifeless. This woman appeared to be an animated corpse, left on the ice for years. Frozen blue crystals clung to her like tiny jewels. The ice and cold had dried her flesh to her bones.

She wasn't Yoran. Her skin looked too dark. Her hair resembled snakes made from black wool, tied back with silver pins and rings. She dressed for battle, all silver chain and sparkling steel. Nothing about her seemed appropriate to the duke's court.

Except her manner, the envy of any sovereign.

Two women trailed behind her, handmaidens to a queen of war.

One of them was Janel.

A shocked silence fell over the great hall.

Xivan Kaen, the dead but not gone Duchess of Yor, began to laugh.

"Oh, husband," she said, grinning with a smile made grisly by how little tissue existed between her skull and skin, "Have they forgotten me so quickly?"

"It's been a long time, my love," said Duke Kaen.

Xivan drew her sword and pointed it to the gathered courtiers, each in turn, before sheathing the blade again. "Did you think you'd kept me down just because you'd murdered me? Did you think it would be *that* easy?"

"Xivan, have you decided to return?" Kaen didn't seem upset or surprised to see her. "You know I've always wanted you here and not in those damn caves."

She chuckled. "Yes, and I've missed you and Exidhar both. I needed time to think things over."

"It's been fifteen years," Kaen reminded her.

"Who knew it would be so hard to reconcile being assassinated? Besides, I didn't think you'd be happy with me if I slaughtered your entire court. But I really wanted to."

"And now?"

She cocked her head to the side. "I'm here, aren't I?"

He swept her into his arms, twirling her around him even as the crowd stepped back in ill-concealed horror at this show of affection.

A wife fainted, or at least pretended to.

Brother Qown, no longer guarded, made his way to Janel. She grabbed at his arm. "Oh, thank the Eight you're all right." She touched his face. "Although you'll need to do something about those bruises."

"It's you I'm worried about. You're bleeding." He glanced over at the other woman. "I'm going to look at her leg, if you don't mind."

"Please." The second woman, also Khorveshan, looked past him and waved her hand to someone behind Qown as if greeting a long-lost friend.

Thurvishar, he realized. She was waving at Thurvishar. He wrested his attention back to Janel. "What did you do—"

"I tripped on the ice," Janel explained, "while running from Aeyan'arric."

Since only the duke and duchess had been talking, and their words had turned to whispers, Janel's pronouncement echoed with perfect clarity throughout the entire hall.

The duke refocused his attention on Janel. "And why were you on the ice?"

"You'll want to ask Veixizhau," Janel responded.

The wife in question put heel to toe with commendable vigor. It didn't save her. Long flowing dresses don't make for good running attire. Soldiers caught her and returned her to the duke.

Xivan looked at the woman, raised an eyebrow, and turned back to her husband. "You can thank Veixizhau for my presence; I'm reasonably sure she tried to sacrifice your young guest to Suless. Isn't that interesting?"

Qown knew Suless had once ruled Yor, as goddess of witchcraft and betrayal, along with her god-king husband, Cherthog. Then after Quur invaded and conquered Yor, the empire outlawed their religions. Unusual for an empire typically happy to fold conquered faiths into their own.

While Duke Kaen might hate the empire, he wouldn't tolerate anyone breaking *that* law. Not when his own grandfather had helped slay Suless and Cherthog. Worshipping either of those old god-kings was the equivalent of openly declaring rebellion against *Kaen,* not just Quur.

Which might explain why Duke Kaen's expression became a scowl. He gestured to some of his soldiers. "Search the wives' quarters. Bring back any signs of the witch-queen you find. Don't take your time."

They bowed quickly and then ran out of the room.

"Please!" Veixizhau threw herself to the ground before the duke. "Please have mercy! I'm carrying your child!"

A murmur carried through the hall.

The duke's expression turned cold. "Wyrga!"

An old woman tottered forward, dressed in stained tatters. "Yes, my Hon?"

"Is she carrying my child?"

Wyrga made her way to the wives, a polar bear cub tucked under her arm. She grabbed Veixizhau by the chin and looked her over. "She's carrying a child," she said. "But it's not yours."

"Damn you!" Veixizhau screamed, flinching back. "You bitch! You—" She put her hand to her throat then, as though choking while trying to say something.

Wyrga cackled and then gave a sly look to the duke. "Would you like to know who the real father is? You'll just love it."

Duke Kaen's stare looked wary. "No."

"Aw, but it's—"

"Quiet!" Kaen snapped. "Not another word from you until I say so."

Wyrga growled, holding the bear cub to her chest.

Ignoring that, the duke turned to Veixizhau. "Who is the father?"

She raised her chin. "You—you are."

"Really."

Veixizhau didn't respond.

A minute passed, with no one talking.

"What are we doing?" Xivan Kaen finally asked. "Besides making the rest of the court very uncomfortable."

"We're waiting," Duke Kaen replied.

"Ah," she said.

So they waited.

After ten minutes or so, the soldiers who had left earlier returned, carrying a chest between them. "Your Grace? You'll want to see this."

The duke looked back. "What have you found?"

The men placed the chest on the floor and opened it. Brother Qown couldn't see what the chest contained, but the duke's expression turned murderous.

"Where did you find it?" Kaen asked the men.

"In a room off from the main gathering area, Your Grace. The door wasn't locked."

The duke reached down into the chest and lifted an animal skull—a carnivore to judge by the solid, sharp teeth. The skull had been singed black and carved with intricate patterns. Long ribbons decorated with beads had been tied to the jaws.

Duke Kaen showed the skull to the crowd. People gasped and then stepped back. Wyrga bared her teeth.

Brother Qown didn't understand its significance. To judge by Janel's expression, as well as the other girl who'd arrived with the duchess, neither did they. The Yorans sure did, though.

"Is that a Suless worship mask?" Thurvishar asked. "I've never seen one in person."

Duke Kaen didn't answer. He did, however, turn and give a hard look to his many wives.

"Is that a wolf skull?" Qown whispered to Janel, although he wasn't sure why he thought she'd know.

"I suspect it's hyena," she whispered back. "Apparently, they used to be sacred to Suless." She glanced over at the old woman, Wyrga.

"Who set up this altar? Veixizhau? Were there others? Which of you worshipped there?" His voice carried through the hall. "Tell me now."

Silence.

Kaen tossed the skull back into the chest. "Kill them all." His voice blistered with anger. "Then return their bodies to their families."

The guards looked at each other. "Sir?"

"Have you gone deaf? I said kill my wives."

"*All* your wives?" The men's eyes widened.

The duke waved a hand. "Never mind. Xivan, they're yours."

Some women cowered or broke out in tears. A few fainted, this time for real. The rest stood straight and defiant.

Qown wondered if those were the ones who had worshipped at their homemade altar to the witch-queen. Veixizhau stood in this last category.

The duke noticed this. "You have something to say to me?"

Veixizhau shook her head. "Not a word, my lord."

Xivan looked curiously displeased for someone who'd brought the matter to the duke's attention in the first place. She cast her eyes about the room as if searching for any other recourse but didn't seem willing to defy the duke's ruling. When the guards stepped forward to escort the wives, she stepped aside.

"Wait!" Janel cried out.

Duke Kaen turned. "Yes?"

"I plead for mercy."

Brother Qown bit down on his fingers to keep from shouting at her. He felt torn between concern and pride.

The hall fell silent once more.

Duke Kaen tilted his head. "What did you say?"

"I plead for mercy, Your Grace." Janel pointed to the chest. "How are we to know who was involved with that? Your wives aren't the only ones with permission to enter those quarters. Senera didn't need permission to enter. Can Wyrga come and go as she wishes?"

That made Kaen pause. "Yes."

Behind him, Wyrga made horrible faces but didn't speak.

"So perhaps the reason your wives couldn't answer your question is because they didn't know the answer."

"Are you forgetting Veixizhau tried to kill you? Sacrifice you to a dead goddess? She at least is quite guilty. And no one tried to stop her either. None of my 'wives' called for the guards. And let's be clear: more than my wives conspired in this. Darzin D'Mon and Sir Oreth are implicated *at minimum*, and then they involved my son. They'd have seen you dead and smiled at themselves for a job well done."

Janel's face set into a stubborn cast. "I seek clemency for your wives," she repeated. "Even if a few wives knew what Veixizhau planned, they couldn't all have known. I ask Xivan to spare them."

Xivan stepped forward. "*Spare* them? Why?"

Qown asked himself the same question. Not that he wanted to see them executed, but Janel seemed to have something specific in mind.

Janel turned to Xivan. "Because they're prisoners. Because they've spent years living in a fine gold cage, and the only power they've ever had is what they hoped to gain by capturing one man's attention. Is it any wonder these women thought their only recourse was to eliminate competition?"

The wives who were not weeping gave Janel odd looks. She might as well have spoken a foreign language for as much as they'd understood her meaning.

Xivan tilted her head. "What are you suggesting, child?"

Janel spread her arms as if to take in the whole court. "You're already training Talea. Why not expand that? Train these women too. Give them a chance to be something beyond hostages and trade goods."

Xivan frowned. "Now why would I do that?"

"How many women did Yor lose when Quur invaded? How many died who could've taken up arms to help defend this land? How is that different from what Khorvesh suffered when the morgage invaded? Didn't the women of Khorvesh take up arms then? Isn't that the reason you and every other woman of Khorvesh wear swords now?"

Xivan blinked. "It's not the same."

"Isn't it? Most of these women are likely innocent, but you and I both know innocence is no shield against a sword."

The duke cleared his throat. "These women aren't warriors."

"Not yet," Janel responded. "But we can change that. Why does Yor lock away the people it forces to be women, when what you should be doing is training them? They should be taking up sword and shield to defend their homes. Why deny yourselves the support of half your population?"*

The duke blinked at Janel in stunned surprise.

Then the whole room erupted in laughter. Mocking laughter, scornful laughter. Janel had made a fine joke. Of the men, only Exidhar looked unhappy. The rest thought she was adorable and hilarious. Woman warriors? Comical.

Every woman scowled.

Finally, the laughter quieted. Janel stood in the center, hands locked into fists.

Brother Qown felt for her. It had been a worthy attempt. What Yoran would ever listen to such a heretical notion? Most Quuros wouldn't have either.

"I like it," Xivan said.

Duke Kaen turned to her. "What?" Then he chuckled. "My darling, it's a terrible idea."

"Why? Don't we need soldiers?" Then she added, "Besides, it's not your decision."

The whole hall seemed to hold its breath.

The undead duchess raised an eyebrow. "You *gave* these women to me. Just a few minutes ago."

"Don't twist my words, wife. I gave them to you for you to *execute*, the same as all the other condemned I send down to the caves to sate your hunger." Duke Kaen held up a hand before Xivan could make any further protest. He turned to Janel. "I'll give them to my wife in truth, but since you're the one asking for mercy, you're the one who will pay the price."

Janel grew wary. "Price?"

"I asked for your assistance in a matter just before your adventure outside the palace walls. Now I want your word that you will give me that aid. I want your vow of loyalty." His smile was dark. "What is it the Joratese call it? Your thudajé? I want your thudajé."

Janel looked like she'd been struck. The court murmured

---

* Because they'd rather have our enslavement, obviously.

among themselves. They were perplexed. Why did their duke care about a woman's loyalty? Even the women seemed to be asking themselves the same question. They probably assumed Kaen was adding another Khorveshan woman to his collection, even though Janel was "married" to Relos Var.

"Well?" the duke said. "I won't ask again."

Janel fell to her knees and bent her head. She said something softly.

"What was that?"

Janel looked up. "I said I pledge myself to your service, Your Grace."

Qown heard a gasp and then realized it had come from him.

"That wasn't so hard, was it, Janel Danorak? But let's do this properly." He gestured to one of the attendants while saying something in a language Qown didn't understand.

Immediately, a large man with a tightly curled beard and shaved head stepped forward. He wore so much jewelry in that beard it was a wonder he could even move his head. Whatever he said to the duke, it was clear the man wasn't happy.

The duke responded in kind, his tone dismissive.

The courtier stormed out of the great hall, and several other men followed.

Meanwhile, the attendant came back with an open wooden box. Kaen reached inside and pulled out a piece of jewelry, very similar in style to the jewelry in his own beard, the jewelry in the beards of many of the men in the room. He separated a lock of Janel's laevos and threaded the band around the base. "Repeat after me: as the winter is cold, I cleave to the protection of my king."

"As the winter is cold, I cleave to the protection of my king," Janel repeated.

Another jeweled band came out of the box, this one slightly different in design. "As the winter is long, I protect my people in his name."

She repeated this. He laced the band around another lock of hair.

"As the winter is hard, I will overcome our enemies." Again, he granted her another jeweled piece as she repeated his words.

"Until the winter ends, my life belongs to Yor." The same ritual repeated.

The whole time, the crowd was silent and wide-eyed. Qown wondered if this was some sort of knighthood, the sort that wasn't associated with tournament contests and commodity trading. That might explain why that courtier had been so furious. Duke Kaen finished lacing the last jeweled band into her hair and then stepped back. "Now I name you hand, extension of my will. Rise."

Janel rose to her feet, looking shaky.

The duke tilted his head toward his undead wife. "They're all yours." The two continued to speak, while various courtiers looked upset or uncomfortable.

Janel rejoined Qown.

"Are you all right?" Qown leaned toward her.

"Ask me again later," Janel said. "Why was everyone staring at me?"

"Because you're the first woman to ever be given that particular honor," Thurvishar D'Lorus said. "My apologies. I couldn't help but hear the question."

Janel started to respond, then stopped and blinked. "I remember you from the banquet. D'Lorus, yes? The Academy?"

"The same," Thurvishar responded. He started to say more but paused and looked toward the duke instead.

At that moment, Duke Kaen turned his attention back to Janel and gestured toward Sir Oreth. "And what about this one? Shall you plead mercy in his case as well?"

Sir Oreth blinked. "Me? Wait, I thought we'd agreed it was the women—"

"Be quiet," Duke Kaen ordered. "Do you want him to live?"

"Him?" She raised an eyebrow, incredulous.

Sir Oreth's eyes widened. "Janel, please—"

"Three times," she told Oreth. "Three times you have moved against me. The first time, you tried to force me to be your mare. The second time, you took my lands. The third time, you tried to take my life."

"Janel, damn it, it wasn't like that! Would you just listen to me? I did nothing wrong. I had nothing to do with this! This is ridiculous!"

She turned back to the duke. Only Brother Qown could see the tremor—rage—moving through her fingers. "No mercy from me. Do with him as you wish, Your Grace."

The duke nodded. "He's all yours, Xivan."

"What? No!" Sir Oreth pulled out his sword, pointing it in the undead woman's direction as she approached.

"I agree. It's better to go to your death with a sword in your hands." Xivan Kaen unsheathed her own sword. She used a curved Khorveshan blade, very different from Oreth's straight sword.

Brother Qown looked away. "I can't watch this."

As it happened, he didn't have to. No sooner had he averted his gaze than metal hit the ground followed by a grunting noise. When Qown glanced back, shocked, he saw Sir Oreth had been disarmed. Xivan Kaen held him by the throat. He writhed and tried to break her grip, without success.

And a glowing light trailed from his eyes and mouth to the duchess while the entire hall watched in silence.

It took seconds or an eternity, depending on how one measured such things. When Xivan finished, she dropped his corpse to the ground. Xivan looked haler already; her skin didn't appear so blue, her cheeks had filled out. She almost passed for someone alive.

"We're done here," the duke announced.

45: THE SPURNED

Jorat Dominion, Quuros Empire.
Three days since Kihrin's story ended . . .
for a little while

Kihrin pointed toward the rings in Janel's hair. "Are those—?"

She shook her head quickly. "No. And my loyalty to Duke Kaen—well, it was always under false pretenses, wasn't it?" Janel stared into her coffee cup. "False pretenses on both sides. Azhen Kaen knew I was a candidate to fit the prophecies for the Hellwarrior, so he wanted to keep me under his eye. Make sure I never usurped the role he wanted for himself. And if he turned my loyalty to him in the meantime, I was much more likely to go along with his plans concerning General Milligreest. Can you imagine the look on the high general's face if Kaen were to show up for a meeting with me at his side?"

"I don't think I like this Duke Kaen fellow," Dorna said.

Janel sighed. "He had his moments. Unfortunately, he then had all those *other* moments."

Kihrin fought back a yawn and grabbed for his coffee cup. If they kept this up, they would end up staying up straight through the night. On the other hand, he'd rather be awake but tired than *sleeping* when Relos Var arrived. "Yeah, but Xivan's the more dangerous one."

Ninavis chuckled. "You have good instincts about people."

"You'd *think* so," Kihrin said.

Janel shrugged. "Yes, I admit I have a problem with Xivan."

"Which is?" Kihrin asked.

Janel sighed. "I really like her."

Janel's Turn. The Ice Demesne, Yor, Quur.

I was numb when I returned to the wives' quarters.

No one noticed, but only because everyone else was equally dazed. Xivan stayed with Kaen. Qown and I were separated. I don't know what had happened to Talea. Guards escorted all the other women, myself included, back to our rooms. No one spoke.

I hadn't realized . . . I hadn't been prepared.

That scene in the great hall had cost me in ways I'd never expected. I had known it would come to this. I had known this was the price I'd have to pay. And yet when the bill came due, I was shocked to find the coin so dear.

How much of my self-worth, my self-image, was predicated on this idea of being a proper noble, an honorable person? Good for my word. Loyal to the empire and my gods. And now that couldn't be true, could it? Either I was a liar or a traitor.

It didn't matter that this was the whole reason I'd wanted to go to Yor. I had *wanted* to infiltrate Duke Kaen's house, *wanted* to lie to him and gain his trust in order to steal the magic spear Khoreval. If I needed that spear to slay Aeyan'arric and stop her rampage through Jorat, then it followed I would do whatever it took to claim the weapon as my own.

The whole point had been to betray Kaen. Right?

Except if my new status—whatever that status was—meant I could convince Kaen not to unleash Aeyan'arric on Jorat at all, then . . . did I even need the spear?

I could gain everything I wanted by betraying everything I was.

I touched the rings now woven into my laevos while women slid past me in the great room. They silently fanned out again through the rooms. I found myself reminded of the survivors of Mereina—all those people in too much shock to do anything but stare at nothing. A wife sat down on one of the couches and began weeping.

Across the room, out on one of those balconies, a motion

caught my eyes. I realized Wyrga was out there, feeding scraps of something to her little polar bear cub. She caught my eye, gave me her feral grin, and winked at me. She put a finger to her lips and made a shushing motion.

I looked around to see if anyone else had noticed her, but when I glanced back, Wyrga was gone. And there was no place for her to have gone—the only exit from that area was either into the main room or . . . or a thousand foot drop onto freezing ice.

A tension settled over the room. I thought Wyrga had entered from another doorway, but as I turned around, I realized the pressure had a different cause.

Veixizhau had arrived.

She crossed her arms and scanned the room. "What are you bitches looking at?"

The woman who'd first greeted me, Bikeinoh, rolled her eyes. "Seriously? After the shit you just pulled? You're lucky we don't kill you ourselves."

"As if half the women here wouldn't have done the same given the chance. I just beat you to it. And don't you dare try to be sanctimonious with me. We were *all* worshipping—" Veixizhau stopped talking as another wife cleared her throat and pointed.

Pointed at me.

I waved.

Veixizhau scowled at me. "What are you doing here?"

"Looking for a bed," I answered. "Humorously enough, they didn't have any other place to put me. But you've learned your lesson, right?"

Her nostrils flared. "Sure. I've learned my lesson. I should have poisoned you instead."

"There's always next time."

None of the other women came to her defense. Veixizhau ignored them and focused on me. "I wouldn't smile, tumai. Because you had it wrong back there. I only told one person what happened to you, Exidhar—and I assume he told the

535 THE NAME OF ALL THINGS 535

others because he wanted to impress his friends. But those friends? They had no part in it. Which means you just fed an innocent man to Kaen's dead monster of a wife."

I did indeed stop smiling. "No, Oreth said Darzin—"

It couldn't be true. Oreth had plotted to kill me. I *knew* that.

Veixizhau laughed. "In any other case, it would have been smart to point the finger at a royal. It's not like the duke would have punished one of *them.* I bet it never even occurred to your Oreth to tell the truth. He thought finger-pointing would serve him better. He was wrong."

"You're lying."

"That's the best part; I'm not. And don't even think about being all righteous with me. You belong to Suless now, and it's only a matter of time before she claims you."

"Suless is dead," I reminded her.

"No, she's not. Oh, I can't wait for you two to meet. She loves murderers."

I flinched.

She saw the reaction and smiled. Then Veixizhau turned, head held high, and swept out of the common area.

All the women were quiet until Bikeinoh clapped her hands. "All right, everyone. Let's have dinner and then go to bed early. I have a feeling tomorrow is going to be a very long day."

"What does *tumai* mean?" I was back to being numb, distracted by minor details.

She paused before answering. "I suppose the closest word in Guarem would be *knight.*"

I nodded. Veixizhau had said it like an insult, but maybe that wasn't the case. Maybe it didn't matter. A different word seemed more fitting.

Monster. Kaen did collect them, didn't he?

Bikeinoh touched my arm. "Let's find you a room."

No gods or goddesses presented themselves to me in the weeks that followed, not god-kings or the Eight. Veixizhau's words proved hollow.

But I couldn't shove her accusation from my mind. Couldn't escape the nagging suspicion that Oreth had been innocent—at least innocent of that crime.

I retreated into myself, speaking to no one unless spoken to first, seeking no company, snapping at polite attempts at conversation. I'd managed to avoid Senera and Relos Var, and while I was in theory now Duke Kaen's man, he'd made no attempt to put me to work. I didn't see Brother Qown either and found myself glad. I wore my anger around me like a coat, and I didn't want to hear Qown insist I was smothering myself.

That lasted several weeks.

"Janel, what are you doing?"

I looked up from the book of Devoran prophecies I'd "borrowed" from the duke's library. "Isn't it obvious?"

We were in the middle of the training yard, which, like everything else in the Ice Demesne, lay deep inside the crystal pyramid. The giant room was divided into sections so multiple groups might train at once, but the large space did nothing to hide the accumulated stench of sweaty bodies.

Xivan raised an eyebrow and pointed to the training mat. "Get in here. I want to see what you can do."

"I'm busy."

All noise near us stopped. Even the nearby men stopped their sparring.

Duke Kaen's soldiers used the same training facilities as Xivan's new recruits; none of the men appreciated sharing those facilities with women. Which meant all the while the women trained, the men watched, harassed, and heckled—or at least as much as they thought they could get away with under Xivan's baleful stare. There had been incidents. Soldiers who had groped or, on three occasions, done worse. Some thought the duke wouldn't mind if someone else helped themselves, if he no longer cared to claim them as his own.

Xivan took those men away, and we never saw them again. After the third "example," the incidents stopped.

But now every eye turned to me.

Xivan's eyebrows rose up. "Get in there, now. If I ask a third time, you'll be fighting me rather than Talea."

Talea, Xivan's apprentice I'd first met in the caves, had started her lessons eight months earlier, which gave her an edge over the other students. I returned to reading my book.

I knew I was being childish, but I couldn't make myself stop. My anger was a slow-burning fury, and the fact I had no clear direction for my rage made it worse. How much easier it would be if I could just hate a special singular someone and not the whole world.

A curved Khorveshan sword landed, dull side down, against the book's spine and then pulled the entire folio from my hands. I had enough time to recognize Xivan sliding another sword within my reach before she swung her own blade toward my head.

She fought with live steel.

I rolled to the side and grabbed the sword, grinning as I stood. The grin faded as I felt the weapon's weight. I'd never fought with a weapon I couldn't swing around like a piece of silk. I could lift this, but only just. Making this weapon an extension of my arm and will? Out of the question.

This was a problem.

"No more smiles?" Xivan mocked.

"I'll smile when this is over." I swung at her, but the force of my blow was inconstant and slow. She blocked me and came inside my reach to nick me on the arm. I hissed.

"When you're ready to start," Xivan said, "just let me know."

Muscle memory and instinct had trained me to fight a certain way. Without the strength of a dozen men, those instincts became pitfalls.

I ran at her again, screaming, determined to at least have something to show for my efforts. She watched my approach with amusement, blocked me without effort, and turned on her feet at the last minute like changing leads in a race. "No wonder Oreth didn't think you should be a stallion. You fight like a mare."

My vision turned red. To the side, someone screamed.

Xivan's tunic caught fire.

She looked down, saw the burning threads, and laughed. Still holding the sword with one hand, she quenched the flames with the other. "Remember that trick, student. Against a different opponent, it might prove a good distraction."

She swung the curved sword, a beautiful ornate dance.

I moved to block the attack, failed, watched my sword fall out of alignment, and instead went to kick the duchess. Her leg hooked inside my own.

I ended up on the ground, Xivan's sword at my throat.

"How can you expect to defeat an enemy when you haven't even mastered yourself?" Her voice was even, the question serious rather than rhetorical.

"I don't–" I found myself at a loss for what to say. I'd fought *stupidly*. I'd turned a practice session into a tantrum. I had no idea how to control the maelstrom of my emotions. I didn't try to stand. I just lay there, miserable, every eye in the practice yard on me, too numb to even care.

Xivan moved the sword from my neck and knelt beside me. "Don't tell me you loved him."

"What? Who?" What she said couldn't have been more startling than if it had been a slap, but at the same time, I felt remorse stab me. I knew who.

Oreth.

But no, I hadn't loved him.

I had *wanted* to love him, though. I had wanted him to love me back too. Neither wish had come true. Instead, his pride had demanded he break me, and my pride–

"The knight. The one I executed."

"No, I–" I shut my eyes, tears welling at their corners. "I just–" My voice came out as a ragged sob. "I didn't. It's all so pointless. So unnecessary. I didn't mean for him to die. I never mean for any of them to die and–" My grief expressed itself as a jagged exhalation. Somehow his death became conflated with all the others–the citizens of Mereina, everyone at Lonezh, the

Hellmarch, my parents, that Marakori man murdered on the bridge to Atrine—

All the people I couldn't save.

"So it's yourself you hate, then." Xivan's voice sounded sad.

I felt like she'd pulled out the last piece from a tottering foundation. A shudder, an ugly clenching feeling, and then the avalanche. Her words ripped through me, until I felt I would be lost in the tumult. Naturally, I hated myself. How could I not, when I always lived? Lived not because I deserved it, not because I'd earned it, but to serve the false games of demons, the commands of generals, and always those damn prophecies. Lived, but never once made anyone's life better for it. I had become a stallion to protect the ones I loved, but I couldn't even protect myself.

What good was it all, then? What purpose did it serve?

I turned on my stomach, away from her, and began sobbing into my hands. Brutal sobbing, and for a time, I couldn't stop. If I faced the world, I'd have to do something about it. I'd have to try to fix it.

I didn't think I could this time.

I felt her hand on my laevos, stroking my hair. "Oh, my sweet little girl. How all those fires in your heart must burn."

I'd reached the stage of a full-on bawl, which is tears and hiccups and too much phlegm. We were in public. I wiped my eyes and nose with my hands, anyway.

"You let all those others define you," she whispered to me. "So many people telling you who you must be."

I couldn't let that pass unanswered. "I've rebelled—"

"It's no different. When opposing forces collide, they define each other. You cannot advance against an enemy without letting them shape you. You push, and you're pushed against. You measure yourself against others, by their approval or by their displeasure, and every time you will find you have given them power over you, whether you realize it or not." She cupped my cheek, and I felt her hand's cold flesh, nothing like living tissue. It didn't horrify me as much as it should have. "You must find yourself, my dear. Find your own heart, your own beauty, your own truth."

She stood and offered her hand to me. "And then we can work on defeating your enemies."

I laughed, a choking near-hysterical laugh even as I grabbed her desiccated hand and let her help me to my feet. Because you see, *she* was my enemy. The Kaens and Relos Var and all the forces aligned to help them. My enemies.

Or my friends.

And I didn't know the difference anymore. Was Xivan nothing more than an obstacle in my quest to steal the dragon-slaying spear, Khoreval? Or was Xivan someone who would help me triumph over Duke Xun and Markreev Aroth, to regain Jorat? Was it better to truly be Duke Kaen's tumai—or do as I'd promised the Goddess of Death and help destroy everyone helping Relos Var?

Ever since Tya, Goddess of Magic, had enchanted Arasgon to join me in the Afterlife, I had been the traitor hidden in Duke Kaen's midst. I'd been passing messages and instructions back to my camp every night while I "slept." Yet still I knew I hadn't truly accepted my role. Maybe Oreth had been right. Maybe I'd never know my place.

I was supposed to find Yor's crimes unforgivable, while ignoring the blood on my own hands.

Xivan Kaen pulled me into her arms and cradled me, while racking sobs claimed me again.

Talea guided me back to my room afterward, arm around my shoulders. She sat me down in a chair by the bed, kneeling next to me.

"Is there anything I can get you?" she asked. "Tea? Something stronger?"

"I messed up back there, didn't I?"

She smiled. "Messed up? Hardly." She turned back the furs on the bed. "You're grieving. Let yourself. I'm still not over my—" Talea must have seen my expression, the question in my eyes. "I had a sister. She was murdered."

Two sentences, thrown out like idle trivia, but the pain in her voice ripped at my heart. "And—" I returned her smile with a much more pallid version. "You're going to kill the one responsible."

She'd always approached her lessons with a rage I'd suspected was personal, as though she pictured a special someone on the other end of every sword swing.

She scoffed and turned around, sitting down on the bed. "I wish. Darzin D'Mon murdered her."

I blinked as the declaration cut through my own numbness. "The royal? The same one who—" I'd almost said, "The same one who'd tried to have me killed," but I didn't think that was true anymore.

"That's what Thurvishar says." She shook her head. "I don't think Darzin even realizes what he did. It was just bad luck. She happened to be at the wrong place at the wrong time, and his assassin didn't want witnesses. Just another bystander caught up in the royal games of empire. And Darzin's done so much worse—" She looked away. "His list of crimes is long."

I moved from my chair and sat next to her, took her hands in mine. "I'm so sorry. Are you going to kill him? Do you want help?"

She laughed and squeezed my hands back. "I appreciate the offer. Ask me again in a few years. I'm told he's phenomenal with a sword, so I suspect I'll need a little more than eight months' training, no matter how amazing Xivan might be."

"When the time comes, it would be my pleasure to help."

Talea grinned. "Thank you. One of these days, I'll be good enough with a sword and Darzin will stop being useful to Duke Kaen, and I just hope I'm there. Or Thurvishar is. I think he might try to fight me for the honor of killing Darzin."

"How can you be friends with a royal? With the D'Lorus Lord Heir?"

She swallowed. "He bought me from Darzin." Talea saw the

expression on my face and added, "But Thurvishar freed me. Right away, he freed me.* He asked me what I wanted to do with myself, said he'd grant any wish I had. I felt like I was in a god-king tale where the peasant girl frees an injured lion from a trap—only the lion is a goddess who can grant any wish." Talea cleared her throat. "Well, I told him I wanted revenge."

"Darzin's still alive," I said, "so I'm guessing Thurvishar hasn't fulfilled his promises."

"He said it would be up to me," Talea said, "but he explained—" She paused, taking my hand again. "He explained what they're trying to do. I may hate Darzin, but they *are* trying to take down the empire. Slavery isn't a feature of Yoran culture— Kaen won't allow it to continue once he's in charge. And what price wouldn't I pay for a Quur without slavery?"

Truly, her willpower left me awed. I felt equally skeptical about the motives of royals. The Royal Houses rested on a foundation of slavery, greed, and pain.† I didn't think anyone whose fortunes rested upon such a base would be eager to undermine the source of their wealth.

Oh, I understood Kaen's motives: Yor felt lashed to a Quuros yoke, so it made sense to smash the empire first, before Yor declared itself free.

The royal families, though? All they wanted was more power. Always more power.

"It must be torture seeing him alive and breathing," I said at last.

Talea shrugged. "Not once I started training with Xivan. I've rarely left the caves. And even then—" Talea chuckled. "He did see me once, when I first arrived with Thurvishar. Can you believe that bastard didn't even recognize me?"

"But now you've left the caves." The idea Talea would now

---

* I assume Thurvishar had thought to bring her back as his bodyguard or the like one day. He is still royal, after all. There's no way he helped her without some expectation of one day having her repay his "kindness."

† Well, she isn't lying, is she?

have to deal with Darzin horrified me. "He's going to be here. He's here rather a lot."

"No," she said, grinning. "I won't be running into him. And I have you to thank."

"You do?"

"The Hon banished Darzin from the court as punishment for his role in plotting to kill you. Darzin may send someone else in his place as an emissary, but he's not allowed here again himself."

I didn't feel like pointing out Darzin might have been accused unfairly. "I'm glad to hear it. I admit I didn't relish seeing him again."

"He's a monster." The bitterness and hate returned to her voice.

Even as a monster myself, I couldn't disagree.

She reached out a hand and touched my cheek, lingered just south of my lower lip. "Would you like me to stay with you tonight?"

I felt a tremor shiver down me from cheek to loins. I hesitated. "Are you asking to share my bed?"

Her smile faltered. "Only if you want. I hope I haven't offended. If you prefer men . . ."

I didn't quite laugh. The desire to pull her to me, to cup her head in my hands, kiss her open-mouthed, and push her back onto the bed felt overwhelming. Did I want this? Oh yes.

I picked up her hand and kissed her calloused fingertips, each in turn. I felt her shiver. "Nothing would please me more."

46: THE SEARCH FOR THE
BLACK KNIGHT

Jorat Dominion, Quuros Empire.
Three days since Janel crossed a really rickety bridge

"I always wondered what had happened to Talea," Kihrin said. "I thought about asking Thurvishar, but I was afraid he'd tell me she'd been eaten by . . . you see, I used to know this mimic . . . Anyway, I'm glad Thurvishar freed her."*

Qown raised his head. "Did you say a mimic? I thought those were myths."

"Oh no," Kihrin said. "Very real and very terrifying. And this particular mimic—Talon—is the same assassin Talea mentioned, the one who murdered her sister, Morea."

"Well, I'm just glad you saw sense and decided to run with mares," Dorna said, nodding and patting Janel on the shoulder. "Talea seems lovely."

Janel rolled her eyes. "Dorna, don't start."

"You run with whoever you like, dear. I will always love you," Dorna said.

Janel plastered a tight smile on her face and turned to Qown. "Start reading. Right now."

Qown's Turn. The Ice Demesne, Yor, Quur.

Brother Qown didn't see Relos Var again for several months,

---

* Oh sure. He was so upset about the idea of Janel being involved with Teraeth, but doesn't blink at the idea of her sleeping with another woman. Typical.

but when he did, the wizard seemed in a foul temper. He paused at the study door, still speaking to someone outside.

"Why haven't you killed her yet?" Relos Var said, looking behind him, and, as far as Brother Qown could tell, failing to notice Qown. "Mark my words, you're going to regret your misplaced loyalty. She's dangerous. She should be destroyed."

Then the Hon, Azhen Kaen, pushed past the wizard. "I have my reasons. This isn't up for discussion, Var."

As both men came into the room, Brother Qown found himself hoping they might overlook him, too involved with the conversation to realize someone was already present.

Luck wasn't with him.

The Hon slapped the table before Brother Qown, making him jump. "You're Var's new apprentice, right?"

"I, uh—" Brother Qown swallowed. *Apprentice* wasn't the right word, considering. But reminding the Hon he was Relos Var's ensorcelled, soul-chained slave didn't seem a good idea either.

"It's fine, Qown," Relos Var said, smiling down at him. "The Hon has asked for our help with a situation in Jorat. And since I'm sure you've had enough time to grow accustomed to Worldhearth, I volunteered your services. I hope you don't mind."

Brother Qown swallowed again, but this time managed a wan smile. "No. Of course not, Lord Var."

"Good," said the Hon. "I need to find out who has picked up the Black Knight's mantle. Someone's assumed that role at the last dozen tournaments—and I'm sick of it."

"I'm sorry?" Brother Qown asked. "How does the same person playing the Black Knight cause a problem? It's a *tournament*. It affects commodity prices and business deals . . ."

The Hon gave Qown such a fierce "you're an idiot" glare the priest found himself fighting the urge to duck. "Pick your reason. When he won the tournament in Praliar, he used his idorrá to convince the local baron to evacuate the entire town afterward— before Aeyan'arric arrived. Or the several occasions where he was so disruptive, the local rulers canceled the tournament and sent everyone home. Or simply the fact that he's sneaking into tournaments, knocking out whoever should be the Black Knight, taking their place and *winning*—often before scattering his prize money to the crowds. Which is making the local rulers look like fools." He growled. "That's supposed to be *my* job, Var. How am I supposed to come in and save these people if this bastard keeps beating me to it?"

Brother Qown blinked and looked up at Relos Var. "Wouldn't it be better to use the Name—"

Relos Var shook his head. "That would require too open-ended a question. The Black Knight isn't a unique identifier. Since it's a role and not a title, we'd receive a thousand names or no names at all. There are times in Jorat where no one is the Black Knight, because no one is playing the role in a tournament. But we've made an initial list of people who've played the part in the last year. It's likely one of them." He untucked the large vellum scroll he'd been holding under his arm and unrolled it on the desk.

The scroll rolled across the desk and back off the other side.*

"We know Janel Theranon played the part when she interrupted our plans in Mereina, but obviously she hadn't been around during these latest events. Find out as much as you can and report back to me."

Brother Qown picked up the paper. Janel's name would be there. So would Sir Baramon's and Captain Mithros's. Ninavis was the last person he saw wear the outfit, although Qown didn't know if she counted since she'd only done so to escape Duke Xun's soldiers. Since Relos Var hadn't given him a direct order, Qown felt no compulsion to volunteer what he knew.

"Yes, sir. I'll start right away."

The Hon stared at Brother Qown for a long second and then grunted. "Good."

---

* It took me two days to put that list together. I had to enchant myself first so I wouldn't need food, water, or sleep.

"Kaen—" Relos Var said.

Duke Kaen paused.

"About the women," Var said. "Your wives."

Kaen sighed and waved a hand. "Ex-wives. And I don't care. You want that D'Lorus royal to teach them magic? Fine. Maybe they'll be good for something."

"Not all of them will have an aptitude for magic," Relos Var said, "but I believe Thurvishar D'Lorus wants to start by teaching them how to *read*."*

"Whatever. You have my permission." The duke swept out of the room as quickly as he had entered it.

Relos Var, however, stayed. He watched the Hon leave, waited a few seconds, and then pulled up a seat next to Brother Qown. He opened a small gate with his usual graceful style and began pulling plates and cups from that small portal. Within seconds, Relos Var had filled the tabletop with steamed rice buns, Brother Qown's favorite black truffle soup, and a steaming pot of tea.

"Oh, this isn't necessary—"

"I rather think it is. You're forgetting to eat, which isn't like you." Relos Var gave him an intent look. "I'm told you had some trouble while I was away."

Brother Qown looked down at his hands, even as Relos Var began to pile up a plate with vegetable-stuffed buns and then ladled him a bowl of soup. "It was fine. Just weak men who wanted to feel strong."

Relos Var smiled. "Yes, weak men are always the ones who cause problems, aren't they?"

Brother Qown had the feeling a trap waited in that sentence, so he didn't respond. He instead spent about two seconds contemplating if wanting to help himself to Relos Var's food made him a bad person. Var had presented proper Eamithonian cuisine, the kind Qown would daydream about while reading in the Ice Demesne library. He decided no man, no matter

---

* Apparently, not a necessary skill for women in Yor. Although that's not really so different from the rest of the empire either.

how moral, could resist such a temptation. Qown began to eat.

The sorcerer put his hand on Brother Qown's shoulder. "I'm also told you have been spending time with Thurvishar D'Lorus."

Brother Qown set down the food. "Is that a problem?"

"Be careful. Thurvishar can't be trusted any more than you."

Brother Qown blinked. Could Relos Var mean—

"He's gaeshed," Relos Var said, just in case there had been any doubt. "Gaeshed by Gadrith the Twisted. If you ever run into a pale, slender man with D'Lorus black eyes, run the other way. He's not your friend. He's not anyone's friend."

"Oh gods," Brother Qown said. "I did meet someone like that. I think—" He shuddered then, remembering the hungry stare of the pale man he'd met at Shadrag Gor. "Wait, Gadrith the Twisted? I thought Gadrith D'Lorus died."

"It is very much to his benefit everyone thinks so. However, his house is useful to the Hon, and his libraries are useful to me, and he has—" Relos Var paused. "He has something important to me. Gadrith knows I won't move against him while he possesses it."

Brother Qown managed not to choke on his soup, managed not to show any reaction at all, but inside, his emotions churned. After all, if a talisman or artifact existed that could be used against Relos Var—and Gadrith had this in his possession—then perhaps Qown could find it—that is, if Brother Qown ever freed himself from Relos Var's gaesh.

"So Thurvishar is gaeshed, and Thurvishar is Gadrith's spy." Brother Qown turned the conversation back to safer territory.

"Yes. Now Thurvishar is even more magically talented than his father, so there's no one better to help you with your studies. Except for that one tiny detail—he'll follow Gadrith's commands, no matter how horrifying or treacherous." He scowled as he helped himself to several bean-paste-stuffed buns. "Sometimes it is useful to know where one stands with another person, whether they be allies, enemies, or, as in this case, both."

"I'm sure they feel likewise," Brother Qown responded, "but you all have a common enemy, right? Quur?"

Var chuckled. "I don't play so small, dear Qown. Let the Iron Circle—Gadrith and Darzin and all those weak-minded folk—think this is about overthrowing Quur and its High Council. The real stakes are larger than they can comprehend."

Brother Qown chewed at his lip for a moment. "So when you came in, the woman you said should die . . ."

Relos Var didn't respond right away. He ate more steamed buns, drank tea, sipped at his own soup.

Finally, Relos Var said, "I'm fond of Azhen Kaen. That doesn't mean we agree on all things. Sometimes you watch your friends make mistakes and there's nothing you can do but let them."

"You mustn't think it's so important a mistake, or you'd stop him."

"He isn't my only game piece, Qown. Not by half."

"Is that how you think of us? Game pieces?" He couldn't hide the heartbreak in his voice.

Relos Var reached out again, put his hand on Qown's, and squeezed his fingers the way he used to when his name was Father Zajhera and not Relos Var. "No, not at all. But I have lived too long and seen too much to let any single person's moral failures or bad choices stop me. What we're trying to do is more important."

Brother Qown wondered if the wizard would abandon that stance if Relos Var himself became disposable.

"'What we're trying to do' makes it sound like you have a plan."

Relos Var smiled at the priest. "Dear boy, I always have a plan."

The list the Hon had given Brother Qown must have taken Senera quite some time to write out. And as predicted, Sir Baramon and Janel Theranon's names were both listed.

So was Ninavis's name. And Dorna's.

And Dango's. And Kay Hará's.

In fact, many names didn't belong to knights or to people one would expect to ever be knights. Brother Qown had a good idea what must have happened, even before he'd used Worldhearth to scry them.

His friends were muddying the waters.

Almost as if they somehow knew their enemy had a way to discover information about them, they had put as many people as possible in the Black Knight's costume. This made it difficult—if not impossible—to find out the identity of the "real" Black Knight.

A thought occurred to Brother Qown, a thought so outrageous he had to stop and jerk himself away from the firepit he had been scrying in Atrine.

Did Janel have a way to communicate with the others?

It seemed impossible, but he knew Janel's consciousness went elsewhere when she "slept." He had always assumed the ability passive, not under her control, even if she'd inadvertently created that spell. But could she somehow use her ability to keep in touch with others?

No, he thought. It wasn't possible. If she went to the Afterlife, she'd have to be able to communicate with someone else with the same ability. He didn't know anyone else with that power besides gods. And possibly Relos Var.

He had a hard time shaking the nagging feeling he'd missed something.

And what if he had? He wouldn't do Janel any favors by ferreting out her secret, only to report it to Relos Var the next time the wizard asked Qown to tell all he had discovered. Better to leave it alone, a truth not confirmed and thus impossible to betray.

As Relos Var himself had said, Brother Qown couldn't be trusted.

He therefore decided to start with the other names on the list, the unfamiliar names not associated with Marakori bandit queens or her forest-dwelling outlaws. It proved difficult to track down the Black Knights, because they lived their own lives while not performing. Nobody spent every hour running around a tournament wearing black and upturning people's ale mugs for laughs.

Then he came across a Black Knight who wasn't trying to be funny.

It had taken weeks, hampered because tournaments didn't happen every day of the week. On days when tournaments ran, they tended to happen all at once, all across Jorat, leaving Qown to try to goat-leap across multiple locations. Additionally, they tended to happen during the day, when people didn't light fires, lanterns, or candles. And kitchen fires were seldom built within viewing distance of tournament stands. All this made fulfilling the Hon's request tricky indeed.

He almost asked Thurvishar for help, thinking a retreat to Shadrag Gor would give him the time he needed. But he decided he didn't want Thurvishar to know.

When he found the right Black Knight, he almost missed him, skipping over the horse and rider. Then he recognized the horse.

Not a horse at all, but Arasgon, disguised and wearing black.

Brother Qown didn't recognize the rider, but the Black Knight seemed far too large to be Ninavis.

A chance arrangement of azhocks allowed Qown to see the tournament grounds from the farrier's forge. Enough to see the Black Knight compete. Not unusual, but the fact that the Knight won contest after contest was—as demonstrated by the muttering and whispered complaining from other knights. Those complaints rode a strong undercurrent of awe.

Word of what had happened in Mereina had spread, where the Black Knight slew a demon on the tournament field. This had mixed with Janel's now-legendary duel with Relos Var, itself often misreported. No one knew if this was a normal Black Knight or *the* Black Knight.

People had started to spread stories, grander with each retelling.

This Black Knight looked well on his way to taking the prize, when a great hue and cry rose from the nearby castle. Someone came running into view wearing the local Markreev's colors. "Fire! Fire! There's a fire at the mill!"

Chaos spread. Brother Qown tried to leap his way back across fires again, but too few existed. He did manage to spy a wagon, parked behind a guard azhock near the stands. People were loading boxes of weapons and armor earmarked for the local Markreev's soldiers.

Brother Qown recognized Dango.

"What are you up to, Ninavis?" Brother Qown asked aloud, even though no one could hear.

The robbery finished swiftly. By the time the guards returned with the happy news that the mill was undamaged, the Markreev's men had been robbed of their martial supplies. The Black Knight made a fast retreat before the tournament finished. And in an impressive display of obfuscation and distraction, his target rode into an azhock and vanished. Arasgon stepped out in his normal black and red. Then the black-skinned smith, whom Brother Qown had first seen in Mereina, started loudly complaining that he too had been robbed.

Everyone agreed it was the best tournament they'd seen in ages.

Brother Qown lost the thieves as they left town, since no one needed torches or lanterns in broad daylight. He saw a few he remembered from Ninavis's party, but he didn't see Dorna, and he didn't see Ninavis herself.

Brother Qown might have thought Dango had joined another bandit clan, returning to a familiar life of crime, if not for Arasgon.

The second time he spotted someone who appeared to be the Black Knight, months later, the circumstances made his stomach turn. An "enterprising" baron had decided Marakori refugees fleeing onto her land could be used to harvest her crops. Whether she paid them was unclear, but Brother Qown suspected not.

She wouldn't have needed whips to motivate them, if they were being paid.

The Black Knight sat astride a steed on the bridge to the baronial manor house after dark. In an echoing, demonic voice, the Black Knight warned if the baron didn't release the Marakori by the next morning, he'd curse her lands with a disaster beyond imagining.

The baron laughed and ordered her soldiers to shoot him.

It didn't go the way the baron had planned, though, as every soldier's bowstrings snapped, and not a single arrow fired.

Then the people hiding in the forest fired back. Their bowstrings didn't snap. More volleys followed that first, softening up the baron's defenses before raiders dispersed throughout the compound, gathering up Marakori.

Brother Qown lost track as the group retreated into the woods, but he hadn't needed to see Dorna to know she'd been there. He knew how her mage-gift worked. He wasn't sure what Dorna would do with the Marakori. But several freed people had demonstrated a skill with the same weaponless fighting style Ninavis practiced, helping in the skirmish.

Brother Qown took diligent notes, but it didn't take long to realize the numbers didn't make sense. He'd originally suspected Ninavis and Dorna had returned to crime, since they both had a predilection for such.

But these activities had involved far greater numbers than could be explained by Ninavis, Sir Baramon, Dorna, and their five or so companions. In the months he'd been observing, he'd already seen closer to several hundred different people, including multiple firebloods, operating across the entire dominion. They seemed . . . organized.

Brother Qown sat back in his chair, exhaling as he reached for tea long since grown cold.

What he was witnessing wasn't some ne'er-do-well bandits with hearts of gold, stealing metal from the rich of Quur to help the oppressed.

He was witnessing the beginning of an organized rebellion.

Following the Black Knight's exploits wasn't Brother Qown's only research project. Several weeks after Sir Oreth had been executed and forty-plus women had ended up simultaneously divorced, a servant brought Brother Qown a box of his favorite chocolate biscuits and a note from Janel.

The note said, *"Thank you for your help researching Quuros war curses. I'm sure it will be invaluable in the future. Also, thank Thurvishar for me as well."*

But of course, Qown hadn't researched Quuros war curses. So he started.

Which *did* require Thurvishar's help.

"How would one go about researching the war magic the Quuros used when they invaded Yor?" he asked Thurvishar when Qown next visited Shadrag Gor.

The D'Lorus Lord Heir had thrown himself into teaching the Hon's wives to read. He was scanning suitable materials when Brother Qown interrupted.

Thurvishar looked up. "Why in all the heavens would you want to know that?"

"Obviously, because it would help Yor." That didn't seem obvious at all, but Brother Qown had a good idea why Janel wanted to know. The weapons unleashed against Yor haunted its land still. Since the Yorans didn't understand what had been done to them, an opportunity existed to gain the duke's trust, gain greater privileges and great access to—well, whatever Janel had come to Yor to do. If someone like Janel—or Brother Qown—presented the duke with information on what had been done, and better yet, how to reverse it . . .

Thurvishar narrowed his eyes and leaned back. "You want to make friends with the Yorans."

"My life depends on being perceived as useful," Brother Qown reminded him. "You do know, don't you? What was done?"

"Oh yes," Thurvishar said. "We unleashed horrors upon these people."

Brother Qown waited.

Thurvishar sighed. "It's not reversible," he said. "The things we did—" He stood up from his chair and walked over to a large book stack. "Here. *Rituals of War* by Ibatan D'Talus. Also . . . *Siege Tactics of the Yoran Invasion* by Sivat Wilavir. Those two will have the most information. But I wouldn't read them just after you've eaten." He set the books down.

Brother Qown blinked at the magician, but he seemed serious.

"Selanol preserve us. How bad was it?"

Thurvishar scowled and looked away. "We should be ashamed. But we aren't. We never are. It is our duty, you see, our destiny. We'll make any excuse that lets us believe we were righteous when we crushed our enemies underfoot."

Brother Qown's mouth felt dry. "Did they deserve it?"

"Define *deserve*." Thurvishar's mouth quirked. "The god-kings Cherthog and Suless were fiends. Cherthog was a power-hungry brute, and Suless—oh, Suless had so much blood on her hands, entire oceans wouldn't wash them clean. Did you know Suless invented the god-king ritual?"

Brother Qown blinked. "What?"

"She invented the process, figured out how to turn a wizard into a god. She was the very first god-king. God-queen, I suppose. The Eight Immortals are much older and didn't come into existence the same way. Even if no one worshipped Argas, as one of the Eight, he'd still exist—because the concept he represents still exists. Same with Thaena and death or Galava and life. The Eight are tied to concepts that give them power. The god-kings, though, require active worship, they require tenyé sacrifices to maintain their power. Without the ritual Suless created, we would have no god-kings, just powerful wizards. She found a way to be more. Then she taught her husband, Cherthog, and her daughter, Caless. Caless taught her lover, Qhuaras—who went on to found what would later become Quur . . ." Thurvishar spread his hands. "The rest is history. Maybe someone else would have figured it out, if Suless the witch-queen hadn't done it first, but she *did* do it first. Think of all the monster races in the world who wouldn't exist if not for Suless. The snake-king Ynis wouldn't have created the thriss. Jorat's Khorsal would never have made centaurs or firebloods. The Daughters of Laaka wouldn't exist. It's a long list. So . . . did Suless 'deserve' to be slain when Quur conquered Yor? Interesting question."

"Even if she did, a lot of Yorans didn't."

"Yes, true." Thurvishar tapped his hands against the table, unhappy and bitter. "There's one spell in there in particular . . . Invented by Henakai Shan about two hundred and fifty years ago, it transforms common rock, igneous or otherwise, into razarras ore, which is . . . deadly. Not even House D'Talus's Red Men know how to work razarras safely anymore.* And it kills every living thing around it. Whole caverns in this dominion can't be used because the ore poisons anyone who comes close. It's not a fast death either. No. When our wizards realized Yorans grew their food in those caves, they cast the curse to break the siege. The poison ruins everything it touches. And it doesn't go away."

Brother Qown felt sick. "Why would—"

He didn't finish the question. He didn't have to. He knew very well why. They did it because they could, because it had seemed like an easy, clever answer to their problems.

He was growing to loathe easy, clever answers to problems.

Brother Qown opened a book. The very first chapter was titled "Suppressing Large Population Centers Using Self-Distributing Lysian Gas." The very first paragraph included a warning about experimenting in areas without adequate ventilation systems. And the very first sentence noted that the summoned magical gas manifested as a pleasant shade of blue.

Brother Qown closed the book, fighting back nausea.

"I told you it would be hard reading," Thurvishar warned.

Brother Qown took several deep breaths. He reminded himself he had, at least on some level, always known Quur

---

* Assuming they ever did. I bet the dreth do, though.

capable of atrocities. After all, one didn't become the largest empire in the world through compassion and a generous spirit. Quur had always crushed its enemies, mercilessly and without hesitation. This was . . . just that. Just another example.

But he had seen this example with his own eyes. And he knew it wouldn't be the worst example he'd find in these books.

"Do you have any more volumes?" he asked instead of fleeing.

Thurvishar frowned at him. "This is dark research, my friend."

"If I'm going to figure out how to cure a curse, I need to understand how the curse works," Qown replied.

"The advanced books are kept locked away in the House D'Lorus archives," Thurvishar admitted, "but since I'm the lord heir, I have the key."

47: THE WITCH-QUEEN

Jorat Dominion, Quuros Empire.
Three days since Kihrin briefly remembered being S'arric

Everyone remained quiet as Qown finished.

"The Academy spends a great deal of time researching—weapons. Spells usable as weapons," Qown finally said. "They've become good at it."

"When I said anyone who would use a weapon like that . . ." Kihrin swallowed and looked over at Janel. "You already knew."

"I already knew," she agreed. "I may hate talk of prophecies, but I will say this: Those prophecies that talk about the Hellwarrior toppling the Quuros empire? Smashing it to pieces? I hope *those* prophecies are true. Quur has earned it."

"Now you sound like Teraeth."

Janel refreshed her coffee. "Am I wrong?"

Kihrin scrubbed his eyes with his hands. He was losing track of what *wrong* meant. Horribly, he found himself agreeing with his brother—with Relos Var rather. Maybe everyone was wrong, and it was a matter of picking the wrong side you found more acceptable. "If the Empire of Quur is as powerful as you say . . . as horrible as you say . . . what chance would anyone have to rebel against them?"*

"Sooner or later, everything falls." Janel and Kihrin stared at each other for a rather long beat, before Janel took a deep breath. "Anyway, I believe it's my turn."

---

* The first mistake most people make is calling it a rebellion. If you do it right, it's just called *being ambitious*.

Janel's Turn. The Ice Demesne, Yor, Quur.

"Bikeinoh, I have a question for you." I leaned over toward the woman while we waited for our turn at the practice yards.

Not all the women had been eager to take up weapons training, but a surprising number had. Even more were eager to learn to read and write and to explore the possibility they might have an aptitude for magic. The D'Lorus Lord Heir had been shocked to discover every single Yoran woman tested displayed a high magical aptitude. He muttered about it being unprecedented. The women laughed and reminded him that they were *Yoran.*

Bikeinoh turned to me. "Yes?"

"Who taught Veixizhau?"

She blinked at me. "What?"

I stared out at the two women who were sparring under Xivan's critical eye. "It's been a hundred years since it was legal to worship Suless. Did Veixizhau learn it from her family? From her mother? Seems like the sort of thing a clan leader wouldn't want to encourage in his own family."

"That must have been what happened."

I raised an eyebrow. "Do you really think that?"

The older woman swallowed and looked to the side. "No, I don't."

I followed her line of sight. She stared at Wyrga, who'd started coming to the training yard to watch the women practice. The old woman had her polar bear cub carried in the crook of one arm while she watched.

"I've been here for almost fifteen years," Bikeinoh said quietly. "She's always had that damn cub. It's never grown a day older than it is right now. Kind of like her."

Wyrga must have felt us staring. She looked back, grinned, and laughed. She was too far away to hear, but I knew her terrible cackle well enough to imagine.

I stood up from the bench. "Thanks. Tell Xivan I wasn't feeling well, okay? I'll be back later."

The woman shrugged. "Sure."

I left to see if I could find a special someone to answer a question.

Senera kept an irregular schedule, but I was in luck. She'd returned.

She answered her door red-eyed with tears streaking her face. Her gray eyes turned flint hard as she regarded me, as if I'd committed an unforgivable sin by witnessing her vulnerability. She walked back to her chair without saying a word, leaving the door open behind her.

Well. I took it as permission to enter.

She sat back down by the fireplace and refilled her tea. Then she watched the fire, her expression blank.

Senera's room turned out to be the same room I'd woken in on that first day. And it contained no more traces of personality than when I'd first seen it.

Senera spent her time and energy in the field.*

Then I saw I'd been mistaken about the traces of personality. Senera had left papers and charcoal pencils on a table, alongside a small doll made from white linen and bleached yarn. The doll appeared colorless except for two silver beads that had been used for the eyes. And the paper . . .

The top paper had been ripped in half, but still showed a young Joratese youth's face. I couldn't say whether she'd captured his likeness, but the boy's eyes shone brilliant and joyful. And I had no reason to think this sinister, except . . .

Except. I remembered the tears on Senera's face when she opened the door, her red eyes. If there had been a tragedy, likely as not Senera had caused it. I tore my gaze away, shuddering.†

"Is there something you want?" Her voice cracked the air.

---

* I'm forced to remind myself she never actually saw my cottage. She must think I actually lived in that sorry little room.

† I don't remember this at all. I would never cry over some Joratese boy.

"Senera, what happened?" I crossed the room to her, but she wouldn't look at me.

"Are you going to make me repeat myself?" she countered.

"I came to ask you a favor, but you seem upset. Do you want to talk?"

Senera turned to me then, and her nostrils flared.

"No, I do not. Now tell me what you want and leave. Or better yet, just leave."

I didn't answer her immediately. I sat there and enjoyed the flames crackling in the fireplace, the scent of hot tea and burning pine needles in the air.

I heard her intake of breath, knew she was about to start yelling at me.

"When is the price too much?" I asked her, looking up.

"That doesn't sound like a favor," she snapped.

"It isn't," I admitted. "But I'm curious when it all becomes too high a price to pay. What marks the line?"

She closed her eyes and muttered a curse under her breath. I'm certain it involved unpleasantries involving my genealogy.

I leaned forward. "How many lives are too many? How many have to die before it's enough?"

She scoffed. "Death is a meaningless term. They go to the Afterlife. They're reborn from the Afterlife and start over. Who cares?"

"Oh no. Did no one tell you? Demons and magic both changed the rules. Souls are only immortal to a point, and past that point, oblivion is real. When Xivan kills someone, they don't go to the Afterlife. When demons eat their victim's souls or, worse, transform those souls into more demons, they don't go to the Land of Peace. The trauma those souls experience is real and, assuming Thaena can rescue them, carries on from one lifetime to the next. Who cares? You do. You just don't want to admit it, because that would mean admitting you're wrong."

She stood up, her face a mask of righteous fury.

"How dare you. Do you have any idea what I went through

when I was a slave? What every slave goes through? And you people give no thought—"

"Any sympathy I might have had for your past vanished when you started wiping out villages and you were willing to gaesh Qown. Willing to gaesh me too, even if that attempt failed."

She closed her mouth mid-protest, eyes bright and angry. Oh, that had cut too close, I suspected, hitting at nerves still raw through guilt.

I dropped my head, turned away. "I'm sorry," I said. "I didn't come here to pick a fight."

"And yet, here you are."

"Here I am. I just . . ." I shook my head. "I'm sorry," I repeated. "These months haven't gone smoothly for me."

"I heard about what happened to Oreth. I'd say I'm sorry, but . . ."

I smiled, looked back at her. "He was an ass."

She nodded. "He was."

"Unfortunately, I also think he was innocent."

Senera sat down again. "You think it was Darzin D'Mon who plotted to kill you? I understand the Hon has forbidden him to come back here."

"No, not him either. I'm sure Darzin is as terrible as they come, but I don't think we should make the same mistake that the duke and his courtiers are making—they're assuming a man *must* have been involved. I think this crime was women only. After all, if Veixizhau meant to sacrifice me to Suless, the men had nothing to gain by helping her."

She studied me. "That's plausible. But may I ask why it matters now? It's over."

"Is it? This wasn't Veixizhau's plan. Someone else was manipulating her. Think how it could've gone: with forty-eight chieftains receiving the heads of their daughters in boxes— accompanied by a note saying they'd been executed for being worshippers of Suless. How well do you think that would have really gone over?"

She exhaled. "I see your point. If I were one of the chieftains—" Senera scoffed. "Kaen's having a hard enough time keeping his dominion united as it is."

"Exactly. That would have been tossing oil into a fire. Now I think I know who's behind this, but I don't want to go to Duke Kaen without proof."

"Ah, so here's the favor. You want me to use the Name of All Things."

"Yes. I want you to use the Name of All Things."

"I make it a point not to use the stone for every damn random question someone asks me. I would never sleep."

"This isn't any damn random question, though. All I want to know is if Wyrga was the one who taught Veixizhau how to worship Suless."

Senera paused, mid-sip. "Wyrga? But why . . ." She trailed off. "Huh."

"Wyrga's more than she seems. She knows things she shouldn't. And I'm not sure why Kaen seems to trust her as much as he does, but I don't think he's being wise."

"What motive would she have? She has no protector if he loses power."

"What motive does she need? This is a woman who tried to feed me foal meat, just because she knew the idea would sicken me. I think she loves to stir up trouble for its own sake." I rolled my eyes. "Honestly, she trains the damn snow hyenas the palace uses for patrols. Weren't those animals sacred to Suless?"

Senera pursed her lips. "That's true. And your question is answered with yes or no. I prefer those."

"So will you?"

"And what do I get for helping you?"

At least that wasn't a no. "Well, for one thing, you get the satisfaction of helping women who are treated as little better than slaves."

She rolled her head back, giving me an amused look. "Oh, so I'd be contributing goodwill and camaraderie? And here I thought I was on the wrong side."

"Wyrga could end up in a lot of trouble?"

Her gaze sharpened. "Hmm. That's more tempting. Relos Var hates Wyrga." She pulled the Name of All Things out from her bodice. "There's very few people he *hates,* you know. She's on an exclusive, short list." She concentrated on the stone, licked her finger, traced a word on the wooden tabletop.

No ink this time. No paper. Those things were performative. She was using the waxed surface of the table to read the result.

"Yes," Senera said. "She did." Then she concentrated again and wrote out another word.

Also *yes.*

"What did you just ask?"

"If Wyrga ordered Veixizhau to dedicate you to Suless."

I frowned. "Xivan said in the old days women would sacrifice their daughters to gain favors from the witch-queen."

"What she was doing isn't technically sacrifice," Senera amended. "*Dedication,* not sacrifice. The women never saw their daughters again, but Suless didn't kill them."

"That's what Xivan suspected. That Suless trained them as her priestesses, as witch-mothers." I leaned over the table. "Senera . . . is it possible that Wyrga is a priestess of Suless? A witch-mother?"

"The Quuros killed all—"

"Is it possible?"

Senera bit her lip. "Let's ask." She concentrated again, wrote out another one-word response. I didn't have to be close to see that it was *no.*

Senera shook her head. "Well, it was an interesting hypothesis. But no, it's more likely that Wyrga's just a nasty old woman who knows enough old stories to lure a bunch of gullible young wives into trouble. She probably did it for a lark so she can crawl back into whatever hole she sleeps in at night and cackle about it to that stupid bear cub of hers."

I startled. Of course. "The bear cub. Ask about the bear cub."

Senera raised an eyebrow. "What about the bear cub?"

"It's just—" I waved a hand. "Someone told me the bear cub doesn't age."

"What?" Senera laughed. "Don't be ridiculous. I'm sure she keeps a cub until she's killed it and then switches it out for another cub."

"Check for me?"

She scoffed. "Okay, now we're getting into silly territory. I don't answer silly questions."

"Just ask the age of Wyrga's bear cub. That's a simple question, right? Harmless? It's not a yes or no, but the answer is precise." I was grasping at straws, but damn it, I knew something about Wyrga was *wrong*, from her knowledge of prophecies to her insistence that she'd known my mother, Irisia.

And the fact that my mother *is* named Irisia. Wyrga had known that information before I had. How many people knew the Goddess of Magic's birth name wasn't Tya?

Senera rolled her eyes as she asked the Name of All Things one more time.

We both watched as she traced a number on the table.

A large number.

"Is that minutes? Months?" I was confused. It couldn't possibly be *years.*

Senera's eyes widened. She ignored me and ran to her desk, pulling out paper and graphite before bringing both back to the table.

She concentrated again and wrote out a single word: *voras.*

That didn't clarify matters. "What does that mean?"

Senera looked exasperated. "I thought Thurvishar was supposed to be educating you lot."

"Don't lump me in with the spurned wives," I snapped.

"Back before the Quuros Empire," Senera explained, "many years before the Quuros Empire, there were four immortal races: the voras, the voramer, the vorfelane, and the vordredd. Each race except for the vorfelane has been forced to give up its immortality in order to keep Vol Karoth imprisoned. The voras were the first; they became *human.*"

"I've never heard of the vorfelane."

"That's because we call them *vané* now." She waved a hand.

"You're missing the point. The cub wasn't born a polar bear. It was born human, or the immortal equivalent of a human. It was born voras." Senera wrote down the large number sequence a second time, this time with charcoal on paper. "Those *are* years."

"Over fourteen thousand?" I said. "How can a polar bear cub possibly be over fourteen thousand years old?"

"It can't. That's why I asked what race the cub was when it was born."

"What's its name? What's its birth name? I don't know what Wyrga calls it, but I'd have to assume she'd lie if I asked."

"I almost can't bring myself to ask."

"Do it, anyway."

Senera concentrated on the artifact in her hand and then wrote out a single word. "If I'm right . . ."

Cherthog.

Cherthog, the Yoran god-king of winter.

We both stared at the word.

Senera said, "Fuck."

After that . . . everything was quiet.

I don't mean to say nothing happened. We continued training. I kept looking for how I might safely pass through the poisoned stone caves to recover the spear. Duke Kaen started asking for my opinion on Joratese strategies, giving me access to his war room and plans. He slowly began testing my loyalty, which wasn't always pleasant.

Veixizhau was hardly forgiven by the other wives, but everyone seemed willing to leave her alone until she gave birth. No one knew what would happen to Veixizhau after the baby was born—it was entirely possible that Duke Kaen would still have her executed for adultery. Because of that impending threat, the other ex-wives overlooked her tantrums.

I avoided her whenever possible.

A week after Senera and I discovered the truth about Wyrga and her "pet," a messenger told me the Hon wanted to see me.

The messenger found me in my room alone. Although Talea

and I continued to be lovers, I firmly insisted on sleeping by myself. I didn't want her or anyone else to realize that my nighttime slumber couldn't be interrupted.

When I arrived at the Hon's private rooms, I saw Senera and Wyrga were also present.

Wyrga was kneeling on the floor. For once, her polar bear cub was nowhere to be seen.

I exhaled. Senera had asked me to wait before going to Duke Kaen about her, and so I had. Apparently, however, Senera had only asked so she might deliver the news herself.

The question was: Just how much had she told him? Had she told him the cub was Cherthog? Had she told him who that meant Wyrga must be? Not a witch-mother, no. The Name of All Things had been right when it had told us she wasn't one of Suless's chosen daughters. No, she was much worse.

Wyrga was Suless herself.

"Close the doors behind you."

Senera looked tense, nearly standing at attention, looking straight ahead, eyes unfocused. I had the feeling she'd been questioned intensely before I entered. Next to her, on the table before the Hon, sat the Name of All Things.

Several pieces of crumpled parchment had been thrown to the floor.

"Thank you for joining us, Janel."

I bowed to the Hon. "Of course, Your Grace. How may I be of service?"

"I think you know."

I straightened and tried to keep my face blank.

I pursed my lips for a moment. "I'm sorry, Your Grace, but I don't wish to assume on this matter. It concerns Wyrga?"

The Hon's expression didn't change. His ice-colored eyes bored into mine. Angry. I had never seen him so angry.

"Yes," he said. "Senera was kind enough to look into the situation that ended with you on the ice. She tells me I have Wyrga to thank. Indeed, I have Wyrga to thank for convincing my wives to rekindle the worship of Suless as well." He walked out from behind the desk, and as he passed the old woman, he kicked her in the stomach.

She cried out and rolled up into a ball, holding her midriff.

I frowned. Had I been wrong? If she really was Suless, wouldn't she fight this? Wouldn't she lash out?

"If you hadn't come to my wives' defense, her plan would never have been discovered. Or discovered too late. I'd probably be facing open rebellion."

"Then I'm even more glad I was there, Your Grace." I tried to smile at him, but I couldn't shake my dread. I'd seen his temper.

Senera looked worried.

No. Senera looked *scared*.

"Wyrga has been in my family's service for many years," Kaen said as he began to pace. The mountains shone behind him like a crown of glory, the sun reflecting off perfect blue-white peaks. "I have been warned many times not to trust her, but I have always dismissed those warnings because she has served us so well. Isn't that right, Wyrga?"

The old woman groveled. "Yes, my lord. Yes, I have always served you. I have always done whatever you've asked of me."

"You're gaeshed, Wyrga," Kaen said, hand around a necklace at his throat. "What choice do you have?"

"None, my lord."

"Gaeshed? But—" I realized my mouth had dropped open. If Suless was gaeshed, that explained a great deal. I just hadn't realized it was possible to gaesh a god-king.

"Do you know who the father of Veixizhau's child is?" Duke Kaen asked me.

"I—" I hadn't expected to be asked that. "No, I don't."

"My son. Veixizhau's baby will be my grandchild."

I blinked. "Really?"

"Yes, really," Duke Kaen snapped. "Wyrga's idea, of course. She convinced Veixizhau to seduce my son, Exidhar, fed the woman some drivel about being able to change my son's child into *my* child. Lies. Wyrga fully intended to reveal what

Veixizhau had done. I'd have killed my philandering wife and Exidhar for that, thus executing both my son and grandchild. Now that was an act fit to feed a goddess of betrayal, wasn't it, Wyrga? *Wasn't it?*"

Wyrga cried out, "Yes, my lord!"

I met Senera's eyes. In that moment, I realized Kaen knew exactly who Wyrga really was.

He already *knew* Wyrga was Suless. He'd always known.

He sat down on the table's edge, shaking his head. "Thank you, Wyrga. It's always best when you tell the truth." He looked . . . hurt. Disappointed. And still furiously angry. "But I hope you realize you will have to be punished."

"My Hon," Senera began. "I must advise caution—"

"I will handle this myself, sorceress. You've done your job. You are, in fact, free to leave."

Senera reached down and picked up the Name of All Things, tucked the stone into her bodice. "Your Grace, please—" But she didn't finish the sentence. Leaving whatever she might have said unspoken, Senera gave me a sympathetic look and walked out the door.

I felt rather abandoned, to be honest.

As soon as the door slammed shut, Azhen Kaen turned to Wyrga and said, "Pluck out your eyes."

I wasn't certain if Wyrga gasped or if I had. Maybe both.

I hadn't truly understood how evil gaeshe were until then. And no matter how I felt about Wyrga, I couldn't stand by while he forced her to do this.

"No!" I shouted, but her hand moved to her face.

I reached for her, grabbed her wrist, but Wyrga shoved me away.

"No," Kaen said as he reached down and grabbed me by my laevos. "You won't stop this."

"Don't *do this* and then be surprised when she plots against you and your family. What do you expect? Loyalty? Duty? You might have gained loyalty if you had freed her!"

"She has no honor or loyalty. She's evil, a force of chaos,

and I should have killed her years ago." He pulled me back against the desk, and I didn't fight him that time. He released my hair even as I heard Wyrga scream. I knew when I turned back, I'd see blood streaming down the old woman's face.

It didn't matter that Wyrga had tried to kill me or that she was thoroughly horrible. She was a slave, and she was helpless. I had to do *something*. I knew better than to attack Duke Kaen, so what could I do? What options did I have? What could I possibly use as leverage?

I did have something. One thing that Kaen evidently valued. I pulled my dagger from my belt and set the edge against the corner of my eye. "Order her to stop, Your Grace, or we'll both lose our eyes."

Azhen Kaen turned back to me, eyes wide with surprise. "You—what?"

I took a deep breath, ground my teeth together, and pushed the edge in.*

The sharp dagger ensured I didn't register the result as pain right away. Cold and wet and unpleasant, a sharp icy claw reaching right through my skull. Something wet and oozing started sliding down my cheek.

I'm told I also set the drapes on fire. And the table.

"Wyrga, ignore your last order! You stupid fool!"

That last part was directed at me.

Then pain spiked through my whole skull and I screamed, folding up into a tight ball. "Help her!" Azhen Kaen ordered Wyrga.

Help is an open-ended command, but Wyrga did something. Everything turned black, and nothing hurt.

When I woke, I found myself in a guest room at the top of the pyramid, the sort with beautiful mountainside views. Perhaps most importantly, I could see from both eyes. I checked. Both were present and accounted for, uninjured.

---

* Talk about being dramatic.

I sat up from the bed, noted I remained dressed, and walked over to the slanted crystal window. I watched the storm-shrouded mountains, noting that someone had put me in a southern-facing room looking out toward Jorat. I couldn't see my adopted homeland from here, but I knew the direction. And as I watched, I saw Aeyan'arric sporting along a ridgeline, a giant sparkling diamond of white death.

"You're going to have to learn magic, you know."

I winced as I turned to face Wyrga—the witch-queen Suless, although for obvious reasons, I couldn't call her such. She stood at the doorway with her polar bear cub—with Cherthog—tucked under her arm. The flesh around her empty left socket looked puffy and red.

So Kaen hadn't let her heal the injury. He at least hadn't let her finish the job either, while I lay unconscious.

"I'm sorry," I said. "I didn't think he'd do that."

The old hag grinned her toothful smile and waddled over in my direction. "Don't let it bother you any. I barely notice it myself. See?" She raised her hand and I saw she held her other eye. The orb rotated in her fingers, a brown cat's eye pointing at me.

"Oh Eight." I tasted bile and turned away, even as she started laughing.

"He told me to pluck my eyes out. He never said anything about not being able to still use them."

"Of course. What was I thinking?" I swallowed down the awful taste in my mouth and wished for water. A sparkling white flash caught my eye as the ice dragon dove down below the cloud line. She twisted herself around to fill up the snow hollow she used as bedding. *At least that's a beautiful monster,* I thought.

But Suless was a monster too. I hadn't moved to her defense because I thought her a wonderful person, I'd done it because I didn't think anyone deserved such treatment.

In a way, I was grateful. Suless had given me clarity. Because when Kaen had given her that terrible command, I'd known for certain I could never serve Azhen Kaen, no matter what rewards he offered. I'd been tempted, but a man who used his power as he had with Wyrga could never be trusted.*

What you protect is what you rule. Kaen was thorra—a bully, someone who used his strength to dominate. Any vows I'd made to him melted in my heart and then turned to ash.

"You're going to have to learn magic if you want to take Aeyan'arric down, you know. Sword skill alone can't kill a dragon, no matter how good you are; you'll never be good enough. Magic, on the other hand, might just keep you alive for long enough. Maybe. If you're lucky."

"I don't know what you mean." My heart hammered drumbeat fast. What questions had the Hon asked Senera? What did they know? How did Wyrga know about my mission? If the Hon realized my goal was to steal the spear Khoreval and use it to slay the dragon he loved sending into Jorat . . .

It wouldn't go well for me.

She set her dismembered eye on the nightstand. "I don't want to lose this. The cub will start chewing on it, and wouldn't that be awful." The old woman turned back to me, pointing at me with a skeletal finger. "Veixizhau dedicated you to Suless. That *means* something. You can't hide yourself from Suless now. She knows all your secrets."

I knew why she spoke of herself in the third person. Kaen had likely forbidden her from revealing her identity. Of course, that didn't change how troubling her words were.

Assuming they were true.

"You know you would be good at magic. Do you think Tya would have a child who didn't have the gift? She breathed it into you from your birth, stamped it into your bones, set it spiraling into your blood. Yet you've done everything but study it. Swordplay? Yes. Strategy? Oh please. Tactics. Yes,

---

* Honestly, I'm with Janel on this one. Object lessons are one thing, but what Kaen did was just unnecessary.

tactics. Your father's gifts. But not your mother's. You reject those."*

"Are you so sure?" I said. "I haven't been here that long."

"I think all you have to do is ask." The way she looked at me emphasized her dowager's hump, her spine's curve. "And your mother would be only too glad to teach you." She reached out toward me with a twisted hand and touched my arm with the lightest sweep. "But she isn't half as good a teacher as I am."

"Any help you'd offer would come poisoned. I'm not the fool Veixizhau was."

Wyrga cackled, like the laughter of her hyenas. "Can you blame me? The abused dog snaps at her keepers. You know what it's like to rebel against your jailer, don't you? Are you so fond of Xaltorath?"

I winced and looked away. Wyrga knew far too much about me. Maybe what she'd said about being "dedicated" had some truth to it. If so, I had even more reason to curse Veixizhau. She had laid my secrets bare to a monster.

Wyrga grinned once more. "Where was your mother when you needed her?"

"Shut up."

"That's why you deny her, why you deny her gifts. She had nothing to give you when you needed her protection, and so now you would deny her the satisfaction of knowing any talent of yours stems from her."

A shuddering exhale escaped me. The fact Wyrga might be right galled me. My father hadn't known I existed, but my mother had no such excuses. Worse, in my mother's eyes, I had been created as nothing more than a tool, not born from love or lust or even accident but purely to fulfill some idiotic prophecy.

Tools can be traded. Tools can be discarded. Tools can be broken.

"I had a daughter once," Wyrga said. "She felt very much

---

* How long had Janel known who Tya was by this point? Oh right, Suless was just messing with her.

the same about me, but in trying to rebel against me, she became me.* Isn't that funny?"

"You're acting sane today. Please tell me what the duke did to you isn't responsible for this pleasant change."

She winked at me. "Don't worry, dearie. It won't last."

I didn't find that reassuring.

She spider-walked her fingers over the crystal wall. Black lines branched out to cover the glass. Writing, but nothing I knew how to read.

"What does it take," I said, "to become a god?"

"Oh, it's not so hard." The spidery glyphs branched out, flowed into passages. The fact I couldn't understand them didn't stop me from feeling like I should. "At least, it wouldn't be hard for you."

"I don't want to be a god," I said.

"Everyone wants to be a god," she retorted, her voice hot. "The reason my 'master' hasn't asked is because he doesn't realize I know how. He didn't gaesh me. His grandfather didn't even gaesh me. You know who did? Cherthog."

I looked over at her, eyes wide. "What?"

Her chuckle turned nasty. "He'd been one of my students. Never liked him. It was just after Vol Karoth killed the rest of the Eight. After I made my breakthrough, Cherthog turned up on my doorstep with this little blue rock, about this big." She held thumb and forefinger apart to demonstrate. "The Stone of Shackles. And that was that." She held up the bear cub with her other arm. "Isn't that right? Who's been a bad boy? Was it you? Yes, it was you!"

She saw me staring at the cub, must have seen the question in my eyes. "You know you can't be too specific with a gaesh command or you'll kill the person, and if you're too vague, you leave loopholes. Cherthog wanted to be hidden from the Quuros. And Suless did that for him, didn't she?" The old crone waved a hand. "To Hell with them all. None of them

---

* Caless? God-queen of lust and whores? Not seeing the resemblance, personally.

appreciate me.* Kaen's no better than Cherthog. He'd make himself a god if he thought he could."

"Kaen hates the gods. He thinks it's his destiny to find Urthaenriel and kill the Eight Immortals with it, remember?"

She continued weaving her words across the wall's clear surface. "Because he thinks they aren't doing their job. Which is a fine way of saying he'd do a better job. When people pull down their idols, they never hesitate to put themselves on those same pedestals."

I started to feel dizzy, looking at the unfurling words . . . "What—what are you doing?"

No cackle this time, but a deep, throaty chuckle, still animal, still hyena-like. She smiled at me like I was a cherished niece. Her remaining brown cat's eye flashed pale ice blue. "Kaen told me to help you, my dear. It was a little vague . . . There was a prophecy about four fathers, you know. You might have heard it. Maybe you haven't. But there's another one about four mothers. A bit of trap, that. Because they don't mean a mother for each of you cute little Hellwarriors, no. Four mothers just for you." She patted her bosom. "I'm the fourth."

"Oh, I don't think so," I said. My protest wasn't as strong as I would have liked.

"Ah, don't worry, little lion. I *am* going to help you. I'm going to give you so much help you won't be able to stand it."

The script on the windows rearranged itself, transformed, and suddenly I could read it.

But it wasn't Guarem.† The words hadn't changed, only my own perception.

Also, I don't remember what I read. I know I read . . . something.

Then the world went black, and this time—

This time I didn't wake up in the Afterlife at all.

---

* That means she'd been gaeshed for thousands of years. I'm almost sympathetic. Almost.

† Voral, you think? Or some other script. I should really find out.

The world looked white, and the sky looked bright blue. Not the sky's normal teal color but Kazivar pottery glaze or House D'Mon blue.

I stood at the crystal pyramid's summit in the mountains, which glowed so brightly from reflected sunlight I couldn't look down without blinding myself. Skulls edged the top of the truncated pyramid, their eyes glowing with ghostly blue light. The air smelled of glacial ice and pine and, faintly, fresh blood and desiccated flesh.

I turned around and saw Suless.

She was still an old woman; I knew she could've been young if she'd wanted. I knew too that we existed in a place of her own invention, and she could've taken on any appearance. Her hair was white fur and her skin made the snow seem dark. She dressed in a style unfamiliar to me, archaic and alien. Yet she still looked like an old woman, wrinkled and sagging, her eyes the same ice blue as the white hyenas who sat at her feet. The hyenas paid no attention to me, more interested in gnawing on skulls.

"This world is controlled by power and will," she said in a voice both majestic and deep. The hyenas perked up and looked at me for the first time, then went back to gazing at their queen.

"Wyrga—" I stopped myself. "Suless. Whatever you're doing—"

"Child." She rose from her crystal-and-diamond throne. As she did, I realized the throne sat off center. There had been a second throne up on this plateau once, now broken or removed— Cherthog's, I assumed. "You're on a quest, and it is a quest you cannot complete without help. If you will be so stubborn as to refuse the aid of your other mothers, then I'll force my help upon you."

I breathed deeply, ignored the way the cold air lanced through my lungs like knives. "I'm tired of being a piece in other people's games."

She walked over to me. Unnervingly, I stood taller than she did. Her pale blue cat eyes met mine. "So am I. But I watch and wait, and I act a bit touched in the head." She smiled. "It's not always an act, I admit. But they underestimate me. Oh, they've always underestimated us, have they not? We have behaved for so long. Played the good servants, the obedient slaves. It wins us no prizes, but they do think we're beaten. Sooner or later, they let down their guard." She reached out and grasped my hand. "Let's see what we can do about that, shall we? Not long now, before all slaves are freed."

"The prophecies?"

"Oh yes. Let's be ready, for we'll have little warning when the time comes." And before I could dodge or pull my hand from her grasp, she grabbed my arm, drew me to her, and set her thumb against the center of my forehead.

My vision shifted, and I saw the universe differently. Suless didn't stop there, though. I felt her slip into my mind, silken and cold and so very painful as she began to change contents. Rearrange thoughts.*

Moving down old roads, long forgotten . . .

I'm standing just off from the main stage, waiting to go on, my nerves so taut I feel like they're about to start making their own noise.

I look across the room and see A'val, and I smile at her even as I curse that she's talked me into doing this. I never intended to go into politics . . . yet here I am.

"C'indrol, it's time."† She motions to me, and then I'm walking in front of the Assembly to give my first speech . . .

I remember when the demons first come, and I remember screaming when they kill my sister and then wear her body like a skin while they chase down my family. I remember the

---

* *This* is a major problem. Suless doesn't sink her claws into someone without leaving wounds.

† I tried to find out any information on this C'indrol, to see if I could verify this. That's when I found out a really interesting little feature of the Name of All Things: it can't see back before its own creation. I must therefore assume C'indrol died before the Cornerstones were created.

pain and the terror. I escape, but I never forgive myself for living, when they didn't . . .

An impossibly bright light flashes through my apartment windows. I run to the door leading upstairs to our rooftop garden. I manage to step through the door when the blast wave's edge hits. Then I remember nothing . . .

I ride on the back of a wagon while we travel down an old dirt road through an impossibly dry, hot desert. I shift my veil around my neck to catch the sweat while I practice chords on my father's harp. One day, I hope to buy my own harp . . .

I'm crying as Valathea takes me into her arms, and the vané woman's lips are soft. I still know this is goodbye. Worse than goodbye, because there's nothing I can do to convince Valathea to stay. To stay living. To make the pain of existing bearable for just a bit longer. She puts her hand on my swollen belly and whispers, "Promise me you'll teach him to play," just before she begins the ritual that might as well be suicide.

I set down the harp once called Valathea on the edge of ruined streets, not liking the way these ruins feel familiar, the way I feel like I've been here before. Worse, I know I'm being followed. I've felt eyes on me for days now. I don't think it will be long before the morgage make themselves known. But I've come here for a reason, and that reason is to negotiate for the lives of my people. I refuse to believe the only path to victory lives on a sword's edge.

There must be another way.

Up ahead I see a large palace, the least ruined structure in the whole dead damn city. Surely if the morgage leaders are anywhere, they will be there. I lift the harp again, muttering that Valathea might have at least waited until we'd left before cursing herself, and head in that direction . . .

Then I remember darkness and hunger and a great, unending

void. I remember a voice, screaming. I remember pain, not my own, but felt as keenly.

I blinked my eyes, waking. I was still on the mountain, still in Suless's dream world. The goddess of witchcraft and betrayal still held me.

"What was—"

"Did you think you'd forgotten the lives you've lived before? That such knowledge is lost? What interesting lives you have led, my dear. I can see why Tya picked you."

I backed away from her. "I don't . . ." I shuddered. "I saw fleeting images. They didn't mean anything."

"Just as well." She wiped her hands against each other. "We're done here for now, anyway."

"What did you do to me?"

"Left road marks." Her smile seemed every bit as feral as I remembered from the normal world. "A foundation for you to build upon. It's much easier when you're a baby, but it can work to some extent on anyone who hasn't finished their neural development. You, for example. And you didn't need much help—either Tya or Xaltorath must have beaten me to the most important changes."

I pulled myself upright. My head hurt; I wanted to throw up. "I don't believe I'll thank you."

Suless grinned and the hyenas next to her did as well, tongues lolling.

"No, I wouldn't expect you to thank me at all. I'm not doing this to help you, but you already know that. I just want to see the look on Kaen's face when you kill his dragon and grab hold of every prize he thinks should be his. When you—oh yes—*betray* him. Oh, what joy."

"Fine. That part I'll be happy to oblige."

She waved her arms, and I woke back in my room.

48: Revelations

Jorat Dominion, Quuros Empire.
Three days since a witch-hunter with the ridiculous
name of Piety didn't return to the Capital City

Everyone stared at Janel.

She sat back and drank her coffee, looking embarrassed.

"Oh, foal, you—" Dorna gave her a look of deep concern. "You didn't really cut out one of your eyes, did you?"

Star nodded slowly in approval. "Not bad."

Janel cleared her throat and looked away.

Qown's Turn. The Ice Demesne, Yor, Quur.

Sir Baramon ended up giving the whole scheme away.

Brother Qown knew Sir Baramon hadn't meant to, but someone was bound to slip up. Over time, Qown had figured out the times and places where he could count on people to be indiscreet, to gossip, to whisper. He lurked invisible in rooms where people knew beyond all doubt they were alone, and people who knew they were alone sometimes let down their guard.

And in Sir Baramon's case? Well, Sir Baramon liked his pillow talk.

One evening, Brother Qown checked in with the knight to find Sir Baramon energetically enjoying Dango's company, much to Qown's embarrassment. Qown left for long enough to check on his normal targets and returned later to find the two men finished with the sex, but not with the intimacy. While the two men cuddled together under blankets next to a burning fire, they talked.

That part, he stayed to watch.

"Tomorrow's going to be rough," Sir Baramon said as he rested his head against the other man's shoulder.

Dango smiled and grazed his hand against the knight's arm. "Ah, now don't be like that, love. Tomorrow's going to be dangerous, but no more so than the dozen times we've done this before."

Baramon sat up, letting Dango's hand slip away. "I liked it better when we didn't have to split up. And when one of us could ride in pretending to be the Black Knight without anyone making a fuss. I can't even do it anymore. And it used to be my real job! All you have to do to make a noble faint these days is mention the Black Knight."

"That's their doing, not ours."

"Do you know I found an altar to the Black Knight set up two villages back? They're claiming the Black Knight is the Nameless Lord."

Brother Qown blinked. The Joratese called the eighth of the Eight Immortals the Nameless Lord. Their name, or lack of a name, for Selanol, Qown's own god.*

"What do you expect? The Black Knight is answering their prayers. These days, you can't ride through a town without seeing a word or two about the Black Knight scrawled somewhere. There's some good songs making the rounds too."

"If we don't split up—"

"Janel said—" And Dango stopped himself.

"How do we know Janel Danorak said *anything*?" Sir Baramon said. "The last I saw Janel Danorak, she lay dead on the tournament floor in Atrine. Talaras would bite my fingers off to hear me talk this way, but we only have Arasgon's word she survived. And now we're supposed to believe he's talking to her every night?"

---

* Huh. You know, since worship often does generate tenyé, I wonder where it's going in this case. After all, it can't be going to Kihrin . . .

"Bary!" Dango's voice was a low warning scold. "Only the firebloods are supposed to talk about this!"

For a long time, Sir Baramon didn't say anything, then he shook his head. "Right. Right. Of course." He smiled. "There's writing about her too on the walls. Warms my heart to see it. Even if it's ridiculous to think she'll come back and save us."

Dango laughed and hugged him. "Don't you see? She's doing that very thing right now. We're her hands and her arms and her sword. We're saving Jorat *for* her."

Sir Baramon tried to smile, but it came at an effort. "What would I do without you?"

Dango pulled Sir Baramon to him. "Be miserable, probably—"

Brother Qown pulled himself away from the divination and sat there for a moment, exhaling, thinking about what he'd heard.

Janel had been using the firebloods to relay instructions and information, knowing no Yoran or western Quuros understood their speech.* She had figured out how to pass notes to her people in Jorat and had been feeding them detailed information on Yoran strengths, plans, and numbers ever since. Everyone knew she couldn't be involved; she'd never left Yor.

Janel Danorak had been controlling the rebellion in Jorat this entire time.

"So," Relos Var said, "find out anything interesting?"

Brother Qown jumped in his chair and sat there for a second, feeling stupid and scared and caught with his hand in the sweet jar. Relos Var sat at the table. The wizard dressed in traveling clothes that would have been inappropriate for the weather here—but of course, he'd used a gate. Var had also brought a late dinner—sag flatbread, vegetable-studded saffron rice, mushroom-stuffed peppers, and a deep red stewed eggplant dish, swimming in oil and spices.

---

* *Or* suspected they were capable of spellcasting. How many firebloods are sorcerers? I wonder.

Then Qown realized he'd been asked a question, and this time he did feel the pain of forced compliance kicking in. He had to answer.

"Yes," Qown gasped out, grabbing the table's edge.

"Oh good," Relos Var said, smiling at the young priest. "Come have supper, and tell me all about it."

Qown felt as if he were walking to his execution as he sat at the table and helped himself to the food. Eamithonian food. Probably made by Loma back at the monastery. Loma never used enough cardamom but still made a delicious stew.

Qown blinked and pulled himself back to the present. "I'm sorry, I didn't . . . you surprised me."

"I'm sorry. We've all been so busy these days." Relos Var ate a stuffed mushroom. "You know, Loma never uses enough cardamom."

"That's what I've always said. I think he's afraid he's wasting it because it's so expensive."

Relos Var waved a piece of sag bread. "That attitude just proves he's clinging to a false notion of material importance." Then he paused and made a face. "Sorry, Father Zajhera would have said that."

"It's fine." It wasn't fine, and nothing would ever be fine. Qown concentrated on eating. He ate without tasting the terrific meal, only able to think about how he'd have to talk before the end of it.

"It must be bad. Look at you. You're shaking."

Qown pushed away his food.

"Tell me," Relos Var said.

"Janel's found a way to communicate with Arasgon while she sleeps. He's then talking to other firebloods and giving them orders and information, which they pass along to human resistance groups—either by gate or by running. Janel's been organizing rebels, interfering with your plans to undermine Duke Xun's authority in Jorat. She's still undermining his authority, mind you, but so it benefits her, not Duke Kaen."

"How? The Joratese must think she'd dead."

"Oh no. Ask your average Joratese and they'll tell you Janel didn't die in your duel. She ascended, or she tricked you and escaped, or Khored chose her to be his champion to save Jorat. How do you kill a legend? We've never been able to spy on her people passing plans, because her human followers aren't the ones disseminating the plans. Janel's certainly told them about Worldhearth and the Name of All Things. They know they're being watched. But since every Joratese grows up understanding firebloods, *they* can relay orders openly. I haven't figured out what they're doing about the Marakori yet, but they must have figured something out . . ."

"Wait, Marakori? How are they involved?"

"They're being recruited in massive numbers. Pulling the same trick Duke Kaen does with his soldiers and disguising themselves as Joratese. So many villages were left deserted by the Lonezh Hellmarch that they're just blending into the countryside, taking over farms. And training. And when the rebellion has seeded enough of these people into a banner, Janel's people Censure the local ruler and put one of their own people in charge. Enough banners turn, and they can take over a canton . . ." Qown shook his head. "I know Kaen wanted to put Jorat in so much danger that it would be obvious to everyone that Duke Xun can't protect his people, but Janel's taking the opposite approach. Starting small and working her way up."

Relos Var leaned back in his chair. "Janel? Our Janel is doing this?"

Qown winced. "Yes, sir. She's been directing the Black Knights since the beginning."

Relos Var looked surprised and then began laughing.

Brother Qown just stared. He looked around to see if someone else had slipped into the room or if a joke involving a morgage, a vané, and a high lord had appeared above his head.

"Oh, Qown." Relos Var slapped his hand down on the table. "That is amazing. I couldn't be prouder." He raised his hand again, pointed with a single finger. "I give you permission to lie to Kaen. Don't breathe a word of this to him. Falsify your next reports to him. Don't tell him what's going on."

Qown blinked and stared harder. "What?"

Var smiled at Qown. "My boy, would I have invested the years I did into Janel Danorak if I had no plans for her?" Without waiting for Qown to answer, he continued, "Now I admit, when she challenged me back in Atrine, I thought she'd made a fatal error. And she's been so . . . cooperative . . . since coming here, I thought she'd just given up. I should have known better. When has Janel ever given up on anything? Delightful!"

Qown felt numb. The pain of betraying Janel felt bad enough, but he had expected Var to be upset, angry. Happy? Pleased? He didn't know what to do with Var's satisfaction. "I don't understand."

Var leaned forward. "If you want to make certain you'll win a horse race, bet on *all* the horses. I have pushed Kaen into uniting Yor and Jorat, because we'll need that strength soon. But Janel has, right under my nose, taken important steps to unite Jorat and *Marakor*—a better result I hadn't pursued because I hadn't thought it practical. Or even possible."

"Quur won't tolerate that . . . as soon as Duke Xun asks for aid, the troops will come in."

"Except Duke Xun won't admit there's a problem. That's admitting weakness," Relos reminded him. "Admitting weakness terrifies our dear Joratese duke. And since Kaen has taken steps to keep most of the Royal Houses from making too much fuss about disturbances in Jorat, Janel's rebels benefit there too. In fact, there's a good chance that, by the time the High Council realizes there is a problem in Jorat, it will be too late, and when they do—" He chuckled. "Oh, I can just imagine the look on High General Milligreest's face when he realizes who he's fighting. How delightful to find my wild filly isn't out of the race yet."

"I thought you'd be more upset," Qown admitted.

"Kaen will be furious. He'll order her execution, guaranteed." The wizard looked rueful and sighed. "Do what you can to help her, Qown. Try not to put yourself at risk, but I think we're approaching a time when I will have to decide if I want to keep saving that man from his own bad decisions."

"You have a plan, don't you? A plan for how you're going to save the world?"

Relos Var stopped smiling. "Yes, I do."

Qown's throat felt tight as he wrestled with emotions he couldn't name, let alone control. "I'll see what I can do to help her. She's, uh . . ." He cleared his throat. "She's trying to learn magic."

"I suppose if she must. It won't do her much good when we track down Urthaenriel, but it will help her in the meantime. I'd rather she focused on her lessons with Xivan."

"Urthaenriel?" Qown sat up. "You're looking for Urthaenriel?" He'd naturally heard of the Ruin of Kings, the fabled magical sword of the Quuros emperors, but he'd assumed it was permanently lost—or decorating the vané king's wall.

"Yes," Relos Var said. "And if it were any other sword, I could just ask the Name of All Things to tell me its location. Which is a pity, because we'll need it soon."

"Why?"

Relos Var laughed in surprise as he stood. "Because its other name is Godslayer, dear boy. And we are, after all, going to kill gods."

49: WINTER TRIALS

Jorat Dominion, Quuros Empire.
Three days since Thurvishar pedantically corrected himself

Janel chuckled. "No, don't be so hard on Baramon, Qown. He wasn't the person who revealed our plans."

Ninavis sniffed and rolled her eyes.

"He wasn't?" Qown looked confused. "But he's the reason I found out what you were doing."

"Yes," Janel agreed, "but Relos Var didn't want you to say anything, remember? No, someone else gave up the game, I'm afraid."

"Who?" Kihrin asked.

Janel reached for her drink. "Oh, that would be me."

Janel's Turn. The Ice Demesne, Yor, Quur.

Suless's eyes turn blue when she casts spells. Not every spell, mind you. Just the enchantments, just the moments when she's playing with someone's mind. It is as though in those precious seconds the old woman named Wyrga cannot help but show the goddess who lives underneath. I'd learned to notice the telltale clues, but given no one else seemed to have, I found myself wondering if I could only see the signs because of what Suless had done to me.

Suless proved good at teaching, but I hated the lessons. With each one, a little more witch-queen seeped into my soul, an infection taking over my mind. So I tried, as much as possible, to learn elsewhere. I studied books, tutored with Qown, and even sat in on Thurvishar's lessons to the Spurned, as Kaen's rejected wives began calling themselves. They deserved their pride. Since they'd begun studying under Xivan, her relentless training had turned them from a gaggle of bored, pampered prisoners into a proper fighting force.

The Yoran men were . . . incredulous. Quite unable to understand or believe how these women—who had just a short few years earlier been nothing more than beautiful furniture—exceeded them for speed, strength, and ferocity. They didn't know about the spells the women had developed to increase their physical prowess to supernatural levels.

The stories I'd told Talea about my own strength had been the inspiration. She'd gone to Bikeinoh, who had figured out how to make the spells work. Then Bikeinoh taught any other woman who could learn.

Most of them, as it happened.

However, no man suggested putting the Spurned into the field. The women became a luck charm, an accessory for the Hon to wear while receiving guests, much like myself. Women warriors both scandalized and delighted visiting royals. Duke Kaen had special armor made for the women, which accentuated their femininity: still no more practical for surviving freezing cold than the old gowns had been. Useless for protecting against sword blows too, since it showed a great deal of cleavage and leg. Still, the stories spread. Maybe it did some good, when more distant Yoran villages heard rumors of the Hon's fighting women.

Maybe.

I learned right alongside them. Thurvishar D'Lorus turned out to be an excellent teacher, although his insight into exactly what he needed to say or do to help me comprehend a spell occasionally unnerved me. He'd turn the book in my hands, say something, point out a flaw in my approach, and it would trigger some great breakthrough in my understanding.

Azhen Kaen grew more and more impatient and temperamental. He had believed Jorat would be an easy victory, and it had turned into a quagmire. Aeyan'arric began attacking more, and more villages emptied before she arrived. "Priests" of the Black Knight—dedicated to the Nameless Lord—began spreading the air sigil, rendering the Lysian gas Senera had used against Mereina obsolete. Senera began encountering Joratese using talismans to shield against magic. Kaen's inability—more so, Relos Var's inability—to track down the rebel leaders causing so many problems rubbed the duke's temper raw. He snapped and bit at everyone around him.

Kaen did not stop sending Aeyan'arric into Jorat.

For several years after I first vowed my loyalty to Duke Azhen Kaen, he tested me. I hated these trials, but he never asked me to do anything too objectionable; I never traveled into Jorat with Senera, for example. He made me a symbol of his future rule—a Joratese taking orders from a Yoran—his promise of things to come for anyone who doubted their duke. I delivered messages to the clan houses, just to be seen. I wore Kaen's rings in my hair and Relos Var's jewels at the neck of a red cloak far too thin to protect anyone else from the cold. The Yoran nobles and courtiers took to calling me Dyono Tomai, or the Red Knight, and I was never quite sure if they meant it as a compliment. I suspected not.

Then came the day when Duke Kaen asked me to do something a little more serious than running errands.

"I want you to clear out the prison," the duke told me over a game of Zaibur. "Xivan doesn't want to take the time, but it's grown too crowded."

I paused and cocked my head. "You want me to release the prisoners?" I hoped I had misunderstood what he was asking.

He snorted. "I want you to execute them."

I remember the moment quite well. The scent of burning wood from the nearby fireplace mixed with the odor of spiced butter tea from the tray next to us. The mage-light lamps cast a yellow glow over us, sparkled against the diamonds in his thick white beard. I stared at him, and he smiled.

Azhen Kaen knew exactly what he was asking me to do. He

was escalating his tests. Would I kill for him? Not just fight for him, but put someone to death just because he asked it?

I bowed my head as I moved a game piece. "Do you wish me to make an example?"

"No. Dead will do just fine. I'll order some men to assist you as you require."

Which meant he'd order some of his soldiers to make sure I went through with it and then report back to him. After all, what good was a test if he didn't have a way to verify the score?

I pinned his god-king piece. "And that's game."

He scowled at the board. "So it is."

The next day, I traveled down to the prison level—still quite a way up from the Spring Caves under the palace—and realized just how bad the test would be.

Unlike Jorat, Yor does have prisons. Or at least the Ice Demesne has a dungeon. It was as dreary and miserable as anything I've encountered outside the Afterlife itself. Despite Kaen's orders, his dungeon didn't need emptying, because he never left prisoners alive for long enough to overfill its cells. This wasn't about executing prisoners. This was about seeing if *I* would execute prisoners.

I'm no stranger to death, but slaying someone in battle and killing someone who is weaponless, bound, and helpless are very different.

The condemned were political dissidents who had been too outspoken against the duke's rule or who had moved against him in some fashion. I had no idea if they'd received a trial, but I suspected not. The dozen men and women all appeared to be Yoran, dressed in the clothing they'd been wearing when arrested. From the looks of them, none had been pulled from their beds; they all wore furs, boots, the normal Yoran cold-weather attire. Since no effort had been made to heat the palace's dungeon, they'd been allowed to keep their clothing. Apparently, the Hon hadn't wanted them to freeze to death before they could be executed.

Which had given me an idea.

I gestured to the men Kaen had dispatched as my escort. I knew their leader, Hedrogha, from previous escort runs out to the clans. "Captain, pull them from the cells and follow me."

"Where are we going?" Hedrogha seemed wary. I wondered what his orders were if I refused to kill the prisoners.

"The kennel," I answered.

The soldier's eyes widened.

The prisoners barely made a fuss as they were pulled from their cells. They looked weak and beaten. If they'd been fed, it hadn't been enough.

I kept my expression blank as we made our way back up to the main level, to the kennels.

Of course, what the Yorans called the kennels would have been called the stable anywhere else. Even though most travel to and from the Ice Demesne happened via Gatestone, a main road did lead up to the pyramid's base. Any conventional travel happened by way of animals more adapted to the cold than horses—namely, snow hyenas and ice bears. Neither animal was ridden, but teams of hyenas or bears often pulled sleds or wagons across the snowy countryside.

This was Suless's (or rather Wyrga's) domain. She trained and took care of the duke's animals. No matter how she was despised, everyone admitted she excelled at her job.

The large hall was constructed from the palace's normal black stone, but here a dark musk scent mixed with blood, offal, and ice filled the air. Hyena laughter and bear growls mixed with creaking leather and the sharp retort of snapping jaws.

I motioned to a handler. "Harness a wagon with bears."

"You're supposed to kill the prisoners," the same soldier reminded me.

I turned to him. "Yorans may tolerate cold, but you have your limits. I'm going to leave them outside to freeze. Or won't that be dead enough for you?"

The soldier gave concerned glances to the large entrance. They didn't want to go outside either—exactly as I'd planned.

The prisoners heard our exchange, so panic set in. They were tied, but several began openly begging for their lives. Others started crying.

"Just kill them here," someone snapped.

I stared at the man. "Are you questioning me?"

"No, just—" He gave Captain Hedrogha a pleading look. "We'll need to change into our winter furs."

I was about to tell them to go get them (which would give me time to take the prisoners out myself) when Wyrga stepped in.

"Or you can let her go alone," Wyrga suggested as she walked over. "What's she going to do, hmm? Help them escape into the mountains? Travel somewhere warm? I'd like to see her try." The old woman had tied a cloth over one side of her head to hide her missing eye. I didn't know what she'd done with the eye itself, which I felt was for the best.

Captain Hedrogha started to protest, but Wyrga locked her eye with him. That eye's color flashed, just briefly, to ice blue.

Hedrogha paused. "You make a good point."

Wyrga smiled sharp teeth and malice. "I always do, dearie."

I suppressed a chill. I'd seen the ice eye flash before: Wyrga had just used magic on the guard. Duke Kaen had forbidden his captive goddess from doing a great many things—harming his family, for example—but she was useless to him if he forbid her from ever using magic at all.

But what could I say? What she had done worked in my favor.

"I'll be back soon," I reassured Captain Hedrogha. "This won't take long."

He didn't even look at me. Wyrga's ice-blue stare still trapped his gaze. His men didn't seem to notice.

The animal handlers readied two of the great bears for me, who I preferred to the hyenas. The bears were terrifying in their own way—they were more than capable of killing someone accidentally—but they liked that I was warm and good at scratching behind their ears. It wasn't at all the same as riding a horse, but since I secretly went riding with Arasgon almost every night in the Afterlife, I didn't resent the difference.

Once all the prisoners had been loaded into the wagon, we set out. I tried my best to ignore their screams.

For me, the difficult part of traveling in the Yoran winter landscape wasn't the cold. I'd long since learned to heat myself up enough to prevent frostbite. No, the difficulty was keeping that heat inside. If I allowed myself to radiate heat, I'd find myself wading through ice water, defrosting equipment designed to work best while frozen, or falling right through snowbanks and ice sheets rendered unstable. I'd found that out the hard way.

I rode out, unescorted, down the main road, not a proper road so much as a line of tall poles staked into the ground meant to rise above the worst winter snowbanks. Then I turned south, traveled several miles off the road, and stopped.

I enchanted coins as we rode. I'd have preferred to use rocks, but finding bare ground in winter was unlikely, so coins would have to do. Fortunately, the Hon hadn't been stingy with his metal, and to my surprise, I had a spending allowance.

And thanks to Suless, I had a few other tricks up my sleeves as well.

I stopped the wagon, opened the door, then backed away and drew my sword.

"Come out," I said, "and I'll explain how this will work."

They looked at me with undisguised fear.

"I don't want to kill you," I said. "You may either come out and I'll explain what you need to do to survive, or stay where you are and give me no choice but to follow through on the Hon's orders. I leave the choice to you."

They all stepped onto the snow and looked confused as I handed each of them a coin. More confused as they felt the warmth emanating from that metal.

"Keep those on you. Those tokens will keep you from freezing to death." I pointed south. "Aim between those two mountains. The pass between them will lead you south. You'll end up in Tolamer. Once you're there, I'll have people waiting for you. Ask for a woman named Ninavis. Understand?"

A tall, thickly built man with dark blue hair shook his head.

"It'll be weeks to make it that far. Even if we don't freeze, what are we supposed to eat?"

I nodded. I'd prepared for this part too, although it galled me that I had Suless to thank for the method. I whistled, then made a barking, laughter-like noise.

The hyenas responded immediately. These weren't the snow hyenas Suless had back at the palace. These were wild. I heard their barking response in the distance.

Hyenas are very hierarchical. Every animal in a clan knows exactly where they fall within that hierarchy—who is above them and who is below.

Really, not so different from Jorat.

In any event, it meant I only had to dominate their queen to rule the whole clan. I could only give the animals simple commands, but I thought it enough to ensure the former prisoners safely escaped Yor.

"The hyenas will escort you out and bring you food. Don't attack them. Don't even try to touch them, but they'll keep you safe."

I suppose I couldn't blame the prisoners for looking scared and nervous. Between the hot coins and the hyena escort, enough of them remembered stories told at grandmother's knee to suspect me of being a witch-mother. I was in no position to correct them.

I closed up the wagon doors and pulled myself back up behind the bears, grown restless with the proximity of that hyena clan. "It's the best I can do," I told them. "Good luck." I nudged the bears to head back to the palace.

I didn't know if they'd make it, but I suspected they'd rather have a chance.

When I returned, everyone seemed to accept I had indeed executed those prisoners. How could it have been otherwise? The soldiers reported back to Kaen, who in turn seemed pleased.

I thought I'd gotten away with it.

At least, I thought so for a little while.

50: WAR RESEARCH

Jorat Dominion, Quuros Empire.
Three days since Thurvishar revealed he wasn't
really Gadrith D'Lorus's son

"What gave it away?" Kihrin asked.

Ninavis and Janel shared a look before the latter waved a hand. "No, no, that would be jumping almost to the end. There's a few more pieces of this story to tell first or it wouldn't make sense."

Qown flipped to a new section of his journal. "We're almost finished, anyway."

Qown's Turn. The Ice Demesne, Yor, Quur.

Brother Qown sat in the library, working on his notes, when Janel came through the door and slid into a seat next to him. She began tapping her foot against the ground in a way that spoke of ill-contained anxiety, like she might break out into a run at any moment. It reminded him of horses, and he winced.

It had been a long time since they'd ridden horses. Surprisingly, he missed Cloud. He hoped whoever now owned the sweet little gelding had treated him well.

"Did you need something?" Qown asked after a long silence. He hadn't seen nearly as much of Janel as he would have liked, and he found himself upset to realize he didn't really know what she'd been doing with herself.

Errands for the duke. Training with the Spurned. Presumably passing messages and secrets to the Joratese rebellion. Not that he expected her to tell him about the latter, but he was sad they hardly spoke anymore.

Janel frowned at him. "You sent a message to me, remember?" Her right leg continued its nervous rapping.

"Oh." He pointed to Janel's knee. "Please stop."

She stilled her leg. "I'm sorry. So why did you want to see me?"

"Ah yes. One moment." Brother Qown stood up and fetched a notebook. He removed the spell making the journal look like a boring treatise on fireblood genealogies of southern Koenis. "I apologize this has taken so long, but it's been difficult research. I've been researching Quuros war magic—I'd have vivid nightmares if I dreamed anymore—but I've finally made some progress."

Janel straightened. "Qown, I asked you to look into that years ago."

He paused, wondering if he'd done the work unnecessarily. "Have you made any progress on your own?"

Her lips thinned. "No."

He nodded. "Honestly, I'm not surprised. Now I've made some assumptions about why you wanted to know about war curses—" He paused to give her a significant look. Janel intended to win over the duke by curing the Spring Caves. At least, that was his theory.

She motioned for him to continue.

"—and as a result, I think what you're looking for is a way to protect yourself from the ore called razarras. You already know how to protect yourself from Lysian gas—that's the blue smoke—with the air glyph, but razarras is different. Quur unleashed this horror without a way to counter its effects. They just didn't care. Since Quur knew how to cure tissue damage, any accidental exposures on the Quuros side would either be healed or considered an acceptable loss."

"Please say you're telling me the bad news, and good news follows right behind."

"I've been able to find several methods of protecting yourself from the effects of the metal. Several reports suggest the risks of exposure to it can be blocked by, well, other metal. Dense metals like gold or lead are the most effective, but rock will also stop the poison. This is why the whole castle isn't contaminated. Although I worry about our water supply. It's only a matter of time before this poison leaches into the water reservoirs—"

"Qown," Janel said, putting her hand on his. "Is there a way to remove it?"

"Yes, but it will require transmutation, which isn't easy magic to learn or cast. Most mages, even wizards, never learn how. Someone would have to undo the magic Quur used to create the metal in the first place—and we'd need to do the same for the witch-smoke. Unless we plan to permanently tattoo that glyph on the entire Yoran population." He paused and looked uneasy. "I, uh . . . it isn't in my normal skill range. It's also slow, so I'd be poisoned while doing it. I tend to work better with flesh and—"

"It's fine," she said. "I'm not expecting you to do this. I will."

Qown stared at her. "What? Janel, you're not that good at magic."

She raised an eyebrow. "How would you know?"

"I didn't think Thurvishar had advanced so far in your lessons, that's all." He cleared his throat, feeling embarrassed.

She looked vaguely uncomfortable for a second, before changing the subject. "You're saying if I go down to the affected caverns, clad in dense metal armor, I should be able to gain enough time to transmute the rocks there? And you'll fix any tissue damage that sneaks through?"

"Janel, you *can't* do this."

"Is that so? And why are you telling me about this, then—so I won't try?"

"Maybe you could learn, eventually—" Qown swallowed. "I'm not exaggerating the danger. This metal kills. People poisoned by it die in great pain. If there was ever a way to handle it safely, no one knows what it is."

"Wyrga—?"

He shook his head. "Don't you think Kaen would have just ordered her to clean up the mess, if she knew how?"

She scowled. "You have a point. He'd have asked her. For that matter, he'd have asked Relos Var."

"Right. Which means fixing this isn't something either specializes in."

"Or just didn't want to deal with, in Relos Var's case. Keeping Kaen hungry and vengeful, and reminding the Yoran people why they hate Quur, seems to be in line with Relos Var's goals. If he just fixed the problem, the Yorans might lose their knife-edge focus."

That made Qown pause. He knew Kaen's allies weren't always trustworthy—he often wondered why Kaen allied with the D'Lorus and D'Mon families. But Qown hadn't given much thought to the idea Relos Var and Kaen might be considered separate entities, with different goals.

"Janel," Qown said, "I have always thought you were a magical prodigy, but what you're suggesting is something people study for years to learn."

"Ah, but I'm cheating." Her expression turned bitter.

"You are?" He waited for an explanation.

She stood, clapping him on the shoulder. "You'll have to take my word for it. Are there any books I should be looking at? Practices that might help put me into the right mental state?"

He nodded. "Yes, I've collected all the notes I could find on the subject." He handed her the journal dedicated to this one project.

"Thank you," she said, and started to leave.

"Janel—"

She paused at the doorway. "Yes?"

"We should talk about what's happening in Jorat."

Her smile turned . . . feral. It gave Brother Qown a creepy feeling. Where had he seen that smile? Not on Janel's face.

"No," she said. "I don't think so. Now you say that I can use dense metal to protect myself from this poison ore. I assume you're not talking about a shield . . ."

Qown shook his head. "It would need to be encompassing. A suit of armor, perhaps. Something custom built . . . and expensive."

Janel chewed on her lip, her expression thoughtful.

Brother Qown sighed. "Do you really think you can learn to transmute razarras ore?"

She met his eyes. "Thurvishar will know how."

Qown leaned back, feeling spectacularly stupid. "I . . . stars. You're right. He probably will. That didn't even occur to me." He raised his hands. "All right. All right. You see about enlisting his help to learn that spell, and I'll see what I can do about acquiring you a very special suit of armor."

It was Janel's turn to look surprised. "How in all the heavens do you plan to do that? Did you take up smithing while I was elsewhere?"

Qown grinned. "You'll see."

51: Dragon Hunt

Jorat Dominion, Quuros Empire.
Three days since most of the Blue Palace
guards were animated from the dead

When Qown paused, he looked around, expecting someone to make a comment or have a question.

But instead, Kihrin simply gave a significant look to Janel. "Well?"

She chuckled and took her turn.

Janel's Turn. The Ice Demesne, Yor, Quur.

Suless proved to be far more invested in magics that dealt with living creatures than inanimate ones, but no one becomes a god-king without being extraordinary at magic on a general level, so she did have pointers on what had to be done.

As I predicted, Thurvishar had more.

Still, it was nearly three more months before I felt ready to make the attempt. Then I was waiting on Brother Qown to come through on his end of the plan: the armor needed to protect me.

I'm sure you can imagine my relief when Qown sent me a message. When I arrived at his room, I discovered a suit of complicated, intricate plates, sewn to thick, pliable material, lying on his bed. Brother Qown stood next to it.

"Qown? What is . . . what is that?"

"Your armor," he replied. "Well, not armor. Remember how I said metal provided excellent protection against razarras?

This is it." He waved a hand toward the suit as though presenting a prize. "I scribed the air sigil on the inside. Between that and the metal, you should have enough time to make your changes to the ore, before the razarras poisoning begins to affect you."

"How did you ever manage—" I tried to pick up the suit and found I couldn't.

It must have weighed several hundred pounds. I wondered how he'd managed to transport it. A team of servants? Some magic spell?

"What is this made from?"

"Lead, mostly."

I just stared at him in disbelief. "I'm not sure where you managed to find this, but I'm even less certain how you thought this would work. I can't lift this, let alone wear it."

"Ah, well, in fact," He cleared his throat. "The fine smiths at House D'Talus made this, on orders from High Lord D'Talus. Or at least, that's what the paperwork the deliverymen brought with them says."

I raised an eyebrow. "Do I wish to know how you managed such a feat?"

"The less you know about that, the better. As for wearing the suit, that's easy. Only a few years ago, you would have been more than strong enough to wear that. So the solution isn't to design a different suit, it's to restore your strength."

I walked over to him and put my hands on his shoulder. "How? The gaesh—"

He gently put his hands on my wrists and pulled my arms away from him. "There are loopholes. I haven't been ordered *not* to take the sigil off your back. And as it happens, Relos Var asked me to help you. Clearly, this is helping you."

"Relos Var?" I stepped away from Qown.

"Yes. A few years ago, truth be told. He never rescinded the order, so here I am, still helping." He grimaced. "Unfortunately, I can't promise this will be easy. In fact, removing the sigil may hurt a great deal."

"What do you mean? Why?"

"Well, it depends. If I can erase what Senera wrote, then it's easy. The difficulty comes if I can't. Then my options for removing the mark become . . . painful. And surgical."

My stomach tightened. "Are you suggesting skinning my back?"

He made a face. "Maybe a little? Just a few layers. I'll heal any injury afterward. I'm much better at healing than I used to be. But there's one other complication."

"Tell me."

"I don't know what this sigil does. I mean on an intrinsic level, I just don't know. I can't find it in any books. Then I realized Senera doesn't need books. She learned this from the Name of All Things, so she's the only one who understands that sigil's meaning. It drains your strength, but what if it also does more? We don't know its purpose, only its symptoms. So I don't know if Senera will be notified if we disrupt this mark, and I don't know if removing the mark will have some other catastrophic effect. I realize you haven't looked at your back through the Veil—"

"That would be difficult, yes."

"Right. The sigil pulls tenyé off you and shunts it elsewhere. Which means if we stop the flow, someone may notice."

"So you're saying that when we do this, we need to be fast."

"And we need to do it soon," he confided, "because someone at House D'Talus will start asking questions—for example, about why they delivered a custom lead-lined suit of shanathá armor to Yor."

"You're going to be in trouble, aren't you?" I found myself feeling a guilt I hadn't felt in years, a reminder that Qown was only here in this mess because of me. And if everything went as planned, I'd very likely be doing exactly what I'd promised I never would.

Namely, abandoning him.

Qown grimaced. "I'll be fine. I'm useful. Relos Var likes my work. Don't worry about me. You have more important things to do."

"I can't leave without you," I said.

"Who said anything about leaving? You just want to explore some caves under the castle, don't you?" He gestured toward the armor. "And if you find any god-king's buried treasure down there, bring it up, would you? Kaen won't be happy when he receives the bill for this. Do you have any idea how much shanathá costs?"

I laughed, feeling the humor like a stab wound. In the years since we'd been brought here, it did indeed feel like Qown had been a part of the Yoran intelligence-gathering community, someone who earned his keep. But he also stood as hostage to my good behavior, and what I proposed was anything but good behavior.

"Qown . . . no. I won't let them hurt you."

He shook his head. "You're going to have to trust me when I say they won't." His crooked smile made it clear he understood the irony of asking me to trust him. "Besides. It's my decision. Leave me one thing that is my decision."

I exhaled, fighting back my own sadness and despair. "Promise me you'll stay safe."

"I'm under orders from Relos Var to try," he said. "When do you want to descend?"

"We're looking for specific circumstances. For one, Aeyan'arric has to be here in the mountains, and two, none of the wizards should be present."

Qown blinked. "Aeyan'arric? Why do you care about Aeyan'arric?"

"Because . . ." I sighed. "You really don't need to know that."

"Wait, I thought you were cleansing the Spring Caves so the Yorans could use them again."

"That's the side effect, not the goal."

"Aeyan'arric wouldn't matter unless you . . ." He stared. "You're going to try to kill her, aren't you? Even if you could—and you *can't*—what good would it do?"

"It will keep her from icing over any more villages in Jorat or attacking any more of my—" I stopped. "It needs to be done. Stop asking questions. When are we going to do this?"

He thought for a moment. "Now."

"What?" I blinked. I wasn't ready or expecting *now*.

Qown nodded. "Now. Relos Var and Senera left this morning. I'm not sure where, but it seemed important—and they left Aeyan'arric. It's as good a window as we're likely to have."

"Thurvishar's not scheduled to have classes with the Spurned, but then he does make his own schedule." I pondered the strange D'Lorus mage. "Still, even if he's here, I don't know he'd interfere. It's not his pasture or his horses. But what of Gadrith?"

We had talked about Gadrith on many occasions, once Qown found out his real identity. We wanted nothing to do with him. There was a sort of sick humor to the fact Xivan kept herself alive in a very similar manner to Gadrith, and yet Xivan was beloved—at least among the Spurned. Maybe because Xivan wouldn't murder everyone around her just because she felt peckish. I guess the fact she wasn't a wizard—who presumably burned through far greater quantities of tenyé due to spellcasting—worked to her advantage.

"Gadrith hasn't visited in weeks," Qown said. "So if you're going to do this . . ."

"Yes. Best to do it now." I looked around his room, which still managed to feel monastic in the middle of a palace. I wasn't ready, but maybe it was best this way. No chance to say good-byes and thus betray my goals. No chance to accidentally let something slip.

Qown cleared his throat. "I'm afraid you'll need to disrobe." He handed me one of his robes for my modesty.

My mouth quirked. As if Qown hadn't seen all of me at one time or another. I turned my back toward him and stripped down so he could examine the sigil and—hopefully—remove it.

"Give me a moment," he said.

"Take all the time you need."

However, it didn't take very long at all. Then I heard him sigh.

"It didn't work?" I looked over my shoulder.

"It didn't work," he agreed. "Whatever's creating the mark, it's not coming off just because I asked."*

"Are you sure cutting off the skin will be enough?"

"Of course I'm sure. I—" I heard him pause. "Oh sun, what if it isn't?"

I half turned toward him. "We'll find out. Hopefully it will be like you said and you won't have to remove all the skin."

"Right. Lie down over here. I'll just, uh . . . okay, I'm going to dull the pain. It's going to feel odd, but it shouldn't hurt."

"I'd say knock me unconscious, but it's nighttime so you wouldn't be able to wake me again."

"Oh, good point."

I felt his fingertips against the skin, and then I couldn't feel his touch at all. It did indeed feel odd, a numbness around the edges of my back, but I couldn't feel my back's center.

"You're going to feel tugging. You might also feel some wetness."

"That won't by chance be blood, will it?"

"It might be, yes. Now let me work."

I put my hands under my chin and tried not to think of how my dearest friend was skinning me alive.

So that was all I could think about.

"Okay, it goes a little deeper than I'd like, but not all the way to muscle. We should be able to excise this. Don't move. When I'm finished, I'll still need to heal you."

"Oh yes, please do. I don't feel like fighting a dragon while missing all the skin from my back."

"Look, about that . . ."

"Me missing the skin off my back? Will it scar?"

"I'm not sure," he admitted. "No, I mean, about killing Aeyan'arric. Have you ever thought about just . . . fixing the poison in the Spring Caves instead? I mean, you'd be a hero. They'd erect your statue in every cave system."

---

* Like I would make it that easy to remove.

"And Relos Var would keep right on asking Aeyan'arric to freeze villages. Damn it, Qown, what's gotten into you—"

"I said don't move!"

I felt his hand shove me back down to the bed again.

"Sorry," I muttered.

"I can't stress how important it is that you don't move," he said after a long pause. "This is tricky work, and I'd like to make sure you don't scar . . . or anything else."

I'll be honest, I didn't like that "anything else."

I stayed still, but I thought about what he'd said. Yor had never been the least bit expansionist before Quur had come in and messed up their entire country. I remember the stories from my childhood about Suless and Cherthog, how necessary it had been to free the Yorans from their enslavement by god-kings. I think Quur was just running with what they knew: slay the god-kings, take their countries, add them to the empire. They'd done it with Jorat (albeit with actual cooperation), and they'd done it (much less willingly) with the city-states that made up the area once called Zaibur, now called Marakor. Of course, Quur had gone on to conquer Yor next. Had there ever been any doubt they would?

How disappointing it must have been to whichever emperor ruled back then (Gendal? I think it must have been Gendal) when all the god-kings had been conquered. South lay nothing but the Korthaen Blight, which no sane person would want, and the Manol, which no sane person would be fool enough to invade a second time.

But back to my point: Yor had every reason to hate Quur, didn't they? Even if being freed from Cherthog and Suless might have been a blessing under other circumstances, Quur had literally poisoned the ground under Yoran feet. How many had died in agony for Quuros generals to break their siege? Didn't Yor deserve to have that fixed?

I felt . . . I felt an odd solidarity. I wasn't Yoran, in many ways didn't understand the Yorans either. And yet, I knew what it was like to be played as a piece in someone else's game. In everyone's game.

I did indeed know what that felt like.

My back felt cold, and then something wet hit the table next to me. And I couldn't look, because I knew what I would see.

I clenched my teeth to keep from shuddering and reminded myself I'd been injured a thousand times. This was no worse than those injuries, some of which had been very bad indeed.

Then my back started to itch.

"Is that supposed to happen?"

"What? What's happening?" Qown sounded worried.

"My back itches."

He exhaled. "Oh. Yes, that's normal. Just ignore it."

"Easy for you to say. I promise you if our situations were reversed, you—"

"Shhh. I'm concentrating."

I ground my teeth together and stayed silent.

After a few minutes, the itch became hot and painful. Just as I started to ask him about it, Qown said, "It's going to start burning. Don't worry, I'm just removing the numbing. I'll do something else about the pain in a minute, but I want to check the nerves."

I felt a sharp, flaring pain that faded into a tingling. "Did you just pinch me?"

"I haven't given you permission to move yet. Okay, that . . . that looks good. Does it hurt?"

I bent forward, stretching my back. Then I twisted. "No. It doesn't."

"Fantastic."

I made a fist. "Uh . . . something's wrong."

Qown looked up sharply. "What? Wait. What's wrong? You said it doesn't hurt . . ."

"Yes, I did, but I also don't feel any stronger." I walked over to where I'd discarded my tunic and pulled it back over me before attempting to pick up the shanathá plate. "No, this is

still too heavy for me to lift." I must have looked panicked.
I felt panicked. "Qown, my strength isn't returning."

He looked relieved. "Is that all? I expected that."

"What? Didn't our plan hinge on the idea my strength would
return? You expected this?"

Qown pulled over a chair and sat down. He looked exhausted.
Apparently, I really was that hard to heal.* The fact that he'd
managed it at all by himself spoke to how his own magical
skills had grown. "Janel, you must have realized by this point
Xaltorath never cursed you with strength."

I froze.

He saw my expression and sighed. "Please. Just listen. You
were a small girl in horrifying circumstances. Anyone's mage-
gift—what others call a witch-gift—would manifest under such
pressure. And yours did. And what you wanted, little girl you,
most of all—"

"You don't know what I wanted," I snapped.

"I think you wanted to be strong," he said. "Too strong for
your enemies, too strong to fall victim to a demon. That's what
you made yourself, even though physical strength had nothing
to do with what happened to you. You became strong because
you used magic to make yourself strong."

I stared down at my hands. "Strong by casting a spell."

I knew how to do that now. I had become the witch I had
always feared my enemies would accuse me of being. That fact
didn't even shame me. But it felt like losing to admit my strength
had been my doing all along. Like admitting I had used the
demons as an excuse—*I'm not a witch, I'm just cursed by a demon.*

No. That thinking led to Xaltorath's logic, her twisting
chasms of guilt and recrimination. She had loved to suggest
everything I secretly wanted caused everything that had
happened. That I only played at being the victim because it
absolved me of responsibility or choice.

---

* It's like she's wearing talismans all the time, and I'm really not sure she's delib-
erately causing this effect.

To which I always reminded her that eight-year-old children don't have responsibilities or choices.

I could do this. More so, I had to do this. If I couldn't, then Aeyan'arric would keep right on freezing towns. Kaen's plans would continue. The situation in Jorat and Marakor would continue to deteriorate. The horrible tainted ore the Quuros wizards had left in the cavern under the Ice Demesne would do as Qown feared—leach into the surrounding water and kill everyone.

Painfully. Slowly.

I shut my eyes as I remembered my childhood. Remembered my fear, remembered my hate, remembered my terror and pain. I felt the rage wash over me and knew that if I wanted, I could channel my rage into destruction and violence so easily. My proficiency at magic would never be anything like Qown's healing. I felt, through a wash of red, one shining moment of connection when I felt Khored. I heard the screaming crows and felt the God of Destruction standing right next to me so I could just reach out and twist my fist around the red swirl of power feeding him.*

Not yet, little girl. Not yet.

I reached over to the table, picked up a goblet, and crushed it.

"Good," Qown said, sounding shaky. "Good. Now let's get you dressed."

As I stood there, staring at the crushed cup, I noticed the other object on the table: thrown there during Qown's operation on my back. Blood-side down, leaving a red smear: a large section of red-brown skin, marked with a black pattern.

"Do you have any plans for that?"

Qown looked startled and then appalled. "Yes, I planned to destroy it so there wouldn't be any evidence."

"Don't. I think I have a use for it."

*

---

* I honestly have no idea how to interpret that.

We made our move in the middle of the night, or rather I did, since we agreed Qown shouldn't follow. Qown would help from a distance, using his Cornerstone.

Good enough. Why carry a nonsentient deity in your pocket if you never use it?

I didn't need a lantern. The caves were dark, but in the three years I'd been studying, I'd learned the trick of making my own mage-light.

I packed the armor into a large bag, each section wedged with dresses, scarves, and cloth to keep it from rattling. Then I made my way down to the tunnels, heading deeper and deeper down until they led to the caves.

I may have mucked things up in this next part.

You see, I hadn't known the Spring Caves under the palace twisted and branched in quite such a tortuous maze of tunnels, chambers, and precipitous drops. My floating ball of mage-light threw harsh shadows against the walls, and I became turned around. I had no idea which direction faced down—let alone how to make it to Khoreval's cave, before making my way outside to find Aeyan'arric. I hadn't been down there in years.

I was lost.

And Qown couldn't help. Qown had *never* been down in these caves. He didn't have a clue where to go.

So not knowing what else to do, I put on my armor (wearing it proved less awkward than carrying it) and set out again, heading down a random tunnel. I was trying with all my might not to fall down a sinkhole, trip and break something, or in general make a bad situation worse.

The armor felt uncomfortably warm, but at least I could breathe fresh air because of the sigil. Qown had given me safety instructions—don't pick up anything but the spear, don't remove my helmet. And when I had finished with this whole business, I needed to throw the armor into a deep crevasse and melt it to slag.

I agreed with Qown on taking this poison metal business with appropriate seriousness, but I already regretted losing the armor. The metal alone would have paid my canton's taxes for several years.

I almost gave up and started forming a *HELP* sign from pebbles so Qown would see it when he checked in. Then I saw a very golden glow reflected against the cave wall before me.

And Khoreval, when I had seen it last, had glowed golden.

I inched my way forward until at last I saw the same break in the rocks Xivan had warned me about, a few years before. Beyond it, I saw the Spring Cave's blue smoke and toxic stone terrain.

Dealing with the smoke was the easy part.

The armor covered my entire body. Then a thin sheet of glass (well, it looked like glass) covered my eyes. Truly, the House D'Talus armor smiths had created a masterpiece.

My strength made climbing easier, but I still worried I might break off a handhold and plummet. Fortunately, on closer inspection, the cliff resembled a sharp incline rather than a straight drop to the main cavern floor.

But bones littered the floor, glimpsed through gaps in the blue smoke.

Small, warty yellow-orange pieces of razarras ore protruded from the otherwise black stone floor. Some of the chunks had broken underfoot too, leaving powdery residue. I began to understand what Qown had meant about destroying any traces of razarras clinging to my suit. Any dust kicked up into the air and breathed in would prove fatal. I walked toward the dais where the spear sat.

For the first time, I wondered if there might be traps.

A large black boulder stood in the cave's center, near the spear. The stone was . . . hot. Red hot, radiating a heat I felt through the armor. I saw no reason for the heat; the boulder didn't sit near lava or a volcanic vent, and no one had lit a fire near it. It just glowed hot.

Then I realized the same symbol marked on my back had been carved into the stone.

I stopped.

The presence of that symbol meant Senera had been here. That meant, as I had once suggested to Qown, Relos Var almost certainly knew how to neutralize the poison here. Yet he had chosen not to, for his own purposes.

But what purpose did the stone serve? Why that symbol?

I pulled the rolled-up skin—my skin—from the satchel. There had been no time to treat or tan it, so it was still a grisly souvenir of my stay with the duke—one I'd also have to destroy.

Although I didn't much care if it turned poisonous, considering what I planned to do with it.

As I looked closer, I saw the two symbols were not identical. Close, but a few marks distinguished them. They seemed to be variations on a common base glyph. I didn't understand what either meant.

I shifted my sight past the First Veil and saw what the Spring Cave had to show me. Not much, to be honest.

The most insidious feat the Quuros had performed was transforming these caves in a way that required no magical maintenance, in a way that couldn't be overcome by a snap of another wizard's fingers. Their poisonous metal ore wasn't magical at all. But the blue smoke? Yes. Magic had powered it, and finally, that magic had begun to fade. If the smoke in Mereina faded at the same rate, well, then, in a few centuries, Mereina would be safe to occupy again.

There had to be a better way.

The large black boulder, nearly an obelisk, held astonishing amounts of pure tenyé.

If Xivan ever came down and found that boulder, she'd never need to execute another Yoran prisoner in order to feed. The boulder contained enough tenyé to power spellcasting of such strength . . . well . . .

Who had created it? Relos Var? Perhaps. Certainly, the presence of the sigil carved deeply into its side suggested Senera's involvement and, in turn, Var's. And as for the sigil itself?

Brother Qown had told me the sigil on my back hadn't just been suppressing my strength but had been siphoning off tenyé to another location. I had a good idea where that tenyé had been going. Three years' worth, stored up right there before me.

My tenyé.

"Actually, mine."

I whirled around in the room and saw my mother, Tya, standing before me.

I didn't even jump.

"What are you doing here?" I asked her as she walked past me, over to the spear.

"Breaking the rules," she said, sitting down on the dais. "But as a wise man once said to me: fuck the rules. Is that human skin?"

I looked down at what I held. "Yes, but it's all right; it's my skin."

She narrowed her eyes. "That's not as reassuring as you may have intended. You don't *seem* injured."

"Qown healed me." I took a deep breath, not wanting to talk to Tya at all. Not wanting her here, even though logically she could be very helpful. "How could Relos Var pull tenyé from *you*?" I shook my skin. "This wasn't *your* back."

She winced at my demonstration, which had splattered gore onto my armor. "Relos knew I wouldn't let him kill you. Which would have happened, if I hadn't lent you enough power to withstand that glyph. So for the last few years, he's been draining the tenyé I've been feeding you and storing it away for a rainy day."

"So you made the same mistake twice?"

"It wasn't a mistake," she insisted.

I scoffed. "You're giving our enemies succor and aid! Xaltorath exploited me to gain favors from you, and now you're letting Relos Var do the same thing. Why?"

She raised an eyebrow. "I just explained this."

"No!" I almost pulled the helmet from my head in protest, torn between the certainty she'd protect me from the razarras metal and the overwhelming desire not to rely on her protection. "Horseshit. I'm not worth you giving in to Relos Var or to

Xaltorath. I'm not worth letting them win! Why do you people keep using me as the excuse to lose?"

I wanted her angry. Oh, angry would have felt nice. Instead, she looked sad. "But you are. Janel, I love you."

"No! You don't even know me. You don't know anything about me. How can you love me? I don't even love me!"

I don't remember removing the helmet, but it had vanished when I found myself in my mother's arms. She smoothed my hair and kissed my forehead. "I love you," she whispered. "I have always loved you. I loved you when you burned your harp on the Blight's edge and prayed for me to guide your path. I loved you when Valathea sacrificed herself to help you free S'arric's soul. I loved you when you marched into Khorvesh, newborn baby in your arms, and demanded no woman would ever be sold to a man there again. And I loved you even more the first moment I held you in my arms, still bloody from your birth—and I screamed so hard no mage on this planet could hear for three days when I had to give you up. I love you enough to humble myself before my enemies so you might live." She leaned away from me for just long enough to look me in the eyes. "But when all is done, when this is all over, I'm not going to lose. I'm not going to lose, because my daughter doesn't lose."

I wiped my eyes and sniffled, choking back an inelegant knot of phlegm. "Three *days*?"

Her smile turned mischievous. "They call it the Great Silence. They've never been able to figure out what caused it."

"How . . . dramatic."*

She smiled. "I was in theater when I was younger."

That made me laugh, even as I still cried. "Apparently, I was too, in another life. Seriously, you couldn't put me in a body who can carry a tune? I can't sing at all."

"Sorry. You get that from me."

"Of course. The Goddess of Magic can't sing." I wiped my

---

* She's one to talk. At least I know where Janel gets it from now.

eyes, aware I'd just killed myself from razarras poisoning unless Tya intervened. "So what now?"

Tya hugged me and kissed my forehead again. "Let's go ahead with your plan. You wanted to do something about the metal and smoke here?"

"Yes."

"I like that idea. Let's do that together. Then how would you feel about letting your mother help you fight a dragon? Just us?"

I had to admit, I liked that idea rather a lot too.

Aeyan'arric played in the snow.

Tya and I stood on a mountainside in the Yoran mountains and watched the dragon below us cavort and roll in the snow like a cat with a feather, grinning and joyous. Except a cat playing doesn't make mountains shake or leave giant grooves in granite rock faces. A cat doesn't start an avalanche and then chase after it like it was a mouse.

She was so beautiful. The sun refracted off her scales, making a thousand rainbows, sparkling against the snow and ice—cold and perfect, winter manifested.

I tightened my grip around Khoreval and wished, just for a moment, that we didn't have to do this.

Taking the spear had been an afterthought, despite all that planning. From the moment I held Khoreval, I felt its extraordinary magic, indeed strong enough to kill a dragon. Still, Khoreval seemed like a toothpick against Aeyan'arric's size and majesty. I felt like an idiot for ever thinking I could fight a dragon without a goddess at my side.

The goddess in question must have been thinking along the same lines, at least about Aeyan'arric's beauty, because she sighed next to me. "This breaks my heart. I knew her when she was a little girl."

"You—" I looked over at her. "Wait, Aeyan'arric used to be human?"

"All the dragons used to be . . . well . . . yes, let's go with human. Aeyan was the daughter of a good friend. As a child, her smiles were like the sun peeking out behind the clouds."

"What changed her into a dragon?"

"A monster. Her uncle."

"Her uncle—?"

"Relos Var. Her uncle is Relos Var. And he murdered his own brother, Aeyan's father, because . . . honestly, I don't know. Even after all these years, I still don't know." Tya's expression set into something unfriendly, and she didn't seem inclined to answer any further questions. "Hide up behind that ledge. I'll lead her beneath you. Jump down and don't miss."

"That's the plan? Jump on her and hope for the best?"

Tya laughed. "What were *you* going to do?"

I frowned and looked down at my bag. I'd planned to give Aeyan'arric a new scale decoration that would sap her strength, but that was before I realized Senera had personalized the sigil she'd marked on my back. So it probably wouldn't work on Aeyan'arric, especially if it meant "steal energy from voras daughters of goddesses of magic."

"You don't happen to know what this means, do you?" I asked Tya, showing her the sigil.

She shook her head, looking rueful. "Strange as this may sound coming from the Goddess of Magic, I don't."

"I'd planned to throw this at the dragon to weaken her, but now I don't think it will work."

"So not too far removed from drop down from above and hope for the best, is it?"

I cleared my throat. "No."

"Move quickly. If it doesn't work, run. You can't fight her with endurance or strength. Aim the spear at the space between her eyes."

I nodded and moved up to the ledge.

Tya vanished.

She reappeared a moment later down in the valley, where Aeyan'arric sported. The dragon reacted immediately, spreading her wings and rearing back, serpent-like. She dispensed with polite conversation and quick banter.

Aeyan'arric attacked, breathing winter incarnate down at the spot where Tya stood. But Tya had already gone, so fast her veils left a blurred rainbow behind her.

I knew the timing would be tricky. I'd have to jump before Aeyan'arric reached me, and if I jumped early, I'd plummet to my death. If I jumped too late, the same result seemed likely.

By then, Aeyan'arric had almost reached my position. I jumped.

I landed halfway off the dragon's neck and nearly lost both my own life and the spear as I scrambled to hold on to her scales and claw my way up. Aeyan'arric noticed me and swung her neck to the side, but she couldn't bite me. She pulled up from her flight, reaching up with both fore-claws to snatch me from her neck.

Tya attacked as soon as Aeyan'arric looked away, filling the sky around us with fire. I felt my skin crack and blister before I raised the proper protection spells. I cursed myself for not thinking to do that beforehand.

Then I stabbed Khoreval downward, into Aeyan'arric's neck.

The dragon screamed. Extraordinary, immense power channeled up from the wound into my body. This wasn't a pleasant sensation. The dragon's tenyé felt twisted and wrong, somehow rotten, as if the normal magical energies informing all creation had broken and realigned into chaos and disharmony. I screamed too, pushed the spear deeper into her neck, and screamed again when acidic icy blood sprayed over me.

Then we were falling.

Hitting the snow felt like salvation, not painful at all but a cool compress against painful burns. Aeyan'arric lashed backward against me, missing me only because I made such a small target. But Tya hadn't left. After her fireball had faded, the Goddess of Magic returned in an instant, unleashing violet energy that began disintegrating the dragon's claws and wings.

I reminded myself that I had more important things to

do than pay attention to the pain, pulled the spear from the dragon's neck, and slammed it down again, this time between her eyes.

Aeyan'arric collapsed.

I did too, covered in gore, dragon blood, and human blood, with injuries I didn't dare to contemplate.

But we'd done it.

We'd slain a dragon.

Tya floated down next to me. She made a noise that reminded me so much of Dorna after I'd come home from playing in the mud that I almost choked. She laid me down on the snow next to Aeyan'arric's head and healed my wounds.

"Wait here. I need to go find out if this worked."

Shock roused me from my stupor. "What? What do you mean, 'if this worked'?" I pointed to the dead body.

Tya shook her head. "That happens every time."

I blinked at her.

"We've killed dragons before, Janel. They recover. They heal. Just like we do. You can't kill any of the Eight. We just won't stay dead. And you can't kill a dragon. They just won't stay dead either." She touched the spear impaling the dragon's head. "Rest here. I'll confirm the results with Thaena. She'll know if this worked."

I nodded even as I sighed and leaned back. I almost told her I'd be happy to check with Thaena myself, but I wanted to stay awake. I felt and heard the tenyé swirl and shift. When I looked up, Tya had disappeared.

I watched the swirling clouds overhead. Storm clouds were dissipating, as if they had only ever gathered because their dragon queen demanded it. Now they could bring snow and rain and life to other fields.

I'm not sure how long I sat there. Not very long, I think.

Then Relos Var said, "When I ordered Qown to help you, this wasn't what I had in mind."

52: THE BREAKING OF CHAINS

Jorat Dominion, Quuros Empire.
Three days since Talon's team won

"I wonder if it's all of them," Kihrin mused.

"What was that?" Qown asked.

"If all the dragons are children of the Eight Immortals. I mean, I spent four years stranded on Thaena's sacred island because her dragon son, Sharanakal, didn't want me to leave. And then there's Aeyan'arric and—myself—"

Qown frowned. "What about Aeyan'arric and you?"

"Uh, never mind. My point is, I wonder if that will prove true of all the dragons?"

"Wow. Uh, now that's a conversation I never thought I'd be having," Ninavis said.

Janel looked at Brother Qown. "I think it's possible. Maybe Relos Var's fondness for going after family goes right back to the beginning."

"Man's got some issues," Dorna commented.

"It changes things," Kihrin said. He remembered comments from both Relos Var and the dragon Sharanakal. They'd recognized him not from his physical appearance, but by the "color" of his soul. If all dragons shared such an ability, then Aeyan'arric might well recognize him.

But was that good? What if Aeyan'arric hated her father?

"Why does it change anything?" Janel asked. "She's still an angry dragon Relos Var is using to trap us here."

He paused and waved a hand. "Keep going with the story. I need to think about this."

Qown's Turn. The Ice Demesne, Yor, Quur.

Brother Qown learned he could even spy on a god, when he realized Tya didn't sense him.* He'd been following Janel since she left, using her distinctive higher core temperature as his heat source. It proved unnecessary after she entered the Spring Caves. The stone monolith ran so hot Qown couldn't stare at it lest he blind himself; it burned with the heat of an open forge.

Like Relos Var, like Janel, Tya ran hotter in temperature than a normal person. Much hotter, and Brother Qown made a note to see if he could find a connection between tenyé and heat levels. Did tenyé have a tangible energy impact? What did this physiological difference signify?

Then Janel was crying and Tya was crying, and Qown wished he didn't have to keep watching. Much more embarrassing than spying on sex, which he'd forced himself to do more than once for fear he'd lose information otherwise.

He watched, anyway. And he watched as mother and daughter defeated Aeyan'arric together.

Brother Qown exhaled. Whatever else happened, Janel would be fine. Her mother would take her away.

She'd made it.

Then something pushed him, knocking Worldhearth from his hand.

Senera loomed over him. "Watching anything interesting?"

"What? I—"

She grabbed him by the shoulder and pulled him from the chair. He looked around and saw her soldiers filled the room. The soldiers were patched and bandaged, as if they'd just come from a fight.

Which they probably had.

"What's happened?" Brother Qown asked.

"You'll find out soon enough," Senera said. "Will you walk, or should I have the lieutenant carry you?"

---

* He probably would have realized it earlier if he'd known Mithros was Khored.

He stood, straightening his agolé as he picked up Worldhearth. "I'll walk."

Together, they marched from the main library, heading upstairs to the great hall. Brother Qown felt his stomach squeeze tighter with each step. They'd been discovered. They'd been discovered far too early. Everyone at the palace must have witnessed the fight outside. And no one—not Duke Kaen and certainly not Relos Var—would be happy to see Aeyan'arric slain. The Yorans would probably kill Qown, but he'd known that would be the price.

He'd always known.

But when he stepped up into the giant crystal trapezoid, he saw a scene he'd expected and two additional details he hadn't.

What he expected: Duke Azhen Kaen stood there, furious and mighty, looking like he had been roused from bed and had not yet had time to decorate his beard. His wife, Xivan, stood next to him, as well as his son, Exidhar. Wyrga sat at her normal place by the fire, accompanied by her pet polar bear cub / ensorcelled husband. The Spurned spread out like an honor guard, dressed in full armor and holding shields and swords. Qown didn't recognize the robust blue-haired Yoran man standing just to the side of the duke, but that wasn't shocking. Most of the Yoran nobles wanted nothing to do with him, and the early hour meant a great many of the normal faces were absent.

What he hadn't expected: Janel Danorak lay on the floor next to Relos Var, unconscious. Her arms had been forced behind her back and were held together by a giant metal band, molded around her hands. And before Duke Kaen, beaten and bloody, stood someone Brother Qown hadn't seen in years but remembered well.

Ninavis.

She was bound with rope. Ninavis also sported a bruise on one cheek, and blood trickled from her split lip.

"Ah, good, everyone's here now," Relos Var said.

Brother Qown nearly threw up, right on the spot. Relos Var

had warned Qown that one day the wizard would have to choose whether to continue supporting Duke Kaen or turn instead to Janel. It looked like Relos Var had finally made his choice.

He studied Relos Var's face for any clue that this was somehow not what it seemed, that Var had found some way to keep Janel and Qown—and possibly Ninavis—alive. Var's face was carved from stone.

"You realize she's coming back, right?" Brother Qown said.

A guard stepped forward to hit him, and Qown fixed his gaze on the man. The guard hesitated.

Relos Var turned around. "Who's coming back?"

"Tya. Did you think Janel killed Aeyan'arric by herself?"

Duke Kaen gave Relos Var a look. "I'm beginning to think killing a dragon isn't as difficult as you've led me to believe."

Relos Var shook his head. "Aeyan'arric isn't dead, Your Grace."

"She killed her," Brother Qown volunteered. "I saw it."

Relos Var sighed and pinched the bridge of his nose. "Yes, you did. But such a death isn't permanent. She'll return." He smiled at Qown. "Janel missed a step."

Brother Qown folded his hands over his arms. "What do you mean?"

"You see, what you failed to take into account—" Relos Var stopped. "Why don't we save the class lecture for another day? Much as you know I love to enlighten the uneducated, you're right. I'm not sure this palace would survive a reunion between myself and my favorite student."

Qown blinked for a moment, confused as to why Relos Var would reference Senera when she stood right there. Then he realized Var meant something else entirely.

The goddess Tya had been his "favorite student."*

"So what are our options?" Duke Kaen asked. "Kill Janel Danorak? Send her to Shadrag Gor? And what about our Black Knight?" He gestured toward Ninavis. "Are you seriously

---

* That boy does not understand sarcasm.

expecting me to believe you couldn't track down one middle-aged woman responsible for all the trouble we've had in Jorat? When *this* is the Black Knight?"

Kaen didn't notice the glare Xivan gave him.

Ninavis raised her head and grinned as she licked blood from her lips. "And I have to say, you lot sure did make it easy. But your man is wrong; I'm not the Black Knight."

The blue-haired man spoke. "She is, my Hon. I know what I saw in Jorat—"

"Or should I say, everyone is the Black Knight now? Killing me isn't going to change a thing. We knew you lot were looking for armies, so we never formed any. We knew you lot were looking for leaders, so we made everyone a leader. We knew you lot would try to find the Black Knight, so we made everyone the Black Knight. Me? I'm just a thief who's good with a bow. Killing me is like taking a cup of water from the sea and thinking you've stopped the tide."

"Shut her up," Relos Var said. "She's just trying to delay—" He paused, and his eyes widened. A dozen emotions seemed to cross his face: anger, shock, outrage, and fear the most identifiable. Brother Qown thought he looked rather like someone who had just been stabbed or poisoned by a good friend, who had just realized how thoroughly they'd been betrayed.

Or maybe Qown was just conflating Var's emotions with his own.

"What's wrong?" Duke Kaen said.

"Someone just killed my brother," Relos Var said.

Then he vanished.

Everyone hesitated. A beat of silence filled the room, and then Duke Kaen turned to his wife. "Did you know he had a brother?"

"I didn't think he was the sort to have a family, to be honest."

"Hmmph. Fine. And now that he's gone—" Duke Kaen drew his sword and advanced on Janel's unconscious body. "I will not tolerate traitors."

"Azhen," Xivan said, "we don't yet know what happened."

The Hon whirled back to face his wife. "We know she's a traitor. We know she disobeyed at least one of my orders, freed prisoners I'd ordered executed, sent them into Jorat. She killed my dragon! She clearly knew who the Black Knight was the entire time and hid that fact from me. I know all I need to know. I had hoped I could trust her. Now I know I can't."

Qown stared at the blue-haired Yoran, who was biting down on a knuckle, eyes haunted. Now that Qown looked closer, he didn't think the man a noble. The man was dressed in simple Joratese-style clothing.

"I agree we will need to do something," Xivan Kaen reminded her husband, "but if we kill Janel, won't that just send her to our enemies?"

The duke paused, consternation in his expression. He had forgotten the reason they made a point of not killing certain people.

Senera gestured. "If you like, I could, um, an enchantment might, uh—" She licked her lips, looking nervous and upset. "I mean, I—"

Qown had never seen Senera lose her composure before.

"No, not you." Kaen looked displeased. "I placed my faith in you and your master once. I no longer believe you've been steadfast in your loyalty. First the Black Knight and now Tya. *Tya?* This should never have gone so far."*

Senera bowed. "As you say, Your Grace."

"What about my family?" the blue-haired man interjected. "You promised that you'd reunite me with my family."

Kaen stopped and looked at the man.

"I mean . . . I . . . please. My Hon."

Kaen said, "Wyrga, take the prisoners and our new friend here down to the Spring Caves. I want you to make sure they can't escape. If anyone tries to remove them without my permission, I want you to destroy them."

---

* He'd gone full paranoid by this point. I mean, he wasn't wrong, but that's beside the point.

"What? But I told you everything!" the Yoran man protested.

Qown had his own reasons for disbelief. He was reasonably certain Duke Kaen had no idea Janel and her mother, Tya, had rendered the caves safe. So Kaen had—or rather, thought he had—just sentenced them all to a terrible and slow death. Indeed, Kaen's vague instructions didn't prevent Wyrga from killing them either, so long as she kept their bodies in the caves. But he'd also made life difficult for her, since the duke had effectively demanded Wyrga kill Tya if the goddess showed up to free her daughter.

And Qown didn't think Wyrga was anywhere near powerful enough for that.

Wyrga must have realized as much. She threw a murderous look at the duke, but he either didn't see it or didn't care.

"Husband, what are you doing? This can't—"

"Don't cross me!" the duke screamed. Then he motioned to the guards, who didn't realize they too were being sent to their deaths. "Take them downstairs."

"You've lost weight," Ninavis said as they were marched downstairs toward the caves.

"Nice to see you too," Brother Qown snapped.

"No, I mean: Are you eating enough? You look like they've been starving you. I liked the baby fat. It was cute." Ninavis glanced around, looking for some way to escape, looking for some opportunity.

"You did?" He shook his head. "No, no. I just . . . I forget to eat sometimes."

Ninavis threw him a concerned look.

They walked down five flights with a guard carrying Janel slung over his shoulder. Then they heard a voice from an adjacent hallway, yelling for them to wait. Senera appeared.

She'd either opened a gate or she'd run. Possibly both.

"How many floors down are we going?" Ninavis asked out of the corner of her mouth.

"You don't want to know," Qown said. "It's a large building."

"Wait," Senera said, holding her side as if she had a stitch. "The duke forgot to have me spell you."

Ninavis groaned. "Oh, it's *you*. I hate you."

Wyrga turned and looked at Senera, smiling sharp-toothed and vicious. "Is that so, little girl?" The old woman motioned for Senera to come forward with a crooked finger.

That smile made Qown pause. He recognized it. He looked from Janel's sleeping form back to Wyrga again. How much time hand Janel been spending with Wyrga, anyway? But he had no time for that distraction.

Senera straightened her back. "What do you want, Wyrga?"

Wyrga grabbed Senera by the neck and brought the Doltari woman down to her eye level. "You've always been one of mine, haven't you? Fake marriage vows may fool the men, but I know one of my daughters when I see her."

Senera ground her teeth. "Let me go."

Wyrga grinned. "Call me *Mother,* darling."

"Let me go, 'Mother,'" Senera repeated.

Wyrga released her.

Senera walked forward. She had the Name of All Things in one hand, filled with ink, and her brush in the other. "This will just take a moment."

Wyrga cackled.

Wyrga knew the duke hadn't "forgotten" to have Senera protect them against the poisons in the caves. Indeed, the duke didn't know such magical protections existed.

Brother Qown shook his head. "This isn't necessary," he whispered as Senera approached. Senera didn't know the dangers had already been neutralized.

"Shut up," she said, looking over her shoulder toward Wyrga. "I know what I'm doing."

"Do you?" Qown looked at the pale-skinned woman and wondered just how much this would cost her. He also wondered if she was attempting to save their lives for Relos Var's benefit or because she didn't want to see them die herself.

She marked the air glyph on everyone's forehead and then

added an unfamiliar second glyph. Qown studied the new sigil, memorizing it.

When she finished, Senera said, "All right, let's go." Evidently, she'd no intention of staying behind.

Which meant she too had caught the loophole in the duke's orders to Wyrga.

The old woman scowled but didn't protest. The group continued until they reached the tunnels underneath the palace. Wyrga clearly knew the way.

Senera took one look at the large monolith in the main cavern and turned back to Janel's sleeping figure. "She removed the sigil from her back."

"I did," Brother Qown confessed. "She mostly just lay there."

Wyrga smirked at him.

Brother Qown felt himself turn red. "I didn't mean it like that."

The old woman walked around the room, seeming to stand straighter with each step. She tsked at the bodies on the ground even as she swept her gaze from side to side like an industrious maid with a broom. "The razarras ore is gone. The smoke is gone. Who's been cleaning my house?" She set her cub down— *Cherthog,** Qown reminded himself—and the little beast immediately began chewing on a corpse's thigh bone.

"Tya removed all the dangers," Brother Qown said. "Earlier."

Senera met his stare. "It's not necessary," she repeated Qown's earlier warning to herself, and then sighed.

A guard lowered Janel to the ground. "Do you want me to wake her?"

"Good luck with that," Ninavis said.

Senera walked over to Janel and frowned. "Relos Var must have her under another sleep spell."

"I doubt Relos Var had her under a sleep spell after the duel

---

* I suppose I should have expected that Qown had figured out who Wyrga really was, either because Janel told him or because we did make the little sneak good at spying, didn't we?

in Atrine," Brother Qown said. "She's . . . hard to wake once she sleeps."

So naturally, Janel woke right away.

Qown and Ninavis exchanged looks. It was still night. Janel normally wouldn't—*couldn't*—wake before dawn.

"Hard to wake, you say?" Senera raised an eyebrow at Qown. She gestured to the guards. "Get her up."

Wyrga ignored them as she ran her hands over the stone monolith, muttering to herself.

"Janel," Qown said. "Are you all right? The situation is a bit, uh—"

"Everything's screwed," Ninavis finished.

Janel blinked as the guards hauled her to a standing position. "Hey, Ninavis. It's been a while."

"You too," Ninavis said. "You know, I'd started to wonder if you were a ghost haunting Arasgon from the afterlife. Looks like I owe Dorna twenty thrones."

"Oh, you know me. Hard to kill." Janel looked around the cave, noting the people present. Her gaze stopped at the blue-haired man. "Why do I know you?"

He swallowed and looked away.

Janel made a face. "You were one of the prisoners I freed."

The man didn't deny it. "I just wanted my family back. I'm sorry, I thought—"

"You thought all would be forgiven if you gave us up to the duke," Janel said. She glared at Wyrga. "You must be loving this."

"Oh, I am," Wyrga agreed.

"We should've switched to fake names," Ninavis mused.

Janel said, "Did Tya come back? Where's Relos Var?"

"He . . . left," Senera replied.

"Who fixed the walls?" Xivan Kaen stepped into the cave. She wore full Khorveshan armor and carried the spear Khoreval. She turned back behind her and shouted, "Don't come in! It's not safe yet!"

The soldiers straightened and bowed to their duchess as she entered the cavern complex. She must have left the Spurned back in the tunnels. And since Xivan had recognized the cave walls and floors no longer posed a problem, the caves could only be dangerous because of two people: Wyrga and Senera.

"Hello, vampire," Wyrga said. "I'm not receiving guests, so leave."

"I plan on leaving," Xivan said, "but I'm taking your prisoners with me. I don't trust you not to hurt them, and my husband isn't thinking. I don't want him doing anything rash." She smiled. "I know how well that works out."

Wyrga sighed. "You don't have Azhen Kaen's permission."

"No, I don't."

Wyrga just stared at the woman, lips drawing back from her teeth, fangs showing.

Qown realized Duke Kaen must have ordered Wyrga never to harm his wives, his family, himself.

But Kaen had also just told her to destroy anyone who tried to rescue the prisoners.

Wyrga couldn't obey both commands. If she attacked Xivan, the gaesh loop started, and the moment Xivan left with a prisoner, it also triggered.

Xivan looked over at Senera. "Are we going to have a problem?"

Senera cocked her head. "Not unless you object to me leaving with you."

"He'll never forgive you," Wyrga growled. "Your husband already feels betrayed. He already doesn't trust his friends."

"Your doing, I think," Xivan said.

"Of course it was my doing!" Wyrga screamed. "He deserves nothing less!" She held out her hands, changing tack, her voice dropping to a more reasonable volume. "I'm helping him, defending him against all the things he's too weak to understand are threats: trust and love and respect. Only when he understands his true enemies were his closest friends will he be ready for my truth."

Ninavis edged over toward Brother Qown. "I'm guessing there's some history here I don't know."

"Just a little," Qown said. Then he blinked and put his hand to his chest.

Wyrga did the same.

Janel frowned.*

"Are you all right?" Ninavis asked Qown.

"I can breathe," he whispered. "By the sun, it feels like I can finally get enough air. What is happening? Why—"

Across the cave, next to the monolith, Wyrga's eyes widened with surprise, joy, triumph. "My gaesh is *gone!*"

Xivan grabbed Janel by the arm. "Run."

They all heard Wyrga cackling behind them. Then the sound of large stones breaking battled with her high-pitched screams. Xivan led Janel, whose hands remained bound. Everyone else—including the guards—followed in her wake. No one wanted to stay and see what the witch-queen Suless would do, freed from her gaesh.

They exited into cold air at the mountain's base. The sky wouldn't see the sun rise for several hours. Tya's Veil spread out over the sky as a ribbon of red, green, and violet above them, just bright enough to reflect off the packed ice and snow. A snow incline led up and away from the palace.

When they had reached the slope's top, Xivan stopped. "We can rest here," Xivan said. "I'll do a head count while you catch your breaths. We'll figure out what happened—"

A deafening roar shook the ground under their feet. Qown felt like he stood right next to a lightning strike as thunder rolled over the land.

"Holy shit," Senera said.

Everyone looked back.

A fire column a hundred feet across tore up through the pyramid, from the bottom to the top, burning up into the sky. It turned every snowbank and mountaintop for a hundred miles orange red. The inferno seemed to pause for a split second . . .

---

* I bet she felt her gaesh break too right then.

And then the column of fire exploded outward.

The explosion surged, ripping right through the great hall.

"Suless," Janel murmured.

Time slowed. Everything happened so fast, but to Qown's perceptions, events crawled at a leisurely pace. He saw the delicate fire flower curl outward from the explosion. The shattered crystal walls flew out in a sparkling, deadly rain capable of shredding anyone standing too close to the palace—and they all stood too close to the palace. The exploding fireball looped up and out and then started to sink . . . heading straight for them. The blue-haired man and several of the soldiers started running.

"Duck—" What Ninavis would have had them duck behind, he didn't know. Probably she didn't know either.

Senera raised up her hands. Her spell kept the lethal shards and high winds from pouring death down on them.

But Qown didn't think she could handle the wall of fire too.

As it turned out, she didn't need to. The fire launched upward and away, melting the snow below them and scorching the rocks.

All over in seconds.

Senera turned around, looking as surprised as he felt. "Okay, who did that—"

Janel had been held tight in Xivan's grip, but she'd fallen to one knee in a half crouch on the stony ground. It wasn't clear if she'd wriggled her way free or if Xivan had let her go. But the duchess just stood there, mouth gaping, staring up at the devastated palace.

"If by 'that,' you mean saving you from burning to death, then you're welcome," Janel said. Steam hissed from the snow as molten metal fell from the band holding her hands behind her back. She stood and carefully pulled free of her restraints.

But after a few seconds, Janel's gaze shifted back to the burning palace. Everyone's did. Xivan's mouth hung open, a look of absolute horror on her face as she stared at the devastated, burning remains of the Yoran palace.

Finally, the guards pulled out their weapons and began to walk forward toward Qown, Ninavis, and Janel. They might have still been in shock, but they still spoke the language of violence.

"Oh, come on," Ninavis said as she noticed their behavior. "It is way too cold out here to fight. Those women look like they're going to freeze to death."

"They always look like that," Qown said. "They're Yorans."

Ninavis waved Brother Qown off as she addressed the men. "Just hold a minute, will you? Let's not forget we just left an angry—whatever that woman is—"

"Suless," Janel provided. "She's the god-queen Suless. And she just . . . she just blew up the palace. Who was up there?"

"Everyone," Xivan said. "Everyone. They're all dead. My family is dead."

"No, they're not."

Everyone turned their heads at Senera's voice. She'd pulled the Name of All Things from her bodice and crouched down, writing in the snow with a finger.

"What?" Xivan woke up. "I left my whole family up in the great hall."

Senera shook her head as she tucked the stone back into her bodice. "I just asked. They were gone by the time the palace exploded. Your family is still alive."*

"Of course they are," Janel said. Disgust had replaced shock.

"What do you mean, 'of course they are'?" Xivan brandished Khoreval, seconds from using it on Janel.

Janel exhaled. "Do you think Suless would give your husband—your son—a *quick* death? Does that really sound like something she'd do?"

Brother Qown's stomach clenched. It didn't sound at all like

---

* I'm not sure you were paying attention, but Veixizhau gave birth to a healthy daughter, whom Duke Kaen promptly ignored after taking the step of ordering Wyrga to stay away from them both.

Mother and daughter are missing too.

something Suless would do. He shuddered. Quur had a thousand stories about what the witch-queen Suless did with stolen children. Ten times as many existed in Yor about what she did with men. She'd always been a monster.

Xivan dragged a hand over her face. "*How* did this happen?"

"That's the question I'd like to know too," Janel answered.

Qown said, "Somehow my gaesh, Suless's gaesh—they've vanished. I have no idea how. It should be impossible. Would you *stop* that?"

The guards had started advancing again.

"Stand down," Xivan ordered. She motioned for the guards to lower their weapons. "Free the Marakori woman. I have no interest in taking prisoners today. Let them all go."

The Spurned exchanged some looks, but no one protested her order. A woman untied Ninavis.

"Oh," Senera said.

Janel turned to her. "Oh?"

"Someone's finally done it. Fulfilled one of the prophecies. Destroyed the Stone of Shackles. That means someone's found Godslayer—Urthaenriel. And so, all gaeshe have been broken, just as predicted."

Xivan started to laugh, a wild, crazed sound. "Perfect. Just perfect. My husband looked for that damn thing for decades, and someone finds it *now*."

Senera rolled her eyes. "Finally."

Janel threw Senera a murderous look. *"Finally?"* Janel turned to Qown. "Didn't you tell me, all the way back in Barsine Banner, that the only thing keeping every demon bound and unable to enter our world unsummoned was a *gaesh*?"

Qown's eyes widened. "Oh no."

"We anticipated that," Senera snapped. "The prophecies made it perfectly clear. Why do you think we had Aeyan'arric freezing bodies after we killed them? Do you have any idea how many souls Thaena has been able to recover from demons because of us? How many demons she's been able to destroy because we left them trapped for her to find?"

"I thought you hated Thaena," Qown said.

"Oh, I do," Senera said, "but I'll still use her to destroy demons. She has to be good for something."

"Don't you dare," Janel snarled through gritted teeth. "Don't try to pretend what you did in Mereina had anything to do with altruism. You and Relos Var are *not* the heroes here. You did this to terrorize the region, so Duke Kaen could walk into Jorat—save the day—and be hailed as the new Atrin Kandor. You weren't sabotaging a demonic invasion, you were waging war."

Senera smiled. "This was always war. At least now we can to stop pretending it was anything else."

"Enough!" Xivan Kaen said. "I don't care about demons. I don't care about my husband's damn war! Tell me where Suless is, Senera. Tell me right *now*."

Senera stopped smiling. "Your Grace, I'd be glad to help, but Wyrga—Suless—knows I have the Name of All Things. She knows what it can do. She's not going to stop moving for long enough for us to catch up with her. And while you're chasing her, what happens to your dominion?"

Xivan's expression epitomized quiet fury. Her voice was soft. "Do you have family, Senera? Do you love someone?"

Senera blinked. "No."

"Someday," Xivan said. "Someday you will. And when you do, only then will you understand. In the meantime, trust me when I say I don't give a *fuck* what happens to Yor. This place was my husband's obsession, not mine. The only Yorans I give a damn about are my family and the people standing right here!"

As if on cue, several dozen women stood to attention. The male Yoran soldiers looked at a loss. Reality was starting to set in.

"Are we free to leave, then?" Janel asked.

"And go where?" Ninavis glanced over at Janel. "I hate to break this to you, but we're not going to make it far without food, water, or winter clothing." Ninavis glanced over at Janel.

"Although I suppose you could keep us from freezing to death with that trick of yours."

Janel turned to Xivan. "I don't suppose you'd—"

Qown broke off reading.

Kihrin frowned. "What's wrong? Why did you stop?"

But then he heard a noise behind him.

Kihrin turned around in time to see a gate open in the tavern's center and Relos Var step through.

PART IV

DEMON FALLS

53: BROTHERS

Jorat Dominion, Quuros Empire.
Three days since Miya discovered that her son
wasn't dead after all and then discovered
that no, he really was

The people sleeping on the ground or lounging on the other side of the tavern room proved they'd just been pretending. They jumped to their feet, reaching for weapons. Janel stood, scowling. Ninavis reached under the bar for her bow. Star pushed Dorna behind him, while Brother Qown inhaled, eyes wide.

Kihrin drew his sword and stood there, eyes narrowed.

"Var, you unbelievable—" Janel started to move forward.

Kihrin caught her arm. "Stop." He pointed at the ground before them. Here Relos Var had created a defensive second portal, which acted like a moat. It opened onto bright teal sky. Nothing but bright teal sky, and Kihrin was sure dawn hadn't yet arrived where they were.

So it was a long way away, with a long drop to the ground.

"There's one other problem," Kihrin said. He grabbed his cup from the bar and hurled it at Relos Var.

The cup passed right through Relos Var and fell through the second gate, which was still open on the figure's other side.

"So now that we've established you can't attack me, shall we talk like—" Relos Var said.

Kihrin turned to Janel. "I'm not seeing whatever you're seeing. Trust me, Relos Var isn't there. I assume he's projecting some sort of illusion."

Relos Var sighed and vanished.

The wizard reappeared. He didn't use a gate this time. Between one second and the next, the wizard simply stood in the room as if he'd always been there.

"Satisfied?" Var said.

Instead of answering, Kihrin touched Urthaenriel to the edge of the portal on the ground, which fizzled out and vanished. Then Kihrin stepped forward, lunged with Urthaenriel—

Janel grabbed his hand and pulled Kihrin back before he fell through a giant gate—which had opened in the air directly in front of him. Urthaenriel could disrupt portals, but only if Kihrin touched the edges with her. Otherwise, the sword could travel through the center of a gate as well as anyone else.

"The wizard's put some kind of gate in front of himself," Dango called out. "Can't get a shot."

"Here too," Ninavis said. "It must be wrapped around him."

Ninavis's people spread out through the tavern. Most of them had bows drawn, but all had the same problem as Dango: no clear shot.

The illusion of Relos Var appeared again to the side, outside the gate barrier, so suddenly Kihrin couldn't stop himself from glancing in the wizard's direction.

"Oh, you can see me now," Var said.

"I could see you last time," Kihrin admitted, "but I wanted to draw you out. There was no point in stabbing an illusion."

Relos Var scowled before turning to Janel. "Do you want to play these games? Because I can easily leave, taking Khoreval with me too. I'll be curious to see what you do when Morios shows up to ravage Atrine, but it won't be my problem."

Kihrin cocked his head. "Did you really vanish on Duke Kaen like that because I died? What were you going to do when you saw my murderers? Shake Gadrith's hand or—?"

Relos Var rolled his eyes. "Don't act like a child. Though I realize that's all but impossible for you. How many times do I have to explain that I'm not your enemy?"

"Explain as much as you like; it doesn't mean I'll ever believe you."

Relos Var continued as though Kihrin hadn't spoken. "It was my fault for not keeping better track of what Gadrith and Darzin were plotting. Thank you for killing both, by the way. Especially Gadrith."

"I didn't do it for your approval."

"I never claimed you did." Relos Var seemed to be grinding his teeth.

"So let me guess—you returned from the Capital before Tya came back from consulting with Thaena about Aeyan'arric," Kihrin said, "and you reclaimed Khoreval from Xivan Kaen—and made a deal with Janel. But explain something for me, 'big brother.' Why do we need Khoreval again? Janel already killed a dragon with Khoreval, and it didn't stick."

"Don't be so humble," Relos Var said. "You've killed one yourself."

"What?" Kihrin blinked. "Uh, no? I'm sure I haven't . . ."

"In the Afterlife," Janel whispered. "You slew Xaloma using Khoreval."

Kihrin paused. He'd like to think he'd remember a thing like that. It seemed important. And yet, clearly, he had some big gaps in his memory of events that occurred in the Afterlife. He really needed to find out how Janel and Teraeth were remembering their experiences in the Afterlife. "Fine," Kihrin said. "I'll take your word for it. And I'll assume this 'Xaloma' will recover too. Seems to me Khoreval isn't that great at killing dragons, so why do we need it again?"

At that, Relos Var smiled. He glanced over at Qown. "You haven't figured it out yet."

Brother Qown straightened. "Figured what out?"

"What the Cornerstones *really* are."

Qown blinked. "What do Cornerstones have to do with—" His eyes widened. "Wait—oh sun—"

Relos Var turned back to Kihrin and Janel. "You need both Khoreval and Urthaenriel because it isn't enough to simply kill a dragon. You must also simultaneously destroy the dragon's heart—what we know as a Cornerstone. And only Urthaenriel can destroy a Cornerstone."

Janel blinked. "Wait. A Cornerstone is the *heart* of a dragon?"

"Not literally," Relos Var said. "It's a metaphor."

Janel looked extremely relieved for some reason.*

"Where's your Cornerstone? Just curious." Kihrin hadn't lowered the sword.

"I don't have one."

"And once again, I don't believe you," Kihrin said.

Relos Var vanished. The portal wall vanished.

Relos Var—the real Relos Var—stepped forward to Kihrin. "Then stab me," he told Kihrin, "but the moment you stick me with that little piece of metal, I'll revert to my true form—" He glanced around the tavern. "Which is considerably larger than this room. So Urthaenriel won't protect you—or your friends—from being smeared against the bedrock. I'll heal. But you?" He shrugged. "Thaena's quite busy killing demons at the moment, but I assume she'd get around to Returning you at some point." Var glanced at Janel. "And you. But probably not anyone else."

Kihrin set the edge of Urthaenriel against Relos Var's neck. "You're bluffing."

Relos Var smiled. "Am I?"

Another gate opened.

Kihrin didn't look away from Relos Var, lest this prove a distraction. But the wizard seemed just as surprised by the gate as anyone else.

Relos Var's eyes widened. "Thurvishar?"

The Lord Heir of House D'Lorus ran through the open portal, which briefly showed a watery expanse and a sky preparing for dawn. He closed the gate, turned around, and

---

* Probably because Kihrin split Xaloma's heart between himself and Janel, at least if Thurvishar D'Lorus's book is to be believed. I have to assume that would have been a largely symbolic gesture. I think.

then drew up short as he took in the scene in front of him.

"Is this a bad time?"

Brother Qown said, "Thurvishar, what are you doing here? You were supposed to wait—"

"I did," Thurvishar protested. "That's why I'm here. Morios just climbed out of Lake Jorat. He's attacking Atrine."

54: THE PROBLEM WITH TRUST

Jorat Dominion, Quuros Empire.
Three days since Kihrin had a realistic
sense of the odds

Before anyone else could say a word, Thurvishar reopened the gate behind him. This time, the point of view was much higher up over Atrine. Someone cursed as the portal framed a nightmare scene.

Urthaenriel's edge left Relos Var's neck; Kihrin couldn't stop himself from staring. The night sky through the portal was lightening gradually—they *had* been up all night—but Atrine itself glowed with mage-light and fire. The flickering light highlighted the edges of a colossal shape, as it demolished a section of the white quartz wall surrounding the city. Screams echoed, audible even from this side of the gate.

If the scale hadn't deceived him—and Kihrin didn't think it had—then Morios towered in comparison to Aeyan'arric. Morios even dwarfed the other dragon Kihrin had seen: Sharanakal. Morios was gargantuan. And once the light hit the dragon's scales just right—

"Are those—are those *swords*? Are those dragon's scales swords?" Kihrin glanced over at Janel. "Why didn't anyone mention the dragon is covered with swords?"

Thurvishar shook his head. "They're not really swords, but they're just as sharp and lethal. But it's not just on the surface— Morios is metal all the way through."

"How do you kill a dragon made from metal?" Ninavis muttered.

The dragon smashed a tower of the duke's palace.* Pieces of stone flew, some hurtling straight at the open portal. Thurvishar waved a hand to close the gate, but several chunks of stone made it through. Janel and Kihrin both ducked to the side as one of the missiles slammed into the bar where they'd been standing, smashing paneling to kindling.

Relos Var turned to Kihrin. "*Now* can we talk?"

Kihrin's sword wavered in his hands.

He lowered Urthaenriel.

"Everyone stand down," Ninavis called out.

Kihrin turned to Relos Var. "Explain how this is *supposed* to happen, us working together here. Explain it to me like I'm hearing it for the first time."

Kihrin knew cons. He knew scams. His adoptive mother, Ola, had been fond of them. So he wanted to see if Relos Var's story would change from what he'd told the others; he also wanted to see how the story *didn't* change.

Relos Var pressed his lips together. "The only way you can permanently destroy a dragon—much as the only way you can permanently destroy their corresponding Cornerstone—is to annihilate both simultaneously. Every dragon has a matching Cornerstone. Unfortunately, while dragons can be slain in a variety of ways, the only method I know to destroy a Cornerstone is Urthaenriel. You can understand why I never bothered telling Duke Kaen where Morios laired; until we had Urthaenriel in our possession, fighting the dragon would have been futile."

"You still don't have Urthaenriel in your possession," Kihrin pointed out.

Relos Var ignored the correction. "We also required the location of Morios's Cornerstone, but since Senera has the Name of All Things, we had simply to ask. We destroy both Morios and his Cornerstone together, they both die forever."

Kihrin felt a chill wash over his skin. "Go back to the part

---

* I'm reasonably certain Duke Xun died with that first strike to his residence.

about destroying Cornerstones permanently—are you saying I *didn't* shatter the Stone of Shackles?"

"Oh, you did," Relos Var replied, "but it won't stay broken. The Stone of Shackles will reform, and eventually, people will realize gaeshing is once again possible. Too late to put the demons back in their cages, unfortunately."

Kihrin ground his teeth. "And the Stone of Shackles is the heart of which dragon?"

"This is an unimportant tangent."

"Tell me, anyway."

"Rol'amar." Var growled the name like it was a personal insult. A fleeting expression of loathing crossed the wizard's face.

Kihrin carefully filed away the name *Rol'amar* for future use.

"Much as I respect your desire to continue your staring contest," Janel said, "perhaps we can indulge later? After evacuating Atrine?"

Both men looked over at her in surprise.

"I never said I'd go along with this," Kihrin said.

Janel cocked her head and stared at him in turn.

Kihrin coughed. "All right, yes. I'm helping."

"We can best help Atrine by destroying Morios," Relos Var told Janel. "If you focus on evacuation first, you're letting sentimentality cloud your judgment."

"No, I'm not. If we don't pull people out of Atrine—right now—we shall soon find ourselves facing a combination of raging fires and terrified, screaming souls. And such a recipe summons a special sort of connoisseur to dinner."

Relos Var made a face. "Demons."

"Exactly. They'll swarm Atrine. I'd rather face one enemy at a time." Janel looked back at Thurvishar. "Can you open a gate to the east Atrine bridge? That's where the Marakori slums are located."

"I see no reason why not. Where's Senera?"

Relos Var scowled. "In Atrine. *She* was supposed to signal me when Morios arrived."

Thurvishar stared at the man hatefully. "You didn't hear from her, with a raging dragon on the loose? And you weren't going to say anything? *Damn* it!"* Thurvishar immediately reopened a portal and started to rush through. He stopped at the last second and turned to the room. "If the rest of you are coming along, do it now, or haggle with Relos Var for the privilege later."

"Thurvishar!" Kihrin said.

"I'm not joking, Kihrin. I'm leaving now—with you or without you."

Ninavis clapped her hands over her head. "All right, people, we've practiced this. Everyone through the gate, right now. We'll regroup on the other side."

Dorna ran toward the stable, yelling, "Arasgon! Talaras! Lead the others. It's time to say goodbye. Palom—Star, help me out here."

Kihrin saw even Relos Var looked bemused at Thurvishar's reaction. Janel and Qown's story had certainly implied that he and Senera had the opportunity to know each other, but this seemed to indicate a deeper relationship. Kihrin found himself wondering if they'd been something other than casual associates.†

Everyone must indeed have practiced this, because they cleared out with a speed and efficiency that struck Kihrin as militarized. Arasgon and Scandal trotted down the ramp, leading the horses, while Talaras was last to catch any stragglers who balked at traveling through the gate.

Finally, the only people left were Kihrin, Janel, Thurvishar, and Relos Var.

Janel turned her gaze to Kihrin and Relos Var with obvious concern. "Don't be foolish, either of you," she warned. "We need both of you right now." She stepped through the portal.

---

* I honestly have no idea why Thurvishar was so upset here. Did he think we'd lose the Name of All Things if I died?

† Absolutely, emphatically *not*. I've barely spoken to Thurvishar D'Lorus, let alone formed an amorous . . . it's a ridiculous notion. I would sooner eat glass than become involved with a royal, under any circumstances.

And yes, I'm aware he's not really royalty and that he was Sandus's son—and that you were fond of Sandus for reasons that escape me. It's still unthinkable.

"After you," Relos Var said to Kihrin.

"You should tell Aeyan'arric she doesn't need to sit watchdog over this tavern anymore," Kihrin said.

"She'll figure it out," Var replied.

"Why are you really doing this? You don't care if Morios is dead or not, and I really don't think you give a damn what happens to a quarter million people either. What's really going on?"

"Can we please hurry?" Thurvishar snapped.

"One moment," Relos Var said. He turned back to Kihrin. "Let there be no lies between us. You're right. I don't care what happens to Atrine, and my feelings toward Morios are at best ambivalent. I'm doing this because I care about fulfilling the prophecies. I also care a great deal what it will mean when Janel stops Morios."

"That's right. You need to replace Duke Kaen as Jorat's rebel ruler, don't you? Janel's the backup plan." It was almost refreshing to hear Var admit he didn't care. The wizard only ever helped when his goals temporarily aligned with others. Var wanted to see some Hellwarrior-related prophecy fulfilled— helped along by Janel overthrowing Duke Xun, by killing Morios. The population would interpret her victory over the dragon as proof of her right to rule them. Which put her one step closer to smashing the empire. And *that* was what Relos Var wanted. As always, he played the long game.

Var smiled. "By the way, if you break Janel's heart, I will make your life a living hell."

Kihrin felt himself flush with anger. "Seriously? You're giving me the *father* talk?"

"I don't see Qoran Milligreest stepping up to do it."

Thurvishar cleared his throat. Kihrin hadn't realized someone could clear their throat *angrily* before. Thurvishar looked like he was seconds from closing the portal on them both.

"Let's go kill a dragon," Relos Var said.

Kihrin walked through the portal.

55: THE DRAGON OF WAR

Atrine, Jorat Dominion, Quuros Empire.
Three days since Kihrin asked questions to which he
already knew the answer—actually, forget this one: that
could be any day in the past twenty years

When Kihrin looked back, he realized Thurvishar hadn't followed. He suspected the mage had opened a second gate, in a far more dangerous location, somewhere inside Atrine. Kihrin shook his head. Senera wore the Name of All Things—and as far as Kihrin knew, any Cornerstone protected its wearer from casual scrying. Which meant Kihrin had no idea how Thurvishar intended to *find* Senera in a city that size, let alone help the woman if she proved to be in jeopardy.

Of course, given what Kihrin had been told about Senera, he also wouldn't have prioritized her rescue. Thurvishar clearly had differing opinions.

Then a deafening roar made the ground shake, and Kihrin put his hands over his ears, wondering how anyone closer could possibly stand it. When the sound quieted, he looked to its source, toward Atrine.

Since Thurvishar had placed them at the end of the east bridge, Kihrin had a reasonably unobstructed view of the city itself, rising too tall to be obscured by the bridge's shanties and slums. As sunrise fast approached, the sky had begun to lighten in anticipation of dawn. He could now see what perched on top of the highest towers of the city—presumably the fast crumbling remnants of the duke's palace.

"Taja save me," he whispered.

Steel and iron, drussian and shanathá—every metal, a thousand metals, all twisted together in sharp swordlike tangles to form the dragon's body. It resembled a porcupine warped into nightmare, formed by an insane and malevolent god. Morios's wings seemed less like tools for flying than weapons to scour and excoriate, lash and annihilate. Nothing about the dragon spoke to any purpose other than slaughter and mayhem.

Morios raked and gnawed and chewed on the stone towers and walls, the duke's palace's spires, akin to a dog with a favorite bone. The ancient granite provided little resistance, crumbling and falling to ruin under his weight. His thrashing tail smashed buildings, and his claws left deep and horrifying grooves through entire neighborhoods.

The first time he'd seen the fire dragon, Sharanakal, he'd wondered how anyone had ever thought they could kill a creature like that. Sharanakal hadn't seemed alive as much as an animated force of nature, a volcano brought to life.

Morios was worse.

Janel shoved Kihrin's shoulder. "Snap out of it. Our priority is evacuating as many people as possible. The Atrine main gates aren't designed to let more than a few people through at a time." She pointed to the bridge, where panicked people were running from the slums.

Kihrin felt his gut twist. He remembered Janel's description of Atrine—a place designed to trap and kill horses. It seemed to him it would do just as fine a job of trapping and killing people. The Marakori forced to live outside the city could run, but Joratese wouldn't be able to escape quickly enough.

"How are we going to—?" Kihrin started to ask.

The firebloods trotted over.

"We'll direct people to this side of the bridge." Janel grabbed Arasgon's saddle and pulled herself up. "Relos Var, follow us. I want you to pull down the wall when we reach the east gate, and open a portal leading to safety. We'll herd people to you."

Relos Var blinked and slowly smiled. "As you say."

Arasgon turned and called out something to the rest of the crowd.*

"On it," Sir Baramon responded as he mounted Arasgon's fireblood brother Talaras. Everyone was following suit, because this was Jorat, and of course everyone had their own horses. Brother Qown had a horse. Even Star had managed to find a horse of his own from somewhere.

Kihrin felt something shove him from the side. He almost raised his sword before he realized it was Scandal, pushing him with her nose.

"Hurry!" Janel yelled. "You have ridden before, haven't you?"

"Oh yeah, riding lessons every day when I was growing up in the slums of the Capital City." Kihrin made a face. "Of course I've never ridden!"

Janel grinned. "Good thing you just need to hang on."

Scandal shoved Kihrin again.

"Fine!" Kihrin snapped. "But don't blame me if I fall off." Urthaenriel murmured angry complaints as he sheathed her, but he ignored that. Kihrin grabbed a section of Scandal's mane for leverage and jumped up on her back. Naturally, Scandal wasn't saddled, and Kihrin felt sure that this wasn't going to make for a fun ride.

He looked over in time to see Relos Var summon a horse out of thin air, a creature of smoke and darkness that looked ephemeral but held his weight perfectly.

"Show-off," Kihrin muttered.

But all of them immediately perceived a problem. The narrow main path through the slums only allowed for one horse at a time, but now it was jammed with people trying to run away from the city. Some of those people were pushing others out of the way, resorting to violence in panicked fear for their lives.

---

* What Arasgon said: "Ride through into the city and lead as many people out as you can."

"Make way!" Janel screamed, but they paid no attention. The firebloods shouted something too, but it seemed unlikely the Marakori had understood them.

"Oh, this is ridiculous," Relos Var said. "We do *not* have time for this."

Relos Var brought his hands together.

A portal opened on the ground ahead of them, spanning the width and length of the entire bridge.

Everyone on the bridge—as well as every building, shanty, and shack—fell through.

Behind them on land, farther down the road leading to the city, Kihrin heard shouts and screams and the accumulated crash of multiple objects. Presumably this was every displaced building, shanty, and shack—all hitting the ground of their new location at the same time.

Scandal said something. So did Star. Kihrin liked to imagine both cursed eloquently.* Kihrin himself could only look, slack-jawed, aware most of the others appeared similarly stunned. Time froze for a moment as everyone stared.

Then Kihrin remembered that this was the man the Eight Immortals had said they couldn't kill. Although technically speaking, Relos Var wasn't a man anymore. And on the plus side, the bridge was clear, and the Marakori living there were now evacuated.

Caring not at all what everyone else thought of his sorcery, Relos Var opened a second, less trap-like portal. "To the east gate," he announced.

After a moment's hesitation, everyone guided their rides—whether horse or fireblood—through.

When Kihrin exited the portal and looked back toward the shore, he realized he'd underestimated the bridge's length. Suddenly, he understood why everyone had immediately gone for their horses, even if Var had then provided a faster passage.

* They did.

The bridge was miles across. He suppressed a shiver, thinking of what Relos Var had done.*

Of course, that same mistake in scale meant Morios loomed even larger than he'd initially thought. Still, once in the lee of the east gate's white quartz walls, Morios was no longer visible. The terrified guards within had little to go on, in terms of protecting their people. They'd just seen the bridge's entire shantytown vanish before their eyes, accompanied by a roar reminiscent of an earthquake. The bridge must therefore have seemed the greatest threat, representing the most obvious and deadly use of witchcraft. So the guards had decided not to let anyone leave.

"You!" a rattled guard shouted. "Identify yourselves!" He looked like he might fire his crossbow without waiting for an answer.

Janel ignored him. "Here!" Janel said, dismounting. "Var! That wall there!" She pointed, not at the gate itself but at the wall beside it.

The wizard raised an eyebrow at her commanding tone, but regardless, he narrowed his eyes at the offending structure. It began collapsing in on itself, as if succumbing to age and the weathering of millennia in a matter of seconds. The crowd behind it pulled back, clearly terrified. Oh, and Morios became visible once more.

"Good," Janel said. "Now I need—"

Several of the guards fired their crossbows.

Relos Var batted them out of the sky before he turned to Janel. "Enough of this! You have a job to do." He held out his hand, and a spear appeared in it, which he tossed in her direction. Khoreval.

Janel caught it. "My job is to protect my people, Relos! I'll deal with Morios once the city is cleared."

"He'll bring the city down around your ears!"

"So distract him," Kihrin said.

---

* I'm impressed, and I've known you for a long time.

Var turned his head. "What was that?"

"You're a dragon too," Kihrin said. "Don't even *try* to pretend you're not. Every person who participated in that ritual to create Vol Karoth was turned into a dragon, *including you*. So you're more than capable of distracting Morios, until we can evacuate. Then we'll talk about killing the damn creature."

Relos Var stared at him, lips drawn back in a sneer. Janel watched, waiting for Var's response.

"Well?" Kihrin said.

Relos Var turned his phantom horse around and galloped to the edge of the bridge, away from Lake Jorat and toward Demon Falls. The phantom horse jumped.

For anyone else, it would have been suicide. But Var seemed to hover for a second in the night air, the magical construct horse vanished, and his form blurred. What replaced him was an extraordinary sight—enormous and reptilian, winged and clawed. He confirmed what Kihrin had long suspected: that he was the dragon Kihrin had seen briefly in Kharas Gulgoth before Relos Var had shown up in person. That indeed, the morgage hadn't been mistaken when they had depicted nine draconic shapes—not eight—leaving the site of the botched ritual that had created Vol Karoth. His hide glimmered with metallic rainbow shimmers in the predawn light.

Gasps and some screams echoed from those realizing two dragons were now on the scene. Relos Var was clearly smaller than Morios, but that didn't make him *small*. And since there had never been such a thing as a good dragon, no one could be blamed for assuming the new dragon's motives were equally malevolent.

Urthaenriel sang Kihrin a song of hate.

"Not yet," Kihrin whispered to her. "Not yet."

Relos Var banked, caught a crosswind, then turned and soared back toward the city. He was silent as he glided in toward Morios . . .

And slammed into the other dragon. Morios's metal spikes screeched against Relos Var's more elegant serpentine armor.

Then both monsters tumbled backward, sailing over Atrine and splashing down into Lake Jorat, out of view.

"You know he was the only one of us here who can open a portal, now Thurvishar's run off somewhere," Janel pointed out.

"He was also becoming impatient with our insistence on 'saving lives,'" Kihrin said. "Now he has something interesting to distract him, so let's help these people, shall we?"

Ninavis trotted up next to Janel. "You have this handled?"

"It's even easier, now that we don't have to worry about the shanties blocking our way. We should be fine." Janel gave Ninavis a significant look. "You know what you need to do."

Ninavis waved to the riders behind her. "Come on, people, let's move!"

The rest of her group rode with her, entering the city even as the last crumbling remains of the wall turned to dust.

Star gave Kihrin a salute as he passed.

"You lot!" Janel shouted at the guards. "Come over here and help with this. Right now!"

To Kihrin's utter astonishment, they did. The dragon was probably just more shock than they could handle, and they would have done what anyone had ordered.

People began streaming toward the bridge from the city—not questioning their sudden lack of wall but fully willing to take advantage of it. Many were bloodied and covered in stone dust from collapsing buildings or were coughing from smoke inhalation.

Arasgon began yelling, since the Joratese at least understood him—and he sure had a set of lungs on him. Then Kihrin saw a flicker of light out of the corner of his eye and saw a second gate open. Thurvishar stepped through, holding a bleeding, unconscious Senera. Inexplicably, she was glowing brightly.

"Qown!" Thurvishar shouted. "Over here!"

The Vishai priest looked up from helping a woman with a cut on her arm. "What? Oh—" He pressed a piece of cloth over the woman's wound. "Keep pressing, like this. But don't stop walking until you reach the other side." The woman nodded and quickly ran off, lost in the rapidly expanding crowd running to cross the bridge.

Kihrin rushed over to Thurvishar. "What happened?"*

Thurvishar set the woman down. Blood matted one side of her head. "She must have been struck by debris. I found her half-buried." He waved a hand. "The glowing part will fade."

"I didn't know you two were lovers," Kihrin said.

Thurvishar's eyes widened. "We're not." The wizard seemed to search for words or an excuse for his actions. Something. "She has the Name of All Things. We're going to need her."

Kihrin nodded. "Sure. Of course. What other possible reason could there be?"

Thurvishar glared at him.

Qown knelt next to Senera. "Give me room." He looked at the woman's eyes, then covered the side of her head with one hand.

Thurvishar turned his head and raised a wall of solid stone ten feet in the air. It curved inward, forming a protective pocket around them.

Qown hesitated. "That works." He returned to concentrating on Senera.

"Thurvishar," Kihrin said, snapping his fingers. "Qown has this. You're with me. Let's see if we can give these people a faster way off the island."

Thurvishar stood. "Did I just see *two* dragons fly overhead?"

"Yes, you did. The second one is Relos Var."

Thurvishar blinked and then shook his head. "It's really a pity he can't be on our side all the time."

"Yeah, if only human life held any value to him . . . He'd be *great*." Kihrin forced his way through the crowds, until he

---

* He must have cast a spell over the entire city that made anyone of Doltari ancestry glow. Which neatly circumvents the scrying protections provided by a Cornerstone.

I'm going to remember that trick.

reached a spot in the lee of a giant piece of masonry that used to be part of the palace. "Let's put a gate right here. Make it as large as you safely can. And put the other side somewhere reasonably close to where Relos Var sent everyone else so families can find each other."

Thurvishar frowned. "Wouldn't we be better off sending them as far away as possible?"

"Do you know *any* spot that's actually safe right now?"

"Good point."

Out near the center of Lake Jorat, a searing beam of white fire soared up into the sky, turning the lake and all the surrounding land bright as day. People screamed and covered their eyes. Kihrin winced and looked away, but still saw ghosts dancing in front of his eyes. A second later, Relos Var and Morios both erupted from the water, clawing and biting at each other.

As far as Kihrin could tell, Relos Var had done no damage at all to Morios. Unfortunately, the reverse wasn't true. Great rents in Relos Var's hide streamed silver blood into the water, and he was clearly not doing well. Normally, Kihrin would have cheered, but . . .

If Morios ended up killing Relos Var, even if it was (as Var claimed) temporary, Kihrin had no idea what the rest of them were supposed to do.

Kihrin shook his head to snap himself out of it. One disaster at a time.

Janel had been working nonstop, herding people toward the now open gate, and it didn't seem like the crowd would ever slow. Scandal and Arasgon both helped, keeping people from trampling each other in the rush to reach safety.

Every time Janel saw a Joratese soldier, no matter whose colors they wore, she pressed them into service.

Kihrin was slowly making his way over to her, when Janel froze. A group of Joratese nobles, resplendent in red and gold, were making their way in her direction with their entourage. Then Kihrin remembered what those colors meant. The

Malkoessians. Markreev Aroth of Stavira. Janel's former liege, Dorna's ex-husband, Star's illegitimate father.*

Kihrin picked out the Markreev easily enough. But Aroth Malkoessian was the man who did a double take when he first spotted Kihrin, probably because his coloring did indeed resemble his son Oreth's.

The Markreev and Janel stared at each other for a silent, tense moment, then Janel motioned for him to pass through the portal with the rest of his family.

He did.

Kihrin let out a breath he didn't realize he'd been holding.

Just in time to see Relos Var's bleeding draconic form fly over the bridge, falling straight over the side of Demon Falls.

---

* As if the Joratese care if people are married. I'm sure Star's claim to inherit is entirely legitimate. Which is a problem, now that I think about it.

56: THE ARMY WITH EIGHT GATES

Atrine, Jorat Dominion, Quuros Empire.
Three days since Jarith Milligreest found out
that his father was an idiot

Morios turned his attention back to Atrine.

The crowd had never been exactly calm about evacuating, but now their panic redoubled. Thurvishar was sweating from the strain of keeping the portal open for so long. Presumably he'd have had a much easier time of it if they'd had a Gatestone, since that seemed to help the House D'Aramarin mages. Then a second gate opened next to the first, and Senera walked through, gingerly touching her head. "We need to leave."

"I can't argue with that," Kihrin said. "Janel, it's our turn! Let's go."

"There's still people—" Janel started to protest.

Above their heads, Morios turned his head and looked right at the bridge.

Kihrin didn't think it was his imagination Morios was looking down at them in particular. He was quite sure Morios hadn't only seen him but that the dragon had *recognized* him. Dragons seemed to pay more attention to souls than people, and his would no doubt seem familiar.

"Arasgon, take Janel out of here!" Kihrin yelled. "Where's Qown?" He spotted the little priest not far from Senera's portal, which probably wasn't a coincidence.

"I'm here, but there's—"

"You're next to a gate. *Run!*" Kihrin shouted.

Morios raised a wicked, spiked claw over their heads, and

people surged for the open portals. Some, knowing they couldn't possibly make it in time, began jumping off the bridge on the Lake Jorat side.

Suddenly, Scandal stood next to Kihrin, and he vaulted onto her back. Janel and Arasgon, knowing they'd also never make it to a gate, didn't even try—they began galloping full out for the end of the bridge. Kihrin and Scandal followed. Or more accurately, Scandal followed, and Kihrin held on for dear life. He could only pray that the others had made it through the gate safely—which he did out loud, in case Taja could spare a second from fighting demons in the Afterlife.

He heard a loud whistling sound and looked back to see Morios's bladed body slicing through the air. Then the dragon's claw slammed into the bridge, making the entire length undulate. The section of bridge under Scandal's feet jumped. He fell out of sync with her, slammed against her back as she recovered, and slid off her side, holding on by a single tuft of mane.

Kihrin screamed. He felt Scandal slowing, trying to give him time to recover.

"Keep running!"

He could hear the metal-on-stone screeching of Morios's claws behind them. Right behind them.

Kihrin reached up, managed to find purchase with his other hand, and somehow pulled himself back up on Scandal's back. She whinnied, and he desperately wished he understood the language of firebloods.

The metallic scream suddenly stopped. The air vibrated behind him, and he heard an enormous *thud.* He looked back to see Morios slam himself a second time against a diaphanous rainbow-hued wall of energy that had materialized behind Kihrin.

Kihrin had seen something very much like it before, and just as he blinked in recognition, the bridge ended and he was on solid ground again. Morios gave one last, half-hearted attempt to break the magical energy field before turning his attention back to the city. Clearly, it was more interesting.

"Introduce us to your friends, Thurvishar," Janel was saying.

Kihrin turned around, his heartbeat still pounding. Several men in imperial military uniforms stood next to Thurvishar, Senera, and Qown. Another group of soldiers were busy leading away stragglers, those who'd made it through the portal before Morios had destroyed it. But Kihrin's focus was drawn to the woman who stood in the middle of the bridge, lowering a silver wand. She was a handsome olive-skinned woman in her forties, lavender-gray cloud-curl hair supporting a plain silver circlet. She wore black, but that color would never be half as deep as the fathomless night of her eyes. The woman saw Kihrin and grinned.

"Hey, Scamp," Tyentso said. "Miss me?"

Kihrin stared. He panicked for a moment, thinking this wasn't Tyentso at all, but rather some monster—the mimic Talon, maybe Xaltorath—counterfeiting her. However, he dismissed the idea as too easy to check.

Kihrin slid off Scandal and swept her into an expansive hug. "Tyentso, you're alive! By all the gods, you're alive!"

She sputtered. "Easy now, Scamp. You can't just go around hugging the emperor of Quur, you know."

"The what?" He blinked and took a second look at the silver circlet on her head, the slender wand in her hand. No . . . it couldn't be . . .

But the energy field that had held off Morios had matched the one surrounding the arena back in the Capital. The same arena where a new emperor was selected, whenever the last one died.

"Oh yes," Tyentso said, "I'm emperor. Empress? We're still figuring out the title. It's, uh—" She grinned again. "Not going to lie; it's *good*. Except having to deal with a damn dragon, two days into my reign, wasn't how I thought this would go."

Janel dismounted. "Go help with the evacuees," Janel told Arasgon. "There isn't anything you can do here."

He started to argue, then tossed his head in a way Kihrin could only assume meant *We'll talk about this later* and trotted away along with Scandal. She seemed perfectly fine with the idea of not staying around for any more fighting.

"Scamp?" Janel asked him carefully as she turned back to the group.

Kihrin held up a finger. "You don't get to call me that. There are rules. Only the emperor of Quur can use that name."*

Tyentso grinned at Janel. "You have my permission to call him that." Then she tilted her head toward Thurvishar. "Thank you for contacting me. As you can see, we moved as quickly as we could." She motioned for them to follow as she moved off the bridge, heading toward a distant cluster of men gathered before a table. Soldiers were busy erecting a tent around them. "This way. We have maps and battle plans and wizards from the Academy to ignore—all the amenities."

"I wondered how you'd arrived so fast," Senera mused.

As Thurvishar gestured toward a portal, Kihrin saw what had missed his attention earlier: the D'Lorus wizard wore an intaglio-cut ruby ring on each hand. One of those had been worn by Thurvishar's father, Emperor Sandus. Which meant the second had to be one of the enchanted rings Sandus had distributed to his secret agents, allowing them to report back directly to him. Directly to Tyentso, now.

"Where did you find a second ring—?" Kihrin started to ask.

"It's yours," Thurvishar said. "From the items Gadrith stripped from you. I suspected it would allow me to contact whoever held the Crown and Scepter of Quur, whether that person happened to be my father Sandus or not."

"May I see one of those rings?" Qown asked.

"Not right now."

"Thurvishar, why didn't you tell me we could—" Janel began, then shook her head. "Never mind. Smart thinking. I admit I had assumed we'd never see the army in time. The normal protocols—"

"Sometimes you have to move faster than the normal protocols," Tyentso said.

---

* Oh no, Scamp it is. It's official now.

"Where's Relos Var?" Senera asked.

"Excuse me?" Emperor Tyentso said. "Relos Var's *here*?"

"Not exactly," Kihrin said. "He went over the falls. Either dead or so injured it doesn't matter."

Senera stopped walking for a moment, grief plain on her face.

"He'll heal, though," Qown said to Senera. "Relos Var will be back."

"Not in time to help," Kihrin replied. "And he hadn't yet told us where to find Morios's Cornerstone. Apparently, we need to destroy that too, if we're to have any chance of permanently killing that damn monster."

"Then you're lucky I have that information," Senera said.

Thurvishar glanced over at Kihrin. "I told you we'd need her."

Imperial forces were leading refugees down the road from Atrine, past the hill where the army was encamped. Kihrin counted no fewer than eight magical portals, each with their own green-clad D'Aramarin Gatekeeper attached. Kihrin started to protest that he knew most sorcerers powerful enough to open a random magical portal, and these weren't them. Then he realized these weren't random. Someone had burned a complex combination of geometric and magical symbols at the base of each gate. Kihrin grappled with a sudden desire to question the Gatekeepers about exactly how Gatestones worked, but quelled the urge. At least someone in the Quuros army knew how to set up temporary Gatestones, and they'd been used to bring in troops and equipment.

The equipment mostly consisted of the imperial war machines known as scorpions. He'd heard about the fabled Quuros siege weapons for most of his life, but he'd never actually seen one, let alone the dozens being marched through the imperial portals. The metal devices most closely resembled their namesakes, except each was the size of a rhinoceros and probably weighed more. The driver used a strange orb with handles to steer, while two more soldiers rode in the back. One by one the scorpions took up positions along the shoreline, turning so the stingers could flip back like catapults. The massive machines settled to the ground, legs digging into the soil and locking into place.

"Here we are," said Tyentso as they arrived at her partially erected tent, a small swarm of imperial staff coming and going.

"Good, you've brought back—" High General Milligreest's greeting came to a sudden halt.

Kihrin counted at least a dozen men, some clearly high-ranking military officers and others wearing the colors of various Royal Houses. And of course, the high general.

"General Milligreest," Kihrin said.

The high general pursed his lips. "I should have known I'd find you anywhere someone's destroying a city." Dismissing Kihrin, he looked over the group. His gaze paused momentarily on Senera. He didn't look at Janel at all.

"Play nice, Qoran," Tyentso chided. She walked up to the table and pushed an Academy wizard out of the way. "Make a space, people. The adults have something to discuss."* She waved her group forward. "Now what was that about destroying Morios?"

Senera stepped up. She eyed the Academy wizards warily, then shrugged. "This is theoretical. As no dragon has yet been permanently slain, we're operating under conjecture—"

Tyentso made an annoyed noise. "Skip the caveats and get to the point."

"Morios and his Cornerstone, Warmonger, must be destroyed within thirty seconds of each other. We think. So we'll need to split up. Kihrin goes with Thurvishar to where the Cornerstone is hidden, and the rest of us kill Morios—which Khoreval should make easier." She pulled two small twigs out of her misha. They were identical, except that one was a normal twig made from wood and the second looked like wrought iron. "These are keyed to each other. The moment Morios has been slain, I'll

---

* Any chance we can keep her?

snap the normal twig, breaking its metal twin, signaling it's time to shatter Warmonger."

"You make it sound so easy," Kihrin said.

"No," Senera corrected. "I made it sound *simple.* It will most definitely not be easy."

"Why does Kihrin go with Thurvishar?" Janel asked.

"I assumed Kihrin would want to be with someone who could make a portal back." Senera turned to Kihrin. "I could do it, but I also assumed you'd prefer someone you actually trust."

"Preposterous!"

Everyone paused and looked over at the man who'd interrupted—an older Quuros wearing green robes.

"Havar D'Aramarin, right?" Tyentso said, eyes narrowed. "Just curious: Which part of that did you find preposterous?"

"I am *High Lord* Havar D'Aramarin," he corrected. "And the idea that this woman could open a freestanding portal beggars all belief. She's clearly lying and you're too naïve to realize it." He scowled. "As for you, don't expect anyone to consider you the *legitimate* emperor, when you didn't even win the right in the arena."

The high general gave Tyentso a warning look. "Don't."

Tyentso smiled. "Right now, I don't give a fuck who thinks I'm the legitimate emperor. I care about saving what's left of Atrine and its population. So unless you're here to help us, why don't you go check on your Gatekeepers?"

The high lord started to say something else, but Qoran Milligreest stepped up next to Tyentso and gave the high lord a look. The wizard turned on his heel and strode away.

"That one's going to cause trouble later," Senera murmured. "There's no way he won't try to have us arrested as witches when this is over."

Milligreest said, "You *should* be arrested—as a terrorist and a traitor."

Senera smiled. "It's nice to know my work is appreciated."

"Worry about it later," Janel said. "In the meantime, we're

missing an important piece of information: *Where* is Morios's Cornerstone?"

"Oh," Senera said as if she'd forgotten an insignificant detail. "In the god-king Khorsal's throne room, under a thousand feet of water, at the bottom of Lake Jorat."

57: Memories of Horses

Atrine, Jorat Dominion, Quuros Empire.
Three days since Kihrin first learned
about Aeyan'arric

Janel stared at Senera. "Khorsal's palace? But Emperor Kandor destroyed that."

"No, just submerged it underwater when Kandor dammed the Endless Canyon," Kihrin said. "There's no reason the palace wouldn't still be down there." When Tyentso blinked at him, he said, "Teraeth told us about it, remember?"

Janel drummed her fingers against the table. "Anything *else* we need to know?"

Senera picked up someone's writing quill from the table and dabbed it in ink. "Yes. Thurvishar and Kihrin need sigils to let them breathe and survive the pressure." She paused to give Kihrin a thoughtful stare.

"They'll work on me as long as I have Urthaenriel sheathed when you draw them," he replied.

"Good."

"I'll need sigils too." Qown stepped forward. "I'm going with them."

Janel blinked. "You are?"

"Someone besides Thurvishar should hold Senera's signal branch. Thurvishar's going to be concentrating on magic portals and fighting off any hostile forces we find." Qown gestured at Kihrin. "And I don't know if the twig will even work if Kihrin holds it. Urthaenriel might block the effect."

Kihrin grimaced. "That's . . . possible."

Janel hesitated and then nodded. "All right. You three will smash the Cornerstone. The rest of us will fight Morios."

Senera moved to each man and drew something on their foreheads. Looking at the other two, Kihrin saw the now-familiar air glyph and a new, different symbol.

"There is one additional problem," Thurvishar said. "I can open a gate, but I don't know where this palace is located. The bottom of Lake Jorat is rather a big place."

"You only need to know the way out. I know the way in." Senera concentrated and wove her magic. The portal she created opened onto something black, the gate's normal mirror finish reflecting . . . nothing.

Kirin bet the watching Royal House wizards were giving themselves fits.

"We're doing this right now?" Qown seemed surprised. He set his satchel down next to the table.

"Every second we wait, more people die," Janel said.

"Why is the gate black?" Kihrin asked.

"Light can't reach that far underwater," Senera responded.

Since Kihrin had already resigned himself to ending up drenched, he walked to the portal. Halfway there, he turned back. "Hey, Janel."

She looked up. The tension around her eyes added a decade to her real age. "Yes?"

"Kick that dragon's ass. Somehow."

Janel smiled. "I will. And you be careful."

"What's to be careful about? I've got the easy job."

Senera held up the metal twig. "Aren't you forgetting something?"

"Oh! Thank you." Qown grabbed the fake twig. He stared at it, and the metal began to glow—like sunlight condensed into one tiny portable object.

"We can all swim, right?" Thurvishar asked.

"If not, we're going to learn." Kihrin blew Janel a kiss and walked through the gate. The others followed.

*

Kihrin's head stayed dry because the air sigil kept water from touching his face. But this proved more annoying than helpful. Instead of the visual clarity he might have gained by sticking his head underwater, it was as if he was "above" water, trying to see into the depths of a continuously moving pond. Kihrin had a hard time seeing, even with the light Qown created.

"This way." The lake water muffled Thurvishar's shout. The wizard tugged on Kihrin's misha and Qown's robes as he pointed toward the murky pillars in the distance.

They swam a ways, and Kihrin found himself thinking about the questions he should have asked earlier. Were there crocodiles in these waters? Sharks? Predators of any kind? He saw fish. Or in any event, saw the silver flash of a scaled hide, before a piscine shape made an abrupt about-face and swam away.

Brother Qown, also dissatisfied with the visibility, summoned several glowing mage-lights in addition to the glowing twig, lighting up wide swaths of the lakebed.

A palace lay ahead.

It must have indeed been a wonder in its time, featuring enormous broad colonnades, raceways, roads, and parks where large animals could mingle. The architecture had faded and weathered, worn down by water, accumulated freshwater reeds, and pond scum. Enough had survived for Kihrin to see that yes, that was a centaur, and yes, those were firebloods. He didn't spot any human statues, but then Khorsal had been a god-king who'd loved horses far more than humanity.

They swam forward, assuming all roads led to the horse king's throne room.

Kihrin saw no skeletons. He supposed if there had been any—if every centaur hadn't all died on the bridge to Atrine—fish would surely have eaten any remains.

Everywhere, the accommodations catered to equine needs: no stairs, no second floors, nothing one might call a roof. As they swam farther, Kihrin caught odd glimpses of architecture unlike the streamlined style Khorsal had favored. As if Khorsal had himself built on another city's ruins.

Then they found the only stairs they had seen in the entire city, leading to a space that was less a room than a formal receiving courtyard, either intentionally open to the sky or made that way through the centuries. The floor had been enrobed in the silt, mud, and muck of ages, interrupted only by sticks and branches sticking up at odd angles.

Still, some details of the throne room's splendor remained. Qown's mage-lights glinted against gold, and four rearing centaur statues decorated the corners. The stairs led up to a large throne, whose back formed a large spike rising several feet higher than the chair. Something was going on at the top of that spike: a faint beam of light led either to or away from that apex.

Thurvishar pointed to the top of the throne and said something.

"What?" Kihrin shouted. "I can't hear you."

As Thurvishar started to shout again, glowing gold lettering appeared, floating in the water before them. The writing said: *I'm removing the water from this area. Be ready to fall.*

Kihrin saw Thurvishar give an affirmative sign to Brother Qown.

The priest concentrated and Kihrin thought Qown must have transformed the water to air, since a vacuum never filled the space.

All three men fell to the ground, Kihrin more gracefully than the other two. He brushed himself off as best as one could while sopping wet and ankle-deep in mud.

"Is that what we're looking for?" Kihrin pointed to the spike behind the throne. The light was harder to see, but still faintly present.

"Maybe," Thurvishar said. The wizard walked over to the throne and used it as a stool to climb up and examine the top of the spike.

Wiping the mud away revealed an eight-sided gemstone. Thurvishar stared at it, concentrating.

Kihrin felt himself grow a little jealous. He missed being

able to see past the First Veil, but Urthaenriel hadn't changed her mind about allowing him to use magic. Of course, Kihrin had his own way of discerning magic. For instance, Urthaenriel continued to scream at him for allowing not just one, but two, Cornerstones within proximity. One near Qown and another near the throne.

Which confirmed Senera's story that this was where Warmonger had been hidden.

"I have no idea what this crystal's made from," Thurvishar said.

"That's a good sign. If you could tell what it was made from, it wouldn't be a Cornerstone."

"So what do we do now?" Brother Qown said.

Kihrin unsheathed Urthaenriel and bade it grow to its normal sword size, a gleaming silver bar. "Now we wait."

58: Assault on Morios

Atrine, Jorat Dominion, Quuros Empire.
Three days since Raverí D'Lorus seriously overestimated
her father's ability to remember everyone he'd murdered

Janel watched as the portal closed and then turned to Senera. "Give me the branch."

"What?" Senera blinked at her.

"Give me the branch. You burned through any trustworthiness I might have felt for you years ago." She held out her hand.

"You didn't used to be this paranoid." Senera handed over the small twig. "Don't break it by accident or we'll be doing all this for nothing."

"I'll be careful." Janel wrapped the twig in a strengthening spell before she tucked it into her bodice. "Now I want you to ask the Name of All Things how to slay Morios."

"You know I hate asking anything but a yes-or-no question," Senera protested.

The high general raised an eyebrow. "The Name of All—what?" He looked toward Emperor Tyentso for an answer.

"I'll tell you about it later," Tyentso said. "Prepare to be unhappy."

Senera gave Janel a glare she promptly ignored.

Janel said, "Ask, anyway. And fast."

Senera pulled out the small slate inkstone. She picked up the brush and ink already on the table and wrote: *Don't fight him.*

Everyone stared.

"Helpful," Tyentso said. "Extremely helpful. Why don't we skip the 'don't fight him' part since it's not a gods' damned option."

"Can you distract Morios for long enough for me to put this spear through his eye?" Janel tightened her grip on Khoreval.

"I don't see why not."

High General Milligreest set his hand down on the table between them. "Let the army soften him up first. We have the scorpions in position."

"Qoran," Tyentso said gently, "that's a good way to lose a lot of your men."

The high general gave the emperor a tight smile. "I wasn't asking your permission." With that he waved a hand toward his officers. "Tell your men to begin when ready. Start with dragon fire."

"Dragon fire?" Tyentso said.

"Coincidentally enough, we call it that, yes," Milligreest admitted.

"What happens if they miss?" Janel said.

"I imagine they'll hit the city," Senera replied.

General Milligreest left the tent, and everyone followed.

Morios still played in the city. Janel shuddered to think how Ninavis and the rest of her crew were doing. With any luck, they'd managed to find the duke and rescue him. And if that didn't work, well . . . there was always Dorna and plan B.*

"Second rank—load!" someone called out.

Janel forced her thoughts back to the dragon. Putting herself in a position where she could stab him in the head would be the tricky part—he was so enormous. Unfortunately, neither Suless nor Thurvishar had ever taught Janel to *fly*.

It would have been so handy.

Even as Janel contemplated options, she heard one of the men yell, *"Going bright!"*

What? Janel looked over at the scorpions. Each catapult-like device's driver had dismounted, bringing with them the same

---

* This. *This,* Relos. She's too damn much like you. Apparently, while you thought she was being sentimental about insisting on evacuating the city, she was using that as cover to move her own game pieces.

spheres they'd been using to steer the scorpions. But now that said spheres had been removed from their protective casings, the undersides were revealed—uncovering painfully radiant light beams the soldiers pointed straight down at the ground.

"Front rank—target!"

As one, fifty light rays converged on Morios as he rampaged through Atrine. A few lights wandered off target but were quickly and expertly corrected. Janel had no idea what that accomplished, given that they were still at least two miles from Atrine. The impossibly bright lights didn't seem to do much more than spotlight the dragon. Maybe they hoped to lure Morios closer?

"Front rank—fire!"

Janel blinked. "That's too far away. They'll never hit—"

Each scorpion tail launched a small barrel up into the air on a trajectory that wouldn't make it a hundred feet, let alone miles. Yet when each barrel reached the height of its arc, it sped away at an impossibly fast speed as if some unseen god had thrown it. Each barrel slammed into Morios at exactly the same point highlighted by its scorpion's light.

And exploded.

Morios reared back. Yellow-white fire clung to his neck and back, throwing out sparks and globs of molten metal. The dragon's scales glowed red hot and began to melt and drip.

"Second rank—fire!"

The Quuros army fired again.

Senera leaned toward Janel. "If you ever wondered how Quur conquered an entire continent, now you know."

The high general smirked.

"And then remember this still wasn't enough to invade the Manol," Senera added.

Morios swung his head toward their position on the lakeside and roared, incredibly loud even from that distance.

Then he spoke.

"Ha!" the dragon said. **"So you *do* want to fight!"** Then in a conversational tone, Morios added, **"It will give me something to do until my brother arrives."**

"Brother?" Janel looked over at Senera. "Who's his brother?"

The witch shrugged. "Who knows?"

Morios began scraping away his melting metal scales, flinging bits of steaming death into the water and out over the city.

Then the scales began to *regrow*.

"Son of a—" Tyentso glared at the high general. "What *else* do you have?"

The high general seemed equally displeased by the dragon's lack of dying. "The normal casket allotment—most of which won't work. We have Argas's fire, but it doesn't burn hot enough to melt metal. And seeing as Morios is made of metal, that would be pointless. We have rhino caskets . . ."

Tyentso growled. "I didn't serve in the damn army, Qoran. What's a rhino casket?"

"Just metal. All it does is hit you, but it hits you hard."

"Perfect. Order your men to load that up and hit Morios with all of it at once. I'll buy them time. Red Eyes, what's your name again?"

"Janel."

"With me, Janel. Morios is bringing the fight to us." Tyentso ran down the slope toward the scorpions as the high general ordered one of his men to relay the orders.

Janel looked back toward Atrine. She'd assumed Morios's sword wings would never support him in flight, but she was wrong; Morios had finished his grooming and now flew straight toward his attackers, and anyone else on the hill. And he flew fast.

"All ranks—casket change *rhino*."

Up and down the line, men hurried to change out their ammunition. Janel ran after Tyentso in time to see her run up to one of the scorpions and demand one of the caskets. The soldiers blinked at her, probably because it took both of them to load the ammunition, which clearly made it too heavy for two women to lift.

Janel just tucked Khoreval under one arm and picked up the casket with the other. "Where do you want this?" she asked Tyentso.

"On the ground in front of me." As Janel set it down, Tyentso asked, "So you're Qoran's daughter, right?"

"*Going bright!*" the caller shouted.

As Janel stared at her, wide-eyed, Tyentso grinned. "Process of elimination. I've been stuck in this too long not to know a few of the prophecies. Cover your eyes—"

"All ranks—target!"

Janel covered her eyes just as the soldiers aimed their lights at Morios once more. They were angled much tighter this time: he was nearly on top of them.

"All ranks—fire!"

Well over a hundred rhino caskets sprang up into the air and then shot straight at Morios. Tyentso bent down and touched the casket at her feet and then raised the Scepter of Quur above her head. A shimmery rainbow force field sprang up, blocking the hail of metal blades that rained down from Morios's mouth and wings.

But another thing also happened: the metal casket Tyentso touched vibrated and then slammed into the nearest metal scorpion, making its operators curse in surprise. A split second later, Morios jerked downward, as the hundreds of caskets Tyentso had linked to hers slammed into his body. The rhino caskets then stuck to his body as though glued in place.* When the targeteers returned their spotlights to their normal position—pointed at the ground—the caskets obediently tried to follow orders and slam into the earth as well, taking Morios with them.

"I'll ground the bastard, you—" Tyentso cut off as both women saw Tyentso's sharp silhouette highlighted against the ground, so black it was as if something had set a piece of the sun behind her.

Or was targeting the emperor with a scorpion's aiming light.

"Behind you!" Janel yelled.

Tyentso threw a portal down under Janel's feet even as a

---

* Hey, sympathetic magic is *handy*.

green glass casket slammed into Tyentso and broke, flooding the area around the emperor with acid.

Janel fell through the portal and landed farther up the hill-side, giving her a perfect view of the emperor's protective shield flickering out and dying. The dragon had been busy trying to resist the pull of all those giant magnets, but when he saw the shield fail, he must have seen his chance. He breathed out again, nearly horizontal with the scorpions. And this time, his deadly rain of blades found their mark as they slammed into equipment and men with equal vigor. Unlaunched caskets stored on the scorpions' backs exploded, setting off a chain reaction. Impossibly bright aiming crystals fell to the ground, pointed in every direction.

Morios screamed as different parts of his body were pulled in a hundred different directions, but with the magnets no longer working in concert, no single direction exerted enough force to control him.

"Run!" Janel was screaming, heading toward the dragon. "Everyone *run!*" She bent down to help Senera stand on her feet, but the witch seemed undamaged except for grass stains.

Morios landed on top of the Quuros war camp.

He raked a wing along the shore while bending down to scoop up a giant volume of earth, men, and equipment into his mouth. As far back as she was, Janel still found herself leaping out of the way to avoid being split in half by a wing feather shaped like a giant sword two feet wide.

Tyentso stood, acid spilling off her as though she were made of glass. She threw a spell at the dragon, but whatever it was, it seemed to have little effect except to draw his attention. Then Janel realized the emperor had done something to those few caskets that had landed on Morios's neck, pulling the dragon's head toward the ground.

The dragon's head would never be closer to the ground than it was at that moment.

It might well be her only chance.

"Senera! Help me reach him!"

Senera snapped out her hands and gestured—and the ground next to Morios surged forward, making a ramp.

Janel sprinted up it and leaped, both hands on Khoreval. She aimed the spear straight for Morios's eye.

Her thrust hit true. She felt the quicksilver metal of his eye give, then shatter as the spear drove deep. Morios roared, the sound loud enough to send a nightmarish stab of pain through her skull. He began tossing his head backward, ripping away chunks of scales and whatever passed for flesh on his body.

Janel faced a choice: either hold on to the spear and let herself be tossed a lethal distance into the air, or let go and fall a much shorter distance to the ground. Tyentso might be able to catch her. Maybe.

She chose the latter.

Janel felt her leg break as she landed, a searing snap of pain.

The dragon roared, and then roared again, and then kept making the noise, rhythmically.

Morios was *laughing*.

"Brilliant! I love it!" Morios pulled Khoreval from his eye. **"This is the most fun I've had in millennia!"**

Then the dragon snapped the spear in two.

59: THREE BRANCHES

Atrine, Jorat Dominion, Quuros Empire.
Three days since everyone in a busy tavern failed
to notice the emperor among them

Kihrin sat down on the throne and leaned back. "So . . . how are the nightmares treating you two?"

Both Thurvishar and Brother Qown raised their heads, looking surprised.

After a long, awkward pause, Brother Qown said, "Awful. I dream of caves filled with families who are choking to death or melting. Or choking to death *and* melting."

"I told you not to research Quuros war curses." Thurvishar shook his head. "I dream of Gadrith. It's so hard to believe I'm finally free of the man."

Brother Qown, who had been pacing around the throne room, looking at the mud-caked statues, turned to Thurvishar. "I'm curious about something. Relos Var once told me the only reason he didn't kill Gadrith was because the man had something that belonged to him. And while Gadrith did, Relos wouldn't move against him. So what was it?"*

"Okay, this conversation just turned a whole lot less 'idle chitchat.'" Kihrin straightened.

"Why . . ." Thurvishar frowned, fingers absently turning the band of his father's intaglio ruby ring. "No. No, I haven't the slightest idea. Although . . . I did often sense Gadrith must

---

* I find I'm curious too, but I know better than to ask.

have had some edge over Relos. But I grew up in the Capital, where everyone is blackmailing everyone."

Kihrin cocked his head. "If it was information, it might well have died with Gadrith, but what if it wasn't? Do you think he might have hidden something at Shadrag Gor or back at the D'Lorus estate?"

"You mean an artifact?" Thurvishar asked.

"Sure, why not? Relos Var claims he doesn't have a Cornerstone himself, but I don't believe him. All the other dragons do. Why wouldn't he?"

Thurvishar blinked. "Wait. Just because he shape-changed into a dragon doesn't mean he is one. Khaemezra did the same thing . . ."

"Yeah, but Relos Var *is* a dragon. Remember the dragon who flew overhead when I was in Kharas Gulgoth? That was Var."

Thurvishar inhaled. "I suppose it might have been."

"Well, If I were a dragon who could only be killed if someone had my Cornerstone," said Qown, "and another wizard had it? I'd reclaim it the second I heard he'd died."

"Yeah, I would too." Kihrin sighed. "It was worth a dice throw, anyway."

Janel stared up, dumbstruck, as the dragon reared back.

It hadn't worked.

It hadn't worked, and she'd done everything perfectly.

"Janel!" She had that much warning before Senera grabbed her, not physically but magically, pulling her from the path of Morios's clawed hand.

"Aw, come back, little girl. We're not done playing."

"I'm so glad I've made a good impression," Janel said, feeling hysterical.

A fractal circle opened in midair next to them; Tyentso stepped through.

"Cover your ears!" Tyentso shouted to Janel and Senera, as well as anyone else in proximity.

Tyentso pointed the Scepter of Quur at the dragon. Janel and Senera both put their hands over their ears. The air distorted as a beam roared from Tyentso's scepter to Morios. A high-pitched, horrid sound emanated from the beam, impossibly painful to hear.

Where the beam hit, Morios's body just . . . vibrated apart, the beam drilling right through him.

Oh, thank Khored, Janel thought. *Surely this will–*

Then Morios laughed again, and everyone watched in horror as the gaping holes through his body healed over.

"I take it back. I haven't had a fight like this since my brother."

But instead of attacking, Morios launched himself up into the air and began flying back toward Atrine. He turned and looked back over his shoulder as he flew, as if checking to make sure his audience was paying attention.

"What's he doing?" Senera said.

"Baiting us," Janel growled. "He knows we don't want to see Atrine destroyed, so he'll force us to go to him. As he said, he's *playing.*"

"Oh, it's worse than that," Tyentso said. "He is going to hover over a crowd so I can't try the magnet trick again." She gave Janel a sympathetic look. "The medics are on their way. It was a good try. Sorry it didn't work out." She opened another portal and left.

"Damn it all." Janel started to stand but then ground her teeth as the pain in her leg reminded her why moving was a bad idea.

"Wait here," Senera said. "I can't heal your leg, you know. Never could—you're a two-healer job. Let me find someone."*

"It's fine," Janel said through gritted teeth. "Help Tyentso. I can take care of this myself."

"Good luck." Senera paused and smiled at Janel. "You know,

---

* You know, I can only assume Qown managed it earlier because he's improved his skills as a healer. You're right; he really is quite talented.

it was kind of fun at the end. Tell Thurvishar thanks for saving my life." She summoned a portal for herself and ran through, tossing something to the side just before she did.

Senera's final words sent a chill through Janel. She crawled over to where Senera had left and felt around on the ground, looking for what the woman had discarded.

Her hand closed on half a twig.

"No." It couldn't be the same twig. *She* had that twig. Janel fished under her bodice and pulled out the stick.

It was broken.

Janel had spelled the branch to resist breaking. Her falling to the ground wouldn't have done it.

Then she realized what Senera had done. What Senera must have done.

There had never just been two branches. There had been *three*. Senera had anticipated Janel confiscating the twig. So Senera had enchanted a twig of her own, sympathetically linked to the other two. When Senera had broken that, she'd snapped the other two twigs, wood and metal both.*

But why? What could Relos Var have gained by sabotaging his own plan to destroy Morios? It had been his idea from the start, so why would he—?

Janel felt dizzy. She couldn't count on any of her assumptions being true. What did she *know*? She knew Kihrin had Urthaenriel. She knew Senera had signaled Qown. She knew Kihrin was seconds from destroying another Cornerstone, assuming he hadn't already.

What she didn't know: what would actually *happen*. Destroying the Stone of Shackles had released the demons, after all . . .

Janel looked around. The army was in disarray, the survivors of Morios's attack gathering the injured and dead. She saw her father—he'd survived—off in the distance in a yelling match with a green-robed D'Aramarin royal.

---

* She got it right on the first guess too. I'm honestly proud of her.

Milligreest would have a fast way to reach Tyentso. She'd just order him to—

Janel stopped herself. She couldn't order Milligreest to do a thing. Khorveshans might not understand idorrá and thudajé, but they sure as hell understood chain of command. *High General* Milligreest knew who was in charge: himself.

Janel put her hand on her leg and concentrated on pulling in enough tenyé from the surrounding ground to heal her broken bone.* Suless had taught her the trick of it. It hurt like someone putting a torch to her bare skin, but it worked fast.

She jumped to her feet. "General Milligreest!" Janel yelled. "High General Milligreest, I need your help!"

The high general paused in the middle of his confrontation with the High Lord Havar D'Aramarin. "Yes?"

"We've been tricked," Janel said. "Senera and Relos Var have tricked us. The emperor *has* to contact Thurvishar—tell him to stop Kihrin from shattering the Cornerstone. Before it's too late. Please, sir, I'm begging you."

The high general gave her a hard look, but then he stared at a ring he wore—not an intaglio-cut ruby ring, but probably the same principle.

After a few agonizingly long seconds, Qoran Milligreest said, "She passed along the message, but he didn't respond."

Janel's heart skipped. "What does that mean?"

"That he didn't respond," Qoran repeated. He turned his attention back to the high lord. "I'd leave if I were you. The emperor won't be pleased with you when this is over."

Havar raised an eyebrow. "She can't hurt me. *Literally* can't hurt me. Have you forgotten the restrictions that come with wearing the Crown and Scepter? She can't so much as lay a hand on any member of a Royal House."†

---

* Huh. Suless taught her that? Then I'd be very surprised if that pulls tenyé from the ground. More likely it pulls tenyé from all unshielded living beings nearby. I wonder if Janel killed anyone.

† Did someone forget to tell the high lords those restrictions were enforced by a gaesh? Whoops.

"Don't say I didn't warn you," the high general said, smiling.
The high lord sneered and started to walk away.
Then the ground began to shake.

60: BROTHERS, AGAIN

Kihrin held up a pair of dice. "So anyone feel like a game to pass the time?"

Brother Qown shook his head.

"Not a chance in hell," Thurvishar said.

Kihrin sighed.

Brother Qown raised his head and opened his hand. The metal twig had broken in two. "That's it. That's the signal. They've killed the dragon."

"Thank the Eight," Kihrin said. He drew Urthaenriel and slammed the edge down against the crystal.

The ground rolled under their feet, undulating.

Janel screamed as the ground tossed her up into the air like a small child playing blanket games. She hit the ground and scrambled to keep hold of something as the earth beneath her continued shaking.

Over on Lake Jorat, a whole giant section of the bridge leading to Atrine broke free and slid away. Then Janel realized she had the scale wrong.

A whole section of Demon Falls, holding back Lake Jorat itself, had just given way.

Not only was Tyentso still fighting Morios, but Janel had no way to reach her to tell her she had just seconds to slay the dragon, if they wanted a true death. And Janel was quite certain that she'd just watched their chance to permanently kill Morios this time slide away, thanks to Senera's betrayal.

Only, what had caused the earthquake?

"I need a way over there," Janel said to General Milligreest. "Is there anyone here you'd trust to open a portal?"

He glanced back in the direction the high lord had left. "No. And I'm not going to risk you or anyone else on the bridge in that condition."

"I have to help them!"

"You *tried*," General Milligreest told her. "There's nothing more you can do."

"I refuse to give up!"

"Sometimes you don't have a choice," Milligreest snapped. "Damn it, you're as stubborn as your brother." He stopped himself and winced.

Janel felt dizzy . . . it had never occurred to her . . . "I have a brother?"

"Not anymore." Milligreest's voice caught.

Her throat tightened at the grief in his voice. She didn't ask what had happened. This wasn't the time.

But then she frowned.

Brothers. Morios is looking for his brother, Janel thought. *Morios thought his brother would* be *here* too. *Why?*

Kihrin had speculated the dragons might all be children of the Eight, but what if it wasn't so specific? Relos Var himself didn't qualify, for example. He was Kihrin's brother. So they weren't children necessarily, but relatives of some sort. Children, parents, sisters . . . *brothers.* What if, on some level, dragons still remembered that familial connection?

Kihrin had said that the dragon Sharanakal was Thaena's son and that he had laired near her island sanctuary. Aeyan'arric had stayed near her uncle Rev'arric, better known as Relos Var. Janel wasn't sure which came first: Had Thaena chosen to stay near her son to keep an eye on him, or had her son chosen to stay near his mother? Had Relos Var stayed near Aeyan'arric, or the reverse? But if the pattern stayed consistent

. . . there *had* been one of the Eight living in Atrine, hadn't there?

"Khored," she breathed.

Her father paid no attention. He probably thought she was cursing.

Janel bowed her head and prayed.

"Khored, please hear my prayer, for your brother Morios is here. Morios, who lays waste to Atrine, a city you love. Please help us, or he'll scour this place to the ground—"

Khored said, "I can't stay for long."

Her father gasped and fell to one knee.

Janel looked up. Khored floated above her, red armor dark as blood, raven-feather cloak blown back by the wind. Everyone around them seemed to realize a god had appeared among them at the same time. She heard people dropping to the ground all around.

"We can't stop him," Janel told Khored. "Nothing's working."

Behind Khored, Janel could see explosions over Atrine. She had to assume Tyentso still fought to keep the dragon from smashing Atrine, and Morios still played.

The God of Destruction said, "Of course nothing is working. My brother is the personification of war, battle's avatar. Combat makes him stronger. Relos Var should have told you."

"Brother!"

"That's my cue," Khored said, looking over his shoulder. "I'll distract him for as long as I can. We can't kill each other. Believe me, we've both tried. Evacuate everyone from Atrine and find safe ground." He waved a hand at Janel.

And the world shifted. She now stood inside Atrine. It was a horror of fallen buildings and crumbling masonry. Far too many bodies were visible in the streets.

Janel had no eyes for such disasters as she stood there, stunned and furious. Relos Var should have told them? Relos Var had *known*? Known combat would make the dragon more powerful, known Morios couldn't be killed by violence?

But of course. Senera never would have betrayed Janel

without her master's approval, would she? This had been planned from the start.

Above Janel's head, she saw Morios, now fighting two opponents. He was having a great time, despite the huge chunks of his scales that had been ripped away from where he'd freed himself of Tyentso's magnetic caskets.

Wait. Why hasn't he healed that damage?

"Don't fight him," she said aloud. The Name of All Things had said the only way to kill Morios was not to fight him.

Why in all the cold depths of hell had she assumed that the Cornerstone gave any answer but the literal truth? Senera could lie, but the Name of All Things never would. *Morios couldn't regenerate the injuries he'd inflicted on himself.*

Janel turned around and began running toward what was left of the Temple of Khored.

61: UNDER THE WATERS

Atrine, Jorat Dominion, Quuros Empire.
Three days since Kihrin made his way to the
Culling Fields invisibly

As soon as Kihrin smashed the crystal, he knew he'd fucked up.

For one thing, the crystal hadn't been solid. Rather than being a single piece of rock, the way every other Cornerstone he'd ever seen had been, this crystal formed a thin, hollow shell surrounding gems, talismans, and objects whose purpose he couldn't fathom. Under Urthaenriel's touch, the crystal had shattered like glass.

For a second thing, as soon as he broke the crystal, the ground began to shake. Violently. Water began to splash onto the three of them, as their cube of air buckled and twisted.

And finally, he felt like he had been stabbed. Not physically stabbed. Kihrin felt like someone had just shoved a sword through his _soul._

"Thurvishar—" Kihrin grabbed the throne for support. "Something's wrong."

He glanced at Thurvishar just as the wizard's eyes rolled up into his head and he fell to the ground.

"What just happened?" Brother Qown asked, running to Thurvishar's side.

"I don't know—" Kihrin didn't finish the thought. He brandished Urthaenriel as she screamed a warning to him.

The water curtain parted.

And Relos Var walked into the throne room.

*

Morios had all but leveled the duke's palace but had left Khored's temple—nearly as tall—alone. As if destroying that would be rude.

Janel wasn't the only person who'd noticed the dragon's reluctance to demolish Khored's cathedral either. As soon as Janel ran inside, she found Ninavis, along with Dorna, Star, and most of Ninavis's people. Vidan looked like he'd taken some sort of head wound, while Kay Hará and Jem Nakijan both sported some ugly-looking injuries that Dorna was in the process of treating.

Talaras tossed his head back in greeting as Sir Baramon rose from where he'd been seated on the cold stone floor. "Count!"

Janel looked around. The inside of the temple was packed, but she shuddered to think that this might be the largest group of survivors.

"Oh, I'm so happy to see all of you," she said, "but I can't stay. Does anyone know if there are stairs to reach the upper levels?"

"Through those doors, foal," Dorna said. "And it's not quite as bad as it looks. We've stashed quite a few people down in the caves."

Janel grinned as she ran. "Good!"

She climbed the stairs to the upper levels of the temple. When Janel had reached the highest point she could find, without scaling the outside of the building, she began shouting for Tyentso.

Morios was now exchanging blows with Khored, but Janel saw no sign of the Quuros emperor.

"Tyentso!"

A portal appeared next to Janel, and Tyentso stepped through. "Did you know, a week ago, I couldn't open a gate at all? This crown is amazing."

Janel laughed. The situation was horrible, the odds grim, and she was laughing.

"Tyentso, could you help me trick Morios into swallowing me whole?"

The emperor stared at her.

Janel tilted her head.

"You're serious?"

"I think I've figured out how to kill him." Janel grimaced. "At least, how to kill him temporarily. If I'm right, I will have bought two days for you and the Academy wizards to devise some solution, melt him down, transport his body out to sea . . . *something*." Janel paused. "And if I'm wrong, the worst that happens is that I die."

"Right. Because that's the *worst* that could happen." Tyentso shook her head. "It's your funeral, kid, but sure, I think I can help you out."

"Did Morios even hurt you?" Kihrin scowled at the wizard.

Relos Var laughed. "Morios doesn't believe in 'pretending' to hurt someone. The injuries were real. Quite painful."

"Good."

"Don't feel bad; I spent centuries setting up all the pieces to this con. Quite a few very smart people fell for it."

With his free hand, Kihrin gestured over his shoulder, back toward the throne. "And I assume that *wasn't* Morios's Cornerstone?"

"Not in the least. You just destroyed an ancient device created a long time ago by a people now extinct. But if it makes you feel better, it would have cracked on its own in fifty years, give or take. I didn't feel like waiting for nature to run her course."

"You aren't leaving here alive." Kihrin descended the steps.

"You think I've never fought someone carrying Urthaenriel before?" Relos Var smiled as he circled the young man. "Please. You're ill-equipped to deal with me."

Kihrin suspected that was true. That trick Relos Var had pulled with the portal gates back in the tavern, for example. That could work far too well, even against someone holding Urthaenriel. But what choice did he have? Running wasn't an option. "I think you talk a good game, Var, but you weren't prepared for me to be the one who found Godslayer. And this time, I'm going to kill you, not the other way around."

Relos Var stopped smiling. "Let's find out."

Which was when Brother Qown hit Kihrin in the head with a mud-soaked branch.

Kihrin collapsed.

"Oh sun." Qown threw down the branch. "I think I've given him a concussion." He bent down to check on Kihrin, kicking Urthaenriel away. Finally, he exhaled in relief.

Relos Var said nothing and watched.

The small open space under the lake fell into silence.

"Why?" Relos Var asked at last, tilting his head.

"You were going to kill him," Brother Qown said.

"I was not," Var protested. "I need him alive for my plans to succeed."

Brother Qown nodded. "Good." Tears rolled down his cheeks. "Because at least you have a plan. Because you're the only one who has a plan. I don't think the gods do."

"Give them some credit. The Eight have a plan. Unfortunately for all of us, it's a really bad plan," Relos Var said. "They want a stopgap measure, something quick and certain to buy them, oh a few centuries at most. But we only have one immortal race left who could seal Vol Karoth back in his tomb. Even if the vané sacrifice their ageless existence to re-imprison Vol Karoth, what will we do then? When this inevitably fails, just as the last measures did?" Relos Var snorted. "The demons will be free. A broken god who wants nothing more than to devour the universe *will be free*. And do you know what the worst part is, Qown?"

Brother Qown wiped the tears from his face. "No?"

"The worst part is those things I just mentioned are *not the worst part*. Every living creature on either side of the Veil will be destroyed long before Vol Karoth sates his hunger. The worst thing isn't Vol Karoth and it isn't the demon hordes—it's a flaw in the universe. And every minute and every second, that flaw grows a little larger. It won't stop until our entire universe is ripped apart. And *that* is our real enemy."

Qown shuddered. He looked down for a moment at Kihrin,

at Thurvishar—both still unconscious. He tried not think about Janel and how the fight up above was unfolding. She'd never forgive him.

That is, if she survived.

Relos Var's expression softened as he smiled at Qown. "Do you really want to help me? It won't be easy. People *will* die. You will be forced to make difficult choices."

"I'm making one right now."

"True." Relos Var looked down at Kihrin's prone body. "Ah, little brother. You should have listened to your instincts. The mistake you and Janel made—even after you knew I controlled Aeyan'arric—was being unable to imagine why someone would unleash a dragon—and then show you how to kill him. You couldn't imagine anyone using a dragon as bait."

Var continued, "Morios only slept under Lake Jorat because I asked him to do this for me about, oh, three hundred years ago. He didn't wake because of any prophecy. He woke and attacked Atrine because I ordered him to. Naturally, it was no coincidence that it only happened now, *after* you'd found Godslayer. Urthaenriel is the only weapon I know that could safely shatter a control beacon, and you performed your role perfectly. Truly, I have missed you."

"Uh . . ." Qown fidgeted. "You know he can't hear you, right?"

Var rubbed his chin. "I make it a point to never correct an enemy's mistakes when they can hear me."

"But wait," Qown said. "If the prophecy wasn't about Morios . . ."

A flicker of disappointment crossed Relos Var's face as Qown failed to grasp what he thought should have been obvious. "*In the twentieth year of the hawk and the lion, beneath the silver sword, the sleeping beast's prison shatters. The dragon of swords devours demon falls as night takes the land.*" He waved a hand. "I told Duke Kaen the entire quatrain centered on Morios, but I lied. That part about the dragon of swords refers to Morios, which is obvious. And easy enough to orchestrate. So what does the rest of the quatrain *really* mean?" His tone turned into something appropriate for the classroom.

Qown bit his lip. "I don't know."

Relos Var gestured for him to continue. "Do better."

Qown shifted. "There are a few inconsistencies. I would interpret 'as night takes the land' to mean sunset, but this fight didn't happen at sunset. It happened at dawn. *Atrin* means *silver sword* in Guarem. That's why everyone thought the prophecy referred to Atrine."

"Keep going. Work it out."

Then Qown blinked as a new thought occurred to him. "But Morios wasn't imprisoned, was he? Just sleeping. And not sleeping *under* Atrine, because there's no place under the city big enough to fit a dragon his size. Those caves we saw under Khored's temple are too small." Qown concentrated as he worked through the problem, forgetting where they were. "So that phrase doesn't even refer to Atrine. And if it's not Atrine, then maybe *silver sword* means something else. Maybe it's a description. If we rearranged verses, then 'beneath the silver sword, the sleeping beast's prison shatters' becomes 'the sleeping beast's prison shatters—beneath the silver sword.'" His gaze settled on Urthaenriel, which had fallen into the mud, but it was still bright, vibrant, *silver.* It had indeed shattered *something* too. Crystal shards lay all over the throne. The light that had streamed off into the darkness was now absent.

"Then . . . that . . ." Qown started breathing fast. "Oh sun. That quatrain was about Vol Karoth, wasn't it? The 'sleeping beast' is Vol Karoth?"

"Technically, *every* prophecy is about Vol Karoth. But yes."

Qown felt his heartbeat drum in panic. "What have we *done*?"

"What did I just say about difficult decisions? And what we have done is bought humanity *time*," Relos Var explained. "I know it doesn't seem as if waking up Vol Karoth is helpful, but think about our circumstances. The last time the demons roamed free, before Grizzst the Mad gaeshed them all just to prove he could, god-kings ruled this whole continent from coast to coast. Say what you want about those little tyrants, but they kept their pocket kingdoms safe from demons. So what did the Eight Immortals do—through proxy Quuros emperors—once the demons had all been tamed? They slew every god-king they could. They only pardoned those who surrendered their old fiefdoms. The god-kings protect *nothing* in Quur now, while the Eight Immortals cannot be everywhere at once. We're overrun.

"The Eight Immortals may be far more powerful than the god-kings, but they aren't omnipotent. Each time some poor fool dies in a Hellmarch, the demons become stronger and more numerous. But what scares demons more than gods or god-kings? Vol Karoth, whose unending hunger is sated just as well by demons as by any other kind of soul. The demons will hide now. They'll retreat. Hopefully for long enough so we may do what we must."

"How can I help?" Qown asked, then paused. "Wait, *can* I help?"

"Of course you can. Never doubt yourself, Qown. I singled you out for special training when you first came to the Temple of Light. That's because I saw the potential for greatness in you. As for how you can help, start by picking up that sword." Relos Var pointed to Urthaenriel. "Trust me when I say it's best for everyone if I don't."

"But as soon as I pick up Urthaenriel, any spells I'm maintaining will fail. The water will come rushing in—" Qown's eyes widened as he glanced at Thurvishar and Kihrin.

"They're perfectly safe. Both Thurvishar and Kihrin are glyphed for pressure and air. Those won't run out. There are no predators interested in humans in these waters. Also, I'm expecting one of the Eight Immortals to check on what happened to their precious control crystal any second now."

Qown gasped. "In that case, we have to leave. Right now!"

Relos Var smiled. "In a moment." The wizard walked over to the throne and bent over, clearing away the muck and mud to reveal a small chunk of hematite. He chuckled as he picked it up. "Don't want to forget this. Morios would be upset if it fell into the wrong hands."

"That's Morios's Cornerstone? Warmonger really was down here the whole time?"

"Of course. One of you might have forced Senera to use the Name of All Things to confirm its location. And I'm sure Kihrin did use Urthaenriel to confirm the presence of a Cornerstone in the vicinity. The only way to satisfy both means of checking was to leave the Cornerstone here. Now why don't we be on our way. We have a *lot* to do and not much time to do it."

Qown picked up Urthaenriel as Relos Var opened a gate.

The water rushed in over the two unconscious men.

Qown and Var stepped through.

By the time Tyentso finished, Janel perched on top of the very highest pinnacle of the temple, had a voice that could be heard for miles, and glowed.

She was also—at least temporarily—extremely difficult to cut.

"Morios! Answer me this. How does one become a dragon? Did you have to make some sort of demon pact?"

The dragon turned toward her, snarling. ***"What?"***

"Janel, what are you doing?" Khored said.

She ignored her god.

"It cannot be so easy to become a dragon," Janel continued, "or they would litter the valleys. Is there a guild? A special password?"

With each word, Janel threw fire at Morios, spells she knew would never ever damage him.

Come on, she thought. *Ignore your brother for just a little while longer. Swing at the gnat. Bite at that snake's wriggling tail.*

Morios breathed at her, but the swirling energy cloud Tyentso had placed around her deflected most of the blades. The few that penetrated beyond that point bounced against her own protections.

"Is that the best you have?" Janel taunted.

"Janel—" But Khored stopped. Perhaps he'd sensed she had

a plan. Perhaps he just couldn't imagine she'd be this stupid otherwise.

Then a look of horror crossed the god's face. Khored vanished.*

Why . . . ?

Morios flew right at her, opened his maw, and swallowed the top of the spire, her along with it.

Janel screamed as the dragon's dark, suffocating throat constricted around her, an act that would have crushed her without Tyentso's protections.

And she should have known; he had razors on the inside too.

She unsheathed a dagger and plunged it into one side, jamming the blade between two razor ridges to gain her a handhold. Morios might have even felt the act, the way one feels it when a rice grain lodges in one's throat the wrong way, because he continued trying to swallow. Janel held on for dear life.

If she was wrong, she was about to find out what the Afterlife was like as a permanent citizen.

She took a deep breath and concentrated. Not on attacking Morios. Not on the dragon at all. She shoved all thoughts of Morios from her mind because she now dwelt in a playground where intentions mattered, where concepts mattered, where purposeful violence and accidental violence were not equivalent. Not so different in some ways from the Afterlife's metaphors, where the realm of the spiritual and mental triumphed over the physical.

Instead of thinking about Morios, or her odds, Janel did something she'd always done by instinct and always done well.

Janel created fire.

In tremendous quantity.

The survivors were gathered at Lake Jorat's shoreline, too numb to do much more than see to the injured and watch as one of the wonders of the world disintegrated.

* I'm guessing Khored had just figured out what really happened under the lake.

Only a small few understood the philosophical under-pinnings of the battle going on above the city. Destruction on this scale fed Khored's power.

And yet, Khored seemed incapable of defeating the dragon who had destroyed his city, Atrine, quite possibly beyond all rebuilding.

But even as some watched in horror and others observed with massive academic interest, the spectators noticed the dragon pull back from the fighting, looking surprised.

He shook his head, as if trying to clear it. Then Morios began clawing at his neck, tearing giant rents in the metal there. He keened to shake the stones as he dug deeper.

The giant tears in Morios's neck turned red. The color rapidly brightened to yellow and then to bright white. Metal melted, sizzling down to the lake water.

Abruptly, Morios's neck and head separated from his body. Both pieces fell, the huge body landing across Atrine, and the head dropping past the city, over the falls. It tumbled all the way down the immense, failing dam's enormous height.

Only a few noticed the small red dot, person-sized, that also fell into the water.

Those few were enough.

62: END GAMES

Atrine, Jorat Dominion, Quuros Empire.
Three days since Tyentso told a high lord to
"stand there and look pretty"

Janel woke, gratified to be alive, fearful of what news the Living World would bring. The Afterlife had been strangely deserted, with no sign of the demon hordes she expected to find snapping at the heels of such a massive event as the destruction of Atrine. The souls of the dead had freely wandered, however. There had been so many.

She staggered to her feet, ignored the concerned looks of military physickers. Outside, smoke turned the normally teal sky a sooty green; she'd only been unconscious for a few hours.

Ninavis waited for her outside the tent.

The woman seemed uninjured, a few smudges marking points on her forehead and jaw. Ninavis gestured toward a Joratese azhock as soon as she saw Janel, and they both started walking in that direction.

"Casualties?" Janel asked.

"We lost a few," Ninavis admitted. "Dango took some shrapnel in his leg, but he'll be fine. Although you wouldn't know that with the way his husband's fussing over him."

"Oh, I can't blame Baramon for that. I'd fuss too. What about—"

"Arasgon's fine." Ninavis held open the azhock flap for Janel. "He's over at the refugee camp, helping herd."

Janel nodded, relieved, and then couldn't help but smile as she entered the azhock and saw the Markreev Malkoessian's pennants. The smile faded quickly. There was only one reason that the Markreev would have set himself up so close to the high general's bivouac: because the duke was in no position to do so.

"I'll assume this means you weren't able to save Duke Xun."

"He must have died in the first few minutes of the attack. We always knew that was a possibility. Plan B, on the other hand, went smooth as silk." The Marakori woman tapped the satchel at her hip.

"Good. That's not all of them, I hope?"

"Oh no. Call it a representative sample."

"Good enough." Janel inhaled deeply. "Ninavis, I need to change the plan. I know what we discussed, but there's simply no way—"

The tent flap moved as Markreev Aroth Malkoessian entered. He halted, shocked. Under normal circumstances, he probably would have had guards enter first, but maybe he'd assumed he'd be safe in the middle of the Quuros army encampment.

He recovered quickly, closing his mouth as he starred at Janel. "I had half convinced myself I'd seen a ghost when I spotted you earlier."

Janel broke off from her conversation with Ninavis. She leaned against the table, stretched her arms up over her head, and smiled. "Oh no. Not at all. So now we really must finish that conversation we once had so many years ago about my 'place.'"

The Markreev's eyes narrowed as he lifted his chin.

Before he could respond, Janel continued, "But first I have an unpleasant task to complete." She lowered her arms. "I regret I must inform you that your son Oreth is dead."

He barely reacted, except his face paled. "Did you kill him?"

"He fell in with the Yorans—"

"So did you."

"I was kidnapped by the Yorans. Not the same thing. In any event, I believe you already know about Oreth's crimes. But after he left, your son found himself mixed up with unpleasantries. Really, it had nothing at all to do with Oreth, but he took the blame. Duke Kaen had him executed. For what it's worth, I'm sorry it worked out the way it did."

He swallowed, eyes bright, and said nothing for several heavy, tense seconds. "Very well." He nodded. "I shall take it under advisement. I assume you've come here to throw yourself on my mercy—"

"No."

Malkoessian frowned.

"I'm here to explain your new situation," Janel corrected. "I'm sure you realize, or must suspect, that Duke Xun is dead. And you likely think that you're the obvious choice to replace him." She shook her head slowly. "Let go of that idea, Aroth. It's not going to work out that way."

"Have your years away made you forget all etiquette? You call me *my lord*."

"No, I don't." Janel's eyes flashed blue as she snapped her fingers in front of his face. "Look at me, Aroth. Look in my eyes."

The rest of the Markreev's admonishment died stillborn. Ninavis gave Janel an odd look.

"No, Aroth. You talked your son into believing that he was entitled to my bed. You gave him my grandfather's letter and told yourself that you were forcing a marriage between us for my own good, for the good of the Theranon family name. Because of that belief, Oreth tried so hard to gain what you'd told him was his birthright that he strayed right into treason." Her smile was cruel as she saw Aroth flinch. "I owe you no thudajé. But you owe me a great deal."

The Markreev's expression cleared. "So you want to be duke."

"In fact, no." Janel stepped away from the table and clapped a hand on Ninavis's shoulder. "Please allow me to introduce you to Sir Ninavis Theranon. *She's* going to be next Duke of Jorat."

The Markreev likely didn't notice the slight widening of Ninavis's eyes, the startled glance the woman gave Janel. Ninavis recovered quickly.

"Theranon? But there are no other—"

"I've decided to adopt her." Janel turned to Ninavis. "Did you know there's no rule that says I can't adopt someone older than myself?"

"Well, I know now," Ninavis admitted, eying Janel warily.

"I'm also abdicating," Janel continued. "I suppose that means she's properly Count Ninavis Theranon. You will, of course, approve that succession. Which should be more than enough title to soothe anyone who would object to a Joratese ruler jumping from knight to duke." She tilted her head toward Ninavis. "Bad news, though. I'm afraid you're going to have to give up the tournament circuit."

Ninavis stared at her hard. "I'll cope."

Aroth sputtered. "You can't just pick a person and declare them in charge!"

Janel laughed. "Yes, we can. We can, and we do. All the time. Now you and I both know that since the duke died without heirs, there will be a meeting of the ruling nobles to pick a successor. You'll find a great many of those nobles will have no problem putting in their vote for the Count of Tolamer. Especially once word begins to spread that said count is the Black Knight. You know, the one who slew that giant dragon? Everyone saw her ushering people to safety earlier while you and your family evacuated with the rest of the herds."

Aroth's nostrils flared. "This woman didn't kill that dragon."

"Oh, but I say she did," Janel corrected. "And as I'm Janel Danorak, I know something about the power of a reputation. However, I never planned on relying on your good grace and kindness to ensure your cooperation." Janel motioned to Ninavis.

In response, the woman pulled a sheet of parchment out of her satchel. She leaned over a brazier next to the desk and set an edge on fire, releasing the sheet as the whole paper caught.

"What was that?" Aroth demanded.

"I do believe that was a lien for fifty thousand thrones given to Count Jarin Theranon," Ninavis explained. "Oh, did you need that?"

"*What?* How did you get that?"

"And this—" Ninavis pulled another paper out of the satchel. "Is another lien, originally between Jarin Theranon and the Baron of Omorse, but you bought that, didn't you? Only ten thousand this time. Still, you have lent people a lot of money, haven't you?" She rolled up the piece of paper and tapped it against the edge of the brazier. "All these loans. Half the empire is in debt to you, Aroth."

"And that's the problem, isn't it?" Janel pursed her lips. "Truth be told, you stopped being a Markreev a long time ago. You're not a Joratese noble protecting his herd; you're a *bank*. A usurer."

"How did you get those?" the Markreev demanded again. He glanced back at the entrance as if giving serious consideration to calling for his guards.

"I should rather think that obvious, Aroth," Janel explained gently. "We stole them. All of them. Every proof of lien you have and all your accounting books as well. It turns out that while this giant dragon was attacking, no one was guarding the Atrine Gatestone, and there was only a token guard back at your castle."

"Which means," Ninavis said, "that as of this moment, you cannot prove you have lent anyone so much as a chalice."

"You won't get away with this," Markreev Malkoessian snarled.

Janel waved a hand. "Think it through, Aroth. Yes, you can bring in Blood of Joras—wizards and truthsayers—to verify your claims, but do you really want to remind your fellow Joratese just how in bed you are with the Royal Houses? D'Aramarin in particular. Your Censure would be quite real. Or you can honor Ninavis's claim, support her, and no one has to know this ever happened."

His nostrils flared, and he didn't answer.

Janel sighed. Again her eyes seemed to change color, flickering into something resembling an ice-blue cat's eye before it settled back into crimson. "I'm making this offer because you're a smart, pragmatic man, and I think you and Ninavis will work well together. Jorat will need a lot of effort in the years to come and our people need strong leaders." She shrugged. "If I didn't think you were the man for the job, I'd have simply killed you and your son Ilvar and let your firstborn son, Palomarn, become duke. But Palomarn's a mare, and I know he'd hate having to be in charge of an entire ward. And Dorna would be upset with me if I killed you."

The Markreev's expression transitioned through a lot of emotions in quick succession: anger, worry, dread, fear, and finally a wary, grudging respect. He gestured toward Ninavis. "Why her, though? Why not yourself? Setting this up must have taken you years. No one just gives away power."

The corner of Ninavis's mouth quirked. "I admit I'm wondering this myself."

"I'm surprised at you, Aroth. I'm not giving away power. I'm delegating. I'd do it myself, but it turns out I'm going to be too busy with more important matters." She raised a finger as Aroth started to protest. "Yes, it turns out that there really are matters more important than ruling Jorat."

Aroth Malkoessian examined Ninavis. "Can you do the job?"

Ninavis laughed. "Compared to Foran Xun? A goat would do better." She shrugged. "Wouldn't hurt to have a good adviser. Someone who's actually Joratese might be nice. None of that Relos Var business."

"Indeed." His gaze turned contemplative. No doubt the Markreev was mulling all the ways he could possibly turn the situation to his advantage. "What about my papers?"

"What about them? I'll keep them safe for you." Ninavis's grin bordered on nasty as she lowered the rolled-up page in her hand to the brazier. "Except for the Theranon debts, of course. It's so kind of you to forgive those. Really, I'm touched."

Janel snapped her fingers again, and the Markreev's gaze focused on her immediately. "Do we have an understanding, Aroth?"

He met her eyes, which flickered pale blue again, then he shuddered. "Yes," Aroth whispered. "Yes, we do. My . . . my lord."

Janel smiled. "Good."

Aroth shook himself.

"Well, you two should find Dorna and start planning how you want to approach the other Markreevs with the happy news about their new duke. I have other things to check on." Janel bowed to them both and left to see who else had survived.

63: RESCUES

Atrine, Jorat Dominion, Quuros Empire.
Three days since Teraeth retained his gift for diplomacy

When Kihrin woke, he found himself lying on a cot set up inside an army tent. He left before anyone had a chance to decide what should be done with him, one way or another.

Outside, a continuous rumble filled the air; the vast, deep sound reminding him of the sea maelstrom called the Maw. Nearby, soldiers busied themselves setting up or tearing down the military camp. No one seemed eager to pay any attention to him.

He rubbed his head, but whoever had pulled him from the water had healed the injury. Kihrin's hand fell to his belt. No Urthaenriel either, and he couldn't hear her singing from nearby.

Kihrin's gut clenched.

Kihrin saw Thurvishar pacing near Lake Jorat's shoreline, looking pensive and miserable as he gazed at Atrine's burning, wrecked remains. Standing next to Thurvishar . . .

Kihrin's breath caught as he saw the Manol vané turn to profile. Then he realized it wasn't Teraeth. The eyes were wrong, the nose was wrong, everything was wrong. Kihrin released his breath, fighting back disappointment. He'd bet metal this was Teraeth's grandfather Mithros—and clearly the camp's soldiers didn't realize the vané was also the God of Destruction, Khored. He had to wonder how the Quuros army—many of whom worshipped Khored—would react to finding out their favorite deity was in fact a Manol vané.

A nearby tent flap opened, and Janel walked outside.

She noticed him right away and smiled. An instant later, Janel was in his arms, kissing him. Which almost made everything better. Or at least made everything a lot easier to forget.

Someone cleared their throat.

Kihrin looked up to see a Manol vané standing next to Tyentso—this time, the *right* Manol vané. Kihrin pulled away from Janel.

"Teraeth," Kihrin said. "I didn't expect to see you here."

The assassin's green eyes flicked to Janel and then back to Kihrin. "Obviously."

Kihrin wanted to kick himself. "Look, I'm glad to see you."

"Are you really?" Teraeth raised an eyebrow at him.

"Yes, damn it." Kihrin looked out over the lake toward the ruins of Atrine. "I've lost Urthaenriel. It only took three days—"

"Well, you do work fast," Teraeth said.

Kihrin sighed. If he'd ever wondered how Teraeth would react to Kihrin becoming romantically involved with Janel, now he knew the answer: *poorly.*

It might have gone that way for a while, but the women had other ideas. "You two can catch up on your flirting later. Janel, how are you feeling?" Emperor Tyentso asked.

"Surprisingly well for someone swallowed by a dragon," Janel admitted. "Have either of you seen Qown? I'd have expected to find him around the medical tents."

Kihrin felt a dozen dull knives settle in his stomach. "Uh, about that—"

He didn't want to be right about his suspicions. He certainly didn't want to explain those suspicions to Janel.

Janel's expression gave way to dread. "He's not hurt, is he? I don't know what happened down there—"

"That's what we came over here to find out," Tyentso said.

"I don't think Qown's injured, but Relos Var tricked us all. You see, I didn't destroy a Cornerstone." Kihrin felt sick. Somewhere out there, Relos Var had just checked off another item on his list, come one step closer to whatever horrible event he was attempting to trigger. Fulfilling the prophecies. As if that were a good thing.

Kihrin looked out over the water. Nearby, he heard people working, talking. Also moans and cries of pain.

Teraeth's expression changed from simmering anger to caution. "Kihrin, I pulled both you and Thurvishar out of the water. Qown wasn't there. Neither was Urthaenriel."

"No, I think Qown took it with him after he knocked me unconscious." It had to have been Qown. Kihrin had seen Thurvishar go down, and he'd been facing Relos Var. Qown was the only person who could have done it.

Janel blinked at him in horror. "No, that can't be what happened. Relos Var must have done something, some trick . . ."

Kihrin pressed his lips into a thin line and met Teraeth's stare. The vané had, at least for the moment, put jealousy aside in favor of being concerned with more important matters. And they had both placed recent events firmly in the "not good" category. Teraeth gave him a single nod of acknowledgment.

"No," Kihrin said, "I don't think so. Qown just figured out whose side he's really on, that's all. I'm really sorry, Janel."

Janel's eyes were wide and shocked. Teraeth walked over and put a hand on her shoulder.

"I know it looks bad," Tyentso said, "but we'll find Relos Var. Everyone will be looking for him now. I may not like the Academy witch-hunters, but they're good at their job. We'll find him—and we'll find Urthaenriel."

"You don't understand," Kihrin said.

"It can't be that bad," Tyentso said. "No one's reported a demon attack in hours, anywhere in the empire."

"Sure," Kihrin said. "Because the demons are hiding."

"I noticed that." Janel's voice sounded numb. "I just didn't understand why. They aren't even attacking the Chasm."

"Scamp, what don't we understand?"

"I felt it, Ty. I felt the moment Vol Karoth woke up. *That* was what Relos Var wanted, what he orchestrated all of this to obtain." Kihrin laughed, dark and hopeless. "Var convinced me he was interested in Janel, that she was his focus, that this was all about her. But the whole point was to trick me into waking up the one creature I would *never* willingly free. Vol Karoth's not asleep anymore."

Janel snarled, "Someday, somehow, I swear I'm going to kill Relos Var."

Teraeth said, "Let's gather everyone. We need to talk."

64: THE ICE DUCHESS

The Borgheva Valley, Yor, Quuros Empire.
Four days since the attack on Atrine

Xivan Kaen scanned the valley as a Spurned marched up the narrow trail toward her, carrying a deer on her shoulders. Behind Xivan, the mountain homestead and cave system of Bikeinoh's clan, the Arsagh, hummed with tension. The steep trail was designed to be difficult to navigate, lined with spikes and steep, treacherous drops. The Arsagh hadn't been thrilled with Xivan's arrival.

Still, she'd only had to kill a half dozen or so men, before the rest agreed to a meeting.

"Hon," the woman said as she passed Xivan, heading into the main structure. The Spurned's face had been painted with a sigil, the same sigil Xivan wore. The same sigil every man, woman, and child in the homestead now wore, now that they understood its significance and use.

One day she intended to clean out the Spring Caves under every homestead, as Janel had somehow managed. In the meantime, the poisoned rock underneath them would hurt no more Yorans. When the chief had realized she offered them this gift, he'd become considerably more amenable to inviting her inside.

Not that it was a gift. More like a trade, but one with a simple price: any news of Suless's location.

Xivan's expression didn't change as Relos Var and his apprentice, Qown, emerged from the portal. Relos Var paid no attention to the cold, but Qown was bundled up in furs.

"You've got a lot of nerve," Xivan said. "Where's my spear?"

Var made a face. "Unfortunately, I'm not going to be able to return that, but I've brought what I hope will be a suitable apology. Qown?"

Qown knelt and set a plain-looking sword on the ground.

Relos Var turned back to Xivan. "How are you doing, my dear?"

"Still dead," she answered. "Almost as dead inside as out now, but fortunately for me, the hate is keeping me warm."

Relos Var winced. "I'm sorry. I know you'll get him back, though."

"But he won't be sane." She paused. "He wasn't sane before, was he?"

Relos Var paused and then nodded. "No. Suless is good at that."

"You didn't stop her." Xivan didn't even sound upset. She merely presented a simple fact. He hadn't stopped Suless. He could have.

"I told your husband to destroy Suless when he had the chance. He refused. I may not have agreed with his decision, but I let my friends make their own choices."

Her eyes flickered, and for the first time, emotion crossed her features. "Really? You've manipulated everyone you've ever known."

Relos Var shrugged. "I won't apologize for making certain options more appealing than others."

"I would kill you now if I could," Xivan said.

"You can," Relos Var said. "The sword my apprentice just placed on the ground is Urthaenriel."

She blinked in surprise as she stared at the weapon. "You found it. You actually found it."

"Yes. Well, my brother found it." Relos Var raised his hands in a "what can you do" gesture. "I think Azhen would have wanted you to have it, if he couldn't wield it himself."

"It wouldn't destroy me?" Her gaze hadn't moved from the weapon.

"Not at all," Relos Var said. "But it will stop you from feeding and thus healing. However, its powers are only active when the sword is drawn, so I wouldn't hold it unsheathed for more than three or four hours at a go. Barring that, I see no reason you can't wield Urthaenriel. And indeed, I think we can both agree you might wield it very well against certain individuals."

Xivan stared at him. "Suless."

"It's not called Godslayer for nothing." Relos Var smiled. "And I do want you to find her. Suless has a talent for unpredictability I'd like removed from the board."

Xivan gazed down at the blade. Relos Var wanted to use her. She knew that. He'd use her for his own purposes too; what she wanted wouldn't be relevant to him at all. He might claim to want her to kill Suless, but she knew the names he really wanted crossed off his list sounded more like Khored, Taja, Ompher, Galava, Argas, Tya, and Thaena. Xivan Kaen had never been fooled by Relos Var's overtures of friendship to her husband. She knew a puppeteer when she saw one.

Xivan picked up the sword.

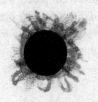

Afterword

And finally . . .

Deep in the heart of the Korthaen Blight, eight streams of light united in the center of a city. Once called Karolaen, now Kharas Gulgoth, the city existed as tomb and prison, maintained for one purpose: to imprison a corrupted god of darkness and oblivion with eight chains of light.

One of those lights had been failing. The same light always failed eventually, the same light always dimmed, each time sooner than the last. Maintaining the chains around a prisoner—one removed from the universe itself—was a strain capable of dimming the very stars in the sky. It couldn't be maintained forever, but that light hadn't yet failed. That one weak link wouldn't have failed for another fifty or so years, if it had followed the pattern.

But we'll never know.

Far to the north, a young man wielding Urthaenriel smashed what he thought was a Cornerstone. But since he had been deceived, what he destroyed instead was an ancient mechanism. A device whose sole purpose had been to feed a single stream of light to a site thousands of miles away, to the center of Kharas Gulgoth.

And so, a stream of light that should have lasted at least a few more decades flickered, dimmed, and finally died.

Eight chains became seven.

The number could not hold.

As a distant earthquake rumbled through the land, waking morgage from their beds, the system broke down. A single link in a corrupted god's chains *snapped*.

Vol Karoth opened his eyes.

APPENDIX 1:

DRAGONS

Aeyan'arric—female—glacially white dragon but does not look like she'd been made from ice. Last seen in Jorat, current whereabouts unknown, but likely Yor.

Baelosh—male—a dragon made from vines and plant material or covered with vines and plant material.

Drehemia—female—described as shadowy, possibly made from shadows, and impossible to view directly. Current whereabouts unknown but has never been seen inside Quur.

Gorokai—female—a chimeric, constantly shape-changing dragon.

Morios—male—metal dragon made entirely from blades, swords, and other weapons. Vague stories about Morios survive from confiscated dreth accounts from Raenena. The creature was previously believed to be fictional. Last seen at Atrine. Cannot be harmed in direct combat.

Rol'amar—male—described as a skeletal-looking dragon whose bones continually break and heal. Believed impossible to kill by any known means. Last seen in the Korthaen Blight.

Sharanakal—male—described as an active volcano shaped like a dragon. Last seen in the island chains between Xherias and the Manol, an area known as the Desolation.

Xaloma—female—bioluminescent ghostly dragon who can move between the Veils of the Twin Worlds at will.

APPENDIX 2:

GLOSSARY

A

Aeyan'arric (EYE-ann-AR-ik)—a dragon.

Afterlife, the—a dark mirror of the living world; souls go to the Afterlife after death, hopefully to move on to the Land of Peace.

Agari (ag-AR-eye)—Marakori clan.

Agolé (ah-GOAL-aye)—a versatile scarf-like garment that can be worn in a number of ways.

Alvaros (AL-var-os)—a ward in Jorat.

Arasgon (AIR-as-gon)—a fireblood, Talaras's brother.

Argas (AR-gas)—one of the Eight Immortals. Considered the god of invention and innovation.

Ash Flower—a Joratese farm horse.

Atrine (at-rin-EE)—capital of the dominion of Jorat, originally built by Emperor Atrin Kandor.

A'val (ah-VAL)—a friend of C'indrol's.

Avranila (AV-ran-il-AY)—a small town in Tolamer Canton, in the Stavira ward of Jorat. Not directly affected by the Lonezh Hellmarch, but depopulated later as its residents moved away in search of better economic opportunities.

B

Baelosh (BAY-losh)—a dragon.

Baramon, Sir (BARE-ah-mon)—an aging knight who works the tournament circuit, primarily in Barsine Banner.

Barsine Banner (bar-SEEN-ee)—a district in Jorat.

Bikeinoh (beh-KEEN-oh)—Duke Kaen's second wife.

Bitsy—an alias used by Dorna.

Black Knight, the—an expected figure in Joratese tournaments, meant to represent the unpredictable hand of the divine, often the only way titled nobles may compete in tournaments. Usually used for comic relief.

Blood of Joras (JOR-as)—a Joratese term for any wizard not of either Joratese, Marakori, or Yoran extraction.

Butterbelly—a deceased fence and member of the Shadowdancers who worked in the Capital.

C

Caless (kal-LESS)—goddess of physical love.

Censure—a Joratese custom by which a noble may be removed from power without bloodshed; at least 50 percent of the noble's vassals typically present the titled noble with gifts, indicating that they have higher idorrá than the noble. Since one must present gifts to a noble in person to Censure them, nobles worried about Censure often travel extensively.

Cherthog (cher-THOG)—a god of winter and ice, primarily worshipped in Yor.

C'indrol (SIN-drol)—of of the past lives of Janel Theranon. Possibly a voras who died during the destruction of Karolaen.

Cloud—a Joratese gelding.

Coldwater—a small village in Barsine Banner.

Cornerstones, the—eight magical artifacts; the Stone of Shackles and Chainbreaker are two of these.

D

Dango (dang-O)—one of Ninavis's crew.

Danorak (dan-OR-ak)—a fireblood who famously rode himself to death, in an attempt to warn people of Emperor Kandor's intention to flood the Endless Canyon (which resulted in the creation of Lake Jorat).

D'Aramarin (day-ar-a-MAR-in)—the first ranked Royal House. House D'Aramarin controls the Gatekeepers, the guild of wizards primarily responsible for running and maintaining the gate system. They are thus responsible for and control almost all inter-dominion trade.

Havar (hav-AR)—High Lord of House D'Aramarin.

D'Kard (day-KARD)—a Royal House, primarily associated with crafting.

D'Lorus (du-LOR-us)—a Royal House, primarily associated with paper, books, schools, and education.

Gadrith (GAD-rith)—Lord Heir of House D'Lorus, an infamous necromancer and wizard, widely believed to be dead; also known as Gadrith the Twisted.

Thurvishar (thur-vish-AR)—son of Gadrith D'Lorus, Lord Heir of House D'Lorus.

D'Mon (day-MON)—a Royal House, primarily associated with the healing arts.

Darzin (DAR-zin)—Lord Heir; oldest surviving son of High Lord Therin D'Mon.

Galen (GAL-len)—firstborn son of Lord Heir Darzin D'Mon.

Kihrin (KEAR-rin)—youngest child of High Lord Therin D'Mon and only child of Queen Khaeriel of the vané. Also, the re-incarnation of S'arric, one of the Eight Immortals.

Therin (THER-rin)—High Lord of House D'Mon.

D'Talus (day-TAL-us)—the Royal House in charge of the smelter and smith's guild, known as the Red Men.

Ibatan—author of *Rituals of War*.

Dedreugh (deah-DROOG)—captain of the Barsine guard.

demons—an alien race from another dimension that can, through effort, gain access to the material world; famous for their cruelty and power. See: Hellmarch.

Devoran Prophecies, the—a many-book series of prophecies that are believed to foretell the end of the world.

dhole (dole)—a form of wild dog, domesticated in Jorat and also found throughout Marakor.

Diraxon (dear-a-CHON)—a quasi-mythical, infamous Marakori clan known for their skill at stealth and assassination.

Doltar (dol-TAR)—a distant country whose people have pale skin and light-colored hair and eyes. Occasionally, they will be sold in Quur as slaves.

Dorna (DOR-na)—an elderly Joratese woman who served as Janel Theranon's nanny in childhood. She continues to travel with Janel.

Dragonspires, the—a mountain range running north-south through Quur, dividing the dominions of Kirpis, Kazivar, Eamithon, and Khorvesh from Raenena, Jorat, Marakor, and Yor.

Drehemia (DRAY-hem-EE-ah)—a dragon.

dreth (dreth)—see: vordreth.

drussian (drus-E-an)—a rare metal, superior to iron, which can only be created through superhot magical fires.

Dyono Tomai (DIE-o-no TO-my)—the Red Knight (Yoran words).

E

Eamithon (AY-mith-ON)—a dominion just north of the Capital City, the oldest of the Quuros dominions and considered the most tranquil.

Eight Immortals, the—eight beings of godlike power created by a ritual performed by Relos Var.

Empire of Quur (koor)—see: Quur.

Endless Canyon, the—an extraordinarily large, deep, and convoluted series of canyons that were used as the god-king Khorsal's refuge and place of power. The Endless Canyon was destroyed when Emperor Kandor dammed the rivers that had eroded it, creating Lake Jorat.

F

Falesini blood sickness (fal-ES-en-EYE)—a hemorrhagic fever associated with mouse urine, sometimes encountered in dry, hot climates such as the dominion of Khorvesh.

Festival of the Turning Leaves—a yearly celebration to the goddess Galava. Here petitioners may, after one year of service to the goddess, petition the goddess to change their biological sex.

firebloods—a race originally related to horses but modified by the god-king Khorsal to possess extraordinary size, power, resilience, loyalty, and intelligence. Firebloods are omnivorous, and although they don't possess fingers, some are capable of manipulating tenyé. They have an average life expectancy of eighty years or more.

Forest—a Joratese legal practice of declaring a wilderness area "outside" legal protection or repercussions. Used as an early form of eminent domain, but with more opportunity for state-sponsored murder. Outside of Jorat, typically just an area of protected woodland, such as the Kirpis forest.

Four Races, the—four immortal, powerful races that once existed. Only the vané still exist in their original, immortal forms, with the other races having devolved into the morgage, dreth, and human races.

G

gaesh (gaysh), pl. gaeshe (gaysh-ay)—an enchantment that forces the victim to follow all commands given by the person who physically possesses their totem focus, up to and including commands of suicide. Being unable or unwilling to perform a command results in death.

Galava (gal-a-VAY)—one of the Eight Immortals; goddess of life and nature.

Gan the Miller's Daughter—one of Ninavis's crew.

gate—a.k.a. portal, the magical connection of two different geographic locations, allowing for quick travel across great distances. Only powerful wizards can typically create Gatestone-independent portals.

Gatekeepers—the guild who controls and maintains gate travel. Ruled by House D'Aramarin.

Gatestone—a specially inscribed section of stone that somehow makes gate travel much less magically onerous. Exactly how this is accomplished is a proprietary, heavily protected House D'Aramarin secret.

gelding—a Joratese term for any person, male or female, who does not fall into "stallion" or "mare" stereotypes. Note that this does not indicate the person is sexually neuter.

Gendal (GEN-dal)—former emperor of Quur, murdered by Gadrith D'Lorus.

gender, Joratese—Joratese define gender socially rather than biologically. So while they acknowledge biologically male, female, and intersex individuals, who is labeled a "man" or "woman" has to do with their societal role, rather than genitalia. There is a catch-all "gelding" category for people who refuse to conform to either extreme. But for the most part, gender is still binary in Jorat and still suffers from many of the same problems as binary genders elsewhere. Joratese gender can typically be determined by outward presentation, with "stallions" dressing in elaborately decorated clothing and "mares" dressing in much more modest attire. See: stallions, mares, geldings.

Godslayer—see: Urthaenriel.

god-touched—a "gift" or "curse" (depending on whom one asks) handed down by the Eight Immortals to the eight Royal Houses of Quur. Besides giving each house a distinctive eye color, the god-touched curse prevents the Royal Houses from making laws or ruling over territory.

Gorokai (GORE-o-kai)—a dragon.

Gozen, Sir (GO-zen)—an up-and-coming knight.

Grazings, the—southern Jorat, where large areas of plains and grasslands are dominant.

Great Silence, the—an unexplained event in which every wizard in Quur (and in fact the entire world) was inexplicably rendered deaf for three days.

Grizzst (grizt)—falsely attributed to being one of the Eight Immortals; famous wizard, sometimes considered a god of magic, particularly demonology. Believed to be responsible for binding demons as well as making the Crown and Scepter of Quur.

Guarem (GOW-rem)—the primary language of Quur.

H

Hamarratus (ham-ar-RA-tus)—a fireblood, previously a slave owned by Darzin D'Mon, also called Scandal.

Hará, Kay (HAR-ah, KAY)—one of Ninavis's crew.

Hedrogha (hay-DRUEG-ah)—a Yoran captain.

Hell—distinct from the Land of Peace; it's where demons come from.

Hellmarch—the result of a powerful demon gaining access to the physical world, freely summoning demons and possessing corpses. This usually results in a runaway path of death and devastation. It typically results from a demon escaping a summoner's control. Before the breaking of the Stone of Shackles, demons could only be summoned to the Living World by corporeal entities (such as humans or vané). But demons quickly discovered they could exploit a loophole by possessing a living body—and forcing that body to summon more of their kind. Demons can also possess corpses in the Joratese/Marakori area but cannot summon more demons this way.

Hellwarrior—a prophesied villain who will rise up to destroy the Empire of Quur and possibly the world. Also a prophesied hero who will rise up to save the world.

I

idorrá—a Joratese concept of authority, dominance, and control. Roughly analogous to responsibility, duty, and authority, idorrá can be lost if the holder fails to protect or defend those under their charge.

Irisia—see: Tya.

J

Jalore (jah-LOR-ee)—the Quuros emperor who finalized the conquest of the Zaibur city-states.

Jorat (jor-AT)—a dominion in the middle of Quur of varying climates and wide reaches of grassy plains; known for its horses.

K

Kaen (kane)—the Yoran ducal line.

  Azhen (AHJ-en)—Duke, or Hon, of Yor, grandson of the Joratese

Quuros general who conquered the region and slew the god-king rulers of the region, Cherthog and Suless.

Exidhar (EX-eh-DAR)—Azhen Kaen's only son.

Xivan (JI-van)—Azhen Kaen's first wife; her Khorveshan ancestry made her unpopular with the Yoran people, and she was eventually killed in an assassination attempt meant for her husband.

Kalazan (KAL-a-zan)—one of Ninavis's crew.

Kandor (KAN-dor)

Atrin (AT-rin)—an emperor of Quur who significantly expanded the borders of the empire; most famous for deciding to invade the Manol, which resulted in the destruction of virtually the entire Quuros army and the loss of Urthaenriel. This left Quur defenseless against the subsequent morgage invasion.

Elana (eh-lan-AY)—see: Milligreest, Elana.

Karolaen (KAR-o-lane)—former name of Kharas Gulgoth.

Kasmodeus (KAZ-mode-e-US)—a demon.

Kazivar (KAZ-eh-var)—one of the dominions of Quur, north of Eamithon.

kef (kef)—a style of trouser common in western Quur.

Kelanis (KEL-a-nis)—son of Khaevatz and Kelindel, younger brother of Khaeriel; now king of the vane.

Khaemezra (kay-MEZ-rah)—a.k.a. Mother, the High Priestess of Thaena, and leader of the Black Brotherhood; Teraeth's mother; the true name of Thaena. See: Thaena.

Khaeriel (kay-RE-el)—queen of the vané, assassinated by her brother, Kelanis. Because Khaeriel was wearing the Stone of Shackles, she ended up in the body of her assassin, and was later gaeshed and sold into slavery to Therin D'Mon by her grandmother, Khaemezra.

Kharas Gulgoth (KAR-as GUL-goth)—a ruin in the middle of the Korthaen Blight; believed sacred (and cursed) by the morgage; prison of the corrupted god Vol Karoth.

Khored (KOR-ed)—one of the Eight Immortals, God of Destruction.

Khoreval (KOR-e-val)—a magic spear believed to have the ability to slay dragons.

Khorsal (KOR-sal)—god-king who ruled Jorat. He was particularly obsessed with horses and modified a great many of the people and animals under his power. Responsible for the creation of the fireblood horse lines and centaurs.

Khorvesh (kor-VESH)—a dominion to the south of the Capital City, just north of the Manol Jungle.

Kirpis, the (KIR-pis)—a dominion to the north of Kazivar, primarily forest. Most famous for being the original home of one of the vané races, as well as the Academy. Also, home to a number of famous vineyards.

Kirpis vané (van-EH)—a fair-skinned, immortal race who once lived in the Kirpis forest. They were driven south to eventually relocate in the Manol Jungle.

Kishna-Farriga (kish-na-fair-eh-GA)—one of the Free States, independent city-states south of Quur, past the Manol Jungle; Kishna-Farriga is used as a trading entrepôt by many neighboring countries.

knight, Joratese—unlike knights elsewhere, Joratese knights are more akin to sports athletes, who fight as proxies to establish idorrá/thudajé relationships. This affects every aspect of Joratese life, from business deals to trials.

Korthaen Blight, the (kor-THANE)—also called the Wastelands, a cursed and unlivable land that is (somehow) home to the morgage.

Kovinglass (KOVE-ing-lass)—a Gatekeeper formerly in the employ of the Count of Tolamer.

Kulma Swamp (KUL-mah)—a lowland swamp area in Southern Marakor.

L

laevos (LAY-vos)—a Joratese hairstyle consisting of a strip of hair down the center of the head and shaved sides, echoing a horse's mane. Some Joratese grow their hair this way by default; it's considered a sign of nobility.

Lonezh Hellmarch (LONE-ej)—an infamous Hellmarch that occurred in relatively recent memory, starting in Marakor and ending in Jorat; casualties were staggering.

Lorat (LOR-at)—an elderly nobleman.

M

Malkoessian (MAL-koz-ee-an)

Aroth (AIR-oth)—Markreev of Stavira, one of the four quadrants or "wards" that politically divide Jorat. Count Janel Theranon's canton, Tolamer, lies within Stavira's borders.

Ilvar (ILL-var)—Aroth's heir.

Oreth (OR-eth)—youngest son of the Markreev of Stavira, who often participates in tournaments as a knight. Briefly engaged to marry Janel Theranon.

Manol, the (MAN-ol)—an area of dense jungle in the equatorial region of the known world; home to the Manol vané.

Marakor (MARE-a-kor)—the Quuros dominion to the southeast of the empire. Politically important because Marakor is the only (relatively) easy entry point to the Manol Jungle. Consolidating the various rival city-state clans, which originally made up the region, has proved difficult.

mare—a Joratese person who identifies as a woman (note: different from being sexually female, see: gender, Joratese) and expresses "mare" attributes such as housekeeping, child rearing, farming, crafting, art, cooking—and embraces teamwork, family, and subordinate values.

Markreev (MAR-kreev)—a noble title in Jorat, just below duke.

Mereina (MARE-ee-NAH)—the capital seat of Barsine Banner.

Milligreest (mill-eh-GREEST)

Elana (e-lan-ay)—a musician from Khorvesh who married Atrin Kandor. After his death, she returned to using her maiden name and journeyed into the Korthaen Blight to negotiate a peace settlement with the invading morgage people; responsible for freeing S'arric. Past life of Janel Theranon.

Jarith (JAR-ith)—only son of Qoran; like most Milligreests, served in the military; killed by Xaltorath during the Capital Hellmarch.

Qoran (KOR-an)—high general of the Quuros army, considered one of the most powerful people in the empire.

misha (MEESH-ah)—a long-sleeved shirt worn by men in Quur.

Mithros (MEETH-ros)—leader of the Red Spears, a mercenary

company selling their services to the highest bidder for tournaments in Jorat; a Manol vané.

Miyane (MY-an-ee)—queen of the vané, wife of King Kelanis.

Morea (MOR-e-ah)—a slave girl murdered by Talon; Talea's twin sister.

morgage (mor-gah-GEE)—a wild and savage race that lives in the Korthaen Blight and makes constant war on its neighbors. These are mainly Quuros living in the dominion of Khorvesh.

Morios (MORE-ee-os)—a dragon.

N

Nakijan, Jem (Na-KEY-jan, JEM)—one of Ninavis's crew.

Nameless Lord, the—the Joratese name of the Eighth of the Eight Immortals.

Nemesan (NEM-es-an)—a deceased god-king.

Nerikan (NAIR-eh-kahn)—a Quuros emperor.

Ninavis (NIN-a-vis)—an outlaw who has gathered together a group of like-minded bandits and exists on the outskirts of Barsine Banner, mostly sticking to the forest.

O

Ogenra (OH-jon-RAY)—an unrecognized bastard of one of the royal families. Far from being unwanted, Ogenra are considered an important part of the political process because of their ability to circumvent the god-touched curse.

Omorse (OH-mors-ee)—a banner in Jorat.

Ompher (OM-fur)—one of the Eight Immortals, god of the world.

P

Prialar (PRI-a-lar)—a town in Jorat.

Q

Qhuaras (kwar-AHS)—a deceased god-king.

Qown, Brother (kown)—an acolyte of the Vishai Mysteries, assigned to guide Count Janel Theranon.

Quur, the Great and Holy Empire of (koor)—a large empire

originally expanded from a single city-state (also named Quur) that now serves as the empire's capital.

R

Raenena (RAY-nen-ah)—a dominion of Quur, nestled in the Dragonspire Mountains to the north.

raisigi (RAY-sig-eye)—a tight-fitting bodice worn by women.

razarras (RAY-zar-as)—a highly poisonous ore.

Red Spears—a mercenary company of Jorat.

Return—to be resurrected from the Afterlife, always with the permission of the Goddess of Death, Thaena.

Rev'arric—see: Relos Var.

Rol'amar—a dragon.

S

saelen (SAY-len)—Joratese word meaning *stray*.

sallí (sal-LEE)—a hooded, cloak-like garment designed to protect the wearer from the intense heat of the Capital City.

salos (SAH-los)—a type of snake native to the Manol Jungle.

Sandus (SAND-us)—a farmer from Marakor, later emperor of Quur.

S'arric (sar-RIC)—one of the Eight Immortals, mostly unknown (and deceased); god of sun, stars, and sky; murdered by his older brother, Rev'arric. Past life of Kihrin D'Mon.

Selanol (SELL-an-al)—the solar deity worshipped as part of the Vishai Mysteries.

Senera (SEN-er-AY)—a former slave of Doltari ancestry, later operating in Jorat as a witch and saboteur.

shanathá (SHAH-nath-AY)—a type of metal.

Sharanakal (SHA-ran-a-KAL)—a dragon.

Sifen family, the (SIGH-fen)—a family of farmers in Barsine Banner, primarily known for their mangoes.

Simillion (SIM-i-le-on)—first emperor of Quur.

snow hyena—a type of hyena adapted to the extremely cold conditions of Yor.

stallion—a Joratese person who identifies as a man (note: different from being sexually male, see: gender, Joratese) and expresses "stallion" attributes such as leadership, assertiveness, guardianship, entertaining, contests, and combativeness.

Stavira (sta-vir-AY)—one of the four quadrants, or marches, dividing Jorat.

Stone of Shackles, the—one of the eight Cornerstones, ancient artifacts of unknown origin.

Suless (SEW-less)—god-queen of Yor, associated with witchcraft, deception, treachery, and betrayal; also associated with hyenas.

T

Taja (TAJ-ah)—one of the Eight Immortals, Goddess of Luck.

Talea (tal-E-ah)—a former slave.

talisman—an otherwise normal object whose tenyé has been modified to vibrate in sympathy with the owner, thus reinforcing the owner's tenyé against enemies who might use magic to change it into a different form. This also means it's extremely dangerous to allow one's talismans to fall into enemy hands. Since talismans interfere with magical power, every talisman worn weakens the effectiveness of the wearer's spellcasting.

tamarane (tam-a-RAN-ee)—a system of Joratese cooking with eight specific styles of heating.

Tamin (TAY-min)—Baron of Barsine Banner.

Tanner—one of Ninavis's crew.

tenyé (ten-AY)—the true essence of an object, vital to all magic.

Teraeth (ter-RATHE)—hunter of Thaena; a Manol vané assassin and member of the Black Brotherhood; son of Khaemezra.

Thaena (thane-AY)—one of the Eight Immortals, Goddess of Death.

Theranon (ther-a-NON)—a noble family from Jorat.

Frena (fren-AY)—Janel's mother, who died during the Lonezh Hellmarch.

Janel (jan-EL)—a demon-tainted noblewoman from Jorat. Nicknamed "Danorak" because of the widespread belief that she'd outrun the Lonezh Hellmarch as a child in order to warn Emperor Sandus of the invasion.

Jarak (jar-AK)—Janel's father, who died during the Lonezh Hellmarch.

Jarin (JAIR-in)—deceased Count of Tolamer, Janel's grandfather.

thorra (THOR-ah)—Joratese term for a person who abuses idorrá privileges; bully or tyrant, lit. "a stallion who is not safe to leave with other horses."

Three Sisters, the—either Taja, Tya, and Thaena, or Galava, Tya, and Thaena, depending on local beliefs; also, the three moons in the night sky.

thudajé (thu-DAJ-ay)—Joratese term of respect, humility, and submission; thudajé is considered an essential and positive Joratese trait. No matter how high in idorrá someone is, the Joratese believe there will always be someone to whom they owe thudajé.

Tiga Pass (tie-GAY)—a pass allowing physical travel between the Great Steppes and the Grazings.

Tolamer (TOL-a-mear)—a canton in northeastern Jorat, ruled by the Theranon family for almost five hundred years.

tournaments—regular contests of skill, usually involving horses in some fashion, which take place as often as possible in various regions of Jorat. Joratese spectators can be passionate about teams they support.

tumai (TU-mai)—Yoran word for *knight*.

Twin Worlds, the—name for the combination of the Living World and Afterlife, when referring to both realms as part of a larger whole.

Tya (tie-ah)—a.k.a. Irisia (IR-is-EE-ah), one of the Eight Immortals, the Goddess of Magic.

Tya's Veil—an aurora borealis effect visible in the night sky.

Tyentso (tie-EN-so)—formerly Raverí D'Lorus, now the emperor of Quur; the first woman to ever be emperor.

U

upishiarral (U-pish-e-ar-AL)—a traditional Joratese dish of vegetables and rice.

Urthaenriel (UR-thane-re-EL)—Godslayer, the Ruin of Kings, the Emperor's Sword. A powerful artifact that is believed to make its wielder completely immune to magic and thus is capable of killing gods.

V

Valathea (val-a-THE-a)—a harp passed through the Milligreest family; also, a deceased queen of the Kirpis vané.

vané (van-EH)—a.k.a. vorfelane, an immortal, magically gifted race known for their exceptional beauty.

vanoizi (vah-NWA-zi)—a style of Eamithonian cooking.

Var, Relos (VAR, REL-os)—a powerful wizard, believed responsible for the ritual that created the Eight Immortals, and also the ritual that created both the dragons and Vol Karoth.

Veixizhau (vex-e-SHAU)—one of Azhen Kaen's younger wives.

Vidan (VID-an)—one of Ninavis's crew.

Visallía (viz-ALL-e-ah)—a march in Jorat.

Vishai Mysteries, the (vish-AY)—a religion popular in parts of Eamithon, Jorat, and Marakor; little is known about their inner workings, but their religion seems to principally center around a solar deity; usually pacifistic; members of the faith will often obtain licenses from House D'Mon to legally practice healing.

Vol Karoth (VOL ka-ROTH)—a.k.a. War Child or Warchild, a demon offspring crafted by demons to counter the Eight Immortals; alternately a corrupted remnant of the sacrificed god of the sun, S'arric; possibly both.

voramer (vor-a-MEER)—a.k.a. vormer, an extinct water-dwelling race believed to be the progenitors of the morgage and the ithlakor; of the two, only the ithlakor still live in water.

voras (vor-AS)—a.k.a. vorarras, an extinct race believed to have been the progenitors of humanity, who lost their immortality when Karolaen was destroyed.

vordreth (vor-DRETH)—a.k.a. vordredd, dreth, dredd, dwarves, an underground-dwelling race known for their strength and intelligence; despite their nickname, not short. Believed to have been wiped out when Atrin Kandor conquered Raenena.

W

Warmonger—a Cornerstone.

Wilavir, Sivat (wil-a-VIR, SIV-at)—author of *Siege Tactics of the Yoran Invasion*.

witch—anyone using magic who hasn't received formal, official training and licensing; although technically gender neutral, usually only applied to women; in Jorat, anyone using magic who isn't Blood of Joras is considered a witch.

Worldhearth—a Cornerstone.

Wyrga (WIR-ga)—an animal trainer in the service of Duke Kaen.

X

Xaloma (ZAL-o-may)—a dragon.

Xaltorath (zal-tor-OTH)—a demon prince who can only be summoned through the sacrifice of a family member; self-associated with lust and war.

Xun, Foran (CHUN, FOR-an)—Duke of Jorat; Xun gained the throne at a young age when his father was slain during the Lonezh Hellmarch.

Y

Ynis (YIN-is)—a deceased god-king.

Yor (yor)—one of Quur's dominions, the most recently added and the least acclimated to imperial rule.

Z

Zaibur (ZAI-bur)—1. the major river running from Demon Falls and Lake Jorat all the way to the ocean, dividing Jorat from Marakor; 2. a strategy game.

Zaibur, the City-States of—archaic name for the collection of divided city-states that populated Marakor prior to being conquered by the Quuros.

Zajhera, Father (zah-JER-ah)—leader of the Vishai Faith / Vishai Mysteries. Personally exorcised the demon Xaltorath, who possessed Janel Theranon when she was a child.

ACKNOWLEDGMENTS

First, I'd like to thank my dearest love, Mike, who continues to be my foundation, my rubber duck, and my first defense against plot holes. Thanks as ever to Karen Faris, for always making the time to give me feedback. Eternal thanks to my agent, Sam Morgan (you didn't have to answer those panicked Saturday-night phone calls, but thank you for doing it, anyway). I also want to thank the extraordinary people at Tor Books—not just my fantastic editors, Devi Pillai and Bella Pagan (and their assistants, Rachel Bass and Georgia Summers!), but the entire cast of often unsung heroes in editing, production, marketing, and publicity whose hard work and enthusiasm helped make this book possible. My readers may not know about you, but please believe that I do (and will be sending you more fudge). Thank you to Lars Grant-West for his fantastic cover art, Irene Gallo for her perfect art direction, and Thomas Mis for his hard work making the audiobooks extraordinary. I'd also like to thank Rachel Fish for her advice in grappling with the often-complicated gender issues of Jorat. And lastly, thank you to DeBracey Productions at the Georgia Renaissance Festival for letting me hang out and ask annoying questions. Special thanks to the surprisingly nice tournament villain, Lee Kirk, and to Dosbergen "Dopka" Kozugulov, whose discussions of the horse games of his native Kyrgyzstan neatly upended all my plans for how Joratese tournaments worked.